THE SPORT OF KINGS

ALSO BY C. E. MORGAN

All the Living

THE SPORT OF KINGS

C. E. MORGAN

4th ESTATE • London

4th Estate
An imprint of HarperCollins*Publishers*
1 London Bridge Street
London SE1 9GF

www.4thEstate.co.uk

First published in Great Britain in 2016 by 4th Estate

First published in the United States in 2016 by Farrar, Straus and Giroux

1

Copyright © 2016 by C. E. Morgan
Map copyright (hardback) © 2016 by Jeffrey L. Ward

C. E. Morgan asserts the moral right to
be identified as the author of this work

A catalogue record for this book is
available from the British Library

ISBN (HB) 978-0-00-731326-6
ISBN (TPB) 978-0-00-731327-3

Grateful acknowledgement is made for permission to reprint the following material:
'How to Identify a Thoroughbred' from The Jockey Club Registry, reprinted
with permission of The Jockey Club. Copyright © 2016 The Jockey Club.
Secretariat's measurements from the *Daily Racing Form* copyright 2016 by Daily
Racing Form, LLC. Reprinted by permission of the copyright owner.

Designed by Abby Kagan

Printed and bound in Great Britain by
Clays Ltd, St Ives plc

This novel is entirely a work of fiction. The names, characters and
incidents portrayed in it are the work of the author's imagination.
Any resemblance to actual persons, living or dead, events
or localities is entirely coincidental.

All rights reserved. No part of this publication may be
reproduced, stored in a retrieval system, or transmitted,
in any form or by any means, electronic, mechanical,
photocopying, recording or otherwise, without the
prior permission of the publishers.

This book is sold subject to the condition that it shall not, by
way of trade or otherwise, be lent, re-sold, hired out or otherwise
circulated without the publisher's prior consent in any form of
binding or cover other than that in which it is published and
without a similar condition including this condition being
imposed on the subsequent purchaser.

MIX
Paper from
responsible sources
FSC
www.fsc.org   **FSC® C007454**

FSC™ is a non-profit international organisation established to promote
the responsible management of the world's forests. Products carrying the
FSC label are independently certified to assure consumers that they come
from forests that are managed to meet the social, economic and
ecological needs of present and future generations,
and other controlled sources.

Find out more about HarperCollins and the environment at
www.harpercollins.co.uk/green

This book is dedicated to the reader.

As buds give rise by growth to fresh buds, and these, if vigorous, branch out and overtop on all sides many a feebler branch, so by generation I believe it has been with the great Tree of Life, which fills with its dead and broken branches the crust of the earth, and covers the surface with its ever branching and beautiful ramifications.

—CHARLES DARWIN, *On the Origin of Species*

CONTENTS

THE SPORT OF KINGS

THE STRANGE FAMILY OF THINGS

Your spirit will spread little by little through the whole great body of
empire, joining all things in the shape of your likeness. —SENECA

Henry Forge, Henry Forge!"

How far away from your father can you run? The boy disappeared
into the corn, the green blades whisking and whispering as he raced
down each canopied lane. The stalks snagged him once, twice, and he
cried out like a wounded bird, grasping his elbow, but he didn't fall. Once,
he'd seen a boy break his arm in the schoolyard; there had been a bough-
like crack of the thick bone snapping and when the boy stood, his arm hung
askew with the bone protruding like a split ash kitchen spoon—

"Henry Forge, Henry Forge!"

Number one, I am Henry Forge.

His father's voice echoed across the warped table of the earth, *domine
deus omnipotens, dictator perpetuo, vivat rex, Amen!* The thick husks strained
their ears toward the sound, but the boy was tearing across the tillable soil,
soil that had raised corn for generations and once upon a time cattle with
their stupid grazing and their manure stench. He was sick to death of cattle
and he was only nine.

Number two, curro, currere, cucurri, cursus. I am forever running.

Silly child, he couldn't know that the plants announced him, the flaxen roof of the corn dancing and shaking as he passed, then settling back to coy stillness, or that his father was not in pursuit, but stood watching this foolish passage from the porch. On the second story, a window whined and a blonde voiceless head protruded with a pale, strangely transmissive hand making gestures for John Henry, John Henry. It pounded the sill twice. But the man just remained where he was, eyes to his son's headlong retreat.

The young boy was slowing now in the counterfeit safety of distance. He boxed the corn, some daring to feint and return, some breaking at the stalk. He didn't care; his mind refused to flow on to some future time when redress might be expected or demanded. There was fun in the flight, fun borrowed against a future that seemed impossible now. He had nearly forgotten the bull.

Number three, Gentlemen of the jury, I am not guilty!

The corn spat him out. His face scraped by the gauntlet, he clutched handfuls of husk and stood hauling air with his hair startled away from his forehead. Here the old land is the old language: The remnants of the county fall away in declining slopes and swales from their property line. The neighbor's tobacco plants extend as far as the boy can see, so that impossibly varying shades of green seem to comprise the known world, the undulating earth an expanse of green sea dotted only by black-ship tobacco barns, a green so penetrating, it promises a cool, fertile core a mile beneath his feet. In the distance, the fields incline again, slowly rippling upward, a grassed blanket shaken to an uncultivated sky. A line of trees traces the swells on that distant side, forming a dark fence between two farms. The farmhouse roofs are black as ink with their fronts obscured by evergreens, so the world is black and green and black and green without interruption, just filibustering earth. The boy knows the far side of that distant horizon is more of the bright billowing same, just as he knows they had once owned all of this land and more when they came through the Gap and staked a claim, and if they were not the first family, they were close. They were Kentuckians first and Virginians second and Christians third and the whole thing was sterling, his father said. The whole goddamn enterprise.

Number four, Primogeniture is a boy's best friend.

He heard the whickering of a horse around the wall of the corn and sprang to the fence that separated Forge land from the first tobacco field belonging to the Osbournes. He scrambled over the roughcut rails. Casting back over his shoulder, he saw the proud bay head of a Walker turning the corner and darted to the first plants risen waist-high and crawled between two, prostrating himself on the damp, turned bed. His face pressed against the soil, which was neither red nor brown like bole when it stained his tattered cheek with war paint.

The horse and the man rounded the corner. The Walker was easy and smooth, head and neck supremely erect, its large eyes placid as moons with the inborn calm of its breed. It scanned its surroundings out of habit, slowing its pretty pace near the fence, then prancing alongside the timbers. A high tail jetted up like a fountain from a nicked dock, then streamed down overlaid pasterns almost to the ground. The tail trembled and betrayed the faintly nervous blood that coursed through the greater quiet of the horse.

"Hmmmm," said its rider, loud enough for the boy to hear in his low, leafy bower. Filip.

Number five, This race was once a species of property. It says so in the ledgers.

The man sat as erect as the horse, his back pin-straight as if each vertebra were soldered to the next. One hand grasped the reins, one rested easy on his thigh. A bright unturned leaf obstructed the features of his face, but the boy could see the high polish of the head under dark and tight-kinked hairs. That head was turning side to side atop a rigid back.

"Aw," said the man suddenly, then reined left, and with one dancing preparatory pace, the horse took the fence with heavy grace, and the startled boy breached the plants like a pale fish, diving deeper into the tobacco field. The horse didn't follow, but paused at the lip of the field, dancing sideways, her ears perked for her rider's voice.

"Mister Henry," said Filip.

Henry scrambled away on his hands and knees.

"Martha White can catch you," Filip said. "Think she won't?" He waited, then, "I'll catch you on my own two feet. Think I won't?"

Henry could no longer tell where he was in the endless tobacco. He curled around the base of a plant and yelled, "I didn't do it!"

"Oh, I know you ain't killed that bull!" Filip hollered back.

"I swear!"

"I know it, you know it. Some other fool done it," said Filip. "Now get out of them plants."

"No!"

"Come on now . . ."

Henry rose on unsteady feet, looking like a refugee wader in the sea. "Father's angry at me."

The man shrugged a stiff shoulder. "Set him straight. The reasonable listen to reason."

"He didn't send you after me?"

"Nah," said Filip. "I seen you light out like a fox on the run, and I made after you."

The boy bit his lip, fiddling with the last tailings of his reserve, then picked his way through the plants to the edge of the field. Filip stared down over the sharp rails of his cheekbones, but did not incline his head as he reached down his large hand, fingers unfurling. White calluses stood out on his skin like boils.

"Where will we go?" said the boy, all suspicion and still calculating the odds of the gamble.

"Where you want to go to?" the man said.

"Clark County," Henry said, the first place that came to mind.

"That right?" Filip said, and a dry laugh scraped out of his burleyed throat. The boy could not make out the meaning of that laugh.

"Step up," he said, and Henry did.

Number six, If you live, you gamble. A necessary evil.

Swung up by Filip's strength and his own leap, he scrambled his way onto the man's lap, straddling the withers. The short, wide neck of the horse shuddered and trembled under him like a dreaming dog. From where he sat, he could see straight down over her black cob and nose to her broad velvetine nostrils.

"Let's go," he said.

"Not yet. I'm going to roll me a cigarette first. Hold this," said Filip, who drew a foil packet out of the breast pocket of his plaid shirt. "Huh, I ain't got no papers," Filip said, patting his pocket. "Want to ride to the store with me?"

"Sure," Henry said, pressing tiny drops of blood from his knees into the bay's neck. He painted them in with one finger and they disappeared into the body of the horse, which was red as deep as wine.

Filip gathered the reins, and Martha White backstepped and squared the fence.

"Up on her now," said Filip, and when the horse sprang from its quarters, the boy clutched up high on her neck in alarm as the man inclined toward the boy's back, and they sailed the fence.

"Don't take me by the house!" cried Henry.

Filip reined hard to the left, and the mare switched back, so they followed a faint trace around the far side of the cornfield along the grassy farrow that separated the plants from the fencing. Henry could just see over the tops of the corn, which reached to his own chest and over the bobbing head of the horse. The tufted tops were plumed and entirely still save for one roaming breeze that grazed the surface like an invisible hand, meandering down from the house to the tobacco basin behind them. To their left ran the zigzagging split rail fence and in its shadow, the remnants of its predecessor. Built seventy years before, the fence had rotted down until it was subsumed by grass and soil. Now it showed only a faint sidewinding mound behind the younger fence.

Henry patted the mane of the horse. "Make her walk fancy," he said.

Filip clicked twice and adjusted the reins and set the mare to a running walk, so her front legs appeared to labor, reaching and pulling the unbent back legs that boldly followed, her head rising and falling like the head of a hobbyhorse. The natural urge to run pressed hard against her stiff limbs, and in that dynamic tension her back neither rose nor fell, so her riders glided forward on her restraint as if on the top of a smooth-running locomotive. Henry leaned back against the wall of Filip's chest.

"Does her head hurt?" said Henry, noting the jerky treadling of her head before him.

"Nah."

"Does she want to run?"

"She ain't never said."

"She's like a machine."

"Huh."

Number seven, Living beings are just complex machines.

They rode on in silence to where the creek discoursed about the southern edges of the property, forming cutbanks and small sandy half-submerged shoals amidst weeds and tall grasses and cane. Broad-trunked walnut and alder sprang up from the creek bed to shade it and to form a secret lane of the rocky waterway.

"Let's jump the fence and ride down in the water so they can't see us," said Henry.

Filip said nothing.

Henry twisted his neck to find the man's face. "Do it," he said.

"Martha White don't want to get her feet wet."

The end of the field was approaching, the house loomed.

"I don't want to go to the store anymore," Henry whined just as, with a sudden gripping motion, Filip slapped the reins hard, his arms fitting over the boy's like a brace over muslin.

"No!" But the Walker was bearing down into a gallop and the boy, unprepared, bounced painfully against the protruding pommel as they swerved hard around the corn's edge to where his father waited on the far side. Henry cried out, struggling as the horse pulled up before John Henry, neck extended and ears flattened away from the kicking, flailing passenger on her withers.

John Henry stepped to the horse, his lips pressed together so they looked like pale scars.

"You tricked me!" Henry cried, twisting around in the saddle to strike Filip with the point of his elbow but baring his neck as he did, so his father snatched him off the saddle by the ruff of his shirt like a runt puppy, and he hung there, suspended, making a strangling noise, his hands grappling up for his father's hands. He was dropped unceremoniously as the bay skittered to one side, sweeping Filip away.

"Nigger!" Henry cried.

"Be still!" said John Henry.

Number eight, Niggerniggerniggerniggerniggerniggerniggerniggernig

Filip reined toward the stables, and the mare sauntered away slow and sinuous, and though Henry's eyes were filling with tears and he could barely see, his mind scrambled for an association, the horse was like, the horse was like: something, someone, he couldn't name how it moved away on its widemold hips, ass dimpling with sinuous inlaid muscle, though he knew it was feminine, yes: it moved like a woman from the rear.

His father yanked him up, his hands an old story.

"I didn't do it!" Henry cried, but his mouth formed words he was not really thinking, his mind having been startled by the strange family of things.

"Up!"

He would not up; he made himself be dragged, forgetting the horse now, forgetting Filip's lying, begging until his voice rose so high that his words destructed into a bleating cry.

Father dragged son across a broad swath of grass to the post by the old cabins, all the while unfastening his black belt with one hand. He struggled to cinch it around his son, but the boy puffed out his belly like a horse tricking a girth strap loose. John Henry just turned him around, face to the post, so all the air expelled in a woof.

"Undo that belt and believe me you will regret it," John Henry warned. The boy's hands sagged at his sides without any more fight, and his head fell forward, cheek scraping the post. He cried without moving.

John Henry placed one hand firmly on his son's crown. "Do you realize you might have died today? The foolish thing you did . . . I'm going to let you stand here a while and think about what that would have done to your mother."

Henry said nothing.

"When I come back I'm going to whip you," his father said, "but not until you've had a chance to stand here and think. Do not touch that goddamn buckle, boy."

"But I didn't do it," Henry parleyed.

John Henry narrowed his eyes and said with thorny quiet, "You're a liar, and that makes you an embarrassment to me."

The boy went to cry or speak.

"I gave you that mouth. I'll tell you when to open it."

He puckered his lips in a tiny sphincter of sorrow, and then his father was gone.

The scotched and furrowed pole had stood for more years than the boy could count. It was half as tall and nearly as thick as a man, long debarked and burnished by the years, its length seasoned by tears and blood and weather, but oh what did it matter, he was strapped like a pig to a spit, but he didn't do it, he didn't go onto the Miller property, where the bull stood with its

Number nine, Man shall rule over all the animals of the earth.

head turned away, utterly still, as if sleeping on its feet the way a horse does, not moving an inch—not for Henry's creeping along the tall grass, not for his striking of the match—until the firecracker burst with a pop and a scream. Then the bull took one startled step forward and slumped stiffly to the ground, its chest seizing and its back legs twitching like electric wires, breath hissing out of its lungs like air escaping a tire.

John Henry was back, standing over him, casting him in shadow. He was broad and red to the coppery blondness of his son, but they were clearly of a kind, bound and separate as two pages in a book.

"I want you to listen to me well," he said, the tart tongue of a crop gathered up in a hand lightly freckled by middle age. "I have a duty toward you, just as you have a duty toward me."

"Father . . . ," low, imploring.

"No son of mine would ever lie to me." He set his feet apart. "I don't care, Henry, that you killed an animal today. An animal is just unthinking matter. I'm not sentimental about that. But you didn't just kill an animal, you destroyed another man's property. Bob Miller's family has lived on that farm for three generations. Do you think he values his land? Ask yourself if we value ours. If he places value on land that bears an animal as relatively worthless as beef cattle and milk cows, how much more then do we value the land we've stewarded twice as long? Our crop is our family. So when you behave in a manner that's beneath us, when you act the fool, then you shame a long line of men that is standing behind you, Henry, standing behind you watching you always." Then he said, "I can only hope you're listening to me. You have no idea what a man sacrifices for his son."

He reached down and tugged the shorts from the boy's hips, so they pooled in a khaki heap around his ankles. His white underpants were sweated through, and the crack of his bottom showed a dark line through the cotton.

"Today I'm not whipping my son, just an animal. Because that's how you've behaved."

Henry pressed his torn cheek to the pole, his eyes bugging behind the lids. But the blow did not come. His father, ever the attorney, asked, "Do you have anything to say in your own defense?"

THE SPORT OF KINGS

To this question, Henry craned his neck wildly over his shoulder, his eyes half-lidded against the coming blow, and cried,

Number ten, I've hated you since I was in my mother! Sic semper tyrannis! "I am not guilty!"

John Henry raised the crop and struck his son.

Far across the road, cattle moaned with longing for a night coming in fits and starts. The air was restless and the crickets thrummed. The hot, humid breath of August was lifting now from the ground, where it had boiled all day, rising to meet the cooler streams of air that hovered over it. Airs kissed and stratified, whitening and thinning as the sun slipped its moorings and sank to the bank of the earth. Its center was as orange as its umbral rim was black. The sky grew redder and redder as the sun turned an earthier orange and less brilliant. Above it, purling clouds showed terraced bands of dark against crimson, and the rungs spanned the breadth of the sky. They stacked one upon the next on and on above the sun until the highest bands stretched into interminable shadow, darkening as they reached the top of the bow of the sky, then drifting edgeless into the risen evening. Blackish blue emerged from the east and stretched over the house like an enormous wing extended in nightlong flight. But day was not done, it shook out its last rays, and as low clouds skimmed before the spent sun, the roaming, liberal light was shadowed and then returned like a lamp dampered and promptly relit. The westernmost rooms of the house registered this call and response—walls now flush with color, now dimmed, now returned to red, the orange overlaid with gray, molten color penetrating the sheers and staining the interiors. Walnut moldings and finials and frames were all cherry-lit like blown glass. Now there was a slight breeze, the curtains moved, the sun sank to a sliver, and in the last light bats swarmed the eaves, fleet and barely weighted and screeching smally. Somewhere, an animal called for its mate. A scale tipped. Then it was dark.

The boy lay on his stomach in his bed. He wasn't sure if he'd been sleeping or not. The light no longer played against the thin film of his eyelids, and his mother had returned. When she tugged the lamp cord, the room flooded with warm light. Henry made a small petulant sound, turning his face to the black window. When she didn't reach out to him, he turned back to see a slender finger wagging in gentle reprimand. His mother wore a pale dressing gown belted tight under her small breasts, and the curls on her blonde head had retired to limp strands in the heat.

Henry only eyed her sullenly.

Inclining her head to one side and staring intently with wide dark brown eyes, she raised her hands palms up at her shoulders.

"I don't know," Henry mumbled.

She bent further to see his mouth. Her brows drew in, folding the pale skin between them, her gaze swallowing him.

Talk, she signed.

No talk, he signed back with the hand that lay curled by his chin, the gestures terse and incomplete, more like flicking than signing.

She scooted forward off the chair and lay down on her side, a sylph, so he had to hold himself back from falling into her. He found the scent of faded perfume and talcum powder and something on her breath he could not identify, but it was not unpleasant, like graham crackers or creamed coffee. She touched the nape of his neck and the top of his back, but not lower, where crisscrossing wales had risen along his waist and lower still, where split raw flesh like a red rope followed the crack of his bottom.

You could have died, she signed with a sad and clownish face, then made her hands flip and die on the mattress.

He shrugged, staring resolutely at the mattress, refusing her. The silk of her dressing gown rippled and washed as she breathed her loud, awkward breaths, the material falling like water from her crested hip to a pool on her inner thigh.

You don't care about me, she signed, and fingered the track of an invisible tear from the inside corner of her eye to her lip.

He shrugged. "Father says I talk too much."

She shook her head against the mattress, a pin curl bobbling loose across her penciled brow.

"He says my mouth is my Achilles heel."

Am I not pretty enough to talk to? she signed, her eyes sparkling, her lip thumbed out.

"Talk with Father if you want to talk," he whined, and his aim was true. Her face evened slightly of expression, a white cloth ironed. But when

Henry saw the sudden stony and monkish reserve that marred her face, he conceded. His father had only learned the simplest signs.

He signed, *Okay.*

She brightened, but before a word was shaped by her hands, he began to cry raggedly. "It hurts."

Nodding, one toe whispering in nylon over his instep, her hand caressing the air above the broken and welted skin, where each thewing lash had landed. The whole of his body was concentrated in the concave of his back and between the cheeks of his bottom, where the painful lines his father had drawn all swelled together in a hot rosette. The pain rose and fell in a syncopation against his breath and the regular beat of his blood. He would not be able to shit without pain for two months.

"He hurt me," he cried softly. His mother scooted against him now, all silk to his pain. She kissed him on the nose.

Darling boy, she signed, *Daddy didn't mean to hurt you.*

"I hate him," he said, tears flooding his eyes.

She pursed her lips. She signed, *Blood waters the vine.*

"When I have children, I'll never be mean to them," he spat. "Never." But when he tried to imagine his children, his only reference was himself. There would simply be more of him, and then he would assume his position in the line his father spoke of, that concatenation formed in the begotten past, one that wouldn't end with him. It.

He wanted to think about It, but he was so tired and the aspirin was working, and his mind kept slewing free, then knocking to rights again with a jolt, and always his mother was there, gazing on him with eyes as deep and dark as mouths. He drifted and sensed her gentle touch on the lines and curves of his face—the ridge brow that would soon emerge from its soft recess, the jaw that would widen like his father's under fine cheekbones, a proud nose, all markers of those men residing in him, forming rings in his bones, rings in the family tree: John Henry by Jacob Ellison Forge out of Emmylade Sturgiss, and Jacob by Moses Cooper Forge out of Florence Elizabeth Hardin, and Moses by William Iver Forge out of Clara Hix Southers, and William by Richmond Cooper Forge out of Florence Beatrice Todd, and Richmond by Edward Cooper Forge out of Lessandra Dear Dixon, and Edward by Samuel Henry Forge out of Susanna Lewellyn Mason, and it was Samuel Forge who had come through the Gap in the old time in the old language:

He was raised up on the graded slopes of Virginia, where the Forge clan had resided a hundred years on a piedmont tobacco farm, far east of the mysterious, canopied wildernesses. But the Old Dominion was too small, too tame for a man like Samuel Forge, and Virginia was fighting for a freedom already hemmed and hedgerowed, so he thought his hands empty despite his wealth, and his restless eye turned to the wooded West. He set out for that expanse, leaving behind for now the woman who had borne his son, Edward, taking with him only a Narragansett Pacer he had raised from a colt and a bondsman he had bought for $350 on Richmond's Wall Street, younger than himself but stronger, fine-speaking, and useful. The black rode a stock roan with feathering over its thick draft pasterns and followed behind, his flintlock rifle strapped along his leftside flap. They crossed the bucolic piedmont, heading west along well-worn roads, over the first blue ridges that wrinkled and buckled up from the rocky flats, until the wide roads narrowed and sparsed to a trace like a roughspun thread through the wilds. The cultivated world of Virginia dimmed to a hum, then fell silent, replaced by the ungoverned noise of hardwood forest. Beyond those first beckoning ridges with their white mist over black deciduous interiors was the promise of infinite land. Forge and his slave both settled into their saddles and checked their rifles. Beyond the last fort they encountered a few starveacre farms with straggling corn patches and children outfitted in woolen rags like worn poppets with yarn hair, unschooled heads atop churchless bodies. A half day beyond these, they encountered a pack of dogs run off from slaughtered families in distant cabins, the dogs now roaming the trace as the bison once had, shaggy and grinning. An acrid sliver of cooking smoke here or there. The sound of chopping wood far beyond the steep escarpments of trees and rocky soil. One day they rode beneath a parrot escaped from its filigreed past, perched now on a chestnut limb, counting one, two, three. Then nothing, nothing but an ever-narrowing passageway through interminable wilderness. They rode on, the black behind the white, neither speaking. The road grew rough as it went sidewinding up the ridges of rock, wet with lichen and moss, and down into notches narrow and dank as graves, the wood and many generations of leaves rotting there as midden. They rode on. Upon besting the highest ridges, the great dissected plateau extended before them, long ridges baring strata of the earth, endless green and blue and gray under the augmenting sky. When the valleys sometimes widened for rills and rivers, the land blossomed bright in sunlight and thronged with birds. There the men would rest and water the horses and then ford the rivers, the last ferry having been many waterways ago.

They took to sleeping on opposite sides of the same tree, their backs to the bark, half-awake even in their deepest slumber. The slave spared one eye for Cherokee and Forge an eye for Shawnee. And every morning they resumed their westward trek, sometimes leading the horses along by their bridles, sometimes mounted and poured flat over the saddles to evade the low raftery of trees. They climbed and weaved and scrambled and hacked, their senses alert for natives. When they had struggled their way through the worst of the trace and were within hope of the valley called Powell's, a man without a horse came staggering out of a crook in the path, and they stood their own horses in amazement as the man took no notice of them at all, but walked past with a torn burlap satchel and a dressing knife, staring straight ahead with wild eyes and murmuring child's talk as he went. Forge tightened the grip on his rifle and spurred on, but the bondsman turned and watched until the man was out of sight, and a long time after.

They came to the Gap in the afternoon, easily traversing the six level miles before it and watching the vast pinnacle loom to their right, the shallower ridge to the left and the low curtsy between. They found a stream and a cave in that open land, and they passed as quickly as possible, and though they did not see any natives, the natives saw them. They rode through the saddle passage and into the hot and humid hills that redoubled their pleating on the far side, so the trail rose and fell with maddening redundancy with no reprieve for days, and their fear was like pain. A horse was snakebit while foraging, and they bled the horse and waited three long days until he finally took the bit again. Then they continued and the next day found a scalped dog in a field of fiddle ferns, a hound. They buried it beneath a sepulchre of geodes and for another week saw no other signs of travelers, only bear, wolf, fox, and rabbit, and at night heard the womanly cries of wildcats.

Finally the land eased, calmed, and they walked in expansive sunlight through a glade. Approaching the crest of one of the last great hills, Forge stopped and gazed back over the fraught land they'd traveled, where in a year's time he would bring his belongings, his will the windlass by which

all the packhorses and the children and the slaves and the mules would
be hauled across the mountains. On this last big hill, Forge finally spied the
knobs that announced the end of the mountains, and they made for them.

Beyond the knobs, they discovered a transylvanic broadening of the
land, where it rolled out its high shale hills and sloped to a distant river
they could not see but expected. Forge stopped on this high meadow and
reached down, scraping the soil with his finger, his heart stalling at the
thin yellow soil reminiscent of clay. His slave said nothing; there was still a
ways to go before they reached their destination. Forge remounted and
slipped his feet into the irons that had borne him across two hundred miles
of agony, and shortly they arrived at the river that snaked three hundred
feet below its upper limestone cliffs. They wondered at the sheer drop and
then clambered down the palisades, the horses shying and sinking into
their quarters as the trail sank, the day and the heat fading. They passed the
exposed musculature of the plateau's rockbed, loose limestone shedding
where cleft plates had formed the canyon; the horses stumbled on these
shed innards as they walked the barely hewn path, blowing air and straining.
At the cool base of the canyon, they swam the green river and remounted
the ramparts on the far side. When they finally regained the summer day
far above the river, they had passed the last great impediment west of the
mountains, and their destination was closing. They were in Lexington by
nightfall of the next day.

But there was a bustling at this outpost and cabins with yards neatly
set, and women walked there in chattering pairs on land already parceled
and named, so spurred by dissatisfaction, Forge set out northeastward,
and they rode quickly on the level forest with its occasional meadows of
clover. They saw no one, though they followed a faint path broken largely
by hooves. Soon, the underbrush grew denser all around until they dismounted and were forced to reblaze the trail.

They crossed streams thick with fish and passed through groves of
maple and black ash and finally came to a river they had heard of, though they
veered south from the settlements there. They passed an outlying chim-
neyless cabin by a stream, where a man named Stoner offered them black
bread and cream, and then there was nothing more that spoke of enclosure
or obligation or entrapment or civilization. Forge's blood rose and in a few
hours' time, they came upon a gently wending stream that fed a long brake

of cane, ideal for battening cattle, with a broad swath of level land to the north. The two men rode east along the prattling tongue of the stream until it slipped deep beneath black lips to an aquifer mouth. In another half mile the even land sloped gradually down to another stream and rose again in the far distance. The men dismounted at the curb of this vast bowl. Their overrun horses stared straight ahead beside them, wasted, their eyes enormous in the shrunken frames of their heads.

Forge raised one hand to his sunburned brow and gazed out over the vast tract of land. Then he turned to the man beside him, nodding and smiling. "This is the land I've waited a lifetime to find," he said.

The slave, who was called Ben but named Dembe by a mother he could not remember, did not need to shield his eyes as he gazed out over the woodland with its streamlets and springs gushing lustily through the dark bedrock.

"A bit karsty," he said. "Perhaps we should turn back."

Forge threw back his head and laughed, then he bent at the waist and snared the lush rye grasses in his hands, reminded once again of why he had brought his favorite slave instead of one of his younger brothers—to properly scout a land only dreamed of, to protect Forge's life at the expense of his own, and to amuse him.

A rough, three-bayed cabin was erected next to the stream that came to be known as Forge Run. This remained the dwelling of Samuel Forge for seven years, then became a cabin for slaves when a team of English masons built a new stone house with two stories, as many staircases, gable-end chimneys, and paned windows. But this house shivered thirty years later when the earthquake made the pit silos collapse like old drifts, when Forge Run splashed out of its shallow banks, covering the corn and standing the startled cattle in six inches of slate water, so they bawled down in alarm at their vanished pasterns. When the water withdrew, the left side of the stone house had settled strangely with one shoulder slumped, and it was soon leveled, and the settler's cabin too. The new Forge home was built two hundred yards north of the stream, a house formed from thousands of pounds of red brick fired by slaves on the land, who packed clay and fired kilns for months. When it was complete, the new house was hardier than its stone predecessor, with a black tile roof and a protruding el porch on its southern side that gazed out over the fields and the creek. Its interior moldings were stained dark, the walls dun, scarlet, and robin's-egg blue with double-hung windows on all sides, and small ellipse fanlights along the eaves. The sun rose from across the bowl every morning and sparked its many windows, then peered down from high angles all afternoon, so that the house did not appear like a house at all but only a pitch stain on the green fields, and then in the evening, a wide, red, optimistic face. This house stood without complaint through the abandonment of corn for hemp, the building of stone fences by Irish masons, the arrival of neighboring families, the War when Morgan's men camped alongside the creek and requisitioned all the cattle and horses, then the eventual reintroduction of corn, the selling of many of the original three thousand acres, and the getting up and dying of seven generations. In this house, Henry Forge was born and raised.

The wheals on his back soon faded to a faintly risen road map of pink, then white, then disappeared altogether. He never once placed a foot in the Miller bull yard again, but settled his debt for the bull's life with a year of remunerative labor in the milking shed. He spent the crisp September mornings in the tie-stall barn, where the dung stench crowded out the clean air as smoke fills a burning room. God, he hated the cows with everything in him. He shuddered when he first gripped the swollen teats, extruding streams of warm milk that whined in the bottom of a tin bucket. He refused to rest his cheek on the hide of the cow as the farmer's three girls did while they milked, but craned his neck to the side to keep from brushing against the distressing mass of the animal. He endured this indignity every day.

On a September afternoon, when the calves' seventy days of nursing were through, it was finally time for weaning. The youngest Miller showed him how it was done—a girl of seven with violently red hair, a face mottled with freckles, and knees as fat as pickle jars. She stuck her little fingers into the mouth of a skinny black calf and looked up at Henry, her own mouth a small O of delight. "This is my favorite part," she said. "I wish I could stick my whole arm in there." She motioned with her free hand for him to do the same. His calf took his fingers into its urgent mouth, and Henry fought the desire to snatch his hand back, but let it stay, worked and pulled by that alien, suckling muscle.

"Pull them down," said the little girl, whose name was Ginnie. They

guided the calves to their waiting buckets until their hands and the calves'
mouths were bent into new milk. Then Henry slipped his fingers free,
and the calf sputtered the white milk, foaming it. This was repeated again
and again until the calves finally drank willingly from the bucket. Henry
wiped the slime and milk onto his jeans and stared at the foam-spattered
face of the calf. It was pathetic how the teatlorn creature so easily traded its
mother for a bucket.

"The only thing better than cows," sighed Ginnie, "is Corgis. The big
ones. With tails."

Henry just moved on to the next calf. The Holstein's baby black turned
a glossy red as a chilling evening light slanted into the crib, casting sudden,
severe black shadows across the barn floor. Late autumn brought these
shadows early now. The lemony light of summer was done, the fruits were
overripe or rotten, the leaves sapped to ocher. The corn stalks were knived
and soon, in the fields, the first frost would stiffen any forgotten remain-
ders, encasing them in ice. Staring at this light, Henry turned ten.

Ginnie said, "Henry, are you gonna get married?"

Henry made a face. "Someday, maybe, I don't know."

"Let's you and me get married!"

"You? No way, you're ugly."

"I am not!"

Henry sighed. "When I get married, I'm going to marry a beautiful
woman. My father says not to waste energy on ugly girls."

Great dollop tears formed in Ginnie's eyes. "A pretty girl won't be half
as fun as me!" she whined, but Henry was distracted by the blooms of his
breath in the suddenly icy barn air.

"When did it get so cold in here?" he said, jogging to the tack wall,
where his winter coat hung from a shaker peg. Through a keyhole knot in a
wallboard, he fisheyed the farm, which was now a snowglobe of white interrupted by the dark shape of the calves grown tall. Not so long ago, they had
gamboled alongside their mothers, but now stood in staggered, snowy
groups. As Henry watched, the dark of the winter wasteland crept over them.

Ginnie, busy shoveling manure in a crib, seemed to have forgiven him
and said, "Maybe you can stay late today, and we can play?" She eyed him
with sneaky delight. "We can pretend your farm is a wicked kingdom, and
you're a baby I save from the wicked king!"

"Ginnie, I'm too old to play." Henry yanked a woolen cap down over his copper hair and was moving out the barn door when something was hurled against the back of his jacket. A cow patty.

He said nothing, it would only encourage her.

"I'll throw more!" Ginnie cried with the passion of young love, which had grown positively anguished as winter warmed under a restless trade wind. When Henry didn't look back or even acknowledge her, she came charging out of the barn with more manure in her hands, but was stymied by snow melting into mud. Dirty remnants of winter remained draped like old, tattered white cloth all about the farm.

"Henry!" she called, as he was moving steadily down the lane peeling off his hat and coat and breaking a spring sweat. The air was raucous and thick with birdsong, the afternoon's light refracted through a veil of pollen. In the field to their left, which bordered the road, the male calves were now cattle, sturdy on their legs and fattening. They chewed their cud with the resignation of age.

Ginnie was panting along behind Henry. "You know what's next for them? You know what's next, Henry Forge?"

Henry risked a glance back and, grinning madly, Ginnie drew a finger across her throat, her eyes wide.

He rolled his eyes. "I have to go, Ginnie. I have lessons with Father in five minutes." The sun was blistering his already red neck.

"Well, my daddy says your daddy thinks his shit doesn't stink! And I think your lessons are boring and stupid!" Ginnie was falling behind now, attempting to scrape ashy, sun-dried manure from the instep of one boot. There were sweat beads on her upper lip, and she was flushed the color of a strawberry.

Henry turned on her. "Stupid? I study Latin and Greek, math, philosophy—"

"Yeah, I know," she said.

"Yeah, you don't even know what that is."

Henry Forge left Ginnie on the side of the road in defeat. She watched as a late Indian summer sun slung his shadow out before him, and just as his feet touched the far side of the country road that separated their farms as surely as any fence, just as Henry turned eleven, she cried out, "Henry Forge, don't you ever have any fun?"

John Henry: Close the door, son.

    Henry: Yes, sir.

John Henry: All the way.

    Henry: Yes, sir.

John Henry: Have you brought your translation?

    Henry: I have, but . . . I was trying to figure out a word, and I—

John Henry: A simple yes or no will suffice.

    Henry: Yes.

John Henry: Did you translate like an automaton, or did you actually use your mind?

    Henry: I did.

John Henry: You did what?

    Henry: I did use my mind.

John Henry: So, tell me—is man the measure of all things?

    Henry:

John Henry: Since you're never at a loss for words, I have to assume that you've come unprepared. Henry, these works can't be read like your modern claptrap. They're valuable only insofar as your mind is engaged. Novel thought to those who think there's value in a pretty phrase that means absolutely nothing. Can you define "aesthete"?

    Henry: No, sir.

John Henry: The fool who finds value in the merely pretty.

    Henry: Mother likes pretty things.

John Henry: I love your mother, but I've never met a truly educated woman. Now, I'll ask you one more time—is man the measure of all things?

    Henry: Socrates says no . . .

John Henry: And why is that?

    Henry: Because, the wind can't be cold and hot at the same time?

John Henry: Because it is impossible to determine anything absolutely based on one man's perceptions, which are subjective. Tell me more.

    Henry: And if some men are mad . . .

John Henry: If man was the measure of all things, then the perceptions of madmen would necessarily be true, and that's nonsense. So, tell me, what would result if an individual man thought he was the final arbiter of all things?

Henry: Chaos?

John Henry: Yes. Sanity begins with knowing your place.

Henry: But if people wrote all these books, then they made up all the ideas. Doesn't that make them the measure of everything they're saying they're not the measure of?

John Henry: Don't interrupt me, Henry. I swear, your mouth is a millstone around your neck.

Henry: That doesn't make sen—

John Henry: Stay on point!

Henry: Well, I like it when he says dreamers are the best kind of men.

John Henry: Why does that not surprise me? Henry, you spend too much time in your mind. Do you want to wallow in daydreams, or do you actually want to understand the order established by minds greater than your own?

Henry: But great men cut new paths. They think outside the box.

John Henry: No—great men pursue excellence, but the standards of excellence were established by those who came before them. You have no knowledge not granted to you by others. Henry, you're always hijacking a principled conversation with nonsense and daydreams, and it's a result of spending so much goddamned time with your mother. She coddles you too much.

Henry: I just want to know how to know.

John Henry: Then I'll share with you what my tutor would have said to me if I'd had the impertinence to pester him. Real knowledge begins with knowing your place in the world. Now, you are neither nigger, nor woman, nor stupid. You are a young man born into a very long, distinguished line. That confers responsibility, so stay focused on your learning. And as far as your imagination is concerned, it should be relegated to secondary status. You'll never have an original thought, never be great, never invent anything truly new, and this shouldn't bother you one bit. There's nothing new under the sun. You just need to know your place. It's unexciting, but the truth is often unexciting.

Henry: And what exactly is my place?

John Henry: Your place is as my son.

Henry: But . . . what if . . .

John Henry: Goddammit, Henry, don't be indirect.

Henry: But what if I have an opinion that's different from your opinion?

John Henry: Then we can't both be right, and one of us must be wrong. And who would that be?

Henry: Me?

John Henry: The first stage of wisdom.

Henry:

Two weeks later, his father taught him to drive.

They were running errands on an October afternoon strangely stagnant and thick under a slant sun the color of ripe tomatoes. By the time they reached the tracks by the Paris depot, their shirts were suckered to their backs, the black hood of the sedan turned into a boiling plate. The air was dusty with the scent of old leaves and the faint cloying scent of a decaying animal somewhere close by.

When his father killed the engine, Henry asked him a question that had been bothering him for a long while. "Father, what made you want to go into the legislature?"

John Henry considered the approach of the train before replying. "It was a natural progression," he said. "There are so few well-educated men, we're all but obligated to serve the public. The world is nearly overrun by idiots these days. There are more white niggers in this world than one can know what to do with."

"Are there any women in the legislature?"

John Henry scoffed. "A few. But the core of femininity is a softness of resolve and mind; reason is not their strong suit."

The train interrupted. Henry watched in silence as the gray and canary-yellow coal cars clacked by, coal heaped above the open tops of the cars, the black nubs glossy in the sunlight. The train, as it rolled against the rails, raised a great clanging noise and the slenderest breeze.

His voice loud against the clattering, John Henry said, "What you don't yet comprehend about women, Henry, is a great deal." He stared at the cars as they flipped past. "I wouldn't say that they're naturally intellectually inferior, as the Negroes are. They're not unintelligent. In fact, I've always found little girls to be as intelligent as little boys, perhaps even more so. But women live a life of the body. It chains them to material things—children and home—and prevents them from striving toward loftier pursuits."

"Well, I wouldn't want to be born a woman," Henry said.

His father just laughed, and for a moment, Henry found himself unwillingly laughing along. But he stopped suddenly, wary. He distrusted his father's laugh and its magnetic draw, how it always seemed to bubble up out of a secret his father possessed, one that might be at Henry's expense.

With a sudden cessation of noise, the train's caboose tailed into the trees, snaking into Fayette County, and John Henry said, "It's time you learned to drive."

"It's against the law," Henry objected. He was only thirteen.

"I trust I can keep you out of federal prison," John Henry said, his brow arched. "Filip wastes untold time and money chasing after your mother's every whim, and I can't be bothered to keep her entertained. I'm certainly not going to hire her a driver. No need when there's a young man in the house."

Nodding, Henry said, "Yes, sir."

"But don't ever touch the vehicle unless your mother asks you."

"Yes, sir."

The older man exited the automobile, stretched briefly with a growling sound of a bear come out of hibernation, and walked around to the passenger side.

With nerves wicking his mouth dry, Henry slid into his father's spot, perched on the front springs of the seat, gripping the wheel and toeing about beneath the dash with both feet.

"First, second, third, fourth," said John Henry, pointing. "Off the gas while on the clutch, shift, on the gas again. It's not difficult."

Henry grasped the stick.

"Depress the clutch, turn the ignition." He did this.

"Clutch down, first." He did this too.

"Gas, and slow off the clutch." The car moved forward on a halting stream of fuel as if it were shy, and they crossed the tracks with an uneven rattle.

"More gasoline."

Henry pressed, but the car emitted a wounded screech, then barked and quit. For a moment there was only quiet, but Henry could feel the temperature in the car rising, then his father snapped, "Henry—this isn't that difficult."

One more attempt, barely breathing as they crept haltingly down the road, closer to where the town evanesced house by house into the rural district.

"Faster." He pressed the gas and the engine sang. They drove for one mile, Henry barely blinking and his eyes stinging, accosted by the late sun.

"I'm considering taking you out of school," said John Henry suddenly.

"What!" He hazarded a glance at his father. "Why?"

"Because your school is mediocre. The students are mediocre." A curt wave of one hand, then John Henry crossed his arms over his chest. "And things are happening right now in the courts. There are changes in the air, changes I don't want you exposed to. I swear the Negroes seem intent on delivering themselves to hell." He passed a hand over his heavy brow. "These men who always seek to improve things rarely know much about human nature. One smart monkey can find his way out of the cage, but that doesn't make him any less a monkey. And, naturally, the other monkeys follow suit. They never realize until they leave the cage that they were warm and well fed in the cage."

Henry had no idea what his father was talking about. "You're not going to send me to school in Atlanta, are you?" he said, his stomach creeping up around his heart. He'd long dreaded the thought of boarding school, of separation from his mother for an excellence whose grammar he could not yet parse, that he was just beginning to speak.

John Henry said, "Your mother has never wanted that. And I've considered her request, because I pity her predicament. You'll be her only child, you know that. I've been considering a tutor instead."

"But you already tutor me."

"I'm not truly qualified. You're not a child anymore. Your mother can prepare a decent meal, but we have Maryleen because Lavinia isn't a cook. It's no different."

At the edge of a tobacco field the car stalled out, snapping them forward in their seats. John Henry sighed, but louder this time, and Henry flinched hard under the whip of judgment. God, how he hated his father, loved him, hated him—regardless, all the tangled roots of his inherited heart grew forever in the same direction: I am his.

The boy stuttered out into first again and the car juddered and spun its tires as it progressed. John Henry finally reached for the wheel, but Henry blurted out, "No, I've got it, I've got it!"

"*Facta non verba*," his father said, and the boy looked at him and thought—not for the first time—that his pronunciation was not all it could be. And then he stalled again.

"Pull over, Henry," said his father, and they switched places yet again. John Henry was releasing the parking brake when, suddenly, in a tone from which all irritation was wiped, he said, "All I really want is to be proud of you." Then, with uncharacteristic hesitation, as if testing the words on his tongue: "There's nothing more vulnerable than a man with everything to lose. Don't disappoint me."

A man reasons his way to irrational numbers. It was a strange paradox. Mother's beauty was never-ending, thus never-repeating, it went on and on and on, an irrationality. Her face was a beautiful math, a womanly number without equivalent fraction: the depth of her brown eyes, which were cavernous in her silence; the sublime distance between pupils, a neat third of the width from cheek to cheek; the plucked half-shell brows, each hair articulate and precise against pale, powdered skin, which was lineless; a nose subtly dished with a bridge as delicate as the handle on a teacup; the philtrum, just a gentle scoop over bowed lips the color of Easter silk, lips that even Plato would have kissed. Perfect.

But they couldn't speak, and the fact never failed to startle. Her physical debility was like a gash across a masterwork, never more plain than when she spoke with her hands, her face contorting with agonized efforts to make herself known—the brow reaching, the eyes bright as solariums, the lips wrenched up. Then her face embarrassed Henry; it became the hysterical face of an actor without any vanity and not the placid face one would want from a mother.

Mr. Osbourne.

He snapped alert from his daydream. "What, Mother?"

Drive me to Osbourne? She signed. *Maryleen made lunch for them.*

Dean Osbourne was their neighbor across the bowl, a short, black-haired man who'd long despaired of the farm he'd inherited, making day wages as a police officer until he became deputy sheriff, farming only at night and on weekends. But he'd been shot one year ago at the First County Bank, and just when the town was collecting half-dollars to pay for a mahogany casket and a flag, he'd rallied and survived. But he'd never gone back to his fields. Now there was talk of morphine and erratic behavior, and the seedman at the store said there'd been no winter order. Someone mentioned Thoroughbred horses.

It was a short drive down the frontage road to the lane that curved around the bowl to the Osbourne place. As Henry fanned his hands over the wheel and scanned the road, Lavinia sat easily beside him, her hands a gentle, quiet knot in her lap. Henry had barely enough time to feel familiar at the wheel before they were parked in front of the Italianate cottage, Lavinia slipping from the car, picnic basket in hand.

But her drop of the iron knocker drew no reply. Henry stepped around her and rapped up and down the door. After half a minute's pause, he turned the knob and pressed the old door as his mother bent behind him, so two light heads peered samely round the jamb. The house was cool in the shade of the porch balcony, the remnants of night still present in the day. But in the quiet, there was some vibration adrift. Lavinia felt it with the soles of her small feet.

She prodded Henry with one finger to his back.

"Mrs. Osbourne?" he called, all hesitation as he tiptoed into the room, his mother a brief shadow trailing behind him. A great thump distressed the floorboards of the upstairs and sent tiny tailings of dust spiraling down.

"Mrs. Osbourne!" he called louder now, but again no reply. His mother tugged at his shirt in inquiry, but Henry shrugged her off, pointing upward.

They had just reached the broad newel of the staircase when a voice barely muffled by its distance from the pair cried out, "Betsy! Betsy! Please, I'm fucking begging you— Fuck!" And then the voice unleashed a stream of obscenities that Lavinia could not hear, but which caused Henry's jaw to drop.

"Open this door, you fucking bitch!"

Henry grabbed at his mother's thinly veined arms, but she just patted his hand off her arm, smiling and climbing upward with her picnic basket before her.

At the end of the second-story hall, Mrs. Osbourne rested on a ladder-back chair in front of a closed door. She leaned forward with her elbows on her knees and both palms to her lined forehead. Behind the closed door, the voice of Mr. Osbourne rumbled forth, words distending into an agonized cry. When the body of the door rejolted against its jamb, Mrs. Osbourne reared up with a start and saw Henry's mother with her picnic basket. She stared open-mouthed for a moment, then she cried, "Oh, Lavinia, the boy!" and she rose with a start from the chair, flapping her hands like small, useless, exhausted wings. "My husband's coming down off the morphine—he made me lock him in that room and promise not to let him out until he's clean! Oh Lord, get the boy out of here!"

Lavinia only looked at her in alarm and confusion, but Henry was already backing up on his own, angling behind his mother like a much younger child.

"Oh, please!" Mrs. Osbourne cried, her voice almost overpowering her husband's agonized complaints. "It's not fit!"

Lavinia turned, bewildered.

Mr. Osbourne's in there—he pointed—*saying bad things*, then hollered, "I'm going, I'm going!" and all but threw himself down the stairs, leaping three at time, one finger to the balustrade. He raced straight to the kitchen in the back, where a rear door opened to the newly fallow fields. But when he reached the door, he lingered suddenly with his hand on the knob, his heart pounding like a burglar's, one ear cocked for Dean Osbourne screaming fuckfuckfuck as if it were the refrain to an obscene song. The raw, unleashed sound of it thrilled him. Then it occurred to him that Mrs. Osbourne would be waiting for the banging sound of his departure, so he yanked open the door and slammed it after him with a glass-rattling clap.

His mind was startled by the absence of tobacco. Without its leafy spread, the land seemed strangely naked, a shorn sheep, all sinew with the bones of its conformation laid bare. The nearest barn was emptied of tobacco, its doors flung wide to reveal an interior newly outfitted with windowed stalls, ones Henry knew were for horses. A paned cupola had been erected on the slant roof, the black boards all painted white with kelly trim. Beyond the barn stretched young green pasture grass carefully squared but not yet fenced, so it beckoned like a park lawn or a pleasure garden. He walked toward it.

Short, abrupt calls from the far side of the barn. Henry turned the corner and saw, situated out of view from the main house, a new round pen. Two men worked there, one standing outside the fence, a boot and both elbows resting on the planking, the other standing in the center, driving a rangy red horse in frantic circles round the pen with a rope line. The horse lurched and kicked, its eyes rolling like marbles in its head. It was oddly rigged in a harness of rope, the likes of which Henry had never seen. The constraint circled the neck, the girth, looped beneath the switching tail to circle the foreleg on one side, but it served no purpose that he could see, its remaining length looped and tethered to itself, draped along the shoulder. The horse charged around the pen regardless of its awkward corseting, fretting and stamping and blowing air, clearly terrified of the thin man who stood quietly in the center. Neither man saw the boy approach, but the horse did, one eyeball trained on him as it made a dust-raising round.

The man leaning on the fence caught the flash of eye and turned. He squinted without a hat, but the broad, overhanging brows made a hat almost unnecessary.

"We're working here, kid," the man said.

Henry made a backward motion, but kept one hand on the pine plank, nailed between two posts made from telephone poles. The man eyed him sideways but didn't shoo him off again.

"You ever seen a horse broke?" the man finally said after a minute of silence.

"No." Henry's eyes were pinned to the place where the horse ran, head low and ears flat, in the pen.

"Well, you got you a front row seat," the man said.

"What kind of horse is that?"

"That's a Thoroughbred—a filly. Mr. Osbourne nickel-and-dimed her off some lady what let her go to seed in a oat field. She ain't had no idea what this horse is worth. You're looking at the next Regret. Wait and see if she ain't. Look at them sticks."

Henry saw nothing like potential in the horse. The filly was immature, stringy, and loose-limbed, with parts that seemed hastily cobbled together. Her long, ungainly legs might have belonged to a moose rather than a horse. Her ears swiveled wildly on a head slightly large for her short, slender neck, which snaked now in a fearful, colicky gesture as she slowed and edged along a far portion of the fencing. Henry didn't know a horse could move its neck that way, as if it were a boneless thing.

The filly trained one moony eye on the man in the center of the pen. He took a single step forward, and she stopped the waving of her neck, blinking warily.

"Aw, see," said the man, "she's just showing out. She's fixing to quit here in a minute. Giving us the devil 'fore we set her straight. Oh, shit," he said, and ducked his head into his own neck as the filly charged the center man, her ears flat, her mouth snapping like a turtle's, neck extending straight out from her body. But the man lined her back to the edge of the pen, where she continued her fretful circling, and, beside Henry, the man laughed an uneasy laugh.

"She looks crazy," said Henry.

"We like to died loading her in the trailer."

"Maybe you can get your money back?"

"Naw, Duncan's the best. Tame a lion, that boy could. And that horse don't look like it, but she's coming around."

"You've been doing this all day?" Henry marveled.

"Shit, son," the man said. "The whole everloving week."

"So, this is how it's done . . . ," Henry wondered, shading his eyes with one hand to cut the midday sun.

"Nah, not hardly," said the man, brushing a bit of chaff from his lip. "Not if you're lucky. You raise 'em up right and gentle 'em, then you ain't got to do all this, but some skirt leaves 'em out in a field, and they ain't never been rubbed and rode, then you got to whip the devil out of 'em. And them's the worst," he said, pointing. "Ain't never seen a human hand. You whup 'em and saddle 'em, but you can't turn your back less they backslide and when they do that, they whup you heaven high and valley low. She's a nasty one, but I seen worse. I done worked the breeding shed up at Castleraine Farms and this stallion one time—a stallion is just bad as sin, you got to eyeball 'em every second you got 'em on a lead. This stallion was fixing to pop this mare and his handler—I knowed him two years 'fore this happened—his handler gone to push his shoulder to situate him, and the mare kicked out just a real little bit, so the stallion, he, uh, toppled out sort of, and lost his foot and fell out and, Lord, I ain't never seen a horse get so riled. And what he done, he turned and bitten the throat off that handler. Jack Houghton.

Never forget that name. He come from England, and they done return shipped him in two parts. Head and the rest of him. All was left of his neck was the spiny part, and that got bitten too."

The man touched his forehead briefly, and his face twisted. "Makes you appreciate beef," he said. "They don't make no trouble. The worst bull ain't nothing but a breeze next to a stallion."

Henry turned new eyes back to the harassed horse, where she stood in sudden, stark relief from her surroundings like a black horse in a snowy field. Her head was long and dished, so the nose tip rose with a pert slope to its bony protrusion, the nostrils stretching wide, cupping air. Her lips were risen off the broad, faintly humorous teeth, already browned at the dog-eared meeting of enamel at pink gums. The teeth clacked like rocks brought together when she snapped. Without realizing, Henry had leaned his head into the pen.

"Back up now," said the man beside him, pulling him bodily from the planks. The filly passed them, but some of her fire was banking, Henry could see that. Her head wagged, lower and lower, her tempo and temper flagging. Then she stopped entirely with just a faint weave in the line of her neck, as though she were a blade of grass moving slightly in the wind.

"Here she comes now," said the man. The man called Duncan approached the horse, his upper body angled slightly out as if listening to a distant sound the horse could not hear, all the while looping up his line. The animal feinted as if to skitter to the side, but remained where she was, blowing and chewing. Now the man unhooked the line and let it drop and untethered the other looped line from the horse's back, holding it in his hand.

"How come she's roped up like that?" said Henry.

"Shhh," said his companion, and held up a stubby finger for silence.

Duncan called out lowly without turning, "Floyd, I think we're ready for some more sacking." His voice was flat and barely inflected, not sliding up and down like Kentucky talk. Henry guessed he was from Iowa or Kansas or some other unlucky place without hills.

Floyd called out, "I believe so, yes."

Duncan remained for a moment at the horse's side, passing a slow and gentle hand along her quivering flanks and up her neck, charming her skin into stillness. Her breath came in short, wary bursts under his hand, but she stood planted. Then Duncan backed slowly to the middle of the pen, stooped, and brought up what looked like a drying line with dark laundry attached. The horse blinked quickly, and her tail snapped. Then Duncan lunged in, drawing taut her loose line in his right hand and sailing out the cloth line with the other, so the cotton rags snapped and fluttered like terrible black birds across her back, and she squealed and lunged forward, her ears plastered to her head and her eyes rolling. When she burst from her quarters, the man jerked her rigging and in a single motion her head was drawn savagely toward her tail, her right front leg was cinched to her surcingled belly, and she crashed all eight hundred pounds onto her rib cage in the dust, which plumed around her. She thrashed and cried and rolled away from the winging birds, then the man was there, snatching the fluttering cloths away and slacking her line, so she could rise to blow and clatter along the planks, her muscles leaping under her skin. But he stayed right with her, returning the furiously flapping line to her back, and she shot out again, an awful sound emerging from her mouth like the squeal from a tortured cat, a heart-shredding sound, but every present heart was pointed, an arrow toward its target. Henry could barely breathe as he watched the horse being chased and overpowered, forced into a submission it couldn't know was permanent. He watched as the filly was rigged tight and rolled to the ground again, where it suffered the birds again, only to jerkily rise, then fall again, and roll again, the man now risking his own limbs to pin hers down, overpowering her briefly before stepping off and allowing her to rise—shaking visibly—to her full height. She was sacked again and again and again until finally, when Duncan lashed her sweaty back, her will followed on her weariness, and she moaned pitifully through her downcast eyes and staggered forward a single step, but did not leap or lunge or fall. The sound she made was unmistakably broken; even Henry's virgin ears could hear that.

"Oh my God," Henry said, turning breathless to Floyd. "Does he ride her now? Can I ride her when he's done?"

The man turned to him with a bemused smile, his arms crossed over his chest. "How many years on you, son?"

"Sixteen," said Henry.

The man laughed. "She'd serve you spiral cut for Sunday supper."

"No, no, I can ride! I know how to ride!" He failed to mention he'd never ridden anything but the Walkers, who were gentle and placid as kine. "Please!" he said. "I'm begging you!"

"Naw, naw, naw," the man said, waving a dismissive hand at him. "Shit. You think you can ride *that*?"

"Fuck yes," he said, testing it out, and found it smarted his tongue only a little.

"Whoo!" The man laughed. "Don't let Duncan hear you talk like that. That man's a follower of Jesus Christ and then some."

"We're all Christians," said Henry, his eye swerving back to the horse, who stood breathing hard, finally allowing the breaker to stroke her, huge eyes cast groundward in search of a self spalled to bits on the round pen floor.

"Some of us is Christian like you's sixteen. Get on now, you got your show."

"No, really!"

"Get," said the man, tested.

"I'm Henry Forge," the boy said suddenly.

Another bemused glance. "Honey, I know it. You got the stamp of your daddy all over you. Now get."

"But—"

"Get now!" Floyd swung out loosely with feigned scorn at the boy, and Henry could do nothing but move off. The horse spared no eye for him as he retreated. He had never before felt so young or useless as he did in this moment, spurned from the Osbourne house, spurned from the events of the round pen. Why was the province of grown men such a secret place? Adults were always misreading his youth for an ignorance he only needed an opportunity to disprove. He glanced back at the horse, at her head hung low and her black mane fallen over her face, obscuring her bloodshot eyes. Floyd offered only the neglect of his back. Adults were nothing but school-yard bullies—they made you beg for small favors, his father most of all! It was only your mother who gave freely—gave her whole entire life to Henry Forge, Henry Forge, I am! He felt his strength rising. Why on earth shouldn't he ride a horse like that—or own a horse like that? He'd seen the ruling strength of the breaker's body, how dominant it was—a man like more than a man—and how quickly the larger, braver thing succumbed to the one who refused to alter his path, the one who offered no concessions.

A man and a horse were a perfect pair. Henry was nearly wild with excitement now, stalking around the shrubbery that bordered the house, kicking out at the grassed lawn in exuberant frustration, his mind in a tangle. Finally, he threw himself on the porch, looking out over the frontage road to the drab cattle farm on the other side, and waited there with hammering impatience for his mother, only occasionally hearing the sound of someone crying out and cursing somewhere in the house above him.

His first memory was of the last hand harvest. The men came from town during the first week of September, a dozen or more, the same who had been coming for years. They swarmed the acreage, hats tugged low, corn knives flashing like mirror shards. He'd been so young—he couldn't remember how young, but no longer in diapers—that he'd chased along after those men, finding himself at Filip's side as he waded into the forest of plants. Filip counted the corn hills as he walked, and the boy chimed beneath him onetwothreefourfivesixseveneight until they arrived at the center, where Filip gathered and tied four middle stalks to a coping vault. Then he stooped and bladed the surrounding stalks, circling and circling from one corn hill to its neighbor and leaning them on the foddershock. By the onset of noon, the shock looked like a fat teepee. Henry did his own work, sawing on a stalk with a butter knife, until Filip came and stood over the boy, casting him into a sudden shadow that stilled his play. Henry could smell the astringent odor of Filip's armpits as he bent and gripped the fibrous trunks, chopping and carrying them away, leaving the boy in a bald patch of sun.

Then Henry's mouth was dry, his knees shaky from the heat, his hands the color of worked leather. The day was flaming when he toddled back onto the shaggy lawn, where his red wagon stood, and also his mother, now carrying a pitcher of sweet tea with their cook, Maryleen, following behind with a tray of glasses, stepping over him. The men were trickling in from the foddershocks like red-faced insects, and soon his mother retreated toward the house and beckoned with her hand. Filip was always there, always there in every memory.

Come, she signed. *Come.*

Filip went. Henry would not go, asked or unasked, remembering this, forgetting that; memory is a combine cutting and mixing everything. He ran toward the men, handing one of them his red ball. The man turned and long-armed it into the corn, and Henry went bounding after it, disappearing into the standing plants. When he returned on this day or another, they were eating their lunch and drinking tea and smoking hand-rolled burley. Filip sat at some distance beneath a maple, a wet blue bandana over his eyes. Henry settled behind them and made cigarettes of grass.

"Twenty-four today I bet," one of the men said.

Another: "Think bigger, boys. I need the cash."

"Shit, son, you just lucky anybody lets you cut nowadays. How much you wanna bet this here's the last time? Nowadays . . . Look at this place, don't tell me he can't afford no picker. He ain't even got no tobacco patch. Rich men can afford to do things sideways."

"Him ain't got no stock neither."

A man said, "Y'all tell me this: You ever seen a man just grow corn and nothing else?"

"Onced or twiced."

"But what does he do with the blades?"

No one answered.

"What does he do with the cobs?"

"They are some horses in that black barn."

"And what about the nubbins?"

No one answered.

One whispered, "Well is he stupid or crazy . . . ?"

"If you're rich, you can afford to be both!" And there was uproarious laughter.

Henry was too young to feel a frisson of shame. Then the talk drifted; some of the men reclined on their backs and slept with their hats steepled atop their faces, so they wouldn't burn. Henry curled around his red ball and slept too. And when he awoke, his mother was carrying him into the house, and the men were scattered in the fields again, and Filip was somewhere else.

By the evening, half the corn plants had been stripped and in their place stood scores of ricks, funereal heaps that would remain for weeks in the sun until the ears and the blades cockled and paled. Henry played among the short stalks when the men went home, the sharp, severed plants scraping at his ankles and shins. He leaned hard against the lee sides of the foddershocks, where no one in the house would see him. Sometimes his mother paid him a nickel to gather the gleanings for a neighbor woman, so he would stuff the raspy blades in a woven basket. He discovered worms and crawling beetles in the dirt and killed them. He tucked a blade in his mouth like an old man with a pipe. And when he slept at night, he dreamed he was climbing the ricks, but in his dreams there was never any top to them, they went forever upward like a magical beanstalk that he climbed under the watchful eyes of that age-old line of men looking down at him, watching him always.

Then the season ended, and the bright roulette of the year spun, and the next fall the men did not come. Only Filip and his teenaged nephew and a shiny new cornpicker with a wagon attachment. The store-bought contraption lumbered across the acres, swallowing ears off the stalks, leaving them upright and stripped in the field. Henry loved the brontosaurus neck of the picker, how quickly it spat ears from its mechanical mouth into the rolling wagon. He wagged and skipped along the line where the grass met the field, dueling the machine as it cobbed two rows in a single run, until one day his father returned unexpectedly at the lunch hour and snatched him from the field's edge and thrashed him on the lawn and yelled at his mother. Later, when it was too painful to sit, Henry stood on his bedroom bay window seat, his hands frogged to the deadlight, watching the progress of the machine, wishing he could ride it like a metal horse. And he would have were it not for his father.

But this September, with the boy turned fourteen, the old picker was retired to its shed, and a new combine was driven through the streets of Paris. It came to devour the acres, threshing its way through their fields with a furious mouth and a fricative roar. Ruthless and fast, it snatched the stalks from the ground, mashing them. It would have handily outpaced the boy, but this year Henry didn't even think about racing it. He was seven days out from the Osbournes' farm and the spectacle of the broken filly. He stood pensive and alone with his back to the old cabins, where the picker was now abandoned, watching the combine as it routed the fields. The machine made quick, wasteless work of the corn and its speed was a marvel— he couldn't deny that. But he also couldn't care. Yes, he liked machines; in fact, he loved them. He was fascinated by the intestinal fittings of the tubes and fans beneath the hood of their sedan, how the bodies out of Detroit were yearly improved and refined. A short time ago he'd admired nothing better than the old picker he'd chased alongside. But he could see now that all these machines ran out of an obligation that was man-made; a thing without a will could run, but never race. Anyway, how much could you improve upon the combustion engine? It was—in some irreducible way— already the perfect fulfillment of its own potential, its invention and destiny the same damn thing.

Suspicion came to roost in his bones, and it tarnished everything. Here was the old dairy barn, its cribs retrofitted for the six Tennessee Walkers. Here were the slatted outdoor cribs, their sod floors still littered with last year's kernels. There was the all-purpose barn, where the tractor idled; and there, the old equipment shed in which he had played as a child, that dank, battened place, sieved of sun, where he had found his first toys: corn knives in rows and hand-turned wood boxes with winches that no longer cranked, bladed objects that had not bored or shaved or whittled for so long that the blades were now thick with a hide of rust, an old plow stretching in the shadows that a boy could only pretend to drive, a boy born too late under the sign of advancement.

But Henry was ready to put away childish things. The bright, shiny apple of his youth now had brown spots. He knew that any beautiful thing not used rightly in its time would rot to its core. Bite the apple, build a better garden. He seized upon this certainty, and he took it to his father.

John Henry stood alone on the side porch, sipping his bourbon from a crystal tumbler, the faint warblings of his record player in one ear, the cleanup clatter of Maryleen's kitchen in the other. Deep evening had draped itself across the burred fields and shrunk the day to downy mist. A full, unblinking moon rose up over the house as fresh night soaked into the grasses.

Slipping quietly, almost stealthily onto the porch, Henry cleared his throat. "Father, I wanted to talk to you. I've been thinking about the farm."

John Henry didn't turn. From the far side of the creek, he heard the whir of a baler working well past the supper hour, and occasionally, a snatch of swinging yellow lantern light shone through the Miller tree line, drawing his eye. It would be one of the Miller girls returning from milking.

"I've been thinking," Henry said again, "that—" but he swerved suddenly from his course and said instead, "How long have we grown corn here?"

His father spared a glance, his head notched to the side, but was slow to answer. "Ever since we arrived here," he finally said. "After the Revolution, any man who came to this region and planted a crop of corn became the owner of that land."

"And the corn was always for—"

John Henry held his tumbler aloft and pointed, the boy nodding. "Good bourbon. Good feed. In that order."

"I think," said Henry slowly, turning away slightly, gripping the porch banister and rocking as if he would almost launch himself rather than continue. "I think—"

"Don't be indirect, Henry."

"The farm will be mine someday."

John Henry nodded once, but his tongue withheld assent.

"I've been thinking maybe when I'm older I'll raise racehorses here instead of planting corn." His voice rose in spite of itself, taking a kind of flight in lieu of his body, attached as it was to the banister by white-knuckled fists, and he was looking up as if his words had been directed to the expansive ear of the sky instead of his father. John Henry didn't reply immediately, only looked at his son. Then he cleared his throat and with a voice low and pregnant with intent, like a man reading slowly from a family Bible, he said, "You are expressly forbidden to raise horses on this land."

Henry's head whipped round. "But—"

"You disappoint me, Henry," he said. "You don't speak up when you should, and you speak nonsense when you do. It makes me alarmed for the future."

Henry's eyes swam with instant, resentful tears.

His father shook his head. "I don't want to speak about this tonight," he said. "You know you can come to me whenever you have a real need, but you've interrupted my solitude, which I've earned, with what I frankly regard as an insult."

He held up his free hand when the boy objected with a sound. "You don't realize what the insult is, I recognize that. And I don't fault you for it." He laid a hand broad as a spade on Henry's shoulder, turned him, so they faced squarely. He patted or cuffed him twice on the bone of the shoulder.

"We'll talk soon. Good night," he said, and he pointed toward the side door.

Henry turned and, without saying a word, slunk to the door.

"Henry," his father said.

The boy turned.

"I said, good night."

"Good night, sir."

"He hates me," he whispered in the half dark, lying there with her original, originating face too close, so she could discern the words on his lips. "Why does he hate me?" Lavinia laid a cool, dry hand over his mouth, but he went on speaking around her fingers, while she shook her original, originating head, *no no no*. He snatched her hand from his mouth.

"Who did he want if not me? What is it that I'm not? He never listens to me, he ignores me, he acts like he's the king of everything!" Tears flooded him again, a young boy in an adolescent body. Still his mother didn't answer, only shook her head and wagged a reproving finger.

"Do *you* love me?" he said, and she kissed him on the lips, hard. Then his cheeks and the adjutment of his chin.

"Mother," he said, "what would you think if I raised horses here someday?"

She followed his lips and her face—watchful, elastic, overfull—suspended all hasty movement like a figure balancing. Her eyes quizzed him.

"I've seen something amazing!" he said. "Have you ever watched a horse being broken?"

She smiled a sorrowful smile and signed, *When I was a girl, I saw a horse killed in the street. A drunk man shot his horse in the belly. Then someone else came and shot it in the head. In front of me.*

"No, no," said Henry, impatient. "When we were at the Osbournes', I saw a horse being broken. Haven't you ever just known something? I *know* something."

A sad little smile emerged, and she took his face in both her hands. Her eyes said, *Tell me what you know.*

Behind the Forge house stood an apple orchard, planted a few hundred yards down the acreage in the direction of the bowl. It boasted a two-acre stand of Yates and Rome Beauty with a line of deep red Foxwhelp for cider making in the fall. The orchard was nothing but a headache for Maryleen one week of the year, usually October, but this time early November, because the apples had ripened later than expected. Now everyone was there in her kitchen—*everyone*: the boy; his mother, who had all the personality of a pillow; Filip, who was quiet, but mostly because he was drunk on white lightning, and everybody in Claysville knew it, because despite his haughty, stoic airs, he had a special talent for public intoxication at festivals and carnivals and whatnot. Apple-picking help even came from the field hands on occasion, because there were simply too many apples, more than any single person could manage. The garden Maryleen handled on her own; the green beans came in first and then tomatoes and the lettuce early and late, so the whole process was staggered, neatly terraced in time. She'd can what she could, freeze just a little in the icebox, but she never needed any help with that, and if she needed help, she wouldn't ask for it, she just stayed late. That way she didn't have to deal with people. That was her specialty, besides cooking—refusing to suffer fools, and most everybody was a fool in her book. When she'd first interviewed, she said with that gravelly voice of hers, "I don't do child rearing." She hadn't said, I ain't no Hattie McDaniel, you see two hundred pounds and a kerchief? She'd just kept that to herself and stuck to her intentions with the rigor of the devout. She only spoke to the child when he spoke to her, and she kept it to "yes" and "no" as often as not, and when nuance was called for, she said "Hmmmm" as if she were studying on it, which she wasn't; she was thinking, Get thee thither, fool. The tall-dark-and-silent Filip, who was supercilious as hell for no reason except he was a colored man with someone he could actually lord over, tried to impress upon her the importance of learning to talk to the lady of the house in signs, because that was the respectful, Christian thing to do, damaged as she was and all. Well, Maryleen wasn't about to do that, not today, not tomorrow, not ever. She could say yes and no with her hands, but she just begged off the rest. After all, didn't they train dogs with hand signals? Better to communicate with nobody at all than to have them flap their hands at you like you were a golden retriever. "Oh no, can't nobody teach me nothing," she'd mouthed like some simpleton to the blonde lady, who always looked at you like she was the doe and you were the oncoming headlights, but the truth was Maryleen wasn't here to talk to anyone. She wasn't here to child rear, or make nice with some white lady, or play the role of kitchen slave to the pink toes and the Filips of the world. She was here to cook. And she was exceptionally gifted at it.

She'd come up in Claysville, the colored enclave, or what was left of it. The place was sagging on its foundations by the end of the war, which was to be expected. She always said, "You let a bunch of colored men run a town where there's liquor to be had, and you might as well turn the keys over to the white folk." What they should have done, if anybody'd had an ounce of brains, would have been to kick the menfolk out—make them live in shacks on the outskirts of town, only allowed in to deliver food or for population replacement (a disgusting but occasionally necessary allowance)— and let Claysville be run by the ladies. Then, voilà! It would become the Brooklyn of Kentucky, Brooklyn being her only reference to a once-little town that had done something with itself, high blackness intact. Or something like that. Her own mother could have run an army if she hadn't been so tired when she came home from work every day. Too tired to be of any use as a mother. So Maryleen had taught herself to read. Well, a neighbor had taught her the letters and sounds, and then she'd figured out the rest. As a result, she'd always known she was smart. "Taught her own self to read," her mother had always told everyone they ran into, as if that was something to brag about. But it had been simple, really, looking at the shapes, sounding them out, fitting them together. It was this drive toward sequential thought that made her a natural at solving mysteries. She'd begun reading them in the library when she was eight years old, and she could honestly say she hadn't read one in ten years that she hadn't figured out by the hundredth page. She always harbored the secret desire to write them when she retired—except what colored woman ever really retired? Anyway, she knew she was gifted. Everyone had thought she'd go to one of the colored colleges in Atlanta or Washington, D.C., which was not something anyone in Bourbon County did, everyone being the child of a farm laborer and whatnot, and she had in fact applied, because, like a peacock, she had some colors to show, but she'd turned them down flat when she received her acceptances. Aside from the getting-in part, she had nothing to prove to anybody—or so she told herself—and, besides, she already knew what she wanted to do. She wanted to cook. She'd taken every Home Economics class available to her (when she wasn't reading her Shakespeare, her Dickens, her Dunbar and Hughes) and then her teacher, Miss Martin, had invited her home after school every day for two months to teach her more recipes and to talk to her, probably because she was a lonely woman getting on in years. Miss Martin had even taken her in for a whole summer when Maryleen's mother was staying nights at her employer's, because there was a child there that had cancer. It ended up dying in August, but Maryleen wasn't sorry about that, because she had spent the best summer of her life at Miss Martin's. She learned to make beef tenderloin with horseradish butter and fried chicken brined in Coke; also chicken divan, citrus Cornish hens, the best sweet pickle relish ever, chowchow, peach cobbler, derby pie, and bread pudding with whiskey sauce. It was during that baking and cooking, when Miss Martin's conversation dwindled from current events to gossip to occasional rumination to companionable silence, that Maryleen's mind became suddenly, startlingly free, and she realized it was here she could make her home, in this deep quiet, regardless of whether it was in some white folks' house or in her parents' home, where her father did nothing but read his Bible and ignore her, and her mother was sleeping every moment she wasn't working. Silence was freedom.

Which was why she hated this particular week of . . . involvement. There was the picking of the apples, which was hard physical work. Then there was the peeling and the piecrust making, the sorting, then the mashing in an enormous old sugar kettle that—she'd bet fifty dollars if anyone actually cared—probably dated from slavery days. Then the boiling of lids and jars, the canning, the sealing, then sauce making, cider making, which meant the addition of crab apples, which she was allergic to, so her eyes swelled up just from looking at them, and everyone said, "Oh, Maryleen, dear, have you been crying?" to which she yearned to reply, "Oh, Massah, yes, I's just cryin' thinkin' 'bout where I'm a go affa Emancipation—oh!" But tongues were for biting. You just did what you had to do to get them out of your hair, which was help them, which was what she was doing today.

They had spent the morning hours up and down like spiders on the ladders plucking Foxwhelp from the branches, so she would be able to start the cider in the morning. She had already gotten Filip to drive her to the A&P to purchase the sugar and nutmeg she'd ordered for the cider, and now they were trundling baskets from the orchard to the kitchen, and she was sweating so much that she couldn't stand the smell of herself. The day was unseasonably hot for November, a put-chipped-ice-in-your-tub-water kind of hot. And she was already irritated enough with the woman helping and Filip and the boy underfoot. If she'd had eight arms, she would have done the whole thing herself and let that be the end of it. But here she was with the white boy tagging after her—well, he wasn't a boy anymore, he was a teenager and not that far behind her in age, maybe five or six years. He was less talkative than he had been even just recently, but he still had plenty of irritating things to say, going on and on about the head of a horse, and wasn't it like the Sistine Chapel, just a marvel of architecture, and he was explaining in detail what the Chapel was (as if she didn't know!), and she was being very careful not to roll her eyes unless her back was to the boy—teenager. And there was his mother, picking apples in heels. Low heels, but heels. When Jesus comes back, everyone will be changed, that's what her father always said. He could not get his ass back here soon enough.

Somehow, during the heat and bustle of the day, she managed to shake them all. She'd gone round front to sit with a glass of tea and then, upon returning to the orchard, there'd been no one there at all, just empty ladders by the trees, staircases that went nowhere. She stood in the pleasing stillness for a moment, holding her empty glass, absorbing what was undeniably the amber beauty of the autumn day, and then, fatigued and finally easy because she was alone, she padded into the kitchen feeling almost pacified. There, dozens of apple baskets stunned the eye with their heaped red, and she heard herself sigh. Except she hadn't sighed. There was a snuffling sound. She thought the boy was crying in the pantry, because he liked to hide there when he was upset, and she was always the one to find him, because she was always the one in the kitchen, though of course she never comforted him, just took him firmly by the elbow and delivered him to his empty-headed mother. Maryleen took a single step toward the pantry, which led off from the kitchen by the stove, and she knew, suddenly, exactly what she would find, because she sensed things, because her mind had been prepared by many novels that taught her everything she needed to know about the human sex impulse (a thing she wouldn't learn from life, because she found men repugnant), and then there they were, Filip and the lady of the house, clutching at each other, the woman making hideous throat sounds against his mouth, probably because she was deaf—God, please don't let that be a normal kissing sound—and with the negative of their black and white scorching her eyes, she fled from the kitchen on the balls of her feet, her white tennis shoes making nary a squeak, her hand smacked over her mouth. She fled around the side of the house, a bright red blooming through the smooth darkness of her cheeks, and, absurdly, in a panic, she crawled between a juniper bush and the side of the old house and sank down on her haunches there, hidden from sight. She breathed raggedly into her palm, leaning back against the bare bricks, her eyes wide. There she remained until her breathing returned to almost normal, though now her fury was risen like a fire that rages once the winds calm. When her legs had all but fallen asleep, she heard the boy walk by talking to himself, and then she could no longer stand the tingling in her legs; she crept out from the bushes, feeling absurd and looking around. There was no one to be seen. She coughed loudly as if in a fit, walking around to the kitchen door. She swooped up an empty apple basket in her hands and said "Lord!" loudly, for no discernible reason. Then she went on into the kitchen, allowing the door to clatter terribly behind her. No one was there. With nothing less than absolute fear, she walked into the pantry, but it was empty too, and she sagged against the wooden shelving closest to her, then reached out and touched the wavy glass of a bell jar, angrily mouthing her thoughts. She didn't know how long she stood there before she heard the sounds of his feet, and she knew they were his because she'd memorized the family's footfalls, the better to avoid them. She flung herself into the doorway of the pantry, her hands clutching the doorjamb on both sides. Her eyes were wide, sloe-deep with fury. Filip started when he saw her, when he saw her face.

"Get in here!" she said, her voice brooking no alternative.

Whether he was startled by her tone, or by the strange fact of youth wrangling age without reserve, he simply did as he was told and stood before her there in the pantry, looking down curiously with that diffident blankness she knew he'd earned by right of his skin, but which she had no sympathy for. Not today.

She raised a straight, slender finger right up to his face. "You idiot!" she hissed.

There was no change in his face, except his eyes narrowed almost imperceptibly, then he made a move to go, so she reached out and grasped up his shirtfront in her fist to pull him back around. Her grip was so hard it threatened the hold of the seams.

"Are you crazy?" she whispered, but to her own ears it sounded like hollering. "You know where you're going to end up? Nigger, they're going to hang you from a tree!"

He refused to answer, refused by turning again to leave, but Maryleen reached up with her free hand, and with a feeling of something near glee, which she would allow herself to acknowledge only later, she slapped him hard across the face.

He just stared at her in wordless shock while she said, "Have you lost your damn mind? Stop this madness! Don't touch her again!"

And then, like an actor showing up late for his cue, the boy was in the kitchen, just standing there slack-armed between the butcher block and the sink, looking up into their faces with his mouth slightly ajar. Maryleen let loose Filip's shirt, and the man was gone in an instant, shouldering past the boy, who stepped aside to let him go, all the while continuing to look up into Maryleen's flushed face. He said, "I just wondered where everyone went."

"We've been right here," she said smartly, moving past him into the kitchen, so that she could reorder her expression without his eyes on her. "Right here the whole time."

The boy turned slowly on his heels to watch her, but he didn't follow. His face was soft, just the faint beginnings of an unreadable expression perched there.

"Where's Mother?" he said slowly.

"How would I know?" Maryleen said gruffly with her back still turned.

"What were you and Filip arguing about?"

"Folks argue," she said sharply. "It's no concern of yours."

"But—"

She turned quickly then, trying to project more passion and less fear than she felt. Her eyes were wide. "He said something nasty about my mother, all right? And I don't care to talk about it anymore!"

Henry said nothing in response to this, only reared back slightly with distaste or wariness, and Maryleen made a quiet drama of calming herself for his benefit, but she could have cried with relief when he finally walked haltingly, sullenly to the kitchen door that led outside. He stood there on the step for a long moment with his hands in his pockets, surveying the orchard, which was quiet now, deserted, and full of ragged shadows. Then he walked out onto the grass lit yellow with the fading afternoon, and he turned suddenly. Maryleen, who'd been eyeing him like a hawk from the kitchen window, thrust her hands under the faucet and pretended to wash, but from the side of her eyes, she watched as Henry cast a wary glance back over the house, looking it up and down. And though she didn't believe in God at all, and certainly not in some white man in the sky who'd sanctioned everything evil in this world, she prayed.

Church: the father, the son, the holy ghost, and his mother—his own original, originating Lavinia!—who always fanned Henry's heavy head when he nodded off, enveloping him in a rosed perfume and the unnamed scent of her person. There was a change in her son, she eyed him now with the wariness of a doe that senses the hunter is afoot. He didn't lean into her on the pew anymore, didn't doze like a child against her shoulder; he no longer smiled.

Dark dissatisfaction ran through him like a coal seam. He no longer cared for the old, unsatisfying stories, the Bible just a crass country cousin to the myths and nothing more. He counted the commandments: Honor thy mother and thy father. Really? Why? So you could climb some rickety ladder to heaven? When he sat in those worn pews and tried to imagine God's heaven, all he could conjure was a glistering expanse of nothingness. Roads of gold stretched without event farther than imagination, farther than forever, until his hope of heaven was a distress, and his heart flagged in his chest. Henry knew you had to make your own heaven—a place where, when your mother said she loved you above all others, it meant that she loved you more than a lover, more than God. He was newly sick to his stomach. Was church the wrong place to pray for the death of a man?

The ride back to Forge Run was an exercise in strained silence, his father concentrating on the road, Henry turned mulishly to the passing fields. The theater of razed greenery was fading before their eyes under the blue autumn sky, death hatching a mottled dun on the withering shocks. Their dying bored him to death. Easy come, easy go. His eyes slashed the back of his father's head, and his tongue felt perverse. Loose. He could not latch it to his better sense, which was silence. He said, "I can't stand to listen to all that preaching about rules." His voice felt like breaking something.

There was no immediate response. His father seemed determined to teach him the rudest of life lessons: there is nothing worse than being ignored.

"I'm tired of rules for no reasons." This time his belligerence was barely contained.

Without turning his head, John Henry said, "That you don't understand the reason for a rule is no indication of its absence."

Henry sulked, his shoulders crouching down around his spine. Then he reached forward suddenly and pressed on his mother's shoulder until she turned.

"Do you believe God answers prayers?"

She raised her brows, her pretty mouth puckered, and they both inclined their heads in mutual misunderstanding like confused dancers curtsying.

"Yes or no?" he said, impatient.

"Leave your mother be," said John Henry, but the boy was staring at his mother angrily and frowning.

Do you understand me? he signed.

She nodded.

Do you understand the preacher? he signed with terse, pithy gestures.

She smiled a smile like an apology.

"You mean you don't understand him?" He said this out loud.

She shrugged.

"Father!" he cried accusingly. "She doesn't even understand what the preacher's saying! I always thought she was reading his lips!"

John Henry said nothing.

"Then why even bother going to church?" he spat, but his mother was swiveling away from him to face forward. He tapped her on her shoulder, hard, and he said, "Why even go, then?" And then she turned and brushed at his hand as if it were a fly and not her own son, and he had never seen her do that. He sat back in surprise.

"Be quiet, Henry," said his father, one slate eye to the rearview mirror.

Henry seethed, clenched his jaw, and locked eyes with John Henry. His mother ignored them both and gazed out her window, refusing them. Henry fairly boiled with irritation all the way home, but when they reached the house, John Henry didn't cut the purring motor as expected, or pull alongside the house. Instead, he idled on the circular drive that traced the front of the estate. He gestured to his wife to go on in without them, so she slid from her seat and stood awkwardly on the drive. Henry refused to look at her, only assumed her place slump-shouldered, and John Henry eased down the lane again. No one looked back to see Lavinia standing still where she had been, a solitary figure with a bright yellow clutch tight in her hands, her face cast in shadow by her half veil.

Henry wanted to ask where they were going, but he refused to speak, so they drove in silence, two men hard and unbending with thirty-five years between them. Henry wrapped his arms around himself, though it was warm enough in the car, closing his eyes and feigning disinterest. When he opened them, he didn't know where they were and recognized none of the farms on either side of the road.

He finally buckled. "Where are we going?"

"I want to show you something," said John Henry, "because of your recent concerns."

"About what?" In the ensuing silence, his regret was instant. His father was always biding his time, withholding answers like scraps from a bitch.

When they turned east onto a new gravel road, John Henry slacked his speed and coasted to the top of a gradual incline, where they attained a broad view of the green, rolling hills. They parked on the side of the road and John Henry pointed, but it was not necessary, because there was nothing else to see but the farm.

The property was situated directly before them, a vast spread of impossibly verdant green that rolled like ocean swells, the bright fields curbed by virgin white plank fencing. The scattered barns and outbuildings were dressed in white and green, all cupolaed and topped by striding iron horses not yet gone to verdigris in the weather. The vanes wheeled and spun in a high wind that seemed to come from all directions at once. The barns were pristine, no dirt or manure to mar their snowy sides, no stray chaff or markings on the sun-sparked fan windows. Brick walks paved paths from building to building, and men led horses into paddocks and out of barns, and the horses were dark and leggy. North of the barns, far beyond the horses, the main house was an astonishment: Ionic-columned and endlessly gabled, shingled in a gray almost white, and built to four towering stories, from which it gazed down on the adventure of its own beauty. The acreage stretched beyond sight in all directions but one, and there a threadbare to-bacco barn stood beyond the last line of fencing, a poor and classless inter-loper, only its upper half visible from its perch on a declivitous slope, where it leaned away from its new neighbors, boards rafting into disrepair, a sorry sight before stupendous wealth.

John Henry sat quietly, his heavy hands on the wheel. "Tell me what you see," he said.

Henry tore his eyes from the groomed land and looked at his father, weighing the truth against the trap he sensed there. "A horse farm," he said cautiously, reluctantly, the words drawn out of him by sheer paternal force.

John Henry's lips pinched into a hard smile. "Spoken like a child with a child's understanding. Henry, I intend to have this conversation with you only once, and then the subject will be closed. Let me tell you what a grown man, a man of discernment, sees. What looks like a horse farm is really a cheap attempt at dignity. All these pretty things before you amount to a heap of goddamn rhinestones. Caveat emptor: significance is not for sale. Dignity can't be purchased, Henry, least of all by these latecomers, these . . . these outsiders, who dress up their addictions in Sunday clothes and Derby hats. People call it a sport, but I'll tell you this: this so-called sport is driven by compulsion, and weak men love nothing more than to abandon them-selves to their compulsions."

He turned to his son now, something raw in his eyes, though his voice remained low and controlled. "I saw that in the war," he said. "And I be-lieve you've seen it in our neighbor, Mr. Osbourne, who's an embarrassment as far as I'm concerned. The man knows nothing about animal husbandry, nothing about the proper raising of horses, and his Wild West simpletons know even less. A gunshot wound, however impressively heroic it may ap-pear to you, is merely the kind of excuse a weak man seizes upon to wriggle his way out of his real responsibilities. The very definition of a white god-damned nigger."

He considered for a moment. "Henry, the education I'm purchasing for

you is to keep you on the established path. Do you understand me? This . . ."
He spread a hand forward toward the fields like an indignant blossom, his
palm a ruddy ocelle, his fingers hard petals. "This is nothing but a rich
man's game, where he bets his better self and loses."

"But *we're* rich," said Henry.

"There are two different kinds of rich, Henry. Our family name depends on your ability to distinguish between the two."

Henry did not respond immediately, but stared ahead at the sweep of
this farm, its perfectly painted buildings shining like white knights standing guard over an emerald expanse. His one ear was trained to his father, but
the other extended itself in the direction of the fields and whatever sounds
might be rising from them, which were none. Nature was manicured into silence. The horses moved slowly in that distant silence as if underwater.

Again, his father pointed out over the wheel. "Look how they're trying
to outshine every modest tradition that the first families established here
two hundred years ago. This is just ostentation. Does your mother need to
dress like a common prostitute to prove her value?"

Henry looked down, startled.

"And look at this one here."

Henry turned to watch the slow progress of a black man stooped over
his mower as he traced the outer edge of the fencing. His face was turned
down against the midmost glare of the sun. He moved as if burdened by an
unearthly fatigue.

"Watch how he slouches around without any dignity whatsoever. Born
colored but made a nigger by being caught up in all this—and he knows it.
He's panning for fool's gold, and it demoralizes him. The black race has
always depended upon our guidance to steward them into lives worth leading. A colored man uses his place of employment as a school to learn the best
of what white society can offer. It's the only place he can hope to better himself, regardless of what the restless voices may shout from time to time. The
irony of Negro intelligence is that it makes them aware of the poverty of their
own intellect. The only proper response to white influence is humility. And
the only right schooling is correction. To whatever degree is necessary."

"But it doesn't have to be as fancy as all this," said Henry. "Mr.
Osbourne just—"

"To condescend to any of this would be to insult your family."

Henry's eyes escaped his father's and returned to the man at his mower. The boy's heart rebelled, but there was a kind of plain disregard in the man's body; he saw that, and it disappointed him.

"There's a long line behind you, Henry."

"I know," he whispered, his mouth and eyes appearing downcast, but they were only distracted by his warring selves.

"Look at me, Henry, when I'm speaking to you."

He looked at his father.

"You need to think like a man, not a child. There's a sore temptation upon youth to discard with tradition, but tradition is learning collected. You're a fool if you forget that and are forced to relearn what so many men before you have already learned. You owe obedience to them and you owe obedience to me, just as I owe it to them, and I owe it to my father, in greater degree than my brother because I am the eldest. All roads have led to you, Henry, and I won't have you throw everything away for a heap of rhinestones. I'm a planter's son, and you're a planter's son. There is no need for improvement, Henry, only adherence to a line that has never altered, because it's never proven unsound. Have I made myself clear?"

"Yes, sir," Henry said thinly.

His father narrowed his eyes. "Say it."

"Say what?"

"Say right now whatever it is you want to say. This is the one and only time we're going to have this conversation."

"Well . . . I . . . ," Henry skated.

"Don't flirt with your words."

"What if," Henry rushed, "what if your father had asked you to marry a different woman?"

John Henry reared his head back slightly, but he didn't hesitate. He saw clear through his boy. "I would have married her," he said, "just as he wanted me to."

"But—"

"I would have married her," he repeated firmly. "But I was smart enough to choose a woman of whom I knew he would approve. She came from good stock, she was beautiful and—"

"Never talked too much," said Henry.

John Henry paused, his shrewd eyes gathering up the meaning in

Henry's face, but then he smiled slowly as if they were sharing the joke. His shoulders eased in his suit jacket. He brought his hands together now, so his fingertips touched. "I told your mother I'd be taking you to dinner this afternoon to a restaurant where I take my clients. They don't normally admit children, but I spoke with them earlier and made an arrangement. Would that be to your liking?"

Henry nodded straight-faced and without speaking, his head bobbing in a mime of obligation. But then he pressed himself back into his seat and tasted the word "children" in his mouth as if it were something too vile to swallow. John Henry restarted the sedan, and Henry didn't turn his head to the left or the right but watched the farm pass from the corner of his eye, so it washed by like a grassy stream through which horses ran.

In the house, Lavinia waited, unable to step away from the window until she saw the sedan pull up the long drive in the interminable stretch between sundown and darkness. Her nails were bitten to the quick. She assumed her old, reliable smile and stretched out her arms when her son walked through the kitchen door. But when she stepped to him, he pushed her arm away from him with startling force and charged up the back staircase, so she felt the vibrations on the steps like hammer blows. Whatever it was that he said in that moment with his back to her, she didn't hear.

In the wintertime, John Henry took his bourbon in the front parlor. He returned home from Paris by five thirty and dinner emerged from Maryleen's kitchen no later than six o'clock. Then, satisfied and regardless of desperate cold or wild easterly wind, he would stand for some time on the el porch, watch the snowy farm weather to gray as the stars spangled out of the black, feeling the night freezing and contracting around him. By the time Venus was setting in the south, he had returned to the parlor, where he could enjoy his solitude for another hour or so before bedtime. He unlaced and removed his black wing tips, placing them side by side on the Aubusson, and selected a seventy-eight for the player. Then he smoked a single Dominican cigar, which he removed from a carved bone box on the mantel, and sat on the davenport to read the *Lexington Leader*. He did this every winter evening without fail.

Henry knew the rule: no one disturbed his father. But this evening he fretted pensively along the front hall, end to end, his weight distressing the old heartwood planks until the record screeched suddenly and his father called out, "Stop that incessant pacing right now!"

Henry peered swiftly around the doorway to the parlor. His father stood there in his black socks in front of the davenport, the newspaper wrenched up in one hand.

"I knew it wasn't your mother. She never makes a sound," he said. To Henry's surprise, there was a hint of smile in his father's eyes.

"May I speak with you, Father?" Careful, discreet, he glanced both ways down the hall.

The smile vanished. "Henry, we will not be discussing horses again."

"No, sir, I know. It's not about that."

"Come in, then. I was meaning to speak with you anyway. I wanted to tell you that I found a tutor for you. He may not look like much, but his credentials are impeccable."

Henry stepped into the room and closed the door as his father regarded him. In his stocking feet, the man was six feet but had grown somewhat thicker through the waist and redder, like the sun was turning him, his freckles now mixed with age spots. The cupreous, stalwart bulk of him was lessened somehow, and his son arrived at the fact of it without sentimentality, with eagerness even.

John Henry said, "I'll give you five minutes, and then I would prefer to return to my reading." He seated himself again on the davenport with the paper, his eyes peering directly over it at his son. Waiting.

"Father," began Henry, and though his body urged him to sit in the wing chair opposite his father, he forced himself to sit cross-legged at his feet like a servant, beside his emptied and stinking shoes. Quietly, he said, "Father, why is everyone so upset?"

"Upset?" His father's large head reared back, consternation on his brow.

"I mean, in the news. There's so much happening. It seems like there's more unrest every day."

"Ah. Yes, that's right," John Henry said, nodding. "It's a distressing time in many ways, an embarrassing time. It will only get worse, I imagine. No one—absolutely no one—remembers their place anymore, and we will all pay the price for this kind of national amnesia."

Careful, steady, his face full of concern. "Is it true that they plan to desegregate the schools? What will happen after that?"

"After that?" his father said, and laughed. "After that, there will be social chaos and a breakdown in the educational system, and the Negro will be the first in line asking us to come back and fix it all. He never hesitates to implore others to come in and clean up the mess that results from his demands. His children, of course, will end up suffering the most. That's what always happens. He is simply incapable of predicting the consequences of his actions. There is potential in some of them, but as your grandfather used to say, the Negro is our Socratic shadow. I think the allusion is apt."

John Henry lowered his paper and folded it. "You see, in the end, Henry, de jure segregation may be stripped in some segments of the society—in fact, it appears almost inevitable now—but de facto divisions will always remain. Segregation is inherent, natural, and inevitable, no matter what the dreamers would like to think, no matter what the town of Berea would have us believe. Bring twenty white men and twenty colored into a new town and within a week, the white men will be successful landowners and the colored will be tenants. Good tenants, perhaps, but tenants nonetheless. Nothing wrong with that. The world always needs good tenants."

"I heard they'll send in the military to force the schools open if they have to."

John Henry shook his head. "If it actually comes to that, there will be decent, God-fearing citizens to block the way. Men like Byrd. There's certainly nothing to be afraid of."

Henry sat up straight, indignant. "Oh, I'm not afraid. Did you hear what Senator Darby—"

"Darby!" snorted John Henry. "Darby's a fool. He makes the Southerner appear the blubbering idiot, which is precisely what Northerners want in order to vilify the South—a vision of the South as mindless cracker. It makes them feel virtuous, when in fact they know absolutely nothing of the Southern situation. Darby!" He snorted again.

"The North—"

"The North is far more segregated than we could be, given the fact that half of our population is colored and we interact with one another constantly—daily. The Negro lives in our very homes and always has. The North can't even fathom. The North doesn't even know what a Negro is.

"You see, Henry, for them the race problem is either a mental abstraction or a romance. For us, as perhaps you're beginning to understand, it is a problem of practice and the everyday frustration of dealing with the colored appetite and intellect, which is entirely different from our own. It is quite easy to imagine the equality of all men when you sit on a high horse and don't have to walk among them in the fields. Indeed, everyone appears the same height from that view. But demount the horse and it soon becomes apparent that there are not merely masters and slaves by happenstance, or overseers and laborers by happenstance, but that these divisions are inherent and unavoidable. God save the mark—there were slaves in the Republic, and these liberals would imagine themselves greater minds!"

Now his voice was rising, the color bloomed in his cheeks. "The problem, Henry, as I have always seen it, is that the Negro is fundamentally a child, and children are incapable of understanding their own inferiority. Indeed, they generally err on the side of grandiose delusion. Mind you, the Negro is naturally playful, with a great capacity for joy, and I can appreciate that. But he's as self-pitying as he is playful, and like a child, he can despise you with as much passion in the evening as he loved and admired you with in the morning. Look at Filip—"

Henry leaned forward eagerly. "Yes, I wanted to talk to you about Filip."

"Filip is, I believe, only five years my junior, but has lived his life in a state of perpetual adolescence. You know him as a quiet and sober man, but that's only because I demand he stay sober in this house—and even then I sometimes have my doubts. My father always said Filip was weaned with a bottle of whiskey. You can't imagine the scrapes your grandfather saved him from time and time again, because the man has the aptitude of a child. He simply cannot fathom consequence. Each bottle of liquor is his first adventure in drinking. Each hangover a fresh surprise. Dealing with the man has been an uphill struggle, but my father was unreasonably fond of him, and my father was not a kind man. That says something, and so here he remains."

John Henry settled back into the curve of the davenport. With one hand, he held his ankle where it rested on the opposite knee. He looked over Henry's head. With his other hand, he rotated his tumbler.

"I once heard a Northerner refer to the South as 'that perplexing place,' and I can't say I disagree with him. Look at you—you're distinctly privileged to be among the planter class, yet you've been surrounded your entire life by Negroes of all manner of quality, and also by your common white redneck. Or, rather, rednecks recently of the hill class, which is to say of no class at all, and saddled with a character so low it can't claim the term. A sensible man would prefer the company of a hundred temperate Negroes to the prattling of one hillbilly. I know I certainly would."

John Henry appeared on the verge of saying more, but then he cocked his head to one side, cleared his throat, and said, "White trash as your grandfather always called them. They have their uses. Their passions have their uses."

"Like the men who cleared our fields when I was younger."

"Yes, exactly," said John Henry, "but I intended . . . Well, the story of the South is long. I sometimes think the Yankees hate us so much because the richness of our story frankly belittles theirs. The original nation is more alive here than it is in the North, and the Northerner resents that. We still know the land, we still know how to treat a woman, we still know the names of all our forefathers. Family actually means something here. Anyway, I was going to tell you a story about your grandfather's activities in the county, but perhaps I'd better not. Let me just say that there are . . . artifacts in the house I pray your mother never stumbles upon. I fear she would never recover. I mean only—to return to the original point—that the poor white serves a useful purpose from time to time. The Klan is comprised largely of these country types, almost unfathomably stupid and passionate. This is the sort of man who would kill a Catholic but couldn't define one. And yet, justice . . . Henry, it may seem a strange thing for a lawyer to say, but the courts can't be relied upon to mete out justice in all cases. Abstraction can paralyze. Trust me when I say I know this better than most. I've seen the failure a thousand times over. The Klan and their ilk, for all their rabble-rousing, often have a keen sense of right and wrong undiluted by relativism, and they can carry out justice with alacrity. Rough justice, yes, but justice. I don't wish to glorify the Klan—they're fools—but . . . as your grandfather used to say, 'Manners are morals. And a gentleman always minds his manners . . . until he can no longer afford to.' That's when the Klan comes in handy. They're more discreet these days than they used to be."

"Okay," said Henry. But then, with an expression like petulance or confusion, he placed his chin in his palm and leaned forward and frowned.

John Henry watched his son through narrowing eyes. "Well, I've been speaking a good while. You came in to speak with me."

"I don't know . . ."

"Don't be indirect, Henry."

"Well," said Henry innocently, "I guess I . . . Well, I just don't really like Filip."

John Henry blinked a few times, drawing his mind round to this tangent. He cleared his throat. "When you were a child, he was my biting dog. It was only natural that you would feel a certain antipathy toward him. But your insolence was a sign of high spirit, and I wasn't unappreciative of that fact."

Henry breathed once very deep, felt his heartbeat in his jaw, looked up into the face of his father. "I don't trust him."

There was a twitch of the lip. "Deservedly so. One ought not to entirely trust a drunkar—"

"I heard people talking."

Into the warm tenor of their talk, a cool wind snaked. John Henry shifted almost imperceptibly, his chin lowering a fraction of an inch. "And what precisely was the nature of this talk you heard?"

"It was probably nothing."

"Don't equivocate, Henry."

Henry's brow furrowed. "I don't know—"

"Henry!"

"I think it was about Mother."

John Henry sat back. "What do you mean?"

"They were talking about someone touching Mother. Maybe Filip."

The silence in the room was total.

Into its vast expanse Henry said, "I'm not even sure what they meant."

His father laid his tumbler aside and sat up straight. "Who is they?"

"I don't know; they were around a corner. Well, I think it was Filip and Maryleen talking? It was a while ago. I'm not sure. But Mother's so clumsy without her hearing, maybe he was catching her as she fell. I've done that myself."

"Have you spoken to your mother about this?"

"No, should I have?"

The response was a curt "Your five minutes are up."

"Oh," he said. "Yes, sir." Henry was instantly on his feet, standing over his father, who was now reaching down for his shoes. His heart was hammering in his chest, but he felt suddenly unable to step back to open the door. With his father's head downturned, Henry had a clear view of his thinning crown. In a strange gesture, Henry reached up and touched his own thick hair gingerly. Then, as if the motion had caught his eye, John Henry looked up at his son, who stood there with his hand to a tendril of his hair in what was a strangely winsome—even girlish—manner, looking perplexed and unsure. John Henry's face was blasting furnace red. He rose up from his seat on the davenport with a suddenness that almost unbalanced him, so he swayed for a moment.

"Henry," his father said, but then absolutely nothing followed on the name, so they simply looked at each other, and on Henry's face plain fear appeared. Suddenly and surely with a force that alarmed him, he wanted to retract every word that had been spoken and rip up the court record, but he heard himself saying simply, "Good night, Father." Then he walked out of the room, feeling as though an enormous, age-old wheel had been set creaking into motion. He moved slowly through the lower halls of the house to the back steps and then climbed woodenly to the second floor. He didn't know where his mother was and, suddenly, belatedly, was enveloped by a supreme panic, certain that his father was going to kill her. That fear was immediately allayed when he felt the reverberations of the front door slamming, and then, just moments later, the sound of the sedan prowled down the icy lane like a big black cat.

The next morning, Filip did not show up for work at the Forge house, nor did he appear any day thereafter, and the code on the white, silencing streets of Paris was that the man had simply left town.

And why not? After all, sometimes black men simply left a small, Southern town. Especially when the snow was falling so finely, and there were elderly relatives to visit in Cincinnati and Detroit and trees to trim down in Jackson, Birmingham, and Atlanta. Sometimes a man just went away for the holidays, and then he stayed. Stranger things have happened. Who can say?

Case in point: sometimes a man didn't even have to leave town to disappear, he just went to the opera like Will Porter, who shot a man in honest self-defense but was ripped from a Kentucky jail, carried high on shoulders like an athlete dying young, down the roiling streets to the opera house. They charged a penny admission and strung him up high over the stage, and the strangling sounds were lost in the blaze of pistol fire from the orchestra seats, and good shots all.

Or a man headed down to the court of public opinion, like C. J. Miller after he allegedly raped and murdered two little girls he'd never seen in a county he'd never been to before. Poor, pathetic killer, half-mad with guilt, they dragged him down to the open-air court, and there were five thousand jurors that day, and all thumbs went down as Mr. Miller, he went up.

Others just burned to leave—like Richard Coleman, a hand on a farm when he rode the black train to Covington for supposed rape and murder. Upon his holiday return, ten thousand good souls were waiting, who bound him to a pole and stoked a creeping fire. All the little children brought kindling and bits of twig and laid them on the hearth of his life and roasted him good and slow. And when the smoke cleared, well, you must forgive the rush for the bones—this was a Kentucky delicacy.

No, this was the 1950s and Kentucky had stopped hanging its black laundry, or so they say. Surely Filip Dunbar wasn't what his mother used to call the Christmas babies, the ones killed at Christmas, his mother born out of the foul pussy of slavery on a Jessamine County farm, where horses now run. Until she died in 1940, she lit candles during Advent for all those who had perished, and even then the count was quietly rising.

December 20: Moses Henderson, James Allen, Mr. Lewis, Scott Bishop, the brothers Da Loach, Clinton Montgomery, George Baily, Cope Mills, Samuel Bland, William Stewart, and two unidentified men.

December 21: James Stone, John Warren, Henry Davis, Henry Fitts, two pregnant women, and three unidentified men.

December 22: Joseph James, Jerry Burke, George Finley, and H. Bromley.

December 23: Sloan Allen, George King, seven men together in

Georgia, James Martin, Frank West, Mack Brown, Mr. Brown, and one unidentified man.

December 24: Kinch Freeman, Eli Hilson, James Garden, five together in Virginia, and fourteen unidentified men in Meridian on this day.

Christmas Day: William Fluid, Calvin Thomas, J. H. McClinton, Montgomery Godley, King Davis, and Mr. and Mrs. Moore and more and

Filip Dunbar was one of the lucky ones, or so they say. Surely he walked out of Paris of his own free will that freezing Christmas Eve night without a word to his wife, without even his jacket or shoes. And the only things left hanging in Kentucky that Christmas were the ornaments on the trees, or so they say.

If Maryleen heard nothing, it was likely because her father had come down with the flu over Christmas and not attended church, so of course her mother had not gone but stayed home to tend to her husband, and Maryleen had not gone because she hadn't seen the inside of a church since she was thirteen, when she'd announced she wouldn't worship a God as cruel as this one. ("Maryleen, you fixing to go to hell!" "I'm sure the food's better there.") As far as she was concerned, all religious foolishness ended right then and there, even if—and she would be the first to acknowledge this—religion had saved the black race from certain suicide. But she wasn't the black race and didn't answer to it; she was Maryleen, and she wasn't nearly as stupid as most folks, black or white.

If she heard nothing, it might have been because December was the busiest month in her calendar; it was hog-killing time, and she didn't work at the Forge house from the twentieth of December until the second of January. Instead, she was busy cooking in her parents' hall-and-parlor cottage on the outskirts of Claysville. Her mother told her with no small amount of resentment curdling her voice that Maryleen was the only colored girl in Bourbon County who got the holidays off, but Maryleen had insisted upon it when she was hired; take it or leave it. They accepted it, because her reputation preceded her, and her trial cooking sealed the deal. She had authentic talent, which she had learned was a powerful bargaining chip, and she used it to her advantage. Plus the white lady had seemed to actually like her a little bit, or perhaps merely sensed Maryleen's dislike, which had worked its strange allure. Lavinia had probably never been disliked before. That sort of thing could unsettle a white woman and make her needy, the way cats only want to be petted by the hand that won't touch them.

If she heard nothing, it was probably because hog killing was an all-consuming chore. Maryleen didn't give a damn about the old-timey ways, and she was certainly aware she could purchase any pork product she wanted down at the A&P, but she did give a damn about her cooking and knew that no store-bought lard or fatback competed with what she could get from hogs fattened on their property by her own hand and then butch-ered in December when the old cutter came down from Georgetown. That man, born in another century to ex-slaves, would wait for a cold snap and the moon to increase; this kind of backwoods superstition and conjuration threatened Maryleen's always tenuous relationship with patience, but she tolerated it with unusual forbearance, because the man could core a pig like it was no more trouble than an apple. His butchering was fast and deliber-ate and neat: he built the scaffolds himself from last year's wood, then death came quick with barely any squealing, then the carcasses were scalded and hoisted up and hung with a gambrel. Even her father managed to put his Bible down for a few hours to aid in the process, and all the while Maryleen either helped with the cutting or stood in the kitchen, boiling coffee for the men. She wouldn't touch coffee herself, considering it a drug no less harm-ful than any liquor and not something a human with good sense would tolerate in the body. The men sliced the hogs so their entrails spilled down like loose mottled sausages into the old copper pots, and from the scaffold-ing the shaved carcasses hung empty like glabrous, translucent lanterns for three days—bright pink with the winter sun lighting them just so—until they could be cut apart. During those three days, Maryleen went to Lex-ington to shop for ingredients, paying for it all herself as a Christmas gift to her parents, and then she spent the last week of the year undressing the pigs and cooking from dawn until dark. She separated the leaf lard, then ren-dered it in huge cast iron pots in what had once been a summer kitchen and which now saw no use except during hog-killing time; various cuts were carved, trimmings rendered down for common lard for when she didn't need a fine pastry flavor; she saved some lean with the fat to be used later in sausage making. Then she laid away middling and jowl bacon seasoned with saltpeter and brown sugar in a meat box, and made her own sausages from the trimmings. Most of the pig couldn't be used right away, but she was now set for a year of deep, bold flavor, at least in her own home. In the Forge house, everything was store-bought with flavors as shallow as an August pond, so she had to work twice as hard to create half the depth, but so be it. She doubted that kind of people could even tell the difference between a well-raised meat and supermarket cardboard. White folk were stupid like the sun was bright. Which was to say, shatteringly.

So she was tired when she walked the three miles to the Forge house at five in the morning on the second of January, 1954. She was sweating through her blouse despite the cold when she finally approached the house, which stood tomblike on its hillock alongside the slushing creek, barely visible against the cinder-colored sky. It was not yet dawn, but normally there would already be at least two lights burning in the upper house and in a barn as well, where a worker would be tending to the horses. But the house was dark. Only when Maryleen slipped into the kitchen did a single bulb illuminate a room on the second floor, but that she didn't see.

The kitchen was so quiet, hollow-feeling, and undisturbed that she did something unusual: she lit a fat, drippy beeswax candle instead of switching on the bulb over the stove. It preserved a bit of the early-morning peace, while she laid out buttermilk and butter to warm for biscuits, and rooted around for peach jam in the outdated icebox. She reached behind her for the egg bowl, which Filip placed on the butcher-block island every morning prior to her six o'clock arrival—but no egg bowl. She swiveled around, staring at the deeply scarred block, exactly at the spot where the bowl should have been, and thought, why that lazy old drunk—

The boy was in the room. He stood there in his boxer shorts and a rumpled white undershirt, which was risen up and showed some of his pale stomach. The sight of his flesh made Maryleen rear back in distaste and alarm. Not only was he dressed improperly, but he appeared ravished and worn, as though he'd suffered some wasting disease over the holidays that left his hair sweaty and deep hollows like blackened lime slices beneath his eyes. Even in the mild, shifting candlelight, he looked like a buzzard off a gut pile.

"What's wrong with you? You ill?" Even her concern sounded like an insult.

Henry didn't move further into the room. He just shook his head, exhaustion lining his face.

"If you've got a fever, I don't want you near me. Make your mama tend you."

"Mother isn't here. Father sent her away to Florida."

Maryleen raised a hand. "That's not my business. Go on back to bed. I need to fetch eggs. Filip didn't fetch them for me this morning." She scooped up a yellow ware bowl, actually glad now that the chore hadn't been done, as it gave her a chance to escape this strange troll of a boy, but he said, "Filip isn't here anymore."

It wasn't just the words, but the way he said them—so deliberately, like something memorized and carefully recited to an audience of one. It made Maryleen stop with her hand on the brass knob of the door with just enough time to note the cool oval shape, how similar it was to an egg only nowhere near as fragile, before her mind reared up. That thing that had been waiting like a stalking cat ready to spring had sprung.

"Oh," she said, her voice oddly cool, disembodied from her beating chest. "Where's he working now?"

His voice wavered, hesitant. "I don't believe he's working anywhere anymore, Maryleen."

The way he said her name filled her with dread. She stepped out the door without another word, clutching the bowl to her belly and walking a few paces, then half running through the dark toward the chicken coops behind the horse barn. Her breath was coming in shallow draws and her face was flushed. She kneeled on shaky legs and reached around blindly in the coop, pushing hens aside impatiently, so they winged about and complained, and she dropped two eggs in her haste, one chicken escaping the hutch, so it required a minute to wrestle it back in. Six eggs in the bowl now, and she was walking back to the house, because she didn't know what else to do. In lieu of proper thought, her legs just ferried her back, the minions of habit. The morning was still dark as the inside of a stove, the sun a long way off.

Thank God the boy was no longer in the kitchen when she returned. She placed the bowl on the butcher block, just as Filip would have done, and without further hesitation tiptoed as quickly as she could to the black phone, where it hung in the hallway. She couldn't call her mother; her white folk didn't rise until seven. Anyway, her mother would have told her if she'd known something. Her father's preacher? No—Miss Martin, her old Home Economics teacher, the woman who had taught her everything she knew about cooking. Miss Martin would be awake; she woke every morning at four thirty for her morning prayers.

The phone was answered swiftly after two rings. There was that reliable, gracious voice with its precise elocution. "Good morning," it said. "This is Ella Martin speaking."

"Miss Martin!" Maryleen rasped with a hand curved around the receiver. "It's Maryleen!"

"Yes, Maryleen. I'd recognize that voice anywhere. What are you doing calli—"

"Where's Filip?" Maryleen interrupted. Into the tiniest hint of a pause, Maryleen whispered, "Filip Dunbar."

"I know the Filip to whom you're referring," said Miss Ella. "Maryleen, he ran off over a week ago, just up and went. Left Susah on her own, which some might argue is for the best. They'd been having a lot of trouble recently from what I hear. My goodness, child, surely you didn't call me at this hour to gossip with an old woman."

"Oh God."

"Maryleen." The voice was curving into a question when Maryleen abruptly hung up the phone and stood there in the dark, her mind sorting and measuring, but knowing she was way too late to the equation. The final numbers had already been calculated by others.

"Who were you talking to, Maryleen?"

Despite the alarm that sent her body rimrod straight, despite the fact that she would whip around and see him standing there like a ghost in the shadows of the hall, her first acid thought was "with *whom*."

"My mama," she lied, her answer formulated before she even turned. There was a frightening stillness in Henry's form, and his face was set in shadows, so she couldn't know exactly what it held. She was sweating now, and her charged breath was audible.

"Today's my shopping day," she said uselessly into the silence, but he didn't respond.

Then she snapped, her voice keening upward from a barely suppressed panic, "Go ask your father how I'm supposed to get to the grocery without a driver!"

"He's not awake."

"Go!" she cried.

For a second, he looked as though he was about to go do just that, but he didn't. He said, "You can't tell me what to do."

Her mind reeled. The last time she'd been in the house, only ten days prior, she could have told him to drink lye and somehow, by virtue of her bandsaw personality or her seniority or just her evil eye, she could have gotten him to do it. But whatever power she had held in her hand at the end of December, he was holding in his hands now in this hallway, in this new year. Wearing a thin mask of frustration over rising fear, she shouldered roughly past him, stalked down the hall to the kitchen, trying her best to appear angered by his eavesdropping.

But he followed her. He stood watching as she banged copper and tin pots around mindlessly. She wasn't a cryer, but the first droplets of grief and fear were wringing from the winepress of her mind.

"I can't cook with you staring at me like that," she finally hissed over her shoulder.

"Maryleen," he said. "Do you think we all eventually get the punishment we deserve?"

"What?" she snapped.

"I mean, if God doesn't exist, then he can't punish anyone. I guess we have to do it ourselves," he said. "See, man actually is the measure of all things. Man wrote all the books, so he's the measure even if he says he isn't. We invented God to tell us to do what we already wanted to do. That's what I think."

"Punishment? You mean men? What?" She had no idea what he was talking about, what he was trying to riddle out to her, but her body made its own interpretation, a trace of cold wending its way down from between her shoulder blades to her tailbone, and the sudden feeling that she had to pee.

"I heard you say Filip did something," he said quietly, and the sound of his voice was the thing that frightened her most of all, the queer way he sounded like a little boy when he said it. When she turned, his eyes were enormous and febrile, and she couldn't stop the words as they rose up from her very belly, passing through the esophagus constricted by fear and then through the ashes in her mouth: "What have you done?"

He reared back, a look of injury on his face. When he spoke, she could see the sheen of tears in his eyes. "Nothing. I was trying to do the right thing. All I want is to grow up."

"I said"—she hissed—"what have you done."

"I didn't do anything! I just told Father what you said."

Maryleen's brow crumpled up in bewilderment. "What I said?"

"You know what I'm talking about."

She stared at him without a word, waiting.

"You said Filip touched Mother. I heard you."

She gasped. "Oh my God."

"Maryleen—"

Her finger was trembling when it punctuated the air between them. "You are evil."

Sudden rage blasted through him like fire. "No, I'm not! He touched Mother!"

Maryleen's eyes grew impossibly wide. "He touched your whore mother," she said, and then leaned so far over the butcher block, she was practically lying on it to yell into his face, "BECAUSE SHE WANTED IT!"

Henry reached out and swept the bowl with its eggs onto the floor, fury undoing what was left of his reserve. "Get out of my house, Maryleen!" he screamed. "Get out now!"

Only later would she look back furiously and think of herself as some slave ordered about by a little boy who had just discovered he would be master someday, talking big at the kitchen girl, who obeyed him, not even stopping to snuff out the candle, just grabbing her jacket and a black goatskin purse she'd spent a week's wages on. The door spun a draft that gutted the candle and left Henry in the darkness behind her.

Maryleen raced down the drive in a flat-out panic and onto the road toward Paris; it was only six fifteen; there was no one about and still no play of light on the eastern horizon. A sense of unreality enveloped her now as she hastened along; had those words really passed between them, had she just imagined the absence of Filip? But no, there'd been no egg bowl waiting, this was real and actually happening. Yet, surely she was overreacting; she tried to calm her mind, she didn't really think anyone was coming after her, not really, there was no lynch mob waiting for the girl cook, though she glanced fearfully over her shoulder for headlights; yes, the boy was just messing with her, she was turning this into something it wasn't, she just needed to calm down. But by the time she was approaching the outskirts of town, sweating through her blouse, she could almost see Filip hanging from a tree right before her eyes, and her decision was made. Later, she would realize there had been a sneaky joy smuggled into her fear, that she hadn't been quite as afraid as she remembered, that she had forced her own panic like a hothouse flower to compel her stubborn spirit to the action for which it had always—always—been intended. What had she been thinking, turning down colleges and ending up in a white kitchen like that? What exactly had she been trying to prove? Or avoid?

Her own house was empty, her mother and father both at work. In the wallpapered room where she had grown up—odd how the ugly trellised pea-blossom paper would soon be a thing she remembered fondly—she shoved two outfits and her spare pair of shoes into an old fabric traveling bag, but then eyed the single line of mysteries on her shelf and removed the extra shoes, returning them to her nearly empty closet. Nine mysteries and her pocket Shakespeare fitted snugly into the bag, all that the space would allow. Quickly, she removed her sweaty clothing and shrugged into a loose-fitting black blouse and a rayon skirt that fell below her knees, identical to the other three sets she owned and under which no hint of a figure could be discovered. With that final task complete, she was down the steps and out of the old house, site of her father's Bible reading, of her mother's weariness, of her own bad-tempered childhood. She didn't leave a note, she would call them from Lexington—no, Cincinnati; first she would leave this bloody borderland behind. She intended to apologize to Miss Martin for hanging up on her, but Miss Martin would understand—she loved her like a daughter; Maryleen knew that. Then as she was shutting the old walnut front door, bag in hand, she suddenly stopped, her swarming thoughts stilled, and she stood at her fullest height, fear vanishing. She didn't know where the certainty came from or why, but she suddenly knew she was going to New York City, that she'd find a job in a restaurant and then figure it out from there, and she felt now that she didn't have a moment to lose, that her very life depended on it.

Oh, Mr. Forge, is your son ill?
   Yes, yes, he is.
   When did he take ill?
   Over the holidays. There was a fever in the house.

John Henry picked up his wife at the Paris train station. He waited on the platform, an utterly motionless figure. His affectless face was outperformed by the fine details of his wool pin-striped suit, his black silk overcoat, gold cuff links, and houndstooth handkerchief, his wedding band, which winked dully. Every hair on his graying head was arranged into a still life, and his absolute stillness was betrayed only by the redness of his ears. It was very cold out.

When the train arrived, it came without urgency, its whistle distorted by the distance, its black flashing brokenly through the trees; then came the falling rhythm of its deceleration, the whine and hush of brakes. When it finally stopped, John Henry half wanted it to roll on, carry her away and fail its engine somewhere else. His head turned abruptly, found the straight black tail of the locomotive and the people who poured from it. They were all embracing. Someone kissed someone. He found their displays vulgar and invasive and turned away. Then she was there, standing hesitantly on the last step, blonde and pale, looking at him with all the native shyness he remembered from when they first met eighteen years ago. The wife of his youth, looking no worse for her obvious wear. He stepped forward, his cold hands helping her to navigate the last step onto the platform. He grasped up her suitcase. His other hand made a small, solicitous gesture at the small of her back. His father, Jacob Ellison Forge, had told him that a woman's bones were lighter than a man's—and may my words alone be a lesson to you in that regard. Only an animal visibly damages its mate.

They drove home in their usual silence made newly entire; they drove in the tame light of dusk and the aseptic chill. John Henry tried not to think of anything, but watched the thrifty sky as it diminished into evening, a sky like middle age, without eagerness or gladness, without the bright light and heat of youth. His wife shifted on the seat beside him. The motion caught his eye, and he looked at her as he pulled the sedan up the drive. She was looking at the house he had given her—she came from a family that had more name than money—in wonder or regret or some other unjustifiable female emotion. When she made a tiny mouselike motion to open the door for herself as if he would not do it for her, as if she had forgotten in her time away that it was the husband's place to open the door for his wife, as if in her absence their marriage had ended, this was too much, and he suddenly reached over and placed one hand firmly against the back of her head. Without explanation, he pressed her head forward toward the dashboard, feeling her resist only for a moment, her left hand darting up once the way her heartbeat would flutter lightly when they made love, then he took up her pocketbook and landed three hard blows against her head, high enough on the back of the skull so the bruise would not show and where there was no danger of breaking her neck. She made no noise but a grunting exhalation with each blow, her shoulders shrinking up around her ears. Then he flung the pocketbook onto her lap and used both hands to turn her now, so that she could see his lips as he said, "Your son is sick. Go tend to him."

And that would have been it. Except that she cried. They had already come into the house, John Henry following after her with her suitcase and pointing her upstairs, as though she were a child. She had walked up the stairs gripping the walnut banister, but then stumbled awkwardly on the last one, looking back down at him with fear wrinkling up her face, and he saw tears on her cheek. Despite her actions, her guilt, what she had done to him, despite the fact that her wet little tongue had no doubt licked the rotten fruit before she had taken it in her mouth and swallowed it, here she stood, crying, and the naïve innocence of her look, which was at best a lie and at worst cuckoldry, made a mockery of his strict dignity, his family, of his manhood. The high heat of rage flooded him instantaneously. He rushed the stairs like a bull, and for a moment Lavinia could only stare in alarm, never having seen him wholly uncontained, before she turned and fled down the hallway, and he realized she planned to escape him by rushing into their son's room—his son's room! He overcame her as she was reaching for the door, twisting her under him, his hands like manacles on her wrists.

He dragged her to their room and kicked the door shut, beyond caring about the clatter they made or their heavy breathing. Her strained grunting and struggling only aroused him, and he unleashed himself. He forced her face-first onto the bed with her arms folded against her chest and struck her with his open hand against the back of her head with increasing force until she mewled into the bedspread. Forcing her tweed skirt above her hips, he was stymied by a hard white girdle and belts and straps and stockings so tight around her—like a chastity belt—that his fingernails scratched her as he ripped them down from her hips. He didn't say anything, there was no need, she understood absolutely nothing of him anyway even after all these years, so this was both his farewell address and a reconfiguration of his vows. He dropped his trousers and shorts and, hard with the potency of his anger, he forced himself into her dry, the rude, fleshy slap of his hips beating against her flanks. He breathed like a gladiator as he stared down at the back of her deceitful head. But when she shifted under him once in pain, he shuddered with pleasure, and, against his will, he remembered suddenly their youthful coming together with a vibrancy like lightning, and he paused midthrust, panting, blinded by the memory of it—the plangency of old delight, of her lost charms, how her eyes had once admired him. But she had changed and turned away and made a fool of him, and he had wasted the energy of his adult life on her luster; it was not so much that he hated her now, but that he respected himself. And with that thought, he was moving again, stabbing into her, fast and with no feeling now, not even anger, in a strict charade of lovemaking again and again in the old, rote motions again and again until she cried out, but not in pleasure.

My darling boy—sleeping there just as you did as an infant—I don't expect you to understand. You are so young, and we have no shared language between us, not really. I held you in my body for nine long months, and I gave birth to you, but you don't know me at all. I'm not just your mother; I'm a woman. I'm telling you something now that I can barely stand to see myself, that I have until very recently been a little girl. Married, pregnant three times and now thirty-eight years old, but still a little girl. No matter what anyone tells you, a person is not fully mature until they can love another human being. I love you, of course, but loving a child you gave birth to is not what I'm talking about. That's effortless. What I'm talking about is the love that occurs between equals, love being something that can *only* occur between equals. I know you don't think of that man as my equal. The truth is I didn't either—he's black and he drinks too much. I can't hear the way he talks, but I can just imagine how rough and rude it is. But what you may never understand, because you are not a woman, is that the first time he kissed me, he didn't kiss me just with his mouth; he kissed me with his eyes. He looked into me. No one had ever done that before. Then I was completely and totally ashamed, but not because of the sex, which is the natural course of things. I was ashamed of the glaring inequality that existed between us. He knew something of which I was completely ignorant, and from that moment on, against every impediment, I strove to become worthy of him, to become his equal.

In blistering dreams, he ascends a ladder out of the brilliant sunlit present into dark, roiling cumulus clouds where the troubled faces of his mother and father recede from countenance to anachronism to chiaroscuro to nothing. There in crumbling, sooty clouds, where the rotten-flesh dead cease their prattling and rutting long enough to point upward, saying, That way, Mister Henry; up, up, step after step into the future. Now over the rumbling of heaven's rusty gears, he detects a tolling deeper than blood: the bells of ambition and desire. Up, up to the very top of the ladder. With feverish effort, he hauls up the ladder and turns it onto its side and makes it a proscenium. So, here they come, advancing along its length, a procession of horses from time immemorial through the Age of Man, only the finest specimens: the dish-faced Arabian, the mighty Clydesdale, the wild Mustang, the cutting Quarter, the stalwart Morgan, and last but not least the royal Thoroughbred, that perfect marriage of speed and strength, of cold and hot blood, of high temper and astonishing speed! This alone is the culmination of the species, of this long, long line as old as the gods, standing behind you always watching you, Henry. Always.

Henry struggled in his sheets, but he couldn't wake. Demeter has returned with gentle hands and nothing to say, touching him here and there and everywhere, hands on his face and at the crux of her legs, and when he says, I've seen something amazing, she points up at the mistletoe above her head, smiling sweetly. But when she removes her painted mask, she's nothing but that bitch Aphrodite.

Father asks, Is the good the pleasurable?

Son: Mother thinks so!

Father: Is the wife the head of the house?

Son: The low seat of the house!

Father: Who made you the man you are?

Son: The long line behind me . . . It.

Father: I gave you blood.

Son: And *quantitas magna frumentorum*!

Father: Why are our voices not in communion?

Son: *Ut sementem feceris, ita metes!*

Henry snapped awake, drenched in sweat and realizing he had crossed some invisible line into adulthood. He knew this, because he no longer found death interesting and certainly nothing to be afraid of. Anyone could do it.

He was waiting for his tutor, quiet and certain as a secret in the downstairs study, sitting behind a stacked rampart of Greek and Latin volumes, his hands folded into a rock of purpose, his bleary head high. He heard the front door open, listened to a deeply polite voice greeting his mother, then sat forward as the footsteps sounded down the hall. The tutor stopped short in the doorway.

"Good morning," the man said, surprised to discover his young charge waiting for him in a soft pool of sunlight that sparked the gold lettering on the spines of the black and burgundy volumes. Dust motes danced around the boy like a swarm of gnats.

"I'm ready to start," said Henry Forge.

The tutor was a slim, slight man, shorter than Henry, who walked with the gentle stoop of an older person. His skin was invalid-pale, but his book-trained eyes were sharp and unsentimental; there was no indecision about him as he stepped into the room and shut the door with a gentle, firm hand.

"Well, perhaps *I'm* not ready to start," he said with the faintest of smiles on his face. "I've only just now walked in the door and met your lovely mother." His voice was deep and flat with no bowing at the vowels. Henry inspected him carefully, as if the precise topography of his Northern home could be discovered in the lines and angles of his face.

"You're not from here," he said slowly.

"Apparently," said the tutor as he took stock of the room—the lazy whir of the ceiling fan, the antique Italian desk at which Henry sat—"Kentucky suffers from a dearth of classically trained educators. But I have to say it's a lovely state you have here. Remarkably green." The man took his time advancing across the room and easing into a chair opposite the desk, crossing his legs with a care that spoke of old injuries or some other infirmity. All the while, he observed Henry with a mild, unblinking gaze.

"Kentucky is the best state in the union."

"Is that right?" the man countered.

"That's right."

"Better than New Jersey even?" There was a twitch of amusement about the lips.

The joke was lost on Henry, whose eyes widened. "People risked their lives getting here to escape states like New Jersey. They banned slavery in 1804 and a lot of families moved south with their niggers to establi—"

"Negroes." The man cocked his graying head to one side, one brow on the rise. "Negroes, I think you meant to say."

Henry made no reply; he looked down at the man's battered leather satchel resting against the sinuous leg of his chair. "Is my work in there?"

"It is."

Henry edged forward. "But I already had an idea of what to start with."

The man sat back against the spines of his Windsor chair and folded his hands at his belly. "Is that right? Enlighten me."

Henry sat up straighter. "*On Horsemanship*," he said.

Now the brow was soaring. "I might have chosen something less . . . esoteric. Something more suited to the educational needs of a young man your age."

"*On Horsemanship* would be good, I think. Did you know that evolution is a ladder to perfection? It's true. You can chart the development of the horse right up the ladder: Eohippus, the dawn horse, which was about the size of a terrier, then Mesohippus, which was about six hands high, then Merychippus, which—"

"Young man," the tutor interrupted. "I don't think your father wants you spending valuable time on something like *On Horsemanship*."

Henry maintained a level gaze, but his tone slipped some. "I'm sure Father would allow me to read anything, so long as I work hard. I can translate it into English, then I can translate it for you into Latin. I need the practice."

The man recrossed his legs, smoothed the pressed creases on his gabardine pant legs, and took his time responding. "Well, it sounds to me as if you intend to work very hard."

"I do," said Henry. "I wouldn't want to waste my father's money." An attempted smile of his own.

"Your father said he's been tutoring you himself in Latin thus far. That's very impressive."

"Well, he began studying Latin when he was five. We were one of the first families to come over the Wilderness Road. We're quite wealthy."

"Young man," the tutor said abruptly, "you look exhausted. Do you get enough sleep?"

"Yes. I really think my father's pronunciation could be better, though." Henry leaned forward again. "I want my education to be very heavy on the classics—not that I won't study math and science; I'll study all of it. I intend to be excellent at everything I set my mind to, but what I want most is to be heavy on the classics. I want to be a classicist. I've already memorized most of the details of classical mythology. But I'd really like to start with *On Horsemanship*."

"All right, all right," said the tutor, holding up a hand. "I do, of course, have a curriculum for you based on your previous schooling and tutoring. But if your heart is set on it, then I suppose we can begin with *On Horsemanship*. What is extant, at least. If that's your . . . inclination, I certainly don't see the harm in it. Though I'm not sure I see the value either."

"When can we start?"

The man didn't answer immediately, but lowered his head ever so slightly, so that he gave the impression he was gazing at Henry over invisible eyeglasses. "Wouldn't you like to know my name first?"

"My name's Henry."

"Yes, I know that. My name is Gerald Price. Of Trenton, New Jersey."

"When do we start?"

The man shrugged with a barely audible sigh. "We begin now, I suppose."

And so his true education began. They studied this appraisal of animals for hours and when the older man left, the student remained exactly where he had begun the day. He grammared and translated and conjugated and declined, then read well into the night in his bed by flashlight and many nights thereafter, making penciled notes in composition books and memorizing Xenophon to the word, so he would never forget that *for soundness of foot a thick horn is far better than a thin. Again, it is important to notice whether the hoofs are high both before and behind, or flat to the ground; for a high hoof keeps the "frog," as it is called, well off the ground; whereas a low hoof treads equally with the stoutest and softest part of the foot alike, the gait resembling that of a bandy-legged man. "You may tell a good foot clearly by the ring," says Simon happily; for the hollow hoof rings like a cymbal against the solid earth.*

And the boy paid keen attention to *the assemblage of a horse's body, particularly the shoulder blades, or arms, these if thick and muscular present a stronger and handsomer appearance, just as in the case of a human being. Again, a comparatively broad chest is better alike for strength and beauty, and better adapted to carry the legs well asunder, so that they will not overlap and interfere with one another . . . Again, the neck should not be set on dropping forward from the chest, like a boar's, but, like that of a game-cock rather, it should shoot upwards to the crest, and be slack along the curvature; whilst the head should be bony and the jawbone small. In this way the neck will be well in front of the rider, and the eye will command what lies before the horse's feet. A horse, moreover, of this build, however spirited, will be least capable of overmastering the rider, since it is not by arching but by stretching out his neck and head that a horse endeavors to assert his power.*

Henry sketched his plans, made lists and calculations. He shaped a horse out of the dark clay of his mind, and it crept forth into the light of expectation: first its destrier head, then its massive barrel chest. From the turned hooves to the cut of the knife-tip ears, its body was designed for forward motion. Bred light, but heavily motored. Flexible, intelligent, full of force and fire, towering in height—not the servant of the Moirai but their trampler—this was a horse that made good on horseness. Tough enough for war, but more beautiful than any woman and even more necessary.

Every morning the tutor greeted the madder-eyed insomniac, saying, "Tell me what you know," and Henry stood before him, maniacal with fatigue, but inlit with consuming desire:

I know that a horse is better than corn, and that a man is better than a horse, and that a boy is better than a man, because he has not become his father yet.

Tell me what you know.

That this farm is just a sleight of land—a play at restraint! But the joke is on John Henry, not Jacob Ellison or Moses Cooper or William Iver or Richmond Cooper or Edward—

Tell me what you know.

That I am a Kentuckian first, a Virginian second, a Christian third. I am the refinement of Samuel's seed. I am a man made for my time, not my father's or his father's. I know that a city untended weakens and falls. Troy will fall, Rome will fall, any great city will fall without a show of strength.

Tell me—

I know that when the Liberators killed Caesar, they stabbed him right through the heart.

A tall and beautiful Henry had just turned sixteen when his cousins made their yearly weeklong visit. They traversed the shimmering Florida byways in the late summer heat, and when they finally stumbled from their Chevrolet onto the Forge lawn, they were sweating like miniature prizefighters, throwing themselves into Lavinia's waiting arms. John Henry was cordial at her side, but their increasingly distracted son was nowhere to be seen. Henry had bicycled into Paris, his Saturday habit now, to pore over books in the public library. There he studied the principles of legacy. He spread out his books of pedigree charts, breeding formulas, family trees that branched crookedly back to the Godolphin Arabian, the Darley Arabian, Byerley Turk. Once he carefully ripped a page from an old encyclopedia, so that he could bring home the Turk, all greyhound head and legs like rose stems. The picture hid gamely under his mattress, waiting for the time when it would finally centerpiece a wall—when Henry was eighteen and matriculated at Sewanee alongside the sons of the South.

Today, he made his scrupulous notes on mare stamping, the intractable tendency of the female to raft her features over the weaker male and mold her get in her image. It was a tenuous and risky task to breed when male strength was infinitely subject to the savvier, prepotent female. Henry was just now learning how to linebreed and inbreed a horse to a desired constitution, delving back to the same female ancestor on both sides, so that the lines rhymed and the foals showed a dam's taproot strengths without being dominated by her. A large heart came through the dam; one could trace its passage from foal to granddam and beyond; it stoked the chests of all descendants, it fueled limbs across finish lines and into winner's circles. The heart was the thing—and how to get it.

Henry cycled back to the house in the amber afternoon with borrowed books crammed into his rucksack, a cap tilted across his brow. He'd nearly run over his youngest cousin in diapers before he remembered that the family had arrived today, that he'd been expected back well before the supper hour. He dropped his bike in the gravel, so the wheels spun with a useless rattle, and lifted the first child he saw to his chest, a small human shield against the remonstration sure to come. But his father was engrossed in conversation with his brother, a man with dark red hair just beginning to gray and the easy, open face of a younger brother. Never close, they were as different as spring and autumn. Beyond them, the girls played croquet—

Henry detected his cousin Loretta among them.

When the new cook, Paulette, called for supper, the girls all dropped their mallets and sprang across the lawn, calling "Henry! Henry! Henry!" as they angled past him toward the house, waving and sparking white and all redheaded in their bowtied dresses. Lavinia, on a step of the el porch, ushered them inside, touching each on the shoulder as they went by in a bright wash, blessing them as they went, but her eyes were on her son, on whom Loretta was advancing like a gay shadow. Henry turned to her, reinforcing his face against her prettiness, which he couldn't remember having seen before. It changed the temperature of his skin.

"Oh my gosh," Loretta said, "what happened to you?" It was a statement, not a question, but Henry looked down at himself as if his shirt were fouled or his zipper undone. His face returned to hers, wary.

She was watching him as if she knew something he didn't, smiling from one side of her pretty mouth as an older person might smile at a child, and propping her white, heart-shaped glasses on the crown of her head. Her eyes were green, disarming, bold. Like his, but more adult, even he could see that.

"You're gorgeous," Loretta said.

If he didn't move, his eyes started somewhat in their sockets, and he fought the urge to turn his head away from the soft blow of her compliment. Instead, he blushed so badly his face burned. Then he did allow his eyes to escape from hers, but they only turned awkwardly down toward the mother-of-pearl buttons on her blouse.

She laughed then, but the sound was young, and so much sweeter and less sophisticated than her speaking voice that he was able to look into her eyes again.

"God, how did you get to be so good-looking?" she said, and she grabbed his elbow, guiding him toward the house. Henry snuck a peek in the direction of his mother, but she was gone, watching them now from a window in the dining room that he couldn't see. Henry and Loretta advanced on the house slowly; she owned him by the time they had walked ten paces.

"You could be in movies, I'm not kidding," she said. "Aunt Lavinia is pretty, but your dad, not so much. So what happened to you?"

He was still blushing as he eyed the exquisite slope of her coral-colored lips. His mind was fumbling for something to say when she said, "Do you have a girlfriend?"

"Yeah," he said. "Do you still have horses?"

She laughed. "Liar."

"No," he said, "I have a girlfriend. I was just curious if you still have horses."

Arm in arm they went and she rolled her eyes and sighed, but said, "A couple."

"Yeah, but real horses."

"Yes, real horses," she said. "I still compete."

Now it was his turn to roll his eyes. "I meant Thoroughbred horses."

Loretta withdrew her hand suddenly from his elbow. "Yes, we have horses. Real horses. Yes, some of them are Thoroughbreds. Mother and I do dressage. You know that. What's your point?"

Henry's laugh was a foil for a secret, and for a moment their ages seesawed.

"What's that laugh supposed to mean?" she said.

"Nothing." He shrugged, turned up his shoulders a bit, allowing a small insouciant smile to play around the corners of his mouth.

Loretta stopped walking altogether. He stopped to look back at her.

"When did you get so high and mighty?" she snapped. "You don't even have a girlfriend. I don't think you have a foot to stand on." Her tone was acid, her face hard, and now she marched past him, all slicing shoulders and high chin, angling for the side door.

"Hey!" he called after her. "I was kidding!" A moment later: "Hey, I don't think dressage is stupid."

Loretta paused with her hand on the screen door and turned toward him, so he had a proper glimpse of her bright copper hair and newgrown breasts, her legs white and gleaming. Through eyes turned to slits, she regarded him without saying a word.

"Don't be mad at me," Henry said softly.

For a moment it seemed as if she was going to turn her back on him again, but then she laughed that childish laugh, and she made a kissing motion at him before she skipped on into the house.

He followed after her like a dog.

John Henry and Uncle Mason sat deep in discussion of the farm and its plantation, their heads tilted together at the breakfast table, their plates pushed hastily aside, so their fingers could make maps of the linens. The girls were a messy, squabbling flock, while their mother, Melissa Jeane, hovered over them, ever the harried hen, too overwhelmed by the task of feeding her brood to eat anything herself. Lavinia sat in the cocoon of her silence as Paulette moved unnoticed at their outskirts, replacing dishes, filling glasses, covering eggs and potatoes in their silver servers. Henry had no interest in any of it; he abandoned the room, grabbing a piece of toast and escaping through the kitchen's swinging door.

He was standing on the porch, surveying the farm drenched in morning's brisk light—his crucible, where a new world would be forged—when Loretta appeared behind him, tapping a smart rhythm with the toe of her shoe. "I'm bored to death," she whispered, and her breath whispered too against the skin of his neck.

"Yup," he said, chewing his toast, and when he made no further response, she stepped in front of him, her robust figure interrupting the light.

"Show me the Walkers," she said.

"I thought you were already bored." He wiped his fingers on his khakis.

"Come on," she said, and reached out to tug at his arm. She was surprisingly strong, but then she was no small girl. She grinned at him, her lipstick nearly worn away by her breakfast.

"I have no interest in the Walkers," he said.

"But," she said slowly, "don't you want to go for a ride?" And to his utter surprise, she swiveled her hips once in a carnal, circumscribed dance for him, which instantly made his insides lurch. Caught in the warm vice of alarm and arousal, he stood there, saying nothing at all.

"Listen, if you don't want to come, that's fine." Loretta sighed and moued, her hands on her hips. "I'll just go find Jimmy then." She marched down onto the grass.

"What?" Henry snapped, flinging aside what was left of his toast and starting after her across the lawn. Jimmy was a teenager from Louisville who'd been passed relative to relative in Claysville for over two years. He'd been an occasional employee on their farm, a handsome and raucous boy, whose laughter was always cut short when Henry came around. Then he would stand mute with dark, bruised eyes, his smile withering on his lips. Henry was startled that Loretta even remembered him.

"Why would you even say that?" Henry pressed, whispering as if someone was close by and listening. "That's disgusting."

"What's disgusting?" Loretta said innocently.

"I know what you meant," he whispered.

"Oh, your mind is in the gutter," she mocked.

"You're the one who said it!" He felt the rising heat of fury on his cheeks.

"I never said coloreds have big cocks," she said, and Henry reared back, shock eclipsing his anger, but she only grabbed at his elbow, that easy female gesture again, and he remained at her side, that easy male acquiescence.

"My gosh, I'm just trying to rile you up," Loretta said, rolling her eyes. "You're such a bumpkin! Who knew you were so . . . sensitive."

"I have standards," Henry said, and snatched his arm back, but they kept on until the syncopated rhythms of their feet formed a unison.

"Father won't let you ride the Walkers," Henry warned when they reached the barn door.

"Oh, I'm not afraid of Uncle John," Loretta tossed back. "Are you?"

Henry paused where he stood, feeling the great, reassuring warmth of the morning pressing against his back, and a prickly sense of discomfort arising. He watched, circumspect, as Loretta sashayed down the row. Then he followed his cousin into the barn, because her hips and lips were warmer than even the bedazzling light of morning.

The horses were immediately aware of their presence. They stirred, collecting one after the other at their stall doors, dark heads swinging over crib doors, drafts of air quivering down the channels of their nostrils.

"Oh," Loretta sighed, "they smell like sunshine and earth." She slid the palms of her hand along one filly's jaw—the yearling foal of Martha White— and stared into her eyes, that dark, confounding space. Then she traced the jagged line of her brilliant blaze, but the other horses blew and stamped, so she moved to each in turn.

"Don't you just love them?" she said.

Henry made a face. What use were the Walkers to him? They were predictable and unsurprising as time, heavy on their bones with their absurdly long underlines. And, too, they were the province of Filip, a man he could not think of without his stomach turning to a hard plum pit.

"Let's ride," said Loretta, whirling around suddenly.

"No way," Henry said.

"Where's the tack room?"

"No, Loretta," he said again, more sternly, he hoped.

"I'll find it myself then." She started off down the row with fresh purpose, horse heads pointing the way, their tails tossing as they blew for want of affection or a ride. One Walker whickered and traced a needy circle in his stall as she passed.

Henry jogged along after Loretta, but just as her hand lifted the latch of the tack room door, and just as he was trying to draw her back, their hands wrestling briefly, the door swung open, and Loretta dragged him inward, slamming the door shut again. Before their eyes could adjust to the swamping dark, her mouth missed his for his cheek, then latched onto his lips. Her hands plied at his shoulders and his bottom.

"Lie down," she said. He felt about with his foot, his heart beating madly, until he nudged the edge of a hayrack. He scooted back onto the bed of scratching hay, and she joined him there and began to work on the buttons of his fly. She half lay over him then, her pliant tongue reaching into unexplored regions of his mouth. The pressure of her breasts was strange and insistent as she rooted around in his shorts. His breath came in ragged draws. Then she schooled him with her hand.

Even before his breathing had slowed, he was shoving himself still half-hard into his khakis and fumbling with the buttons. Loretta lay beside him, wiping her hands on the hay, but only found that it clung to her palms.

"Do you think I was good at that?" she said.

He nodded, but inside him he discovered an awkward twinge of disappointment. Was this some kind of farewell address to childhood? It felt less than spectacular.

"Guess where I learned to do that," she said.

"I don't know," he said.

"One of my teachers; he's my boyfriend." She waited for his response, which didn't come. It was all he could do to get his pants buttoned in the half dark. His hands were leeched of strength, the buttons downright disobedient.

Suddenly, a small sound caused his blood to leap like a lasso, and he started up from the hay. "Relax," Loretta hissed, "no one's coming."

She was right. They waited, but the only thing Henry could hear was the untaxed rhythm of her breath. There was nothing out there; even the horses were silent.

"I have to say," Loretta said, staring at his face in the dark, "you really don't look like you get enough sleep."

Henry sighed. "Well, I read a lot," he said. "I have plans."

"Plans for what?"

Henry was silent for a moment, finding his cousin lacking in seriousness and unworthy of his private, curated thoughts, but under the spell of this new relaxation, he went on. "Nobody knows this, so you need to keep it a secret, but someday I'm going to turn Forge Run Farm into a Thoroughbred operation." He tried to ape the calm of an adult, but his eagerness pressed through. "All this corn farming is ridiculous," he said. "It's a waste of this farm's potential, a waste of this family's legacy! Do you know how long we've been here? I mean, you're in Florida now, it's almost like you're not part of the family anymore—"

"Hey," Loretta said, but listlessly, and he barreled on. "This is what happens when you get complacent, when you don't have the courage to dream big or grab the opportunities that are right before you. I mean, Tennessee Walkers? Give me a break. This is Kentucky—this land is destined for Thoroughbreds."

"Thoroughbreds again," Loretta sighed, and rolled her eyes.

Henry bullied her down with a rising voice. "You're all the same! None of you know how to think big! I can't stand the way Father's running this place! It makes me crazy! We're like runners in the middle of the pack. Why even compete, what's the point? Run out front or quit."

Loretta shrugged and rolled up to a sitting position to check the buttons on her blouse.

"Hey, where's my headband?" she said suddenly, and turned over on her hands and knees, scouring the hay, but Henry didn't move. He just spoke to her back.

"Everybody thinks there's so much chance involved in horse racing, but that's not how I see it. It's about controlled usage of every resource. 'Chance' is a word ignorant men use when they don't know how to plan and take calculated risks. Life is ten percent chance and ninety percent willpower and intelligence. Think of—"

"There it is," Loretta said, and she returned the checkered band to her hair.

"—Signorina and Chaleureux. Their meeting on the road might have been chance, but the breeding of Signorinetta was anything but. A great breeder has to know when to seize the opportunity to get the dam's heart."

"Shhhhhh!" Loretta said, and she sprang suddenly up from the hay, tipped forward on her toes with her hands out to her sides in the attitude of a startled dancer.

Henry lost his thought in an instant and flung himself up, fumbling in the dark to secure his clothing. Loretta was raking wildly at her hair, all the gold straw drifting around her shoulders when the door opened.

They were confronted with a man's embarrassed face for only a moment before they tumbled out, Henry fairly flying down the row, but Loretta stopping suddenly and saying, "Hey, you're not Filip."

Henry was light-blind with one foot out the barn door when he realized she wasn't following. He said "Loretta!" hard, as if he were her father.

"Who are you?" Loretta said, gazing up with consternation into the white man's face.

"Uh," the man said quietly, looking anywhere but at the door the two had exited from, "I'm Robert Forester."

"Where's Filip?"

"Loretta!" said Henry sharply again.

"I reckon he don't work here no more," said the man with a shrug.

"Well, that's odd," said Loretta. "He'd been with this family since forever." Baffled, she turned and walked slowly out of the barn into the now harsh light of the risen sun. She looked at Henry and said, "Why on earth would you let Filip go? He was my favorite."

"I never could stand that nigger," Henry said.

Now it was Loretta's turn to rear back. "I get the feeling you can't stand anyone! And don't say nigger. It makes you sound like a bumpkin."

"And you sound like a nigger lover."

"Oh, I'm just a lover," Loretta said airily. "I don't even see color. I'm beyond all that."

Henry scowled at her, and she said, "Don't be such a stick in the mud."

Then she spotted their fathers now on the porch, still in conversation, John Henry's back rimrod straight with his strict dignity, which never altered. Loretta grasped Henry's elbow suddenly, so that he almost stumbled over his own shoes. She whispered, "Don't tell about . . . okay?"

"You really do think I'm an idiot," he snapped.

"Ha!" She laughed, tossing the fall of her hair over one shoulder. "I think you're pure as the driven snow!" And she flounced on ahead of him toward the house.

"Henry Forge!"

No. He wouldn't go. He was stacking boxes for his mother in the attic, where the family history lay organized and covered in sheets under the roof, where birds roosted as if on thin black soil, calling as his father was calling.

"Henry Forge!"

Who died and made me your slave? His insolence was a physical delight.

"Do not make me find you! Now!"

It still owned him. It. His lace-ups clapped the servants' stairs, one after the other; they beat out the steady rhythm of John Henry. His only disobedience was his desultory pace.

His father was standing at the rear door off the kitchen, his pale blue striped sleeves rolled up over his freckled biceps, the short red hairs glinting there. By now, the hair on his head was completely gray. It always startled.

"What took you so long?" he said, turning to open the door to the backyard, where the morning was rioting in the dew and sparking off the crisp grass and the hedges. "Come along."

As Henry descended the limestone steps off the back door, half-blinded by the acid light, his father picked up clippers and a saw from the ground. He said, "Fetch a ladder, please."

"What for?" The words slipped off his truculent tongue before he could stop them. Even now, at the threshold of his adult life, he was just a little boy asking for answers from a man who wouldn't answer.

But this time John Henry replied. "We're cutting mistletoe from one of the trees. Apparently, if you want a job done correctly, you can't hire men who are too busy rolling their own damn cigarettes to do any work. You have to do it yourself."

By the time Henry had found the twenty-foot ladder in one of the old cabins, his father was a solitary figure in the orchard. Henry followed after him as best he could, clumsily balancing the shaky length of the ladder on two pinched palms. Before him, the wild fecundity of the orchard bloomed in the light wind that sluiced gently through the avenues of trees. The wind seemed to come directly from the sun, a perfect globe of red risen confidently out of the laden boughs. That globe commanded all the life of the garden, the many million blades of grass, the thick stalks of the trees with their secret rings, the gradations of green flourishing off the dark limbs and in their shadows, and the red, hanging apples.

John Henry stopped before one tree, about twenty deep, where the house couldn't be seen and where the privacy was nearly primordial. He pointed upward. "Mistletoe," he said. "Poison," he added.

At first, Henry could detect nothing but bright fruit and limitless green punctured by the sun, but then, squinting, he discerned there, among the healthy branches, a smattering of pale seeds like tiny pearl onions or white trinkets clustered in a bush of hardy leaves. It had the look of a wildly disordered bird's nest. The tree branch was suffering under the leaching plant, which drained its natural strength. With care, Henry positioned the ladder next to the blighted branch.

"My hope is that it can be merely clipped out. I don't want to lose my tree, or any tree."

"Well, one tree—" Henry began.

"I planted these two rows of trees when your brothers were born."

It was as if the sentence had been said by someone else, so foreign was its meaning. At first, Henry simply stood there, staring stupidly as his father adjusted the clippers in his hand and set his hands on the ladder, peering upward.

"I don't understand," he said.

Looking up at the mistletoe clump, where it encircled the branch in a draining embrace, John Henry said, "There were two children before you were born. The first died right after birth, the other died in its second month. There was a great deal of rejoicing, then a great deal of bitterness."

Henry's astonishment wrote red across his cheeks. There was a pained accusation in his voice when he said, "Why didn't anyone ever tell me?"

"Because it almost killed your mother, and it wasn't your business," came the reply. "So I have my reasons for preserving this orchard." And after one deep breath, girding himself with self-assurance, John Henry placed one foot on the first rung and slowly began to climb. Henry, his outrage growing even as he held the ladder steady, blurted, "Why do you always treat me like a child?"

This time there was no reply as John Henry hesitated on the second rung, his brow furrowed and a trembling causing his khakis to shake.

It was the subtlest of movements, but Henry grabbed instinctively at his father's strong, bunchy calf to steady him. "Are you okay?" He saw the steeling of his father's jaw, the way he thrust his chin forward toward a rung of the ladder to gaze resolutely skyward, and he started in surprise. "Father, are you afraid of heights?"

Only a grunt as a reply. But his father seemed to inch up the ladder, rather than climb, each motion slowed by hesitation. What door had been opened on conversation was closed again, and the room of their understanding was silent.

Father, I didn't know you were afraid of anything.

Oh oh but perhaps I did

For a moment, he wanted to say, Why don't you let me do it, but he was spellbound by those strangely enfeebled movements his father made as he climbed and, toughened by his sense of injustice, he scraped the last bit of love off his tongue with his teeth. Presently, the gray head disappeared into the ceiling of green. Then the voice—the authority that had circumscribed his life for sixteen years—called down, "It's too late. It's gotten into the vasculature and the branch is stunted. Goddammit. Hand me the saw." And the clippers dropped down with a thud to the ground.

Henry picked up the saw by its serrated teeth and, because his father had climbed so high, he ascended the first two rungs of the ladder. John Henry, watching him come, reached down with an awkward, curtailed gesture, still clinging with desperate force to a higher rung. Henry felt the ladder shake with his father's shaking. It shook its way right past his fingertips into the muscles of his chest.

John Henry grabbed the saw and placed its teeth about two feet from the infestation.

"I hate to do it," he said.

But of course you will, his son thought with a wintry scorn. His father began to cut away the injured limb to save the tree, draw after grating draw until it came crashing down with its mistletoe intact, bright green.

Henry watched it come down, but John Henry still gazed upward into the fragrant compass of the tree. Then he began his slow, unnerved descent, one painful rung at a time, as Henry said, quietly, "Take it slow," as if his words were an encouragement and not a slap, and his father came, his breathing audible, the ladder trembling, until his feet were on firm ground, and he simply stood there, gripping the ladder sides, breathing like a gladiator.

John Henry turned his flushed face to the side and said, "What we talked about today, don't mention it to your mother. She never wanted you to know."

"Yes, sir." The polite words were alloyed by a stingy metal in his voice. John Henry turned fully and looked into the ever-increasing mystery of his son's face, as if to determine whether this was sarcasm or straight, and the indecision in those aging eyes was a tiny glory to behold. He said, "Leave the ladder, and drag that branch back to the yard, where it can be chopped."

Would his insolence get off so easy? He had only moved ten feet, when John Henry intoned three words: "And young man." When Henry glanced back over his shoulder, John Henry's right hand, that clamp, wrench, hold, vise, that old beater, was pointing at him: "I've been watching you."

A depth charge shook the boy, and the whole of his sexual misdeeds were laid out in that moment, as if his father had been there in the tack room as Loretta had sucked on his tongue and worked her salivaed hand between his legs until he shuddered wretchedly and gasped, and instantly, in his father's presence, before he said anything else, Henry's mind was on fire with shame.

John Henry stared directly into his son's guilty eyes. "Don't chase after just any bitch in heat."

"No, sir." His mouth was sandy.

"You're better than that."

"Yes, sir."

"I don't believe I need to waste any more breath on this conversation."

"No, sir."

"Manage yourself."

Henry stared down at the ground, conquered.

"Or I will manage you."

John Henry: Son, what is desire in a strong man? Do you remember what I told you?

Henry: Desire is a draft horse, harnessed by tradition, working in service of the line.

John Henry: And desire in a weak man?

Henry: A Thoroughbred, wild and dangerous.

John Henry: And eros?

Henry: A blindfolded youth.

John Henry: Which results in mania.

Henry: Yes, *but*

Oh, Father, you hypocrite! Enfeebled and blind! Your Argument from Authority fails! Choke to death on your words—Mania transforms! It makes the cuckold the lover again, it makes the blind man see, it ripens the fruits that reason can only plant! Madness lays waste to shame! Even Socrates hid his face over his stupid speeches! Hide your own!

Paulette carried trays piled with pineapple-glazed ham with mint garnish, corn pudding, and dusky dinner rolls; chardonnay for the adults, virgin mint juleps for the children. But Henry's silver cup sat sweaty and untouched, finely engraved with its curlicued *F*. Lonely Lavinia tried to catch his eye, and Loretta grinned her grin full of secrets, but Henry had eyes only for his father: how his straight spine formed the axis of the room, around which the entire earth revolved. How, once again, the men inclined their heads toward each other, speaking in a fraternal enclosure that excluded the bustling table of children, which unjustly included Henry. But he wasn't cowed. His shoulders were as square as his jaw. He had grown to his full six feet one this summer and could look Uncle Mason in the eye. He was strong as new rope.

John Henry said, "We've rarely seen a worse drought, but I have faith it will rain soon."

"We're feeling the effects as far south as Florida," said Uncle Mason. "I don't believe it's rained in twenty-seven days now."

"Is that right?"

"But you're worse off, to be sure. Much worse."

"There has been some talk of families leaving the area," said his father, but then he shrugged. "Many of these men have mishandled their black years, so my sympathies are limited to say the least."

"Well, I'd hate to see that," said Uncle Mason. "When an uneducated man leaves the only thing he knows—"

"There are lateral moves to be made into manufacturing. Not to mention there's security in the factories that these farmers can only dream of," said John Henry.

Loretta glanced up suddenly from her food. "They should move to
Florida if they need work," she said. "There's a lot of work there, isn't that
right, Daddy? I always see men standing on the side of the road when I go
to school."

John Henry stared at her, blinking, and her mother hissed, "Loretta."

"What?" she said, swiveling toward her with a blank look. "It's true."

Uncle Mason cleared his throat and glanced at his brother. "Well,
Kentucky's always been a corn deficit state. Are they bringing down
surplus from Ohio?"

John Henry shook his head. "Even Ohio is baling corn this summer."

"It's like when we were kids all over again."

"Yes," John Henry said, and now he eyed the table round, his look a
warning, as if they all should remember, though no one else could, except
Lavinia, who watched him and nodded, sensing a strange energy in the
room, but unable to parse it.

"Well, you have to wonder how many of these family farms can hang
on," said Uncle Mason. "What did Grandfather always say? All you need is
a good gun, a good horse, and a good wife? It's not enough these days,
apparently. Still, it's a sorry sight to watch farms go under."

"Well," said Loretta brightly, "when Henry's raising horses here you
won't have to worry about any of that ever again." She grinned at them all,
but the table plummeted into silence around her; then something stilled in
her eyes, her broad smile contracting slowly to a line of poised alertness.
She glanced at Henry, but he was not looking at her; he simply took another
bite of ham as if by continuing to eat, as if by pretending he hadn't heard, he
could distend time and stave off what was to come.

"What did you say, young lady?" said John Henry. His voice was stony
and low. Loretta looked at him, eyes wide, but said nothing at all into the
raw, charged quiet of the table.

Then John Henry brought his utensils down to the tabletop, one in
each hand, and it caused the table to rejolt with a crack like a branch breaking. "What did you say, young lady?" His voice was rising to a roar, and
Loretta visibly started and cowered back into her chair, instinctively scoot-
ing against her mother. Mason laid a steadying hand on his brother's upper
arm, but that arm sprang loose from its cocked reserve, pointed out across
the table at Henry, that hand the detonation, so the voice that followed was

only a report. "I haven't sacrificed everything so you could waste your god-damned life! I haven't raised you to be an idiot!"

What other words were flung across the table at Henry he could not later reconstruct, not in their entirety. He simply rose up from the table with a strangely disembodied calm on his strong, new face, a face built for the future. Lavinia whipped around in her seat, reaching for him, but she was too late.

"Don't you dare leave my goddamn presence, boy! Not without my permission!"

But Henry did just that, passing out of the dining room, walking faster and faster until he was almost jogging, leaving the assembled family with their mouths gaping and John Henry storming up from his chair, so that he knocked the table, causing the china to dance violently and the younger girls to cry. Loretta had already fled into the kitchen when, freeing herself from a tangle of chair legs and crying girls, Lavinia chased after John Henry as he stalked to the front hall. When she grabbed at his shirtsleeve, he lashed out blindly behind himself, striking the fine flesh of her cheek with his Sewanee class ring, so that she was bleeding even before she sat down hard on her bottom on the polished floor.

Henry, who was just rounding the foot of the staircase, saw his mother fall, and he screamed out to his approaching father, "I hate you!"

"Get back down here," John Henry warned, not running, but also losing no ground as he followed his son, who was skipping stairs now in his haste to reach the second floor.

"Get back down here," he barked again, trying to rein in his voice, but there was weakness in the repetition, and he seemed to sense it, because now he cried full-throated, "Look at me when I speak to you, goddammit!"

Henry whirled at the top of the stairs, sixteen years of fury wrenching the contours of his face. His lips rode back from his teeth like an animal's as he pointed down accusation at his father.

"You're a fucking tyrant!" he screamed.

"And you're behaving like a fool, Henry. Control yourself." The words came low and rumbling.

"You're nothing but a coward!"

His father shook as he raised a meaty hand and pointed up at his son; even his jowls shook. "You're embarrassing yourself in front of your entire family."

"No, I'm just embarrassing you!" Henry cried. "There's a difference!" He was stringing his arrows, now setting the bow. "You've always been afraid of ever trying to be truly great! No war medals, right, Father? Maybe the General Assembly, but never the governorship! And, oh, don't touch the farm! Nothing you could ever fail miserably at! You weren't even enough for your own wife!"

For a moment, all rage slacked, and his father looked at him as though at a stranger. "I made you to break my heart?" he said.

Henry spread his arms like wings. "Whether you like it or not, this land will be a horse farm."

"I would sooner you die," came the leaden reply from the foot of the stairs.

"But I'm not going to die," Henry said, gasping for breath. "You are."

John Henry's face grew apoplectic. "Then I will not die!" he screamed, and the house shook.

But he did die. He collapsed from a massive stroke in the spring of 1965, and Henry immediately returned home from his graduate studies and let the fields go fallow, then reseeded with fescue and clover in the fall. The next year he bought his first horse at a claiming race in Florida, a mare called Hellbent. She was a spirited horse, fast, and almost perfectly formed. She would become his taproot mare.

INTERLUDE I

The following colors are recognized by the Jockey Club:

BAY: The entire coat of the horse may vary from a yellow-tan to a bright auburn. The mane, tail and lower portion of the legs are always black, unless white markings are present.

BLACK: The entire coat of the horse is black, including the muzzle, the flanks, the mane, tail and legs, unless white markings are present.

CHESTNUT: The entire coat of the horse may vary from a red-yellow to a golden-yellow. The mane, tail and legs are usually variations of the coat color, unless white markings are present.

DARK BAY/BROWN: The entire coat of the horse will vary from a brown, with areas of tan on the shoulders, head and flanks, to a dark brown, with tan areas seen only in the flanks and/or muzzle. The mane, tail and lower portion of the legs are always black, unless white markings are present.

GRAY/ROAN: The Jockey Club has combined these colors into one color category. This does not change the individual definitions of the colors for gray and roan and in no way impacts the two-coat color inheritance principle as stated in Rule 1(E).

GRAY: The majority of the coat of the horse is a mixture of black and white hairs. The mane, tail and legs may be either black or gray, unless white markings are present.

ROAN: The majority of the coat of the horse is a mixture of red and white hairs or brown and white hairs. The mane, tail and legs may be black, chestnut or roan, unless white markings are present.

PALOMINO: The entire coat of the horse is golden-yellow, unless white markings are present. The mane and tail are usually flaxen.

WHITE: The entire coat, including the mane, tail and legs, is predominantly white.

—*Jockey Club Registry*

The master of color is the gene. The gene is found inside the cell on the chromosome, coiled material formed in arkan pairs, a chain provided by each parent with the allele a blind toss from dam and sire to foal. Genes, like many tyrants, are small but manifest in a multiplicity of forms. Allele pairs dictate the genotype, which, due to the vagaries of expression, may or may not correlate precisely to phenotype: black, brown, bay, dun, grullo, buckskin, chestnut/sorrel, red dun, palomino, silver dapple, cremello, which subdivide to reflect allelic combinations of jet and raven and summer black; or dark and light and seal browns; slate, lobo, olive, smutty, or silver grullos, and so on; also the white markings, which increase upon the infinite with roans, or the gray of age, or rabicano, frosty, paint, or tobiano; this is to say nothing of the effects of dappling, foal transition, seasonal change, & Etc.

Nature manipulates her colors—or color happens, insofar as the gene has no Mind to mind the gene—either as alleles occupy loci in homozygous and heterozygous pairs, or through the wily machinations of epistasis, where brute dominance shoulders its autocratic way through the old blood-lines, while recessives wait in genetic shadow, eyeing the dominant pairs and biding their time until, in tandem, the recessives in a surprise move—

No, perhaps it's better to render genetics a descriptive but meaningless math as it concerns the hard colors, these colors being chestnut, black, and bay:

ee
EE or Ee
&
EEAA, EEAa, EeAA, or EeAa

But math won't satisfy. Why do we always want the story? A dominant allele storms the House of Agouti and seizes half its resources, producing a bay horse, *AA* or *Aa*. Most recessive combatants will ultimately join forces with the house to produce the expected black *EE* or *Ee*, but sometimes a chestnut, *ee*, emerges victorious from the House of Extension, outmaneu-vering the blacks and dominant bays of Agouti.

One would imagine that mastering the houses—Agouti, Extension, Dun, Silver Dapple, Champagne, and their meddling servants Pangare, Sooty, Shade, Flaxen, Brindle—would allow for the rational construction of color, including the dilutes that form from the hard, fundamental colors. But then there is white. White is less a color than a superimposition. It is a pigmentless pattern, a roan or gray intrusion upon all the hard colors and their various configurations. A white is the only horse without pigment, though even the white horse has dark eyes, *WhW*. White serves to mask color, though color lives forever in the genes. Therefore, a white horse—or what seems a white horse—is capable of great reproductive surprises.

Ultimately you may breed for color just as you may breed for conforma-tion, speed, strength, & Etc, but the organism itself exerts no will to form. The natural dispersal of color is neither random nor intentional. Which is all to say that there may be tyrants with no ambition for power.

THE SPIRIT OF LESSER ANIMALS

On the principle of the multiplication and gradual divergence in character of the species descended from a common parent, together with their retention by inheritance of some characters in common, we can understand the excessively complex and radiating affinities by which all the members of the same family or higher group are connected together.

—CHARLES DARWIN, *On the Origin of Species*

There was a culling of resources: which represents tolerance of risk, a form of courtship display, i.e., the organism's ability to assert itself in the war of sexual selection. So, the detritus of the old plantation was sold away: the slump-shouldered plow, a corn planter with its four ugly teeth, jointers and froes and poleaxes and chisels and a thousand antiques lined out for appraisal and bidding on the side lawn, all sold to strangers on Valentine's Day 1966. Even the old Tennessee Walkers were auctioned off, but purchased by the Millers, so the six were led in a head-hanging line down the drive like bewildered cow ponies off to their first cattle drive, while Henry stood on the el porch, bourbon in hand, watching without regret. At this point both of your grandparents have died.

There followed a reorientation of remaining resources: Stallion paddocks were arranged in two-acre units near the house with a yearling barn erected some way behind a stallion barn. The old whipping post was not uprooted in the redesign of the farm, but left to stand perversely in the path of an emerging thicket windbreak, so the evergreen bushes grew up around it like a rose around its thorn. The Osbournes' land was purchased when they went bankrupt in the summer of 1968, so the old land of the silt bowl, which had once been Forge property before being sold in William Iver's generation, was Henry's and yours once again, and it came with a brood-mare band and a foaling barn only thirteen years old and the assurance of hardy grass over limestone; also a sweet-tasting Stoner Creek streamlet that pooled in the bowl, glimmering there like gray ice on cloudy days.

Another note on display: Your father paints the plank fences wedding-dress white instead of black, an unnecessary expense. However, in the wild, male suitors often develop brightly colored, highly ornamented tails or wings that display genetic excess, which is to say wild tolerance of risk (see above), in order to secure a suitable mate and reproductive success. The female, frequently the choosier of the species, selects. Note how in this schema, the male and female are merely avenues to reproduction, dispens-able agents of futurity.

A note on the 1 percent: The human is an organism defined by its 1 percent genetic difference from the chimp, which involves improved hear-ing, protein digestion, sophisticated speech, and all the other necessary conditions of humanity, not least of which is hope: in this case a horse. Hellbent is well balanced with a head neither too large nor too small, situ-ated nicely on her neck over a slim swell of belly; driven by quarters that are strong but not stocky; legs set neither forward nor back but perfectly straight; unimpressive in her first races, but intriguing on paper; a gamble, your father's roughcut gem, a daughter of Bold Ruler, showing some of his high temperament and nerve, if not his power at the mile and beyond.

But there follows disappointment: dejection at the frustration of design. During Hellbent's life the broodmare band was expanded then culled, stallions were purchased and sold, mares crossed out and inbred, but there never came a horse that made the farm, or made your father. Hellbent her-self became a solid producer of horses, including stakes winners, though a few broke down, overextended in distance by overeager trainers, and one died of colic in the pasture, its guts twisted like engorged ropes, striking its head against the ground in vain attempts to rise, so it had beaten itself to death before the vet could arrive.

Disappointment is compounded by perfection: Henry sees Secretariat, the big red colt by Bold Ruler out of Somethingroyal, at the 1972 Laurel Futurity, then again at next year's Belmont, where the chestnut springs from the inside and establishes a lead along the backstretch against his rival

Sham and ahead of Twice a Prince and My Gallant, firing out the first three quarters in 1:09⅘, at which point Sham begins to fall away under the scorching pace—*Secretariat is widening now, he is moving like a tremendous machine, Secretariat by twelve, Secretariat by fourteen lengths*—with Turcotte wild-eyed and asking for nothing and the grandstand rising with an oceanic roar around Henry, who stands transfixed as Secretariat takes the only purse of real value, greatness, charging under the wire thirty-one lengths ahead of Sham in 2:24, a record that stands even today.

But your father procured a mate that fateful day in Saratoga: a woman thin as a pin with a glassy blonde bob and lips painted burgundy, displaying near-perfect conformation with only minor defects: pigeon-toed with a hard voice; but also restlessness, the quality of perpetual dissatisfaction, a state which represents a subtle but very real threat to young prior to the age of separation; see Bowlby's work on maternal deprivation, also Ainsworth, Winnicott, & Etc. You call this woman Mother. She is one-half responsible for your corporeal organization, your particular form of accumulated inheritance. Together with your father, she is a conduit of the great law, the Unity of Type.

And so you were born: into the Conditions of Existence. Our ignorance of the laws of variation is profound.

The Quarter is a cutting horse and the Morgan is a generalist. The Kentucky Saddle is a smooth ride, the Connemara a great jumper, the Mustang an independent. The Mongolian is an ancient primitive and the toady Exmoor is exceedingly rare. The Akhal-Teke has endurance, and the Belgian Draft the strength of ten. But only the Thoroughbred can claim to be the fastest horse in the world—and here it was resident in their lush spring fields, bathing in the sunlight, calling antiphonally over Henrietta's head as she spent herself each and every day on her father's holdings, his very earth.

Her eyes were always open.

She saw wheat rounds as they rolled off the tongue of the baler.

Doves lined into the air when a cat came and parted the grasses.

Clouds were piled and red-tipped like a sunshot mountain range inverted.

The faces of the tall horses were riddles.

Perhaps her parents could discover their meaning? Her father was not in the stallion barn, not in the orchard, so she ran in search of her mother and found Judith in the master bedroom, reclining against a landslide of silken pillows, magazines fanned around her, speaking urgently under her breath on the phone to one of her sisters. With her pale skin and blonde hair, she almost disappeared into the sheets the way fences vanish into snow in the wintertime.

Henrietta barnstormed the room, her arms wide. "Mother, I want to know why—"

Judith shrank into her pillow, covered the receiver with one palm, and said, "Jesus, Henrietta. A little warning next time."

"I want to know—"

"Hold on," her mother said into the phone, struggling to sit up straight and pressing the receiver between her breasts. She gathered herself, arranging her good-night smile, cheer like bright paint over irritation. Then she leaned over, offering her cheek. "Henrietta, you know I don't like it when you yell indoors. Now kiss me good night. Did you say good night to the horses?"

Henrietta sighed, her question abandoned. "Yes," she said very simply, leaning over the magazines, crumpling their glossy pages as she kissed her mother's cheek.

"Good girl," said Judith, clearing her throat. "Now go to bed, and your father will be in shortly to tell you a story. Go on."

"Okay."

But when Henrietta straightened up from the bed, her mother said very suddenly, "Henrietta, wait—tell me, did you have a good day?"

"Yes."

"And did you have fun?"

Henrietta shrugged. "Yes."

Then, Judith's crystalline blue eyes narrowed. "But—are you happy?"

Henrietta laughed the evergreen laugh of the very young; of course she was happy. It was the natural state of childhood.

"Well, good night."

She was almost through the door when a hard, desponding voice halted her one more time. "But you would tell me if you were unhappy, right?"

Impatiently: "Yes, Mother."

"Promise?"

"I promise." Then only a dark, empty space remained where the child had stood. Sighing so loudly that Henrietta heard it on the threshold of her own room, Judith said, "Yes, I'm still here."

This is your story, Henrietta. It was 1783, during the waning heat of the Revolutionary War. Thousands of soldiers had already died on the field, or were injured in their drive to beat back the British. Your great-great-greatest-grandfather was one of those injured at Yorktown, and he received a bounty land warrant offering him surveyable acreage west of the Blue Ridge Mountains. This whole area was part of Virginia at the time, and that's why we are Kentuckians first and Virginians second and Christians third. Well, Samuel Forge was more than eager to go. The state of his birth was too populous and too loud, and he was saddled with a pioneer's roving mind, which demands space. So Samuel set out west and brought with him a slave, who was smart with black magic and a very fine cook, and together they traversed the mountains. But those mountains were dark and forbidding. The two of them followed the old buffalo blaze and battled mightily against the elements, wary of Shawnee to the north and Cherokee to the south, because in those days a scalp was very valuable. The way was rough and full of dangers, but Samuel persevered. When they finally reached the Gap, they discovered a cave, an opening right there in the sheer wall of rock. Now his slave had a special feeling about this cave and wanted to explore it, but first they needed protection from the gods, so they sacrificed four bulls that they found wandering around in the open land around the Gap, and then his slave led the way down into the dark. This was a cave that led to the underworld. They wandered in the dark past Dread and Hunger and Want and Sleep and Toil and War and Discord, who had wild, long, horrible hair and was the worst thing Samuel Forge had ever seen, and they walked past the Tree of Dreams, but it didn't catch any of Samuel's dreams. He was too slippery and his dreams too big to be caught. Down, down, down they went until they came to the milling crowds of the unhappy dead that gathered on the bank of a river as wide and muddy as the Ohio. A boatman rowed them across the river, and they walked onto the fields of heaven, and all the noble dead were alive like gods. They crowded around him with stories on their tongues, but Samuel Forge had come to look for only one man—his father, Andrew Cooper Forge, who had died back in Virginia and never again seen his son once he'd set out to make his own way in the world. Samuel wanted his forgiveness for past wrongs, and he did indeed discover him there on the green underground fields of heaven. The old man was making a census of all his descendants, and had in trust all their futures and their fates, everything they would be and everything they would do, all the Forges, who in their time would march out of the cave into the bright daylight on the Kentucky side of the Gap. He was gathering his numbers, and I was there and you were there, even though we hadn't come to be yet—

Are you awake, Henrietta? When you lie so still like that, it's as if you're dead and if you're dead, then I'm dead too, because you are the very pupil of my eye. Are you listening?

Yes, Father. I'm awake. I'm always listening.

"All I want is a little pleasure."

Pleasure: a sensation of enjoyment, satisfaction; the indulgence of appetite; sometimes personified as a female divinity. Considered by most to be the opposite of pain.

What was there to do for pleasure on a Sunday in Paris, Kentucky, 1983? The only thing that didn't drive Judith completely and utterly insane was to spend a quiet hour in the Paris Cemetery. The space reminded her—granted, in peacefulness only—of the Tuileries and the Jardin des Plantes, which she had enjoyed when she was pregnant with a teenager's hope and limitless expectation but not yet pregnant with Henry Forge's child. She had at first tried to take Henrietta to the park in the center of town, but the girl was relentless, pressing endlessly for a push on the swing—One more push! One more! Mother!—then Watch!Watch!Watch!—so Judith couldn't read the real estate section of the *Times*, and she was forever stubbing out fresh cigarettes to attend to the girl, who made a mess, an absolute, irredeemable mess of her own clothes and her mother's sanity. What she was coming to realize, but what no woman was allowed to utter aloud, was that there was no guarantee your child would be adequate compensation for the life you gave up to have it. More and more, life looked an awful lot like a hoax perpetrated on women and designed to further men's lives at the expense of their own.

"All I want is a little pleasure."

What did Henrietta know or care about any of this? She had plenty of pleasures, such as the cemetery's Gothic chalk gates, white as the Cliffs of Dover, through which broughams and phaetons once rattled under the old sign: It is appointed unto men once to die, but after this the judgment. When her mother stopped their Mercedes to light her first cigarette of the hour, Henrietta—free, unmolested, wild—would run out among the graves to trample on the dead, skipping over their complaints and concerns, their dreamy chatter and arguments of confinement, their hate bred by close quarters, not so different perhaps from her parents' ferocious arguments, which she heard when she was tucked in her bed at home. The dead had nothing to break or slam except their dull coffin lids. Her mother had the dishes of life and the doors of happenstance. And a voice for shattering windowpanes.

"Jesus," Judith said, "this place is just unspeakably boring. It simply defies words." A great, trembling ash broke free from her long cigarette and floated alongside the car.

Henrietta looked about in confusion. "The cemetery?"

"Everything, Henrietta. Every last thing."

"Mother, why do you smoke?"

"It keeps my weight down," Judith said distractedly. "I mean, please explain to me how I ended up here. I lived in Paris, honey, the real Paris. The only Paris. Sometimes I can't believe I bought Henry's pack of lies and . . . traded Paris and Deauville for this." She shook her head and lowered her chin. "Just promise me that when you grow up, you'll know exactly what you're choosing between when you make your choices. Men like naïve girls, and there's a reason for that."

Henrietta gazed up at her mother's delicate profile. "Can I have brothers?"

Judith's finely sculpted head snapped round, her brilliant eyes nearly sewn shut. "Did your father tell you to say that to me? Did he put you up to that?" she said.

"No—"

"God, I can't stand men. It's always all about them. They'll even use their children to further their own ends."

"Daddy says—"

"Go play, Henrietta! Please! Just give me a few minutes of quiet."

Yes, go play among the graves, turn cartwheels over those tucked into their grass bedding, snatch at any excitements they left behind. Find the sloping declivity with Lavinia's cenotaph, under which she lies with dusty eyes closed, hands folded on her cancerous breasts. What pleasures she once flung away in her dying, Henrietta, take up now in your mouth.

The time-tattered granary loomed across the road.

When she approached birds, they all fled heavenward.

Chips of cloud formed scissors. They threatened to cut every thread in the world.

In joyful horror, Henrietta grasped up a single flower and raced back to the car. Her mother sat resting with her chin on her hand, her elbow on the window chrome. Her face had regained its equilibrium, but as the girl approached, her brow drew tight.

"Henrietta—have you been lying in the grass?"

The girl slowed, her mood suddenly veiled, her lips pressed together so tight they puffed out, showing a faint belligerence.

"Have you been lying in the grass?" This time the voice was not so sharp, but it seemed to shake with a strange and mysterious grievance, which the girl sensed but could not understand. "I'm not interested in putting you in a new dress every hour of the day. Why do you always do that?" And then turning to the windshield and saying to no one: "Why does she always do that . . . ?"

Henrietta said, "I brought something for you." She held out a yellow carnation, soft as a horse's muzzle, its edges already curling and tea-stained with decay.

"Henrietta," Judith admonished, "did you steal this from a grave?" but she reached out and gently lifted the flower from her hand.

"No."

Her mother couldn't help it, she smiled. "Get in the car," she said, and her daughter came round dutifully and slid in beside her.

"Grandmother says hi," Henrietta said as she struggled with her seat belt.

Judith reared back slightly. "Don't say things like that," she said. "It's creepy."

"Okay," said the girl. Then she said, "Did you know that if there were only two elephants in the world and they mated, in five hundred years there would be fifteen million elephants?"

"You're only seven," said Judith. "Why do you know anything about mating?"

"Daddy told me. Mother, what if you had to spend your whole life being chained to a tombstone, and you couldn't get anybody to unlock your chain?"

"My God, Henrietta, what awful things you think of," said Judith, the delicate plane of her brow wrinkled up in distaste.

"Probably nobody would want to be around you, and wild dogs would come and try to eat you."

"Well," said Judith, starting the car and remaining attentive only by an anemic and diminishing force of will, "maybe you could train the dogs and name them and then they might leave you alone."

"Wild dogs don't have names, silly!" Henrietta cried, and she laughed uproariously, and her mother just bent her head slightly away from the sound of that shrill and disruptive laughter, a sound she herself could not remember ever having made.

But their horses did have names. In the early spring of each year, Henry led his daughter out to a pasture at the rim of the bowl, where three or four mares were turned out with shiny new foals—copper and bay and a dappled gray almost white. Unlike their dark and calm dams, they sprang about, bouncing here and there and spending their small energies. They were comically, even absurdly, composed with root beer barrel knees and cannons thin enough to snap over a grown man's thigh. Their eyes, like their legs, were set awkwardly wide, their tails as short and bushy as the tails of rabbits.

Henrietta was reading by her fourth year, and by the time she was eight, she was attendant to the namings, standing beside her father with a stenographer's notebook and a pencil, marking down his choices like a small actuary. She balanced her book on the second plank of the fence while Henry rested a loafered foot on the first, his freckled forearms crossed on the top plank, as he gazed out over the dams and foals. Casuistry passed near, her foal peering curiously around her, its head already framed by a halter, though it was merely days old.

When old Jamie Barlow appeared beside them, leaning on the fencing and flicking up the frayed brim of his ball cap, Henry said, "What do you think of this one? He's by Motor Running over at Dale Mae Stud."

Barlow was sanguine as he considered the foal. "I'd say that's a mess of feathers, but no bird."

"I was asking my daughter," said Henry, and if there was anything in Barlow's silence then, Henrietta was too young to sense it. "What do you see, Henrietta?"

With her pencil tucked behind her ear, she said, "He's okay, I guess?"

Henry shook his head. "A horse I see, but horseness I do not. He's in-bred to Casuistry's line, but he looks hackish, pedestrian. I don't see the right balance of bodily weight and light bone."

His daughter was barely listening. At her feet, the grass roiled and shook with its invisible machinations, teeming with life's orchestra. The blades of grass were little bows making its music. The green there was so sincere, so undiluted, it rivaled the sun for intensity.

Henry reached down and, with a gentle but firm hand, turned her head forcibly back to the matter at hand, and it made her squirm. He was too enthusiastic, like a candidate on the hustings. "See how thick his legs are already? That's cold blood and not at all what we're aiming for. This is selective breeding we're engaged in, nothing random about it. Evolution is a ladder, and our aim is to climb it as quickly as possible. We'll most likely geld him."

"That Motor Running ought to be a kill shot," said Barlow, shaking his head. "Don't know how come we can't get a winner out of him."

"Call the foal Castrato," Henry said suddenly. "Write that down. Castrato out of Casuistry."

Kastroto, she wrote, sounding out the word with the tip of her pencil.

"Now, take a close look at Hellbent's foal."

Henrietta peered between the planks. Hellbent's foal was darkly red as a steak with a blaze and two white kneesocks. She bucked out with gangly legs and lunged gamely at the neck of her dam, who brisked and shone in the light.

"That's a mighty good-looking filly right there," said Barlow.

Henry looked down at his daughter. "I've been waiting for the right mare to send over to Secretariat, but I've wanted the best materials to work with. We'll have to see if she runs as good as she looks. I'm sure they'll think I'm breeding too far up the ladder—"

"Nah, she's got the Bold Ruler look, good hind end, smart face—"

"And perfect legs."

Barlow reached down and with no warning swung Henrietta up and positioned her on the top plank, so she was facing the man, who smelled of dusty hides and cigarettes, which she was soon rooting for in his breast pocket. She discovered one, slipping it from its pack, but he playfully knocked her hand away, said, "That ain't Christian. You be good or I'll take you home and let my old lady straighten you out. She always wanted a little girl."

"No," she said, grinning.

"Oh my, yes," said Barlow. "She'll fix you up. Raised four wild and woolly boys, think she can't handle you? You ain't got any kind of wicked she can't bring to Jesus."

"No!" she cried.

Henry reached over and ruffled her reddish hair. "You'd still be my little Ruffian."

"What's a Ruffian?"

Henry turned a considering eye on her. "The best filly to ever run the race. You'd have to go back to the turn of the century to find another one like her."

"She was smart?"

"She was beautiful."

"Can I go see her?"

"No . . ."

Henrietta's brows gathered to a V of disappointment. "Why not?"

"Well, honeypie, she broke down," said Barlow.

"But doing what she loved most," Henry interjected.

Barlow grinned. "Blessed are they who run in circles, for they shall be called big wheels."

Staring at his new filly, Henry said, "For the great, death dies."

Henrietta sighed and looked up at Barlow, who was gazing down on her with a curious expression on his face. Smiling ruefully, he hoisted her off the plank fence and into his arms, so she was enveloped in the physical warmth of a grown person. She looked over his shoulder in the direction of the green expanse of the bowl with its promise of free play, and because Henry caught her longing glance and it worried something in his mind, he reached down and rapped gently on her head. "Knock, knock," he said. "Are you there?" She nodded, and with her feet returned to the fields of Henry's confidence, she did as she was told, taking her pencil from behind her ear and writing down six potential names for each foal, names that they would then send to the Jockey Club for consideration. Their first choice for Hellbent's foal was Hellcat and in a few months' time, they learned the name had been accepted.

Henrietta would remember the storms that came two years later in the spring of her tenth year, not because the farm was so altered, which it was, but because her mother did not come home. Around dinnertime the sky grew flavid and discontent and earth colors seeped up from the soil into the atmosphere, where clouds gathered, mossed with the green cast of tornado-laden storms. A siren wailed in town, the sound bowing in and out as the gaping mouth turned to the four corners of the county. Everywhere horses pranced with their ears up to catch the rising wind, barn cats skulked for shelter, cows bellowed in alarm. The trees shook and flung their glossy leaves into the changing light and the sun, a useless and retiring thing, slinked away. The farm was swallowed into the dark of the storm and it was terribly still, then the silence was staved in by a mighty crack and the rain began to fall. In their stalls, the horses cried. Lightning forked across the sky and inflected downward to the earth, where it lashed its electric tongue on trees and housetops and cupolas and lit the rolling eyes of the animals and the entire achromatic world.

In her bed, Henrietta listened to the storm as it battered the house, its soughing sounds like the moaning of many anguished people. She watched the water cascade from the coping inches above her window and nursed a seed of panic for her mother, who had not yet appeared. Tears gathered in the girl's green eyes. She strained for the sound of the phone ringing for as long as she was able, but being young and tired, she was asleep before she knew it, and then it was morning and the rain was gently washing the brick skin of the house and its windows. She ran into her parents' room, but neither one was there. From their window gazing down, she could see their three resident stallions being led, frantic with nerves, into waiting trailers. Down beyond the white barn, the stream was wildly gray and belling out of its banks, sweeping fronds into its current, where they waved like tangled hair. She spotted her father and the figure of Barlow. She flung off her nightclothes, leaving them in the hall as she ran back to her own room, where she struggled into jeans and a sweater, racing downstairs even as she was dressing. She was cramming her feet into boots and looking for a rain jacket when Henry came stomping into the kitchen. She flung herself at him, taking him by surprise and knocking him back against the door he had just shut. It was like embracing a tree in a rainstorm, but she didn't care. She was instantly wet through by the outdoors he had brought in with him.

"Henrietta, honey," he said with surprise.

"Where's Mother?" she said. "Did Mother come home?" There were tears in her voice that startled him. He blinked rapidly as she stared up into his face.

"Your mother is fine," he said slowly, carefully. "She just couldn't come home last night."

"Why not?" Henrietta said. "Did she get in an accident?"

"No," he said, and he cleared his throat. "She's fine. She stayed in Lexington."

"Why?" she said, and as a ghost of suspicion flitted in her eyes, Henry thought, she's nothing like her mother; there's so much of me in her.

"Well," he said, "your mother . . ." Then he paused and waited for something to come into his mind and when it didn't appear, he winced and hurried on. "Your mother has an apartment in Lexington, where she might want to stay sometimes."

"But she's coming home." The words seesawed between question and insistence.

Henry looked down into that worried face and his mouth struggled momentarily as he redirected his words. "Soon," he said, and brighter: "Soon!" But his own smile was alloyed by hesitation. She pressed her face into the flat of his belly, and he heard her mumble, "Good."

Outside, there was the sound of the first trailer rumbling down the lane with a frightened stallion kicking inside.

"Where are the horses going?" she said, her voice muffled.

"To a training center just until the creek settles. We don't want it to rise and carry them away."

In her mind, the black and brown horses were swept off in the raging current of Forge Run, open-mouthed and screaming shrilly in the frothing stream, their eyes rolling in terror and their bodies battling in slow motion against forces stronger, much stronger, than themselves.

"No," she said. "Please keep them all safe, Daddy."

The storm continued for three days without abating. The creek flashed out of its margins, spilling over half the paddocks and into the stallion barn, though it was sandbagged and wrapped to three feet in heavy plastic. Hay and straw floated out on the rising tide and swirled in a gray mass that soaked the earth. The sky was sodden and tiresome, the earth was sodden and tiresome. Henrietta watched it all from the kitchen and from her parents' room as she waited for the phone to ring.

When the rain finally stopped, the clouds thinned and were wicked from the drying sky as quickly as they had come, and the creek began to fall back with a sigh into its banks, leaving behind little pluvial courses like open veins in the soil. Henrietta ventured out in her mother's polka-dotted galoshes and explored the paddocks that oozed water with each step. She stood on the edge of the creek, where it continued to shrink back as if newly shy absent the blustering weather. She could not move about freely without slipping and sliding, so she just stood there and stared, and in her silence and in her fixity was some hint of a pained dawning. There was a change coming, and its germinal moments arrived not when she lay in her bed with panic in her breast, but here as she stood staring dully at the surface of a creek too muddy to see into, too dull to divulge its contents or reflect back anything of the world—not even her own face. She glanced back at the house, wondering whether she would hear the phone ringing down here.

She wandered down in the direction of the road where the rain-sickened creek was still engorged, swirling around the lower line of the old stone fence. A few of the limestone slabs, craggy and cut thin, had tumbled into the water and then either settled into the soil or slipped back into the current, where they lay camouflaged with their neighbors on the streambed.

On the western, Perry side of the stream, the gray hands of the water had pushed the fence until a portion toppled over fully intact onto its side, as neatly fallen as it had previously stood for over a century. Henrietta labored on the Forge side for a few minutes, returning limestone chunks to their spots in the wall and reordering the top vertical stones, so they were stacked together again in a line like books or a row of neolithic dinner plates.

"Miss Henrietta!" a voice called to her, and she straightened up abruptly with a hand shading her brow. There were some few straggling clouds now, but the atmosphere was thick with the moisture of the storm and the light seemed to come dully from everywhere and nowhere. Henrietta saw their neighbor, Ginnie Miller, plump and redheaded, waving one arm above her head and calling, "Miss Henrietta!"

Henrietta remained where she was on her side of their fence, affectless and staring.

"Come here, child," said Mrs. Miller with a beckoning gesture. Ginnie was the youngest of the Miller siblings, but had married a man named Marley, so she was Ginnie Marley. Her husband was quiet and when he drove past them on the road, he lifted only two fingers from the wheel by way of greeting. As if his lack of a first name rendered the marriage null and void, everyone still called her Mrs. Miller, though Henrietta could not recall her father referring to the woman at all.

Henrietta crossed the wet road and stood next to this woman she'd only seen from a distance. She was winded, as though coming from a dance, and her hair, slightly gray with voluminous curls puffed up from her face, re-sembled petals framing the rosy heart of a flower. It was the ruddy face of a life lived outdoors, her cheeks red as if sunburned, though it was only the middle of spring.

"My goodness," the woman said, "you're just a little slip. I guess it runs in the women of your family." She was leaning down slightly, and Henrietta saw her eyes were the color of dark chocolate. She said, "Well, I need your help. A couple of my cows got past my water gap, and my husband just took both my girls back to college. I need you to help me guide them back along the road. Can you do that?"

"Yes," Henrietta said.

"Then let's you and me go get us some beeves."

Henrietta followed her down the road away from the Miller drive, along the cow pasture, which spread to the west, inclining mildly to a hillock about a half mile away. A concrete waterer had been poured there, topping the rise like a crown on a grassy head. Black-and-white cattle were scattered about here and there, lowing a deep and dolorous sound.

They passed the spot where Forge Run ran dark-complected and swollen through a galvanized culvert under the road, running its course along the Miller property. The water gap was just two steel hoods from old cars chained across the creek to form a primitive stanch. One of the hoods still bore traces of its original red paint like old blood. On the far side of the artificial barrier, she saw the bulky figures of two black-and-white Holsteins steeping placidly in the muddy water. The water rose up past their hocks, but no further. They stood there appearing drowsy and mild until the two figures approached, then they bawled in tandem.

"How did they get out?" asked Henrietta.

"Well, when the water all rose up, the water gap went so"—Mrs. Miller raised her flattened palms so they were parallel to the ground—"and they just sort of squeezed on through and went about their merry way."

"They didn't get very far," said Henrietta.

"I think they used up all their fighting spirit just getting through the water gap."

They stopped at the top of the bank and looked down at the cows.

"Hello, my pretties," said Mrs. Miller, and then turned to Henrietta. "So, here's the plan. I'm gonna go on in there and move them up your way, and I just need you to head them off down the road toward the house."

"Okay."

"So set your legs apart like you mean business. Now, don't be scared."

"I'm not scared," Henrietta snorted. She set her legs apart like a sawhorse.

Mrs. Miller waded on into the creek upstream of the cows and the water plashed around her legs and filled up her green galoshes as little eddies spooled grayly away from her. The cows eyed her warily and were already making their first lurching motions toward the bank when the woman came up behind them, shooing. They jolted forward with real force, fat harlequins clambering out of the water, which shook in coffee droplets from their shining black limbs. They were clumsy on the rocky bank, slipping and lunging, their quarters jolting under the skin as they climbed.

"Just direct them," Mrs. Miller called, and Henrietta faced them down with her arms spread.

"No sudden motions now."

Henrietta made subtle pointing hand gestures as if they were wet airplanes being directed on tarmac, and they went easily as directed, trotting heavily, but veering for the middle of the road. Mrs. Miller came scrambling out of the creek, wet to above her knees, and moved on past Henrietta in a hustle to the first cow that was heading Forge-ward.

"Don't let them get in the road now," she said over her shoulder. "I want you between that cow and the car. I can afford to lose neighbors, but not cattle."

"Okay," said Henrietta.

She looked over her shoulder. "Honey, I'm kidding."

Henrietta walked beside the second cow with both her hands out toward its flank. It moved steadily along as though it were a wholly unremarkable event to walk on the wrong side of its pasture fence with the larger body of the herd gathering now as a congregation to watch. Mrs. Miller kept casting over her shoulder to check on their progress. As the Forge paddocks came into view, she said, "Guess there's a lot to keep a girl busy on a horse farm, huh?"

"I guess."

"What does a girl like you like to do?" she said.

Henrietta shrugged, a strange new mood was on her; the rains and her mother's absence had brought it on. "Study diagrams."

Ginnie reared back. "Diagrams! Of what?"

"Animals and plants. The history of their evolution. That sort of thing."

The woman hooted and looked back over her shoulder again with a different expression on her face, as though just discovering a different child in Henrietta's place, one who deserved a second glance. "Is that right," she said.

Encouraged, Henrietta said, "Did you know there are fifty thousand species of trees? That number's going down. They come in five shapes— round, conical, spreading— What's that?"

Mrs. Miller turned to see that Henrietta was pointing at the cursive *M* on the cow's rump.

"That's a brand."

"What's a brand?"

"We burn our family letter into them so if they ever get out like today, everybody will know they're ours and bring them back to us. Just like puppies."

"You brand puppies?"

"No, honey," said Mrs. Miller.

They were now approaching the squat Miller bungalow, where begonia pots hung in bursts of color from the scalloped porch trim and the flower beds stood pert in a wealth of watered soil.

"Run ahead and unlock the gate," said Mrs. Miller, and Henrietta did as she was told, pulling the pin and springing the gate, so the woman could pass on through with the two cows just as the herd was beginning to gather in a mass around the sojourners. With the cows captured, they stopped and watched the reunion, their forearms resting on the top steel rung like two old cowpokes, the older barely taller than the younger.

From this place, Henrietta had a new and clear vision of their home across the road and the black stallion barn atop the rise. Their stone fence was trim and neatly kept except where it had been rearranged by the swollen stream. The Millers' fence was crumbled and tumbled out of its original form along its length, limestone lying everywhere in heaps.

"Our fence is prettier than yours," Henrietta said.

Mrs. Miller snorted once and shook her head. "A good-looking fence is not high on my list of priorities. In my opinion, some people mind a little too much about how a place looks and not enough about how it runs." She looked very pointedly at the girl, but Henrietta was looking across the road to their fields, the grass mowed just so, the fences white as cotton bolls.

"Good looks are an evolutionary mark of health," she said. "That matters when it comes to mating. I read that."

Ginnie cocked her head. "Based on my cows, I'm gonna say that's probably not the whole story. In fact, that sounds like something a man would say to a woman just to get the upper hand. Both of my daughters are dating right now, and they're running into all sorts of foolishness like that." Ginnie leaned down and grasped one of her galoshes by the shank and gave it a tug. It came off with a sucking sound and brown water poured out in a stream like old tea from a kettle stroop. Her socks were gray and sodden. Then she said, "You know, I used to have a big old crush on your daddy when I was about your age."

"Really?" said the girl. "Did he want to marry you?"

Ginnie laughed again. "If he did, he had a poor way of showing it," she said. "But things turn out the way they should. Just think, if I'd married your daddy, then I never could have married the man who holds the Guinness World Record for the least words ever spoken in a marriage."

Henrietta's eyes widened. "Really?"

"Honey, I'm kidding," she said. "But you know," she went on suddenly, turning toward the girl with a level gaze. "Mind how you grow up. Strive to be a good egg. You're gonna have to watch yourself. You're kind of swimming upstream if you know what I mean, which you probably don't."

Henrietta just stared at her blankly. Then Mrs. Miller reached down, took her time removing her other rain boot as she gripped the gate with her free hand, and said, "I'll tell you another secret."

"What?"

"Your daddy tried to buy us out. Twice."

Henrietta's eyebrows rose up in little arcs of surprise. "He wanted your cows?"

"Well, I don't expect that was the attraction, no," Mrs. Miller said. "But he wouldn't offer anywhere close to what this place is worth. My own daddy wasn't very fond of your daddy, truth be told. He'd have sooner sold it . . . Well, I probably shouldn't tell you that." She sighed, struggling her feet back into her floppy boots.

"Why?"

She turned a mild, considering eye on the girl. "Well, I don't know," she said. "I really don't know. I suppose it's just the truth when it's all said and done." Then she said, "How old are you?"

"Almost ten."

"That's why. You're just a little slip. You're too young for the workings of the world. The world can be a pretty crappy place. Just have a good time being a little girl." She sighed.

"I like your cows," said Henrietta.

Ginnie Miller actually blushed a bit when she smiled. "Well, they're not Cardigan Corgis, but . . . yes," she said. "I'm very fond of them myself. I really can't eat beef anymore. I think I'd consider eating my husband before one of my herd. That was a joke." Then she cleared her throat and said, "You know, sometimes the apple falls pretty far from the tree. And if it's

really brave, when it grows up, it can get up and walk over to another orchard. You know what I mean?"

"No."

"No, I suppose not." She smiled, and Henrietta realized suddenly the
hour was late, and her father would be wondering where she was, so she
moved toward the wet black ribbon of the road and the house beyond.
Then Ginnie called out, "Henrietta Forge, did you have fun today?"

Henrietta didn't even have to hesitate; she turned and, walking backward, she called, "Yes, I did!"

She lay there on the davenport in the front parlor by the phone, her hands
still smelling of the damp outdoors, but resolved not to move until the call
came. No one bothered her, her father still out with the horses and the
cleaning lady polishing and vacuuming around her. When the phone rang
in the early evening, she had only to reach over her own head without rising
to grasp the receiver. It was her mother.

"I've been missing you," Judith said in a voice too gentle.

"You have an apartment in Lexington now?" Henrietta blurted. "But
you still live here, right?"

"Is that what your father told you?"

"He said he wants you to come back home right now."

There was silence on the line.

"When are you coming home?"

"Well," her mother said, and sighed. "I think I'll come out to the farm
tomorrow."

"Why can't you come right now?"

"I'll come tomorrow, darling."

But her mother didn't come the next day. She came the day after that,
and she arrived wearing a dress Henrietta had never seen before, her hair
cut in a glassy blonde bob, and with a pained twinge the girl struggled with
a strange, phantom sensation that Judith had been gone not three days but
three years. She was altered like a heap of coins melted down and newly
minted into a foreign currency. When they hugged, her mother's arms were
painfully thin, but maybe they had always been so? Henrietta heard a kissing sound above her head but did not feel the press of lips anywhere.

Her mother said, "You look good, Henrietta." Even her voice was music playing in another room. "Why don't we go out to the porch?"

"Where's Daddy? I want him to come too." Henrietta managed to turn herself halfway around, looking wildly behind her without letting go of her mother.

"I'm not really sure." That old, barely suppressed irritation was audible.

"Daddy!" she called out into the house, and she felt her mother flinch as the word came echoing back.

"Henrietta!" Judith snapped, and then softer: "Your father's not here right now."

"Where is he?"

"He didn't want to be here for this."

Now it was Henrietta's turn to be silent. She stared mutely at her mother, and where the older woman expected to see confusion, there was only a dark kind of withholding, which was new. The girl let go of the hem of her mother's jacket, which she had wrenched up into the sweaty heart of her fist. Judith smoothed it down and Henrietta saw her manicure was the color of a ripe raspberry. She used to bite her nails, but that was different now too.

"Let's go out to the porch," Judith said. "I always hated the inside of this house."

"Well, I like it."

"You don't even know what you like yet," her mother said. "This house is like living in another time. And not a good one."

They went out and they sat on the porch swing, but Henrietta's legs were not long enough to reach the wood planks, so she was forced into a lulling motion by her mother. She clung to the chain for balance but it was rusted. It left visceral stains on her palm.

For a long time Judith just swung them in silence and her face appeared undisturbed, as if she were alone in the world with her thoughts, as if she never had any intention to speak at all.

"Well, I don't have an apartment in Lexington is the first thing," she finally began.

"Then Daddy lied." Henrietta stared straight ahead at the road and the Millers' property, her face devoid of feeling.

"Let's do this nice and easy, Henrietta," Judith said.

"Where's your apartment?"

"Well, I don't have an apartment, not exactly. The thing is I've met someone. Someone I really love and who really loves me."

"Daddy loves you," Henrietta said abruptly against the swift and sudden closing of her throat.

"Daddy loves *you*," said Judith while looking down at her shoes, her yellow heels. She turned a foot this way and that, as if admiring the motions of her own ankles, but her face was downcast and carved close at the cheek. "Listen, Henrietta, I could be angry and, believe me, I have every right to be, but . . . frankly, I'm too young to waste all my good years. I'm not going to sit around here the way your grandmother did, waiting for death to end my awful marriage. God, that poor woman. I'm sure she went slowly insane here. We're trained from childhood to behave like dogs who sit and stay and wait for scraps." She looked up suddenly. "Everyone has to find a way to be happy. When I was a girl, I always, *always* wanted to get married. I was so naïve I thought that if a man married you, then that actually meant he loved you, not just that he wanted something from your body. The reality is you never really know a man until he marries you and thinks he's got you trapped. Then you find out if you really are his prize, or just his prize heifer."

She sighed. "What's funny is I used to model wedding dresses. I mean, for God's sake—that was my niche! I was only high fashion when I starved myself, but I couldn't keep that up. But I actually liked catalog work. I thought it was fun. And now, I mean, look at me. My stomach is ruined. I've just finally woken up, and I want nothing more than happiness. I don't care if it comes in an imperfect package. I don't care where I have to go to find it. It just . . . Henrietta, it has nothing to do with you."

"Nothing to do with me," the girl echoed flatly.

"Nothing at all. I promise." Judith sighed and looked out over the sloping lawn and the frontage road. Softly, she said, "I was really so happy when I was a little girl. There has to be a way back, there *has* to be. Or else what's the point of all this . . . of life?" She sighed again. "The truth is men aren't interested in your happiness; they'll make you think that's the case, they'll treat you really great for a while and make all sorts of promises and give you all their attention, but they all reach a point where they can't pretend anymore. They're just selfish animals, and in the end, animals can't hide their nature."

"But you're happy here with me," insisted Henrietta, her words reaching out with both hands.

Her mother fished around in her pocketbook and removed a black book with blank pages. "Look. I bought you a journal. Since I won't be here for you to tell them to, you can record all your most precious thoughts here." She set the book on Henrietta's knees and smiled sadly. "I know this probably isn't . . . adequate, but . . . God, there's really no good option here." She smiled sadly.

"You're smiling," Henrietta pressed, ignoring the book.

"I'm smiling, sweetheart, because the man I've met is really wonderful," Judith said. "He actually loves me for who I am, not for what I can give him, not for how I look on his arm. He's involved in horses too, so he and your father have a lot in common. And he has sons. See? You'll have brothers now like you've always wanted. The only thing is . . . he lives most of the year in a town called Donaueschingen."

Henrietta looked at her blankly.

"It's in Germany," her mother said.

Still there was no response.

"That's across the ocean. Do you know where Germany is?"

Henrietta knew the DNA of a bacterium contained hundreds of millions of nucleotides; that horses and humans had the humerus, radius, ulna, carpals, metacarpals, and phalanges in common; that Mendel's pea plants held all the secrets of genetics; she knew where Germany was. But instead of answering, she looked out across the road where only two days prior, she and Mrs. Miller had led the cows back into the pasture. That pleasure was already beginning to rot, and there was no way to reconstitute it into joy, not even through memory. She would have to find a new pleasure altogether.

Watching a dawning realization on her daughter's face, Judith reached over to grasp her hand, but Henrietta jumped up from the swing, not slapping away her mother's hands as they reached toward her and not casting a hateful glance over her shoulder, just leaving with the black notebook clutched to her chest. She let the front screen door slam behind her as she went into the house, going nowhere in particular, but very quickly.

"Henrietta," her mother called, then gave chase, so the girl heard those staccato cracks on the wood floors, a sound that somehow seemed to perfectly match the woman herself. The sound caught her in the kitchen. Judith gripped her shoulders from behind and then, with real force, turned her around and pulled her to her body. The girl felt her shivering with a sorrow that came in little waves. Then Judith reached down and took her face tightly in her pale, skinny hands.

"Henrietta, this isn't selfishness—"

"Please don't go."

"—it's survival."

"Stay," Henrietta whispered.

Her mother's eyes bored into her. "Can you even remember the good times?"

Henrietta's mind fumbled for the right answer.

"See?" came her mother's strained but triumphant whisper. "Neither can I."

"Henrietta!"

"Henrietta!"

He found her slumping down the stairs from the attic, where she'd spent hours curled on an old linen-draped divan, surrounded by the boxed and labeled artifacts of her ancestors' lives. They stank of mothballs and of lives extinguished.

His grip on her shoulders stopped her short. "Henrietta, have you been in the attic? I've been looking everywhere."

She tried to look him in the face, but it was too much to bear. There was a strange, fresh exuberance there, something overly bright, a mania impelled by grief. It was like a door swinging open wildly on one hinge.

"Mom went away?" was all she could choke out. Downstairs, as if in affirmation, the tall clock chimed for two.

Now, Henrietta, see how you are swept against your father, the air crushed from your lungs? Head torqued to the side, you are confronted with a yellow wall and two portraits of men who bear your noble nose, the fine cut of your cheekbones, your eternal eyes. Every corner of the house is filled with the purpose of your father's life. Which is . . . you . . . or a horse.

"Please make Mom stay," Henrietta blurted.

"I can't." She felt his exhalation on the top of her head.

"Why not?"

It took him an eon to reply. "I take responsibility for this, Henrietta," and once again with both hands to her shoulders, he drew back to peer into her wrenched face. "In so many respects, I chose poorly. I was so . . . It reminds me of something my father once said—a damaged beauty is the only kind of beauty capable of gratitude. But when I met your mother, I was too young and easily impressed by her . . . conformation to really understand the truth in what my father said. To be honest, I probably didn't believe him." He laughed wryly. "If I'd been wise like Boone . . . do you remember me telling you how Boone chose Rebecca?"

Now it was Henrietta who pulled away; she didn't want a story, a history, a textbook.

Henry hooked a finger under the strong bone of her jaw and raised her chin. "When he decided to court her, he took her out to an orchard, where they could sit in the grass and get to know each other. While they sat there talking, Boone started to toss his knife into the ground, blade first. But this wasn't just absent-minded fiddling. He was testing Rebecca to see how she would react. Again and again, he drove the knife into the ground closer and closer until it was in the fabric of her skirt and almost slicing her thigh. Rebecca saw what he was doing, but she didn't run, she didn't tell him to stop, she never even said a word. And that's how Boone knew he had found the right woman. A woman who doesn't flinch is one in a million."

Henrietta stared straight at the pearl buttons on his shirt, bewildered and barely listening. *I am a hybrid seed. A parent form has disappeared from the record.* She tried to translate this into a configuration another person would understand. "I want my whole entire family," she said, her eyes filling with tears.

"You and I are family," Henry said with too much force. "Blood and treasure. Listen to me, Henrietta. I created this world with my own two hands, and I am going to leave it all to you—the acreage, the buildings, the horses, everything. It's lying in trust for you, because you are my real family. And when you have children, all of this will be theirs in turn. Everything you need is already in this house." That old music again, his dark, fathomless pupils a spinning record, playing the old refrain, playing It.

"Tell me your great-great-great-great-great-great-grandfather's name," he said, staring into her eyes.

"Daddy—"

"Tell me."

"Samuel Forge."

"Samuel Henry Forge and Edward Cooper Forge and Richmond Cooper Forge and William Iver Forge and Moses Cooper Forge and Jacob Ellison Forge and your grandfather, John Henry Forge, and me, Henry Forge. And now you. You. *You*—"

"I know," she said to interrupt him, her mouth trembling. "But I'm a girl."

"Well, then you won't be like any other girl," he said, his voice suddenly sharp. "I won't let you."

She needed a girl to stand behind her in the looking glass, to part her reddish hair down the middle and scrape it over her ears into a bun coiled through with black ribbon and covered with a square of black lace; to ease her grieving limbs into white cotton drawers and a long chemise; to snap her stockings into garters and cinch up a corset until it was too tight for her to draw breath, much less cry; to secure the caging crinoline; to tug over her head a dress of flat black, strangling at the neck but with sleeves like church bells; to slip her feet into black boots so she could totter here and there, tapping out unspoken grief on the plank floors in the long-lost code of broken women; but she didn't have twenty yards of black Parisian cotton or a veil or a colored girl, and, alas, people would say this wasn't a death, just a divorce, but they were all mistaken, because it was a difference of degree, not of kind. The pain was almost the same. And because she didn't have that girl to rail against, to beat about the head and shoulders, because there was no one weaker, she flung her black bonnet against the walls of her mind and clattered about like a drunkard and wailed at the vaporous absent bitches hate sonofabitchspoilevilrottenfuckfuckniggers, because there was no one else around smaller and weaker than she was—

For example:

Class, what is the capital of Kentucky?

Frankfort.

And who works hardest for Kentucky's economy?

Horses.

And who built our world-famous limestone fences?

Niggers.

Mrs. Garrett, after her face righted itself, spun Henrietta out of the classroom like a top, spun her round so quick she felt bile rising in her throat, standing there unsteady in the nauseating green hallway—green as a swimming pool—her head swooning back against the cool tiles as her teacher towered over her, leaning in so close that Henrietta could smell the tuna from lunch on her breath as she said, "There is only one appropriate word for a black person that begins with an *n*, and it has one *g*, not two. Young lady, do you understand what I'm saying?"

"A river in Africa?" the girl said.

Mrs. Garrett just stared at her for a moment with an anger so righteous and consuming, it was almost erotic, peering first into one pupil and then the other, as if trying to discover which eye was the source of this evil. She said, "First of all, the walls were built by Irish stonemasons. Second of all, if I had one black student, I'd be marching you back in there to apologize. But seeing as there are none, I'm sending you home straightaway, because I've had enough of your attitude. Believe me when I say that I'll be speaking with your parents."

"Incorrect usage," Henrietta said.

"Excuse me, what did you say?"

"You used the plural instead of the singular. I'll be speaking to *your* parents, Mrs. Garrett." She was spun forthwith to the principal's office, where her singular was called on the telephone, and then spun again out to the broad concrete steps of the school, where she rested dazed and relieved, like a prisoner suddenly released from years of hard, useless detail. She preferred to sit out here alone. Almost as soon as her mother had left, she'd decided that she would no longer tolerate humans, especially the barely bipedal variety by which she was surrounded: their relentless chatter, the strong smell of their bodies, their dumb games. She classified them far, far down in the family of tailless primates. School had long been a matter of sitting blandly for the duration, eyes locked on the proceedings with your mind flatlined, maybe rereading your textbooks for typos and collation

THE SPORT OF KINGS   123

errors. She'd begun to spend her time in the bathroom, picking at her nails or counting the holes in the pegboard ceiling there. She'd gone so frequently and stayed so long that Mrs. Garrett had finally called the farm with a concern that she needed to be examined. She was sent to a urologist at the University of Kentucky who, after numerous tests and return visits, was the first to simply ask why she went to the bathroom so often, to which she replied, "To be by myself."

"Right, but you're peeing a lot," he said.

"No."

"You're not urinating?"

"No."

"You're going to the bathroom to be alone, but not to urinate?"

"Yes."

"Jesus!" he'd snapped, and dropped his clipboard down on the examining table beside her, then rubbed his eyes for a long while without bothering to take his glasses off. "This is why I'm not a pediatrician," he said through his hands. "I don't speak childese."

"Me neither," she said. He took his hands away from his eyes and looked at her in consternation, and then, fifteen minutes later, her father was driving her home along Richmond Road, saying, "I don't understand what just happened here," and Henrietta said, "I don't want to talk anymore."

Now she sat very still on the school steps, motionless as a dial casting time's shadow. She was waiting for her remaining parent, her immediate genetic antecedent, the Forge who had forged her, but it was old Barlow who showed up in one of the rattling farm trucks—a white 250 with a toolbox in the bed, shedding farm chaff in a swarm as it braked before her. Barlow reached over and popped open the passenger door, his wizened face etched with concern.

"You sick, honeypie? Your daddy sent me up to fetch you."

Henrietta just shook her head and crawled up beside him as he lit a cigarette and pulled out of the school's drive. They were silent as they passed the glassed storefronts of Paris, the antebellum homes with American flags snapping smartly from porch roofs. Through the glass of the windshield, through the bitter brown lacework of the trees, the sun meted out an autumnal afternoon, weakening even as they watched.

She turned to Barlow. "Who built the stone fences?"

"Boy, um . . . the Irish, maybe? I think I heard that before."

"Are you Irish?" she said.

"I don't really know, darlin', I'm just a country mutt."

As they passed the courthouse, on the other side of the road, the familiar sight of three old black men on rickety metal chairs. They sat there every day shaded by their Kangol caps, cigars and folded newspapers in hand, paling of white hair on their cheeks. One glanced at her briefly as she passed, but in another instant, the dark round of his face was gone.

She turned a speculative and careful eye on Barlow. "Did you know n-i-g-g-e-r is a bad word?" she asked.

"You ever hear me say it?" said Barlow.

"No."

"There you go. Guess I knew it then."

"Yeah, but who decided that?" she pressed.

"God did . . . ," he said, flipping his cigarette butt out his open window. "God hath made of one blood all peoples of the earth."

"There are four different kinds of blood," she said. "It's a medical fact."

"Well, I don't know anything about that."

She expected no further response, and she didn't get one. Barlow just nodded with a considering face and drove easily beside her. He was a man who had stayed married forty years and raised four bullheaded boys by holding tight the gunnels and steadying the boat. He was content with his holdings and not inclined to fight.

They drove for a time behind a truck loaded with tawny, bundled tobacco, the cured and withered leaves making small, abrupt motions in the breeze like yellow hands waving. The flatbed turned into the low redbrick tobacco warehouse on East Main, where Henrietta could see, stacked and heaped in golden sheaves, the harvest prepared for auction. The dead plants were even more beautiful than plants in the field—crisp, sculptural, turned by curing to the brown of baked bread. For the first time in weeks, something stirred in her as she gazed at what had to be tobacco's heaven.

"Why don't we grow any tobacco?" she asked.

"Kinda slow out of the starting gate," was Barlow's dry reply as he rooted around in his breast pocket for another cigarette. As always, he got the small smile he was aiming for. But then Henrietta shifted wearily and

Barlow turned to her and said, "You wanna tell old Barlow what happened at school today?" but she just shook her head, staring out the window.

As they pulled into their own drive, she said, "I hate school." She stomped once on her book bag, where it lay in a heap on the floorboard of the truck, and she crossed her arms. Acid tears smarted her eyes.

Barlow cocked his head and said, "I liked it so much I stayed all the way to the eighth grade. Come on." He eased out of the truck, careful on his feet, which were arthritic, a far cry from the day he first went to work on a farm as a spry ten-year-old boy Friday. But Henrietta remained where she was, watching him with a sullen expression. Barlow circled around to her side of the truck, unlatched her door, and drew it wide.

"Come on, honeypie," he said.

"Carry me," she said sullenly, laying her head back in a faint manner on the headrest.

"Huh—do what?" An eyebrow cocked with amusement.

"Carry me."

"You're too heavy—why, you're practically a grown woman!" He laughed.

"I'm nine."

"Well."

"Carry me." She pulled herself up by the plastic ceiling handle and stood balancing on her toes on the side of the runner, her face turned down to his, because he wasn't very tall. "Come on," she whined softly, and he made a mock roll of his eyes and shook his head, but said, "Fetch your satchel then." She yanked it up in one hand, and Barlow gripped her under her skinny knees and shoulders and raised her up. She was lighter than a newborn foal. Henrietta wrapped her arms around his neck and laid her head on his shoulder and closed her eyes. The expression of spoiled petulance on her face settled into something like sadness. She jostled against his chest with each step, and her book bag struck him lightly on the back a few times before she let it drop to the ground behind him. He didn't notice. He just said, "You are one funny valentine."

Of course Henry fielded the phone call, and of course it flung him into a rage, and of course his daughter came home with a hangdog droop and eyes like dull brads. What rage it aroused in him! This was his child—*his* child—the fruit of his loins, the hope of his age, the apple of his eye, and his own. She'd never been as much child as other children were, already possessed of a natural disregard. There was something aristocratic about her, and since her mother's departure, she'd become even chillier and less soft. She broke the mold, and Henry knew it. She didn't like the commonality of school, she didn't like to mix. Her spirit didn't rhyme with the spirit of lesser animals.

Hadn't his own education, prior to his tutoring, been a waste? Even at Sewanee, he'd had to fight for the relevance of his education to his true life as a horseman. Formal education had always seemed a war of attrition designed to starve him of his own history and bring his culture to its knees. But the farm was a whole round world, and Henrietta was a product of that world—she'd one day take ownership of it. It was his bounden duty to reverse the effects of her miseducation.

He placed a hand on each slumping shoulder and said, "Look at me, Henrietta." He noted the wrinkle of worry between her red brows, the lashes made by tears into little black spikes. He said, "Were they very hard on you today?"

She nodded once.

"Tell me who built our fences," he said.

"What?"

"You heard me. Who built the stone fences?"

"The . . . Irish?"

"No, goddammit, our slaves. The impolite, inconvenient truth, but there it is."

"I said a bad word."

"You got a bad education! Consider yourself withdrawn."

She reared back. "What?"

"Henrietta, you've suffered the misfortune of being born into an age of political correctness, when a polite lie is the truth, and the truth is anathema. The simple reality is what no one dares to say: Blacks are inferior and it's always been that way. It's a genetic reality. People police words to avoid grappling with reality."

"Daddy, I don't think—"

"Henrietta, listen to me. Consider this your first

Lesson

Is a horse a blank slate? Is each animal sprung from the forehead of Zeus? Is a foal a patented invention? No, the horse is a house we build from the finest materials of the previous generations. How can we accomplish this with any reliability? Because biology is destiny, that's why. Gold from gold, and brass from brass. Secretariat wasn't born from a hack and a knacker; he was from Bold Ruler out of Somethingroyal, winning horses from long and respectable lines. Secretariat never had the option to be slow. Speed and stamina are heritable. The animal bred true.

Oh, I can see the objection in your eyes that a horse isn't a human. Fine. But the human is just as subject to his biology by fate. Now, I'm not going to bore you with the histories of the polygenists and craniometrists, but I will tell you that Morton's skulls are a fact; the White brain is bigger than the Black brain. This should appeal to your little scientific mind. Just as musical skill and athletic prowess are inheritable, so is intelligence. How could it be otherwise? The average African IQ is 70; the average White is 100. And that's a fact even the Marxists can't avoid! You can find exceptions, but the exceptions don't disprove the rule. And how did racial difference develop in the first place? Think about it, Henrietta. The human populations that headed north contended with difficult weather and living conditions that demanded the development of higher intelligence and organized societies in order to survive. Those left near the equator could get away with investing no attention in their innumerable children, and ignoring social development. The laxity of the elements created a species of indolence, and what no one will say out loud is that Blacks were decreed different by nature. The ascendance of certain races is, in fact, proof of the wisdom of nature. You don't have to be a madman to acknowledge the obvious.

I'm going to tell you what my father told me: throughout the history of this country, we have saved an inferior people from themselves, and now that they've won everything they clamored for, they can't manage their own freedoms. They're the kings and queens of dissolution. They're ruled by base instincts, but lasciviousness is so intrinsic to their nature, most don't even see it as abnormal anymore. Look at our cities—Black women can't keep their legs shut, and they've run the country down with their endlessly multiplying, uneducated spawn. They still live off the White man's money, only now they don't even have the protection they once enjoyed on a plantation or in a small town. They get to live like rats in their projects, because they don't possess the genetic wherewithal to make anything productive of their lives. They're seemingly incapable of the abstract thought required to plan for the future or even to detect a suitable mate. It's not 1860, but rest assured, there still has to be a White man making sure they get enough to eat and that they have a roof over their heads. The reality is White men saved Black people in this country. They saved them from themselves.

The most painful irony is that Blacks clamored for a freedom that can never be. So long as they are bound to bodies bequeathed to them by their ancestors, they can never taste true freedom. They're enslaved by their own materiality, and no White man anywhere has the power to free them from that.

Over her drowsy head, the daily war of morning ensued: dews rose, shrugging off their sleep and skimming briefly over the fields in the shifting dark. After a long night of sleep in the underbelly of the earth, the armored sun rose and charged the horizon, pressing against the dark with long arms until night fell back, wounded and floundering, to earth's antipodal edge. Now the lingering armies of dew turned to mist, mustering over the great house and muffling the voices of animals. The sun cast great handfuls of heated light, looting what was left of shadow, and the dew dispersed, not retreating toward night but fleeing in all directions.

Henrietta shambled down from the upstairs at six thirty, pouring the cup of coffee her father now allowed her to drink and turning into the study where he waited. There, the books were spread wide before him, so it appeared he had been sitting, waiting here for his student all night. He gestured toward the black Windsor chair beside the desk. Her education was under way:

They began with the classics, working through *The Iliad* for the third time in Henrietta's life, and soon thereafter Xenophon and Aeschylus, Sophocles and Euripides; then science through the esotery of pedigree charts and animal husbandry and the variables of genetic inheritance; mathematics through word problems exploring the numerical influence of a mare if she appeared four times in a foal's chart; but also by working with

Beyer's numbers, then the basics of handicapping. Anatomy was equine form, and soon she could parse the elastic maze of musculature, which through endless acts of flexion, extension, and adduction made the horse an animal of tremendous power and speed, and drew men to race it. History was the tale of the Greeks, their branched and ill-fated houses; and also the dynasties of speed and conformation—the lines of the Darley Arabian and his Eclipse, Sir Archie, Sir Gallahad III, War Admiral, Native Dancer, Danzig. The families branched and then their limbs curled back again to their source as bloodhorses were bred back into their own lines, so the families grew deep and redundant with inbreeding, their limbs twisted. For Henry, recalling his own earliest years in study, these recounted histories were so long and tangled; they became confused in his mind, all houses the names of myth, so the horses became indistinguishable from the Greeks and the Greeks from the horses, or the horses became attendant somehow to the fall of the houses, like night-bred furies saddled by fate and ferrying black messages from the gods to men and back again. He often confused their names and misspoke, but his daughter could intuit his meaning. Through it all Henrietta asked no questions, said no unnecessary words, eyes strict on the page, listening, absorbing, memorizing. The first four hours of the day were spent side by side in this manner, heads bent, poised between past and future. There were no breaks until her coffee dried in the mug's white well, and then it was dinnertime. What she could not manage to learn in these four hours of the morning—what she did not learn of the rest of the world—she did not learn at all, and a year passed.

On many days, she shadowed her father on the grounds as he consulted with Barlow, called his bloodstock agent, his lawyers, read the *Racing Form*, and made his travel plans around the racing season. He sent her off with one of the female grooms, who taught her the duties of the broodmare barn, how to muck the stalls and change hay, how to lave the horses and pick their hooves, to detect when the mares turned temperamental in estrus. Henrietta often accompanied Henry to Keeneland to watch Forge horses in their early-morning workouts, the animals wheeling in and out of the cool mist, their breath blooming. The pair made an odd couple of railbirds: the man tall, thin, and talkative, the girl tall, thin, and quiet, both sipping coffee from paper cups. The girl held a silver stopwatch in her free hand and soon knew the horses by their gaits, the track speed by the report of hooves, the trainers by their curses, the jocks by the curve of their spines as they bowed over their mounts, and a year passed.

She took thrice-weekly riding lessons on the other side of Paris; this was something her father demanded. The other girls arrived with their hair scraped back into neat tails, their high boots shined to a gloss. Henrietta's boots were caked with old, dry manure the color of mastic. She was deeply tan to the others' schoolkept pallor. She lasted there only four months, by then a rider equal to her instructor, a seeming natural with no fear of the animal, but no discernible love either. She rode as though she were walking, the horse like the ground beneath her feet, and another year passed.

Only Henrietta's nights were her own. During these hours, while lying in bed perusing the old books, she discovered the ultimate luxury, which was solitude. She tried her best to like the poetry that her father admired, but the Greeks bored her, and, besides, that was all part of her morning lessons. She tried the poems from an anthology she found and liked some, especially those that made no claims, strove for nothing but the revelation of a small, beautiful thing—a vase or a blackbird. But she read no novels, finding them a waste of time. She resisted how they worked on her, asking her to suffer on someone's behalf. If they had no madness in them, they were useless; genius doesn't speak with the limited tongue of sense. Her father taught her that.

What roused her to an almost pained interest, what caused her to copy down long passages into her notebooks and stay awake into the night, her mind running like a stallion on a track, was the mystery of the earth's composition and all of its inhabitants. She devoured the books that had belonged to her great-great-*in-aeternum*-grandfathers—atlas volumes, topographical maps, weathered pamphlets from the Geological Survey, the tomes of Lamarck and Darwin and Lyell; also physiographic diagrams, strata illustrations, and expedition records, which together told the brute story of geology, how it grew continents and plant populations, gave them life and dug their graves. She slowly discerned that Kentucky was a strange and abundant place, half-mad with a restless and protean geology, secreted away under a cloak of limestone and swaying seas of timothy and bluegrass. She came to believe that the earth longed to be known. So she pressed one ear to the lip of its mouth, listening to tales that babbled up from its karsty throat, from jagged fissures in the sandstone hills, gurgling streambeds and salt licks. She learned how the primordial state had formed itself from the mystery of swirling sedimentary detritus under Paleozoic seas: sandstone out of inky silt and sand; clay and black shale from viscous mud that settled like a pitch lime on the Devonian beds before millennial tides rolled back and forth; also layers of friable igneous rock, bits of charred matter that traveled from the hot center of the earth; gravel and nameless shards scrabbled together into conglomerates; delicate, fluted shells forming sleek, packed limestone that made up the thickest strata, four hundred million years old and counting. Casket-gray and underscoring half the state, the preterite limestone founded the old Mississippian plateau with their faulted escarpments and the steep barrowing knobs, which Samuel Forge had spied as he stood with Ben at the verge of what would be Madison County, surveying the thin soils of the Outer Bluegrass, which was itself cinched tight by a belt of Eden Shale. It was in the core of the Bluegrass that limestone, sandstone, dolomite, and shale were pressed together like the layers of an earthen cake, until a massive upwarping formed the Cincinnati Arch, where the young, thin stones were soon eroded by ferocious winds, and the limestone found itself naked before the elements, runnelled and pocked by water until it had transformed itself into karst, a tumulous landscape of sinking streams, sinkholes, caves, and soil so wildly fecund that men lost their religion for a share. It was a rolling dreamscape, a heaven for the raising of crops and horses—better than the modest farmland of the Pennyroyal plains, the coalfields, and Western embayment, which sloped down to the alluvial foreshores of the Mississippi River.

In the Appalachian Mountains, the oldest mountains on earth, a different tale was told. There, organic matter had compressed into bituminous coal. Five hundred million years before Henrietta was born, those mountains extended all the way down into the extraterrestrial deserts of West Texas, pressed into being by the clashing of two young continents, which closed the Iapetus Ocean—an ocean so old it gave birth to the Atlantic—thrusting the abyssal plains and all their doomed marine life into the air like an offering for the gods. As the mountains rose and heaved and eroded, generations of saplings tumbled into the swamps, and hairy grasses too, seed coats, stamens, involute gondola leaves, chips of bark, white and chocolate roots, mosses mixed with stringy vines, hardy stamens, and even the gentle, primordial flower beds in the height of their flowerage fell too soon like the mayflies, dropping their leaves and tumbling into the self-heating morass, which, under the slurried sediment of Mesozoic seas, turned all the fallen vegetal world to rich, flammable peat. But the peat was covered and itself compressed and, with a mountain atop it, vanquishing its air, was tamped and starved into coal, thin, glossy, striate seams of carbon between dingy Pennsylvanian stones, thin, dark pages in a long, long book—

You can close a book, which she did. But then she would just lie there charged, apprehensive, electric, confused. She knew that men extracted coal and sometimes died in the mining. She wondered at their deaths. Was it childish to ask why? How many mountains had been uprooted to light a home like hers? And all the churches dotting the state? Fathers felled the world their children were supposed to live in, Tantalus eternally slaughtering his Pelops. Was it worth it? Was this farm worth it? Was the human nothing but a machine that extracted coal from the hills and horses from the fields? Civilization stood at the ready with its answers, but she bypassed those answers for a deeper, stranger question: What was the earth itself? This teeming, generative thing, which forced human life in a hothouse, only to turn that life like compost back into the soil. She was thirteen, but geological time was 4.6 billion years old. She had just gotten her period, only to discover there was nothing fixed in the geographical world. Even the poles moved. She discovered in her a deep, deep dread, but it wasn't like a horse, you couldn't just assign it a name. You had to discover its name. She suffered from the realization that others had been asking these questions long, long before her, but to no avail. The old books all agree: God is a terror.

On Valentine's Day when she was thirteen, Henrietta saw her first mare bred.

That morning, Henry had called over to Claiborne and spoken with a manager. He said, "My mare is due to be covered on Thursday."

"Yes, sir, we've got Hellcat on the books, and Big Red's in good form."

"I'd like to be there."

"You're welcome to bring her up, but—"

"I'd like to be in the shed."

There was a polite and cursory silence on the line. "Mr. Forge, all due respect, we don't permit owners in the breeding shed for safety reasons.

I'm sure you understand. But everything will be videotaped, and you've got her insured to the hilt. You know we've got your interests in mind at all times."

"Regardless, I'd like to be there, and I'd like to bring my daughter, who's—"

"You— What? Your daughter?"

"My daughter is involved in our operation and I'd like—"

The curt laugh severed his sentence, followed by two words: "Mr. Forge."

"If I can speak with Mr. Hancock, then—"

"Now, Mr. Forge." The voice was louder, parental. "If you want to chat with Mr. Hancock, that's fine. But I'm telling you right now you'll get a no that'll break the sound barrier. So let's just get your mare up here to get her covered, and with a little luck and godspeed, we can meet your daughter at the Derby in three years' time."

Henrietta had never seen her father so angry, not even when her mother left. He was stiff-necked with fury when he steered her, one hard hand on her shoulder, out the kitchen door and toward their small black breeding shed, erected a quarter mile back from the broodmare barn.

"Where are we going?" she asked, craning her neck to see him, hot coffee splashing out onto the tender flesh of her hand.

His only answer was, "Those assholes have no right—no right—to tell me how to handle my own property, or what I should allow my daughter to see."

"Who? Who did that?"

By way of answer, he drew up short and pulled her round, leaning abruptly at the waist so they stood eye to inherited eye. He tipped her chin up with one finger. "Breeding is the heart of this business and you are the heart of my operation," he said. "You need to know how this business is run. I have no tolerance for these idiots and their ideas of what's age-appropriate. I reject their shame—I reject it unequivocally. Do you understand me?"

"Yes," she said, drawing back slightly.

"Henrietta, listen to me," he said. "The sex act is an amoral action of the body designed by nature to perpetuate the species. It should be harnessed and controlled for that purpose, not because it's shameful. It's not morally different from shitting or eating. What's perverse is our attachment of religious mores to a simple, biological act! Be very careful, Henrietta," he said, suddenly straightening. "The world is trying to turn you into a stupid, conventional woman. Don't let it happen."

"Okay," she said, bewildered, because she didn't recognize this strange and lofty tone, John Henry having died a long time before she was born. But she did as she was told; in an instant she rejected this thing, this shame she knew nothing about. She wouldn't become that woman. But a new thought occurred to her: "Daddy, why don't you ever have a girlfriend?"

The question took Henry by surprise. He looked around him suddenly at the brisk morning, considering the question. "Most men throw away their sperm on inferior women. An orgasm is a cheap thing; you can get one for free." He tapped a finger to his temple. "But a wise man harnesses his energies and expels them in a manner designed to improve his line, not dilute it. That's how I got you. Your mother, for all her faults, was a damn fine piece of property."

Henrietta stared at the ground in consternation. "Can I ask you something else?"

"Of course."

"Well, I was reading about linebreeding, and I read that it can produce weak horses, that incest—"

Henry waved his hand, dismissing the thought. "They overstate the case. Yes, you sometimes produce a genetically weak animal from inbreeding and linebreeding, but there's no surer way to hit the jackpot. Breeding a line back to its own line can produce the perfect horse—and that's worth every risk."

"Okay," she said softly, her face flushed. "Evolution by artificial selection. Darwin on pigeons." But in her deepest mind, she asked: Who are you?

In the barn, three grooms were waiting beside a large, thick-legged mare with an ass as broad as the stern of a boat and a tail that swished gently. The men barely looked up as Henry strode into the barn, but all reared back in a collective startle when they noticed Henrietta following behind, her ponytail swinging. One blond man named Jonathan, who held the shank of the mare, actually hauled himself up on the withers of the placid creature to gaze wide-eyed at Henrietta. He said, "What the hell?"

"Good morning, gentlemen." Henry's voice was brisk.

"What's *she* doing here?" Jonathan demanded, pointing accusingly with one hand and coming around the horse now with the shank still gripped in his fist. The brown-eyed mare turned too, peering through the tangled mass of her cob as if to see to whom he referred.

"My daughter will be joining us this morning."

One of the other grooms spoke up now—Henrietta knew him only by the name Sandy—ducking his curly red head in a tentative, preemptive apology, saying, "Yeah, I don't know, Mr. Forge—"

"That's dangerous!" Jonathan barked, and passed off the shank to the third, silent man standing nearby, who stared resolutely at the ground as the tension in the room rose. Jonathan came at Henry with a wash of wondering disbelief on his face. His gaze slashed briefly through Henrietta, who snugged up instinctively against her father's side. But that thing—that shame—she rejected. Her chin jutted out.

"This is no place for a girl!" Jonathan said with open disgust. "It's barely a place for a grown man! Jesus Christ, you can't ask us to do this thing in front of a kid." He stood there with his hands on his hips, staring up at her father in a way Henrietta had never seen another man do. For an instant, she couldn't breathe, afraid the confrontation would come to blows, or, worse, that her father would step down.

But Henry stepped forward instead, his voice steely, low, and final: "If any man is uncomfortable with the situation, he can leave my employ. Now."

There was a heavy, hateful silence in the barn. Henrietta sensed rather than saw the other two men look at each other for a very, very long moment, speaking to each other with their eyes in the manner of the long married. Jonathan continued to stare at Henry with such force that Henrietta thought she could detect the spidery red veins brightening on the sclera of his eye. Then he took a single step backward without once breaking his stare, peeled off his old gloves, rough as gunny, and tossed them onto the wood chips at Henry's feet. Then he snatched the Forge Run cap off his head and flung it at the barn wall behind Henry's head with such ferocity that her father flinched, and Henrietta stepped aside, her heart banging. Then he stalked out of the barn in the direction of the equipment shed without another word.

"Jonathan!" Sandy called after him, "Jonathan! Hey!" and the mare tried to turn again.

But Jonathan was gone, and as Henry walked in their direction, Sandy shook his head and said in a voice barely audible, "Oh, man." The other groom just continued to stare at the floor, mute as the mare.

"Forget about him," Henry said. "I expect you boys to do your job and that's all. If I want your opinion, I'll ask for it." Sandy nodded twice, three times, but the other groom said nothing at all and just stood there with his lower lip sucked in and his brow wrinkled.

Henry took up the lead shank out of the man's hand, saying, "I've got her. Now, Henrietta, I want you up against the barn wall, and be ready to run out of here if something goes wrong."

"What goes wrong?" she said quickly.

"Nothing, nothing," he said. "But Magic Man has never done this before. It's a test run. Just be ready to run back to the house if he gets rough. He'll be here any second."

And he was. The enormous bay stallion rounded the wall of the breeding shed between his two handlers, his tremendous bulk eclipsing much of the early sunlight and casting the shed into abrupt shadow. As soon as the pliant musk of estrus reached his nostrils, he sank into his quarters, the muscles of his flanks trembling spasmodically, the phallus beginning to protrude from its sheath. His dished head traced small circles in the air as he eyed the mare. She, in turn, twisted away from the trammel of the lead shank to find him, her nostrils widening as her hooves danced on the tanbark floor. Henrietta pressed herself against the yellow padded wall. This is when the stallion handlers spotted her.

"What the fuck!" one of them said, and no apology followed on the curse.

The man nearest her turned now, craning his neck awkwardly, never unaware of the thirteen-hundred-pound hormonal creature barely managed at his side. He was a short, black-haired Irishman, maybe thirty. He rarely spoke, never smiled. He looked at her and his lips parted. "Jaysis," he said softly. And then he did something she'd never seen him do before; he laughed. And his eyes glittered over her from top to toe with the brevity of a lightning strike before Magic Man cried and Henry said, "Don't mind my daughter. Let's get this done."

"I can't do this in front of a girl!" the other man said in an echo of Jonathan's words, but when no response came and the horse moved forward between them, the matter was settled by necessity. Henry and the other men situated the mare before Magic Man as she began to chomp and jerk for the shank. But even as a handler tightened the twitch about her lips to wrench them up, forcing her into a churlish cry, her legs moved apart and her bright vulva pulsed like two clapping hands, as if she panged, despite rough handling, for the sire. Magic Man simply stood behind her, dancing in confusion. He crouched involuntarily again and again, but couldn't manage the lurch, and he went nowhere.

Sandy laughed awkwardly, his red brows ridden up. "This fool"—a dismissive gesture at the awkward stallion—"he don't know what end is . . . up." His eyes cut briefly to Henrietta, who was staring directly at him, so he blushed with painful ferocity to the roots of his bright hair, and the other mare groom, the one who had not spoken at all, turned away completely now, so that all she could see was the blank wall of his back.

The black-haired Irishman said, "Come on, my boy, let's get cracking—nowish," and he smacked Magic Man once on the rear so the stallion reared high over the whinnying mare and took two steps, and because the Irishman guided his phallus with one hand, he managed to penetrate her. The underlying mare immediately stilled her irritations. The stallion thrust once, then again, but seemed to carom off her rear the second time, so he fell out on all four feet, shaking his head, his tongue protruding stupidly, his head wobbling at her side.

"Watch she doesn't kick!" someone cried.

"She ain't never kicked," said Sandy in reply, though he'd made certain her ankles were padded heavily with blue tape.

"Ah, no, ah, no," said the Irishman with another smack, and Magic Man stood again and remounted, and the men steadied him square on her back so he was rafted up over her properly, his neck bowed like a dark sea creature over a smaller boat. This time, the Irishman circled to the stallion's rear and pushed heavily on his flanks with each massive thrust, so that the horse pressed boldly into her and bit savagely at her ears, while she accepted him placidly, braced on her sturdy legs. Then in a moment it was done. The stallion convulsed and his tail spun once. The mare hung her head and he rested his terrible, crushing weight on her back. He wound his neck against hers, rubbing and sniffing. He licked her half-drawn eyelid.

There was an embarrassed silence in the shed. Without a word, the handlers pulled on Magic Man, so he fell back from the mare onto firm ground again but stumbled awkwardly there, the handlers dancing back a pace to steady him. A great tremble reversed, like water flowing backward, from his shanks up the ridge of his back along the bow of the neck to his head. Even his lips shook as his head swung in an arc of surprise in the direction of the mare's broad flanks. But she didn't even look back. Henrietta saw how she shifted her weight, her body slow and easy, the stallion's presence useless to her now—as good as forgotten. Sandy slipped the padding from her delicate ankles, and she tossed the hank of bang out of her eyes. Magic Man took a single step toward her, but his legs shook visibly, and his handlers again rushed in to cradle both sides of his wide belly in the event of a faint. When he settled, the lead shank drew him forcibly from the mare, and though he cried out once with a plaintive, bewildered whine, he went. The whole thing took three, maybe four minutes.

The silent mare groom checked the shank's attachment, then managed to turn her toward the exit.

"That went nicely," said Henry as he crossed to his daughter and wrapped a damp arm around her shoulder. "See what I told you? Nothing but mechanics."

Sandy eyed the two of them, then sidewound to the wall and gathered up Jonathan's gloves and cap, which still lay there. "If it goes all right . . . ," he said softly, as if to no one. Then he pressed his lips together.

Henry turned to him. "Tell Jonathan I don't want to see him around here anymore. And that's final."

Sandy shrugged. "Okay." He twisted the ball cap in his hand.

The other man, the one who had not yet spoken and was now leading the mare out, made a chuffing sound just shy of a laugh. They all looked at him. His words were said directly to Sandy but aimed elsewhere. "That boy won't be around to tell it to twice. Trust me. He's got three daughters." Then he cleared his throat, stepped out of the shed, and led the mare into the unimpeded daylight of the early afternoon.

In her notebook Henrietta wrote:

> *Living bodies are machines programmed by genes that have survived.*
> *R. Dawkins*

> *Life is synthetic. It gathers its raw materials from everything that has already existed.*

There are maybe 8 million species. Homo sapiens have found and
classified 1 percent.

can't classify chaos

Just as the sexless card of girlhood was trumped by budding breasts and
widening hips, just as the organism was to be overburdened by the arrival
of the future and all its implications (menarche, coition, gravidity, parturition), Judith, in a moment of intuition, perhaps charged by memories of her
own development and the bittersweet advance of adolescence, called for
her daughter. It was time to go to Germany.

Henrietta would leave with Henry's demands ringing in her ears—don't
become tiresome like your mother; remember that excellence is a habit of
action—and ten pounds of books in her suitcase. She selected with care
from the old library; there were two pamphlets from the Geological Survey, the dog-eared Bartram, *Beagle*, as well as the oldest copy of Seneca
they possessed. When she held this last crumbling tome in her hand, marveling over the ragged sheer of its cut pages, her gaze fell upon the long
black line of bound books. The ledgers. They extended from the Long
Knives to the present day; her father still made notes in them. She drew one
away from its neighbors, looking inside for evidence of a previous time
etched in loping words on vellum. She glanced back at the library door as if
caught in the act of . . . she didn't know what, some venal thing. The ledgers contained mostly lists and mathematical figurings, and yet something
about the names and figures, the uniformity of the books—their titleless
secrecy—drew her private mind close round. She discovered on one page
the draft of what looked like a will scrawled in a curly, filigreed script.

The page read:

Forge Will: 23 September, 1827
    Appraisal of Estate of Edward Cooper Forge, aged 54 years
    One negro Man named Yearlye, $900
    One negro Boy named Denis, $600
    One negro Man named Benjohn, $1000
    One negro Man named Scipio, $1000

One negro woman named Prissey, $500

One negro girl named Senna, $350

One negro woman named Phebe, $300

One negro Boy named Adam, $700

One negro Boy named Akin, $700

One negro Boy named Corey, $700

One negro Man named Prince Sr., $400

One crippled negro girl named Tilla, $100

In event of wife Lessandra Dear Dixon's good health, the negro woman Prissey shall be returned to Stowne Farm of Fayette County, Kentucky, site of birth, along with son, Scipio, and his increase.

In event of wife Lessandra Dear Dixon's decease, the negro woman Prissey shall bequeath to Richmond Cooper Forge with son, Scipio, and his increase shall remain at Forge Farm.

Beneath the names on the page, the ledger listed furniture: a walnut secretary purchased in Lexington, as well as a Hepplewhite cherry cupboard from Nashville. Then the page ended midappraisal, and there was nothing on the back of the page when she turned it, only the shadowy stamp of the words in reverse. She made a hasty copy of the page in her notebook.

By then the heat of the thing was threatening to scorch her fingers. What to do with this remnant of another century still hot enough to burn? Put it away. Which is exactly what she did. The names, whispering repeatedly out of the flames, were dampered by the closing book and then the black ledger was returned to the shelf, where she would soon forget about it entirely, this page from the history her family had made.

The whole thing had cast Jamie Barlow into a blue mood of remembrance— close kin to melancholy, but not exactly the same thing. Good grooms leaving the farm, Big Red being put down, the girl off in some foreign place for almost three weeks like she was finally grown and gone away for good. Then Mr. Forge's foul mood while she was away. But especially the horse's death. It sank his boat a bit, poked a hole in it at least. And being in the airport too, that turned up things he'd not thought of in a long while, of all those times he flew with the horses, though he'd always preferred to drive them. Those turboprops made him kind of uneasy, he wanted a little more plane between him and the ground. And, anyhow, he liked staying up all night with a thermos of coffee and a road map, the trailer thumping along behind the dually, the horses swaying in their sleep, off to Saratoga or Churchill Downs or back to the farm or wherever. But today was his last day—who would have thought Big Red would sign off on the very same day? He didn't know whether that was an omen or what. He hitched his jeans, sat in one of the plastic airport seats, eyed the arrivals from Cincinnati. He took his hat from his head but neglected to run his fingers through his hair, so it suckered to his skull except for a gray ring that sprung up in a wave all the way around. He sighed. When a horse like that passes on . . . when you see all the best things go before you do . . . well, there's a selfish part of you that wants to go first. He thought of Deena and then those old eyes sought out a flock of young girls prancing by with their high behinds and their ponytails swinging. It was a good enough day to retire, but it was odd. Off the farm, fetching the girl and all, not even rubbing the horses, not stomping the dirt. Deena was going to pass before him. In a million years, he would not have thought that would be so. He had smoked a lot of years, also drank quite a bit when he was young. He shifted, rolled his eyes around once like they were sore in their sockets, moved his hat from the empty seat on his right to the empty seat on his left. Ovarian cancer wrapped around the colon, stage IV with six months to live, the doctor said, and she'd reached out, hand on the doctor's forearm the way Jamie had seen her do a thousand times with the boys to keep them peaceable, and saying, "It must be very hard for you to have to tell people these things." Well. All in all, he'd been lucky, really lucky. And luck was all it ever was. Of the four girls, he'd asked the one with the biggest tits to dance, and it just so happened she was plucky and smart—always had been smarter than him. Helped bring his reading up to speed, so he could take the high school equivalency test, which, actually, he never bothered to do. But that was no matter at all. You rub horses, what do you need tests for? He nodded his gray head in unwitting pantomime of conversation. He didn't even particularly like horses, he was just good with them. When the McCourys took him in, they'd always said, Send the Barlow boy, he's able with a hoss, he don't need no saddle nor string, the hosses is sweet on him. And all that. But you didn't have to like a horse, just be good to it. Same with people. Here he'd been working for Mr. Forge for twenty years and he couldn't say he cared for him, he just worked for him, and if there was one thing a person could say about Barlow, he was true. Loyal like no coon dog you ever had. With a will to work and the strength of a wheel hoss. He didn't need good pay and didn't ask for it when he deserved it, nobody got it anyway. All he needed was some old routine he was good at. You liked it or you didn't, sometimes it rained, sometimes it poured—either way, you worked. You went on home for the things you liked. He liked Deena. He'd been a rough boy, he'd put sin to shame, and that was the truth. His parents had made him that way and that wasn't an excuse the way young people always liked to make excuses nowadays, that was just the God's honest truth. But Deena had changed him. He would have been ashamed to cuss or act big in front of her, the way he'd done before. At first he could barely say a word in her presence, just trying to refigure how to be, like learning to toddle and walk all over again, so he let her take the lead. Because he knew this: a good woman was sure to rub her goodness off on you if you let her, but there wasn't enough angels in heaven to protect you if you rubbed your badness off on her. She'd turn it on you, she'd take up what was left of your own life and beat you with it, and an angry woman could do a sight more damage than any angry man he'd ever met. They used psychology on you. Deena had also brought him to Jesus, or at least in the vicinity, and made him want to learn and to be better and kind of chipper in his way. It got so he sometimes thought he'd always been good, always looked on the bright side, but no, that was her. And tough enough too. Here was a woman that got thrown from a horse onto her side and all she said was, "No, no, I'm all right, just let me soak in Epsom salts!" She'd refused to go to the doctor. She walked into the house on his arm and got all sunk down in the tub and it wasn't until she passed out in the water that he finally took her to the hospital, where they said her leg was broken in two places. She wasn't a crier, not really, not the sentimental type, though she was warm. It was Barlow who was the crier. Except when Deena went through the change, when she skipped her first month, she'd cried then. Four boys survived to be good men, religious men—except for one hellraiser just now in the process of coming around—and here she was crying, because she never got a girl of her own to raise up. She'd said some hard things that day, things that he would probably never forget. But she was a good person. He laced his sunspotted hands over his belly, closed his eyes. He thought of her on that long-ago day at the dance in her blue skirt and white blouse. Deena in the blue skirt and the white blouse was pretty much the chorus of his life. He recalled the little sweat stains he saw when he twirled her, how hard that had turned his dial. Someone had said once that you wanted a girl who could get good and wet and he'd had no idea what that meant at the time, he'd been so ignorant, but when he saw those stains under her arms, he went a little crazy on the inside. They sparked off each other the whole night at that dance. She wouldn't let him do it to her until they were engaged, but when she'd finally let him, Lord, he'd taken no prisoners that night. Like a dog on a bone, he worked every angle he could think of. At one point, there had been so many arms and legs and whatnots pointing in so many different directions, it seemed like there were more than two people in that bed. "What are you trying to do to me?" she'd said, and she had laughed at him, and though a woman's laugh could wreck a man, it wasn't like that. Deena laughing was a good thing. It meant you were on your way, and sure enough, they were.

Barlow looked up, found the arrivals sign, checked his watch again. He stood now, but he didn't spring up; he weighted his knees first before his hips followed and his chest found its center. It was time to retire, whether or not Deena was ill. His arthritis was a misery.

He saw the girl then; she emerged from the tunnel gripping a backpack and a yellow blanket he'd not seen before, something she must have got from a stewardess on the plane. He watched how she scanned the crowd of people, and realized she was a lot skinnier now than she'd been when she left, just skin and bone. Everyone passed her as she stood there like a lone rock in a stream. She would be looking for Mr. Forge, he thought, so he raised one arm, the arm that wouldn't open all the way anymore after it took a kick, and she saw him and for a second looked disappointed, and old as he was, about-to-retire-seen-it-all-tried-it-all-survived-it-all as he was, it hurt his feelings just a little bit. He had to smile at himself and when she saw him smile, she half ran to him and stood before him, looking like the mostly grown thing that she was, though still curveless as a boy and probably always would be, poor thing, and she tucked her chin and leaned her head into his chest. She didn't hug anybody full body anymore. It was a mystifying and sad thing to watch little girls grow up.

"Hey, darlin'," he said.

"Hi." She gazed up into his face. "Your hair looks funny. Where's Daddy?"

"Well, he planned on picking you up, but . . . he's kinda under the weather." He looked over her head as he ran his fingers through his hair and he saw the open mouth of the tunnel that led back to the plane, thought maybe there was a chance he would never be on a plane again. It wasn't the worst thing he could think of.

"Is he sick?"

"Well, no, he ain't ill exactly. He's in a foul mood is all. He got some bad news. Everybody got some bad news today." He didn't say that he'd seen Mr. Forge blow up, or tell her some of the things he'd said, the whole emotion of the business embarrassed him when you got right down to it. But maybe he just couldn't understand, maybe he just never cared for horses that way, what did he know? He was a pretty simple guy.

"What bad news?"

"Big Red expired today—Secretariat expired."

Henrietta's eyes grew wide. "What? How?" The horse had only been nineteen.

"Laminitis. It just started to rot up his leg and they had to put him down today."

"Oh shit," she said.

"Well, no need for slang," he said. Then: "Yeah, he made a real good horse with that one." He was undertalking, of course; the horse had been the best thing he'd ever seen in his life, and he'd seen some marvelous horseflesh in his time.

She said, "I guess Daddy's really upset?"

"Aw, kind of. He'll be fine. Thought I'd better pick you up, though." He smiled.

She sighed then, and he patted her on the shoulder. They made their way to the baggage claim and they were standing side by side when she said, suddenly, "I guess it's a good thing Hellcat's pregnant."

"Suppose so."

"But what if it's a filly? Daddy's praying for a colt."

"Well," said Barlow, and then he said something he wouldn't normally have ever said, seeing as it might read as criticism. "Your daddy ought not to pray for a thing like that. With people sick and dying and all. You ought to be happy with whatever life gives you." But then he thought immediately of Deena, of her crying on that day fifteen days ago, and he thought, Well, I'm probably wrong, you also ought not to cast stones at your employer, even if it is your last day on the job.

"Daddy has to have a colt," Henrietta insisted. "If he doesn't, he'll never leave me alone about it."

"How come's that?"

"Oh," she said, "when Daddy gets worked up, he gets mad if I spend too much time away from him. You know, taking walks and reading science stuff or whatever."

"Well, it's your life," Barlow said suddenly before he could stop himself, his tongue apparently just doing whatever it wanted today.

"I guess . . . ," Henrietta said slowly.

"Honey, you just go on and do what you want. You can grow on up to be anything you want to be." Now he actually laughed out loud for a moment, and then he coughed so that she turned to watch him strangely. Lord Jesus, he thought, shut my mouth. Barlow the evangelist. I'm getting old and sassy. Time to retire, indeed.

"I'm like Zeno's arrow," she said.

"You're too smart for me," Barlow said, shaking his head, and then the older man put his arm around her and looked as though he were helping this younger girl through the airport to the truck, as if she were the doddering one with the ruined hips and knees and not he.

As they left the airport, they both gazed out at Keeneland as they passed, at the vast green pastures, the tracks, the fences, the shattering blue of the sky overhead. Cars streamed from the acreage following the afternoon races.

"I'm missing the fall meet," Henrietta said, but Barlow didn't reply, concentrating on reaching 64 to avoid the city, the traffic, and all the changes that had occurred there in his lifetime, things he didn't care to see today. He cleared his throat, pictured again that big, beautiful red horse, dead now, and then shook his head. He was like a fish today, like a fish that kept getting reeled back in. He'd get cleaned and cooked soon enough.

The girl beside him closed her eyes and seemed to sleep and he looked over at her occasionally and he thought kind thoughts about her and he drove her most of the way home in silence.

When they reached the farside outskirts of Paris, she yawned and stretched and opened her eyes.

Old Barlow said, "I ever tell you about the best night of my life?"

"I don't think so." She yawned again.

"Well," he said, and he paused, because the onset of the memory felt good. And also because he thought, Well, my wedding night ought to have been the best night of my life or the births of the boys, and those were almost the best, but this was really the best, and that was just the truth. "Well," he said, "when I was about your age, I was still living with the McCourys, they raised me up. My folks weren't dead, but the McCourys raised me. Kind of complicated, but never mind that. Anyhow, one night, one summer night, they had to get thirty head of cattle to Mount Sterling to sell at the market there. They lived just a couple miles from your all's place. So me and one of the older boys, we saddled up two horses—they had quarter horses—and we drove that thirty head of beef to Mount Sterling. It took us from just after sundown till morning." Then Barlow paused.

"Did something fun happen?" Henrietta said.

He looked over at her in surprise and slowed just slightly, downshifting as he tried to think. It sounded like almost nothing when he put words to it. "Well, I don't know," he said. "I guess what I'm saying is . . . Well, the moon was pretty full, so it was light and it was the summertime, so it felt pretty nice out. And those cattle didn't give us any trouble at all. The other boy rode along the middle and I brought up the rear and we ran them right up the middle of the road. Nobody passed us the whole night. I guess it was kind of like breaking the rules. It felt pretty good."

"Did somebody pick you up when you got there?" Henrietta asked politely.

"Nope, I guess we just rode on back. It didn't take too long without the cattle."

"You must have been tired."

"I suppose so. I don't really remember that part."

They were pulling into the drive, and he was downshifting in earnest now and the horses were gazing at them and old Barlow thought, here

I come for the last time. He looked over the spread of the farm, where he had spent the last twenty years of his adult life. Now he would go home to his wife, who was passing.

"Oh," he said.

"What?"

He shook his head and said nothing. Then when his eyes cleared, he saw Henry standing in the door of the el porch, holding a glass of what looked like bourbon or iced tea in his hand, and he wasn't doing a thing but standing there on the porch, but an odd thing happened. Old Barlow's stomach suddenly twisted up, and he suffered such a pained sense of misgiving, one that was so strong and so foreign to him that he would tell his wife of it later and she would say, "Maybe Jesus wanted you to say something to that poor little girl."

He stopped the truck abruptly, far shy of its destination beside the el porch. It stuttered on the idle. He didn't turn to Henrietta; his eyes were locked on the figure of her father, and it was true, something else seemed to have his tongue, something had had it all day, he couldn't own it anymore, he felt like crying. "How old are you, Henrietta?"

"Almost fourteen."

"Well," he said, "that's almost grown. It's old enough to have a boyfriend."

"Okay," she said quietly.

He said, "Plenty old to start thinking about what you want. Someday you'll have a family."

Growing embarrassed, she shifted. "But what if I don't want to have a family?" she said.

Now he turned and looked at her and she was amazed to see tears in his eyes. "Sometimes . . . ," he said, "sometimes you don't even want the thing that you got to have in this life. That you absolutely for the sake of everything got to have. And only from the other side, you see it saved you. You get me?"

She shook her head slowly.

"Well," he sighed, and laughed suddenly, and it was as if he were clearing cobwebs away from the tiny room of their conversation. "Yeah, I reckon not. I don't know I get me either. I'm having a funny day. It's my retiring day."

"Your what? You're retiring? You're going away?"

"Yeah. I'm going home to my wife. Just the other side of Paris, though. Almost to Middleburg."

"Oh." Henrietta looked down at her lap. She too felt the stare of her father from the porch and when she looked up, his posture had not changed—his lean against the porch frame remained exactly the same—but his body was angry, somehow she knew that.

"Barlow," she said, "can I come visit you?"

"Honeypie, you can come visit old Barlow and Deena anytime you want."

She leaned over then. She pressed her lips to his old cheek, and the wrinkles felt like old leather against the soft skin of her lips.

"Daddy's waiting," she said.

"Yeah. Yeah, I guess he is."

She tried to hold herself apart, though she hadn't seen him in nearly a month. She didn't know why. She thought it was because he was angry.

He said, "You go away and, I swear to God, the world falls apart."

She stared up at him, into the blistering reproval of his face. It almost snatched her breath away, the flush of emotion she saw there like a port-wine stain covering his too-familiar face. She could only whisper, "It's not my fault Secretariat died."

"I didn't say it was your fault," he snapped.

"Then why are you blaming me?"

"Why three weeks away and not a year? Three years! Anything Judith says—"

"Well, Mother wanted . . . But you agreed!"

"I never agreed! Your mother thinks she can just—"

Now she looked through him, her ears blunting his words, the tiny whorls cinched tight. Mute, stony, intransigent, cold, stonewalling. For the first time ever, he was refused entry, and he saw the change, the quiet mutiny, and it shocked him.

"Henrietta," he said, and he reached out and grabbed the girl by the shoulders and pulled her to him. As soon as he touched her, she felt against her will just how long she'd been gone, and she hugged him back as if she would break him and was overcome with homesickness, though now she was finally home. Home at last. She did not look up, did not look down, but her face was pressed directly into his chest so that she could not breathe, feeling his hands against her back like irons. When he was like this, when his face was like this, she'd rather be against him than gazing upon him. But eventually she had to breathe and she turned her face up. He leaned down and kissed her on the mouth, and his lips were parted and her lips were parted too, because she was dying for air.

Child, it's simple, really, in the broad, inexorable scheme of biological diversity, and its oft-assumed corollary the pursuit of perfection: blame the isolating trait. The Forges, once a distinct subspecies, are quickly becoming a closed gene pool with a natural history all their own. You didn't ask to be a part of this taxonomic unit, yet here you are, little redheaded rosebud, ransacked Ruffian, Daddy's little girl. Once upon a time you might have interbred with another subspecies, meandering from the fold, discovering the strange scents of bodies on the verge of a foreign range. But bred long enough, a subspecies becomes a species in its own right, possessed of its distinct mark, the isolating trait. Soon you will begin to emit a sour smell; soon the other animals will recognize your difference, show you their tails, and race away. But don't blame your father, even if he is the author of your isolation; he too is a reservoir of genes he didn't request. He too is a machine designed for survival.

"Henrietta!"

She was not asleep, had not even closed her eyes, and she was moving the moment he called her name, rising even as the word was echoing down the halls. She slipped down the back stairs with her sheets clenched around her like pale cerements, her face drained of color.

He was in the back study, his tan face perfectly calm. He was the same, always the same, his face like a banquet table all grandly arrayed, full of every good thing. She wondered for a moment whether she was mad, her memory faulty.

"Come here, sweetheart," he said. "I've been waiting for the right time and now is that time . . . I want to show you what's going to be yours—now that your mother has decided to consort with a German Jew."

Henry began sorting through the stacks of files and paper on his desk, tugging out a few documents and handing them in her direction. She took her future in her hands just as the heaters kicked on with a monitory rattle. The house breathed in her stead.

"Is this your will?" The calm sound of her voice surprised her. It seemed to come from a distance, from a body other than her own.

He looked up at her over the silver rim of his reading glasses. "In a few years, when you turn eighteen, I'll revise the will and you'll be named my sole heir in the event of my death. You'll have power of attorney if I were ever to become disabled. And these," he said, reaching for another file, "are current copies of the insurance paperwork for the horses."

There were policies for mortality, prospective foal and first season infertility cover paperwork, fire/lightning and transportation insurance, general liability. The premiums ranged from $5,000 to $25,000 each. She calculated the number of mares, stallions, and foals on the farm.

"You have to pay this every year?" she said quietly, stunned.

"That's only the first half," he said. "This is the house."

The stack of papers he handed her was as thick as a dictionary and just as heavy. She had to rest it on the leather top of the desk, which she discovered, as she began to flip through the documents, was made in seventeenth-century Italy of mahogany with secondary veneered rosettes in the shape of pinwheels across its front apron, its appraisal value $150,000. She'd never even looked at it before, not really.

"The leather has been replaced, and that's impacted the value. But it's an unusual piece for the house. Almost everything we have is American and English," he said.

She read on. Here was the leggy chest of drawers in her bedroom, beneath which she had once played as a toddler, no longer a toy but a mahogany highboy of Boston provenance, worth $20,000 at the time of its appraisal eight years prior, worn jeans and underwear now stuffed to overflowing in its drawers. Her bedside table from the 1780s, New Haven. She flipped through the pages of abundance, of surfeit, that reached into every corner of the house, so that the sideboards—all six—were found not just in the dining room but in the hallways upstairs, one even in a guest bedroom, where it housed linens in its burled drawers, plus a dozen old Boston piecrust tables in various rooms, six more beds than people, Georgian secretaries and Regency chairs, lyre tables, mahogany-veneered butler's desks, a Sheraton chest of drawers with carved acanthus leaf columns and turned leonine feet, there were Empire lounges with velvet upholstery, two she had not ever lain on because they were in the attic, alabaster lamps, black marble lamps, a thousand first editions in the two libraries, Wedgwood pottery, mirrors from Philadelphia and London, claw-footed tubs, English brass flowerpots, three sets of Spode china, none used in her lifetime, and four Kentucky sugar chests, together worth over $40,000. Four sugar chests? Her mind balked. She could only think of the one in the living room with Nelson County bourbons tucked into its planed wells. She had no idea where in the great expanse of the house the others might be. Her eyes had overlooked them, overlooked all of this, because they had simply always been here like the lay of the land or the fact of her father.

Henry was watching her carefully as she read, watching the mysterious, obscure movements of her face. "This is your inheritance," he said carefully. "I've saved this for you. I was aggressive with the investments and reversed the retrenchment of my father. Our money dates from at least the Revolution. It's survived five wars and untold market crashes. I hope I'm making clear the kind of obligation you'll be taking on. Do you understand?"

"Yes," she said in a whisper.

"Henrietta, sometimes what looks like a big risk is actually controlled usage," he said. "It's what I've striven for all my life. Orient all your internal resources to amplify your external resources. You walk the tipping point between disaster and perfection. Everything—I mean everything—is used for a greater purpose. Do you understand?"

But this time Henrietta was looking down at a page again, her eyes widening. She said, "Oh my God."

The old print of two blue birds—had she ever imagined its worth? She turned and walked from the room, rushing through the hall, where she became suddenly and sharply aware of the ivory-inlaid sideboards, the sconces twinkling like unlit, dusky brown diamonds, the Aubusson runners damping the sounds of her passage to the parlor, so she was indistinguishable to the ear from any Forge who had come before. She felt her way to the light switch and, when she flipped it, realized how it brought to life a half dozen lamps and sconces simultaneously, so the room was bathed in the rosy ambient haze of a constructed evening. The parlor was perfection, curated like a museum, its complexity distilled and severely fine. She stopped before the print, where it had hung over the burgundy davenport for as long as she could remember. Columbia jays perched on a dead branch, both heads downcast in naïve ignorance of their own charm, oblivious to their dark martial crests and blue velvet coattails. The beauty of their blue pained the eye. Had the painter copied this pair from life or from death? Perhaps he had killed the birds for his picture. That sort of thing was done sometimes; people killed the very thing they professed to love. And maybe, just maybe—though Henrietta would only think this many years later, when she was pregnant with her child—the painter had imagined his own creation to be more beautiful than creation as he found it. Why, she thought now, could no one leave a thing alone?

"I found this in Philadelphia for twenty-five thousand dollars. First edition. A Kentucky original belongs in Kentucky, don't you think?"

She didn't turn, only felt the smallness of the two of them in the overriding catholic luxury of the house.

"This is yours," he said again, and then she turned and, perhaps for the first time, really looked at him.

In her notebook she wrote:

You think you're so smart, but you're wrong. You're antediluvian. You're proud to be a Megatherium but, Father, a dinosaur is still a dinosaur. You're propagating the wrong memes, and the wrong ones parasitize the mind as well as the right ones.
—"Race" is a word, and someone made up the word. "Supercalifragilisticexpialidocious" is also a word.
—Racial categories are inconsistent, because what they measure is inconsistent. What's inconsistent isn't really real in any categorical sense.
—See, traits don't have distinct boundaries. There are gradations of every trait, including skin tone. Genes flow the way a glacier melts. Slowly.
—Racial groups aren't homogenous at all; 85 percent of variation occurs within any ethnic group.
—IQ? Men and women have different cranial capacities with no correlating IQ difference. Everybody's known this forever.
—The anthropologists beat the eugenicists a long time ago. Supposedly

immutable traits are malleable under the forces of environment. "Genes have given away most of their sovereignty." E. O. Wilson
—Difference is real, but the issue isn't racial difference. We're talking about tiny genetic differences created by transmutation under the limits of geography and climate. The limits change constantly, so the descriptors change constantly. Agassiz actually called blacks and whites separate species! Static definitions aren't useful.

Father, did you know they used to think there were only two kingdoms of life? Plantae and Animalia. They actually reduced the whole wide world to two. Then it started to look more complicated, and they decided there should be five kingdoms. They split Plantae into three additional groups: Monera, so bacteria and algae were together, Protista for eukaryotes, and another for the Fungi.

They used to think the big divisions occurred only between the higher plants and animals and everything else. But the closer you look, the more you see that big divisions occur between every two beings. It's an ontogeny/phylogeny problem. There are visible differences, but even more we can't see down at the chromosomal level, and every new life contains mutations—so the potential is always there for more. There should be 6 billion kingdoms on earth.

Two weeks after she returned from Germany she gave herself to the Irishman, and he took her. She didn't have to do much to make it happen. She simply followed him around the broodmare barn and gazed at him unblinkingly until he couldn't help but notice, and finally he curled his finger at her, and she followed him around a corner into the feed room. He kissed her breasts a little, told her she had a good body, and then lay down on her and did it to her that way. She said nothing at all. He lay on her afterward, bent awkwardly at the waist with his jeans pooled foolishly around his work boots, and then he had smiled at her—only the second smile she had ever seen on his face. But she recoiled from that smile. She was already renovating the act in her mind—how it could be different, better, how she wouldn't let anyone do it to her quite like that again. And she didn't. When the Irishman came to her the next time with his knowing grin and his game eyes, she stared right through him and began to walk away, and when he caught at her sleeve, she said, without explanation, "Just leave me alone."

She tried it with other grooms, the ones who did not shy away from the unexpected advances of their employer's underage daughter. The few who accepted seemed doubly aroused by their own illicit desire and fear. These were the ones she had to battle against—they tried to pin her under their demanding, oblivious weight—to climb atop. She figured out quickly to take what she could get, because these men would offer her no pleasure of their own accord. She had no way of knowing that these men were the least worth having, the gates of their inhibition irreparably broken, any native compassion trampled by baser instincts. She didn't know how to want something better. Nothing mattered beyond the landscape of their hard, alien bodies, which she slid over, around. When she moved on them like that, she discovered that the old way of making herself feel good could be moved inward to some dark place that no one could see and no one had ever named for her. What had been up front and tinny and immediate was now shuddering and agonizingly deep. A birthing in. It was the only thing that was hers alone and it required no thought, and so she became addicted to it. But she had to have a man to do it. She had to have a man to bear down on.

She dutifully called her mother every other Sunday. When Judith picked up the receiver, before Henrietta could say anything more than "It's me," her mother would burst into tears in a manner uncharacteristic but increasingly frequent. Her voice was urgent across the transcontinental air, the trackless air.

Judith: Oh, Henrietta, was I wrong to leave? Tell me your father's good to you.

Henrietta: I guess.

Judith: You guess? God, he better be. Sometimes I feel I should have fought for custody, but I never could have won against him. Sometimes I . . .

Henrietta: What?

Judith: I—I don't know . . . I don't know what I think. I guess I . . . it just seems like men aren't interested in knowing women. Even the decent ones. Everything is lonely after the excitement. Do you ever get lonely?

Henrietta: Not really.

Oh, Mommy...

Judith: Even though I'm not there?

Henrietta: No. I have Daddy. I guess I miss old Barlow.

Judith: Oh.

Henrietta: Don't cry, Mother.

Mommy, there's nothing here at all.

Judith: It's just . . . Why do you have to lose everything to understand just a little? I feel so powerless, like nothing ever really changes. You just trade one thing for the next thing, and it ends up being exactly the same thing. Whatever you do, Henrietta, don't grow up. I swear, they've rigged the whole game so women can't win. I don't know why they hate us so much.

Henrietta: I don't think I get to choose anything, Mom.

Judith: I wish you didn't know that yet.

Henrietta: Can't you come back?

Judith: Do you know I love you even though I'm all the way over here?

Then why did you leave me in this black breach?

Henrietta: I have to go now.

There are people ahead of us and people behind us, but there's no one else at all in the breach.

Judith: Oh, honey. They should have named me Regret, just like the goddamn horse.

She withdrew from the house and began to take long walks to be away from people. She wandered down the road past the Miller property where the curious, bellwethering cows streamed in her direction, following until they could follow no further, stopped short by the perimeter fencing. A coal-eyed, affectless crowd. She wondered what they would say to her if they could open their closed throats, what they would ask.

She discovered that 150 acres had been placed on the market a mile down the road. The property boasted two creeks and a white mansion on a slight rise of land like a white pillar on a plinth, near analog to the Forge land, though this house was even grander, and the land did not depress to a bowl behind the house. The family had left for Florida without waiting for a buyer. In their wake, winter had come. Every morning she hiked up the driveway, huffing frigid air in her exertions until she made her way to a frosted wall at the rear of the mansion where she could spy through the windows the gleaming glassed cabinetry of a white kitchen with its white tiles, where dusty boot marks remained from the movers who had last walked there. She would lean against the outside wall, pull her woolen hat low over her ears, stuff her winter-crimsoned hands into her parka pockets. Then, perfectly still in the freeze, she paid the land mind. The old pastures were deadened by winter—she liked that the season had no scruples, it swept out most of the life to be found there, leaving only spare, hardy, scavenging birds and some winter hares that foraged. The spent grasses waved, and the sky impoverished of clouds sent cold, furious, wasted breezes, far colder than the resting air, to toss the weeds, which were brittle and arthritic. Some days they appeared candied with light snow. She could remain a long time against that frozen wall, not moving, part of the motionless winter statuary that included the stolid trees, the black fencing now white, and the barns, only closing her eyes when the winds came in a flurry. Many hours would be spent in this manner.

But by late April, the "For Sale" sign had been taken down, and one of the abandoned pastures had sprung up a mass of rye as tall as her hips. Still there were no people to be seen. She went wading into the pastures and was soon wet with dew, as wet as a wader in the sea. With her jeans heavy and suckered to her thighs, she could watch morning rise. The fringed rye shook and shimmied, its braided feather tips strung with beads of lit dew glazed white like the hides of those long-gone winter hares. The sky conducted, its windy arms swept low as waves of rye moved in a rustling choral. At this particular hour between first light and the sun's emergence, the birds didn't sing, they screamed for morning, as if the wait itself did some kind of violence to them. Then when the sun began to grow a crescent on the horizon, the birds were calm and easy again and began to call for mates now that the first matter, the matter of survival, was settled. The world was renewing itself and it sustained the birds with their small fears and sustained the girl who stood motionless, chilled to the bone and watchful.

Then one morning Henrietta arrived in the early hours to find two white SUVs parked in the driveway of the mansion behind a moving van. And two days later, when she chanced by with her father, she saw that the front paddocks had been mowed and horses installed, horses that turned to watch with dark, extinguished eyes as she passed.

On a mild winter night in 1990, Hellcat gave birth to a foal. It was not a colt but a gentle, bug-eyed filly that Henry, in his initial disappointment, could not bring himself to name. Henrietta called her Seconds Flat, in honor of her sire, Secretariat, and, hopefully—pray gods and goddesses—her propulsive, thundering, unbeatable speed.

The life of the racehorse unfolds: first there is the bright newness of the suckling, all dawn-eyed and gawky with legs too long for the body. Seconds Flat was even more awkward than most, her legs just brown crutches she stumbled upon, suggesting a height she would not ultimately deliver. As a weanling, she was still tethered to Hellcat, but haltered and handled now and beginning to explore the limits of her paddock. In the blink of a breeder's eye, she was turned out in a fresh field with the other motherless foals, skittish and afraid, tracing bereft circles in the grass and gentling to human hands, turning yearling under the watchful eye of her handlers, settling into tender legs and attaining slowly a hint of the conformation of her sire. She was still small with a lady's legs and a trimmer waist, but possessed his sharp head, the same steely, intelligent eyes, and a haughtiness that made her bite. The grooms knew to be wary of her, and when, as an eighteen-month-old, she was shipped to a trainer's farm to begin the process of saddling and bridling, they remained circumspect, careful. One man forgot and nearly lost two fingers, but he never forgot again. Her life in training there was a regular one—a pattern of feed and water and stall work, walking in circles, learning to bear the saddle pad and the corset of the surcingle. She snapped and whined when a man lay like a sack across her back for the first time. She fought against the bit as well but ultimately took it, and when the saddle came again, this time with a man atop it, she bucked, emitted a piercing cry that made the other horses dance with anxiety, but then took that too, as they all would, each in their turn. They were broken now and learning to canter on the outdoor track, then jogging singly, sprinting in packs, and the filly began to show the long reach of her inheritance—the balance, self-assurance, stamina accruing like money in the bank.

The second year in a Thoroughbred's life, the watershed year, begins quietly. Seconds Flat was released to pasture to gain weight. The stem of her neck elongated, the buds of her eyes brightened, then she surprised them all by not growing taller but filling out with a sprinter's cabbagey, bunched muscles. As the weather turned and her winter coat began to shed, she returned to the track for conditioning. She galloped hobby-horse miles and dropped her winter fat, so dappling sprung up on her hide like sunflung shadows. She learned to slice through mere slivers of air that separated horse from horse in a pack, and to hold her power in reserve, then finish with decisive strength. But she was a young gladiator with one terrific weakness: she balked at the starting gate. She would rear and buck and snap as four men forced her from behind into the padded enclosure. Once inside the panic box, she shook and whined until they led her out again and back around. The pushing, crying, and straining was repeated until finally, when they were all exhausted, man and horse equally, her resistance failed and she managed herself at the exhausted brink of terror just long enough to qualify, then leaped clean from the gate at the bang of the bell and was issued her gate card. She was gleaming, muscled, dappled, fearsome, and terrified; she was ready to race.

And race she did. They never did discover the distance her pedigree promised, and she remained clumsy if propulsive out of the gate, but grew to be a terror in the half mile with the speed of a young colt, a jetter, a fast-twitch bitch, as Henrietta liked to say. Never as elegant as her sire, she chopped the air with her forelegs like an overeager dog, so that Henry would cover his head with his *Racing Form*, his cheeks bright red, but she won—four first-place wins in her juvenile year, and as many seconds. By the spring of her third year, her Derby year, she had no more fear of turf flung into her eyes or slippage on wet dirt tracks; what tremblings had existed the year before had been burned from her in the refining fire of competition. Her speed was only increasing. The Derby was in sight for Henry Forge.

Henrietta, at nineteen, could remember the names of every horse she'd ever seen place. From enduring stars like Silver Charm, Unbridled, and Thunder Gulch to those who shined brightly in a single classic, then fell away swiftly from the public eye, they were all locked in her memory. It wasn't love or passion, but the taxonomical principle of her mind at work.

It was life between the races, the quotidian details of a horsewoman's day that had become indistinguishable, save the strange or startling detail. She recalled one day in the saddling enclosure when a horse reared in fright and fell backward, breaking its own skull, so its blood unfurled like a red flag on the brick—it was euthanized on the spot, its tongue bitten in half between its clamped teeth; there was the man she'd had sex with in a private bathroom upstairs, only to find out he was an old friend of her father's and in the Assembly, no less; the day she'd been overcome with food poisoning on the back stretch and run to kneel behind a stable, vomiting into the dirt when a tiny Peruvian jockey known only as Minnie Ball rounded the corner and found her. He'd held up an apologetic hand and said, "No problem. Me also. I do this also."

And, of course, she remembered all of the Derbys, though like most in the business, she was interested in the results and impatient with the festivities, which rankled like overeating store-bought cake on a full stomach, all sickly sweet layers of drunkenness, celebrity, and overexposure of every kind. She wasn't one to mingle in Millionaires Row, watching men shake hands and clap each other on the back, standing dutifully beside her father in their hermetically sealed box. She spent some of the afternoon checking in on Seconds Flat on the backstretch, then braving the crowds at the betting arcade and the food stands, where bettors jostled cheek to jowl and the offense of hot burgoo, sweat, and treacly perfume was undercut only by the persistent and oddly comforting odor of manure. The celebrities were mostly up top in the grandstand; down here the mildly monied pressed against one another in a crush, their cheer tinged always with the tang of violence—and the drive to perpetuate the species. Nowhere else outside a Nevada brothel could you see so many bosoms on display down to the edge of puckering areolas. Coral and red lips and chalk-white manicures, precipitous candy-colored pumps. Men with their penguin chests puffed, strutting dandy before the women, purchasing wine and Cokes and waving stubs and pretending to a knowledge cribbed quick for the first Saturday in May. At the Derby, every male was an expert, so long as there was a female in the room.

Without really intending it, Henrietta wound up near the rail with the other onlookers. She realized suddenly it was almost four thirty, and the Turf Classic was complete with the winner in the circle. She ought to make her way back into the interior of the marvelously white grandstand—white spires looming over white porticos and white pillars under white clouds—and over to the saddling paddock, where, under the Longines clock, the little jocks would come lining out from their official portrait to be tossed onto their mounts at the call: "Riders up!" But it was too late.

the sun shines bright on my old kentucky home tis summer the darkies are gay the corn tops ripe and the meadows in the bloom and the birds make music all the day the young folks roll on the little cabin floor all merry all happy and bright by and by hard times comes a-knocking at my door then my old kentucky home good night

The rising roar of the crowd was a 747 engine on the ascent. The horses, including a nervy, prancing Seconds Flat, were emerging from the tunnel with their lead ponies and silked riders, some skittering in fright, some perking before the attention. Henrietta made a quick decision—if she left now to return to the box where her father waited, she would likely miss the race. So, she remained where she stood, hands on the rail, eyes locked on Seconds Flat, their tough, gritty, game, and slightly ridiculous girl. Even at a walking pace, her inelegant gait was clear; any amateur eye could detect it. She danced and overstrode on skinny scapes, a seeming galoot amidst nobility with only a smart head and big ass to show for herself. She still careened from the gate like a drunk, but she was loaded with talent and ran hungry; once balanced, she was all head drive and forward motion. And one thing was certain: she was a hell of a closer.

the head must bow and the back will have to bend wherever the darky may go a few more days and the trouble all will end in the field where the sugar canes may grow a few more days for to tote the weary load no matter twill never be light a few more days till we totter on the road then my old kentucky home good night

The postparade took its perennial course counterclockwise to the green gate on the backstretch, where the crew forced jittery horse after fractious horse into their coin slots. The jocks, starved and sweated down to weight, were perched with their goggles strapped six deep, crops in hand.

Blood coursed quick for both man and animal, but time crawled, then slagged, then stopped. No one breathed.

The bell rang, and the gate clanged wide.

The crowd glassed the field in a single motion. Seconds Flat launched herself with furor from the gate, but as always, she moved more sky than earth, more the ungainly deer than an elegant Thoroughbred. She corrected quickly under the seething ministrations of her jock, who locked on her mouth and piloted her forward. They settled into a solid, unremarkable sixth when Henrietta, who had no binoculars because she'd never meant to stand at the rail in the first place, lost her in the mix of bays and ruddle reds attenuating to a shifting line on the backstretch. The track was slick with earlier rain, and the muck soon transformed the horses to dun and the jocks to gingerbread men—their cornflower, scarlet, and sienna silks splattered until identical—as they tore goggle after goggle from their browning faces, half-blind as their mounts jostled and edged neck to neck around the precipitous turn.

The second horse, Major General, running hard at the lead's shoulder, didn't go down on the curve, where he bore along under the eightfold drag of centrifugal force, straining the tiny, countless fractures he'd sustained from running too much as a juvenile, unable to heal because the heart heals first, then striated muscle, then bone, and bone only if the training regimen allows. Instead, he went down on the straightaway when, with an arrow's unerring attack, he began to stretch out of the pack, his nose edging toward the distant wire, his mane a flag snapping in his jock's joyous face. When he had barely gained a head, his cannon bone fractured through the flesh with a resounding *snap!*, his right hoof flopping suddenly behind in a gruesome, dismissive backhand to the field. His bulk toppled hideously onto his outstretched neck, which broke without a *snap!*, tossing his jock forward like a child from a bike, too stunned to protect himself as the two horses directly behind tripped on the fallen horse and went down themselves, one with a fractured skull, one with a shattered shoulder, the latter screaming for the four minutes before all three could be euthanized with a syringe to the jugular.

"Oh!" cried the man beside Henrietta, his beer sloshing over the lip of its cup. "They totaled the car! It's a fucking smashup!"

A fourth colt careened wildly to the outside and pulled up in front of the whitened faces of the shocked railbirds, who only now, as the full meaning of the *snap!* registered, began to groan as if they and not the horses had sustained the injuries. Seconds Flat, sixth at the turn and still accelerating where her peers stumbled or veered over the prone, stunned bodies of the fallen, simply used her natural, instinctive chop to leap over them—horses and jockeys all—more like a champion jumper than Secretariat's get.

Still accelerating, she passed second under the wire.

"It's nothing short of a miracle these three jockeys are alive," Henrietta heard the announcer cry. With broken arms and ribs and concussions, they crawled like toddlers back to their mounts, one of which had now sprung up on three legs to hobble frantically about, head jerking manically, so saliva was slung around its neck like a necklace, but two of which could not move at all save the stunned thumping of a tail. Two of the jocks sat in the mess of churned mud, crying like children over their broken horses where they lay, listening as the colt with the injured shoulder screamed.

Henrietta watched with her hand over her mouth as a screen was erected around the horses.

The track ambulance spun up, followed shortly by the vet's truck with its mobile clinic, and three horse ambulances. A hundred thousand strong and mostly drunk, the grandstand waited in muted, tipply shock as one entered willingly, confused, and white-eyed into the ambulance, the other two euthanized and winched even before the weeping owners could say—still out of breath from racing down from their air-conditioned boxes—"Do the right thing."

Only when a door slammed for the third time did Henrietta turn abruptly away from the rail. She had to find her father, who had surely left the box by now to find Seconds Flat. He would be furious, she knew; a second-place finish was a deep disappointment under the best of conditions, but with the best in the field down, it amounted to nothing at all. It added not one letter to the family name. Where was her father? Hands clutching his skull, no doubt, and cursing his fate.

"Slow down, Henrietta."

He felt like an invalid with his daughter on his arm this way, all but held upright as they walked from the barn on the backstretch, where Seconds

Flat, uninjured but to Henry's eye a wasted thing, was now being washed and hotwalked, and where the jockey had gripped his arm, saying, "She just flew, Mr. Forge! She flew over them like an eagle!" and where their trainer met them with not the proper solemnity but smiles of relief that they'd been spared—and second place!—though the man soon fell into a faltering silence when confronted with Henry, who looked out at the horseflesh all around them and, for one gaping moment, could not determine what he looked upon, or his place in it. His hopes were dashed, and his accrued wealth amounted to nothing. He gazed in wonder at his daughter beside him, at that chilly mantle she assumed at all times. She wore it so well, like some kind of birthright, cold in any weather. It was a strange thing to admire in your own child, to watch her perfect what you could not, that regal indifference.

Henrietta was guiding him past the stiles that demarcated the backstretch when he caught sight of a man he had been introduced to once. Akers, or Akins, his blasted mind could not remember which, but this man, this charlatan with what looked like a prostitute at his side, made his money from electronics stores and chicken restaurants, *this* man had a Derby winner in his stable. *This* man's stallion covered every game mare in North America for six months and then was flown south in late summer to cover the other half of the known world. It was ludicrous, preposterous, proof that life favored idiot strivers. It sickened him what stupid men could achieve in this life.

"Mr. Forge, hold up a minute."

They were in the parking lot now, trying to find both their Mercedes in a lot of silver Mercedes. He was slow to turn, though he recognized the voice immediately. Mack Snyder. He'd seen him a hundred times on television, and occasionally in person from a distance. On any other day, he would have drawn himself up to his fullest, most self-assured height. Today, he looked like a man peering out from beneath a cowl.

The man came on, smiling slightly in a pinched way, but the smile didn't suit, like too-tight Sunday clothes on a roughneck. His shirt was damped through the armpits with sweat, and a bolo tie swung with an orange Zuni cabochon. He was a stocky man with a perpetually sunburned neck and hard, unkind hands pinched by two signet rings. When he held out one hand, Henry noted they were hard and calloused, but his nails were evenly clipped and perfectly clean.

"Mack Snyder," the man said. Or the Hillbilly Horseman, as Bob Costas had dubbed him during his first Derby—and the sobriquet had stuck. If he'd shed some of the Letcher County syntax, his vowels were still broad enough to swim in. That roughcut voice rose and fell like the head of a rocking horse.

Henrietta touched her hand to Henry's upper arm, a protective gesture.

"Good to meet you," said Henry.

"You're just the man I want to talk to," Mack said, and for a moment he set his thin lips together, hard, as if he was hesitating, as if he was the kind of man who hesitated. "Listen," he said, "I would congratulate you, but I'd bet you aren't the type who takes kindly to congratulations on a second-place finish."

"Ha," said Henry tiredly. Mack held up his hand as if to forestall further response. "Let me just say this: your filly ran a good race against the boys, and that's in spite of a hard bump and a clusterfuck of epic proportions. Always interesting when a girl doesn't know her place."

Henry stood there listening, but he was beginning to focus with as much energy as absolute fatigue allowed. He waited.

Mack said: "She spends her energy, though. She's missing that smart gait her dam had, but you can see the resemblance once she settles in." He nodded once, hard, agreeing with himself.

Henry cocked his head to one side. "You remember Hellcat?"

"Damn right, I don't ever forget a horse. Not a bad choice for Secretariat. Unconventional, sure, but not bad."

"That's what I always said."

The man nodded again. "The race didn't go your way—it didn't go anybody's way—but I think you got a strong filly worth working with."

"Yes." A soft grin of resurrection spread on Henry's face; he breathed in, almost imperceptibly.

Now Mack took a single step forward toward him, his shoulder effectively angling Henrietta from their conversation, though she stood mere inches away. He lowered his voice slightly. His attempt at small talk was over, the air was charged.

"Mr. Forge," he said quietly, "do you know how big Secretariat's heart was?"

Henry nodded, but Mack continued. He spread his red hands for emphasis: "Twenty-two goddamn pounds."

"What?" Henrietta said. She had never heard such a thing. It was hard to believe.

"And whose side does a monster heart like that come down through?"

Henry nodded again slowly, the light of recognition kindling in his eyes.

"That's right," Mack said quietly, firmly. "Down the female line. I believe you're understanding me now, but let me be real straight. If there's one thing you need to know about me, it's I'm a straight shooter. I live a fast life and you don't want me for a best friend, but I *am* the man you want when you need plain speaking." Snyder turned suddenly and positioned himself squarely in front of Henry again. Henry could smell the sweat of the man, but was pinned by the intensity of those eyes and the hands that rounded before him as if the man were holding a crystal ball between them. He said, "What these folks—what all these folks—are doing wrong is a result of one thing: failure of nerve. They get their piece of Secretariat, and they go fishing around in other lines trying to improve what was already perfect in the first place. They're milking tits on a bull. What do you think Danzig is bringing to the table, or Nearco? Nothing, that's what. You can't better what's already perfect, you can only water it down. Are you following where I'm leading?"

"I believe so—"

The man was not done: "It's a failure of nerve. Let me cut to the chase—if the old boy were alive today, we'd breed her right back to him. Seeing as that's not possible, we do the next best thing. We wait for the half brother with the best distance, maybe even a colt with a little Hellbent in the line if we can get it, and then we breed the best to the best. But we don't hope for the best like the rest of these yokels—we just wait three years, 'cause we know we got our ace in the hole."

"Yes," said Henry slowly. "Yes, I understand you."

Mack fished a card out of his breast pocket. He handed it to Henry, his eyes slashing through Henrietta once before he said, "Call me or don't. It's your choice. But this is the most I'll ever bend your ear. I don't talk, I just get the job done. I cost more than that guy you're working with now, but I believe my record shows I can return dollars on your pennies."

"I will consider what you're saying," said Henry, though already the reserve of ambition was replenishing, almost as if the day had never happened. His hopes, like healthy horses, were scrambling to their feet.

"Well, I wouldn't expect less. But you ought to know there's a reason I'm approaching you, and it's not just because you got a very fine filly, which you do. Frankly, I think you've got balls." He didn't apologize for his language, but tilted his head in Henrietta's direction. "I'm just telling the truth."

They shook hands, and then the man was moving off as abruptly as he had come. Henrietta watched as he moved into the swarm of people, a contrary figure pushing against the bright, well-heeled crowd as it departed. Every single one of them instinctively stepped aside and made a path for him.

Henry was quiet, considering. "You know, maybe this is just what we need right now."

For a moment, Henrietta was tactful. "They say he's hard on horses."

"Trainers are butchers," he said. "You just have to find the best one. But what do you think of him in particular?"

She watched the punchy figure disappearing now into the crowd. She thought of Seconds Flat, the way she had been as a foal, gentle as a harp. She remembered her tender mouth before the cold rolled steel of the snaffle bit, and the sight of broken horses on the track. She said, barely stifling the anger in her voice, "I think he's a fucking hillbilly."

She drove east toward home, toward the fulsome springtime mountains, but even their ancient presence wouldn't be enough today, because—my God, now that she was alone, she could let loose the wail in her mind—everyone seemed out to break the world. It wasn't just horses that humanity was destroying, but everything they chanced to lay eyes upon—even the world's oldest mountains, which were just now appearing on the horizon. What comfort could be found in them today? Humans were reducing those hills to slag. They'd been hellbent on destruction almost from the time of their arrival, tunneling deep into the mountain walls or sloping in at the surface or downshafting like wellers in search of black water, because the old country had wanted chugging trains in all directions and delicate, filmy cages for tungsten filament. They called for the farmer and hunter and drew them to rickety, newborn towns with promises of canned food and a wife in white cotton; the promise of promise itself. So down trappers and diggers and spraggers, down drivers and mules that brayed in their underground stables, their cries echoing hoarsely in the bord-and-pillar chambers that the blasts and the timbermen built. Down vein after slit vein, down into night, down into blackness without recourse, down where they chipped and picked for decades before the next generation arrived with their rotating drums and toothed bits to chip the coal; then the shearing longwall machines, which collapsed the mine shaft as they moved. Those early miners emerged from the driftmouth, black as coal and poor as dirt. Desperation breeds dreams, and dreams trade for desperation in the company store, no tab. The only cash in town is a man's life.

Calm yourself, Henrietta, is what her father would say. You are expected at home.

But, after what she'd seen today, she didn't want to see any foals fresh in their fields, didn't want to watch them run their rounds, didn't want to press repeat. Right at this moment with the mountains before her, she couldn't quite figure how she and her father were any different from the kings of coal who sent miners underground, who underpaid and overworked them, who sentenced them to suffer from black damp, white damp, after damp, stink damp, fire damp, and necrotic lungs and basic want. Miners who died when the roofs failed over them, having long forgotten their native terror of the underground. The bosses got those men coming and going, because aboveground it's death by a thousand cuts as the slag finds streams, the mine tailings drain acid to aquifers, dams break and slurry spills in black apocalyptic floods, and the men drink it and the women cook with it and the children play in it. And the country just flies high over Kentucky as they travel coast to coast, tracing the same route Henrietta and her father took when they bought horses. Kentucky looks like nothing to the coastal eye, just anonymous mountains that subside and slump into a thousand depressions over countless coal-black bodies, the men and the animals alike, both infinitessimally small from the sky, the black bodies of men and animal bodies, the body called mine, or man's, mines, men—

You are expected at home, Henrietta.

She thought suddenly of sporting plants, how their tiny offshoot buds assume a character so different from their parent plant, emerging as a genetic

anomaly from a shared root family. They occur rarely in nature, because—
it seemed to her then—all the busy machines of evolution conspired for
similarity. Sameness is safe. Sameness is survival itself.

Suddenly, Henrietta cranked the wheel to the right and with a savage
kick to the gas singed blacker marks onto the black interstate. The whining
engine overpowered thought as she sped down 75, passing cars and trucks
and horse trailers and the vast farms with their overwrought houses, which
seemed to wriggle and wave luridly in their ostentation. She had half a
mind to drive down to the old town of Berea and hike in the foothills of the
springtime Appalachians—that was a beauty without thumbprints, where
the mountains were not blasted, there the spring grass would be punching
up like knife blades through the soil—but ten minutes later, after darting
erratically through the interstate traffic, she exited on a whim at Man O' War.
To her shock, she discovered that the old Hamburg Place stud farm, where
so many extraordinary horses—Nancy Hanks; Plaudit; Lady Sterling, dam
of Sir Barton—were buried, was being leveled and graded. She hadn't been
here in ages. How was this possible? The farm was an institution, a monument to the sport that had not built the town but had made it matter. A low
string of buildings, what appeared to be an outdoor shopping mall, was
being erected over that fertile bluegrass soil, now degrassed and drained.
She idled the car at the edge of the construction site, watching the enormous mechanical birds swooping for soil and spitting it out again—detritus
now—in red, cloddy heaps behind the rising structures. The birds flying
lazily, searching for prey, swinging low on the steel wing and snatching.
She thought soon all the land would sound like nothing, and no one would
know it had once made sounds, that small civilizations had thrived in the
grass. It would never register with life again. And what was coming? Concrete. Glassed fronts and sale signs and cash registers. And with it all,
people in a torrential surge, carnivorous men and women looking to smear
their skin with colors and creams, to bleach their hair, to shave their hides,
to cinch themselves breathless in order to think themselves beautiful. The
idea of it redoubled her horror at the day and its losses. But the indignation
was easily banked by resignation. What was the point in mourning what
couldn't be stopped? And it truly was unstoppable, the swollen stream of
humanity's consumption, strong enough to take the old horses' bones—
animals so perfect they had become things of myth—and displace them

forever, God knows where. No, wait, right there, hidden in trees, at the edge of a Walmart parking lot.

They should have just barbecued Secretariat, because no one ever really gave a fuck. Cry with joy when he crosses the line, then eat him. There were no more true believers.

She didn't know what to do. How best to forget a day like this? Henrietta reversed and peeled out of the lot, heading downtown toward the stunted high-rises of this provincial town, a city that first repelled Northern aggression and then strengthened itself on a genteel aggression, smiling on its own smallness and petty prettiness. She felt herself to be nearly in a mania. Out of nowhere, clattering hail fell and, jarred, she watched the tiny balls of ice pop and bounce on the ground and percuss on the steel hood and roof of the car. She lifted her foot off the gas, aware she had been speeding; she was no longer in Paris, where she could always say, "I'm Henrietta Forge," where a policeman might peer into her face, note the resemblance, maybe grin and tease her as though she were nothing but a troublesome child.

On the far side of downtown, she found a parking spot by the Ledger, one of the older horse pubs. She had changed out of her dress in Louisville, resumed her uniform of button-up smudged with the grime of horses, her worn boots caked with fulvous dirt, her clothes and her ponytail slightly damp from the weather. She stood in the front of the bar, surveying.

"Can I get you something to drink, miss?"

Yes, they could get her something to drink. Yes, she was thirsty. On the first Saturday in May, the Commonwealth got drunk early and stayed that way until Monday morning. With a beer, she walked the bar with cold purpose, inspecting the men who remained there. In a side room, she noted the old careworn men weighted on their pool sticks as if they were crutches, a small huddle of men in suits doing business, horse business she knew from their Irish brogues. She spun on her heel, returned to the main room. She spotted a blond man at the bar. Broad shoulders, nearly bald. He smiled at her sleepily and nodded once. He had seen her come in, and she had seen him see her.

She walked directly up to him, stood there a moment. "What are you doing?" she said.

"What—me?" He smiled, but the smile failed at his blue eyes as if he'd encountered a trick question. "I'm drinking?" He tried to sound cocksure, even mocking, so taken aback was he by her approach. She did not respond. In a moment, he had unstartled himself, and his smile gained its ground. He said, more seriously, lower, "What are you doing?"

She registered the wavering in his face, the play at confidence. It tested her patience. Why did men always make this play for boldness? They came off like little children pretending to be grown. Why bother lying to a woman, who could read an expression before it formed, and know its source and its source's source?

She said, "Let's go somewhere."

His eyes widened in honest surprise. "Really?" Then he held up his left hand, where a little gold band winked.

She just shrugged. It all seemed like bad acting.

And that was all it took, it was that easy. He started off his stool but headed in the opposite direction of the front door.

"I'm parked out back," he said. "I work in the kitchen."

She followed him through the single swinging door, through a grimy kitchen where a line cook peered out from under the warmers to watch in surprise as they passed, and then out the back doors, where they stood in a two-hundred-year-old alley where the bricks had worn down to nothing from wagon wheels and horse hooves and the heels of the forgotten who once traversed there. Rain was falling heavily now, painting red on the brick, weaving small rivulets around the crumbling geometry of the bricks.

The man held a hand to his brow and peered at her heatedly. "Where to?" he said.

"Your car," she said. The rain fell down her cheeks.

He skipped toward his car, but as he was reaching his keys to the driver's-side door, she peered down the dank alley once and back at the door to the bar's kitchen, and then she said, "No! In the back!" The rain killed any echoes.

So he climbed, almost bashfully, into the backseat, fumbling with a condom he pulled from his wallet, and she climbed in, wet, beside him and stripped her jeans off one leg and undid the zipper on his, and then in another moment she climbed on top of him. He was gasping under her. She braced her forearm against his sternum. He told her to take her top off. She didn't, and he couldn't get to her in the tight space crammed with milk

crates and old clothes. She said, "Don't come, don't come." Already the
fury was easing. He grabbed at her where he could. "Don't come," she said.
When the lightning flashed, she could see his face with startling clarity.
The rain drummed on the roof of the car. It reminded her of something she
couldn't name, but it was better that way. If you haven't named it, you
haven't killed it yet.

She became a familiar sight at the Ledger, McCarthy's, Second Wind, the
Hare & the Hound, Breakers. A skinny woman with her reddish hair
pulled back and a too-direct gaze. She came in for one drink and one man
and tried to make it a simple transaction. The men obliged, not because she
was pretty—she was handsome at best—but because they were willing to be
had and, for once, here was a woman willing to take them without fuss. What
more is there to say about those years? She could shoot and her aim was sure.
She was after pleasure. What is pleasure? It is not the opposite of pain.

At first, she sought out beautiful men, thinking that beauty would naturally make for more pleasure, but she found a thing of beauty was a joy for
not very long. These were the kinds of men who loved to take off their
clothes, who loved their own arms and abdomens sculpted by exercise.
They wanted her to watch them, and they composed their male faces
sternly for her admiration, but she didn't want to watch them, she wasn't
there to admire. The point of fucking was to crush the pearl, not polish
it. But they polished and polished, and then she understood—they thought
they were the pearl!

She learned to stay away from the men who talked too much, who asked
her all the polite and proper questions that men ask women, questions they
thought she wanted to answer, which she did not. They pretended interest
in her private mind, a thing too many women squandered on unworthy
men, seeming to think their inner lives no more valuable than a penny. She
wouldn't divulge it. These were the ones who drew her to them softly and
gazed at her in the warm, bland imitation of romance, the ones who tried to
nestle dutifully against her later, as if they actually preferred this farce of
intimacy to drinking alone in their apartments, free to look down at wet
city streets as pleasantly empty as themselves, as happily deserted.

She avoided the artistic types with their self-congratulation, their misapprehension of their own strangeness, their pride in their small arts, and their disdain for the world, which looked plainly like fear. These men, thinking themselves so unusual, were often the most predictable, the first to ask her why she had no husband and no children. They thought her older than she was, the lines of summers past already lining her face. At first bold and brash, they scuttled back into their shells after the last quiver of orgasm, afraid to be netted. Not so strange, not so different after all.

When she tired of the search, she would stay at home for a period of weeks. But by midcycle, she was dying, wasting on the inside, a slave to her body. She could not spend an easy evening reading, and shaken by her desire out of that cashmere life, she would head to the city. She had to find a man, and she decided she wanted a big man—a black man. She didn't care if there was pain; more pain meant less feeling, and that was fine with her; less feeling in the cunt, less feeling in the heart.

But in the end, she settled for any good body, willing but unremarkable men who wouldn't bother her later. Some shy with the erotic poverty of young men, some older and beaten down in spirit like cuffed dogs. Their age didn't matter when she was in search of something a man hid from you until the very last moment when, while straddling them, you could feel your own cruel power rising up in you stronger than any orgasm, the power to sentence a man to shame, the power the judge holds over the cocksure criminal—no, better yet: the power to judge the judge.

She had only one friend during those years, a man she met in a bar. She'd driven to McCarthy's one night when she was twenty-three and ordered a whiskey while standing at the register, taking quick stock of the men in the room. It was a Wednesday night, there were no women in the half-lit place, and voices were murmurous and low. What men were there were mostly playing pool, smoking and eyeing her through the dimming slat of drunkenness. A shot was missed, and a ball went clattering across the barroom floor. There was only one man at the wooden bar, hunched over his Budweiser, taking occasional sips. His black-and-gray hair was gathered back in a ponytail the width of a horse's tail, and it hung down to within inches of his waist, as thick at the bottom as it was at the band. He was dressed like anyone else in jeans and an old T-shirt, but he was taller and thicker, she could see that, despite his poor posture. When she sat down on the stool beside him, he turned and looked her plainly in the face, then turned away again without a word. He could have been thirty-five, he could have been fifty, his face wasn't telling.

The bartender said, "Penn, you need another?" and the man nodded.

When she didn't turn away and he felt her staring, he turned again and she noticed now the very tan skin, the heavy, dark brows, the broad nose. But once again, he turned away with no expression at all. When he peered a third time, with one eyebrow arched, she said, "Hi," smiling only slightly— as if she needed something from him, and the smile was for politeness' sake, which it was.

A long pause in which nothing transpired on that neutral face, then he said softly, "Hi."

She stared at him without blinking, her small smile not budging, but just as he turned back to his drink, no puzzlement or awareness or anything showing on his mute and impassive face, she said, "Why don't I come home with you." It was not a question.

He sighed, and without looking up from the twinkling amber of his beer bottle, he shook his head slowly and said, "Listen . . ." His voice trailed.

"What?" Her face revealed only careful curiosity, still polite.

"I . . ." He took a long breath and looked straight into her eyes now. "You want to come home with me . . . ," he said.

"Yes," she said, the smile slipping now, replaced by her true face, which was not friendly, just plain.

"Listen," he said, "the truth is, I don't think I . . . can handle a forward lady tonight."

"Oh," she said abruptly, and sat back on her stool, looking directly ahead of her at the wall, which was a mirror so she was looking at herself. She felt him turn likewise to the front. She was mildly affronted, but not enough to move. She'd never thought of herself as forward, only direct, the type of person who knew what she wanted—but then what exactly was the difference? Inside her mouth, she bit her tongue lightly. The man had a strange voice, like he had learned English as a second language. Low and flat and uninflected, like Native American voices she had heard. After a minute or so had passed, she said, without looking at him, "Are you Indian?"

A long pause. "Um, a Melungeon, I guess."

"What's that?"

"Poor man's Spaniard."

"Sounds greasy," she said, and he laughed. But she didn't turn to him again, and he didn't turn to her. She finished her whiskey, and when the bartender looked at her with his brows raised, she just made a defeated face.

But she was watching her neighbor from the corner of her eye, and each time he reached for the neck of his beer, she detected a foul cut along the inside of his hand, extending across the palm to the vale between his thumb and index finger.

"What did you do to your hand?" she asked into the silence.

"I was seeding bluegrass and got cut," he said slowly. She realized that he probably always spoke this slowly, as if feeling his way forward in the dark toward each word. It didn't seem an effect of the alcohol. He would have sounded simple, except that his voice was careful and thoughtful.

"You cut yourself on the machine?" she asked, and now she turned to him fully, because she was honestly curious. She couldn't picture how he'd done it.

"No," he said, and paused, so for a moment she didn't think he was going to answer at all. Then he looked at her, and his eyes were very dark brown, and he said, "I've got a hand seeder."

"It must be very old," she said, frowning.

"Yes."

"Why on earth would you use a hand seeder?" she asked.

"The machine doesn't work so good. You get too much plant in with your seed." He swiveled slightly on the stool and made an upward sweeping motion with his injured hand like he was scooping something up. "With the seeder, you just get the pure seed."

"And there's a market for this . . . ?" she said.

"Pity for it anyway."

Now it was her turn to laugh. Then she said softly, as if to herself, "Seems like we ought to have old tools like that around."

"Farm girl?" he said.

"Yeah."

"But rich."

She blinked in surprise. "I guess so," she said. "So what?"

"So nothing." He turned back to the bar and drained his drink, knocking the bottle back down to the wood. He looked at her and with that not unkind, expressionless face, he sighed and said, "You can come to my place if you want."

"Okay," she said. She hadn't brought her pride along with her.

"But I live all the way down in Jackson County."

"I don't care," she said with a shrug, and there was such an inadvertent tone of despondency in her voice that she didn't hear but he couldn't miss, that he instinctively offered her his hand to help her off the stool.

In the morning she awoke on an old mattress on the floor with the warm sun striking her full across the face. In an instant, her heart was roused to panic. Somehow she had fallen asleep and slept through the night, a mishap she'd never made before. She always, always went home to her father. An extraordinarily heavy arm was now flung across her midsection. She slid sideways along the sheets to free herself, heart pounding. She snatched up her clothes and escaped to the living room with a thought to dressing in private away from this stranger still sleeping. Through the sun-silty windows dressed in faded patchwork, she saw pastures of cows and what looked like a lone goose wandering open-beaked through the yard under an enormous pass of sky, strenuously blue. The house around her was a musty old inherited thing, and while it was not clean, it was tidy. Everything looked to have been found in a garage sale or secondhand shop, except for the bookshelves, which she saw, upon closer inspection, were planed by hand. They had not been further sanded down, so the hard hairs of wood sprang up spikily from the natural grain. On these shelves, poetry books were lined and stacked. The uppermost spines grazed the ceiling. She forgot herself and was reaching to pull a volume from the shelf when a voice called, "Lady, what are you doing in there?"

She turned at the sound, irritated that the man had woken. In an instant, she remembered the expression on his face when they'd had sex—not surprise exactly, but a pleasant mystification, as if he couldn't quite figure how he'd ended up in such a pleasant spot. He had been a gentle man; she was not accustomed to that.

She walked back to the bedroom door, stepping into her jeans on the way and tugging her shirt hurriedly down across her chest.

"You're dressed," he said.

"I have to go home. I slept late."

He sat up very quickly but he didn't say anything, just looked at her.

"What?" she said.

"Are you married?"

"No!" she said. "But I have to go."

"Why are you going? I could make you some breakfast."

She didn't answer, she just turned to walk through the door again, pausing momentarily to tuck her shirt into her jeans. There were photos and magazine clippings taped to the gray plastered wall by the light switch. Photos of a black-haired couple from the 1950s. A series of yellowed shots of a coal train passing by the photographer, the images shaky and ghostly blurred. A few photographs looked to have been taken in a desert setting. The young man in the photograph had short black hair and a military uniform. There were no lines on his face, but it was unmistakably the same man she'd just spent the night with—twenty years and twenty pounds ago. The same distinctly broad nose that reminded her somehow of her neighbor Ginnie Miller. Vaguely leonine.

"What made you go in the army?" she asked suddenly.

After a pause, during which it sounded as if he might not reply at all, he said, "I was a marine."

"Why'd you enlist?"

"I was dumb," he said flatly.

"I'm serious."

"I am too." She glanced at him. He sighed and laid a meaty forearm over his forehead, so he couldn't see anything but his own self-made darkness. "I don't know," he said, "it's just what you did around here. I think I had a hero complex when I was a kid."

She'd forgotten her need to leave. She stood there in wrinkled clothes with her arms hanging at her sides, so that she looked not so different—he would have seen if he'd looked—from a freshly woken child.

"Like . . . ," he said, and sighed again but with some irritation this time audible in the breath. "You grow up reading comic books and things, and you think you know what a hero is . . . that you have to save everybody . . . but then you grow up and you find yourself killing people just to follow orders. It's like growing up means you cross some invisible line where all the rules get totally reversed. I guess that sounds sort of weird to say out loud . . . but it seemed original to me when I thought it."

Henrietta was about to interject when he went on, "The worst thing, though, is killing's not actually as hard as you think it's going to be . . ." He made a quick trigger motion without taking his forearm from his eyes. "You think you're going to be all messed up about it, but . . . I don't know. They diagnosed me with PTSD. But sometimes, I almost feel like . . ."

"What?"

"I don't know . . . I always get the feeling they want you to be more tore up than you really are, so people can feel okay around you. Nobody wants to know that it wasn't actually that hard."

She came to, realized the time. She said, "I do have to go."

"Was it something I said," he sighed, but she was already out the door.

Henrietta felt only dread at the thought of what Henry would say, but when she stepped from the porch, she'd seen the vast unfurling of Madison County to the west where the mountains dropped breathlessly away. Against her will, she walked past a stagnant-looking cattle pond, where cane sprouted up and cattails wagged in the smart morning wind as it raced toward the cliff like water at the edge of a waterfall. Her hair flew into her face. She passed an old tobacco barn, but there were no tobacco fields up here that she could see. A few spare, dark cattle. A deep, karsty sink that looked like a drained pond with boulders in its belly. The farm was situated at the top of such a precipitous drop that the earth seemed to penetrate the sky here. The clouds were as close as viewing gauze, and there was a frighteningly swift wind. She passed away from man-made markers, she passed trees that in their cliff clutching had over time grown wary and bent, as if the spiraling wind spoke through them of how precarious it is to live, cliff or no, how one day all the winds might by fate or chance converge in one place, maybe even this place, and send them all tumbling roots over finger-tips, because the world was full of faceless, random happenings; or the love affair of earth and sky would end and the rain, their congress, would also end, so all the green family of life would starve and shrivel, their roots con-tracting and withering so that all the bodies would fall, senseless, cliff or no. So the trees bowed to the cliff's lip, which also spoke. Henrietta could hear that. She approached the lip, felt the sickening lurch of open space. She edged gingerly onto a rock outcropping like a dais in a church with the annular remains of old trees petrified onto its ancient face. At this edge she peered over, her hair streaming ahead of her as if some part of her wanted to jump. Everything fell away, and the sky rode down a thousand feet like the falcon dropping. No ease here, toeing the crystalline seam of firmity and nothing. And the sense came, intuited perhaps for the first time, that the earth itself was predatory, inbuilt with dangers, and it suddenly made sense why people wanted to pave it and smother it and sell it to render it the simple past. Maybe they saw the beauty, maybe they could look out here to the west and admire the old knobs, the soft, bosomy remnants of the mountains, so lush in the soothing sunshine, but their genetic memory was far-reaching and wise and avenging. They knew the beauty of the earth rendered a fugue state, and while they gazed in blissful wonder, forgetting their own names and the names of their children, they froze in the Arctic chill and died of pustulent boils and rotting diseases, and sometimes they drowned or burned like bugs under glass or died of exposure, and some fell. So tamp the earth, burn the earth, pave the earth with abandon. Of course they did. Of course they would. It was their only revenge upon this wild, heartless theater.

She practically leaped away from the edge, stumbling back into a headwind toward the farmhouse, where the man was waiting for her in only a pair of orange bulldog boxers, each of his limbs trying to wrap around another limb for warmth. His eyes were half-lidded against the risen sun, his hair long down his back. He held a cup of coffee in his hand.

He said, "My grandmother had a horse once that ran itself off that cliff . . . She said it was in love with a cow. They sent the cow off for butchering, and the horse was so . . . upset, I guess, it ran itself off the cliff. Or at least that's what my grandmother said."

"Where am I?" she said.

"Jackson County."

She made an irritated face.

"Big Hill," he said. "Go out to the right and drive down Big Hill, and you'll be in Madison County, and you just follow 421 up to Richmond and catch the bypass to 75."

She gasped and turned once again toward the cow pond and the cliff's edge that she had just left. "We're in Big Hill? Where Daniel Boone . . . ?"

"Yeah," he said. "This was it. Sight of the promised land . . . last hurrah of the mountains."

"My forefather walked this," she said urgently, unable to turn her eyes from the view of the knobs and expansion of the Bluegrass out of the Wilderness Road. This view was the original splendor, the boundless promise, that thing left alone. Only the sky was more singular.

"Samuel Forge walked this," she said. "My great-great-great-great-great-great-grandfather."

"Yeah, yeah," Penn said, looking at her curiously. "I recognize that name."

In Lavinia's last days, when the cancer in her breast had reduced her muscles to rope and her mind to ash, she was too weak to raise her hands. She could say nothing, only lie there, looking hugely at the ceiling with bone-dry eyes. Henry sat by her side day after day with her foundling hands in his, and it seemed to him that the whittled contours of her once elastic face were begging for something—Henry thought forgiveness, but in actuality relief. But soon, vacancy took up occupancy in those forever features. Her feet grew icy at the toes, the instep, the heel. Her cheeks and lips were packed with lead. Her son touched her brow, unable to look away from the horrifying inevitable. Again and again, he signed to her, but little darknesses intruded like the flickering in a silent film, until finally her lids fell and would not raise up again when she wished to see her son one last time. There was total dark. She died with her lips parted and her brow creased as if she had been expecting something more.

And of all the minutiae of his younger life, that is what he remembered most. His mother had died looking not at him, her son, her accomplishment, but into the well of herself at something. And that something was emptiness. He had felt its sucking draw. And felt it now.

Where in the hell was his daughter? He was flying out to Saratoga with Mack in two hours and he needed her to conduct interviews in his stead. But she hadn't come home, and here he was panicking like an orphaned child.

And then she was there, his dear, duplicitous mother, his first love—no, Henrietta, his troublesome, guileful girl, padding in on the balls of her feet as if she wouldn't be detected at nine thirty in the morning, as if she hadn't been missed, as if she wasn't one-half of his own damn self.

The cool air of morning accompanied her, and it was a good thing. His insides were like kindling threatening to ignite. Any number of battles were lost by the man who lost his cool.

His voice was level when he said "Henrietta." She whirled with a gasp, took in the sight of her father in the disheveled clothes of yesterday, his face marred by a complicated fatigue. His graying hair fell forward into awful eyes, where tiny bright roads of blood traveled the curves of his sclera.

"Where were you?"

"I was alone," she said abruptly.

A warning: "Henrietta, you can't just hell around . . ."

"A-lone!" she snapped as two words, and then raised a hand to her own lips as if startled by their rebellion. After coming atop last night's man, after teetering at the edge of the allowable world and staring down its heights, something had changed. The old poets knew all along: the wilderness has an awful tongue, which teaches doubt.

Henry just smiled down at her, trying to appear easy and loose, though his shaking hands belied his calm. He said, "My little Ruffian, all alone in the big, bad world." He smiled tightly. "Are you too old for one last lesson?"

God! Was there really no escape? She looked up toward the ceiling as if perceiving many people through those storied floors, the Forge quorum pacing, observing, advising, alive. They were as real as scars on old wood. With a sigh, she said, "Sure, Daddy." But her mind asked, Am I not a grown woman?

Lesson

You aren't like them, my little Ruffian. You'd like to think you can find real companions out there, but you can't. You'd like to think you can discover a mate, but you can't do that either. You imagine you'll be understood by people less intelligent than you are, because you don't actually believe they're less intelligent, but they are and, believe me, they don't understand you; they're incapable. Gold attracts gold. A natural aristocracy exists.

You should be proud of your position. Do you think history was actually made by ordinary men? History is made by the highly particularized, the ones who are intractable, stubborn, relentless. Men who are willing to become something other than their fathers. Yes, I know you're a woman, but you're a man in mind. They are the ones willing to risk everything, even their own sanity, maybe necessarily their own sanity, to achieve greatness, and greatness is absolutely and always contingent upon individuality. Are you listening?

I don't know where you go, with whom you spend your time, and it doesn't matter. What matters is that you understand that this notion of community life—this ridiculous, sentimentalized idea of a commonwealth, whatever you want to call it—is bankrupt. The ugly truth is that, despite the philosophical spoutings of a few founding fathers, men aren't created equal, not even close. So a community of equals isn't possible. A good sentence meant more to Jefferson than the truth. That's the definition of an aesthete!

Ask yourself this: How many kinds of genius are there in the world? I'll tell you: two. The first assimilates, because it lacks the willpower to stand on its own in isolation. It understands that the world will spare exceptional people, but only if they feign normalcy, live unremarkable lives, and don't threaten anyone with their difference. Of course, most of the time the masses have no idea they're even being condescended to; they're so ignorant, they don't even recognize genius when it's in their midst. The second kind of genius understands all of this, but is so extreme in its unique intelligence that it couldn't assimilate even if it wanted to. It's a born outlier. An individual is not necessarily a genius, but every genius is an individual.

If you remember nothing else I ever tell you, remember this: you must be completely yourself in order to achieve greatness, but you may have to lose yourself entirely in the process. That's the paradox I'm willing to endure not just for my ideals, but for you.

For Henry so loved the horse that he gave his only begotten daughter, so that whosoever believeth in perfection shall have everlasting life, which is fame among men.

Fine. Go ahead and laugh. But do you understand me when I say that the community will offer you comfort and friendship, but in turn you have to give the community your very life?

Do you understand me?

Force of habit prised Henrietta's teeth apart: "I do."

It's strange. One day you're a child of six with the taste of grass in your mouth, and the next you appear an adult with your father's face on your face but a child's heart in your chest, however stupefied, however late to waking. You can't decide whether to climb back onto his lap or crack the black letters of your name. No one in the world speaks to you but he, father and king. Because there never was a world beyond the white plank fencing, not really, just a quick, brutish struggle for existence. So you run in circles on your tiny allowance of earth, a species artificially selected and fenced, and open your horse mouth to say, This is the kingdom come and it is his, I am his, I become his, *Regnum meum est*, I become It.

The three men arrived one after the other in the sunny late morning. All three smelled of tobacco, bore cheerful, local faces, and were reasonably capable with a horse, good workers with solid records from decent farms. But by noon, with the interviews complete, Henrietta had to employ some effort to distinguish among them. Which had been at Three Chimneys with Silver Charm? Which had been at Clairborne for two years? She was exhausted, her thinking a moil, and she was flipping back through the résumés at the kitchen table when footsteps approached on the cupped planks of the el porch. They stopped and a low voice, an unmistakably black voice, said, "I'm here for a interview."

With a swiftness that looked distinctly like alarm, she turned to face the man who was just a dark outline, featureless against the day as startlingly bright as shattered crystal behind him.

Blinking rapidly against the light, she said, "Come in."

When the man stepped slowly into the kitchen, she saw first the middle brown of his skin, and the surprise of it registered, stumbling on the heels of that low voice. Then she could look at nothing but his face, which surprised her with its burden of deep seriousness. Or perhaps something different—anger? Stopping as he did directly beneath the hanging light, his eyes were shadowed under the ledge of his heavy brow.

"You are?" she said, embarrassed by the hesitation in her voice. She cleared her throat.

"Allmon Shaughnessy."

With an abrupt motion, she fanned the résumés with her fingertips, as if for some purpose he would be unable to detect. With a name like Shaughnessy, she'd been expecting an Irishman. As she stared down in consternation, she caught him sneaking a glance around the room as if he couldn't resist its luxury, its stamp of wealth. But he did resist. He appeared to catch himself, and with the tiniest start of his head looked at her instead. When she reached out to shake, his hand was slick with sweat. That also surprised her.

"I'm Henrietta Forge," she said. "Thanks for coming out."

His heavy brows drew together, and he looked almost comically from side to side, as if for someone else.

"My father's out of the state on business today," she said, and as she looked at his skull-cropped hair, his shirt not buttoned to the top, that dark face, she couldn't help but think, And that is a good thing for you, my friend.

"Make yourself comfortable," she said, gesturing toward a kitchen chair. As he sat, she took quick, momentary stock of his body. He was perhaps her height or taller, boxy through the shoulder, the rest of his form hard to detect under the voluminous cut of his clothing. He was neither thin nor thick, and she would have found him an unremarkable thing and not noticeable in a crowd, except for the severe and unfriendly cut of his cheekbones jutting from the grieved hollows of his cheeks, sharp enough to cut glass. They sapped the possibility of softness from the rest of his face.

"Which position are you applying for?" she asked.

He placed his oversized hands on his knees and breathed deep once and said, "Night watchman, or stallion barn. Either one, both. I never worked with yearlings. I'm good with tough animals, the mean ones. I'm good with stallions."

"Either, both?" She had to laugh. "If we were to offer you both positions, you'd be working around the clock. We're not trying to kill anyone."

Now it was his turn to clear his throat and shift in his chair. As he did, her first sense of the body proper—his shape, his fitness—emerged from behind the shield of clothing. She could detect it without her eyes ever really leaving his face, and, as if he sensed this, his own eyes found the soft middle distance between their knees.

"Well," Henrietta said, "we don't need any stallion grooms at present. Though if we hired you and my father liked you"—her mind laughed at this, and it sparked something in her, so a tiny light was lit—"you certainly could be moved to stallions when a position opens. We have a normal turnover."

He nodded once, curt, without looking up. He was three feet away from her in the chair, but the distance seemed great. The quiet grew heavier and more distinct.

Though the information was right before her, she said, "And how long have you been working with horses?"

"Three years."

"That's not terribly long. What do you have to recommend you beyond your limited experience?"

"I'm good," he said simply.

The briefest smile from her. But he remained serious, intent, unaltered, muted. Still refusing her direct access to his eyes.

"That's very confident of you," she said.

He shrugged.

"Well," she said. "It says here that you were with Blackburn the entire three years."

He shifted again in his seat. She saw one foot in a black gym shoe press down on the toe of its brother.

"Blackburn . . . ," she said. "I don't believe I'm familiar with that operation."

"It's a vocational program," he said.

"Vocational program . . ."

"Yeah." His voice was husky. "Yes."

"Where? In Kentucky?"

"Lexington," he said. "Blackburn Penitentiary." He looked up now from where he had been staring with a gaze so direct and penetrating, she had to resist the urge to lean back.

"Oh," she said quickly. "So why were you there?"

"I am not obligated to divulge that information," he said, his voice so formal suddenly, it was clearly something he had memorized. When Henrietta's eyebrows rose in disdain, disdain he sensed before her face even changed, because that change in register is felt more than seen, he suddenly blurted, "Give me a chance. I'm good with horses. Really good." He brought a large hand down over his knee with a hard, deliberate motion, and she saw something both plaintive and coiled in him, something that she would not ever be able to precisely name but that her body misnamed: erotic.

"Where are you from?" she said.

"Cincinnati."

"I'm sorry," she said as a joke, but when he did not smile in response, she said: "Interesting topography up there. A lot of Ordovician outcrops . . . Well, anyway, welcome to the Commonwealth."

But even as she spoke, she thought, Has there ever been a black man in this kitchen before? In their house? Some memory was rattling around in her mind, but it wouldn't stand still. She thought of her tall, copper-headed father with his linen shirts, his bourbon, his horses. She thought, What paradox are you willing to live for greatness? She looked at this man, at the breadth of his shoulders, the size of his hands, the face annealed and hardened. She fought the urge to smile but couldn't check herself. While the cat's away . . .

She sat up straight suddenly and said, "All of your references are from Blackburn?"

"Yes," he said.

"If I call them, what will they say about you?"

He didn't have to consider. He said, quietly and quickly, "He won't ever give up."

"How do you mean?" she said.

Looking up now and speaking louder: "He's got drive. He knows how to work hard for what he wants, and he won't stop. He won't ever stop till he gets what he wants."

"And what exactly is it you want? A job on a horse farm?"

He paused for a moment, then made an obscure gesture with his hands held palms up, as if to hold something broad and round. Like an orange or something bigger, a globe.

"All of this."

"And these people will vouch that you're a whiz with horses?"

"I'm the best." He seemed to make some effort to restrain his hands as he said it.

Henrietta looked at him quizzically. "And how do you know that?"

For the first time, there was a hint of a sly, playful grin on his grave face. " 'Cause I've seen the rest. And they got nothing on me." She couldn't help but smile. And then she surprised herself: she reached out suddenly, impulsively, to take his hand in hers and without knowing what she intended, her body carried her into the contract and instead of saying, "You're hired," she simply said, "Yes."

INTERLUDE II

L *a belle rivière*: the Great, the Sparkling, the White; coursing along the path of the ancient Teays, the child of Pleistocene glaciers and a thousand forgotten creeks run dry, formed in perpetuity by the confluence of two prattling streams, ancient predecessors of the Kentucky and Licking—maternal and paternal themes in the long tale of how the river became dream, conduit, divide, pawn, baptismal font, gate, graveyard, and snake slithering under a shelf of limestone and shale, where just now a boy is held aloft by his beautiful father, who points and says, "Look!" and the boy looks, and what he will remember later is not just the river like a snake but also the city crowding it, and what a city! A queen rising on seven hills over her Tiber, ringed hills forming the circlet of a crown. A jagged cityscape of limestone and brick and glass with a bright nightless burn. The buildings never shut their brilliant eyes to the river where not so long ago, a teeming white mass came floating down to topple trees between the Great and Little Miamis and garrison pike-forts and sling tart, poison arrows at the wegiwas, those brown beehives up in flames. What freedom to rename the named! Losantiville, or Rome, or Cincinnatus after that noble man who would not stay in Rome, but returned home to his plow on the grange. In his stead, they crowned themselves and an American queen was born, one free of Continental dreams, the first to climb off the king's cock. Visionaries and confidence men alike launched down *la belle rivière* in droves. Lawyers and stevedores and sawyers and preachers and masons and Methodists, Lutherans, Baptists, and all the rest; the pious came with the venal, the wealthy with aspiring merchants, and the poor came by the thousands as well, passing women lap to lap on flatboats crammed with china, bedsteads, chests, and hogs to the gunnels that dipped and threatened to tip as they rounded broad bends in the river, curving down through the Territory to the Miami Purchase with its terraced bottoms and towering heights. More green than will ever be seen again, and the chance—now forgotten—to peer straight down through the pellucid Ohio, so sunshot and numinous and strange, it was like peering into bright time itself, right into the eyes of an engorged staring catfish not of this age but of millennia before, darting momentarily through a dream no Boston or Philadelphia could offer. Sooty, city-ravaged fingers dip into the cool river water, then the fish darts off and is disappeared forever, and the Kaintuck at the pole cries "Coming! Coming nigh!" and there she is, the city—fat, pale, concupiscent, a white intrusion into the billowing green. The newcomers drive all their pigs into her. The swine befoul her and roam wild into the seven hills and beyond, where they breed: doubling, trebling, making a second city of swine. On the low banks of the river, blocks south of the new brick residences, the citizens build their first abattoir and in the years to come rangy drovers will drive tributaries of pigs down off the shale hills and out of surrounding valleys, make fat rivers of flesh in the streets so wealthy women will refuse to leave their homes for all the shit. The drovers come hollering and the pigs, thousands upon many thousands of them, squeal in pink and brown and black waves until they reach the muddy river embankment, where they surge around carts, wagons, barrels, and horses only to be beaten and funneled stiff-legged onto a wooden ramp that runs up the full four stories of the meat house. Whacked steadily from behind by the drovers' staves, each wave of squealing hogs pushes the hogs ahead of them to the slaughter, scrambling and pressing up the stinking ramp made slippery with green shit. Now the first hogs smell base blood over excrement, but are forced ahead into the shadows of that first and last chamber. A bloody-aproned man moves in menace at their far reaches; then one animal is gripped at the pastern above the cloven hoof and dragged, screaming, its left leg clasped in metal, now hauled up by a pulley with a shattering cry, its own weight ripping ball joint from socket so it hangs distorted at the thick hip, screeching its final confession, eyes bulging wide as its neck is sliced and blood jets from its jaw and runs into its eyes. Unable to pass through the slit trachea, the air whistles uselessly. The pig jerks madly and is soon drained pale, eyes bald of life. Now the next one and on and on. All hanging in a line, swaying side to side along the pulley as their bodies are opened, showing waved lines of rib and vertebrae like the keys of a warped piano, the heads sawn off. Now to the disassembly: a drop onto the table, then quick mechanical thudding, the fall of cleavers, the flinging of component parts—hock, shoulder, loin. In sixty seconds, the hog is gone and meat is made, the dumb passage of life.

Up city, up boomers, up commerce, uphill the city is built. All the hands of Bucktown come to build it: the escaped, the manumitted, the somewhat free who live in the Bottoms between Sixth and Seventh, backed up against the putrefaction of Deer Creek. After the barrels of pork are shipped to South America and the Continent, the abattoirs haul the remnant, decaying offal up the hills above the creek and make a foul graveyard of the fresh, verdant hillsides; blood and bone and bits of mottled porcine matter tumble down the hills with each rain and make a hellish clog of the creek. Bucktown smells like an open coffin.

The workers emerge from the neighborhood every day; the women walk north away from the tale-telling river to clean and cook at the stately homes on Sycamore and Broadway, and the men gather near the market to be selected for work. The Bavarian contractors survey the stock: here are talented roustabouts and stewards and draymen, but all previous lives count for nothing toward the task at hand. Bucktown will be the builder of the first truly American city. He builds the storefronts on Main, the townhouses on Race and Spring, where, when he stands on the upper scaffoldings and stretches upright with his hands to the aching small of his back, he can see the dark, whispering river in the distance. He labors. He labors and the city grows. But whenever his own numbers swell, he's chased back into Bucktown, his clapboard home burned, some of his number left swinging from lampposts. And when the smoke clears on his dream of the North, he returns to the work site, built red Music Hall side by side with the Germans, who will celebrate their symphonies and sopranos within its soaring halls after hours when he is back in Bucktown bedded down with his wife. Through wars and decades, he labors: Richardsonian stone and Queen Anne, Flemish bond brickwork and brownstones until the city is built up the sides of her hills, the new century's clapboard houses rough jewels in the Queen's crown. Any man working on the bluffs possesses a commanding view of the wide river, and beyond it, the fretful, historied amplitude of Kentucky, that netherworld. But soon enough skyscrapers will interrupt that view and they grow so thick, like a forest of glass, that no one can see the river anymore unless they stand on the fossilled outcroppings that jut like limestone and shale parapets from the very tops of the hills where, now, the little boy is visible under the momentary aegis of one Mike Shaughnessy, truck driver, halfhearted lothario, collector of children, poor Irish agnate, known in high school as that fucking Irish fuck. This man possessed of a rare and undeserving beauty, the one man his mother had the misfortune of loving—end and beginning and middle of story. And now the boy, as dark as his father is light, gazes down at the city and its brown river that seems far too wide and far too deep to be swum but, oh children, it was swum.

NOTHING BUT A BURNING LIGHT

I'm going to ask the question. Please answer if you can.
Is there anybody's children can tell me what is the soul of a man?
—BLIND WILLIE JOHNSON

In this act, Allmon comes up on the streets of Northside, down in the Mill Valley with its meager, misfit creek, squeezed between the university hill to the southeast and College Hill to the north, which has no college despite its name, just modest white houses portending the suburbs to come, white fingers pointing up from the city's palm, pointing the way out. But Allmon never goes further north than Northside, because his mother, Marie, never does. Marie the sweet, Marie the naïve; Marie, the first in the family to escape Over-the-Rhine with a high school diploma and an associate's degree and a dream of being a teacher—she wanted to teach children just like her own son—before she got sick. But now she's still tall and straight, small-footed, large-breasted, she wears her hair in its natural twist behind a patterned scarf. Lipstick the color of a plum with Vaseline smeared over it and a child at her side, a beloved son born on her own birthday.

Just east of Northside, the Procter & Gamble factory runs day and night churning kernolate, chloride, silicate, sulfate, and, once upon a time, pork fat. The gray fumes rise and draw down the sky to a low lid the color of aluminum, so that even on the clearest day the Mill Creek runs gray beneath it. Cars tunnel through the smog-drift in the late afternoon; in pairs they descend over the viaduct and pass through the graceless valley on their way to the suburbs, leaving only fumes which rise and, look, the sun is setting now, rosy fingertips sliding down dirty glass. It fractures the filth in the air and makes a hundred thousand rainbows of it. Sherbet, roses, and cantaloupe orange, wedding pink, sheer white. The first thing Allmon will think of his small purchase of sky: I want to eat it. The streets, from Knowlton's Corner north to the rise of College Hill, are turned rich metallic from a sunset that announces only the midmark of second shift in the factory with its gray leaden windows and turrets streaming banners of smoke. Inside, little white bricks of soap drop from the cooling mold to be wrapped in white wax paper, then gathered by the half dozen and rolled down the clattering line to a box, then sealed in the heart of Northside.

In the valley, asthma is rampant, and Allmon will suffer from it when he's young, his body twisted by crowing fits as he takes his evening strolls with Marie down Hamilton Avenue, both mirrored against the windows of the brownstones and storefronts, their faces rosy with reflected pollution, copper-sulfite highlights in their hair. Marie sings under her breath as they walk. No one has ever said she is beautiful, but she's young and that is a kind of beauty—still unlined, still so upright. Some people driving by will think fondly of their own mothers. Some will think, black girls have kids way too young. But name one who thinks, oh God, in a heartbeat this moment will pass and the young women will be cut flowers, as Marie and her son walk south to where Chase intersects Hamilton Avenue, the site of their first apartment, the first place Allmon will call home.

But again, the valley: they lived in the little valley, four miles from the river, and whenever the waters rose, as they did in 1884 and again in 1937, the gray river coursed along the low arteries of the city and swamped the heart of Northside. The wealthy lived on Cincinnati's seven hills, and when the flooding came they gazed down from their heights, troubled.

On Chase, Marie and Allmon lived in a hundred-year-old building with thirteen other families in two-room apartments. In that first provisional place, summer came like an Egyptian plague, and Marie drew the blinds against the broiling heat. She took off her dress and paced the apartment in her underpants and nothing else and when she breast-fed her boy, she simply sat cross-legged on the floor like a worn, hapless Buddha, the child on her thigh. The plants drooped in the darkened air, the sun-rimmed blinds moved not one inch. She soothed his heat rash with creams and kissed his sweating head. Sometimes she cried over his pertussive crying and crushed him to her despite the heat. And when he napped, she sang a hush song, sang Hush a bye don't you cry go to sleepy little baby when you wake you shall have all the pretty little horses blacks and bays dapples and grays coach and six white horses, hush.

Sometimes, there was a man in the house. He was a white man; he came and went. When it rained, the streets smelled faintly of the distant river.

They lived in that apartment until 1984 and just as Allmon was shaping memories out of the clay of his life, they moved. They moved because the white man came around less and less, and when he did come, there were fights. He was not tall, but he was beautiful despite a painful thinness, with a red-brown mustache like a fish draped over his lip. He had long, dark hair, a brief nose, County Kerry eyes, and cigarettes in his back pockets that made white bands of the denim there. He and his son napped together. The man was like a dry bath; to lie against him was to feel empty and sure, clean, though he smelled of cigarettes. Allmon's mother placed green glass ashtrays all over the apartment so that when he came, he had only to reach over Allmon's head to find the ashtray and tap the butt to the glass. Allmon said, "Where you been?" He said, "North and South Carolina, Georgia, Florida. I just spent two days on Lady's Island. You know what they got there?" He didn't. "Ladies!" He laughed, and his son laughed. "And I went to St. Augustine. You know what they got there? All the things you don't know shit about."

His arrivals always came unannounced, then his checks grew irregular, then the visits stopped, and boxes gathered in the center of the front room. The pots missing handles were gathered, along with the oxalis planters, Allmon's many small shoes, and then his mother is hunched on the sofa, gathering her hair in her hands, her fingers clawing deep into her hairline.

"Momma, what's wrong?"

"Nothing."

"Momma—"

The look in her eyes stops his mouth. "I can't do it. I can't lose nobody else . . . I can't do this by myself."

So they left their apartment on Chase and moved down seven streets toward the turbid, southern end of the neighborhood, the cheaper end, where the viaduct crossed the sewage-strewn Mill Creek to Knowlton's Corner, an intersection of five streets, where the commerce had once been so heavy a hundred years before that on any Sunday afternoon the crowds spilled off the sidewalks, shoppers forced into the streets as they milled past the butcher's and stationer's, grocer's, the coffin maker's, the pharmacy, souls all shoulder to shoulder. But when the city grew, the Saturday crowds drifted north, up the hills to the suburbs, and the southern end of the neighborhood went to poor working white, then to a checkered mix, now they just called it black, and Knowlton's Corner took on the look of a place that once had been. The intersection was as careworn and antique as a wagon wheel, its spires strewn with broken glass and cigarette butts and glimmering oil, its hub home to a decaying costume shop, a gas station, a White Castle, and a corner store. It was here that Marie rented another two-room apartment, a tiny place, but loud with the sounds Allmon would associate with his early scenes: the freakish wail of sirens, the gruff fall of male voices, the Metro buses gusting by, dogs on the loose. In July, he would look down from their bay window and stare at the passing Independence Day parade. In the winter, the snow went gray as tobacco ash the moment it touched the street. And it was in this apartment that when Allmon would say, "I miss Daddy," his mother would still say, "Me too, baby."

Down behind their building, down the shaft of the back stairwell was the cement garden, the hollow heart of the turn-of-the-century tenements that formed their block. The buildings towered forty feet high on every side and made a shady grove where the neighborhood girls played in the summertime. A Rottweiler lay chained in one corner, snoring with its caramel chin on its paws. Girls streamed from the building every morning—one always climbing out through her kitchen window—to argue and dance and scream and double Dutch, but retreated from the noon sun that heated the cement to a skillet, because once a turner had suddenly dropped her ropes, her head lolling like a bobblehead before she pitched face-first to the ground, and she still had the scabbed cheek to prove it. At noon, the girls huddled beneath a lintel and sucked on orange popsicles until the two o'clock shadows canted across their playground, and play resumed.

Allmon maintained a blinkless vigil from their second-story window for many months before he found the courage to creep out of the building to the cement garden. Even then, he was seized with a reserve so crippling that he simply stood on the doorjamb, gazing at the girls through the veil of his lashes. They were jumping and singing and calling while a girl skipped through the lines, her hands perched on her lean hips, her beads up and down and clacking. As Allmon watched, a tiny bunch of foil fell and two beads sailed off and spun away on the cement.

"Your hair! Your hair!" the girls cried, and the jumper leaped out of the eggbeater, her hands to her head, and spotted the boy. Two fingers pinching the braid tight, she cried, "The baby!"

"The baby!" Seven girls, all sweat and brightness and exhilarated jostling, pressed in toward him, though he hung back in a shy twist of limbs. The beadless girl was the first at his side, smiling down and petting him on the head as if he were a sweet dog.

"He has a face just like an old man," she said as she inspected the preternaturally heavy brow, the knife-jut cheekbones, the hollow cheeks.

"Danelle, why you always talk so white?"

"I don't!" the girl cried, wounded, whipping around.

"Yeah, you do!" in a chorus. They were circling him now, or her.

"Danelle wanna be white!"

"I don't!"

"Danelle wanna—"

"Shut up and make the baby jump," another girl interrupted, stepping forward, their tall, unspoken leader. She still held the end of the fallen ropes in her hands.

"I ain't no baby," Allmon said.

"You got a white daddy?" someone asked, and eyes all swerved to him again.

Allmon's tongue was suddenly confused.

"I heard you got a white daddy!"

"Are you white?"

In the middle of those arms and legs and cocked heads, the lie was pure instinct. "My daddy black."

"I wanna white daddy," someone said.

"Naw, you don't. White people don't use no washcloths."

The girl petting Allmon narrowed her eyes. "Is your daddy *really* black?" she asked, but Allmon, under the impress of her hand, could only nod.

"Jump, jump!" someone cried, and they took up the chorus and then they were reforming and slinging a single rope. He stepped forward—a muscular little boy in a ragged white undershirt, his hair poufed slightly out of form from soft neglect.

"I like coffee, I like tea," they sang, "I like the baby boy to jump with me. Double Dutch!" Both ropes rasped now in duple. Allmon's little knees pumped, his hands splayed, his face was angry with concentration. A shadow of cloud swept their playground and the turner—who bobbed her head with the rhythm of the ropes, her little pink tongue caught between her pressed lips—looked up. Allmon judged the descent of the rope and faked a hop and went down with a thud and a false "Ow!" and rolled on his back for the welcome, his arms wide.

They were on him. Oh, they laid their bodies over his and took his face in their hands and kissed on him, their breath hot and their mouths sticky.

"Allmon!"

The girls sprang back from his prone body and there, silhouetted against the sky, was Marie, leaning precipitously from their kitchen window, calling down, "Don't you all molest my child!" The girls just studied the ground, and then one in their midst said, "Ain't nobody molested nobody," and Marie leaned even further out the window, so that she looked near to tumbling out, saying, "That wasn't you on top of my boy? That child is four years old! Don't put your greasy little hands on my boy's business." Someone tittered. Then Marie yelled, "Turkey vultures!" and the girls evaporated, fleeing into the shadows. But when Allmon looked up, Marie was smiling. "Get on up here," she said. "I've got good news for you."

Marie was crouched to his height when he ran into the apartment. She was grinning, and her dimples were deep enough to fit a thumb. "Guess what?"

"What?" he said, shy of surprises.

"Daddy's coming to visit and y'all are going to the Northside carnival!"

"Ah!" he screeched, and would have run, but she snatched him to her, lifted him against her chest.

"Listen now," she said into his ear. "You know how long it's been since your daddy was up here? Oh God," she said. "Forever. Forever. But he's coming back. So I'm begging you. Allmon, your momma is begging you. You need to get some good behavior and be on it, be my little lamb, because—"

Allmon watched her face grow grave.

"—I need this family," she said, barely above a whisper. "That man's got my heart in his body. So just be good is all I'm asking. If we stay on our best behavior, maybe we can get him to stay a while." With gentle hands now, Marie returned him to the ground, lifted his chin with a thumb, and said, "Be my best."

"He be gonna stay?" he said, and the openness of his face, and the uninsured hope she saw there, caused her heart to stop. But all she said was, "Quit that baby talk, Allmon."

He came on a Friday morning, bounding up the stairs with an enormous box in his hands, a box that contained a new, stainless steel cook set. Marie was preparing for work, but she stopped rummaging in her purse when he walked in with the late-summer air around him and pressed herself against the length of his body. Allmon could barely manage his joy. This man's face, so wondrous after a long absence, brought the mystery of his beginnings. He wedged himself between his parents' bodies.

"Now, I'll be back at five," Marie said, and, with a finger against his father's chest, asked, "Want me to bring you dinner?"

"Yeah," Mike said, shrugging. "Bring me something from the Fifth Amendment."

"A pastrami sandwich? I know how you like that."

He made a face and rolled his eyes. "Naw. Bring me a burger. I'm tired of that pastrami shit." He looked down at Allmon, grinning crookedly and reaching for his cigarettes. "You tell somebody that you like pastrami, then—bam!—it's pastrami all the time till you can't stand the smell of it. God, woman." He laughed, the tiniest dart of a glance in her direction. His long, straggly hair was gathered back in a ponytail to reveal his freckled cheekbones, stark from underweight.

"Now, Allmon gets a snack at ten and then—"

"I know, Marie."

She smiled. "I know you know. I'll shut up." She kissed him, and he offered her his stubbly cheek.

"Have fun," she said. "Be good . . ." A pointed glance in Allmon's direction and then she was gone.

"Well," said Mike, and he heaved his skinny shoulders up and down once, glancing around the sunny room. He made his way to the couch, but had only stretched out for a moment, not bothering to remove his shoes, when he perked up his head above the backrest and said, "Allmon, lock the door." And Allmon, excited, watchful, dutiful, dragged a kitchen chair to the door, clambered atop it, and turned the latch. Then he turned around on the chair with his hands behind his back, grinning.

"Good boy."

"When we—"

"Whoa." Mike laughed. "Whoa, whoa. We're not going nowhere till way after lunch, so shut it down."

Allmon clambered down and crept around the side of the couch where his father lay, first his dark, unruly hair showing, then a single eye. His father, drowsy, couldn't help but laugh.

"You're silly," he said.

"What kind of animals is at the carnival?"

Mike ran the fingers of one hand lazily over Allmon's Afro. "Bears," he said. "Snakes, and horses and, like, um . . . They had baby crocodiles once, I think."

"What's that?"

"Oh fuck, I'm so tired. I got like three hours of sleep last night. I drove from Kansas City. Um, a crocodile is like a fish with fucked-up teeth and legs."

"Ah!" Allmon made a frightened face.

Mike tucked his hands into his armpits and closed his eyes. "Wake me up in two hours," he said.

Allmon immediately snatched a pillow from the couch and lay down on the floor in imitation of Mike. "Tell me a bedtime story," he said.

"A story?" Mike said, settling further into the cushions, his brow furrowed. "I don't know any stories. I'm no good at that. No, wait—wait. Okay, here's one. So once there was this football game, and it was like really, really cold. Not just any cold, I'm talking like forty below. This shit was crazy; the guys couldn't feel their fingers and toes, and the field was pretty much ice, so every time there was a tackle, it was cutting through their uniforms and shit. Guys were bleeding all over the place, they were fumbling punts, Green Bay's kicker was missing the goddamn field goals, 'cause he couldn't feel his feet. So fourth quarter, they're all hypothermic as fuck and it's about to be over, and then—tada—make way for Bart Starr."

"Star?" said Allmon.

"Yeah, man. Bart Starr was the man, he was Jesus Christ. The great white hope. It's the fourth quarter, Dallas is up three, Green Bay's third and goal and this is it. Starr calls a time-out, and he's got to make a decision. They're really close, but Green Bay's falling apart. And Bart Starr knows what's what: sometimes you gotta bleed to drive the thing home. So what's he do? Quarterback fucking sneak. He fucking dives in headfirst and burns Dallas down to the ground." He yawned, so his face stretched horribly. "Best moment in football history right there. That's how you win when the chips are down. Sacrifice yourself for the team. End of story."

Mike wasn't sleeping, but his eyes were closed again. "So, hey, Allmon," he said, and he yawned another deep yawn that shook his body. "You know what . . . someday I'm gonna take you . . ." And then he was asleep.

When Allmon awoke, the sun was insistent, it pressed smothering heat into his face, causing itchy rivulets of sweat to travel into his hair. He reached up and touched the white hand of his father, which had fallen into the air between them. He gripped a finger and the man woke, his eyebrows starting.

"Hey, kid," he said softly. "Did your ma buy me any beer?" His face was weary and worn as if he'd aged twenty years in his sleep. Lines from the pillow ran ridges along his cheek.

Allmon brought him two. He drank the first in two drafts. The second he drank lying down, in slow sips, while Allmon watched the sliding motions of his Adam's apple.

"How's your ma been?" he asked.

"Good," said Allmon brightly.

"What time is it?"

Allmon only made a confused gesture and Mike said, "Oh shit," but he didn't rise. "One more beer," he said, and Allmon's grin was slipping, and then, "Two." And then, after drinking the first, he was asleep again.

Allmon looked down at the body of his father on its berth, the man's thin hands crossed on his chest. In a moment, Mike began to snore, a lumbering, unhealthy, grown-up sound. With an expression on his face like dawning suspicion, more rudimentary than anger, Allmon placed his small hand on his father's shoulder. He shook him once, then again and with increasing force until the man was rolling on the couch like a log in heavy water. Finally, Mike brushed Allmon's hand away. "Let me sleep," he said thickly, without opening his eyes.

So a new scene begins, though the action follows through. Allmon simply unlocked the door, gripped the waxy banister as he navigated the creaking stairs, and then the full light of the sun was on him—and on his twin, impulse. The crowd on the street absorbed him as it flowed north toward the intersection, where the trucks had driven in with their animal cargo, though years ago the animals rumbled in on boxcars from Pittsburgh, halting just west of the main drag, so as the evening sun was setting, children in their beds heard the grieved crying of the leopards and the hollow hooting of monkeys.

At the roped-off intersection: snakes in grimy glass cages, a panther slinking in a boxcar, a bald red cat in a harness hissing at passersby, a giraffe in a cage half the height of a building. All around, the people of the neighborhood were drunk on beer and freedom, kissing their girlfriends in broad daylight like men on leave, carrying their children on their shoulders, those children held aloft like trophies, calling to one another in contented, proud recognition and cooing at the animals.

They were shoulder to shoulder, sewn together as a great, continuous garment. But look there beyond the tidal wave of people, beyond the ruction, at a horse. It isn't impressive, just a nag snatched up by a carnie for forty bucks at the slaughterhouse in Peoria. She stands there with a ragged cob in her eyes, a disheveled thing perched on tender, surbated hooves. Her back scoops in at the middle and her rear legs pigeon inward. She's missing hair at her sides, as if a saddle has long rubbed her permanently raw. Her eyes are very blue, eyes void of protest or argument, full of calm, momentful existence, maybe without memory, the eyes of an animal accustomed to the rowel on her bit and a man's hard hand on her headstall. When she turns her head, one blue eye settles on Allmon.

"Guess how many hands high," said the man who reined her, and in his shyness, Allmon said nothing at all, just twisted on one leg, staring up.

"How tall?" the man said again.

"She got a name?" said Allmon, pointing.

"You'll get a prize for guessing how high."

"A hundred," he said softly.

"Huh?" said the man, his face ratcheted in irritation.

Then a woman's risen voice said, "Who's that child belong to?" In another moment, a woman halted him with a hand on his shoulder, saying, "Honey, where's your parents at?" In an instant, his shoulder slipped her grasp and he was on the run, propelled by fear and wicked delight, skidding around bodies and trash cans until two victorious minutes later, the door closed and locked, he stood breathing raggedly over the snoring body of his father, the horse almost forgotten in the yeasty gloam of the room. He tallied seven gold cans on the floor by the couch, one only half-drunk. He stooped and studied his father's face with care: the sharp, sure lines of his cheeks and chin, his brow creased even in sleep, his freckles like tiny brown smudges of dirt. And white skin—white the color of flour, of paper, of snow, of pearls, of stars.

"Wake up," he whispered, and, when there was no response, he balled his hand into a fist and with all the strength he possessed, he struck his father on the bone of his shoulder. The snoring ceased and Mike's bleary red eyes opened. They focused slowly on Allmon's face. Then one hand reached forward and stopped a tear as it tracked down a cheek.

"Hey Jude," he said, "don't be sad."

In the morning, his mind undressed by sleep, he padded along the old cupped floorboards to the kitchen, where he found Marie standing at the stove. The two casement windows on either side of her fired the room with sun, banking her into silhouette, as if she were standing in a tunnel of light. Her hair, inlit with red, curled out to one side, the other side still smashed tight to the shape of her head from sleep. Her right hand gripped the chrome handle of the oven door with whitening strength.

"Daddy here?" said Allmon sleepily.

She didn't turn around, her hand on the stove didn't move. He stepped forward then, and with a tiny motion he touched her hip, a touch as soft as a cat's paw. Her hand came to life then, springing off the stove and smacking his own hand away with such force that he was too startled to cry out, he just hopped back, drawing his wrist to his clavicle and staring up at her in shock, pupils huge with misgiving.

"I don't need a man touching on me right now!" she hissed. Her eyes were deep as a bruise, her face stripped of everything that made it her face except its familiar shape.

"I mean, why?" she blurted suddenly, then her voice rising: "I just want somebody to tell me why!"

Allmon only stared.

"What's wrong with me?" she cried. "I do everything right, I have his baby, I love him! No one loves him like I do! What's wrong with me? He can't stand my ugly face? Who's here for me? Who? Tell me!" She was sinking down and crying openly, sobbing great senseless, wracking sobs, her T-shirt catching on the stove knob as she slid down, so it raised up over her soft belly, showing the white striping of old stretch marks. One hand clutched the folds of her belly and one hand held her breast, low-hung and braless behind the T-shirt, her legs sprawled crookedly before her.

"How come I have to do all the loving? Huh? Just tell me that! You all take all of me! And you don't give anything back!"

Allmon bumped back into the doorjamb, turning to flee as her anger collapsed into tears. "I just want my momma back. How come God's got to take everybody away from me? How come everybody just goes away and leaves me alone?"

Allmon's feet were agents of release, they sped him down the back staircase and spilled him out into the cement garden. There it was cool, a good place for tears. The chained Rottweiler looked up at the sound of Allmon's crying and grinned, his caramel brow dots bouncing. Looking up, Allmon saw only the grimy redbrick enclosure on all sides and then a perfect square of crayon-blue sky without cloud. There were no birds flying there. He stared so long, the shed tears ran into his ears. Finally, a woman's voice said, "The hell is wrong with you, child?" and when he turned to see who had said it—a woman whose tremendous girth filled her entire kitchen window as she leaned down to peer at him—a bird flew directly over his head in the patch of blue. It flanked suddenly, swerved down, and perched on a water tower, glowering at the blaring traffic below and executing a tiny side step that looked like an aborted dance. Then it proceeded to sing a song louder than any country cousin, because it had so much to sing against. No creature comforts here. A bird's only defense is its own body and that you can break with your hand.

That afternoon, when the mood was settling like ashes on a burned-out fire, their neighbor Beanie came visiting, blunt tongue and motherwit at the ready. She wore her sweats pushed up under her chubby knees and a Bulls jersey with armholes so deep, her white bra showed. Her hair terraced down from her crown in a series of tight rolls that graduated in thickness until the final curl at her nape was thick as a toilet paper roll. She wore one or two gold-toned rings on every finger, and they glinted as she smoked; she always smoked. She found Marie at the kitchen table, staring into the window fan with a scraped plate of food before her.

"Where's my favorite baby boy at?" Beanie said.

"I don't know," Marie said softly.

Beanie chuckled. "You know that child got a fierce face. Gonna scare the hell out of some white folk when he gets grown. Bone structure, you know what I'm saying. Bone motherfucking structure."

The corners of Marie's mouth lifted, but she couldn't smile. "I was awful this morning, and he ran off. He's probably out back. I can't blame him."

Beanie eased down heavily into the other chair with her legs stiffed out before her. "Okay, look at me. Look at me, girl." Marie glanced up warily, as if expecting a blow. "I'm sick to death of you crying over this motherfucker. You know I am. This shit getting to be like clockwork."

Marie wiped her nose on her hand. "He promised to take Allmon to the carnival, and then he just sat right there on that couch and drank himself silly."

Beanie made a sorry sound in her throat and shook her head.

"He couldn't even sit up straight, he was so drunk, and then he tells me he got some girl pregnant in Chicago, and he's moving to Chicago now. And I was like, 'Do you love me?'"

"First, don't be asking no man if they love you. 'Cause that's just pathetic."

"And all he said, you know what he said? He was like, 'I love you, but I got a sweet tooth.'"

"Mike, the white boy?"

Marie nodded.

Beanie sighed. "Who even knew white boys was worthless as these niggers up in here."

"He left me his car. But I don't even care. Beanie, Allmon shouldn't have seen me like that."

Beanie sighed. "Yeah, well, somebody's got to put you in check. You act too soft all the time. You let a man run all over—"

Marie laid her hands down flat on the table, her face all affront. "Now you sound like the Reverend saying I act like a white girl."

"Ew, nasty!" Beanie held up a shielding hand. "I ain't meant it like that, 'cause I ain't that mean. I ain't never met no white girl over age thirteen I'd save out a burning building."

Marie sighed and looked hopelessly around her. "It's like I got to be some tough-ass bitch to actually be black around here—"

Beanie's head cocked hard. "Who you calling a tough-ass black bitch?"

She got what she was looking for. Marie bowed her head and laughed through her nose, then swept up Beanie's free hand in her own. "I'm just saying . . . it's like somebody's always ready to tear me down for just being me. The Reverend thinks I act like some whiny white girl, men think they can walk all over me if I just act myself instead of playing some hard-to-get game, and all these girls here act like I'm a race traitor 'cause I was with Mike—"

Beanie waved her hand. "Oh, it don't make them no nevermind, they're just talking shit, 'cause that's what assholes do—"

"No, it's a fact, and you know it. It's like you've always got to playact and pretend to be someone else to get love in this world. Well, I don't playact with men. I don't try to seduce people. I'm just me. And so everybody's out there tricking people into falling in love with them, and I'm all alone."

"How come that is, you think?"

Marie stared straight into her eyes. "Because they're cowards. Men are cowards."

Beanie waved smoke away from Marie. "Okay, well, you ain't got to play-act. Ain't nobody saying that. Just . . . just don't nobody want to see you crying over these spineless, tired, worthless motherfuckers. Ain't nobody ever told you ain't no man alive worth crying over?"

Marie closed her eyes, said, "Children need a father."

"Okay, see now that offends me a little bit," said Beanie, pulling back her hand. "Both my girls is doing good, and where's their fathers at? Where's Derron at? Who the fuck even knows. At least we all know where Omar's at, you know what I'm saying. But both my girls doing good, star students at SCPA, playing in band and doing ballet, all that. Marie," she said, but more gently, with a sigh, "you don't need no man. Open your eyes and look around you. Who you see in this building with a man? Who?"

"Cara."

"Oh. Yeah, okay."

"Diane."

"All right. Shit."

Marie stared in sudden consternation at the fan, watching tendrils of smoke slip into its draw. Then she said, "And that girl with the twins I always see out on Knowlton's Corner. I don't know her name. I see her out with that big stroller."

Beanie reared back. "Oh!"

"What?"

"That bitch? Oh shit! That bitch a one-woman jizz factory, she got dicks clocking in and out every hour of the day. She ain't got no man, Marie—she got a pimp!"

"What? No! She's a prostitute?"

"You ain't know that? Goddamn, Marie, you so ignorant!"

"But—I, I can't help it—I grew up in church!"

Both women howled. And once started, they couldn't stop, so Beanie had to fling her cigarette out the window and stomp her feet, and Marie ended up slipping off her chair onto the floor, leaning her head back onto the chair seat to cry. Then she was too weak from laughter to stand, so Beanie had to stand over her and, hauling her up with both hands, said, "Well, get Allmon on down to church then. Get him a dose of the Reverend."

———

The Reverend lived in an old four-story brownstone on Sycamore, one in a row of five on the block, all in a state of disrepair. The façade was pink as adobe punctuated by black architraves that made pointy eyebrows over windows and black shutters, a few of which swung loose and hung precariously by a single hinge, threatening passersby below. The stoop was concrete, the corbel and cornice painted gray to look like stone. The peeling house rained old paint flakes on the stoop, where once upon a time, when Marie was young, there had been rectangular planters filled with geraniums and oxalis. When her mother died of cancer, the planters and their flowers had disappeared. Now there was nothing on the stoop but the deep wear in stone of a hundred thousand footsteps impressed over the course of a century and more. It swooped gently like the seat of a cold gray saddle.

Marie and Allmon drove up Sycamore in the Escort Mike Shaughnessy had left them, but it was hard to find a spot downtown, so they parked down a side street barely wider than an areaway, crowded with black trash bags and tires and forsaken furniture. As Marie cut the motor, three men who had stood huddled together at the end of the alley scattered like jacks.

"I don't miss living down here," she sighed, but her eyes were on Allmon in the rearview. "Honey, listen to me," she said, pinning him with a serious gaze, "I need you to get some Jesus here, all right?"

He nodded.

"That's all I'm asking of you."

"Okay."

She held up a finger. "And I don't want any talk about your daddy. You hear me?"

"Uh-huh."

"Ain't no uh-huh. I'm serious. Yes, Momma."

"Yes, Momma," he said.

When they rang the doorbell, a Chinese man answered the door. Marie started back in surprise. She looked at him without saying a word, this pint of a man with long, thin hair like a horse's neglected mane, who wore an old white painter's jumpsuit splattered with bright color. He was ageless, bedraggled, a man who hadn't bathed in a long while and who probably didn't care. He took one look at them and said, "Who are you?"

"I'm Marie," she said, indignant. "Who are you?"

"Oh, ha!" the man cried. "The Reverend's daughter, Marie. Of course! Come in, come in. I'm new here. I didn't realize."

He waved them into the building with two quick flaps of his hand, and they entered the soaring foyer, where the balustraded staircase rose steeply to the second floor. Above, the drift of radio chatter and men's voices. The bang of something dropping and raucous laughter.

"I think the Reverend's in his office. Yeah, there he is. Listen, if you're staying the night, I'd like to share with you my witness, how Christ changed my life."

"Uh-huh," Marie said, steering Allmon toward the parlor.

"I was a dead man walking before I let him in my heart. I used to live down on Broadway; you can't even call it living what I was doing. But I'll tell you all about it later. It'll be a warning for your kid."

"Yeah, okay, sure."

The man ushered them over the threshold into the parlor of what had once been a grand Cincinnati row house, now a fraying thread in the tapestry of the city. The Reverend presided, stiff and upright, in his usual place on his busted crimson leather chair, his Bible open on his lap. All over the chair, white stuffing like cotton bolls extruded from seams and tears and from under duct tape patches. When the Reverend looked up and saw them, he closed his Bible, laid it aside, and stood. He was tall and broad with nothing extra on him, shoulders like a box under his neatly ironed secondhand shirt, which was tucked in tight and buttoned to its starched collar. His enormous hands hung at his sides, the fingers fidgeting subtly, forever in motion, his old gold wedding band catching the light dully. It was not so much the man's size that commanded attention but his head and face—the tight, short hair sprinkled with gray above an enormous forehead, dark as a chalkboard with deep lines written across its surface. His nose was wide and sloped steeply beneath the heavy, mannish brows that Allmon had inherited. And set deep, deep beneath those brows, tawny eyes burned bright as lanterns. The Reverend never just looked; his eyes bored into the object of his concern.

"Hi, Daddy," said Marie with a pittance of a voice, sounding not much older than her boy.

The Reverend nodded. "Always late. You missed supper." His voice, enormous even when conversational, filled the shape of the room. His aurous eyes dismissed her with an unreadable expression, then settled on Allmon. Allmon smiled up into that familiar face, which did not smile in return. Nothing was said for a long moment, but just as Marie was drawing her breath to speak, the Reverend intoned, "What're you doing to this child's head?" After fifty years in the Queen City, rural Arkansas still rolled off his tongue.

"What?" said Marie, and she reached down to touch Allmon's hair, which had grown all out of order like a hedge unchecked. "It looks good. I like it like this. It's kind of free."

The Reverend cocked his head and when he spoke, every word was slow, declarative, his vowels as broad as fields. "May I remind you there's a difference between free and sloppy? You think your child looking unattended-to is free? Folks see a child like that, they think he doesn't have a mother. They see a just-so Negro. May as well give him a dashiki and a blunt."

"Daddy!" said Marie, laughing. "Four-year-olds don't need to look like lawyers. I mean, what decade is this?"

"Apparently, the decade where don't nobody care if their children look homeless. This business . . . this ain't even in style." A derisive flap of his enormous hand.

"In style? You really think you should be lecturing me about what's in style?" Marie turned left and right to appraise the Reverend's holdings, which amounted to a wrecked house, dilapidated vinyl furniture, a parlor room with books to the ceiling, and two identical Goodwill suits. She sighed. "Anyway, you know, some people like it."

"Like who? Like White Mike, that's who!" The Reverend turned his back to them and raised up his hands in exasperation. He took a few halting steps toward his chair and said, "Jesus help me learn there ain't no sense arguing when the milk"—and here he paused between each word—"done. Been. Spilt." Then he lowered himself into his chair with pronounced fatigue, like a man much older than his sixty-five years, and said, "Y'all just sit down now. Just sit down and visit and no more bickering."

So they sat, Marie and Allmon on a sticky gray vinyl couch facing the Reverend, who seemed not particularly inclined to say anything more.

Allmon reached up and found the swell of his hair; he noted for the first time how it stuck out past his ears. His grandfather turned that keen, un-breaking gaze upon him and said, "How you doing, young mister?"

"Daddy was here!" said Allmon, his hand still to his Afro.

"Aw . . . ," moaned Marie. "Aw, Allmon . . . dag." And she just leaned forward and put her face into her cupped hands.

"Aha!" said the Reverend, looking at Allmon with an appraising eye. "Children always speak the truth! Now, how long it's been since the good Michael Shaughnessy graced this child with his presence?"

Marie said through her hands, "He was here this weekend."

"I mean before that."

She paused. "Nine months."

The Reverend's head was a deep bell, swinging side to side but making no sound. He didn't have to say a word.

Marie raised her own head and took a deep breath. "It was an okay visit, really." Still the Reverend said nothing, and her eyes filled suddenly with tears and she said, "Actually, it wasn't very good, Daddy."

The Reverend cleared his throat and said, "Don't be crying in front of your child." Then he stood again, removed his worn white handkerchief from his breast pocket, and handed it to Marie.

She took it but crumpled it in her fist unused and whispered, as if All-mon wouldn't hear a whisper. "I don't really know if he's gonna come back."

The Reverend stared intently into her pain-wrinkled face. Then he cleared his throat and said softly, "You pick up white trash, your hands gonna get dirty."

"Daddy . . . ," she said.

Allmon sprang up from the couch suddenly, all defense between them. "He be g—"

"Allmon, quit that baby talk," Marie said roughly, but when she drew him back onto her lap, her hands were gentle. She spoke over his head. "Things are all right—"

"Now, I don't believe that's the truth."

"—but, you know, we might be looking for another place before too long."

The Reverend's eyes narrowed. "What I'm hearing is he ain't sending you no money."

Marie looked up at the cracked ceiling. "I don't want to force anybody to support me."

"I ain't telling you what to do."

"But, actually, you know," Marie said, "they've been talking about cutting my hours down to thirty-five at the dentist's office. I don't know how I'm going to pay my bills. It costs me a fortune to take care of his asthma." She gestured at Allmon.

The Reverend's face betrayed nothing. "Should have got that teaching certificate, Marie."

"I had a baby, God forbid!" she snapped, but then the tiny fire banked, and she said quietly, "I'm just tired, you know. I don't know what to do. Maybe I . . . I don't know. I'm trying to be a good mother, and I don't know why that's not enough in this world. The way I am just never seems like enough."

No reply was forthcoming.

"But so, I . . ." She looked up, her eyes wide, lenitive. "You don't have maybe a little room for us down here, do you?"

The Reverend looked honestly taken by surprise, dark lines drawn between his brows. "This ain't no place for children, and you know it."

Marie's voice was soft, but her gaze was steady. "Not anymore, I guess."

There was a pained, headlong silence in the room as Allmon sat on his mother's lap, staring at his grandfather. His grandfather's eyes were headlights and now the headlights returned to focus on him. The man drew a deep breath and stood abruptly, his hand reaching out for his grandson's as he said, "Lord help me, I can't take it no more, I got to fix this child's head. Allmon, come with me."

Marie opened her mouth to object, but the Reverend just held up that hand, and she thumped back into the sofa with a sigh, crossing her arms over her chest.

The Reverend led Allmon to a pink-tiled bathroom near the back of the first floor, past the kitchen and dining room, past the tiny side bedroom barely bigger than a closet, where he and his mother slept when they stayed over, and just before the Reverend's bedroom. He flipped the switch and knocked the old toilet lid down, placed his hands in Allmon's armpits, and lifted the child up onto the flimsy seat. Then he gripped Allmon's spindly legs and pried them apart, so he was standing secure on the edges of the lid. "Stand like so," he said. "Lord knows I can't have you falling in-side this toilet. You looking rinky-dink enough."

Then with steady hands, he took hold of Allmon's chin, turning the boy's head this way and that, tilting his chin up and appraising the land-scape of his hair. He clicked his disapproval behind his teeth. "Don't no-body know the meaning of pride no more," he said. He reached over and drew open the medicine cabinet and removed a set of clippers from a crack-led pleather bag. "Just a five-letter word that don't mean nothing to nobody. May as well be a cuss word."

He fiddled with the clippers until they came to life with a gentle grind-ing noise, but he didn't do anything yet. He just stood there, looking thoughtful. "It ain't always been like this, believe you me. You think it's a coincidence that we was looking sharp and taking care of the black body till the Reverend King got himself shot, and the president got himself shot, and then all a sudden, the apparel was getting all goofy and the hair was getting wild? You think that's a coincidence?"

"No," said Allmon.

"They call it free, I call it giving up. Because that's what it is. Unlike most folk, I tell it like it is."

Allmon gazed up into his grandfather's face, discovering the tracings of age in his mottled color, the gray in his five-o'clock shadow, the deep ladder lines above his brow. "Grandpa, you gonna die?" he said.

"Huh—what?" The Reverend drew back, startled, holding the purr-ing clippers to one side. "I ain't even that old," he said. "Besides, the Lord can't afford to kill me. Who else he gonna get to do his work? There ain't enough Christians in the world, just a bunch of folk who go to church."

With care now, he applied the clippers to Allmon's hairline and made a single stripe down the center of his head like an inverted Mohawk.

"Anyhow," he said, "like I was saying, everybody thinks if they're doing their own thing, then they're free. Now, they don't know the first thing. Young folks forget more than they ever learned, and they're too ignorant to even know it." He sighed. "Young ladies now, they don't know they need a man to raise up boys. But tell me, how else you expect a boy to learn? These streets, they're just full of broken-down Negroes. A boy, he needs to know a man in order to become a man. He's got to follow him and watch and learn. I had a father, that's how I know. Women don't know how to grow up men."

"I wanna live here," said Allmon, following on his mother's lead.

The Reverend shook his head in irritation. "A halfway house? Like I already said, this ain't no place for children. Anyhow, your mother done dug herself into this fool pit, now she's got to dig her own self out."

"There's a bunch of men in this house," Allmon said.

The Reverend nodded. "Children of God."

Allmon said, "This ain't no place for children!"

At this, the Reverend did something he very rarely did: he smiled. "Well," he said, "my daughter thinks she got it bad, but these men here, they really got it bad, and I got it bad 'cause I got to take care of them, and when a man's got the poison of liquor or cocaine or whatnot in his blood, he brings the devil in the house. So they bring him in, and I run him off, and they bring him in again, and I run him off again. It's a full-time job, and I already got a full-time job. It don't never end. The Reverend always pushing his boulder up the seven hills. The question I always got to be asking is—who suffers the hardest? 'Cause Jesus says I got to minister to the least among us. Your momma ain't the least; she just thinks she is, loves to play the victim. My wife spoiled her rotten."

He sighed and shaved along Allmon's left ear, so it vibrated and tickled.

"Ow!" cried Allmon with high drama, but it didn't hurt. He leaned into the vibration like a cat into a hand.

The Reverend ignored his complaint, focusing on the task. "Well, God never said I was gonna end up satisfied if I followed him, no he didn't. He only promised me the cross. I got a daughter running around with white boys, and my wife, she's been dead ten years. I got disappointments like some individuals got dollar bills."

One last swipe of the clippers and Allmon was shorn like a spring sheep. His head looked about half its usual size. The ledge of his young brow loomed ever more prominent.

The Reverend looked down at him pointedly. "But when a man gets that old temptation to throw in the towel, you know what he says?"

Allmon looked up expectantly.

"Praise Jesus and be not afraid," the Reverend said evenly, and he passed a clearing hand over the curves and ridges of Allmon's skull.

Allmon grinned.

"What's he say, young man?"

Allmon quit the grin. "Praise Jesus."

"And be not afraid. Says it a bunch of times in the Bible. Got to live by it." With all the lingering hairs swept to the floor, the Reverend fell suddenly silent and his warm, dry hand remained resting on Allmon's head. A soft, comfortable silence crowded around them and, for the better part of a minute, they stood enveloped in its haze, utterly still.

Then Allmon reached up and put his hands on the Reverend's shoulders. "Grandpa?"

"Huh?" the man said, startled. In his deep-set eyes, there roosted a faraway look, as if he were contemplating something in another room or another time. Then he said softly, "Jesus is coming into my mind. That's how it is on a Saturday night, I get to thinking, and he gets to speaking. He comes like a trouble in the mind you got to sort out."

He turned and laid the clippers down gently on the pink windowsill and, without really seeing him, lifted Allmon off the toilet seat and set him on the floor.

"I'm listening," the Reverend said vaguely. "Ain't I always listening? I ain't no eyeservant."

Then he nudged Allmon with a hard finger. "Get on now," he said, "I got to converse with the Lord."

Allmon turned to leave, passing a tentative hand along the short hair where his Afro had been. He glanced down at the black tumbleweeds on the cracked tile floor and felt a new, strange feeling. That hair, once a part of him, was discarded, flung away . . . His stomach made a funny, unexpected flip.

"Son," the Reverend said suddenly, seeing him hesitate. "Jesus loves you, but the world don't. The important question is—you look black, but are you colorfast?"

Then he closed the door with a clap and locked himself in the bathroom to pray.

Now in the spare bathroom down the hall she's looking in the mirror as she gets ready for bed—what it was, what it was . . . Something isn't there, she frowns, she turns to the side, it's just hugging up on her face like . . . nothing, it doesn't have a good shape, if her eyes were just a little more open, less almond-shaped, and lighter, if her whole skin was just like a shade up from this, she didn't want to be white, she just wanted to be pretty; she sighs, don't cry, the reality is you live so long, the fact your momma told you you were pretty gets showed up for what it is, just pitter-patter baby talk, just the things you say raising kids; you tell them what they need to hear, and then later they grow up and look at this ugly potato nose and fat cheeks and go, oh yeah, money don't buy you love, but pretty does. And I got nothing in the bank.

She sees him staring up at her in the mirror, his eyes full of something he's seen, but when she turns, he's gone. For a second she didn't recognize him without his hair.

In the morning, Marie dressed Allmon in a gray striped button-up and his blue rayon suit, and together they walked the four blocks west to Race Street. From the corner of Race and Liberty, gazing south along the city blocks toward the river, all that you could see of the church among the relic brownstones slumming on their past glory was the gray steeple topped by a white cross. The church was an old Flemish bond structure built by Tennessee Presbyterians in 1849 when they fled the South for abolition's sake. It had stood abandoned all through the fifties before the Reverend decided to establish the House of Sanctuary Christian Church there in 1962 after a visit from Abernathy in the spring of that year. A fearsome angel of the Lord, the Reverend had stalked the suburban churches for months, guilting funds from the city's affluent blacks until he had just enough to purchase the dilapidated building for a song—a song and a tap dance for the Fancy Black, as he called them. The church's roof needed repairing, which never came; its sanctuary was a shipwreck—pews toppled and water-stained, glass windows replaced with frosted Plexiglas, the lectern dismantled and heaped like kindling on the dais—but it didn't matter to the Reverend. His churchgoers in the early years were those he'd salvaged from whatever the drugs left on the streets of Over-the-Rhine. They wouldn't have been comfortable in a sanctuary anyway, so he led his sheep to the dank basement, where they could listen without cringing shame. It was there in the concrete basement under the fluorescent lights and cracked ceiling that grown men wept and women sang themselves hoarse, and all manner of sin was burned and sucked away like smoke up a flue. "The hull is ugly," the

Reverend would say, "but the fruit is ripe!" The Reverend had little formal schooling, but he had wisdom in abundance and will as well, so his congregation grew. The spirit was in the building, they said, and word soon spread up the hills of the city, all the way to the suburbs. Soon, the crowd that gathered on Sundays mixed Over-the-Rhine with folks from the distant neighborhoods—the streets of flight, as well as the men from his halfway house. But no matter the provenance of the sinner, no matter how blue-chip the dress or the shoe, the services remained in the basement. The Reverend wasn't budging; it was the principle of the thing. He had built his church on a rock, and the rock was himself.

The congregation was already settling when Marie and Allmon arrived, squeezing down a row to claim two folding chairs in the middle. Allmon hopped up on his chair for a moment, eyeballing the crowd. There, at the front of the sanctuary, his grandfather sat in a chair as if asleep, his hands folded on his belly, his chin tipped steeply to his chest. He might have been asleep for how still he was. Close by, a rangy youth stooped over a keyboard, pressing out chords Allmon immediately recognized: there is wonderful power in the blood; power, power, wonder-working power in the blood of the lamb; power, power, wonder-working power in the precious blood of the lamb. The sound grew thick and his heart pulsated to the rhythm until he stomped his legs to assuage the biting joy there—and his mother tugged him down onto his behind. The Reverend had risen slowly to his feet, pointing up to the ceiling just like the white hands atop all the steeples of Over-the-Rhine, and as the hymn poured out the last of its blood, he cried, "Let the holy spirit fill this room!"

"Amen!"

"Help me preach, Lord," he said, bowing his head again.

"Amen."

"Bring down the words in the voice of my brothers, not the voice of the schools."

"Amen!"

" 'Cause ain't no school ever taught me right from wrong."

"No . . ."

"Bring me the truth in the words of my father and his father."

"Amen."

"And the Holy Father, Amen."

"Amen."

"All right!" the Reverend cried suddenly, sharply, and raised his head with a ferocious gaze. But immediately the severity of his face eased as if he was about to make a joke, and his voice was dangerous, slippery when he said, "So . . . how many y'all sinned this week?" Behind that half smile, there was the hardness of carbon that his humor broke itself upon. There was only silence in reply, sudden and heavy. The quick enthusiasm he'd drawn banked.

"Ha!" he cried out into the surprised silence. "Wasn't expecting that, huh? Thought I was gonna warm y'all up, say something pretty about how Jesus is watching out for you and all that. But, oh, Jesus is mad—can't you hear him storming up there in heaven? That's the sound of Jesus in the temple, just mad as can be." He held a hand to his ear and cocked his head. "Now, I asked how many y'all sinned?"

He raised his own hand, peering at the people turned out in their Sunday best, ironed and perfumed, fake-pearled, lipsticked, hair straightened and curled and oiled. "Ain't nobody sinned? Well," he said with his arms stretched wide, "it's a miracle."

Then a low voice said, "Reverend, I sinned."

"Who—what? Who sinned?"

A man stood quietly in the midst of the congregation. He wore a western shirt washed thin as parchment, his stained wifebeater showing through. Some of the women in the front rows turned right around in their seats to stare at the man with eyes wide. He locked eyes with the Reverend and passed a nervous hand up and down over the pearled buttons of the shirt. He said again, with gravity, "I sinned."

"Well, did you like it?" asked the Reverend.

"Uh . . ." The man's eyes slid corner to corner.

"'Cause if you ain't liked it, then it wasn't sin!"

The room broke up and the man said, "Aw," like a scolded child, and then, with a grin that turned his somber face brilliant, he said, "I liked what I can remember!"

"Ha! That's sin! That's sin! If you sin, sin like you mean it! Sin bold!" The Reverend pointed a finger straight at the man's chest, the man who was seating himself again, and he began to pace excitedly side to side directly in front of the first row of chairs, in front of the old watchdogs in the

amen corner who murmured and nodded. Now the sermon was really beginning, now the Reverend was shedding the weight of his person, his voice
rising, his face illuminated by a light from within and without. He looked
simultaneously fierce and overwhelmed with joy. He said, "That there is a
child of God! A true child of God! If you love Jesus, then you own up. You
say, 'I'm a dirty old sinner!' Now, I hear you all laughing, but who else
sinned? Huh? Tell me. Who else sinned?"

He turned on them and the room fell quiet and Allmon yawned and
leaned across his chair into the warm side of his mother. He felt the first
blurring of sleep coming on the steady waves of her breath. Fatigue and
morning heat lulled him. Marie stared unblinking at her father.

"Mmmmm, it got so quiet in here all a sudden." The Reverend laughed
a grim laugh.

No one stirred.

"Ain't nobody gonna speak up? Oh, I see, I see. Y'all are just mad at
me. I can hear you now," he said, and shifted onto his hip suddenly, wagging a finger, and in a creaky little voice: "Aw, now, Reverend, you always
be so *hard* on us. Your Jesus ain't *no fun*." He straightened up. "Well, that's
right—Jesus wasn't no fun. His disciples was ignorant and couldn't make
no sense of what he was saying, and the people was even more ignorant,
and sometimes he got mad like a snapping dog and stormed through the
temple, laying it down, and then, you know what? They assassinated him.
They strung him up. So, that's right. Jesus wasn't no fun. What part the
cross don't you understand?"

Allmon's jaw loosened, then he slipped into sleep.

"No, wait, wait, now I know why ain't nobody fessing up," said the
Reverend. "I know what y'all are thinking: We're so tired of all this sin
talk, all the struggle stories. Isn't it time for Easy Street? After all, we
ain't the generation that got dragged over from Africa. No, we ain't the generation that slaved and slaved for the white man. We ain't the generation that
creeped up under cover of night from Mississippi, Georgia, Louisiana,
when they was still sending your sorry behind back on the L&N with a note
said 'Property Of,' that generation like my great-great-grandfather's who
swum across that muddy river"—he pointed behind him at the claybank
wall, that muddy yellow space an intimation of the river beyond—"and
once he done established himself and got himself a family, hung himself

in a white man's attic from a rafter he done raised with his own two hands! Now you think that man—that Scipio—when he was swinging from the rafters, he was busy paying your all's bill? Well, now you say, things are so different now. They're all so different now. The last century paid the bill. Or maybe y'all think the cotton pickers paid the bill? That come up to Chicago, Detroit, to Toledo, right here to Cincinnati? Like how I come up with my own dearly departed folks from the little town of Shelburne, Arkansas? Brothers and sisters," he said with his hands on his hips, his eyes carefully surveying their faces, "did the good Reverend pay your bill with his own hard life? Was my generation paying the bill when we was young men marching in the streets of this fair city and Selma and Birmingham and the capital of this nation? When the dogs was biting and the hoses was baptizing, when the streets of this country was running with black blood? Let me ask you: Was the Reverend King paying the bill on your all's life when he got shot down on that day in April? Maybe y'all think 1968 was busy paying the bill. I got to admit, that's a awful nice way to think. The bill paid by your forefathers, paid by slaves."

Now he stopped and turned forward, wily eyes on the congregants. Very quietly, almost shyly, he said, "Oh, Lord Jesus." Then louder, with his eyes cast up, "Oh Jesus, forgive all the little children. They try to love you, Jesus, they do, but they're so ignorant! Just like in Bible times, so it is today."

Now he strutted and mocked: "Ah, no, Reverend! We just think the times, they changed! It's 1984. We ain't Negroes no more, we're Afro-Americans. We vote, we got white friends that invite us over, nobody calls us names to our face no more, some of us is vice presidents of the company, some of us even lay down with white men." He stumbled here, his voice stuttering. Marie glanced wearily down at the floor.

"Well, good for you!" the Reverend spat, resuming his back-and-forth walk but pointing at them. "But your brother in the city ain't up there with you! He's still stuck on the ghetto plantation with the overseer at his back, he's still trapped up in the Jim Crow prison! Think about it! While you're laying down with the lion, you ain't tending to no lambs, and Jesus, he loved the little lambs. There wasn't no lions in that shepherd's flock. If the lion's even tolerating you in his presence, maybe you're doing something wrong! Maybe he's just pitying you. You ever think about that? 'Cause ain't it the nature of the lion to eat the lamb? So what're you doing with the blond-haired lion in the first place? Ain't nobody paid the bill for you to lay down with the lion! Fancy black folks always wanting you to hush the struggle story! What part the cross don't you understand?"

"Amen . . ."

"I say don't stand on the middle ground, stand on the holy ground!"

"Amen!"

"I said not the middle-class ground—the poverty ground!"

"Amen!"

"For there stands the living Christ, Amen! Yes. I'm gonna tell you a secret now, and if there ain't nothing else you remember, remember this: Jesus loves the poor, because they suffer, and them that suffer is the only ones that love Jesus, 'cause it's only when you suffer that you see the truth and Jesus, he's the truth! You understand? It's a perfect circle. So why are you trying so hard to not be poor? Jesus said only in heaven is the lion gonna be laying down with the lamb. And this—*this* ain't heaven." He laughed a derisive laugh, then turned to them with a single finger held up in the air as if a thought was newly dawning. His brows were risen high. "But maybe some of y'all think heaven *is* here on earth, it just ain't here in Over-the-Rhine. Ooooooh," he said slow, looking carefully, pointedly from face to face. "Ooooooh, you think heaven is the American Dream."

"No, Reverend."

His eyes narrowed. "Now come on, you know what I'm talking about, don't be looking all innocent. The big old American dream: buy cheap, sell high, forget the past 'cause it's dead and gone, chew up your brother till he ain't nothing but crumbs, smile big, dance real fast, fight their wars, and when in doubt, go white."

"No!"

"You heard me!"

"No!"

The Reverend held his arms wide. "Well, I hear y'all saying the righteous words, but when I look at my brothers and sisters, I got to ask—how many y'all got a credit card burning a hole in your pocket? How many y'all use that credit card till you're so far in debt that every dollar you make you sending off to some white man like you all are his sharecroppers, and he's living up in the big house? How many y'all go to work every day and check your black baggage at the door, saying"—and he stiffed up and spoke with a whittled falsetto—"'Yes, Mr. Smith, I'm just so ashamed of how most black folks behave. It's truly an embarrassment to the rest of us' . . . ? How many y'all want to leave out the neighborhood and live up in Hyde Park, so you ain't got to see your black brethren suffering in the city, looking so darn much like . . . YOU?'"

Suddenly the Reverend clapped his hands to his mouth and, with his eyes wide, whispered, "Ooooooh. I get it now. I see. Y'all think Jesus was white. Ooooooh, you think Jesus was white? Children, what part the cross don't you understand? If you're in America and you think Jesus was white, then I'm here to tell you today, you don't understand the cross and you don't understand the color. If they string you up, if they hang you from a big old tree, if they ASSASSINATE you in the name of your brothers, then: You. Are. Black. Abraham Lincoln? Cracker most his days, black in the end. Young Brother Emmett? Black. All them dead Jewboys scattered through the Southland? Even them, black. Reverend King? Black. Malcolm? Black. JFK? Black. His brother in the kingdom? Black. The great-great-grandfather of my dearly departed wife? That man was black through and through, 'cause even though they all say he hung himself, I'm here to tell you that man was a child of God, and that man was assassinated. Bounty on his head from the day he was born!"

The Reverend stopped his pacing and faced them squarely.

"Listen, now," he said, "I know y'all think you're free, but your aspirations are gonna tell if you're free or not. If the mind ain't free, the man ain't free. And if *my* mind ain't free, then *your* mind ain't free, 'cause we was born just days apart. *Days* apart. How many thousand years man been on this bloody earth? Slavery was just last week!

"So don't be living the lie, chasing the dream, thinking some dead Negro done paid your bill. You ain't earned the right to forget! You ain't earned the right to live in the greenest pasture! You ain't earned the right to lay down with the lion when the kingdom ain't even come! Y'all act like Jesus is dead! Well, let me ask you this: Is Jesus dead in the ground? 'Cause I heard a rumor Jesus done rose up from the grave!"

A woman cried out, "He rose!"

"And how come he rose up out of that dark and nasty grave?"

"Tell me!"

"How come he said, 'Eat my body and remember me'?"

"Tell me!"

"And how come Jesus is so angry up there in heaven?"

"Tell me!"

"Because my Jesus, my Jesus is the original Negro, and he said, only I can pay the bill, but he ain't paid no bill for no Easy Street, he ain't paid no bill for no credit cards and mortgages up in Hyde Park, he ain't paid no bill so you can forget you was made in the image of God and THE SON OF GOD IS A NEGRO."

Now the Reverend stopped suddenly, plucked a pink handkerchief out of his suit pocket, and mopped his streaming face, and when he spoke again, his voice was conversational: "Now eventually somebody's gonna tell you Jesus ain't had no brown skin. And you know what you're gonna say when they tell you that? You're gonna say: If Jesus wasn't born no Negro, he died a Negro. What part the cross don't you understand!"

A woman in the corner began to stomp her feet, laughing with her arms raised. "Yes!" she said, and "Yes!" the Reverend said right back, leaning forward at the waist.

"Brothers and sisters," he said in a voice ratcheted high in exasperation, "train your hearts on Jesus!" Now the whole corner was risen up and dancing and the sprigs on hats shook and there was sweat streaming from armpits and the metal folding chairs were being scraped about on the concrete floor. Tears began to flow. The scrawny youth had resumed his position at the keyboard without anyone noticing, the music once again rolling out in brightly augmenting chords, rising and swelling through the Reverend's words as he said: "Let us close with the truth."

"Speak the truth!" they called.

"You ready for the truth?"

"Yes!"

"The black body is a temple!"

"Amen!"

"The white man's been trying to tear down that temple forever!"

"Yes!"

"God said speak the truth, but America's asleep, so we got to yell!"

"Amen!"

"Wake them up out of the dream paid for with black blood!"

"Amen!"

"Jesus is the lamb! He sacrificed himself so this broken world would wake up and see the truth! You ain't sleeping when you with Jesus, children, you're RISEN, you're standing in the light!"

"Amen!"

"So stand in the light with Jesus!"

"Only Jesus!"

"Jesus!"

Marie kept her secret for three years; she held it in her hands. The secret wasn't fear, though she was terrified when they decreased her hours at the dentist's office, so terrified she'd taken the news without dignity, dissolving into jittery tears in front of the white man in his white scrubs. And the secret wasn't shame, even though she'd had to go down to the Ohio Department of Human Services on Central Parkway and withstand the interrogation with the monotone caseworker, then the information session with all the other hangdog applicants, most too ashamed to look up at one another. She left with her first month of paper stamps and a mouth full of sawdust. Write the word "failure" on the contract of her life.

It wasn't any of that. It was pain.

She'd come home that day from the Human Services office intent on fixing the one thing she could: the apartment. She filled the tub with sudsy water and pushed a scraggly mop over the old wood floors, removed all their clean dishes and washed them anew, replaced lightbulbs, polished their old television, which got three channels, and swept the tenement steps. It was when she went to return the broom to its closet that her hands rebelled, maintaining an iron clutch on the handle. Staring closely as if she could peer beneath the skin to the bone and sinew, she detected a strange, altered sensation—her knuckles felt spongy and swollen, as if packed with cotton wool. She stood in front of the bathroom mirror and raised her hands up to see their reflection. Strange that they didn't look different, though the internal swelling beat with the beat of her inflamed heart. What was this? The strangeness didn't even have a name. It was like an infant, some newborn version of pain, something too fresh to know.

And then the building rattled with his approach: her boy was home, tumbling through the front door and trumpeting that word, that one word containing all the world's needs but never her own: "Momma!"

In the first scene of Allmon's tenth year, a girl dies in the cement garden. Her name was Gladys Gibbons, just a tiny little thing on the third floor opposite with skin the color of chalky, churned-up river water, a soft cheek and a pert ski-slope nose like a white girl's, maybe the kind with money. That nose made her a beloved pariah, as despised as she was envied by girls who didn't yet know what envy was. She had the stamp of difference on her face, and that stamp was a pass. The girls in her building put their hands to the skinny vale between her shoulder blades and shoved. Knocked her against banisters, into doors, down onto cracked sidewalks and onto her knees. She thought: I'm ugly. And there was no grown person to tell her otherwise. So the wind of natural confidence died.

A decent man knows how to comfort a wounded girl, but there's a kind of man who only wants the wounded, who can only desire the flagging child. A loved girl is bright like a lamp, and he'll fear that incandescence. But this girl: the one who thinks she's ugly, whose shoulders sag, who looks down more than up and never meets the eyes, the one who wears hurt like old clothes— she's soft and needful, penetrable. You don't have to work very hard to get inside a child like that. And you don't have to wait very long for her to hug you back, for her to parrot your words, for you to believe you're welcome inside. You'll be the lucky first to tell her what the world means by love.

Gladys ascended the back stairs, one after the other until that brief road ended, and she didn't pause to look down but stepped off the roof, twisting at the last, so she fell backward down. How high is too high? Forty feet. Allmon had just stomped out of the dank vestibule of their stairwell when she fell. She landed in front of him like a sorrow dream in daylight, faceup on the concrete, the back of her head flattened where her skull had broken and collapsed. Her lips twitched. Allmon lurched back into the shadow, swayed there like someone hypnotized, then turned and walked with wooden limbs up the staircase, seeing hearing saying thinking nothing until he was standing in the warm familiar mother world, his face blanched.

From many worlds away, he heard his mother's voice. "What's wrong, Allmon?"

No word, he pointed there there there over there her body was there, twitching like an electric wire, her eyes still open, black pupils busted to red sclera, staring at him. Oh God Oh God Oh God Oh God his mother's scream, it rose and fell, and then his own wail dashed over the edge of his teeth, and Marie's scream was another woman's and another's, so the building was filled with screaming, and the stairwells beat their panicky rhythms, phones shrilled, sirens came spiraling over the viaduct, and his sweating mother was scooping him up, even though he was awfully big now, and folding him in half against her body as she sank onto the linoleum floor, saying, "Don't look! Don't look!" He tried not to look, but the memory of the dead girl was falling up, she was slipping into the scream stream.

"Oh," said Marie, and it was such a groan, like childbirth. "Oh God, how can you let a girl hurt so bad . . . God, why can't you protect the little children?" And then, as if the words came from another person: "Fuck this world!"

Allmon hid his head from the cursing.

Her voice belled with a righteous anger. "There's a war on women in this world! They're killing us left and right, and when they don't do it with their own hands, they do it with ours!"

"Momma—"

"At least they'll know now! Allmon, you got to go out with a bang if you want to send a message to this world! Make it so nobody can look away!" Then her words bent into a moan, and he could feel her huffing breath on his face. Allmon reached for her hand without looking, brought it up to his face, covered his eyes with her fingers pressed tight together. He didn't hear her gasp from the pain of her swollen joints wrenched up in his grasp.

"Don't look, please don't look," she said uselessly and too late.

He nodded but didn't answer; inside he was busy passing his mind away to a sure set of hands that tucked it and ran. There was no goal, it just got farther and farther away until he couldn't remember to watch for it anymore, and then the watcher was asleep.

Marie's heart hurt, and it was no metaphor. There had been tinges and winces of pain, but when the muscle suddenly seized, it did so with such force that it sent her doubling onto her keyboard at work, blasting out nonsense letters, a message from the place she was going. She grasped instinctively at her chest as if she could wedge her fingers behind her ribs and cradle the offending organ in her hands. She rocked and moaned but was unable to utter a word. Searing pain steals language.

In a moment, the dentist's arms were a band around her shoulders and she recognized the crude, jarring sunlight of the front vestibule. Then—in front of God and everybody—she was half carried, half dragged on a halting journey across two city blocks to a Northside doctor. She was dimly aware that she looked like hell and knew her mother would be horrified; as a girl, she wasn't allowed out of the house with so much as a wrinkle in her homemade skirts.

Down the pain-crowded corridors of her mind, the dentist's voice echoed, "I think she's having a heart attack," and some female in return: "We need to call an ambulance." Only then did Marie struggle back into herself, pain overmanned by panic, to bellow, "No!" Then she was bent again, huffing, "An ambulance cost . . . a thousand dollars . . ."

Then she was seated and falling forward until she could fall no further, and she knew the doctor was with her, because she was leaning against his white coat. When he spoke, she groaned, and when he probed, she groaned again. With the whole of her being, she wished her mother were here to hold her.

When the coat spoke, its voice was warm, mellifluous, calm, unaffected. "Her oxygen is fine, and women don't usually have heart attacks with these symptoms. My guess is pericarditis, possibly gallbladder, but we'll need some X-rays. See how leaning forward eases it? That makes me think pericarditis. A dose-pack of prednisone should bring down the inflammation."

"Well, that's good," said the dentist.

"Interesting fact—the heart continues to grow throughout life. It's not much bigger than your fist."

"No kidding," said the dentist. "Your fist, huh."

Her mind jolted round with a fresh pain. Two white men were watching her sweating like a pig with her body all wrenched up. No, her mother would not stand for that. Get up, Marie. Get up right this second and look smart! She struggled to mobilize her pain into action, but she simply could not.

"Marie, is this the first time this has happened?" said the doctor. "Do you have a history with this?"

She shook her head, dazed tears slipping soundlessly down her cheeks. Her shame was now total.

"Anything else I should know about?"

In the strict economy of pain, she made a small, terse gesture with one hand.

"What does that mean?"

"They hurt."

"Your hands hurt?"

"All over. All the time. Every joint in my body hurts."

"Ah, is that right," he said. It was a long sigh, the sound of new understanding, and it made her feel suddenly, prematurely safe. Pain was a lock, and surely this doctor held the key. Suddenly, she didn't want the man to take his hands off her shoulders; she didn't care if she looked like hell. Her momma would just have to deal with that.

"This is sounding autoimmune. I think you'll need to see a rheumatologist, someone who specializes in inflammatory and rheumatic diseases."

She whispered, "Any take . . . low income?"

"I honestly wouldn't know about that."

Her momma, Claudia Jeane Rankin Marshall, daughter of Momma Rae, painter of nails, braider of braids, curler of bangs, the one who made her look smart, was trying to cover her mouth, but she struggled away and said, "All I have is seventy-five bucks. I need help."

Oh, Marie. How could you?

"I can give you prednisone," the doctor said with that warm, mellifluous, calm, unaffected voice. "But that's really all I can do. I'm just a doctor. I didn't make the system and I can't change it."

They made you memorize it for gold stars, even before you could spell the words, even if you were the king of Capitoline Elementary, high on your limestone throne with your pencil scepter in hand and your crown perched on the out-of-bounds Afro your grandfather despises. Allegheny, Monongahela, Beaver, Little Muskingum, Muskingum.

He could just see it when he was twisted around at his desk like so, his chin almost on his shoulder. There it was: muddy, milky, marvelous brown. Little Kanawha, Hocking, Kanawha—

"Almond—sorry, Allmon. Allmon."

Guyandotte, Big Sandy, Little Sandy. Did they still have names once their bodies entered the body of the big river?

Two gentle hands—on the king?—pulled him round, though he came slow and with much resistance as if there were rust on his hinges, and his head turned last to look blankly at Frau Meier. With a start, he realized all the other children had left the room; the day was done.

Scioto. Little Scioto. Little—

"Allmon, you're not in trouble. I just want to have a little chat." Frau Meier's blonde pageboy curled tight under her chin, and the irises of her eyes were two different colors. "I've just been a little concerned about you lately. Where do you live? Are you and your mom up here in Fairview Heights?"

"Northside," his mouth said, but his ear was watching the river as it wound through the green-grass hills of Kentucky—the river like a snake. Little Miami next.

"Ah, Northside." She sighed, nodded, looked down; she didn't appear surprised. "I drive through Northside every day on my way to work. I always think of it as less a neighborhood than a collection of bars and used-furniture stores. It was a wild part of town back in the day. Do you know what they used to call it? Helltown. Because it's where men would go to . . . well, drink after work, I guess."

Allmon looked at her blankly.

"What does your mother do down there?"

He shrugged. "Sleep on the couch." Licking, Great Miami.

Frau Meier's laugh was a hiccup—a proper laugh aborted by the solemnity of the child's distracted face. She leaned toward him earnestly.

"Allmon, I'm very concerned about this story assignment you wrote."

He tried very hard to corral his attention and draw it round to his teacher. She was holding the story he'd written about the little girl who fell—a true story! With a touch of embellishment, of course. Still, he sought the Salt River and wondered how someone could paddle a river of salt granules.

" 'Gladys lived up the top floor,' " she read. " 'A raper throwed her off . . . Who done that? . . . He be like . . . They be like . . .' " Her voice drifted. "Almond. Did you make this up? Did this actually happen?"

He studied her face and tried to discern his answer there—was he in trouble or not? He opted for the safest course: he gazed out the black-silled window, past the fossil-strewn embankment with its aluminum fencing, down the crumbling escarpments to where the Kentucky and the Green flowed anonymously past.

"You're not in trouble, Allmon," Frau Meier said again, and then, as if to prove the point, she permitted a silence to grow between them while she studied him, deciding her next move. She watched a tiny pulse beat madly under the skin of the boy's torqued neck. What was he looking at so intently?

"Well," she said softly. "You can only know someone as much as they let you know them. But this I can fix; *this* I can fix."

There was a rustling of paper and she pried the pencil out of his sweaty fist. When he dared a glance, she was scribbling something on the back of his story—pencil marks over the red marks showing through from the other side.

"First, verb-noun agreement. This is very important if you're going to learn to communicate properly:

"I am

"You are

"He/She is

"It is

"They are

"We are

"Allmon, it's never I be or They be or We be. No one will understand you if you say that."

He stared down at the paper mutely. He tested "Be" in his mouth, chewed on it, rolled it between his teeth. Suspicion centered between his brows. But the Green and the Wabash *be* there—not sometimes, not used to be. Always. *Always. Be.*

"From now on, I want you to look up every single word before you write it down. And I'm going to make that possible. This is my gift to you, Allmon. I've used this since I was in college."

Saline and Cumberland, don't forget those.

She hefted a red, hardbound dictionary onto his desk, marked and well thumbed, and even as she was slipping his story with its corrections between its thin pages, he was pulling it across the desk, drawing it into his chest. He was going to look up the spelling of the Tennessee River.

Frau Meier laid a staying hand, perfectly cool and white, over his. He stared at it. "The truth is I found your story very disturbing. There were things I'm not likely to forget. But I really liked how you wrote about all the funeral roses. You know, under all this mess"—she made a wave of her hand to encompass his spelling, his be's, the whole of his talk—"there might be a poet in there."

Then she was rising, towering over him, releasing the king of Capitoline Elementary, and he was standing up perfectly straight, even with the weight of the dictionary tugging him down. Heavy like a river.

I *am* not. I *be*.

Through the window, he caught one last glimpse of the Cache, which was indistinguishable from the Ohio, which imprisoned it.

Childhood is the country of question marks, and the streets offer solid answers.

An ungoverned wind, a bulldog wind, swung heat through the streets of Northside, cranking the dial for an early summer. Allmon got off the bus a few blocks from home, walked those streets at a half pace, wind brushing his cheek, tangling in his hair. He held his new prized dictionary to his chest. He delighted in the familiar—the trash was confetti, graffiti the truth, church steeples accusatory fingers, the winter-worn sidewalks cracks in the heart. The young hand draws fresh maps on broken landscapes. But the grown man tells tales too. When he says we didn't know we were poor, it's not the truth; it's code for my mother raised me right, she loved me and love is a shield. When he looks back on the Northside of his youth, his nostalgia is anger, and his yearning is hate. That's the building where the cops shot Raejohn, that's where I spent every summer night eating ice cream on the stoop. The old men were pickled on malt liquor, my mother was a warrior, up on Apjones I learned to drive in a stolen car, that's when you could walk through the hood and hear the Reds game the whole way—

"Young."

Allmon turned.

A man stood on the stoop of a row house on Chase, a beeper in one hand and a Pepsi in the other. He stood under the coping out of the sun, so at first Allmon saw only the glint of his gold ropes, but as his eyes adjusted, he noted the wide, full lineaments of a bold face, the thick nose and light green eyes—calm, cold, appraising—and turned on him.

Unhurried, on the low, the man said, "What you got there?"

Allmon tried to peer behind him into the house, into the clubhouse darkness where he detected the dampened, private sound of grown men's voices. His crew. But he couldn't see anything. He just said, "A dictionary," and hitched the book higher onto his chest.

The man's mouth half smiled. "Ah," he said, "we got a smart niggah up in here. You got a name, Smartie?"

"Allmon."

"What you eleven, twelve?"

"Nine."

"Oh, damn," the man said, and laughed a baritone laugh under his breath. "I thought you was older than that. You look older." The man licked his upper lip, then bit it and gazed up the street, squinting as if he were turning something over in his mind. Then he said slowly, "You know who I am?"

Allmon shook his head, and the man just grinned. "I'm Aesop. And I seen you running all over this neighborhood, all over this motherfucking place. That's some nice speed you got—you gonna play ball?"

Under that careful, watchful gaze, the child shrugged but blushed hard.

"You black, you tall, you play ball, right?"

Shrugging again: "Yeah."

"So you Marie's little man?"

Allmon's eyes widened in surprise. "Yeah."

Now the man leaned toward him slightly, his head cocked. "You want to make some rolls?"

"Huh?"

The man's mouth laughed like it was funny, but those green eyes were serious, steady, and sharp. "M-o-n-e-y. Spell it in your dictionary. You want to make some c-a-s-h?"

"Yeah," said Allmon, startled, an electric grin jolting across his face.

"Then I got a proposition for you, Smartie. But first I got to see how you run for me."

"Run? Like now?" said Allmon, the meaning whipping right past him.

"Yeah, all right. Like now," the man said, laughing in his throat, his tone half-mocking as he glanced behind him into the shadowy building.

When he turned around, Allmon was gone. He had taken him at his word and sprang away from the stoop with impulsive delight, clutching the red book as a marathoner's bib and tearing down the street, leaving only the impress of his speed in his place. He was going to run over to Mad Anthony, down to Knowlton, then back up Fergus to Chase, where the man would be waiting, where the man would say, "Young, you mad quick," and then hand him a ten-dollar bill or something. He'd never realized how fast he was before this moment. Even with the dictionary at his chest, he was fleet, particular, his knees pumping in perfectly timed intervals. He was rounding the corner onto Knowlton, barely out of breath, when his foot slid on something and he nearly went down in front of a shotgun house, so he had to catch himself with one hand on the gate, crying, "Whoa!" but it was really more of a screech, a girlish sound, so he looked around, abashed. When he took a step, his shoes clicked. He limped around the corner of the black wrought-iron gate, so he could stand on a patch of grass, out of the brilliant afternoon light. With the dictionary perched on his hip like a baby, he twisted his leg so he could rest his left foot on his right knee and inspect the bottom of his shoe.

"Oh, dag," he said. Lodged into the sole of his high-top, which had come to him in almost perfectly new condition on a very lucky day from Goodwill, was a two-inch-wide curved shard of green glass. It looked like a piece from a Mountain Dew bottle. With extreme care, so he wouldn't slice his fingers, he pried the convex glass out of his sole. Then, after carefully inspecting the curious gradation of green along its sinuate edge, he flicked the shard out into the street, and just as he was about to turn back, just as he was easing his leg from its awkward position so that he could properly balance his weight on both feet, and he was wondering whether the man would still give him money, a woman appeared on her tiny porch, pointing at him, her face cinched up with hate.

"Nigger, get off my lawn!"

He sprang back in shock before his face even came round. At first, all he saw was her mouth, a rictus of scorn. She didn't know him, but then she seemed to realize his age, and some contrition, or the ghost of contrition, arose there. He saw it in her eyes. But her finger still trembled with accusation in the air.

Before thought, before decision, his body took off at a frightful pace down Knowlton. *Nigger.* He ran with his mouth open and the dictionary clutched to his *nigger* chest. Across Langland without looking to either side, then Hamilton, where he had to dodge one car that screeched, the driver jerking forward with her palm to her chest. He came sprinting up to the apartment, on the back side of the block up to the building where Gladys threw herself off the top, round the side of the building and someone who knew him called out his name hey *nigger* why you running, God there was trash everywhere why didn't anyone use trash cans white folks did then three guys standing out front the building in conversation he was normally afraid of them but today he cried "Move!" and they laughed uproariously as he runs up the stairwell in through the front door slams it wakes his mother they think she's *a nigger too* sleeping on the couch in the middle of the afternoon, Allmon! she says, Can't you respect I'm sleeping? He has to pee so bad it stings but he can't do it can't go into the bathroom where you can look into the mirror at yourself he just stumbles into the bedroom where there's no light on and there's no windows so when he shuts the door and feels his way to the bed he lies down his blood is up flying he's still running his legs spasming he lays his migraine head on his pillow for rest he's a crier not anymore he is not crying—he reaches out snaps on the bedside light shocks the room and opens his new dictionary smudged and leafed by the white lady's hands flips through the pages for what he is looking for and reads niggler niggle nigging niggery niggerwool niggerweed niggertoe nigger-shooter nigger pine nigger in the woodpile nigger heaven niggerhead niggergoose niggerfish nigger daisy nigger chaser nigger bug nigger baby and finally there it is *nigger*: to divide by burning.

In the morning, when his mother said, "Allmon, why are you looking like a zombie?" he had a one-word answer at the ready, but it pooled like hemlock on his tongue. He couldn't open his mouth or it would spill out.

He made a halfhearted gesture toward school, taking up his backpack and leaving the apartment, but he just circled the block with its cement heart, and when he was sure that Marie had dragged herself to work, he climbed the stairs again, unlocked the apartment door, and lay on the couch for four hours straight. He stared at the television the entire time, watching horses run in meaningless rounds. He didn't get up to eat or even pee.

Then at one, he rose and left the apartment, waiting no more than a minute on the corner before the number 17 bus came drafting up. He was undersized, dishevelled, and groggy, so the driver looked at him askance, but took his change and with some kindly misgiving said, "You all right?" Allmon just nodded, his eyes flat.

In fifteen minutes he was downtown, standing on his grandfather's stoop, pressing the bell repeatedly and with such force, the color drained from his fingertip.

It was the Reverend himself who answered the door. He looked down at the boy in honest surprise, his nostrils flaring once, and said, "It's a weekday. How come you ain't in school, boy?"

Allmon had no words of excuse. He just stared ahead, not daring to look up into the Reverend's face, only at the buttons on his shirt. His lips formed an inscrutable line.

"Well, get in here," said the Reverend, and reached forward and cuffed the boy lightly on the back of the head, where the skull sloped to the neck. He came into that old house, which smelled like the decay of another century and like the lives of men when there were no women around. It was the smell of work, loneliness, boredom, and old books. And of cheap food pitifully prepared.

Then he was in the parlor, then he was at the vinyl couch, sinking, offering up his weight to the first thing that would hold him. He curled half on his side with his hands pressed flat against his chest, his slim legs tucked up. Boy as turtle.

"What on earth . . ."

Allmon could not reply, his tongue was thick and risen against his soft palate as if something were choking there. On his face, an old riddle was working itself out. The Reverend loomed over him, his thorny presence a comfort: the penetrating stare, drawn brow, the perpetual climate of mild irritation on the old man's face.

"Boy." In the Reverend's voice, the first leavening note of concern. He took stock for a moment. Despite the appearance of surprise, the Reverend wasn't surprised, not in the deepest parts of him. He was a man who had come to expect the worst, who had learned to almost enjoy the arrival of disasters, because those things tested ultimate faith, and he had that in abundance. He distrusted ease, which was the bedfellow of sin. Of course, there had always been the suspicion that a day would come when the boy would show up half-broken about something. Because the boy was too tenderheaded by far, just like his mother.

"Don't cry," the Reverend said, but he sat down heavily beside the boy and, with a gruff hand, patted him twice on the behind. It was his brand of gentle. "Sit up," he said.

Allmon didn't sit, but he rolled further onto his side with his knees still pinched up. His face, always preternaturally mature, appeared ashen and old with the look of no blood. That did not surprise the man either.

"Now," said the Reverend. "Now . . . I know what's pressing your spirit down. You're sad your momma's sick."

Allmon's heart stopped in his chest.

"I don't know, child," the Reverend said heavily, and scratched at the white stubble sprouted along his jawbone. "They call it lupus or rheumatoid or what have you, call it what you want. But I say, autoimmune? You're talking to a literate man! I know what the word means!—means your body's tearing its own self down. Now, if your body's tearing itself down, only reason is because you ain't tended the body, which is the temple of the Lord, the vessel. If you give the body care, the body will flourish, and that's the truth. Only person can tend that body is you." He jabbed the air with a pointer finger like a man poking angrily at dying coals.

"But what can you tell a woman? A woman thinks she already knows everything there is to know about feeling, about emotion, like she got a monopoly on the whole enterprise. I should know: had one wife and one daughter, both stubborn as mules. Show me the woman that leaves a man some breathing room, acknowledges he might know a thing or two about the human heart, and I'll show you a rare and happy man. Your momma, she don't listen to nobody. Oh, she acts like she do, but she don't. Her life's her own fault; you run with stupid white boys, you gonna get the horn and then some."

He crossed his arms over his chest, leaning back slowly against the creaking sofa.

"Your momma was always wanting pity. Acting like she couldn't get enough love from this corner and that corner. That ain't how you earn respect. When you don't love the self, which the Lord hath made, then the self goes out looking for pity, because it don't know the difference between pity and love. But let me tell you here and now—pity, that's just the poor country cousin of love. There ain't hardly even a family resemblance."

The Reverend said slowly, almost under his breath, as if it was an after-thought: "Autoimmune, huh. I tell the truth: destroying your own self."

In a small voice, stripped of emotion: "Momma's gonna die?"

"Not if she gets herself together she won't."

Allmon squeezed his eyes shut, and a sudden, severe fantasy was born with all the devouring force of a blue fire sucking oxygen. If Momma dies, Daddy'll come back. Will he recognize me? Desire bloomed in him.

The Reverend sighed and looked up at the cracked, watermarked ceiling and the dust motes swimming in the yellow light. He said, "I ought to send your behind back to school." But then he said, "He giveth power to the faint and strengthens the powerless. Even the youths shall faint and be weary, and the young shall fall exhausted, but those who waiteth for the Lord shall renew their strength; they shall mount up with wings like eagles; they shall run and not be weary; they shall walk and not faint." Then he sighed loudly. "Be not afraid," he said. "Let's you and me go for a walk. I'm old, but I ain't too old to walk my own city."

He poked Allmon in the shoulder blades until the boy stood there half-lidded with his shoulders sagging. He looked as if someone had poured half the spirit out of him, like the flies were about to settle on him. He'd grown quite a bit since the last time the Reverend had seen him, which was just two months. Was he ten now? Within a few years of looking like a teen-ager, and that filled the old man with an apprehension born of things he remembered all too well. He wouldn't ever forget that bleak and confusing time, when the world began to see a colored man in the body where a child still resided. And the child begins to feel the change—not in himself so much as in the very air around him.

"Come on now," the Reverend said gruffly. "Let's get out the house."

The pair walked through the city as the afternoon began its languid westward slide, a small breeze boring up toward the east. With the hills on three sides, the city rose around them—brownstones and tenements re-placed by the towering heights of skyscrapers, their mirrored windows re-flecting only one another. As they were crossing Main and Ninth, where traffic grew heavier, the Reverend took up the boy's hand and held it. They were two tiny figures walking on an ancient floodplain, though the river was obscured. They meandered past cars with horns blaring, men in suits, women steering shopping carts, watchful police. There was a ball game in progress and occasionally they could hear the roar of the crowd in the coliseum. At one point, the Reverend bought Allmon a bag of roasted peanuts and said, "Now don't ask for nothing else. I ain't got no more money on me." Then they were passing the old fountain with her white hands frozen in welcome, and the river was imminent, they could smell it. The riverboats were honking, that fetish from the last century, chugging through the spooling eddies, old figures of expansion and promise.

When the pair arrived, they saw the river was gray and plain and polluted, greased with oil rainbows.

They walked the Serpentine Wall, the terraced concrete path that wended past the muddy shallows and the trash-strewn banks. The Reverend cracked the peanuts, and Allmon plucked the meat of the nuts carefully from the shell. He was livening up a bit, there was some blood in his cheeks. Every now and again, Allmon stooped down and placed a halved shell on the concrete like in the fairy tale.

When he grew tired, the Reverend seated himself slowly on a concrete step, his knees cracking. "You probably ain't gonna believe this," he said, patting the concrete for Allmon to sit, "but when I was your age, I got the gift for mimicry. I could do black folk and fancy white folk—just about anybody. Still can. But I choose to talk with the Lord's talk, because the Lord made me, and I ain't aspiring to nothing in this world." He cleared his throat. "I tell you what, though, I could make my momma laugh so hard she was fit to bust. She was always going on, how I was gonna end up onstage. In a manner, I suppose."

Allmon wasn't really paying him mind as he rooted in a peanut shell and crossed his legs Indian-style. He said absently, "This one time Daddy said that we was gonna—" But he felt the sudden stiffening of the Reverend beside him and promptly clamped his lips together. He drew his father back into him, as if sucking in a white smoke.

They both looked out across the river now, where the late sun was flinging glass shards of light, all spangling briskly. Light popping here and there without sound. Waves swinging.

Allmon said, "The river's like a big piano playing itself."

"Huh," said the Reverend, peering into the distance. He thought of Scipio, wishing he could picture his forefather's face, but there was nothing to picture. He felt a flash of the old anger. Nobody talks about a suicide; it grinds generations into the soil of time. That kind of dying tells a tale bigger than one man, and people ought to talk about the how and the why.

Across the river stood the historic rows of Covington and Newport, the staunch antebellum houses glowing in the coming evening. They were proud and stately and serene. White as eyeballs rolled back in the head.

"Who lives in those houses?" Allmon said.

"Funny," said the Reverend, not really answering, "how the best homes, they're always on the bloodiest ground. But then if your body's all covered with ugly scars, I guess you're gonna put on fancy clothes and try to fool everybody."

"You ever been over there?"

"I ain't been across that river in over ten years."

" 'Cause you scared?"

"Huh?" said the Reverend with disdain, and looked at Allmon like he'd lost his mind. "I ain't scared! It's the principle of the thing. Lord have mercy." He wiped the offended lines from his forehead and said, "When I was just a tad bit older than you, I was coming up from Arkansas. I was already knowing a thing or two, so when I crossed that river, I just said, 'Devil, get behind me.' I'm talking about the principle of the thing."

Allmon said, "A bunch of white folks live over there, huh." Mike Shaughnessy was heavy in his mind, and the sudden surge of longing was overpowering. He looked down as though searching the ground for something.

The Reverend was watching his face, he saw the slide into memory written all over it—the minute lift of his brows, the way a face looks when it's reaching.

"You know how I know God exists?" said the Reverend suddenly. "Because I need him bad even though he ain't around to see." Allmon looked up sharply. The old man had struck a blow to his private heart. He blinked rapidly.

"See, the human, he knows what perfect is even though he ain't never gonna find a perfect thing on this earth. Now, understand, I done spent my whole life chasing justice. But you think justice is here on earth? Child, I don't see no justice." He swept one hand before him, as if he were putting those fancy white houses on display. "But I know justice is real and perfect, and it's another name for Jesus, and I give my whole life to him."

"But Grandpa," said Allmon slowly and with misgiving, "then how come Jesus let all the bad situations happen?"

"Justice ain't done that."

"But how come Jesus ain't never stopped it?"

" 'Cause justice, that's a perfect thing, but justice can't make a human being do something or not do something. Jesus ain't gonna force your hand. He just lives in you like a hope and shows you what he looks like every day, and you get to decide if you're gonna make your life look like justice, even though you can't see him nowhere, or if you're gonna make your life look like fame or fancy things or money and whatnot. Now most people, they choose fancy things and money, because you can see all them, you can hold all them in your hand. But all them things you can't see is what matters most. They live in the mind and the heart. The perfect things, like justice."

"But if it ain't even here, then how you know it exists?"

"Because the lack, child! Lack's the most real thing there is! My wife is dead, but she's real, and don't you know I feel the lack!" He struck his chest with his fist. "You ain't gonna miss something that don't matter or ain't never had the possibility of existing in this world."

Allmon turned his questioning face away from the river flirting with light, his eyes stinging with unsummoned tears. When he closed them, he saw worse things, much worse, than he wanted to see. He opened his eyes and said, from a wound more powerful than longing, "I don't like Jesus. He don't care about nothing."

"Hush!" said the Reverend disdainfully. "You ain't even listened to a word I said."

Allmon glowered.

Then, without warning, the Reverend was praying. "Dear God, look at this child growing. Being a man is a heavy, heavy burden. Help his heart, Lord Jesus. Help him be not afraid. Help his heart to justice, even if the road gets rough and he's got to drag a cross to Calvary. Bless all the little children, even the ones that don't know you yet, Jesus. Amen."

Without opening his eyes, he nudged Allmon. "Say a prayer."

Allmon said, "Who—what? Me?"

"Who else you think I'm talking to?"

"I thought you was talking to Jesus!"

"I'm done talking to Jesus! Now I'm talking to you!"

"Oh."

"So say a prayer."

"Oh! Uh . . . ," said Allmon, and after a considerable pause, he said, "Thank you for the peanuts and the river. Thank you, God, thank you, Jesus, thank you, Martin Luther King."

"Ha!" cried the Reverend, and coughed down a laugh. "Yes, thank you for the river! Long as you living, Lord, the river ain't never gonna dry up, 'cause the river of justice always flows. Amen . . . Say Amen."

Instead, Allmon said, "Grandpa, I don't want to grow up."

What could the man say? With Kentucky before them and the city behind them, he couldn't find consolation. His heart was full. "Just say Amen," he said gruffly.

"Amen," said Allmon dutifully, but his eyes were open, and he was already looking behind him for his trail of peanuts.

Back through the city they came without a word. It seemed an even longer walk on their return trip, or perhaps the Reverend was simply tired from the long day, from too many long days. His footfalls, usually so martial and direct, were heavy and slow, and Allmon found himself slowing his own tempo to match. Now and again, the Reverend would stop entirely and gaze up into the flagging sky, where tiny flecks of unmoored cloud skittered here and there. Dirty night was on the eastern sky like soot on the hem of a blue skirt. The easterly breeze was gaining strength now, ushering the day's odors out of the city and sending bits of litter kiting along the pavement.

The Reverend passed a faltering hand down his shirtfront. "Them peanuts made you sick?" he said.

"Naw," said Allmon, squinting up at him.

"I don't know, I don't know."

They passed municipal buildings, parking lots empty of the day's cars, and buildings built just before the Civil War. Allmon peered into the bars and storefronts they passed, but the people inside didn't notice him or his grandfather, because the evening light made a dazzling show on the plate glass, rendering them invisible.

When they had walked up the length of Sycamore and neared the rec center across from the School for Creative and Performing Arts, the Reverend suddenly said, "Let's sit," and eased his body down with an unsteady motion onto a low concrete wall. He leaned his dry, ashened elbows onto his knees. His thighs were thick and round like tree trunks, but the trees were shaking. Allmon saw this and it struck him severely, suddenly, filling him with alarm; it was like watching a grown man cry. He immediately sat down beside the Reverend, closer than he normally would have, so close he could smell the coconut oil in the man's hair.

"Reverend," a voice said, "how you doing? You all right?"

They both looked up into a face as round as a moon. It belonged to a young man with a livid white scar that ran from the corner of his left eye all the way down to his mouth, bifurcating the lip. His lashes were spiky and glossy and made a charming show of his chestnut eyes. He was leaning down toward the Reverend's face.

"Tired, young man," said the Reverend.

"Aw, all right," the man said, straightening up again. "I was thinking you was ill, the way you was sitting there."

The Reverend reared back in indignation. "I ain't been sick since 1973!"

"All right, Reverend, all right." The man laughed and offered his hand. The Reverend reached out—Allmon saw his hand shake too as if from shyness—and grasped up the man's hand in greeting. But he didn't let go. Looking up, the Reverend said, "Young man, I ever tell you guilt's something much, much worse than being under somebody's boot? I ever tell you that?"

With his hand held prisoner in the Reverend's, the man glanced up the busy street toward Liberty, then down toward the river, and grinned softly. He didn't attempt to extricate his hand. "Yeah, seems like I heard that from you before."

"And?"

The man sighed. "And you know I got to do what I got to do."

"Really, now?"

"And you know where I'm about to go soon's you let go my hand. If you ever gonna let go my hand."

They laughed, and the Reverend released him.

Those slightly wary eyes were warm when they settled on him again. "But you praying for me, Reverend."

"Of course."

"And I thank you for that. 'Cause I ain't got my mama to watch out for me no more."

"Don't thank me with words," said the Reverend. "Thank me by quitting all this. You know you're just playing right into their trap. You think this ghetto happened by accident? They use this ghetto like they use the police and the prison."

"Oh, I know they use the prison, right." The man chuckled ruefully.

"So, quit this then! Make your mama proud! Your mama walked with Jesus till the day her shoes wore out, and you know that's the truth."

But the man was just shaking his head gently. "Reverend, ain't you never heard you can't never go home again?" He smiled and then, with a shrug of the shoulders, he looked at Allmon and said, "Take care of this old man here. He all sorts of trouble."

"I am trouble," said the Reverend.

"See y'all later," and the young man moved on down Sycamore, limping slightly, adjusting his pale blue drawers, which peeked out from his jeans, but not looking back.

The Reverend watched him go, and when the man turned left into the heart of Pendleton, he said, "God bless and keep him, that man's already spent half his life on the new plantation. Unless he changes his ways, he's gonna spend his whole entire life under state control. Kids with nothing got nothing to lose." He looked hard at the four-story terracotta building across the street. His hand shook when he pointed. "You see that school right there? You know how many brothers was hiding themselves in tunnels under there trying to escape Kentucky? Levi Coffin lived right there, that's right. Tunnels and cellars all over this neighborhood. We figured how to get out the South, but we can't figure out how to get out their ghettos and prisons. But what you gonna do? If you can't burn this whole country down and start over, what you gonna do?"

He sighed and rubbed his brow. "Child, don't grow up and be no white man's black man. Don't grow up to be no . . . stereotype. God's given you all the raw materials, and I gave you all my tools."

"Come on, Grandpa," said Allmon, and he stood and tugged on the man's shoulder. The Reverend rose slowly, unsteadily, and when he reached out suddenly to right himself on Allmon's shoulder, his weight was a grievous thing the boy almost stumbled under. He looked terrible and drawn, almost unsightly. Not how a man would ever want to look on a public street.

"You gonna be sick?" said Allmon, trying to urge him along.

The man shook his head silently, but with a vaporous look in his eye, as though he wasn't really listening. They crossed the street but were moving slowly. When they were ten feet from the stoop, the Reverend said breathlessly, "Lord, I pray . . . ceaselessly."

Allmon was trying to be patient, trying not to drag him forcibly up the stairs and into the house. He said, distractedly, "How you do that when you talking and walking and stuff?"

"Because," said the Reverend, "I pray . . . with my body every minute . . . the day. How you treat the least . . . that's how you pray . . . Jesus' name . . ."

His voice drifted, and he stared down at the steps of his stoop pensively, as though they were a problem of philosophy he was trying to solve. He looked angrily at them, then longingly, then emptily. Then he proceeded to ascend them with a long moment spent on each. He leaned painfully on Allmon and panted audibly.

When they came into the dining room off the parlor, they startled the group of eight men who were current residents of the Reverend's halfway house.

"Hey!" said one from the midst of the group, rising from his chair, a napkin tucked into the collar of his T-shirt. "We wasn't intending to eat without you, but— Hey, Reverend, you all right? You sick?"

Allmon stood between his grandfather and the men around the table, and he held up one hand, even as he struggled to hold up the Reverend, barking in a voice he barely recognized, "Can't you see the man's tired?"

"But—"

"Y'all eat! Just leave him be!"

Whether stunned, or amused into silence by the little boy acting the man, they did as they were told, standing by as he hobbled the Reverend from the room. Someone said, "Well, goddamn."

They passed the tiny bedroom, where Allmon and his mother slept on an air mattress when they spent the night, they passed the pink-tiled bathroom, they passed under the hall bulb, which had not had a fixture since the 1960s. But just before the bedroom door, the Reverend faltered, then stopped altogether and leaned away from Allmon against the cool, uncompromising wall. "I just figured it," he said, and he placed both his hands gently on the wall as if it were a soft and lovely thing and not grimy from years of neglect.

"What?"

"God is love . . . and when you worship love, you worship God."

Allmon reached out and drew him forcibly away from the wall and said, "You got to keep moving. The bed's right here."

It was like leading a blind man. Allmon could barely walk under the grievous weight of the old man's life, but he felt strangely emboldened and strong too. He was growing inches taller in his mind, even as the man was shrinking before his eyes, the thick knees buckling so he keeled sideways onto the bed. He sighed a sigh that sounded like crying and rolled over onto his back. "I ain't good," he said. His hand reached out. "Never a good man by nature."

He looked up at the dim ceiling, seemed confused, and then looked around, almost fearfully, as if he no longer recognized the room, until finally he found the anchor of the boy's wide-eyed gaze. "But the Lord . . . he used me anyhow," he said. "That's the miracle."

Allmon just stared into the depths of the man's eyes, which were recessed and recessing, unknowable. The man looked and looked at him as if he'd never truly looked before, as if the boy were a strange species coming suddenly into existence in front of him. His eyes were full of wonder.

"You look so much like your momma."

"No," said Allmon, too sharply, drawing back. "I look like Daddy."

The Reverend sighed through parted lips. He knew that the child didn't know what he had meant, couldn't understand the import. His chest clenched, nausea and exhaustion taking him over. Allmon held his gaze angrily and then two things happened: the Reverend closed his eyes in defeat, and Allmon seemed to understand he had won a victory at his grandfather's expense, and the knowing filled him with shame. He immediately reached out and placed his hand on his grandfather's chest and said, "Grandpa, you ain't washed your hands and feet. You can't go to bed all dirty."

"Mmm-mmm . . . ," said the Reverend, as if he were trying to speak through lips that had been glued together. Then he rasped out, "I been tired . . . since . . . forever."

"You got to get up and wash."

But the Reverend didn't reply, his brow creased, uncreased, creased and his left hand opened, closed, opened like a great bud trying to decide whether to bloom or not. The child was watching the changing weather of the man's large face with a rapt attention. The face wasn't paying him any mind now. He shouldn't have said anything about his daddy, he felt almost sick about that now. "You mad at me, Grandpa?" he whispered.

With effort the Reverend said, "I ain't . . . never been mad . . . a day in my life. No. The Lord, he just . . . been getting mad through me. He maketh the spirits his messenger . . . and a flame of fire his ministers."

For a moment, there was silence. "I ain't nothing . . ."

Allmon fought the urge to shake his shoulder. "You Damien Emerson Marshall."

". . . but a burning light," he said.

"But—"

"Ain't I said I pray ceaselessly?" he said upward with confused irritation.

"Don't go nowhere," said Allmon, though it was a silly thing to say; the man's body was weighted down by a weight heavier than all the water in the river. The nausea was easing somewhat, but he was indescribably tired. He'd had pneumonia once in the long-ago past and this feeling was not unlike that. But that sickness had been almost pleasant. He had worked on a sugar-beet farm starting when he was eight, but when he got the bout of pneumonia his father, Paul, and his mother, Jenny, had put him to bed for two whole months and fed him garlic soup and raisin biscuits. That child—the child he had once been—rested for two months from his labors. And then the labors returned, and they never went away again.

The man's mind was loose and roaming by the time Allmon returned to the room with a raggedy pink washcloth and a pan of water sudsy with Ivory soap. He moved as stealthily as a mouse, because he could detect motion behind the Reverend's heavy lids, the obscure, private motions of his eye-balls. But the Reverend wasn't asleep. He said, "Every day, Lord," accusingly into the silence, as though that silence itself had dared to question him.

Allmon took up one listless, heavy hand, which had fallen over the edge of the bed. Allmon placed the warm, wrung washcloth over the hand, and

the Reverend opened his eyes once and looked at the boy in blank curiosity; he didn't even seem surprised, only watchful, and didn't resist at
all. Carefully, Allmon scrubbed the long fingers and the swollen knuckles,
round and dark as buckeyes. Warm, wet across the palm to the wrist, which
bore the striping of years in wrinkles. Then he placed that unresisting
hand back on the bedspread and, picking up his pan of soapy water, circled
round to the other side of the bed. He repeated his task on the Reverend's
left hand.

Through this the Reverend's breathing was deep, calm, and even like
the beat of an easy heart. His eyes opened and closed occasionally, but
when his eyes were open, they were fixed on the ceiling cracks, crowded
with black speckling mold.

When he was done with the left hand, Allmon climbed up on the bed
on his hands and knees and untied the skinny black laces on the man's
dress shoes—he always wore dress shoes from Bakers—and pried them off
his large feet with some effort, followed by the socks. His grandfather's feet
were startlingly ugly, with deep, flaky calluses all around the edges of them,
the bony tops covered in risen veins like worms. His feet stank of vinegar, so
Allmon tried to hold his breath as he scrubbed around the flaking heels, in
between the toes and over the nails, which were ridged and thick and dis-
colored. He noted the wiry gray hairs on the topsides of the knobby toes.

When he finished, he returned the rag to the water and eased himself
slowly off the bed, so as not to disturb the man who had now fallen asleep,
and he took up the tray in both hands. He crept out of the room, turning off
the light with the tip of his nose. He considered saying good night, but didn't.

Now he was tempted to be lazy and just leave the dirty water in the pan
on the bathroom floor, but he expended the extra effort to empty the pan in
the bathtub, where the water swirled darkly away. Then he walked down the
hall to the kitchen, the bright lights reintroducing him to life. Two men were
still sitting at the dining table, which was just a metal banquet table, probably
a cast-off from the church basement. Allmon blinked in the fluorescence and
held a hand to his brow, and he experienced the strangest feeling that he was
just waking up, emerging from a deep and placid dream. The men seemed to
look at him strangely, as if they'd never seen a kid before and didn't know how
to behave in the presence of one. They appeared almost shy, but Allmon
wasn't feeling shy himself. There was power in him tonight.

One of the men cleared his throat and said, "The Reverend all right?"

"Yeah."

"You fixing to spend the night here, son?"

"Naw," Allmon said, but he must have sounded hesitant, because the same man said, "How you getting home? Gonna take the Metro bus?"

"Yeah," said Allmon, and made a move toward the parlor and the front of the old house.

"It's dark. Let me walk you to the bus stop," said the man, making a move to rise from his folding chair.

But Allmon felt beyond all that. He didn't even look at the man as he moved past him, saying only three words: "I ain't afraid."

The next morning, when the Reverend did not appear at breakfast, one of the men in the house ventured into his room and found him there with his eyes half-open, a glass of water spilled over the red Bible on the nightstand. He had died of a heart attack sometime in the night.

When Marie heard the news, she sat for a long time on the plaid couch without moving, whipsawed, saying nothing with her blanched hands pressing down on her hair. Then she stood and with no tears in her eyes, said, "Now we got nothing. Now we really got nothing."

She wouldn't let him go to the funeral; she didn't want him to see another body. So, lying on the old mattress alone, he made a list of who had left so far: (1) Daddy; (2) the Reverend; (3) Momma—she had gone off to the funeral but should have stayed, because he was still here, Allmon was still alive! A groundswell of original feeling surged upward from the very center of him, but he fought it with a clamping of his heart and pressed his palms to his cheeks until his face hurt. A headache formed along the tender contours of his skull, but he welcomed it. It was different from the Reverend dying, different from being abandoned. Still the Reverend rose up in the dim circlet of his pain and presented his stern, inscrutable face and his hand that opened and closed—now a bud, now a dark fist—and the ache set the child's teeth on edge, and then Mike Shaughnessy's pale face, all knife-cut angles, said, "I'm coming for you, because you are my son in whom I am well pleased." Allmon's heart finally gave in and, with abandon, he tasted the saccharine sweet of self-pity for the first time in his life, but without any sense of the bitter aftertaste to come.

She was standing over him, exhausted beyond endurance, her eyes dry ever since the disease had wrecked her tear ducts, and held a telescope and a bag of children's books in her hand. It was all she'd taken today from the Sycamore house, which the Reverend had left to the church. She had no idea why her father had even owned a telescope—he was a man who talked about heaven but trained his eyes on the earth, because heaven didn't matter, only the kingdom. While she stood the tripod by the bed, her son couldn't move, caught in the vise of his migraine, but the sound of her movements echoed down the hallway of his mind. Marie wanted to say, "I tried to protect you, but I can't do it anymore. All I have left is pain," and he wanted to say, "Please don't be sick," and she wanted to say, "His eye may be on the sparrow, but he must love me less than a little brown bird," and he wanted to say, "Don't ever leave me alone again," but all she said aloud was, "Allmon, now you've got to learn to love yourself more than me—by any means necessary."

In a moment she's asleep, and he's dragging the leggy Celestron to the front window that overlooks Knowlton's Corner and, using his own body-weight as leverage, he tilts the stiff black arm high, so when he peers through its narrow aperture he can see the sky. But he only catches the white street-light across the street, and in the transforming miracle of refraction, the light shatters into a rainbow of spectral color with no recognizable form. He rears back, spooked, but realizes it's only the streetlight—a boring white light boring into the boring dark. As if not sure what to trust, he peers and watches it explode out of itself again. His heart begins to beat loudly at the door of something: this light in the telescope is wilder, bigger than what he can see with his own eye. Had his art teacher not said white was the presence of all colors, that it contained all the visible world? Only now in this moment does the Reverend truly dim and die like a match going out, and in his stead the white grows deeper and more real. He's grieved and confused in this world where the stars are up and down, where everyone has fallen asleep, where his father doesn't come, where he stands in what he has no words to call the intermundane black between heavenly bodies. Up high, the moon sheds its small light for the world's unintended children. He remembers the word Scipio, and he thinks maybe it's the name of a star.

Seventeen months and three days after the death of the Reverend Marshall, a small white envelope arrived. The presence of Marie Marshall was requested at a pre-appeal disqualification hearing in the investigation of her involvement in attempt(s) to defraud the welfare system. Marie's mind balked—she didn't sell stamps, she worked her regular hours, never more, and she'd always been prompt, polite, showing up with her paperwork at her reevaluations and—

Oh shit, the car. The car that Mike had given her that she hardly ever used except to buy groceries in College Hill, because the IGA in Northside was so awful, the car that had sat there with Chicago plates in an unused alley two blocks away, unnoticed by anyone until a towing sign appeared, and she finally had to hustle up the money to reinstate her expired license and buy plates and insurance. She'd been unable to make the payments after a few months but kept the car for emergencies. You weren't allowed a resource worth more than $1,500. But what was she supposed to do? Throw away her only real resource? No, maybe it wasn't about the car after all, maybe it was some kind of technicality. There was no need for panic yet. She just needed to show up looking proper—her hair straight, clip-on pearls—and keep her damn mouth shut.

But showing up to anything was getting harder and harder. Work had become a farce of trying to look busy and efficient when she could barely function. It hurt her hands so much to type that sometimes she just cried at her desk. A consuming fatigue had filled her from the inside out, and no amount of sleep repaired it. Because her tear ducts had stopped producing tears, it felt as if acid were being poured on her eyes every moment of the day and night, all the thousands of nerve endings exposed to the air, her eyelids turned to sandpaper. She made just barely too much to qualify for Medicaid but couldn't afford private insurance—not that they'd insure her now anyway, given her current symptoms. Most of the time, she felt she'd been invaded by an alien. She didn't know how to get it out of her body since she hadn't allowed it in in the first place. It just arrived one day, like she was accidentally pregnant with her own dying. It was pain's version of the virgin birth—you never did it with death, but somehow he screwed you anyway.

The number 17 bus got her downtown by ten, and she only had to wait an hour in the loud, overcrowded lobby before being called into the windowless hearing room, but that was about an hour longer than her nerves could take. When they finally called her name, sweat rings had soaked through the lining of her suit jacket.

Two people sat behind a table—a black woman and a white man with a beard like Santa Claus. The white man was opening a three-ring binder, reading from something that looked like a script.

White man: Sit down.

(Defendant sits, smiles; tries to look innocent and calm)

Black woman: You've been called for this pre-appeal hearing—

Defendant: I thought this was my hearing.

Black woman: Let me finish, please. You've been called to hear the charges against you and respond if you choose to and begin preparation for the hearing, which will be held in five weeks' time.

(Defendant nods, compliant but clearly worried)

White man: We have reason to believe you've defrauded the welfare system by owning, but not declaring, a late-model vehicle. We know that you recently reapplied for a license and were fully insured on that date. Would you care to respond at this time?

Defendant: No! (turns to woman) I mean, no—listen, someone gave me that car! I didn't pay for it myself—I wouldn't have money to pay for something like that on my own! My ex gave me that car.

Black woman: So you own the car.

(Defendant closes her mouth, realizing her mistake)

White man: (clears throat) Ma'am, your hearing will be held in five weeks' time. Until then, your benefits will be suspended.

Defendant: My what? No, wait! (scoots forward on metal chair, turning from the man and staring earnestly into the woman's face) I've got a boy. I've got a very, very good little boy. I need to get those stamps or he doesn't get enough to eat. Listen, please, you need to believe me.

Black woman: This paper says you still work for Dr. Herman Bischoff in Northside.

Defendant: I do, but it's not enough hours. It covers the rent, and I can't hardly even do that! Listen to me, please—I am sick. There's something wrong with me. I know you don't understand, but you have got to believe me. I'm sick, and I can't do anything about it, because I'm broke, and I can't go to a specialist. I promise you, it's a fact. I've got nothing in this world right now! No parents, no brothers and sisters! I'm so sick I can't hardly work, but I can't stop working or what—or what? What are we going to do? Does the world just want us to roll over and die?

(Long silence, then the black woman looks down at the paperwork. The defendant, instead of crying, turns stonily to audience, proceeds monologue, barely audible:

Lady, I was looking at your face and I was trusting in the familiar, your plum eyes and wide nose. Your color. I thought it was a homing beacon, that brown—like it was saying, talk to me, I'm dark and lovely too, talk to me, my ears are open like God's ears are open, and I speak your language, because we're family.)

Black woman: Well, I don't know much, but I do know that if people like you would spend half as much time seeking better employment and education as you do crafting your stories, your children would be a whole lot better off. And that, Miss Marshall, is a fact.

(Defendant, still facing audience, concludes monologue:

I pray there's a God—and he disowns you, you black bitch.)

A long time ago, she had called out, I've got a surprise for you! Your daddy's coming home! But that was long, long ago—why was life so long? Now she called out with a voice that had lost even the memory of buoyancy, and her son came to her dragging his feet like he could intuit some imminent loss. He stood there before her, twisting on his legs the way he used to when he was younger, but he wouldn't look up. He directed his dread at her feet.

God, the twisting! It set Marie's teeth on edge, and she wanted to grab him, make him stop, force him to understand without having to say the words. Her eyes were burning with an acid that was driving her insane and, God, here was this child she had given life to and he had no sympathy for her at all, didn't know her at all; children thought only of themselves and their own needs. Love and resentment infected her maternal heart in equal measure. She wanted her own mother so powerfully then, more than she ever had. It was such a goddamned lie that time healed all things!

She just said, "We've got no more food stamps."

Allmon looked up at her in surprise. "How come?"

"That's not your concern," she said. "You're the child; I'm the mother."

He said nothing, but she saw him recede into the worried space behind his eyes. Where he had been twisting, now he just looked straight ahead. When her hand made a move toward him, he jerked away.

Her hand hovered in the space between them as she said, "We can't stay here. I can't afford it. We've got to get out by Friday."

"Where we going?" he said smally.

"I don't know," was the only honest reply.

Tears filled his eyes and he said, half question, half accusation, a word he had never said in her presence before: "You fucked up."

The involuntary strike of her open hand across his cheek coincided with her cry: "Don't you speak to me that way! I'm your mother!"

Then, like a bird, he was gone in an instant. But it was only when he reached his bedroom and slammed the door that his composure, so tenuous, shattered. He abandoned himself to the tears that really belonged to the Reverend, tears that had been dammed up for months. He cried and cried until there were no tears left and when he finally looked up with swollen eyes, the sun had slipped low and flung the room into shadow. The sounds of Marie's bedtime rituals were long past, so he rose. Then wall by wall, item by item, he worked to memorize every detail of the apartment, because he knew he would never be here again, and then he got down on his knees on the hardwood floor and prayed to his father, something he had never tried before. Please come. Please come this Friday and save us. And, balanced on the slenderest plank of hope, he waited on Friday for Mike to come—for Mike, for God, for anyone to save them, but nobody did come, because nobody does.

The only place to go was down—down past the useless, spinning wheel of Knowlton's Corner, down near the Mill Creek, which stank of feces and oil, down where the neighborhood disintegrated at its shiftless edges into Cumminsville, a noplace crumbling under the black shadow bands of the viaduct and I-74, where the houses were shambling, filthy, and few, over-shadowed by the behemoth brownfields looted of their industry, windows shattered by rocks and bullets, down into forgottenness where few families lived and the ones who did lived in decay, in the bowels of the city. What's worse than Helltown? This.

Marie and Allmon took up residence in a tiny shotgun on Blair, a narrow side street three blocks southwest of Knowlton's Corner. The tenant had just died of pancreatic cancer and the rent was $400, lowered a hundred dollars by the landlord—a distant cousin of the dentist Marie worked for. The house stood fifteen feet wide and three rooms deep: a dank front parlor and kitchen relieved only by a nicotine-browned window facing north, furnished with an orange, mildewed couch where Marie would sleep; a middle room, where Allmon would inflate a twin air mattress; and a bathroom in the back with a tiny square window that looked onto a tiny plot of shattered glass and nameless weeds. They had brought only what they could transport in the car, then the car was sold for two thousand dollars, and the money was gone in an hour, five months of rent prepaid. There was simply no way to move their old mattress or their dressers, which were left on the street and carried off by strangers. Allmon had brought his telescope, but he didn't need a telescope to know that they had reached the edge of the world.

Allmon stretched a polyester sheet across his mattress, taped a Bulls poster to the wall, then set the Reverend's telescope in the bathroom to train its eye up and out of the tiny window to see what could be seen. That first night the sun fell like something wounded, and a triumphant night came up in all directions.

Without his hearing, Marie stepped up behind him in the darkness of the room and with her gentlest voice said, "Allmon, I believe we're going to make this place a home."

Without surprise, without turning, without otherwise acknowledging her presence, Allmon said, "You believe what you want, Momma. I don't believe in nothing."

Hope and reality were at cross purposes. The new plan wasn't good or bad, just a plan. After school was dismissed, Allmon got off the bus at Chase and counted the doorways as memory dictated until he found what he hoped was the one, then he slipped around back and knocked on the rear door. There was no answer. He knocked once more, rapping hard, and when still no reply came, he stepped off the back porch, squinting up at the redbrick edifice, his hope flickering and dimming. "Come on," he whispered softly, but he realized it was probably a stupid idea anyway—kick the pavement, curse the sky, crawl back into the barrel of the shotgun—

"The fuck you want?"

He whipped around and detected dark bands of face through the pale slatted blinds on the eastern side of the building. He could barely mutter the words through his nerves. "Aesop around?"

"Get the fuck out of here."

"Hey." A deep, calm voice from a second-story window; Allmon recognized the slow sound immediately. He craned his neck and saw a shadow delineated by interior light. "It's cool. Come on up."

In a moment he was through that back door and ascending the stairs, gathering his courage around him like a shawl, the clay mineral smell of a basement almost overwhelming him, a damp cool suckered from last night's air. The creaking stairs led to a single wooden door, and he didn't have to knock; it opened away from his fist, and the man was standing there in a wifebeater and black Bengals sweats, a suspicious look on his face.

"Duckie sent you over here?"

"Huh? Naw." Allmon shifted awkwardly, staring at the doorframe, wishing suddenly he hadn't come, but then blurting out, "This one time, I was walking around here and you was like, 'You wanna make some money?' and I was thinking maybe—"

"Oh shit—Smartie!" And the man placed both his hands on the doorjamb and leaned back so the muscles of his biceps leaped under the skin, and he hollered laughter. "I remember! That was so motherfucking funny, I was like goddamn—you was running so fast! Yeah, I remember you. Like Carl Lewis and shit. Oh my God . . ."

At first Allmon couldn't tell whether he was the target of this laughter and his spirit quailed, but the man reached out, touched his shoulder once with a quick, guiding prod that was not unfriendly, and said, "Get on in here," so Allmon entered the apartment, and the door closed on his old life.

The man was still half laughing, but the laugh was no longer in his appraising eyes: "So now you back and you wanna make bank. How old you now?"

"Twelve."

"Damn, time fly! Why ain't you come back sooner?"

Allmon shrugged.

"What, you can't talk?"

He just shrugged again. "When I got something to say."

The man grinned slowly and glanced at his compatriot. "Respect, respect. Ain't nothing wrong with that."

"You think you maybe got something for me to do?"

The man lowered his chin fractionally, peered at him. "Maybe," he said, then his hands reached forward and clamped down on Allmon's shoulders. "You can run, you know what I'm saying. But not like *run!*" And he threw back his head and laughed, a laugh that bounded out from his belly with so much eruptive force that tears sprang to his eyes, and for the first time Allmon saw in that broad, cold face a real warming. He felt the gears of his own heart scraping into motion.

Aesop wiped a hand over his eyes to stanch his laughter and eased onto a plastic seat at the kitchen table, his legs splayed and his elbow coming to rest on the table. "Motherfucking funny," he said, and looked at Allmon sideways. He sighed and said, "When I'm like I need you to run Northside, I mean you need to run my shit. We cook over by the cemetery. You run from the factory to my boys, keep your eye on my lookouts, they let you know when the five-oh roll. But you got to work without drawing no attention to yourself. You understand what I'm saying? I don't want you to *run*, motherfucker. I need you all calm and walking around and shit. Don't be sneaking, don't be nothing. You got to look like a niggah with no purpose."

As he took in these words, Allmon's face was calm and only a slight twitching at the brow betrayed any fear. But there was no real surprise; his head might be trying to play naïve, but his heart had made its decision weeks ago, and his body had brought him here on that underground resolve, which registered only as a vague plan to make some money.

From the table before him, Aesop picked up one small vial and rolled it between his fingers. "You run good for me, you make like a hundred a day."

"For real?"

Aesop swagged his head, laughing with his friend and making mild fun. "For real."

Allmon just ducked his head, abashed.

"Listen, Smartie," Aesop said, and waited for him to look up. "You run hard, be sharp, you deal in a couple years. Then you make mad bank and chill on the corner, you feel me?"

"Yeah."

Then the man's face grew very still, his eyes hooded. He pointed at the table where his gun lay. He said, staring into Allmon's eyes, "This my piece, Southern Comfort. 'Cause it comfort the Southern brother." Then he grabbed at his crotch. "And this here my big dick. 'Cause it fuck all the white bitches. And that shit comfort the Southern brother too!" His eyes brightened and he laughed a raucous laugh and pointed at his friend in the doorway, who just smiled and shook his head ruefully with his arms crossed over his chest. Then Aesop turned to Allmon, suddenly serious again. "You think we all thugs? You think you a thug?" he asked.

Allmon didn't know what to say. So he said, "You gonna give me a gun too?"

The man scowled. "I don't need no schoolkid wannabe thug round here. I don't do stupid and messy, you feel me? I need smart niggahs. I know Marie ain't had no stupid kid. If you do math, know how to long-range think, understand psychology, all that shit, that's valuable to me, because I'm a entrepreneur. I run a successful business here. For real, I run this motherfucking hood, I govern. Fuck the police, you know what I'm saying, I'm the mayor."

Allmon nodded, but he was staring at that gun, at its cold black grace.

"So couple years, yeah, then you get your own gravedigger. But you too young for that shit right now. Ain't no need, just a accident waiting to happen. Now run hard. Be sharp. Who knows, maybe you be my accountant someday. Get all the bitches you want."

Allmon grinned.

The man leaned in. "But don't fuck with me, little man."

"Huh?" Allmon looked at him in alarm.

And then in the quiet voice that in one sentence would delimit his future and fence it tight: "Don't fuck with me, or I'll fuck everything you love. Every. Thing. Every. One. I'm the mayor and the mafia and the motherfucking love. Understand?"

Yes, Allmon understood, but he was already reaching out to shake the man's offered hand. He'd already decided that life was a gamble and his best odds were in this house.

Marie never left the shotgun anymore, except to go to work, and when she returned, she slumped on the couch with her face to its back and didn't move again unless she was forced to. She was beginning to miss more days than she worked, and she didn't cook anymore. It took all of her energy— every ounce of self she possessed—simply to survive the pain that had engulfed her life. The change was breathtaking. This wasn't the journey into adulthood she'd imagined as a young girl, the one that involved a husband and children. This was a journey with only one companion—illness—and it had taken from her everything that she understood as herself and replaced it with shattering pain.

Allmon carried on as best he could without her. He became the cook of the house, sticking to a plain white diet bought cheap at the IGA: potatoes, rice, white bread, corn, eggs, and milk. And while he cooked, while he playacted the normalcy of a steady home, he turned an increasingly worried, surveying eye on Marie. He began to discover thick clumps of her wavy hair in the shower. At first he thought, Probably straightening made it fall out, but he was kidding himself. Marie had straightened her hair once about a year ago and hadn't done it again. He noticed how she no longer painted her nails or wore lipstick or did any of the things he knew a woman did if her spirit was tilted toward the world of men. And now her hair was falling off her head, and he could see the ground of her scalp through what was left. What he saw was ugly, and he couldn't pretend it wasn't.

When he had saved three thousand exactly, he wrapped it in a rubber band and brought the roll to her, placed it on the coffee table. He said, "Momma."

Slow, slow, with enormous effort that made his stomach wrench with misgiving, Marie rolled over on the couch. Her eyes were red, raw, her face distorted by unmanaged pain, her hands like claws clutching at her collarbone. For a moment she squinted at the roll on the table, uncomprehending, then she looked right at him.

Her voice was scratchy but clear: "No."

Allmon reached forward and pushed the bundle toward her and nodded his head once, a stubborn assertion.

She shook her head. She shook it hard again and again. "Take that money back where you got it, Allmon, and don't ever let me see it again."

"Momma, you know I can't take it back."

Marie's breath hitched. He couldn't tell whether it was a gasp of astonishment or an aborted sob of a woman who'd long expected what was coming. Either way, she stared at Allmon through burning eyes and, despite the terrified pounding of his heart, enduring the stab of her complicated disappointment, he spoke up one more time. "It's enough for the doctor and six months of rent."

Marie began to cry and pushed the money off the couch onto the floor and rolled over on her side on the couch again. Although she wouldn't look at him or talk to him for two days, she didn't say no again.

Doctor: Marie, how bad is the pain?

Marie: It's so bad, I can't think anymore.

Allmon: She can't really open her eyes.

Doctor: Well, you came up negative for Sjögren's for now, but you really need to see a corneal specialist. These things tend to appear in clusters. Have you been using drops?

Marie: They only help for like thirty seconds. I feel like I've got acid on my eyes.

Doctor: How are you still able to work?

Marie: I don't have a choice. My bills . . .

Doctor: Well, I wish I could tell you more from your tests, but there are so many rheumatological diseases and it's not completely clear which one this is. We'll probably know more at a later date. It's normal for it to take a decade to show up more clearly in the blood.

Allmon: What's that mean?

Doctor: It means your mother has a lot of the soft criteria for lupus, but not the hard criteria. But we really don't need to worry about that. We'll treat the symptoms. The diagnosis isn't really important.

Marie: No! The diagnosis is important! I can't get disability without a diagnosis! I can't keep going—I need that diagnosis!

Doctor: Well, I'm sorry, but I can't give it to you. And, frankly, you probably don't want to mess with disability anyway. Even with a solid diagnosis, they almost always reject my patients the first couple of times, and it can take years to get through the appeals process if you get through at all. And that's with a lawyer who knows what he's doing. For now, we'll just get you on a cocktail of drugs and—

Marie: I don't have insurance.

Doctor: Oh. I see. And with these medical records, you're ineligible. Well . . . the only other thing I can suggest is that we get you started on prednisone. It's cheap and it works. Of course, sometimes the side effects of the drug can be worse than the disease.

Marie: There's nothing else?

Doctor: Not really. Lupus doesn't get much research. Mostly, colored women get it. There's really nothing else to do but take steroids. We're all still following a script that was written fifty years ago.

On the bus ride home, Marie leaned against Allmon with her eyes shut. Jostling next to him, she realized for the first time that the hard press of his shoulder blade was a smidge higher than hers. He was almost tall now, he might even grow to be six feet, but he was still too much the little boy, too much the child. Soft. That was her fault.

"Momma, I don't even know who I come from," he said suddenly, his voice cutting into her thoughts.

"What's that supposed to mean?" she said, without opening her eyes.

"I mean, I don't even know who Grandpa's grandparents was."

She sighed. "Allmon, honey, I can't remember their names right now. The Reverend was good at remembering that stuff, not me. You grow up and you forget things."

"See, that's what I mean!" he said angrily under his breath, and the edge in his voice surprised her. She steeled herself against the pain, then opened her eyes to look at him.

Allmon crossed his arms and continued, "You don't know who you are if you don't know where you come from."

"Oh, that's bullshit!" Marie snapped with genuine irritation. "That's just some black-pride *Roots* bullshit, and it's always some black man saying it. You show me a black man who knows a single thing about real pride and I'll give you a million dollars! Always thinking everyone hates them, always acting like thugs. Most white folks don't hate you, Allmon; they just don't care about you." She made a dismissive sound and waved her stiff, swollen hand. Then her own words slotted home, and she thought, *Maybe that's worse.*

"You ain't even listening to me," Allmon said sullenly, and turned away from her, looking so much like the little boy he used to be—hooded eye, puffed-out lip—that it caught her breath. She felt the whooshing of time like a physical thing speeding past her and wanted mightily to turn and hold her baby boy, her little lamb, say everything's going to be all right. But she couldn't. She closed her eyes again and sat up straight on the pole of her spine. She breathed deeply and said, "Allmon, you think you need to know about the past? Why? 'Cause you don't know enough about hurting yet? You think you need to know how your great-great-great-grandfather Scipio got himself out of Kentucky only to hang himself? Really? 'Cause I think staring down the past won't get you anywhere. You need to grow up fast. Focus on the here and now. I want you to take that test and get into a good magnet school. And listen to me now: Whatever happens, I don't want you hovering over me, you understand? I don't want to see you crying or carrying on or dropping out of school. Become a doctor or lawyer or something. I let you get away with being soft for a long time, but that's over. Now you've got to be a man."

He refused to look at her lest he cry. "Yeah, Momma."

"Yeah, okay, then." And she leaned away from him into the cold of the bus window, where the condensation dampened the flushing fever on her cheek.

He did as he was told; he rounded up what remained of his boyhood and forced it into a shadowy pocket of his heart. It kicked and pounded for a while, but he closed his ears to it and his spirit soon evanesced into wounded silence. Instead, he studied on Aesop (caps, glocks, swagger, wit, threat, diamond signet ring on his pinkie), who his mother didn't know a thing about, but then she didn't know anything about being a man, what it was to be in your body, how you were born into obligation. A man's whole life was a haymaker. So he continued to run in the afternoons after school.

Sure, you weren't supposed to lie, to cheat, to bribe, to hit, to sneak. But increasingly, the world of rules was being shown up for what it really was, a rigged system, a fixed game. You should be good, definitely—but only until you couldn't, until everything you loved was on the line. It just made him want to kill someone if he studied on that too hard. So the key was to not study on the truth—the madness in the center of everything that was called common sense in a white-ruled world.

Relax, Allmon. Relax, loosen your mind, free your body, it's lunchtime. That's when they let you out of the classroom, and you run silly and wild on the blacktop basketball courts, because you're still a child even with your fourteenth birthday only weeks away. Your feet pound the pavement, you flail your longish arms, impressed with their new wingspan, you discover the interesting ways you're growing into your body, just like you discovered the secrets of your right hand a few years back. Yeah, sure, maybe you got an average face, an average dick, but wonders never cease, and the best ones come from inside you. You feel smart realizing that, then Keeo's talking shit—that kufi-wearing motherfucker never knows when to quit—and there you go, the two of you kicking across the court in a madcap fifty-yard dash, and you own him, you tear him up like a paper curler, reaching the chain-link fence five feet ahead of him and barely sweating, just taking your air in fitful bursts.

Suddenly, there's a white man in your face and you rear back, startled.

"So you're Allmon Shaughnessy," the man said, holding a clipboard against his chest and staring you down. His drawl was surprising—thick, like beef stew over biscuits.

"Yeah," said Allmon, trying to recover himself, trying to look cool. He realized now where he'd seen the man before; he'd been at their gym class last week, talking to their teacher and watching them run.

"So, Allmon," the man said, "tell me something. Were you going all out just now, or were you holding a little something back?"

"Naw . . . ," Allmon said diffidently, trying to rein in the uprush of pride, "I don't got to go all out 'cause ain't nobody here can beat me."

The man smiled with one side of his mouth. "That's what I thought. Listen, I'm about to offer you some free life advice: when you're headed toward the goal line, you go all out every time. Every single time. No matter who you think you've got beat." He looked at him with an evaluating eye. "Because you never know when you've got some big white defensive end right on your ass."

It was a gamble, and Allmon was surprised for a second, but then he grinned, a little abashed, and the man grinned in return, watching him closely all the while.

"Where are you going to high school next year, Allmon?"

Allmon hesitated and wove once before saying, "Um, Walnut Hills if I can get in."

The man whistled. "Wow, that's a good school—great academics. But you certain that's the right move for you, son?"

"Yeah . . . I don't know."

"Well, I'm going to be blunt. You've got a great body, kid, and I'd say there's a pretty good chance it was made for other things. Look at these mitts. If I may . . ." He reached forward and lifted Allmon's left hand by the wrist. He had his grandfather's hands already.

"You've got monster paws, Allmon, and you just told me I haven't seen the extent of your speed. Your teacher tells me she thinks you have the makings of an All-State and that the only reason you didn't go to competition this year was because you were home sick that week. I have to tell you, as a coach you make me sit up and take notice. I'd like to see you at the Academy for Physical Education next year, be a varsity Lion. Who knows, assuming you can catch a ball, you could have NFL running back written all over you. You never know."

Allmon perked up. "Maybe quarterback? My dad loves football. He's a Packers fan."

The man looked at him through the slat of his lids. "It sounds like your dad's a smart guy. Myself, I never made it to the NFL. I wasn't fast enough, but I did play all four years for Alabama, and it was the best thing that ever happened for my relationship with my dad. We always had something to talk about, you know? Even when things got tough. Sports create a bond."

"Right." Allmon nodded.

"So why don't you talk to your dad about it . . ."

"All right," Allmon said evenly, and then he couldn't contain his child's smile. "I think I will."

––––––––

On the Friday before the admissions test, it snowed. He stood in the bathroom, peering out the tiny square window at their backyard, which was no backyard at all, just a patch of woebegotten earth littered with glass and fenced by chicken wire. Behind their shotgun house, the old bottle factory towered with its shattered, jagged windowpanes, its interior breached by the raw weather and the swiftly falling snow. Maybe it was a trick of the light, but the snow looked gray and crumbly as tabby—as if even the snow couldn't be white on this side of town.

He thought, Maybe it'll snow too hard to get to that test tomorrow.

He thought, Fuck all those white kids on the East Side anyway, with their floppy haircuts and their Walkmen and their wheels, their fucking bullshit easy lives. Why would he want to go to their rich-kid school? He thought of his mother on the couch. He thought of his father.

He thought, nothing ever works out anyhow.

Marie was dead asleep when Allmon slipped into the front room and opened the fridge. In the freezer, there was some United Dairy Farmers ice cream and an old scarlet-label vodka bottle. He grasped up the frosted bottle and walked straight back to his room.

He sat cross-legged on the air mattress for a long time, the bottle between his legs, his mind full of nothing. He heard the little feet of the snowflakes as they landed on the sill. The tiniest whistle of air seeped out of the mattress in the few minutes he spent sitting there silently. Then he started to drink. He didn't mix it, just drank it, and when he got drunk enough, it did actually occur to him that he wanted to go get a real education, but he couldn't remember whether he wanted to be a teacher or was it an astronomer, and his last thought he had before he passed out was: The test is at nine. Don't be late.

He woke in his own vomit at ten to the sound of Marie crying, "Allmon, Allmon, what have you done?"

––––––––

And so it was the Academy of Physical Education. By the first day of training he'd forsworn alcohol forever, but threw up more over the course of the next six months than he ever had in his life. Two-a-days began on August 2 at seven in the morning; at weigh-in, he was hefting 175 pounds on his five-ten frame, broad through the shoulders but otherwise sapling slim. They would have to build him from the ground up.

The offensive coordinator, a big white guy with a face as pocked as a waffle iron, said, "How big's your dad, scat?"

Allmon had no idea, but he didn't blink: "Six-two."

The man nodded. "What I was hoping! You're a baby power back. Let's see if we can't get you through the crawling stage real quick."

The coach, in his first talk of the season, said, "I'm not here to teach you a game—I'm here to make men out of boys. That means I need you big, fast, and I need you mean, because your ability to hurt your opponent is no less important than your ability to memorize plays or catch a pass. If hurting someone isn't in your nature, get it in your nature. Right here. Right now."

With no ceremony whatsoever—and everyone calling him fucking Almond—they moved him into his new home: the weight room. Mondays were legs: squats, leg curls, and extensions, followed by Wednesday's chest, back, and shoulder day: bench press, lat pull, and dumbbell military press until his arms were screaming and his teeth fit to shatter from clenching, all followed on Thursday with explosive fast twitch work: power cleans and box jumps until he was crying on the inside and—every damn time—throwing up. On the field, he struggled to maintain his weight after long days under full pads and gear. *Speed and agility*, they screamed until his own mind turned coach: *Speed and agility!* All hours of the day. Did he intend to make varsity? Fuck, yeah, he did. College? Pro? Yeah, sure. Well, maybe . . . he didn't know. There was Aesop and the work and the money. There was his momma. And there was a starter jacket he wasn't allowed to wear at school and a five-hundred-dollar watch he had hidden under his mattress. He hadn't really worked his whole life out, he didn't really know what he was doing. And he didn't have the calories to burn for thinking between endless tire drills followed by ladder drills—hopscotch, one-foot laterals, backward laterals, crossovers and reverse shuffles, ladders in his sleep, ladders descending to hell—and dashes up and back with the stopwatches clicking and the offensive line coaches barking: Ladies, it's four-eight-forty or nothing! Then at the tail end of practice, when Allmon's body was broken and his spirit rattled from all the screaming, the coaches led them to the hill a half mile behind the school and made them run suicide hills until the entire team was dropping, starting with the linemen and ending with the sprinty little running backs, all of them on their hands and knees puking onto the desiccated autumn grass. Then it was a shower and off to run the neighborhood.

"Get in."

It was Drone behind the wheel of Aesop's Jetta, gesturing with a fat thumb toward the backseat. Allmon had just been walking back from school in Winton Terrace, minding his own, so he was surprised to be accosted in the street by his crew in the middle of the day, or to hear the normally quiet Drone giving orders; he was just a hatchet man for Aesop, big as a bouncer, natural authority like marrow in his bones. He barely ever had to use his booming bass.

"Get in."

Slant late-afternoon sun, whipping spring wind, it felt so good out, so why was he hesitating? He just had a crooked feeling. Don't get in, Allmon. Don't do it.

"Get in, boo." Aesop was leaning over in the shotgun seat, his eyes offering no alternative. Quieting his body, Allmon slid in beside Andre and Dox in the back, but perched on the edge of the seat with his hand on the frame of the car out the open window like he was ready to spring. The air in the car was full of needles.

"What's going down?"

"Over-the-Rhine's about to burn!"

Allmon said nothing, just waited, feeling the hard, fast bloom of dread in his gut.

Aesop twisted around in the front seat, the customary reserve of his face distorted, grim. His chin jutted beneath whitened lips. "They shot Simpson. They shot my boy in the motherfucking back."

Allmon reared back. "Who?"

"Who you think! The motherfucking police!"

"He was running?"

Aesop sneered. "Bitch, he ain't ran. Shut your fucking mouth."

He didn't bother to ask where they were going, because he knew. He knew when Aesop passed back a 9 mm Glock, all black and smooth with its dull sheen. He shoved it inexpertly down into the waistband of his jeans. Aesop once said, You ain't grown till I say you grown, so was he grown? Boom, yes—just like that. He was old and bold. Something electric, like a whole house power surge, replaced his dread.

They flew through Knowlton's Corner, through Cumminsville near the house he now called home, the place where his mother lay on the old sofa, then into the wasteland of the old west end, long routed by the interstate, with its meatpacking plants and its brownstones, its nothing. You could follow that line of nothing all the way to the river, but they veered east with squealing tires onto Liberty and crossed into Over-the-Rhine. Smoke from a fire was rising somewhere to the east when they crossed Central Parkway, that street built on the old drained canal—the Rhine—over which the Germans had crossed into the heart of the city, the Reverend's now ailing Queen.

"Get out, get out, I'm a find y'all," said Drone, and they tumbled out, loped like loose-limbed vigilantes down Vine, joining the people pouring out of their apartments and houses the way smoke was pouring up into the bruised sky.

He flowed, they flowed, everything flowed toward the fire. The streets were full of fight. He was jostled and bumped as he ran and there was the high chatter of shattering glass in the distance. The Glock was cold and hard in his pants like some kind of industrial dick. With sharp vision granted by fear or excitement, he saw as if for the first time the old streets made new, the towering walls of these Italianate buildings with their massive moldings pitted by time, wavy glass windows amber in the falling light. The city was crashing down and a rowdy night was rising. He was back in the world of the Reverend, the old city. He sensed vaguely through his excitement that the Reverend wouldn't be in this river of madness, wouldn't be following the people as they ran now toward the smashing and looting over on Sycamore. His grandfather had tried to save this old neighborhood. He'd said, "As busy as Manhattan back in the day! This city was freedom, and don't you forget it!"

Now Over-the-Rhine was indeed preparing to burn. Men and women milled in the streets, laughing and hollering along Sycamore, hurling hub-caps and old stones from the edifices of these old gray giants into glass windows, smoke rising in three directions now. There were sirens looping out of the precinct house, and they'd be here any second, noses trained to the scent of unrest. The sound of them jogged something; Allmon snapped suddenly out of a fever dream. They'd all be rounded up, or there'd be blood, or both. The thrill was gone and the dread was back.

He would have stood there paralyzed on Race if someone hadn't pushed him into the old Schroeder electronics store, where the televisions were mute with alarm and the radios could only perk their ears as they were snatched from their carpeted plinths and carried out into the wilds. He realized that somehow, somewhere, he'd lost his crew. He ran back to the front of the store with a thought to look for Aesop in the sea of looters, but he didn't; he just looked north. There was the Reverend's old house that he'd left to the church, now derelict. The sirens were mourning louder and louder. Holy shit, it was a flat-out mob, and he was in the middle of it. How the fuck could he get out of this—not just the looting but his whole stupid life? In an instant, a wild dream swooped up in him; all he had to do was get back to the hood, grab his mother and whatever cash he had, and get them both to Chicago on a bus. Abandon this fucked-up life! He wasn't a fucking dealer, he was just a fifteen-year-old kid. What kind of game had he been playing? Enough wrong turns and you run in a circle. He needed to find Mike Shaughnessy and Mike Shaughnessy would welcome him. His white father would want him—that was a given. Allmon took off running.

He was veering and leaping around the opposing team the way he did on the field. All around bricks were being thrown through plate-glass win-dows, so they shattered inward and great guillotine plates came slicing down, then the people streamed through in a great cascade, and the sound of their shoes on the glass made him want to scream. With a spastic crack-ling, the streetlights opened their accusing eyes and the faces all around were horribly exposed in the garish light. He realized that he too was recognizable.

Now Allmon sprinted up Race, already halfway up the street before he suddenly realized he was a black boy running with a gun, so he flung himself into an alleyway, crouched behind a metal trash can, and jerked the

Glock out of his jeans, slid it beneath a trash can. Fear was hammering him from all sides. Aesop would kill him, but maybe he'd come back for it, whatever, he couldn't think about that now; he just needed to get out of this situation. His breathing came in drafts as he waited. And waited.

The river swung lazily back and forth a half mile south.

A wry moon sprung up with its mouth of sham alarm.

Invisible geese rowed the black sky.

A terrified hour passed. The city was only louder, the violence even rosier in the sky, so there was no point in staying; it was only going to get worse. He crept out of the protective dark just as tenebrous voices passed, five figures, and he fell in behind them, thinking he'd follow them north to Central Parkway, then walk up into the parts of the city that weren't crashing down. But a wild whooping commenced, followed by more shattering glass, and he realized with a start that he was standing in front of his grandfather's church. The front windows, long replaced by thick Plexiglas, remained opaque and untouched, but someone had smashed the old glass at the back where Jesus perched on a pearl-white cloud with his arms spread wide like the genius of water. Allmon heard intruders prowling around the interior of the church, hollering and cursing in the sanctuary where the Germans had bent their heads and prayed for God's light, a light now flickering in the dark. It licked the darkness, flirting, spreading itself, warming the night air.

The church of his youth was burning. He stood in a trance before his grandfather's face and the tawny eyes— Be not afraid! It's the principle of the thing! The fire was filled with raucous laughter, voices conspiring with all the glee of children because they were children, as was he. Then the rear of the church was engulfed in orange flame, and black silhouettes went streaking by him and even the river couldn't have put this fire out, it was so strong. And hot as the sun. He bellowed out pure, instinctive rage. The feeling of himself was suddenly enormous, and with impotent, unbearable force, he swung his arms in the dark, strangled articulations emerging from his throat, his eyes burning from the acrid smoke. You're burning the wrong fucking building! You're burning down my life! He couldn't hear the sirens over his own screaming, nor their approach as he stalked around with otherworldly energy before the burning relic, before the billowing smoke and collapsing rafters. It was only when a policeman wrenched his arms behind him and threw him chest-first onto the glass-strewn pavement that he threw out a single word like a shield. It was his grandfather's name, but it offered no protection at all, not anymore.

It didn't take long—they were processing the juveniles from the riot at the speed of light, and his adjudicatory hearing was arranged in just two weeks. Allmon was first up on the morning calendar call, his name boomed out by the PA into the hallway of the courthouse, thick with young defendants and their parents.

In that dingy courtroom, where half the windowpanes were replaced with plastic that dulled the light, they threw the book at him. But he didn't need to read it, he already knew all the words by heart. The judge sustained the petition of the prosecutor—juvenile felony arson—and at the disposition hearing, they ordered him to camp for two years of firesetter education and rehabilitation. He never had the benefit of an attorney or even the offer for one, so he couldn't pretend to be surprised when they sentenced him. They were calling the next case before he'd even risen to his feet in his borrowed dress shoes.

Marie came every day for two weeks following the disposition hearing. She dragged her aching, swollen body across two bus routes and five neighborhoods, using up an hour and a half and all her energy to get to the new redbrick facility on Auburn Avenue. When she finally collapsed in a plastic chair across from Allmon in the visiting room, he could smell the sweat of her exertion, her exhaustion. When she took his hands in hers, her trembling caused his hands to tremble.

She spoke with her eyes closed against the sawing agony of daylight. "They'll keep you in school?"

"Yeah," he said, nodding. "They got school here every day. It ain't so bad—this new building they got is pretty nice. They bring you dinner, so you ain't got to go to a cafeteria or anything."

"So they feed you?"

"Of course they feed me, Momma. I mean, they ain't gonna let us starve." The food was actually pretty good, much better than the white diet he'd been feeding them at home. It was damn near a relief if he was going to be honest. And that relief made him sick with guilt. He swallowed hard.

"I'm sorry," Marie said suddenly.

He shook his head resolutely. "Nope. Nothing to be sorry about."

"I feel like this is all my fault."

Allmon sat back suddenly, retrieved his hands to his lap, where they fiddled with the fabric of his jeans. "Ain't nobody's fault. Especially not yours." But he was looking above her head and far beyond her.

Marie reached forward to pull his hands back to her, but when he refused, when he drew his hands right back to his person with the flashing irritation that men are quick to master with women, her eyes became shot with lightning streaks of red and tears welled. "If I could have given you a father that you could have relied—"

He waved a hand and sighed and said, "Whatever. Don't worry." But the small, unstill voice said, Why the fuck can't you keep a man? You should have fought harder! You should have fought for my sake!

"I know you think about Mike—"

"Fuck him," he blurted.

"Wow," Marie said, and sat back, but there was no anger in the word, just a kind of wonder that sounded to Allmon's ear like self-pity.

"Momma," Allmon said suddenly, clearing his throat, "I think it's time you didn't come back and just let me do this."

Now it was Marie's turn to sit back in offense. "What are you saying? You can't just tell me to be away from you. I'm your mother."

Allmon held up placating hands. "Listen, I know how hard it is for you to get out here, how much it takes. And, anyway, in a month they're gonna send me out to camp. You won't even be able to get out there. I'm in this, I'm gonna do this. You need to take care of your own self."

"No—"

"Momma—"

"No."

"Momma!" he barked. Then with a tic of his head, calm again. He said, "Momma, if you come back here, I won't see you. That's just how it's gonna be. I want you to go home and take of yourself, get healthy, get back to working more. That's the most important thing. Don't waste none of your energy on me. Please don't come back."

Then he looked down, because she wouldn't, and he didn't want their eyes to speak anymore.

So, there was school. In two years, he learned:

1. A black line extends infinitely in white space. Put a point on a line and you can name it anything you want.
2. You are a threat to the safety of others.
3. *Not exactly a part of the talented tenth, or you wouldn't be in here, now, would you?*
4. The lights on the dock are a symbol. The lights are a symbol! *Do you know what a symbol is, Allmon?*
5. Yours was a maladaptive and antisocial crime, its causes multi-dimensional. Family dysfunction factors were paramount.
6. A symbol is a metaphor. A symbol is when you stand for something.
7. *I'm sick of you all thinking you can speak improper English in my class. You think the Oakland School Board's given you permission to be ignorant? Not in my class, they haven't! Not under my watch!*
8. You can get a .38 revolver for like a hundred bucks on the street if you know where to go and who to talk to.
9. *Race is a social construct and you kids just want to keep it constructed so you can whine and complain and play the victim. I'm here to make you functional in society, so you won't grow up to be parasites on the system. But you have to choose to move beyond race. It's your choice. You want to be a victim forever?*
10. The fact you're not a murderer right now is just dumb luck. But luck runs out.
11. Firesetter as sociological type: poor, black, broken family, unsupervised. Significant problem with aggression.
12. I am a victim. I am not a victim, a victim, not a victim. I am black. Not really, though—my dad is white!
13. Let us be sacrificers, but not butchers, Caius.
    We all stand up against the spirit of Caesar;
    And in the spirit of men there is no blood:
    O, that we then could come by Caesar's spirit,

And not dismember Caesar! But, alas,
Caesar must bleed for it! And, gentle friends,
Let's kill him boldly, but not wrathfully;
Let's carve him as a dish fit for the gods,
Not hew him as a carcass fit for hounds.

14. It's possible to jump a car in forty-five seconds if you practice.

15. *You made your choices; now you need to face the consequences.*

16. *Allmon, what do you want to be when you grow up—a hoodlum? A thug? No. Well, what then?*

17. Sleep. School. Basketball. Eat. Homework. Sleep. Repeat.

18. The firesetter responds maladaptively to ongoing stress, begins ideation during crisis, makes decision, gathers tools, sets fire. Elation then replaces anger.

19. When I get out of here, things are going to be fucking different. I'm going to make a new life for myself. The power is mine. All I have to do is choose.

20. You know why they killed Caesar? Because he wanted to be king.

You haven't seen the Queen City in two years, you've been stuck out in the sticks at camp, so this Metro bus, it's like a boat ferrying you from hell back to life. In your mind, the ashen neighborhood has turned in two years' time from the dank, grimy Helltown into a shimmering Atlantis all paved in gold, yellow as a lemon diamond, where your mother is wearing a polka-dotted apron with a quarter sheet of cookies in her hand, saying: You're a man now. And you say: I was adjudicated delinquent but have turned my life around, I was dissociated but now I feel, I do not have a father, but I do not need one to become my own man, I know there is dignity in poverty, I am not a product of my environment, I am responsible for my choices, I get to choose who I will be and now I choose to walk a straight line, I will stay away from the streets and gangs and report to my PO, because I have a future as bright as these city lights.

He wondered whether his father had visited during his absence.

When he slipped off the bus with his duffel at Knowlton's Corner, the wind battered him. Unseasonably warm, with the force of a train, it slung a mad cesspool of flyers and candy wrappers, it turned leaves to razors and branches to spears. The neighborhood was still the color of ashes. Jesus. He tried not to think: everything looks the fucking same.

No, I'm changed, I'm grown, I'm seventeen.

Bent into a headwind, he pressed past the old church, past the gas station where two men were hollering at each other across their cars with gruff voices, past the furniture shops filled with cast-offs no one would ever buy, past a restaurant that hadn't been there before, and down along the row houses, stunted like children who didn't get enough to eat, starved of sun in the shadow of the overpass. And there was the shotgun. It too was unchanged, its gray paint peeling, its wrought-iron gate swinging by an ancient hinge, but that was all right, who really cares, because he was all right and his mother was all right, everything was going to be all right. He was clinging to the new person he was implementing in his mind, and as he approached, his feet hurried him forward without direct orders.

Momma. He was immediately assailed by the scent of rank mildew and stale cooking and something else, something lower and more personal, something animal, the odor of an unwashed person, her old, familiar smell enlarged and made pungent. Allmon stopped short in the doorway, hesitant as a first-time visitor, his pupils adjusting and one hand reaching forward in lieu of sight. First the marmoreal gleam of the linoleum, silver and gray, then the edge of old shag, then the sofa and Marie lying there with her back turned, her arms drawn up between her chest and the sofa back. His mind was jolted by time's tricks. Had she not moved an inch in two years?

Momma. He had said the word out loud, and she started from her sleep or her daze. She came round abruptly on the sofa, rolling her weight, which spread ungainly over the entire width of the cushion. Her old shape was all wrong in the dark.

"Allmon?"

He was prepared for a new world. He was prepared to stand in that doorway like a valiant soldier returned or like a husband, all solemn and sure. But he rushed into the room like a child, flinging down his bag and actually shoving the coffee table out of the way, and as Marie was struggling her way to a sitting position, he was on his knees before her, pressing his face into the side of her arm.

"I didn't know you were coming today. I thought it was tomorrow."

"I'm home."

"Babydoll."

He looked up into her face as she was bending forward, like a groggy animal, struggling to orient in the woken world.

"Momma?"

He switched on the end-table lamp and looked at her, and it took all of his effort not to shrink. Something, some great force of life or death had come and distorted her. It was pressing her essence out of her, turning her into a balloon about to burst—her pendulous breasts and enormous, distended belly, even her cheeks, which were blooming with an unnatural, febrile red. Her eyes were cracked slats, and the few eyelashes that remained were mere black spikes. Her hairline had inched back from her temples, the lineaments of manhood forced upon her once feminine face. And worse, far worse, were the gross lines of pain etched on the face that had murmured once upon an endless time in the forever ago, Hush a bye don't you cry go to sleepy little baby when you wake you shall have all the pretty little horses blacks and bays dapples and grays coach and six white horses, hush.

He sat back on his heels, surprised by the anger in his voice. "Momma, when's the last time you went to the doctor?"

"That's the first thing you say to me?" She turned slightly away, but her scold was shame, as if she couldn't look at the impossibly robust, vital, searching face of her boy not even in his prime. His very life burned her.

"Momma, what's going on? What's happening to you?"

"It's fine. Better now you're here." Her voice was lower than he remembered, husky with disuse. She closed her eyes, and her lips pressed together.

"You still going to work?"

She just shrugged.

For a long moment he just stared at her, corralling love, rage, fear, and disgust into language. Then he said, "I'm here to take care of you. I'm gonna call that doctor we saw, gonna get you fixed up. Seriously. I promise."

She nodded, looking straight ahead.

"We're gonna get back on our feet. I'm gonna get some cash. Don't worry about nothing."

She didn't look at him, she didn't soothe him. She just rolled back to her position with her back turned, and her only reply was a sigh that had no more force than a hush song.

At 7:00, he was standing on the old, rain-slickened stoop. At 7:01, he was being ushered upstairs by someone he didn't recognize, some midget in a fucking Cleveland ball cap. At 7:04 Aesop was clapping his hand over his own mouth and crying out with feigned glee like he actually missed him, like he didn't have a hundred kids ready to join his army—"Oh shit! Smartie!"—shaking his head in amazement like here was the miracle of Lazarus, the last and greatest of all the miracles before the crucifixion, and he was actually witness to the kid crawling out of the tomb, still wrapped in his grave clothes, and gazing confusedly about at this world he thought he had left behind forever.

At 7:24 Allmon was back at work, this time as a dealer, this time with a beeper and a Glock 17.

The days were brief as the bursts from a flare, and the nights were long as everloving fuck. He was back at the Academy of Physical Education and couldn't miss a day or show up late without his PO riding his ass, so he played that game. But then he punched the crack clock at five and worked the streets, standing on corners, hitting a couple of reliable houses until eleven or sometimes on into the deepest hours of the night, what his father had once called—

Daddy, you like driving the truck at night?

Eh, nigger's hours.

All he needed was a solid week of work under the wheeling February sky cluttered with clusters of eyebright stars that made no sense, even less than their names—Betelgeuse, Rigel, the Pleiades and Hyades, the Orion Nebula, upstart Castor and Pollux—to raise some cash for a doctor. Then they'd get it sorted out. This was his herculean labor. This. He was supposed to be straight, he wanted to be straight, but if he looked too close the catch-22 started looking like a noose, like God himself had an APB out on him. So he refused to think. Instead, he worked the familiar streets of Northside, dealing and daring under the schizophrenic Marias, the sea of tranquillity, the sea of chaos, the sea of serenity, the ocean of storms, the ocean of indecision. Door to door on an earth not fixed, waiting for the sun not fixed, in the Milky Way, also not fixed. The goddamned galaxy itself hurtled through black useless space at three hundred kilometers per second toward no real destination, no real purpose. Every object was loose. In this mayhem, he gave himself one week.

Like that was ever going to work. He was back in it in every way—running, hanging with the crew, pocketing change, wearing a bomber Aesop gave him. He was even standing here in the kitchen again, cooking for Marie, just as he had before they threw him in 20/20 and packed him off to camp. Sly, sassy time messing with his mind, is it 1997 or 1995 or 1985 with Mike Shaughnessy about to walk in the door? No, it's now. It's Tuesday, you've been home five days, you're cooking brats and sauerkraut, it's just crazy how you slip into your old gambling seat at the casino, start stacking chips like you never even went anywhere. This is how addicts must feel raising a bottle to their lips after a long dry spell. He wasn't going to lie, being on the loop again felt damn good. Both awful and good. That was probably the definition of crazy.

"Momma!" he said in his bang-the-pot voice, too loud for the space. "Time to eat! Get up!" He turned and looked at her lying there, facing the couch back. Barely ever moving. Impatience was gasoline in his veins. You know what else was crazy? How he couldn't harness his mind, how it vacillated from compassion to . . . Fuck! He didn't know why she couldn't be tougher! How she'd ever let Mike Shaughnessy get away, why she didn't know how to fight—weren't women supposed to be so strong?—why wasn't she hard? Stand up and play the bitch! Their life could have been so different if she'd had a fucking backbone like the Reverend, then Allmon wouldn't have to run all over like a pretend thug, throw his life away, be the fucking man of the house—

He wiped a hand over his face, changed roles. He cleared his throat as he carried over a plate. "Momma."

Leaning over her, he realized with some embarrassment that her gown had fallen away from the upper slopes of her breasts, the skin there inlaid with faded stretch marks. In the room nearly overridden by shadows, he saw that the irregular lesion she had on her right hand—scarlet red and scaled with a scurfy, livid white—was repeated across the skin of her upper chest.

"Momma," he blurted out, and the sound of anger in his own voice made him want to smack himself. But his hand was still gentle as a child's when it touched her shoulder.

"Huh?"

"What the fuck is this? You got these all over?"

Marie came round slowly, turning clumsily, like she didn't know where she was, or what he was saying. She could barely open her eyes. "Why are you cussing at me?"

"How long you had these sores, Momma?"

He reached down and exposed the skin around her clavicle. From her throat, down her sternum into the ribbed vale between her breasts, her flesh was a mottled landscape of enflamed, crusted, flaking sores. Her body looked beaten, or rotten.

"Holy shit, Momma," he said, rearing back. "The fuck is this? I'm calling a ambulance right now!"

That seemed to awaken her properly, and her hand shot out to grip his wrist.

"No!"

"Right now!"

She wrenched up his wrist with all the force she possessed. All her life blazed in her eyes, everything left. "Don't, Allmon. Don't. I'm telling you no. The ambulance costs a thousand dollars—maybe more. I'm fine."

"Then I'll get a taxi!"

"No."

"We got to do it, Momma. Listen—"

"No, you listen to me," she said sharply. "I'm not going anywhere. I'm not on the hospital's charity anymore. I missed their deadline. I was sick, I was running some fevers for a week or two and couldn't get to the paperwork."

"Somebody'll take you."

"Who? We'll end up with crazy bills! You can't ever escape those bills!"

"Momma—"

"No!" she said, and then: "Listen, it comes and goes. Sometimes it's bad, sometimes it's not so bad. It'll pass like it always does. It hurts, but I'm used to it. I'll take a shower and it'll help." And she tried to struggle up and appear more alert, clamping the fabric of her gown between her breasts. "I'm just tired and need to rest."

"This is crazy," he said.

"Allmon"—and she looked up at the ceiling as if seeking for the words there—"go . . . do what you do. I'm not even going to judge you. You're young, you're free, that's the greatest gift. Go be in the world. I'm not young anymore. I don't even want all that anymore. I just need rest. I just . . . Don't you owe me that?"

"Owe you what?" He couldn't make sense of her.

Her eyes burned into him. "You owe me your good life. I mean, give your whole life to good things. Help others."

"Shit . . . I . . . ," he stammered, looking stricken. "I don't even know what good is most of the time, Momma."

She smiled. "Whatever helps people. The ones you love. That's the good. That's why I'm saying go on."

"I don't know."

Now she was rolling over on the couch again, face to the back. "I can't rest with you looking over my shoulder and worrying me to death. Go on, Allmon. I just need to rest my eyes a while."

He backed away from the couch, knowing he was being ordered out. He reached the door and opened it half-unwilling, terrified yet somehow, strangely, sadly, in the deepest part of him, eager to go. As he stood there hesitating, Marie said, "But don't walk out of this house without saying I love you."

He looked back somberly over his shoulder and said, "I love you, Momma."

The pain—once as small as a mustard seed—had grown so large, it had become her. She'd been young once and full of light, pure! She had been so full of love as a girl. She had adored her mother, her father, and Mike Shaughnessy. With compunction, pity, longing, desperate fear, and a river-tide of longing, she remembered the girl she had been, the body she had once lived within, so hopeful, so light and slim; long before her period and the swelling of her breasts, she had been free. Then the ironclad change of womanhood had been forced upon her, and it had taken so much from her. It had made her breasts hurt, her guts wrench, it had made her bleed. Then the boys had pinched her swelling breasts, the black boys on her block grabbing her with their eyes before they grabbed her with their hands, even though she wasn't really pretty, maybe they touched her more because she wasn't pretty, like a vase of no value a man can handle carelessly (you look better in the dark); men are only awed into good manners by women who are like art, and she wasn't art. How she had longed for a clean-speaking, sensitive boy who didn't act or talk black, who didn't grow up in the neighborhood, but when she found that white boy, he used her only to feel good, and a baby—a whole new life—was what he called an "accident." He used to say he loved her body. He never said that about her face, and while she was pressing all her hope against him, he'd already been looking for the next girl.

Her momma was the only human being who ever truly loved her. Her father cared more about the suffering of strangers than he ever cared about her. But she'd taken her mother's love for granted all the days of her life. Claudia Jeane Rankin Marshall had raised her and watched her grow into her late girlhood with pride—but only now did she recognize the wholeness of that love. She'd said, Momma, I'm scared to grow up. Because the boys were hanging around like vultures, and her momma had pet her head and said, I understand, baby, I understand. And she had understood! But the cancer moved into her body when she was forty-two years old, and then she was gone in a moment, so Marie was all alone, and no one knew how pretty she was on the inside or how she longed, prayed, oh, how she had prayed to God, please bring me a man—in her mind he was white and clean-speaking and good and didn't look or sound like he was from the neighborhood— who will love me. Please.

Her temperature was rising, is rising, the wick burning brighter as it burns low, fighting for life in an invisible draft. God, I brought a boy into this world for the love of Michael Shaughnessy and gave him his name. But he left anyhow. Daddy always told me wind is the breath of God, and woman is a flame bent in the wind towards man: Why did you curse me with this female body? I'm begging that you free me of it, make me anything but a woman in heaven. Make me an avenging angel, so I can look down on the world with inhuman strength and no feelings at all. Make me an animal, so I won't know anything. Make me a man, so I won't give a damn about anyone.

Lord, I never asked for this body, and I only had it a moment before the baby came, and he tore it up—I traded my breasts and my waist and my smooth skin. I traded my body for his life. I lost the love of his father, who only loved his own pleasure, because you didn't give me any other beauty to keep him! You named me Ugly. Why am I even praying to you? Shame on you for letting me suffer! And shame on you for stealing my mother from me when I needed her most! God, I hate you more than I hate the devil! You demand that I love you? Is love and hate the same thing in heaven? Folks always say the Lord is wonderful! Who wrote that? They all must live in some quiet, safe world where no black folk live, no poor folk. The Lord isn't wonderful—he's cruel! He looks at the suffering of his own children like he's watching television, and if he isn't cruel, then he's re-tarded and doesn't understand the world he made, doesn't know that little girls get their legs forced apart, boys got pockets full of dope, mothers sell their children, parents die! The Lord is wonderful? If the Lord is alive, the Lord is a pimp, letting life violate you, because your desperation buys him your belief. No? Then prove I'm wrong!

Oh God, forgive me. Forgive me and ease my suffering, help me and help Allmon. He's just a boy and doesn't know a thing. Forgive him for everything he's doing! I wish I never had him to suffer. Momma, I pray to you, I pray to Daddy. Please forgive me for whatever I did to make you go away from me, that made you desert me! I don't know why I'm alone. I tried to love Mike, I tried to love my child, but they took all of me and didn't give me anything back. A baby doesn't even love you, just uses you to get on with its life—and I loved so hard that I broke—

God, please hear your Marie.

God, my lungs hurt.

God, these are my breasts, empty now.

These are my eyes you ruined.

I want my momma.

God, I tried to love me, but I don't know how.

God, please watch over Allmon.

God, please speak to me.

Please.

If I ever heard one word from you in my life, I didn't know it.

Please, I am a thread, please sew with me, I am a candle, please light me, please love me, please tell Momma I miss her every day and I forgive her for dying, God, I am a house for a little boy, let my boy live in me forever, oh I'm afraid of the dark light me I'm scared to disappear God oh God I am a thread sew me to me I am Marie I am your little girl I am a body God you made

He was gone from the house for exactly two hours and three minutes. He walked out with the gun stuffed down his drawers like he was in the movies, but then he was afraid he was going to blow his own dick off, so he switched it into his cargo pocket, the weight tugging on him, bumping his thigh, an off-tempo drum beating against his rhythmless life. He had a plan, he was going to go borrow money off Aesop and take her straight to the hospital, but the man, ever shrewd, saw the way fear sketched in the lines of Allmon's face, so he just tilted his head and said, "Work tonight, then I break you off what you need." He couldn't wheedle, there was no point, and there wasn't any other option, so he just went through the frazzled motions—holding the curb down near Fergus, the old faces grown gaunt and routed from two years of using now filing past with his lookout all jumpy half a block up. Then he was winding his way through the streets and interstitial alleys of the hood, vial after vial after vial, pocket twenty bucks, pocket thirty under the moon obscured by faint clouds, the moon stricken like its own panic was growing. Momma. Holy shit, he was standing on someone's porch—these white dykes that held down good jobs but who used like fucking fiends—when he realized he could hardly breathe. The aperture of his pupil was swiveling shut. Her sores were festering on his own flesh, her flesh was his flesh, and now as he handed a vial in exchange for a tiny roll, tears came unbidden to his eyes. Was this a panic attack? By the time he was back on the sidewalk, panic bloomed full-bore, and he was racing down Hamilton Avenue as if someone were chasing him, cops and traffic be goddamned, until he was standing, heaving air before Aesop, where he dropped the returns and said, "Listen, I got a bad feeling. I need cash now, like right now. My momma's sick. I got to take her to the hospital," and Aesop was rearing back: "Why the fuck you ain't said something? I'd a flushed you when you come in," pressing rolls into his hands, much more than he needed. Then he was running way down Hamilton Avenue, across the wasteland of Knowlton's Corner, down where the smell of the Mill Creek announced its foul presence under the viaduct, and back into the house.

He found his mother seizing on the couch, her right hand twitching and flapping against the floor where it had fallen, palm open and still pink with the fever of life. No thought, Allmon just wheeled away from the house and ran to the Fifth Amendment without hesitating—no time to feel—and he called the ambulance, he didn't care about the cost. Yes, her name is Marie and this is Allmon Shaughnessy, yes, she's my mother!—but by then it was too late. His mother's kidneys had failed, and she died under the care of the shocked ER physician, who took one look at the lupoid lesions that had ravaged her neck and torso, and said with his hand over his surgical mask, "Jesus Christ. Who let this happen to her?"

That night Allmon didn't dream of his mother. Instead, the Reverend appeared for the first time in many years. In the dream, the old man was standing in a field where nothing was sown, and he was kicking at the fallow soil and poking it with a long stick like a shepherd's staff. All around his head, glimmering stars swarmed like gnats, and he batted them away with his hands, which were even larger now than they had been in life, nearly the size of dinner plates.

As Allmon approached him, the sun was setting to his right and warming his skin. The Reverend looked up suddenly, and Allmon saw he had drawn a line in the dirt with his staff.

"Stop!" the Reverend said, and the stars stilled about his head, hovering. He pointed a gnarled finger at Allmon. "Don't you step across this line, boy! This line got drawn for you, and only the Lord can take it away!"

"But—Momma—"

"Time is short! You better pray you discover yourself!"

And in the dream he tried to do as he was told, but when he bowed his head, he couldn't pray, and only cried and cried.

———

This time he came to the funeral and sat in the very front row, shivering like he wouldn't ever be warm again. His PO officer loaned him the suit he wore—gray gabardine, too small in the shoulders, too long in the leg. From the periphery of his vision, the glossy gray box of the casket imposed itself. The half dozen people in the room were staring into that space, but he couldn't look up, he couldn't look at the last vision of his mother in this world. She was his only holding. His hands trembled like there were fevers breaking across them, and if he would just look up, maybe it wouldn't be so bad, not as bad as he imagined—

That was his mother. Lying there in a gray box. Her body. He surprised himself by not making a sound, just looking at her stony, painted face, the still thing that looked like her but wasn't her at all—all that remained of her birthing him, taking him in her arms, schooling him, hushing him, yelling at him, crying over him. He watched closely for her breathing until his eyes blinked of their own accord. Surely, her chest would move just a little bit if he stared long enough. Whereas before he couldn't bring himself to look, now he couldn't look away. It had the appearance of her, and yet didn't. Her face was sunk into itself slightly, hollows around her eyes despite the spackling of makeup. He wanted to stand up suddenly and say to someone, everyone: "That ain't my momma!" But he remained utterly still, both body and mind. Then, into his emptiness came a flood of images—his mother in the kitchen cooking, the coppery brown of her eyes, the lines her worry made, the laugh she had laughed a long time ago that no one else could laugh now. His only inheritance was memory.

He turned around suddenly and looked at the people in attendance. There was a little old woman from Lexington, who'd introduced herself as the cousin of a cousin or something, and who offered out of the blue to let him come live with her; there was Marie's old employer, the dentist, who had paid for the casket, as well as a man who introduced himself as a friend from middle school, and a few people he had never seen before. He stared impolitely into the dentist's white face and the spinning roulette of his emotions settled on fury—who was this white fuck coming here, thinking he could just show up a day late and a dollar short? Same white fuck that wouldn't let her work enough to get health insurance. Same white fuck that didn't let everybody get health care. He hated that white face. Fury was a blood blister waiting to burst, and when his mouth opened, he felt the arm of his PO cradling his shoulder, turning him around again.

Shhhhh.

God's finger touched her and she slept.

His mother was so still. For a moment, grief and uncomplicated love flared in his eyes, and the roulette swung, and he was a boy again with a mother at home and a father due in any minute on eighteen wheels. The tenor of his grief shifted downward. Tears were acid on his eyes.

The funeral was held in the smallest parlor of the Chase Brothers funeral home, in a small space carved from a larger room by partitioning walls made of a heavy gray nylon. The sitters were seated on folding chairs; someone got up and left before the service even began. The service itself consisted of just a minister standing before that unreality in the casket, which was his mother, Marie Marshall, daughter of Damien Emerson and a grandmother Allmon had never met, all gone now. With horror, he realized he could no longer remember the Reverend's voice, only his righteous anger. What had he said to him that night? The night he died and went away from Allmon forever, evaporated into nothing, leaving him alone in the world—

The preacher, paid for the occasion from Marie's minuscule life insurance policy, said, "What do we do when we lose someone too soon?"

no idea

"What words do we cry to heaven in our grief?"

no words

"Even in the midst of grief, we must know that Christ is watching."

not really no

"Because what do we believe?"

nothing

"We believe that Christ raises all believers from the grave."

nothing

"Until then, the dead are alive in our memory and in heaven, thank Jesus."

nothing

Bow your heads and pray. The Lord is my *nothing*, I shall want *nothing*. He maketh me to lie down in *nothing*, he leadeth me beside *nothing*, he restoreth *nothing* yea, though I walk through the valley of *nothing*, he leadeth me in the paths of *nothing* for the sake of *nothing* and I will lift up mine eyes unto *nothing*—from whence cometh my help? My help cometh from *nothing* which made *nothing* and *nothing*, oh *nothing*, why have you forsaken me? Why do you take your little ones and bash them against rocks— where can I go from your *nothing*? Where can I flee from your *nothing* if I go up to the heavens you are *nothing* if I make my bed in the depths *youarenothingandJesusneverdidcomebecausenooneeverdoesamenhavemer cyuponyournothingamen*

He stood alone in the waiting room adjacent to the showing parlor. He wavered before the foggy window that looked out onto Hamilton Avenue and breathed in the gaseous scent of the paperwhites splayed on the sideboard beneath the damp sash. Leaning forward slightly against the cold, wet window, he stared into the street. The snow had turned to mush, cast gray by the weak, borrowed light of winter. Cars slushed by, fanning blackened snow. The people all walked with their heads down. The world looked like old wallpaper.

In these streets, he looked for his prospects and found none.

He turned slightly to gaze back into the other room at the paltry mourners and the woman—that old relative who said her name was Sophia—was turned in her seat and looking at him with such a deep and abiding intensity that he had to turn away. Grief was a hand at his throat. Don't cry. Think. He could barely even do that. He stared into the streets, reading the script and intuiting the ending. These were the killing grounds, he knew that, a cemetery for boys like him. If he stayed here, he had no options but one: to become what Aesop had told him he would become, what he himself had chosen as a twelve-year-old, before he even knew what choosing was. His fate seemed set. How could he escape this life? Every day they spun the wheel of death and someday the ball would fall in his unlucky pocket, probably sooner rather than later. Except . . . He looked over at the old woman who was watching him, his own gaze as intense as hers suddenly, then he leaned in toward the street, listening. He pressed his ear to the glass. The street spoke.

His PO came up beside him, wrapped an arm round his shoulder again, saying, "You're doing great, Allmon; just get through this day. Just make it through this, and then you can—"

He turned to her with a ferocity in his eyes that stopped her short. "Get me out of here," he said.

"Now? Okay, sure, we can go if you really don't want to stay. I can get you something to eat." But her steadying arm remained around him.

"No," he said urgently, shaking off her reassuring touch. "Get me the fuck out of this neighborhood. Get me out or I'm gonna be a statistic."

"What? Allmon. No, Allmon, listen, this is grief—"

"You listen! That woman over there, she said I could come live with her in Lexington. She's my granddad's second cousin or something. Let me do that! Let me go!"

"What? Who? Okay, Allmon, wait—if she's a relation, we can talk about that, but right now you're under Ohio jurisdiction, and if you move to Kentucky, there are legal issues that take—"

"No!" he cried, and all heads in the room turned. "Now! Get me out of this fucking neighborhood! Get me out of here, or I'm gonna die here too!"

"Allmon—"

"NOW!"

The bus crossed the river as it flowed under the Roebling Bridge, and then they were on Kentucky ground. Cincinnati was a sheer wall of light behind them, disappearing behind the cut in the hill as 75 curved south into foreign ground, the land of forgetting, the place where nothing had existed for Allmon before. He shuts his eyes and only sees Marie. Open, and the land is green and rolling like the rolling of the sea you've only seen on TV. Close, you can hear someone's private music pounding across the aisle; beneath the bus your one duffel bag, that's all. Open, and this is Crittenden. Close, open, this is Georgetown—you've never even heard of it. You wonder if they have an accent here, like the Reverend had a fierce accent. What was the name of his father and grandfather? All you can remember is the word Scipio, but you forget who that was if you ever knew. Drift off for a second, wake with a guilty start to the sound of your mother saying, Allmon, what have you done? It's like she knows you left the old telescope in the house on purpose. Only an idiot would do that, or someone intentionally trying to get lost.

In the closing scene, the lady's house is arrayed in lavender from the kitchen curtains to the soft toilet seat that puffs air when you sit on it. Tiny hand-crocheted doilies underlay white plastic lamps, and clear plastic covers the two sofas from Rent-A-Center. The carpets smell of lilac carpet cleaner, and they're so thick, he can't hear the sound of his own feet as he steps across them, almost as if he doesn't exist anymore, as if he's lighter than air. On the lady's hearth lies a taxidermied cat, before which he stops and stares. He's so numb, he can't even be terrified of it.

The lady called Sophia—second cousin by marriage once removed and adopted on top of that—was bustling around him, taking his duffel stuffed with his few belongings, taking his jacket. Are you hungry? Are you thirsty? Are you losing your mind?

"Your cat . . . ," he said, lacking even the energy to point.

"Oh." She smiled. "You don't get rid of your baby just 'cause he passes on!" And then she had him by the elbow and was guiding him into a tiny bedroom, where two twin beds were dressed in sweet violet coverlets with pink heart pillows that said *Home Is Where the Heart Is*, and she was show-ing him the tiny closet and the empty dresser drawers, saying, "This is your room."

No. No, this doesn't look like my room. Where did my city go? Where is my mother? My mother is my city.

And then the lady—a tiny thing next to him, a child really, except he was the child—was helping him sit stiffly on the bed and patting his shoul-der and saying, Let a old lady help you, babydoll. You had a big shock, the worst kind of shock, but you're a good boy, you were a good son to your mama, Sophia can tell, she can recognize a kind heart when she sees one; I don't know how we survive these awful things, but we do, I promise we do, and a better day is coming, but first you got to cry for your mama and for yourself now too, you're in a safe, warm place, yes, babydoll, you're safe here. If he'd known they were the last kind words he would hear for years, that this was perhaps the last woman who would touch his shoulders and hands like he was a precious gift of God—a treasure to be had—he would have tried harder to memorize every detail of the moment and of her and of her simple home, including the yellow fall of light, the dust motes advancing through that light, the timbre of her ancient voice, even the smell of her old-lady breath. But his grieved mind was frozen like a fly in amber.

He was lying down now, his feet free; the woman had removed his sneakers and brought him a glass of grape juice and buttered white bread. Eat this, babydoll, you need to eat something. He couldn't. If he moved one muscle, memory would swamp him and flood his body.

She was in, she was out. She was touching his forehead, saying, Eat.

He listened to her watching television in her lavender living room; it was all happening in another country in a language he couldn't comprehend. Then she was vacuuming. Glasses were washed, the toilet flushed and then ran uselessly for a while, there was the sound of the woman humming, then proper night fell, and darkness engulfed the house.

He lay there in nothingness. The blackness was total, and the only thing he could see was his mother rigid in her casket, and nothing else. He started, his heart pulsing weakly. His hand faltered over his breast, then met the other hand, folding in the attitude of the dead. His eyes were open, her eyes were closed. Either way, darkness. What should he do now?

A candle he thought guttered was burning low, and his mind caught the light. Yes. He was rising suddenly. He was rising in the dark to go back to Ohio, or anywhere north, because that's where they were all waiting for him—all of them.

I am going to find my father. His name is Michael Patrick Shaughnessy. His father's name is Patrick something Shaughnessy and his mother's name is I don't actually know and their parents' names are
and   and   and   and their parents' names are
and   and   and   and   and   and

He was slipping his feet into his shoes and lacing them, his eyes unblinking. He was no longer confused. He felt around for his duffel and found the nylon strap. When he hefted it, he was hefting his whole life, and it weighed practically nothing. He couldn't find where the lady had put his starter jacket, so he simply left the room, bumping twice into a wall in the pitch black, and then he was in the living room, where a tiny eye of light remained on the television screen. It illuminated the keys on a side table. He snatched them up and let himself out of the lavender house, where the old woman would have held him and helped him cry if only he'd known how to do those things without remembering.

For the life of him, he could not figure out why he had been born.

The Cadillac started in an instant, and he did everything the way Aesop had shown him. Lights on the left, release parking brake, reverse, and away you go. He crept down the street, his hands clutching the wheel, looking neither right nor left, but applying the gas and departing forever from this way station.

He had no idea where he was going. He passed AA cemetery no. 1 without even knowing it was there, then the old train tracks, and when he saw a man on the street, he screeched to a halt.

"How you get out of Lexington?"

"Where you headed, son?"

"North."

"Got to head up the hillbilly highway. But watch out for New Circle, it's like a big old wheel."

He was speeding and heading home. The car swerved madly as the gas jetted through the carburetor, and a honking horn wowled past him, but he didn't hear it, because it took all his effort to not remember, because the world had gone retrograde and now ran counter to sense. The stars were slung under the horizon and hell was high. Life led to nothing, and he was arcing now toward that future faster than he ever had before, because every impediment was gone. His speed was tremendous. A horn blared, then more, the bright lights of this city entirely foreign, and then the policeman who had lodged his cruiser between two juniper bushes on the barn end of a Thoroughbred operation actually laughed out loud as he switched on his lights and sirens. What kind of idiot did eighty-seven down Winchester Road—and in a purple fucking Cadillac at that? His partner said, mildly, "Good God." Then their lights were swooping red and blue across the blacktop before them, and damned if the purple car didn't actually speed up for a few seconds before it pulled over, and they saw a man fumbling at the wheel—possibly black, yeah, definitely black—so the cop behind the wheel was pulling his gun even before he was under twenty miles per hour. It was the fumbling he really didn't like; it didn't bode well.

The loudspeaker boomed out, causing Allmon to jump, but then he heard a voice with its sawn timbre saying, "Get out of the vehicle, and put your hands on the roof."

For a moment he reached for his wallet, but he didn't even have it with him. And what good would it have done? All he had was a high school ID. Whatever. Nothing mattered. There was no meaning in his frightened eyes, or in the thumping of his heart, and there was no meaning in the words that said louder this time: "Exit your vehicle with your hands up! Now!"

In the rearview he saw a black guy—and for a moment entertained a faint and foolish hope—but then it didn't matter, because the man's hands were on him, and he was face-first against the hood of the car, his own hands splayed there, as unfamiliar as the contents of someone else's pockets. "Where's your license?" He shook his head, his thoughts as distant as Ohio, and the other cop, a white guy, was going through the car now, rifling through his duffel bag and, "Now what's this?" Two vials. And, "Mark, there's a weapon here," and the black man behind him tightens his hold but needlessly, and if this is his last embrace, he'll accept it; he's not resisting. The black man says, "Stupid. Incredibly stupid. Where did you think you were headed?" Tries to say Cincinnati, but it comes out "Shh-hhh," and the man says, "Well, wherever you were going, you're not getting there tonight, son." Son? No, not that. "Hey, kid, what's your name?" Allmon can't answer the question, because he's not sure what that even means. Hey, I'm just a kid! Just kidding! I'm nobody's kid. And the white guy says, "You don't want to answer questions, fine. Bullpen for you," but he's still refusing to answer any questions when they ink his fingers and photograph his expressionless face downtown. When he walks into the holding cell bullpen tank meatcan, three concrete walls with bars at the Fayette County detention center, he doesn't say a word, can't think over the piss smell, cigarettes, barnyard stench, thrumming music, eyes staring at him, through him; same bewildered silence later when he's arraigned for a fitness hearing and transferred by the juvenile judge to adult court as a youthful offender, and only with his harried defense attorney he meets five minutes before his five-minute hearing does he finally say, confusedly, "When can I go home?" Then with further prompting at his hearing, he begins to haltingly describe the unwound spool which is his life, but when, skeptical and unmoved, the circuit court judge asks him, "Do you understand the nature of a Class C felony?" he can only nod his head yes, because it's true, he does know—Aesop told him. He's seventeen but sentenced as an adult by an angry, exhausted judge: ten years for possession of five grams of crack cocaine, with an extra two years for motor vehicle theft and possession of a weapon and resisting arrest, eligible for parole in six years, and spending his first four months in a detention center before he's transferred to that hellhole Bracken for three years, followed by three in minimum-security Blackburn, where he will learn to groom horses, but in both facilities, he is a strange and terrified boy in a strange and terrifying no-man's-land, where on the first of 2,190 nights, when they cut the fluorescent lights, he begins to cry and longs hellishly for home with the fever-pitch concentration of the damned, aching for the city of his mother, for the ghost of his father, his young and original self; for that place where the skyscrapers are steeples under which the Reverend preaches, divulging all the arcana of manhood and warning him away from Kentucky, which is just a cell Allmon yearns to reach out and unlock, swinging open to a free vista of the seven hills and the river now a fable, a river flooding its banks and telling tales, which Allmon cries to on his knees: *Tell me a story. Tell me about my past. Tell me about a place where the lights don't go out*

A voice says, Shhhhh
tell me a story where no one goes away
Shhhh . . .
tell me a story about me
Scipio says, Listen now:

INTERLUDE III

That man there is a blood man. He stands at the edge of the Kentucky hills where they slope to the prattling river, imagining his children and their children not with his mind, but with the will of his body inclined toward freedom. He has come from the heart of Kentucky, a place that boasts one slave for every white man, and he is one of those slaves, or so they tell him, though he won't be for long.

He is an independent man and enterprising, though never formally educated, a man solitary and suspicious by nature, with no friends but his mother, who died in the spring of this very year, so the yoke of love has been lifted from him, his spirit now free to make his body free. Hate and desire bear him aloft from the outskirts of Paris like a seedling on fresh wind seeking fertile ground. He leaves his master's farm on a Saturday with a pass to attend a dance at a farm in Winchester in the company of ten other bondsmen, but when they reach the fork in the road that turns south toward Clark County, he takes his leave without a word, slipping from their jovial pack and disappearing into the woods. He cinches sacks of crushed Indian turnip around his calfhide brogans to throw off the scent and then crashes deep into the undergrowth of shrubs and thorny bushes. He knows of the famed railroad—all but the most ignorant backwoods slaves know of it—but he long ago decided to seek no help, none at all, refusing to follow another, black or white of any political persuasion, because he will be a man who makes his own way.

His first night is pure and blinding panic, sure the bloodhounds have been loosed, sure there are white men behind every oak tree, every maple. He remembers a nursing woman he had known as a child, one who ran off only to be hounded against a tree where the dogs ripped the breasts from her body; she had lived long enough to be whipped with the tooth side of a handsaw. Now, in fear of patrollers, he steers clear of the road to Mason County and Maysville, and won't travel as far east as the Lexington–Cincinnati road, and on that blessed day when he arrives in the Queen City, he won't go knocking on the door of Mr. Coffin's Grand Central Station. He considers himself unschooled but not reckless—he won't seek the aid of a strange white man, no matter his reputation. No, he'll go straight to Bucktown and throw his body and his soul down on the charity of the first black church he sees: there is no safe place in this world, but a black church is the closest thing. His mother taught him that.

He plunges into the nocturnal edge of the county, racing a desperate, diagonal line north, hoping, if chance and property lines favor him, to emerge at the river a full day's walk to the east of the city, a good distance from the Lexington–Cincinnati road. As he stumbles along in the dark, he clings to the rock-strewn streams that branch along the forest, where cold, plush water gurgles up from the soil, and for two hours becomes lost in a labyrinthine terrain of towering limestone hallways, which veer this way and that beneath the black rooftops of the trees. Eventually freeing himself, he passes along a series of tended pastures, just a dark wraith along the split rail fencing, an unsafe passage to be sure, but no other humans are about in the deep of the night. All around him, the dark forest is alive, vital, a black lattice before a white moon. Things unseen touch his face in jest and curiosity. Every step of the way, the owls question his route, his choices, his odds, and the night critters speechify and debate, but never once does he hear the clipped voices of white men or the brute, pitiless baying of distant hounds. He stays the course until the break of the next morning, when he climbs a sugar maple and expends a jittery, sleepless day at the tangent of limb and trunk, staring wretchedly into the vast green canopy.

Then night again, and no aid, no friend, only the North Star to conduct him. He walks on and on, eating only small bites from a satchel containing fatback, hogmeat slices, and crumbling cornpone. Two more days and his overshoes of turnip have fallen away, his hair is peppered with bits of leaf like green ash, and he has lost weight he didn't have to spare. He begins then to traverse during the day, still fretful, almost forty miles from Lexington now, and safer, he knows, but desperate to cover more ground. The waking world seems to have changed in the four days since he has seen it. The light is shocking and the land is fertile with late summer—the bright corollas of flowers, the winding vines loping tree to tree, the cool and pungent drafts of pine, ginseng here and chanterelles there and everything covered with a green, fair moss like verdigris on copper. He eyes the beauty with bitterness; yes, he thinks, this whole world ain't nothing but a bad penny, keeps turning up and going to mold.

In the muddled brew of his worry and overwhelming fatigue, he grows careless and the next morning stands accosted by a tiny white woman in a stove-black bonnet so enormous and overhanging, he can only see the tight sphincter of her mouth as she says, "Nigger, I got eggs."

He's half-asleep and so surprised by her sudden appearance that, despite the instincts of his legs, he doesn't run, his eyes locked on the eggs she's carrying in the gaping pockets of her tattered linsey-woolsey pinafore. She reaches down and holds out three eggs to him without ever once looking him in the eye.

She says, "Now, my husband he preciated the niggers, but I ain't concerned if they live or die. Still my husband preciated em, so I give em to ye to have. Here now."

With care and fleet glances in all directions, he takes the three eggs from her hands; they're the color of boiled chicory with new milk. "Grateful, missus," he whispers.

"Tain't no difference to me," she says. "If they hang ye or hightail ye back to Africkay, tain't no business of mine. Them's fresh eggs. They'll keep."

He runs then, cradling the delicate, knocking eggs in his shirt until he reaches a distance of a mile or more, and when no one seems to be following, he cracks the eggs and drinks them down. Then he moves on through what he hopes is the center of Harrison County, and on that very same afternoon, after having not seen anyone in four days except the woman with the eggs, he spies a second woman—this one from the back and from such a distance, he just watches her creep shakily along for a breathless minute before he realizes she's colored. He can hear her crying now from where he stands, but he makes no sound at all, resolving to melt back into the under- growth and shield himself from her eyes; he can afford no joiners, least of all a woman. Then she turns jerkily, suddenly, like a deer that senses rather than hears its predator, and he sees that her belly is as big as a sugar kettle and now her black eyes are on him. Deep as coal rocks, full of lustrous tears. She reaches out one hand to him, her mouth aslant: "Help me! Help dis poor gal!"

He takes a step backward from her call, but he can't look away, and she comes forward a few broken paces. He is set to run, one foot behind him, his weight ungrounded, a bird preparing for flight.

"Help me! Help us get north!"

Warily, he whispers, "You got to shift for your own self."

"Please, mistah!" she pleads. "You talk fine, I can tell you a smart nig- ger. Help dis ignorant gal and dis here baby get dey freedom!"

He rears back in distaste and manages one deliberate step backward, but she stumbles forward, grasping up his shirtfront now in her dirty fist; her touch is what he had most wanted to avoid, even more than her desperate voice. Her distended belly is inches from his. Her eyes burn into him. "Iffen you leave us, dey gone kill us. Dey gone kill dis baby."

No, no, no, Scipio wants to scream in frustration and anger—unwind the clock, unspool time—but these eyes, this belly . . . sweat springs up beads on his forehead and upper lip. He wants to curse every step that brought him to this particular spot. All his effort was for him alone! He eyes her angrily and tries to press back his conscience, but it's no use. In another instant, the thing is done and they are a pair, Scipio plowing through the woods at a frightful, angry pace; the woman drying her tears and skipping along despite her bulk, her rounds of thanksgiving and grati- tude devolving into pleas as she falls back now and again with Scipio saying only, "Keep up." And when they stop at a burbling spring to drink, she whips off her headrag and falls to her knees, saying, "Praise de Lord for . . . what dey name you?"

"My name ain't no consequence."

She blinks. "I's Abby and dis baby gone be name Canada when it come. I's gone live in dere, I is."

"Listen here now," Scipio says, "I'll take you two days and then you got to aim east on your own and walk to Mason County. There's a man there what got a yellow barn. He'll skiff you across the river to Ripley. He'll know you by the password 'Menare.' I promise you that's the truth. But I ain't going there. I got my own plan to swim that river, and I can't be shaked from it."

"I's gone where you's gone," she says.

"You ain't doing no such," he growls.

"I is!" And to this vehemence, he doesn't know what to say, he can only glower at her and then they walk on for another day, she at his heels like a bulky terrier, pestering and questioning him and thanking him again and singing and moaning until he feels sure she's soft in the head and he regrets her more and more each step of the way. Finally he whips about and, with a finger to her face, says, "Don't talk, don't ask, don't touch! Just follow!"

And Abby does follow, gradually quietening and walking with her forearms cradling her enormous belly like saddle straps to hold it secure. Scipio is at first grateful for her silence, but once or twice as they walk during that second day, he glances back and sees silent tear-trails tracking through the grime on her face. It gives him pause, he thinks of his mother. It slowly destroys his resolve.

That night when they've sat down side by side, preparing for sleep under the spread arms of a tree, Scipio takes up his case again, but gentler this time.

"Listen here, Miss Abby," he says. "In the morning, you got to strike out for Mason County on your own. I aim to swim the river and you can't swim it with that belly a yours. You hear?"

"I can swim," she says, staring at him mulishly.

He rears back. "God almighty, gal!" The wick of his impatience is lit now. "You gone and lost your mind? What kind of crazy gal runs off when she needs to be laying in? I planned this escape nigh on three years, choosing the month, the day, the very hour, and I won't have no crazy gal getting me shot on the riverbanks with Canaan right there in my sights!"

Scipio expects her to begin crying again, an act which seems nearly as natural to her as speech, but she just hangs her head for a long minute, like she's studying deeply on his words. He begins to wonder whether she's even understood him when she says, so quietly does he have to strain to understand her, "My mammy name me Abby. I am taken from my mammy when I'm age thirteen. I never forget de day. My mammy she done wrapped up my nubbins in a old linen rag so nobody see em, but de speclator come and he seed I got de age on me and he teared me from my mammy and I never forget, she say, 'Be good, Abby, don't give em no cause to whup you,' and I ain't never done no such. I never seed my mammy anymore. Well, dat speclator man take me to Lexington and he stand me up on de Cheapside block. He den tear off my woolens and de mens come and look and pinch and de speclator cry me off. Dis one man, he pay twelve hundred dollar for me. Ignorant nigger I is, I thinks how lucky I is, a rich man gone pay dat kind a money for me, he gone take right good care a me."

Abby stops, she seems not to know what to do with her hands as she speaks, pressing them into her hair now, which is wild and unkempt, her rag long fallen away. She will not look at Scipio, she just rocks her knobby hands into her hairline.

"Well, come find dat white trash man ain't rich," she says bitterly. "Don't know how he paid dat kind a money. He only had him three niggers and only one dem's my age and he done make me de wife a all three."

Scipio makes an involuntary jerking motion with his hands. He almost asks her to hush, but she continues on.

"Now, here he don't make me work in no field like I's expectin, no, he lock me up in dis quarter, ain't no bigger dan a root cellar and ain't got no window. He lock me on dis bed with one chain on de wrist and one on de ankle and den dey come messin with me and sometime de Marster he watch de niggers mess with me and den he mess with me. I don't know how long I's livin dere, den I get swole up big and he say, 'You gone have you a baby, Abby,' and I got de amazement cause I don't know nothin and den dat baby get borned. Den he let me out and I gets de run a de place, cause he figure if I got a baby, den I ain't gone run. And he right. I ain't gone run."

She looks at Scipio then and she appears crazy to him and he wishes all over again that he could have avoided her somehow, or left her along the way. Cruel as it is and against his own will, he wishes she were back where she'd come from, but still he utters no word.

She says, "Den I seed he got him a Missus. A Missus! Why he messin with a nigger gal when he got a Missus? I don't never understand. But dey both am mean as devils. Dey chained de niggermens to dey beds at night and dat Missus she whupped em in de morning with a leather switch out a pure devilment. Forty lashes ever day. Dey ain't never run, cause de Marster say he kill em if dey do and dey knowed it de truth. De Marster have him a old nigger name Perry and one day Perry say, 'I's too old, you can't make me work no more, I's got to rest,' and de Marster, he say, 'Dat sound all right, you slowin down,' and when Perry turn away, de Marster crack him over de head with de hoe he holdin and drop Perry stone dead. De Marster make de niggers wait to bury him five days and den without no stone. So us all knowed dat true.

"Now, on dis farm don't a body never visit, no preacher never come, no family never come, just us all de time shiftin for usselves. Well, I gets a string a babies and when dey six or seven year old de Marster, he sell each em away for de money and I ain't even say no, see, I pray God dey get sold to a good white man. I knows dey's lots a good white folk in de world like my mammy's Marster. He ain't hardly whupped on his niggers and only when dey deserved it.

"But—but den it finally happen. I gets me a white baby and den de Missus know de Marster messin with me and she open hate on me all de time. She pullin my hair and lashin me and de Marster tell her, 'Quit,' but den she just do it when he ain't dere. It am a misery. Dis bout de time my Sarah die a de fever and I only got William who age six and my white baby, Callie. Den one terrible day I brings de sheets in de house for pressin and I fetch de iron out de fire and I got—" She screws up her lips, her whole body shaking.

"Hush!" Scipio whispers, fear and horror curdling in his belly. "Quit talking now, Miss Abby."

Abby raises up her eyes. "Oh Lord, dat day I got Callie on my arm and she cryin and William, he complainin like he hungry and needin fare or some such and I leave de iron on de sheet and it burn a big black mark. And de Missus, she see dat mark and her face get real funny and Callie squawlin and den de Missus say, 'Hush dat nigger chile!' and den she reach over and pick up dat jingling iron and she strike dat hot iron against my baby Callie so hard she break her head in. I never forget how it jingle. My baby don't even cry, she only open her broke mouth like she a baby bird, her face ruint and broke in and she gasp just like dat and shake oncet and den she

die in my arm. Right dere in my arm. Oh God, Lord—I so pained I runs out
de house and de Missus wailin to de Marster what she ain't meant it and he
come a-runnin and a-shoutin."

Scipio has lost the will to quiet her, unable to take his eyes from her
stricken face.

"I runs through de yard with my poor Callie and I can't make no sense a
nothing and I screams and I don't know what, but finally I understands my
baby dead and I gots to bury my baby, but my William, oh Lord, my William, something done shaked loose in dat little soul. He snatch my Callie
away from me and hold her like he got a nubbin for milkin and he singing to
her, and den he cryin and he make like he playin and talkin to her, and de
Marster, he come sneak up on him, but William see him and stop and
screech like he done lost ever wit, 'Go away you ugly nigger! God hate you,
nigger!' He callin de Marster nigger, he so distracted, and de Marster, he
start to cryin too. Den he smack my boy so hard he fall and de Marster
bring me my dead Callie. Den William, he runnin and skippin bout like a
dog gone ill and de Marster tell me, 'You ain't nothin but bad luck, Abby.
Dis here baby dead and now your son, he gone plum crazy. I done lost one
thousand dollar dis day.' And den he done gone off and leaved me to bury
my baby gal. I buried her with dese hands. But I ain't seed where William
runned off and I never seed my William anymore. I gone lookin in de
woods for him dat evening, and I heared him talkin nosense but he runned
away from me, and two days later one a de other niggers come on him in
de deep part a de creek where he drownded. Dey all suspicioned de
Marster drownded him, but I disbelieve dat. I disbelieve dat! God, I pray
my son done put hisself away like a good boy and ain't let dat dirty white
trash hold him down one instant! I heared once God don't favor de man dat
put hisself away, but I disbelieve dat. You hear me? I disbelieve dat! God
got righteous mercy if dey six year old!"

She weeps openly and loudly and Scipio scoots over through the dry,
rustling leaves, reaching around her, but not to embrace her, only to clamp
one dry hand over her mouth. "Hush," he says. "Hush your mouth. Don't
make no sound now."

She sobs against his hand, staring up into the blank sky at something
beyond his eyes. With an utterly lost feeling, he looks around them at the
butternut trees, at the stones, the dumb soil, all the while holding her, rocking

her. He keeps that hand on her mouth, feeling a deep burn in his soul, and finally, when he senses that her tears are only coming harder and won't ever abate, he says, very quietly, "Hush now, hush. Let me tell you something what'll make you feel better. I got a story for you. This a story about a young buck named Scipio. Miss Abby, you know who that is?"

Her chest still heaving, Abby shakes her head against his hand, her brows drawn in wretched sorrow. "That's me, you understand? My mother, she named me Scipio. Now, when Scipio was just a young buck, he was mighty good friends with Master's son, named Richmond. Richmond and Scipio was running all over the place, through the fields, up the road, and all in the great house. Being friends with Richmond, Scipio didn't never get whipped, cause he never made no trouble, and he got some education on the sly. Nobody learned him to read, but he listened to the white folks talk and he learned plenty that way. He figured enough to know that the black folk was property in Kentucky but free in Ohio, and that got him to thinking. Got him to thinking hard. Now, Scipio's mother was the cook for the great house and Scipio, he was brung up to do the carpentry. The years passed until Richmond was near bout a man, sixteen or so, and four years older than Scipio. Richmond begun watching Scipio's mother and then one day he tried to interfere with her. Now, Scipio's mother wouldn't tolerate that kind of treatment from a pup and she slapped him away. But Richmond thought he had got the right to Scipio's mother! Richmond was so mad then, he put a wedding gift fire poker in the quarter Scipio shared with his mother. All the great house was searching for that fire poker and when they found it in the cabin, they raised revolution. They intended to whip Scipio's mother. So what you think Scipio done?"

Abby blinks and tugs his hand from her mouth. "What you done?" she whispers. He grins angrily, feeling strangely loose from his old self, almost disembodied; he has never told this story to a soul. His life has always depended upon it.

"Why, I hollered, 'I done it!' and then what you think happened?"

Abby is silent, saucer-eyed, but her tears have stopped.

"Why, they whipped Scipio heaven high and valley low and then they poured brine on his back and then they done it all over again with the stock end of the whip. But don't you worry, Miss Abby—the story don't end there. Don't you believe that Scipio wanted revenge? Oh, yes, he did, you know he did. But he couldn't get no revenge on Richmond, cause that was too easy to figure. No, Scipio decided he was gonna work revenge on the whipping man, that dumb overseer, who ain't had no sense a smell and was half-blind in the one eye. That man was just mean as a snake. So Scipio waited real patient for his chance. He waited three long months, counting every minute. Now, he knowed his way all around that great house and he knowed the overseer smoked a ivory pipe alongside Master every Thursday evening in the front parlor while they talked the business. Well, Scipio done made a show of acting real sorry and sad and like that, but when nobody was in that great house, he sneaked in there with gunpowder he stole from the gun cupboard, and he packed that gunpowder in the overseer's pipe nice and tight under the tobacco. It smelled real strong, but the overseer, he ain't had no sense a smell at all. See, Scipio just sealed it good and tight and he ran back to the quarter and for a whole day suffered the awfulest fear that maybe he packed the wrong pipe and Master was fixing to blow hisself up instead, but no, come the next evening, there was the biggest bang from the great house and all the colored folk and all the white folk, they was running all over the yard, the Missus was hollering and they took that bleeding, jaw-busted overseer near sixty miles to a special doctor down in Perryville and he stayed gone nigh on seven weeks. When he come back, he hadn't had no tongue, his head just crooked as a scarecrow's, and nobody was the wiser, but they all knowed he was the most ignorant white man there ever was, packing his own pipe with gunpowder. And, sure enough, he also knowed he was the most ignorant white man there ever was, cause he whipped on the wrong nigger, but he done whipped on so many, he ain't even knowed which one."

Laughter erupts from Abby, a piercing bright sound of delight before Scipio clamps his hand down on her mouth again, saying, "Hush!" but she's laughing, her breasts heaving, her belly shaking, and he has to cover his own mouth with his free hand, because he too begins to laugh; he's laughing so hard it rocks him, but he also thinks of his mother dead and cold in the ground, who used to say to him, "You my onliest love and de whole world ain't no count if you ain't in it," and he can't tell whether his tears are laughter or despair, they burn his eyes like acid just the same.

In the morning, their laughter has echoed away, and he doesn't mention Mason County again, or the skiff, or her need to veer east. They resume their northward trek, Scipio in the lead. He pushes ahead with renewed vigor, passing through open pasturage at times, sensing—knowing—that the river is not far now, not if they have covered close to ten miles a day, what would have been twelve or even fifteen without a pregnant woman at his side. But that is no matter now. Because of her story, or perhaps because of his, she stays close to him, sometimes grabbing out at his shirt when she stumbles or trips, but he doesn't seem to mind; she's broken him. Scipio will keep them safe. He will conduct them to the far side.

At midday, as he's gathering berries for them, she makes a deep, chesty sound, what he initially mistakes for singing under her breath, but when he turns, she's bent and hesitant, sweating, her hands spread for balance in the air. When he goes to her, trouble on his brow, she straightens up and blanks her face, says, "I's fine. Walk on, Scipio."

On the last day of their walking, the land grows increasingly hilly and curvaceous, much more so than Scipio had expected. No more obliging fields with forest enclosure, but hikes so steep that Scipio is hauling Abby up the inclines and her whole body trembles with the effort. She speaks no words today, as if every faculty she possesses, including speech, is sacrificed for this last consuming effort and it is the last, because at the break of the hill, she stumbles into Scipio, who has stopped suddenly. Through a natural window in the trees, they spy the Ohio River down below, that dark dividing line made by God but named by men, and they are standing at the watershed where all of life flows north to freedom. Scipio raises his arm and points and she peers around his shoulder with a hard sigh. He realizes with some dismay that though he can see the red brick and smoke of Cincinnati to the west, they are some distance from the city and there's nothing to be done about it. They'll swim from the bank directly below them.

He searches the northern slope of the hill, where sweet gum, mulberry, and beech trees congregate in clusters, until he finds a thick limestone berm, where the hill just begins its precipitous, gravelly fall to the river. The thin, level space is sheltered by the broad cordated leaves of plants so tall on their scapes, he initially mistakes them for trees. A mass of verdant foliage encases the ledge, making a cool shelter there.

He says, "This is where we gonna spend the night. I aim to wake you when it's still dark, and then we gonna climb down and swim. Save your strength, Miss Abby."

She nods her head and Scipio detects the sharpening of fear in her eyes as she contemplates the hillside and the rustling river far below, but when he sits under the leaves, she follows his lead meekly and is almost instantly asleep, snoring gently, though fitting and starting, her mind darting here and there just beneath sleep's surface—he recognizes the motion, because he sleeps like that too, his spirit riven by fear. His brief dreams are like jars shattering. For twelve days, he has lived in terror. He shudders, turning his head away from Abby's bedraggled, restless form and huddling deeper into himself, feeling not just weary but crippled in his pained exhaustion, so that if a patroller were to point the snout of a rifle into their leafy hut, Scipio would be altogether unable to run, or even rise. But they are well hidden in the foliage and though he can just spy the quick river below, the vegetation shuts out the light, forcing an early evening in their bower, over which evening slowly descends: First, a crepuscular smudge at the edges of eastern time and the sky is brushed with crimson and damask, then shadows are knit from the darkest remnants of day, the dark sprawls, daybirds mourn and nightbirds vivify, bony egrets sweep along the tributaries of the river and their flapping wings sound like brown paper crinkling, and bank swallows burrow in the dirt banks, the falling light is gay laughter in another room, the waterside plants hang sorrowful heads from slender petioles, the river speaks in low, brooding tones, the river is a coal seam exposed in a hollow, the river is black velvet unspooled from its bolt, the river is a vein opened, the river is decay, every fine line grown indistinct in the gloaming. A bird trills from the southern shore and the northern shore echoes the call, near intimates but never intimate, now a single lush billow of wind suggests rain and a muggy wet woolen is tossed over the shoulders of the land, the river valley swaths herself in wedding gauze, misty evening hums, this is a shroud or a mother's shhhhhhhh, a droning prayer, this river is a lullaby and a dirge, this river is a promise made in daylight but upheld by night, and soon there will be no color because the night is coming on and nameless animals now call roll for the absent overseer and beneath the crenellated edge of the dew-soaked plants, Scipio's eyes are draping shut against his will. But the crooning of a mourning dove or a mockingbird— the latter so infinitely variable, who can distinguish them—pierces the air and starts him from his momentary rest. He forces a final reconnoitering glance at the river, which holds one last fistful of scattered light, and he thinks, it ain't so wide after all, and then he grasps the absurdity deep down in the marrow of his bones, how this very night the mask of slavery will be lifted from his face by geography, this arbitrary fact of twelve hundred feet, this quarter mile God laid down for beauty's sake. Your humanity depends upon the ground beneath your feet. You cannot straddle this river. You must choose a side.

Later, he wakes from fitful sleep in the dark but forces himself to be still, waiting for that precise moment when the night has grown late but the morning star is yet to rise. He waits and waits, until he can't bear it another minute, and then he wakes Abby. She comes to with a soft cry.

"We got to go now," he says, and they slip out from under the shelter of the plants into the dark, which presses them from both sides. They are suddenly electric with wakefulness. Hand in hand, they navigate the descent to the flat plane of the river, stumbling on exposed roots and the frangible soil of the hillside, the slippery spots where exposed limestone is slick with dew and the scat of animals that passed here just hours before. Through masses of tangled vegetation, Scipio catches brief snatches of the river, and he knows it is the river only because it is blacker than any other black in the night. Just as planned, he has arrived on a moonless night so there is no light to play on the water, or to light their figures for any patrollers who might be waiting and watching.

Abby cries out suddenly and Scipio whips around to shush her, but she is doubled over, gripping her belly with fingers that appear carved from stone.

"Miss Abby!" he whispers, but she doesn't reply, doesn't move. "You close? You can't cross with no baby pains!"

Still doubled, Abby grapples for his shirt and grips him firm to keep him from leaving, but he has no intention of leaving, no intention at all. He can't run away from this woman. He has a vision of them crossing, it's firm in his mind now like a story told to him a long time ago, a story which he now believes with all of his heart.

Abby rises up to her full height and, for once, she isn't begging: "I told you I's crossing dis night. All my chilluns gived me de pain for three days fore dey come. Dis de same, and I's swimming."

"Miss Abby, you're fixing to drown if you cross this river with the pains."

She breathes through her nostrils rapidly, shoulders quaking, but fixes him with a wide-eyed stare, which is only half-wild. "Iffen I pain, den you hold me up. You hear?"

He stares at her a moment, then says, "Miss Abby . . ."

"You hold me and dis here poor baby up."

"Yes."

"Move den," she orders, and they move down the last stretch of oak-clogged hill, which slopes to an alluvial flat pierced with branchless, leafless tree stumps like fat spears in the ground, and finally, sweaty with effort and fear, they stand at the edge of the moving water and Scipio is staring down at the great cinereous boulders scattered on the beach as if a kindly god has placed them there for a man and woman to hide alongside. Abby says, "Thank you, Lord, I's brung to de River Jordan and I's gone wade in de water. I's never gone be de slave a de white man no more, only de slave a God."

Scipio turns his head from words so distasteful to him. He whispers only, "Pray this river to carry us across." He knows it will—look how low and still it is, waters pulsing easily with the river's own calm, even breath. He can already feel his ball-and-chain spirit becoming no heavier than a feather. The patrollers are just a fading nightmare of childhood, the speculators too, the great house, and his life there, even the death of his dear mother. And see there, in place of that old dream, how near stands the opposite shore, night eliding distance, so a man can reach out strong swimmer's arms and almost touch it.

He's been wasting time gawking; he hunts hurriedly around the shadowy shoreline for driftwood and finds, instead, the moldering remains of what might have been a rowboat's stern—he guesses from the angle of the sawn edge of the wood in his hand. Very little of it remains.

"Now swim with this in the crotch a your arm," he says, and wedges it awkwardly into Abby's damp armpit. Then he unties his tattered, sand-caked brogans and leaves them on the shore; he does not want to wear the shoes of slavery on the other side.

He grasps up Abby's hand, says nothing more, and guides her stealthily from boulder to boulder, both of them slunk down low, though she can barely bend with her protruding belly. She grunts audibly as she walks.

The Ohio River is icy cold and in a moment it swallows them whole. Only their heads show and he thinks, Carry us, carry us, carry us, carry us, and then the rocky bed swoops away from under their feet, the hungry current carrying them as they plow through its eddies, both of them good, strong swimmers, though Abby slower because of her bulk. Scipio, slightly ahead, fastens his eyes on the black tree line on the far side, the river itself hastening him there, the current sweeping him closer to Ohio, closer to the dream, closer to Bucktown and a church of brethren who will help him, closer, closer now, ever closer. They cross the midway point of the river, the only sound their own labored breathing.

"Oh," Abby says once, somewhere behind him.

"Hush," he whispers back, plowing on with wide, chopping strokes.

"Oh," she moans, and then her voice is full of water. There is a brief thrashing sound, another gasp, and she slips below. She doesn't cry out again, but her hands crash once more on the surface like the sound of two oars smacking, and Scipio tears his eyes from his salvation and ceases his powerful swimming to look back, only to find the white ructure she's made on the surface of the water. He drifts for a moment in pure panic, unsure what to do, pulled powerfully between two worlds. Then with an involuntary cry, he swims back to her. Once again Abby finds the surface, and he sees for one moment her panicked eyes in the faint light of the moon, and he will never forget the sight of her desperation. Then she slips below. She fights against the swamping weight of the water, thrashing violently, striving for its glistening black surface, but her body clamps in on itself as if the child were struggling mightily within her. Her legs draw up suddenly in a wrenching spasm, and her arms whip wildly about and spin for purchase until she finds Scipio's leg, which she grips with all the life force bestowed upon her by right of her own birth. Without warning, she yanks him beneath the surface, and with blind horror, Scipio kicks downward. Quick as lightning, guided only by instinct, his foot finds her belly. Her hands release, and like a stone, Abby drops away.

Now Scipio fights for the shore as if the devil himself were after him. He's weeping in horror and drinking the river as he goes, sick with panic and making no effort at all to conceal his passage but only trying to escape death, which would drag him with its iron shackles down to the bottom of the river. He crashes desperately through the sucking current until he finally feels the stony riverbed beneath his bare feet and lurches out, stumbling like a drunk among the rocks and fallen branches. On the bank, he looks like a madman, his hair matted and soaked with the spit of the river, his jaw loose, his eyes horribly wide. He touches his face with a shaking hand as if startled to discover that he is alive, but God, she is dead and he has killed her! He whips around once in disbelief to face the water. How he has longed for this moment since he was a child and now . . . The river is speaking to him, its words a curse. He stumbles back, away from the sound. Ten steps and the words are a mere prattle. Ten more and the prattle is a whisper. Ten more and the whisper is just a river flowing silent and black, no more dangerous than fiction, no more true than myth. Trembling, he whips around toward the thousand firelight twinklings of Cincinnati a mere mile to the west. His broad, white-latticed back is a curtain drawn on the crude festival of the South. But oh, reader, now Scipio has found something worse than slavery, and will live fifteen more years trying to forget it. There are tales that are remembered and tales that are forgotten, but all tales are born to be told. They demand it; the dead become tales in order to live. Their eternal life is in your mouth.

THE SURVIVAL MACHINE

What god requires a sacrifice of every man, woman, and child
three times a day?   —YORUBA RIDDLE

reathe.

B   Her graying hair was wrapped in a messy bun, her coffee was
black and hot, her gear bag packed with syringes, tail bandages,
Therapogen, and thermometers as always, but the truth? Lou didn't want
to go. And it wasn't just because leaving her husband's side at four in the
morning was akin to leaving the warmth and safety of the womb. She couldn't
shake the dream she'd woken from with a start: the numinous horse, off-
white as a shell's nacre, the way it opened its sickeningly lopsided mouth
and emitted a hellish sound like the shriek of an old steamboat calliope,
that failed music designed to replace church bells in Cincinnati. And then
to be woken by the girl's voice—the Forge daughter, now the farm manager
for her father, his right hand. Flat, affectless voice, cold like a stone you
couldn't warm even if you tossed it in a fire. She'd called to say Seconds
Flat had been streaming milk down her legs for two days and was agitated
now, though she'd shaped up nicely over the last week. The girl—no, the
woman, she was probably twenty-five—was smart and not prone to drama;
if a 4:00 a.m. phone call was necessary, then Lou was needed directly.

Be in your center. As she drove, Lou welcomed the dark morning into her lungs and thanked the world for this offing day with the old meditative habits: witness, gratitude, devotion, coffee. But deep down, she knew she was just dragging her heart along like an old can on a string. There was a dread in her belly, and her body never lied, just as an animal's body never lied. It had nothing to do with a difficult parturition, which could leave everyone exhausted and heartbroken if an animal was lost, and everything to do with where she was going. As her husband—a man who'd lost his filter many years ago—liked to say: Those Forges are motherfucking nuts.

Breathe.

She switched on her brights outside of Paris, casting the rural world into cameratic relief. The old fenced oaks made strange figural silhouettes, a stray horse caught her headlights with globular luminescent eyes, the colorless January frost gleamed—and she breathed in the peace, this dark reservoir of quiet free to those who worked third shift and poor souls like her, who worked any and all shifts every day. But her peace was brief; she was slowing down along Forge Run Creek and the turnoff. She used to come here as a shy teenager with her father, the famously irascible and opinionated Doc Jenkins. Back then, everyone had called her Lulu or Baby Lou. When she'd announced at the age of fifteen that she intended to become a vet, her father was at first dismissive, then disbelieving, then truly angry. "Women don't have what it takes to be veterinarians!" he'd yelled, and then listed her faults—too sensitive, too quick to tears—none of which she could deny and none of which deterred her. He'd forgotten that she was also stubborn, practical, and taught by five older brothers to move directly into a headwind. When her emaciated little mother, worn half to death by rearing six children and smoking two packs of Burleys a day, had pulled her aside and in her exhausted way said, "Do whatever you want to do, Louisa, but don't tell your father I said so," they were kind but wasted words. Lou's mind was already made up.

Vet school at Cornell had solidified her character as much as it had her understanding of anatomy and chemistry. She wasn't stoic by nature or tough, couldn't joke about awful things to lighten a room the way men so often did to blunt their feelings, and everything from dissection to pinching her first foal had moved and frightened her to the limits of her endurance. But she loved animals, and she'd learned another secret from growing up around her brothers: jump in first; the water's only cold for a few seconds.

She had done just that, immersing herself in experience and developing a calm appended of self-assurance, which made her the envy of everyone she worked with. She was the clearest thinker, the quickest diagnostician, the steadiest hand, the eye in any veterinary storm. And if anyone had asked her the secret to her success, it was simple: feel your fear but don't give it any undue respect.

Breathe and be awake.

Forge Run Farm spread darkly before her now as she parked her F250 under the coping of the broodmare barn. Like a muted invitation, yellow light seeped from the door and window fittings. She slipped between the sliding doors with a cursory "I'm here," shedding her green Carhartt jacket and scrubbing up to the biceps at the work sink, while the Forge girl was managing Seconds Flat. The mare had backed her rump against the stall wall, and Lou was about to warn them when she saw how Henry Forge stood at the girl's side, marginally too close, one hand on the neck of the agitated horse and one low on his daughter's opposite hip, so they were touching ankle to shoulder like a sewn seam.

Lou turned back to the sink, startled, and gazed down unseeing as the water rushed over her cracked and weathered hands. She blinked a half dozen times. She only turned again when she heard—or felt—Henry's approach. His face, a face so beautiful it was made for movies, was taut with worry and fatigue. He said, "Her water bag broke as you were driving over. She had three hard contractions and then nothing. We got her up, and we've kept her there."

Now this was something other than mere agitation, this was not a pregnancy gone too long, this was indeed a reason to hurry. Lou darted past Henry, the moment of that strange touch already forgotten, angling toward the stall where the oak partition had been removed for the foaling. There, the musky bloom of animal odor was cut by the astringency of antiseptic. Without apology or explanation, Lou took hold of the headstall from Henrietta and drew the mare forward into the space away from the wall that could interrupt the extension of a tiny foreleg.

"Bring that foal out at any cost," Henry said from beyond the other side of the stall. "I'd rather lose the mare than the foal."

Lou's brow wrinkled: a foal is not a dividend. If you need a durable investment, get a dog or a cow. A horse, like a cat, is delicate. A horse is just four legs and a will to die.

Breathe.

Seconds Flat came forward, febrile sweat beading where her stomach bossed out, kicking up a bit with her front legs at her own foundering labor. With a gentle and confident touch that belied the race against time and dwindling oxygen, Lou drew the massive dam down onto her stout belly, then rolled her onto her side, so her legs stiffed out in a porcine manner. A moment later, Lou was crouched at the rear of the horse, drawing the wrapped tail aside and reaching in past the vulvar lips. There she felt the slippery gray sac that contained the foal. The problem was immediately apparent and simple—well, simple if the foal was still alive—the leading hoof was wedged tight like a support beam against the roof of the birth canal. With care, Lou slit the opalescent sac with her gear scissors, then cupped that sharp little hoof with her hand and waited. There was the briefest of pauses, then an involuntary movement as the leg realigned itself, then a contraction pressed in from all sides, wringing the foal so it inched forward. It was clear now it was still alive, but Lou reported nothing from the deep privacy of concentration. When the bony nose appeared, she curled the sac away from the nostril. A healthy little blue tongue protruded. Another contraction and the foal slid forward, wet and dark with a marmoreal gleam, its sculpted head draped down motionless into the straw, fluid streaming from the nostrils. No one dared breathe until it jerked once and inhaled raggedly. Lou continued to roll back the sac until the foal was free—discrete, sound, and separated from its mother save for the long, pulsing rope of umbilical cord.

While Seconds Flat remained prone, the filly blinked and pawed forward, struggling to acclimate to the pungent, chilly world of the barn. She gathered her spindly legs, situating them beneath her girth, and sloped up to a stand, her surprised hind legs following unsteadily on her fore. After an awkward, lurching step, she discovered her balance and stood before them.

All around, sharp indrawn breaths.

Even with moony newborn eyes and soaked with amniotic fluid, the stark, crystalline beauty of the animal was clear. She had a fine head with a sharply dished nose and an intelligent, curious face. A coat of miscegenated depth, neither black nor brown with a white marking between her eyes—not a star, almost an aborted stripe, a slash of white like a fissure. Her new body was large and muscular for a foal, the legs straight and strong and full of run. On each pastern a skinny low sock was visible, a mere striping of white above the coronet, so her hooves appeared rimed with ice. She observed them with preternaturally alert eyes.

"My God," said Henry, startled. "She's gorgeous."

He reached over then and touched the small of his daughter's back—that too-intimate touch again. Lou saw it from the corner of her eye, but only stared down hard at the foal, a sense of unease rising like gall, but she reminded herself that the intimacy of other families was not something she understood, their lives so separate they might as well be distinct species. Her own family was something of a black Irish carnival. *I do not understand what I do not understand.* It was a thing she often said when her husband was itching for a fight. It irritated him to no end, but it was the truest thing she could say. Lou, how can you reconcile eating meat with all your veterinary work? I love animals and I love myself, but I didn't invent the circle of life. *I do not understand what I do not understand.* Lou, how can you trust your husband since he's an ex-addict—aren't you always worried about a relapse? I love my husband and that's that. *I do not understand what I do not understand.* Lou, how can you spend so much time around Dad, that pain-in-the-ass son of a bitch never shuts up! I love Dad. If I didn't talk to assholes, there'd be no one left to talk to. *I do not understand what I do not understand.*

From a conserve of strength always remarkable in an animal after parturition, Seconds Flat was rising, the placenta ejecting in a stringing mass down onto the straw, that draped gray membrane inlaid with calcareous white strands. Intact and breathing well with the process of ejection complete, her life would return to normal soon. Lou planned to give the new mother a week of involution and repair before her first postnatal uterine exam. But for now her work here was done and, and with a disquiet urging her on, Lou was eager to get off Forge land.

She shrugged into her coat and slipped out the door with only the quietest goodbye, then paused in the emergent morning when she saw a black man walking a mare across the brick chip lane about fifty feet away. Surprise arrested her movement. In her entire life—forty-three years—she'd never seen a black person on these premises—never a farrier, never a visiting groom, certainly not a Forge employee. She was staring openly when Henrietta strode purposefully from the barn, headed in the direction of that man. She nearly ran into Lou.

The warmth of the birthing chamber behind them, Lou could feel the chill radiating off the girl—like an impersonal dislike for everyone and everything—no less real for being unspoken. But Henrietta surprised her by saying, "I want to thank you on behalf of my father. He's disappointed it's not a colt, but I think even he realizes this is an extraordinary filly. She's an evolutionary gem."

Lou cleared her throat and surprised her back. "Actually, horses are the product of an evolutionary failure."

"My father's— Wait, what?"

Looking at the surprise on the young woman's face, Lou said gently, "Horses may be the most beautiful animals on earth, but— Hold on." Her cell phone was buzzing in her pocket with a text that read *Come back to bed. Those people are craaaaaazy* . . . and with haste, she said, "I'm going to head out, Henrietta," then she checked the lock on her Bowie slide-in and yanked open the door of her Toyota.

Breathe.

For a moment, she thought the better of leaving so abruptly—after all, this was a girl whose mother had all but abandoned her as a child—and turned back, but Henrietta was already striding away under the screaking of morning birds, moving in the direction of the distant stallion barn, or perhaps the man Lou had seen, momentarily passing the amber doorway where Henry was staring, enraptured, at the perfect foal being gentled by its exhausted dam, all while the sun rose with a pitiless red and the shuttle rattled across the ancient loom and, somewhere, Maryleen sharpened her pencil to a knife's point and began to write.

It's 1945 and the farm is an old man, and the old man is a babe in arms. It's 1950 and the servants are stealing the silver, his mother riding easy on a trotter; 1973 and the Old Man is a downed timber in a casket; 1976 and She is the seed flowering once again; 1980 and the Old Man is a husk, nothing but a rotted memory, and you're running the show. Now it's 2003, and what has really changed? Black is priapic drive, confidence man, skin-shifting fright, hellion, killy on a hook and his daughter is biting.

Henry stared at the filly before him, all pert and innocent on stalk legs borrowed from a dam and sire of the same line, a tight constellation of traits to be passed along in due order—perhaps only four short years. Henry's whole life, every breath of his lungs, every firing of every synapse, was a wordless plea for an enormous heart. This shock of a filly was the horse he'd waited for for sixty-one years. She was inbred to perfection, and he knew it with his whole body. And yet where was his daughter, his right hand? He stalked to the sliding barn door and stood at the edge of a feeble white morning.

Rage simply erupted from him. "Henrietta!"

The early light was silent.

He could hear his life echoing emptily around the farm.

Maybe little girls think their fathers don't notice when their hearts raise a cold shoulder. Or maybe—trickle of cognition—maybe it was meant to be noticed. His own reckless young self cast a shadow across the clear vision of a backward glance. That was the game of youth, wasn't it—murdering one's father? At first, the horses, like any weapon, are mere handmaidens to the battle; only later, in the maturity of open war, is the weapon transformed into an art itself. From the lowest calling to the highest. But Henrietta's was a ridiculous game, not even a battle. And he could beat her at it; after all, he had played it before and knew all the tricks. Some men win women with animal brawn, but the fittest is the smartest, the wiliest. Odysseus with his craft and his cock in his hand. A father was born for himself, and his son was himself in perpetuity, *et alii*. The First Cause was existence itself, and the body made morality a servant of survival. He knew how to play on her weakness for his name's sake, and he knew her weakness because he had made it himself.

"Henrietta!"

It was the smell of him that had slain her.

The first day he'd shown up for work, she'd noticed it as she led him to the stallion barn where he would groom. A cutting scent of his body so strong that at first she found it almost distasteful, like sun-ripened sweat on the body too long, until it wended past her nostrils into her lungs and turned to a strange distraction. Then it moved along the corridors of her mind to rooms deeper than thinking: indisputable. It made promises that her whole body responded to with assent.

She was seeking him out in the stallion barn, where he would be mucking stalls in the cool of the morning. She went ostensibly to tell him about the foal, but in all honesty, she couldn't help it, she felt she had no choice, her body was ferrying her there, the selfish hum of the blood rising in pitch. She wanted to open his exotic mouth and press herself into it, to discover what he was naked. But braided into a moment's fantasy of entanglement, painfully expressed in her breasts and between her legs, resided a subtle, old confusion.

"Henrietta!"

Goddammit. The oaken barn shrank to the size of a bird's cage. Henry Forge, father and keeper. She paused at the door and sighed. What did she know? That the horse has true and false and floating ribs. That it has 205 bones in its body, the chestnuts on the backs of the limbs being remnants of the ancient horse alive in the modern; that, like a human, the horse sweats when it's nervous. That I am as trapped as any Thoroughbred.

She walked back across the gentle sloping lane, alongside the apple orchard, past the rear outbuildings, the old whipping post hidden, a hand clapped over its mouth in the thicket, into the broodmare barn.

The tableau remained as she'd left it—potentate presiding over his horse. The filly was dewy and uncertain as she suckled at the heavy teat of Seconds Flat. An evolutionary failure? Is that what Lou had said? But, God, look at the thing! This foal was a golden mean: a straight nose with bold nostrils, curious eyes, a deep chest with a short back and elegant through the fores and gaskins. Henrietta's irritation evaporated in an instant.

She said, "God, that's a beautiful foal. Totally black."

Watching her, Henry said, "Seal brown."

"No, it's black."

"Daughter, I wonder if you're color-blind."

Winter was in residence: "Maybe I am."

"Come here," Henry said abruptly.

She didn't move.

"Come here." And without waiting for her response, he drew her to his side and kissed her hard on the cheekbone, and she thought, Coals are black, but when lit they shine bright as roses. You taught me that.

————

Allmon lived for the daylight. For four months, he'd shivered nights alone in a back room of the old Osbourne house on the far side of the bowl, barely able to close his eyes, the night still something to be survived. Every night was the first time you walked along the tier of your unit, peering terrified into your cell with its skinny steel bed and steel toilet attached to a steel sink. There's a little window that doesn't open out and next door a big swinging dick on the top bunk jacking off under fluorescent light. You still want to sleep on the concrete under your bunk, anus to the wall, a shank fashioned from a Coke can in your right hand—stopstopstopstopstopstop

Don't forget to forget what they made you do.

His mind clamored for space, but his body hated it. His body wanted three walls and a door that couldn't be locked. The day they transferred him out of Bracken into the open world of minimum security, where he could see the trees and the grass, it made his mouth go dry. His first insane instinct was to get back into the pen with the loudspeakers and screaming, the beatings, the hole, the labyrinth of gangs, all the hustlers, even the Aryans, the murderers, the thoroughgoing motherfuckers of every conceivable stripe. For one mad moment, he'd seriously thought about how he could deliberately fuck up and get sent back in. It didn't make any sense, but it had been many years since anything made sense. They forced your hand, turned you into a man your own mother wouldn't recognize. The walking dead.

So he quit sleeping alone in the back room at the Osbourne house, took his sleeping bag up to the stallion barn, and bedded down in the tack room under a peg rack of saddle blankets, surrounded by the stamping snorting urinating sound of animals. It reminded him of minimum, where fifteen men slept in one room. He stayed there, because he needed his rest. More: he needed his wits if he was going to plunge his hands into the white world, if he was going to learn to draw up their rivers of wealth and drink it, like he'd seen a crazy nigger in the pen do—slit the throat of a white dude and opened wide his mouth to catch the blood spurting from his artery. He could think of that now without shuddering, because

There were stars overhead, but he wasn't looking up.

There were graves under his feet, but he wasn't looking down.

The mask looks straight ahead. Don't forget to forget.

He spent those first months in prison rearranging the components of his face so it looked like a man's and could not cry any longer, then the body froze to match his face, hardened by the cold that comes when grief itself dies. His body survived that first year inside, but that brought no relief, because the mind was still alive and spawning thoughts like cockroaches. Real survival is learning to misremember disremember unremember everything as you follow orders, scramble, bargain, fight. Especially fight. Survive by any means necessary and just deal with the shame, because they left you no other choice. So what if your own heart bled out over time? Eventually, when they sent him across state to minimum, emotion was nothing but a long-dead sensation of a long-dead body. Then they told him that he could rub horses, pull himself up by his bootstraps, distinguish himself, play the sport of kings. He wasn't naïve or romantic, he saw through it pretty quickly: horse is just a different kind of drug, horse is heroin. See, the rich hustle too, but they think their gambling is just a game without real consequence. He, however, would go in with his eyes open. So he read everything he could get his hands on, he studied hard, and then they selected him, because he alone knew the difference between hot and cold horses, snaffle and spoon bits, the Byerley Turk and Godolphin Arabian. He knew the meaning of prey animal.

The first day of his life was February 14: They led them all out to the barns in pairs like animals to the ark, the old cooled-down hats and Allmon, the youngest, now twenty-two. A white man was standing there, an ex-trainer, with a massive chestnut on a lead, a reschooled Thoroughbred. The man's words were the first words of Allmon's life:

"Happy Valentine's Day, gentlemen, and welcome to the first day of Thoroughbred boot camp. If you've made it into this program, that means your correctional officers, as well as the committee of the Groom Program, believe you've shown potential and enthusiasm for this line of work. You're one of the chosen. Let me be very clear: We don't care what you did to get incarcerated. We only care how you've conducted yourself inside thus far. You will be released from Blackburn in about six months, and, in order to prepare you, the next half year of your lives will be devoted to everything equus—their history, grooming, and feeding, their care on and off the track, basic vet science.

"Gentlemen, the hundred horses in this program come from all over the country; we have claimers who've put on two hundred pounds since

they arrived, we have your second-tier racers that were made to run on broken knees and bowed tendons, we have some graded stakes winners,
whose names you'll be familiar with if you read the *Racing Form*. The one
thing they all have in common is they were purchased out of the auction
bin, headed for slaughter. About a hundred thousand horses are slaughtered in this country every year. They breed Thoroughbreds to the tune of
thirty thousand a year, so for every stakes winner there might be two hundred draggers who get shipped off to the meat house when they can't earn
their keep on the track. What happens is they slam a four-inch nail into
their foreheads to knock them out, then they hoist them up by a rear leg and
cut their throats, bleed them out. I want you to keep that in mind while you
work with these horses—you're here in a life-saving capacity. Being a groom
is a special vocation. The breeders are breeding bigger horses on weaker
legs, the owners rarely live around the horses and most are in it for the
money or the bragging rights, the trainers and the vets are shooting them
up with drugs and running them injured, and the jockeys are making big
bucks on their backs. You'll hear all of them say they love horses, but as far
as I'm concerned, the only ones who earn the right to say that are the
grooms. You feed a horse, you brush a horse, you pet a horse, then you can
say you love it. We have an old saying in this sport: Treat your horse as your
friend, not as your slave. That's what I'm talking about. Now come on up
here and meet your first horse."

Allmon, when you walked up to that gelding, your heart was banging
in your ear, sweat streamed into your eye, your hands were shaking in front
of God (the great nothing) and everybody when you grazed the horse
on his muzzle, just barely. Then, digging deep for whatever boldness you
possessed—the thing that got you through—you placed both palms on the
flats of that long face. The horse jerked smally, as if startled, then released a
long, ruffled breath and lowered its head like it was bowing to you.

And the trainer said, "Well, hey, kid. That's a nice touch you got there."

Inch by inch, day by day, you learned to master your fear of the animal.
First you took up the currycomb and rubbed the horse from the massive
shoulder around, tracing circles and trying not to leap out of your skin the
first time you passed the rump of the horse with its jackhammer legs. You
used the dandy brush to raise whirlings of dust and swipe the fields from
its hide. Then you took a girl's brush to the mane and tail, a dollop of

ShowSheen, and a braid. You learned to scrape deep into the hooves with a question pick and to bathe the horses with a soapless wash to preserve the skin's oils, to dab balm on hock scratches and check teeth between dental exams. You wrapped swollen fetlocks in blue bandage and disinfected tools in antiseptic. Then, finally, they were hoisting you up on the animals; you, a city kid from a forgotten life, now a horseman. More than that, they were calling you a groom, even calling you gifted, telling you what you could have if only you wanted it bad enough. Which you did. You were a man apart, not like these others, who were just looking for the simple and steady. The future came and wrenched open your eyes when you were just a kid, and once your broken eyes healed, the only thing you could see was: horse.

On the last day, three weeks before your release, that trainer—the one who'd been watching you for six months, took you aside and said, "Allmon, you continue to impress me. You've got good hands, some real talent. What do you intend to use it for?"

You say, "Do my thing." It's nobody's fucking business how you intend yourself.

But he says, "I've got a feeling you're looking for more than that. You feel like you've got something to prove?"

Quiet and steely a moment. Then you turn on him, on that white man who doesn't know you, doesn't know who you are, what you're capable of. Whatever's in your eyes must burn too bright, because the man rears back a little. "Yeah, I got something to prove. I ain't asked to be here, but here I am. And now I aim to play the man's game better than he can play it. I aim to make something of myself."

The trainer doesn't say anything for a moment, just looks at you, very quiet and evaluating. Then: "So I'm going to offer you some advice. As someone who was inside."

This time it's you who rears back, open surprise written on your face.

The man lowers his chin, eyes unblinking. When he speaks, his voice is harsh but low and not unkind. "Allmon, whatever you had to do to get by inside—leave it inside. Don't ever breathe a word of it to anyone. Accept that you have to be a devil to fight the devil in hell. But you're not in hell anymore, kid. You're in Kentucky. They're already going to call you nigger; don't give them a reason to call you devil too."

You're still trying to comprehend how this slight man survived inside, then you comprehend his words, let them sink like a rock into your stomach. You nod finally. "Yeah." And exhale audibly. "Yeah."

The air clears, the man smiles almost ruefully. "So, you've got real talent. I take it you want to be on a good farm under someone with real ambition, not just some dilettante."

"That's right." Gladiator words, but shame enflames your cheek; you have no idea what dilettante means.

"Well, I know just the place. Forge Run Farm is hiring. Their star is on the rise."

Now that—*that*—is what you wanted to hear.

Because Memory is a faculty of Mind, and Mind is what most consider the man.

Which is why the wandering radical said, Die unto yourself. Love me more than your father, mother, wife, children, brothers, and sisters— even more than your own life.

And why the acolyte went to the master and said, my mind is troubling me, and the master said, I can fix it if you will just hand me your mind, but when the acolyte went to give him his mind, he couldn't find it and was enlightened. But that night, when he lay down to sleep, the acolyte felt a great love for his mother, and he lost his enlightenment, and said good riddance, got up the next morning and went to market.

Because the path—well, it's as difficult to find the words as it is the path.

The foal knew nothing but milk and play. It lolled and scratched its new ear with the soft bundle of its leaf-layered foot, it flung itself through timothy grass in fits of exuberance, darting beside its dam and nipping at her long tail and forelegs. It knickered its fresh song at everything.

But it wouldn't let Henry come near.

When he approached, the foal first stood warily apart, its ears pert and sharp as two attenuated thorns, and when he reached out his hand in the gesture of every man who ever offered an animal food and then tamed it, it sprung loose from its trance, spindly spider legs carrying it away. Then, as if aware of a new game, it would slow and turn at the center of the paddock and watch Henry with a kind of evil delight. It stood there, so fine and full of itself, it robbed Henry of his breath.

So: "Henrietta!"

That seemed to be the refrain of his living these days. It's what made the world go round—men chasing women. He was always chasing his.

He stalked the shed row, empty now, the broodmare band all turned out in the southern paddock, tracing maternal circles around their foals. The stalls were redolent with the musk of horseflesh and sunlight heating once-living grasses and old, oiled leather. The place was quiet, no grooms, no business, no daughter.

"Henri—"

They came face-to-face, he and the man who'd been haunting his barn these four months. They'd never spoken; he was the cause of a row such as there'd never been before in the Forge house. Henry would be the first to say he was no longer imprisoned by the hotblood hate he'd felt in his youth, but he objected to this new world of unequal opportunity, a man hired being a man unfireable. In his father's time, under the old dominion . . .

"Where's my daughter?"

"I'm Allmon Shaughnessy."

Henry simply turned from that tough face, all overhanging brow and unblinking eye, and hollered "Henrietta!" under the open blue sky. Allmon used the moment to size him up. The rich tan, feathery copper brows, box jaw. A blue linen shirt casually wrinkled, a brown leather jacket, belted khakis. Wearing good clothes around animals. Like money was water and there was an unlimited supply.

"What do you need?" Allmon said, an edge in his voice that scraped at Henry's patience.

"I don't need your help," was the acid response. "I've got a jumpy foal I need haltered—I'm looking for my daughter."

He stalked off in the direction of the broodmare barn, but his heart was galling his throat. He couldn't stand the man's city voice. It was as though his daughter had taken a marker and drawn a black line down the center of his farm.

He didn't find her, and when he came rounding back along the side of the broodmare barn again, his tongue curling her name in his mouth, he stopped abruptly. At first, he thought that the man was hurting his foal, cinching her in a stranglehold. But then his disconcerted mind knocked right, and he realized Allmon was cradling her in his arms as if just waiting for the bridler. Textbook.

"I got your foal," Allmon said needlessly. Slowly, Henry slipped back into the paddock, the bridle dangling at his side. His eyes were on the man's enormous hands, which caged the gangly foal without any gentling whatsoever, just even pressure, so the foal was easy, quiescent.

Henry's eyes narrowed. "Have you ever worked with foals?"

Allmon shook his head.

"Well, they're infants, not just tiny horses." Now Henry stepped in, so there ensued a small contest of bodies and their shadows tangled, but Allmon did not retreat, maintaining his hold on the horse and taking the bridle right out of Henry's hand. "I got this."

"You need two sets of hands."

"I got this."

And he did. He let loose the foal, but instead of running it stood still, a soft, volitionless statue. Allmon slipped the nylon straps over the long, narrow bones of the nose, under the velvetine jaw, and secured the buckle behind the skull. The filly stood, curious, and after the cinch was checked with the width of one finger, it shook its head as if to test the permanence of its new restraint, and then sprang off, its mane snapping like a flag in the breeze.

Allmon straightened up, his face unmistakably triumphant, almost smug. Henry crossed his own shaking arms over his chest and said, his voice slung low with anger, "I want you to look at that horse, young man."

He turned slowly, casually with a kind of cool disregard in his body, but he turned nonetheless.

"That horse you're looking at is two hundred and fifty years old."

Allmon's brow contracted, and Henry went on. "That horse came over the Wilderness Road when it was a death trail, it broke the ground you're standing on, it built that house I live in, and it bred itself. It's entitled—do you understand me—*entitled* to exist in its own flesh, because of its history. And if you ever so much as look at my two-hundred-and-fifty-year-old horse again without my permission, you can kiss this job goodbye. Do you understand me?"

If he was looking for fear, for a cowed spirit, Henry didn't find it. There was only a deepening concentration, as though the man was memorizing his words for some purpose invisible to Henry.

That made his voice pitch up with irritation. "Do you understand me?"

"Yeah, sure." Insouciant.

Henry's voice was steely. "Let me be very clear. My daughter hired you. I would not have. I'm not interested in having convicts on my property."

No change on that stoic face.

Now Henry smiled a hard smile. His words were clipped, surly. "Why are you even here anyway? What do you want?"

With an almost imperceptible tilt of the head, as if he was honestly surprised by the question, Allmon said, "I want what you got."

Henry's scornful smile died. He drew himself up to his full height and said, "All my life, I've made my name. It's the most valuable thing I have."

"And I got the rest of my life to make mine."

Without a pause: "You can't make a name from nothing."

And just like that Henry was walking away on his money legs in his money shoes, and Allmon just stood there watching him go. Behind them, the filly shook her head again and again, trying to ascertain the nature of a halter.

He damn near lost his head in a rookie grooming accident, but it got him exactly where he needed to be. He'd been picking Acheron's left rear hoof when the bay gelding—usually calm to the point of soporific—stamped his hoof free and swung his belly weight into Allmon, knocking him so hard against the stall wall, he saw stars for the first time since he was a kid. He didn't even register the cry that erupted from him as his own until he felt the unmistakable swill of blood tracing down his temple, seeping warm and wet into the neck of his polo.

In the next instant he was crabbing instinctively out of harm's way, scrambling into the aisle, when he felt hands at the neck of his shirt, and Henrietta was hauling him up as if he were nothing more than a plank board she was raising. He wasn't a lightweight; she had crazy strength for a slim woman.

"Can you walk?"

He turned, but her face was distorted by his fun-house pupils. He took one wobbly, wasted step.

"Let's go outside," she said, "and get some fresh air. Try not to bleed on everything."

She had one arm wrapped around his shoulder as she led him out of the barn into the shocking, undiluted light of day. Allmon could barely open his eyes against it. When they didn't stop immediately, when he sensed their general trajectory toward the white farm truck, which was parked in the precipitous noon shadow of a barn wall, he began to resist.

"Let's get you to the hospital," Henrietta said.

Allmon didn't reply; he just wrenched his arm out of her hands and shoved his back against the barn wall, inadvertently knocking his head against the boards. The air went out of him in a surprised puff.

"Whoa," Henrietta said, watching as Allmon sank down against the spiky grain of the wall, breathing hard, blood still trickling. He squashed bright splashes of marigold beneath him as he sank into the mulch.

"No, no, no, no way," he said.

"You really should." Henrietta curbed her tongue and didn't say, It's more for our protection than yours. She said it through the distraction of the sharp smell of his sweat and the muskier underlying message of his body.

"No!"

The word burst from him, as hard and abrupt as a bark, but it was the unexpected look on his face that truly surprised her—ferocious, but with some mysterious, angry passion. There was no arguing with it. So, perplexed, Henrietta sank down on her haunches and took his face in her hands. When he tried to pull away, she snapped, "Stop." Then, gentler: "You've got a pretty deep scrape. I think either Acheron hit your nose or you bumped it on the wall. Either way, you'll have a black eye tomorrow."

He made a dismissive face.

"Well, you need to stop the bleeding."

She made a move as if to rise, but he wrenched his polo up in his fist and pressed it as a bundle to the side of his head. The skin of his belly was exposed to the cool air and in a moment he was covered in goose flesh.

Henrietta was unsure what to do then, half-risen, but then settled beside him in the mulch with her forearms resting on her knees and her fingers shredding the delicate lace of a fern's leaf. For some time, they simply sat there in the sunlight until she said, "Are you tired of us yet?"

"Who?" he muttered.

"Southerners."

He was kind of dizzy; he had no idea what she was talking about. His disordered breathing had just begun to settle into its regular rhythm.

"We're incredibly annoying," she said, watching as one of their colts was led out of his paddock by a long-term employee. "If you can listen to our tall tales for more than fifteen minutes, you're a saint. But it's all just rocksalt and nails." She looked at Allmon sideways. "I'll let you in on a little secret: we're just an insecure species in a vanishing ecosystem. A conquered nation. The only power a Southerner really has is to never forgive and never forget. It's not worth much."

Allmon closed his eyes to stave off nausea, which Henrietta saw only as a dark listening, a quiet absorption that fed something in her.

"Honestly, though?" she said. "I think Northerners are worse than Southerners. They think they're better than us because they survive the world's shittiest weather and they're convinced of the religious retardation of the South. They're ignorant but arrogant. Southerners, on the other hand, know perfectly well they're ignorant; the problem is they're proud of it." She cleared her throat. "My mom had the right idea—she just left the country." Henrietta looked down; there was much more than an ocean between them now after all these years. Monthly phone calls were the height and breadth of it.

If she wasn't going to stop, he might as well get something out of it. Allmon said, "When'd your father get this place?"

She sighed, capping her head with her hands and looking out wearily at a paddock. "A long, long, long time ago."

Carefully, he said, "What's he like?"

She looked at him with irritation. She didn't want to talk about her father.

"Ask me why I do what I do," she said suddenly.

"What do you mean?" He tried to turn his head, but pain swamped him and he cringed. He maintained the pressure of the polo to his temple.

"Why do you think I do what I do?"

Allmon didn't have to hesitate. "'Cause you got family."

"It's less noble than that," she said, shrugging. "Maybe it's because my father didn't want me to go to college, and my mother left me here to my own devices, and I don't know how to do anything else." Another sigh and then she said, "So have you figured out that my dad's a huge racist?"

Allmon reared back slightly, almost laughed from a whole different kind of discomfort.

She shrugged. "He's from a different generation. We're not all like that."

It took every bit of his strength and self-control for Allmon not to roll his eyes. Oh man, white girls and their . . . His mind paused. He leveled a long, considering glance at the house. This information felt like a little key in his pocket.

He was quiet so long, it was as if he'd forgotten Henrietta. She chewed on her pink lip, her face querulous. Then she looked in the opposite direction, away from the fences and horses, toward the generative east and the earth that lay rumpled there like something discarded. She said cryptically, "It used to be wild here. And green."

Green, exactly! His first day on the farm rolled around again like a bright white horse on a carousel: the green had hurt his eyes like it was hurting them now; everything was lime and kelly and forest, with trees and grass and streams in every direction, just so much . . . green. These folks—people like her—could walk out into all that green anytime they wanted because they owned it. Green was white.

"Are you feeling much pain?" she said, then she reached out and, in a gesture that felt unfamiliar to both of them, gently touched his shoulder.

He surprised her by laughing abruptly. Not just a chuckle, but a laugh that transformed from a cough to a rough sound that rolled out of the center of him. His shoulders shook and tears sprang suddenly to his eyes.

"What?" she said warily.

"You think this is pain?" he said. "Shit. Let me tell you, when I was in two months, I saw a man get killed right beside me. Like far away as you are. We was—were walking down the hall to the yard and some dudes were coming back and this brother in front of me reached out with a shank and just sliced this other dude's belly open. Like left to right and up. Opened up his belly and his guts came out."

"Jesus," said Henrietta in a whisper.

Allmon didn't even notice. "Your guts ain't red like you think they'll be. They're gray. And not big."

Then two things happened at once: he realized Henrietta was staring at him with a gaze as bright as a shadeless bulb, and he remembered his vow to never breathe a word of his life inside. He clamped his eyes shut and she said, much to his surprise, "Your life has been hard."

Set against the backdrop of his existence, it was absurd undertalk and should have made him angry, but it didn't. It was just simple, true. When she reached forward and lifted the polo away from the cut to check the bleeding, he didn't open his eyes, but he didn't resist. She said, "Do you know who Darwin was?"

Now he opened his eyes and looked at her sharply from the side.

"Right, sorry." She cleared her throat. "Well, there's this story about Darwin that's always stuck in my mind. You know, he came up with the theory of evolution in part because of finches he studied from the Galápagos Islands. But when he first got to Chatham Island, it was really more a disappointment than anything. It looked to him like . . . a furnace, like a geological furnace. It looked stripped of life; there was ash on the air and it was inhabited mostly by lizards. But it was in a place that first struck him as a hell on earth that he found the key to the best idea anyone ever though up. He found the key to life."

Allmon was listening carefully, but Henrietta suddenly shrugged and looked away, as if she too had divulged something a little too personal and now felt rather foolish.

"It looks like you've stopped bleeding," she said suddenly. "You can get a clean shirt in the office. If you need to take an early day, that's fine." Then she rose and was moving abruptly away into the sweet, Southern glamour of the property—barns like summer blacktop, coins glittering in the streams, and, of course, the house: solitary, steeped in morning light, proud, and perfect. A thing built to last. How he burned to go inside.

"Hey!" Allmon called out, sitting up straighter, the sudden movement striking his nose and forehead like a fresh blow.

Henrietta turned and lowered her head. "What?"

"You should come back and talk to me sometime. You got interesting things to say. I appreciate that." And he smiled the first smile she'd ever seen on his face, however unsettling.

He made a point to watch her from across the fields, from the far end of the barn, from the next stall. And when she turned to look, he didn't turn away.

Lou had come again with her quiet hands and reassuring voice, checking the articulate muscles of the foal's neck, palpating her velvet jaw, walking watchful circles, probing the recesses of her mouth back to the slick muscles of the jaw. But there was nothing to be found except the undeniable fact of excellence; the foal was exceptionally fine. The mouth problem was not a problem at all, just a tic.

And yet Henry was uneasy. He called Henrietta down after Lou left, fretting and insisting that she see it herself.

He said, "Her dentition is perfect, her bite is good. But look."

Henrietta watched as the foal, now almost ninety days old, turned aside, fixing them squarely in the big globe of her brown eye, then tossed her head with her mouth working. Her lips curled out and back twice, then fluttered loosely, almost comically on the breath.

"Good God," she said, "is she grinding her teeth? Is she in pain? These inbred horses—"

"No, no. Lou said she's just working her lips and jaw."

"So she's just mouthy."

"I don't like it," Henry said, folding his arms across his chest. "And I don't like that she still doesn't have a name."

A small smile grew on Henrietta's face. "Why, Henry Forge, maybe she's trying to talk to you."

"She needs a good name. She's going to be a beast."

"I wonder what she's saying . . ."

"Bold Ruler was tough and Nasrullah was wild, so—"

"Oh!" Henrietta said, laughing.

She's out of Hellcat by Secretariat

Out of Seconds Flat by Second Chance
She speaks just like Xanthus, Achilles' charger
This is Hellsmouth, Father
"Let's name her Hellsmouth."

Henrietta didn't wait very long; it was nature. It was the epithelium, dark
with melanin, stretched taut over the soft architecture of muscles, striated
and smooth, the fine wiring of the nervous system firing north and south,
east and west; it was all that living bone, full of mineral and marrow and
run through with red coal seams; bones stacked neatly to craft his six feet;
the golden eye under the ledge of his brow under the strong vault of his
cranium, its twenty-two bones so neatly placed they seemed arranged by
hand; it was the curvy stack of the spinal column, the aborted wings of the
scapula, the sharp clavicles and the belling ribs; the long fall of the arms;
the hands and the feet, each a bony masterpiece of locomotion wrapped for
travel in four muscular layers; the long pinnate muscles along the tibia, the
strong bunching along the thigh; it was the basin of the pelvis, false and
true, and the organs of generation, conducted by muscles and ligaments
and fibers, the hanging scrotum, the vesicles, the prostate and Cowper's
glands; and the sheathed root of the penis, the defiant, erectile body, the
tender extremity with its timeless tunnel back to the seminal testes with
their millions upon millions waiting in the dark.

She found him seated on an old mustard bench in the tack room, the
bare bulb above him directing bright light onto his body but carving dras-
tic, obscuring shadows onto his face. Tack was spread in all directions on
old saddle blankets. A gallon of thick conditioner lay open and Allmon
reached his hands into it, scooped out the white grease, and then worked it
into the old bridles and saddles, their hides thirsty from neglect.

She saw him start when she upended an empty meal bucket to sit opposite him as he worked over the noseband of a bridle. He glanced at her
askance and saw her scorched earth eyes. She seemed to burn at a higher
temperature than everyone else. It made sweat prickle on his neck.

"You done working?" He'd saved up interesting things to tell her, but
he couldn't find any of them now. His confidence seesawed.

"Yes," she said. He nodded slowly, intent on his project, but her gaze was just steady, unrelenting, and she saw it clear as day when his breathing grew uneven.

"Tell me something," she said.

He waited, the muscles of his shoulders bunched so tight his hands felt numb. Some premonition pinched the nerves along his broad back. He'd been looking for an in; was this it?

"You've spent some time with my father by now. What do you think he wants the most?"

It wasn't what he was expecting. He looked up quizzically as if she'd just offered up a riddle.

"Tell me as someone who's only just met him. Does he want a legacy, a family, a . . . what?"

Allmon actually stopped what he was doing and considered what she was asking. His voice was very quiet when he said, "A legacy. He wants folks to remember he was like a great man."

Henrietta sighed. "Why do men care about that so much—to the extent where they're willing to breed horses to their own siblings, their own mother?"

"You take the risk," Allmon said, "because a legacy is forever. They can take everything else away from you."

Henrietta's smile was small, barely a crack under her flushed cheeks. "That's where you're wrong. They can take your legacy too. There's nothing permanent in this world."

He stiffened up, wanted to say, You don't know what the fuck you're talking about, you don't know how much those words weigh, but before he'd even decided to keep his mouth shut, she had risen with some impatience and stood close to him under the light. "Do you know what I want?"

A sidelong glance at the door, and she looked too, checking to see whether anyone was there. Only a vacancy, so she stepped over some of the tack toward him.

She said, "People spend their lifetimes pursuing things that don't even really give them pleasure in the end—just the admiration of strangers. I think that's a fucking waste."

He glanced up, startled, but she was sinking down onto her haunches before him and staring into the shadows where his eyes were recessed, inaccessible. The shadows excited her terribly. She said, "There are three things I like the most about fucking. I like the first moment, when you push your cock in and I can feel everything—everything—intensely. Men like to say that women don't have much sensation, but that's not true. That's just a lie they tell themselves."

Allmon's hands had come to a standstill on the leather as if soldered there. She could tell he was hardly breathing, and there was the faintest trembling along his neck.

"Give me that," she said, taking up the bridle. Then she rose and in a moment had turned and settled herself backward on his lap, nestling his legs between hers and settling in against his groin. She laid the leather aside and said, "The second thing I like is to fuck like this." And she rocked back into him just barely, listening for the sure-inevitable-easy-math-look-ma-no-hands sharp intake of his breath. He was inert under her as if all his nerves were severed. "I like this because I can feel the big ridge on the head of your cock against the front. When I do it like this"—now she was rocking against him with aching slowness—"I can build up until you're begging me, you're fucking begging me to fuck you harder, and you're trying to get deeper, but I keep fucking you shallowly just like this, even though you're begging me, begging me to fuck you deeper, and this"—she grasped up his hands, forcing them up her shirt to where her elastic bra could be simply pushed aside—"you have to fucking grab my nipples; no, grab them, that's what I like—grab me harder"—and she placed her fingers over his and forced them down hard around her nipples, rocking harder when she said—"and then when I come on your cock, I'll finally let you fuck me really deep, but only when I say so."

She leaned back into him fully then, wound her neck against his, so she could smell him, so that natural-order home scent of him filled her nostrils, and her breathing was rough when she said, "That's what I like."

And then she was off him in an instant, adjusting her bra and pulling down her T-shirt, turning abruptly and handing him the bridle, which he took up numbly, confusedly in one hand.

"But I'm discovering there's a third thing I like," she said, "and that's waiting for it. But trust me when I say I don't like to wait too long. What is it you want, Allmon?"

He was hard, so it wasn't entirely a lie when he looked straight into her eyes and said, "You."

Because there is hunger. Like any desire, it's only temporarily satisfied, which calls into question the reliability of satisfaction and whether such a state can be said to exist at all. Anything we eat knows us more intimately than a lover. Not merely the inside of our mouth but the esophagus, stomach, alimentary canal, upper and lower colon, sphincter. Everything we desire, we shit out and leave behind.

So there is thought, which is ought and should and will. It's a great mill wheel spinning in the mind, all the minutiae of the world swept along in the millrace, plundered and broken by the wheel, detritus to drift away. The wheel spins and spins and spins, going nowhere, despite ceaseless activity.

The amygdala is the seat of elemental emotion. Shaped like an almond, it lies behind the smooth skin of the forehead, the cranium, the rapid eyes. When sensing threat, the amygdala stimulates a cascade of hormones for flight or fight. In a thousandth of a second, this is done.

But before the action, before the clamor and heat of the fight, there is a pause. The body freezes, the slower neocortex not yet aware of danger. In the pause, the body gathers its energies, prepares itself. As of yet, there is no action. But this quiet state is only temporary.

There is also love, which looks like hunger but is not. The fewer words said about it, the better. Language is the charnel house of man.

Allmon crept into the dark stall. He waited until the nightman had fired up the 250, gassed the thing once for good measure, and the lights had fallen away into the black pit of the bowl before rising on its other side near the old manager's house.

Why are you here? Henry had asked.

Allmon touched the animal on its soft, bony head, found the tufted tip of its ears, its subtle sway back and rough tail. Then, careful not to hug on the delicate neck, he bent over and simply wrapped his arms around the chest and rump like he had that first bridling day. He took care not to burden her with any of his weight. This hurt his back, but the animal was warm and passed its heat along without grudge. Then it grew curious and wended its neck back toward him. He felt the warm shallows of breath against his side. In and out, in and out, and for a few moments he didn't realize the press and lull was in him too, that it too was rising, rising steadily until the wave overcame itself and, with crushing force, swamped him. Suddenly he was drowning in the old grief again: he would give anything— anything—to have his momma back for two minutes, one minute, even thirty seconds! Anything! They could cut off his fucking legs if it meant he could hold her hand just one more time! Nothing was anything without her. He was a drowned man.

Then, restoring some of the sand under his feet, the wave receded as he had long ago learned it would, and he straightened up slowly, ancient tears in his eyes, but not on his face. Why was he here? To grasp the very things that had been stolen from him, the things he wasn't allowed to touch.

So you go on working your job, the old life and all of its emotions packed carefully away, trying to keep yourself steady, because the girl's coming back, the redhead, the thin-lipped girl, some kind of future. There's something about her, something interesting, but to do this right, you need to be hard in every sense of the word. You've got something she wants, she's got something you want. You prepare yourself with carnal thoughts, which slip from your brain pan in bubbles. You see that from the top of the room where you take your ease, watching your body below rise up from its sleeping bag, which smells of your own distinct months-long musk. She swivels those little hips through the door, the boss girl, the employer, the owner's baby girl. You don't know exactly how to do this, but you're going to do it, definitely yes. That girl is a door.

A harsh whisper: "Where's your father at?"

The white girl just shrugs, like she's slipping a weight off her shoulder. "I'm not my father's keeper."

Then she forms a noose of her arms and slips it over his head, drawing his body near. From way up there, his breath catches as he leans down, watching very carefully. He wants to see this, how a man and a woman do this. He kissed some girls as a kid, but he was shy and stupid. This is what a real kiss looks like. It makes sounds that discomfit, but it fascinates. Until she slips her hand down the front of his night drawers and he concentrates up there, wills his life to life—really, now is the time, really (!), but no matter how she touches it, it remains soft and cute as a mole. Then the breeder, the enthusiast, the appraiser really goes to work on him, and his mind could explode with the force of his effort; he's a man; he's supposed to leave coins in her purse, cream in her cup, diamonds in her ring. She raises his hand to her breast, but her body is so cold to him, he wants to snatch his hand back. Maybe it's the way his body jolts or maybe because it's been too many minutes now, but her snowy papery white face, which had been peering so intently into his, proceeds through a string of subtly drawn transformations, from confusion to vague disbelief to consternation and now flaring indignation. When he says, dully, "I don't know why I . . . ," she peers at him. "Is this always a problem for you?" "Naw, I just . . . it's not my fault, I don't know." She draws back her hand, real offense on her face. "Are you saying it's me? Are you gay or something?"

She doesn't know the history in his words, what that means to a man like him. His arms, his defenders, his weapons just reached out and pushed her back into the chaffy wood of the tack wall, and the wind went all out of her in an audible woof. From up there, hissing: Don't hurt the woman, the house, the horse, your chances. Then the little white woman was up in his face, her words whipping him. "You know what the problem is with people like you?" she spat. "Self-pity. It's always someone else's fault."

"People like me?" he said, rearing back, incredulous. "Like what—like black? Well, you know what's wrong with people like you? You're all spoiled inbred racist motherfuckers, but you don't even know it! You're so blind, you can't tell when the person standing in front of you is half-white! Which I am!"

She scoffed. "I'm sorry, but if you don't look white, you're not white. At least in the real fucking world."

You know what rage is like? It's like a fire that blooms from your feet to the crown of your head in an instant. He knew what rage could do—she had no idea. He lowered his head like a bull and stared her down. When he intoned, "Fuck you," it wasn't a roar, it wasn't chaos, it was a deep, mortal hatred that rolled up from the center of him. Unmistakable. It caused her to shrink back like physical violence never would have, her face suddenly stripped of its anger and recast with fear. Regret was instant on his tongue. "Shit!" He said, "Henrietta," and reached out for her, because he needed this in a thousand different ways. But it was too late. She'd already turned on her heel, a complicated roil of feeling growing like sickness in her stomach, alongside a determination not to touch him again. And she didn't, not for many months.

It was summer on the wheel again, and Henrietta and Allmon were tasked with driving a pair of two-year-olds to the training center the day before the yearling sale. It was a wet Friday morning with continual, sourceless mist obscuring the lineaments of the buildings, so that the horses and grooms and riders seemed to traverse here and there behind a damp and billowing veil. They were quiet as librarians in the haze, shushed by the soft weather. This was a sly rain, never hard, yet insinuating itself until everything was saturated. The sideways, gossamer weather made continual inroads against the indoors—moisture seeping through dykes of hay to dampen the earthen floors, concrete slickened and made dangerous, tiny runnels steering around bits of straw and manure toward cracks in the doors and stall walls. The grooms shivered in their work, though the day was not cold. The horses smelled like wet dogs.

Outside, the world was a headlong green, a green that weighted the trees, the leaves heavy on the boughs like mossy green coins gathered dangling and dripping in suspended nets. It called to mind Irish days Henrietta had seen when she traveled to Coolmore Stud on prospecting trips with her father. Everyone spoke of the incomparable green of Ireland, but it was no more green than Kentucky. It was a color to crack the code of life.

When they reached the center, Allmon unloaded the fillies one by one, he and Henrietta speaking no unnecessary words. They had long maintained a terse working space in which nothing warm grew—glances dropped before eyes met, conversation withered on the vine. If Henrietta's desire wasn't dead, it was dormant, and familiarity had dulled the sharp edges of their history.

She waited for Allmon beside the truck until the mist began to form fat droplets that threatened a downpour. Just as she was stepping onto the runner, about to swing herself up into the driver's seat to restart the engine, a hesitant voice caught her. "Miss Forge?"

She turned and eyed a slim man of indeterminate age, his face marked and lined by a lifetime of working with horses in the elements. Raffish blond hair fell forward over thick brows but did nothing to obscure the nervousness in his worried eyes.

"Yes?" she said sharply.

"I, uh—I . . ." He edged forward into her airspace. "I'm wondering if I might could show you something. I'm Tony. I've worked with some of your horses."

"What do you want to show me?"

He shoved his hands down into his jean pockets then and indicated with his head. "On the other side of the training center. It'll only take a second."

"The other side of the—" she said. "What is this? I'm busy."

Allmon's voice interrupted them. "What's going on?"

"Oh." Tony looked surprised, discomfited by this other presence. His eyes swung between the two of them, hesitating briefly, but then he continued on down the path he had chosen. "Listen," he said. "I got to tell somebody who can do something about this . . . situation. A woman, you know."

Henrietta found herself pinned by the severity of this man's gaze amidst the bustle and business all around them. "Well . . ." She glanced briefly at Allmon, who shrugged blankly. "I guess," she said, "but we only have a minute."

He nodded. "Meet me at the utility entrance on Rand Road in ten minutes."

Two minutes later, they were idling on the far side of the training center, eyeing culverts converted to streambeds choked with hairy grasses and leaves. A heavy mist moved slowly forward and back as if the air itself were breathing. Light escaped the clouds and found the wet on everything and sparked off each blade of grass. Just as Allmon was beginning to shift around impatiently in the silence, the man appeared, his face flush with color, his pant legs soaked from running across the acreage. He stood there huffing while Henrietta cut her engine and Allmon slipped from the passenger seat with his brows raised.

Tony popped his ball cap once and wiped his forehead. "I got to show y'all a horse."

Henrietta made a face. "A horse?"

"A beat horse."

"Do what?" said Allmon. The hair prickled at the back of his neck.

The man nodded. "You know that new trainer under Mack? That dude they brought out from California with the horn-rimmed glasses? Well, he beat the shit out of a horse yesterday. Tiny Tim. We couldn't get him to work the gate and he was biting all the handlers. Well, this dude fucking took this bat thing and beat the everloving shit out of him. Cracked him over his head, right between his eyes. I saw it myself, I mean I was standing right there, just standing there. I guess I was in shock, you know?"

Incredulous, Henrietta said nothing, so the man gestured toward Allmon, who started forward immediately, and the three of them moved toward the outbuildings on the rear of the property.

"It was nuts," the man continued. "The dude bit his ears when he went down."

"What?" Henrietta laughed an awkward, disembodied laugh, and Allmon cut her a hard look. The laugh made him sick to his stomach.

"You don't know that old trick? To get a colicky horse to stand up? You tug on their ears. Well, he bit him."

Now they were standing at the side of a small white stone stable Henrietta and Allmon had never seen before, far beyond the concentric dirt tracks of the training center, past the hay and grain storage. It was clearly never used, with ragged sheets of old white paint peeling from the grimy stone walls and soggy, blackened hay scattered down the aisle. Tony made an abrupt, rotating turn on his heel, glancing furtively in all directions, then led them into the dank and shadowy barn. It smelled of old, wet wood and housed four stalls, three unoccupied. The fourth contained the horse. Quietly, carefully, they approached. At the sound of their feet, the massive creature whined and struggled to press his enormous, quivering bulk into the far corner of the stall. His rear legs bent as if he were trying to force himself into a box half his size. He appeared ready to sink down into the straw.

The man beside them pointed at him needlessly, uselessly.

Henrietta couldn't see the front of the horse, only the trembling croup, the trembling legs, the trembling sides. Later, in memory, even his hooves would tremble, chattering like teeth. It seemed like something other than an animal, a wretched, discordant orchestra of fear.

Allmon leaped back, stricken, his forearm horizontal to his face, so his mouth was contained in the crook of his elbow. "Oh shit," he whispered. He'd seen worse, he'd seen . . . No, no, no, no—

Henrietta remained rooted where she stood. "Hey," she said very gently, low on the breath, so for a moment the horse stilled and drew his head round from the corner, seeking after the soft, womanish sound. But when he saw their figures, he rejolted and cowered with such force that his nose struck the wall. In the brief moment he was turned, the bleak wreckage of his face was revealed—the torn ears, broken lips, the lids of his eyes swollen like old black fruit with bright broken blood vessels around fathomless pupils. Everywhere his flesh was covered by a patchwork of black stitches.

"Oh my fucking God," said Allmon.

Henrietta just stood still, rooted.

"Yeah," the man said, exhaling. "Yeah. I just stood there and watched, you know? I can't get it out of my head."

Allmon was recovering from the surprise of the animal, slowly lowering the shield of his arm and pointing at the crude crazy-quilt stitching. "Some vet did this shit?"

The man just shook his head ruefully. "On-site vet did that. They brought him back here, 'cause this part of the center doesn't ever get inspected. Three hundred and seven stitches."

"That horse ain't gonna live," said Allmon.

"He won't."

"This is someone's investment," Henrietta hissed. "Does Mack know about this?"

"Nah, he's barely here during racing season." The man pressed his lips together, as if he wanted to keep further words from escaping his own mouth. They had not been standing there even a full minute in pained, horrified silence, staring at the croup of the ruined horse, when they suddenly heard the sound of men's voices approaching. Allmon instinctively grasped Henrietta's arm, and they sprinted out the opening of the barn through which they'd come. To escape from sight, they ducked behind a holly windbreak and, nearly snow-blinded by the light, ran half-stooped back in the direction of the Chevy.

When they achieved the far side of the truck, the man said, "Hold up," and sank down on his haunches, fumbling for a cigarette out of his rear pocket. It was smashed and flat, but it lit. For a moment he said nothing while Henrietta stood over him hauling air. But there was electricity in All-mon's limbs; he couldn't keep still. You stand still, you remember things you can't afford to remember. He paced back and forth in front of the truck, muttering, "Shit, shit, shit." Don't forget to forget.

Tony remained crouched by their truck, gnomelike, one hand ferrying the shaking cigarette and the other shielding his eyes from the light.

"Man," he said finally, "it's a fucked-up situation."

Henrietta had no response.

Tony looked up at her: "I knew I had to show someone who could do something about it."

She looked at him sharply. "What can I do? I don't have any power."

Allmon abruptly stopped his pacing by the truck and turned to look at her.

Tony stood up, openly surprised. "People like you are the *only* ones with any power around here. I'm worth less than a fucking boy Friday. So is he." He gestured at Allmon.

"You were the witness to this," Henrietta said, "not me."

"Me? Listen, lady, I don't have the freedom to risk my job. This is all I know how to do. I got kids to think about."

She shook her head, obstinate. "You're the one here with a story to tell."

The man just stared at her in wonderment. Then the wonderment turned to disgust, and he looked at Allmon, raising his arms in a hopeless, disbelieving gesture.

"Listen—" said Henrietta, but he interrupted her.

"I've done what I can fucking do." He spoke with such open scorn that she had to fight the urge to shrink. Then he walked away from them both, kicking at the ground as he went; birds were aloft in a flurry. He didn't bother to duck his head now, stalking along the holly back in the direction of the training center and moving his head with expostulations that she couldn't hear. Not knowing what to say or do, Henrietta just got in the truck and reached numbly for the gas. She realized then that she was utterly chilled from the mist; the only heat she could feel was the spot on her arm he had touched. Allmon.

He had stopped pacing but was still outside the truck, his back to her, staring out at the pastureland without seeing it at all. What had started as a kind of panic at the sight of the horse had become a hard, dark bud in his chest. What he knew beyond any doubt: people like the Forges deserved whatever the fuck was coming to them. No mercy. The world would go up in flames before it cracked their white shell. That knowledge was akin to hate. So he was thoroughly surprised when he turned around to yank open the truck door and—maybe it was the light shining on her red hair or the way she looked at him, suddenly quizzical and unsure of her own decision— he felt something inside him lean precipitously toward her. It made no sense. He was so taken aback, he stood there motionless for a moment. Then he met her eyes for the first time in a long time, and when he climbed into the truck, he did so with the sinking sensation of someone moving slowly into deeper water.

For a while—he could admit it—he'd been worried. Every time he turned around the man was there, standing too close to his daughter as they leaned against a barn, swinging fifty-pound bags of feed together, riding side by side when Henrietta drove him back to the Osbourne end of the property, his golden eyes always on the house. The temptation to speak up had been great, but he curbed the desire. He was circumspect, smart; he knew his daughter well. He was working out how to newly reframe an old law when . . . it stopped. Sure and sudden as a summer storm; one minute she was glued to the man's side and the next she was back in the house, writing in her notebooks, driving off to Lexington or God knows where, but no- where near the man with the hungry eyes.

And like a barn cat, Allmon was everywhere. Even here—brown like a bay, Henry thought—at the yearling sale in the Keeneland pavilion. There were occasional glimpses of him in the parade of horses brought to the auc- tion block, where the auctioneer presided ten feet high on his dais, flanked by his relay men, whispering and pointing, their eyes trained on the pro- ceedings below. The auctionable flesh emerged stage right, passed to the black ringman in his coat and tie, the yearling striding to the center with a hip number trembling on its quarter, eyes bobbling with fear; there was occasionally some churlish rearing and shitting, then stage left, leaving the black sweep—black like roofing cement—to his job with a broom and pan. Henry and Mack sat in their place in the amphitheater, wedged between a sheik and a drunk County Kildare man whose brogue was so thick as to be unintelligible. The rabble and much of the press were sequestered in the rear atrium, peering in through the glass at the money.

Henry sat up as his yearling Deep Spring emerged onto the plank boards of the auction block, passed by Allmon to the jacketed handler, the bidding set to begin.

A flash of annoyance: there was that age-old black man's stance, something he never could abide. Physiognomy is truth! The form was avoidant and resentful, shoulders rolled in as if to shield a secret, but the secret was insouciance and unceasing rebuff. Allmon had an ability unique to his kind: to affront without saying a word.

Mack leaned over. "Who's your groom?"

Henry crossed his arms on his chest. "Allmon Shaughnessy."

"Well, there's your black Irish. Any good?"

And there precisely was the rub: "Better than good. Great with my stallions." He couldn't say otherwise.

"Where'd you get him?"

"From wherever they grow America's criminals."

Henry laughed but Mack didn't smile. His eye twitched.

"Blackburn, apparently," Henry continued. "Henrietta hired him."

"Well," said Mack, shrugging, "I got nothing against a man with a past. I don't give a damn what you've done in your life, I don't care what color you are—black or brown or illegal or whatever. I've had a few kids from over there."

Henry raised a brow. "From where? Blackburn?"

"Yeah. They train up good grooms," Mack said with another shrug. "How's your filly?"

Henry broke into a radiant grin. "Amazing. Better and better by the day."

"Well, if this kid is as good as you say, assign him to her. Send him to me when Hellsmouth is ready. I don't mind the prison kids. They know how to fucking work."

The light of new thought roosted in Henry's eyes.

"You're up," Mack said with a nod in the direction of the dais.

The bidspotters paced slowly here and there, eyes sweeping over the sea of trainers, bloodstock agents, sheiks, and local hands. Henry stared hard across the lot of them. A flap here, a wave there and the bids rose, the spotters' heads swiveling like the heads of owls, the patter of the auctioneer rising until the last umpish "Hiyah!" when Deep Spring sold for $200,000. The ringman led the jittery yearling away to the left, one gloved hand on the lead shank, the other on the deep neck of the colt. When the left door opened, Henry leaned forward, actually passing a hand before his eyes with some irritation as if shooing away gadflies and barely cognizant of the sale—yes, yes, there he was, grasping the lead shank, the man. Allmon Shaughnessy. Interloper, user, everywhere at once, brown as river mud.

She couldn't stop thinking about the beaten colt. A phantasm, a shivering grotesque cramped in the corner of her eye, he vanished every time she turned to confront him. Again and again it happened, stoking her pulse, but each time it was some other dark horse from the sea of endless horseflesh: ripe but untested, ungainly but salable and all fresh for the auction— somewhere among them a sales topper, an avatar of free forward motion. Vets darted from one exam to the next, trainers stood like lighthouses in a fog of tobacco smoke at the glass doors, their watches flashing as they scratched out hip numbers. Henrietta put her own free hand to her forehead, feeling slightly unbalanced. The way that horse had turned to her voice in its stall with its black, burst-fruit eyes. Slashes across the atlas bone. She knew the velvet of a horse's muzzle was as tender as the flesh of a woman's inner thigh.

Allmon emerged as a solitary figure in the crowd, Deep Spring at his heels. Henrietta slowed. She was having trouble remembering how she had once spat at him from the catbird seat and put him in his place. What she remembered was the way he had grasped her arm at the training center, the surety and heat of that hold. Now she stopped altogether, staring: My God, his body was perfection. She had been avoiding it, but there was no escape. He was a mathematical proof of hard beauty, symmetrical and proportioned for perpetuation. The expressive organs of the face—the full lips and golden eyes—occupied an even third of his face between the smooth forehead, the wide expanse of jaw. The height of his head equaled the size of his hands, which now grasped the lead shank of Deep Spring. The strong length of his chest to the top of that head, the hair of which he now kept shaved to show the smart, round lineaments of the well-turned skull, was a quarter of his body, exactly the width of his chest to the crook of his arm and so also the diameter of his head. His body abounded in architectural relationships: From the knee to the ground equaled his forearms to the tips of his fingers. He stood eight heads high. His foot too was as long as his forearm, articulated now by the effort of managing an irritated horse, and, she knew, nestled in these symmetries, the foci of perfection: the cock and navel, the old compass points.

Her genes rattled stupidly, purposefully, when his eyes met hers.

They traded Deliria for Deep Spring. Her hand brushed his, or his hers, action and reception indecipherable. She could feel the wordless animal in her. It didn't matter that he hadn't really wanted her once. She still wanted him.

"Go well?" she said coolly.

Allmon nodded. "Two hundred grand." They spoke in the measured, level tones of the unsure.

"To whom?" Her words mattered no more to her than the fleeting of distant bats. When Deep Spring tugged against his lead, she barely noticed.

Allmon shrugged. "Some Irish guy." And then he seemed to realize that Henrietta was looking at him, that the temperature had changed, and looking up, he was confronted by an intensity in her face that caused him to step back right into Deliria's shoulder.

A voice shattered their moment of public privacy. "Henrietta Forge!"

Allmon slipped away in an instant, his heart banging an abrading rhythm, as Henrietta peered under the arched neck of Deep Spring. She noted first the dusty Justins, dark jeans, a Wildcats jacket, then the blowsy face and rosaeic nose, the wondering eyes so wide that they showed white around the edges of the brown irises.

"Henrietta Forge? I believe it *is* you," the man said. "You're older, but I'll be darned if you don't look almost the same." The man had rounded the front end of Deep Spring and stood gazing at her with a kind of helpless pleasure, shaking his friendly head in disbelief.

"I . . . ," she stalled.

"Dan Barlow," he said, sticking out his hand.

"Barlow—"

"Jamie Barlow? My dad was your all's farm manager from back in '73 until—"

"Oh my God!" Henrietta cried, her eyes widening. "Old Barlow!"

"Yeah, that was my dad."

"Oh!" Her gasp was quick and involuntary, the tiniest spear piercing the brittle veneer between past and present. One hand rose trembling to cover her lips as she took in the look of this man, stout and sure like his father, but redder and thicker about the middle. "Oh, how is your father? Tell me how he is," she said, her words like a plea.

A mild surprise registered, and the man shifted his considerable weight. He passed a hand down his satiny jacket front. "Well, Dad passed back in '93. Uh, he, you know, he didn't last too long after Mother went, which was, shoot, back in . . . well, that was in early '92, I reckon. I'm so sorry you didn't know. I called your dad myself to give him the news."

Old Barlow was dead? Her eyes filled with fast, unbidden tears. The man had always called her his strange bird, his funny valentine. He had looked at her as though she were the most interesting and precious person in the world. And never once had he told her who to be.

Now his son said, "That happens a lot, you know. One passes and the other can't hang on too long. Dad always relied on Mother to keep him on the path. Maybe a little too much. Lost his spark a bit when she went. I think he didn't have as much purpose without her."

"I never visited him," Henrietta said. "After he retired. I told him that I would." Guilty tears threatened to spill down her face.

There was surprise on the man's face again. He observed her tears. "Well, now," he said, and inched closer and, with the awkward kindness of an aging bachelor farmer, slumped his heavy hand down on her shoulder and patted her stiffly but gently. "You were just a kid, just a little girl. You had no cause to worry about visiting an old man like that. Besides, Dad's last couple years weren't pretty. He wouldn't have wanted you to see him that way."

Henrietta couldn't speak at all, so he just patted her shoulder again and went on, "Dad sure did care for you, though," but then his own voice

caught, and they looked at each other, bewildered by the density of emotion building in the midst of the Keeneland crowd. "Yes, he cared for you
very much. I remember he always said if he had a daughter, he'd want one
just like you. Said you were smarter than he was when you were still in elementary school. He always did admire a smart woman. That's why he married
Mother."

Tears slipped raggedly down Henrietta's unguarded face. Her voice,
when it emerged, sounded young. "Do you"—she said—"do you think he
forgave me?"

"For what, honey?"

"For forgetting . . ."

The man, anticipating the gravity of her reply, had leaned in to offer her
his good ear, but now he faced her squarely and said, "You got nothing to
worry about. Dad was good with horses, but he was even better with people.
He was a very loving man. I never saw him hurt a fly."

"Yes, but do you think he forgave me?"

The man's brow was furrowed, and he said, "Why, I believe forgiveness and love are the same thing. Don't you?"

Partially awake: soft and gray as old ashes, doves bob on the windowsill,
warbled faintly by the rilled glass, so their contours flex and bell beyond
their actual shape. They touch beaks as if kissing and their elegant heads
merge, partially distorted. She's barely aware of watching them until one
dove taps the glass with its slate beak, and the sound carries, as well as the
sounds of the woken world.

Mourning doves mate for life; she's seen evidence of it herself. One day
when she was fourteen years old, she discovered a dead dove on her morning walk. A mess of chine and feather and chalky eyewhite, the thing had
been done in by a prowling cat or some other predator. Above, on a phone
line that swooped along the edge of the property, a gray dove cooed, very
much alive. She thought nothing of it; there were birds everywhere. But the
next morning, the violent bed of feathers remained, and the perched dove
cooed overhead—and the next morning and the next, that bird sang its persistent, increasingly dreadful song. It remained there above the disappearing body of its mate for three whole months until only a beak remained and

all other bones had long been carried away. For all she knew, it remained there still. She had learned not to look.

If Jamie Barlow, that good and kind man, was dead, then truly every other being would also die. Death must be real and not just some story people told.

An old vase—a family antique—had been tottering on its rim for a long time. Now it finally broke.

She didn't make herself pretty; she never had any interest in anything like that. She just went to him. She found him exactly where she knew he would be in the stallion barn, mucking and grooming, cleaning up someone else's mess. At first, he was unaware and moved with the ease of the unobserved, and then, some near-dormant animal sense alerted him, and he turned with the smallest of starts. He looked at her, then beyond her, through the drawn sliders of the barn door toward the house, which was enormous, almost overpowering the constraints of the aperture.

"Can we start over?" she asked, but at first he didn't take a step toward her, because if he moved, he would no longer see the house. But when she tugged on his hand, he followed.

She saw how his pupils were big, voluptuous. She was on her knees before him in the hay, the smell of tack stronger than the smell of two people with their blood rising. He stared down at her, almost repelled as she took him in her mouth. What he felt most keenly was the cold air on his buttocks. Denuded in the almost dark, he shivered. He didn't want her to see his body, but he dissolved into the shadows of the room, and he could only know himself to be where her hands traced. She was moving on him, as if trying to suck up the very source of his male life while he leaned against the door, straining against into away from her, then sinking down, and she was shimmying out of her jeans, opening and widening.

Shocked by his own nudity, he felt—was—inexpert and extremely cold.

"God, you have a beautiful body," she said. It made him cringe, because she thought it was a compliment.

Then he was falling into her and again and again, entirely unsure, and there was almost no pleasure in it, only imperative, the body driving toward its denouement. The anxiety of it snuffed any pleasure. He didn't know how to do this, and yet somehow he did. It was the most natural thing in the world.

She was under him and she remained under him, receiving him without a sound, as if she was curious or amazed, ushering him into her with an undulating tight that made him make sounds like a low song, sung just for her, rising in tempo and volume with each refrain of desire or need or force until he drove into her as if he would break her, the smacking sounds alarming him as much as they turned him on, and then he was done, hunched over her and sweating, his arms trembling with rageful exhaustion and confusion.

She held him tight until he withdrew, and only then did she make a sound, one long, low, lonesome moan, which sounded more like desire than any sound he had made.

He couldn't move; he remained hunched over her, catching his breath for a stunned and exhausted time, inadvertently letting her look at him. He only escaped her gaze when he eventually returned to the workers' quarters on the far side of the property, submerged himself in a tub of water, and covered his face with his hands. Then he was too tired to beat back an insistent memory and recalled someone saying to him somewhere sometime long ago: "Son, the common language of God and man is morality."

It's an old story, how on a late summer evening, Daniel Boone was out with a friend hunting deer at the edge of a farmer's field. They were shining the eyes—which is to say, his friend was carrying a flaming pine torch as he rode along on his horse, directing the light at the forest and its thickets, and attracting the shining eyes of all the species within. As the horseman moved slowly along, Boone followed behind on his mount, his rifle at the ready, trained on the shadows in the woods.

Suddenly, Boone saw a pair of bright eyes. He made a quick motion for his friend to stop, then slipped silently from his saddle. He trained his firearm on the spot where he had seen the animal, steadied himself, and prepared to take the shot. But something stayed his hand—a too-long moment of hesitation, suspicion, or some strange intuition. He withdrew his finger from the trigger and pointed the rifle at the ground.

Soon there was a rustling in the thicket. When the deer emerged, it was wearing a dress. There stood the neighbor's blonde daughter, Rebecca, in plain sight of her would-be murderer. She was beautiful. They were soon married, of course.

So there were trysts, but the trysts were preceded by words, which at first sounded to Allmon like some old song-and-dance routine directed by overheated white girls who needed you to shuck and jive before they'd moan and writhe beneath you, asking you to pump the pump of you until you spilled your come. The first few times he was always watching from up in the rafters— What the fuck are you doing in a barn, Allmon Shaughnessy, son of Mike Shaughnessy, lothario, Irish agnate, collector, and disregarder of children, you fucking half-white fuck?

This was supposed to be what a man lived for—sex machine. So why could you only feel it in one little spot, the head of your dick, while all the rest of you was tied up in old rope. God forbid that rope begin to fray or loosen—holy shit, then his whole life would come spilling out of the shape of him; he would start to feel forbidden things in his body, like the kisses she began to press against his neck, or the touch that was maybe not just desire but something softer than that. Or the look in her eyes, which was softening too, more with each encounter. No. NO. He wasn't fucking her, he was fucking *through* her keyhole into the house on the other side.

"Tell me where you come from," she said.

How can I tell you? No one ever told me.

"What were you like as a child?"

Ugly.

"What's your mother like?"

A tisket a tasket, a gray and glossy casket.

Tell me, tell me, tell me, tell me

Shut upShut upSHUTUP!!!!!!

The real questions were his, shining around him like a whitened, heated aura, and he tried to hang on to them with what remained of his dwindling reserve: How much is that house worth, how much are you worth? How come you think you deserve all this when I don't? I had a white father too, but nobody's handing me shit. How much do you think I need to buy one good mare and one share of the best stud? What were you doing the year I turned seventeen? How much do you think I'm ever gonna tell you about my life inside? Nothing, that's how much. Nothing, nothing, nothing. Because you deserve nothing.

But it was as if she wanted to eat even his silence. She grasped hold of his empty answers, invited them into her, begging him for pleasure or perhaps something else that had begun in the shape of pleasure but was swiftly outgrowing it. She was moving steadily over him, asking and asking and asking to be let loose from the awful hames that constricted her, and then she was coming with great cries and convulsions into openness without care for who heard or knew. She wanted it all—the heavy, burdened brow, his face like a secret, his dark, long chest with its trembling inhalations, his cock, the contours of which she could draw with her tongue. And sometimes as she was moving over him, Allmon's body betrayed him and he was suddenly lost, swimming in the new space that opened up between two bodies but that aroused a terror even stronger than desire—he was losing his purchase on his old resentments, and he couldn't relearn his resistance. Something was growing in him too. In desperation, he tried one last trick: he learned to play the old, instinctive game of postcoital sleep, so that when she resumed her questions, finally asking, "What was it like in prison, Allmon?" his only reply was silence, and when she turned her head to inquire again, he was asleep, his chest so still, it appeared he was dead.

But he couldn't last; he broke. She came to him one morning at seven, an hour set brazenly in the light; he realized she had walked straight across the property, abandoning any need for privacy, his or hers. She had always been so secretive before, and yet here she came, tugging off her clothes in the daylight, naked before she was even on his bed.

"Allmon," she said, and that too struck him as a new curiosity, the way she said his name. It was big and round like a dipper that could hold him. When he looked at her face, he saw what looked like wonder or the joy of discovery, something as bold as the morning light itself. It jarred him; he looked away. But she reached with both hands and turned his face toward her, so he could see her as she undressed him. It was so clear that she was taking joy in this—in him—but that was too much, almost repugnant. He tried to turn away, but then she climbed over him and pressed him into her. She was entirely concentrated, her body so open, they were soon one strong rhythm, and he felt he was becoming her or maybe the other way around. Then she was pulling him over her, and it was Allmon who was making sounds now, release pressing up through reluctance, some kind of desperate song as she was saying please, please, please like the only thing she wanted in this world was for him to come inside her with nothing between them, and the rise and fall was coming—but it wasn't orgasm this time, it was the other wave, the great worst wave from forever ago, suffocating and dreadful, about to crest over him now, and he was off her in an instant, hunched over and dry heaving beside her, his body wracked.

"My God," Henrietta said, too surprised at first to move, jerked from the sex and the warmth into the cold. Then she recovered herself and reached out for him, but Allmon extended one forearm and pushed her back, shaking his head like a wounded bear.

"No," he choked, swallowing hard, struggling to hold himself in.

"Allmon." Henrietta's voice was soft—that change had come once they started having sex; it was a woman's voice like he had never heard before. "Allmon, what's wrong?"

He just shook his head, back and forth, back and forth, hunched. Henrietta lay there on her side and observed him for a moment, the only thing he would allow her to do. She took her time considering all the confounding details of his downcast face, then said, "Allmon, tell me why you're not free with me."

It was so unexpected, so absurd, he laughed from his hunched position— but it was an ugly sound, like a bark. Wholly dismissive.

"What?" she said, but not rearing back.

When words came, they were as cutting as any knife blade: "White people—!" he blurted.

"White people what?"

He was ready—even wanted—her words to be sharp too, but they weren't, and when he looked over quickly at her face, it remained open, curious. He didn't know whether to believe in the openness he saw there, or whether it was some kind of trick.

"Y'all don't get it. You really don't," he muttered, hate now beginning to stanch his tears.

"Get what?" she said. "I don't understand you."

When he spoke, he spat. "No, you don't!" His words were launched arrows. "Y'all fuck up our lives for fucking hundreds of years and then tell us we aren't free? What the fuck! Can you even hear yourself?"

Henrietta didn't defend herself, and he didn't know what to do if he couldn't get her to fight, to hate him back. So he waved his hand abruptly, confusion suddenly present, regret tannic like blood in his mouth. "I don't even know if I mean you anymore," he said, but he did, because she was like a white pebble on a white beach that ran all the way around the world, containing all the oceans she had seen and he hadn't.

Henrietta's touch interrupted the roiling of his mind. Something was moving in her, emerging out of shadow into consciousness. She was seeing the real Allmon, and she knew it. Her hand was light when it stroked the hard slope of his shoulder, then tugged insistently at his arm.

"Tell me about prison," she said, but her words were salt in that wound.

He didn't even hesitate. "No. That ain't never gonna happen."

"Why not? Don't you trust me?"

He shook his head. "I can't trust myself."

"Trust yourself to what?"

Still looking at the ground, he said very deliberately, "If I said my life out loud, I don't know what I'd do. So don't push me."

She didn't. When she did finally speak again, she said simply, "Allmon, I just don't want you to be unfree with me."

He made a hateful, smirking face.

"What's the most unfree thing about you?"

He half laughed, still dismissive, but wouldn't look at her face. "I don't even know what we're talking about. Forget it. Seriously."

"Allmon, what's still holding you prisoner?"

The blood rushed to his face. It came so fast, he felt dizzy. He shook his head, looking at the ground.

"Tell me. Please," she said, and only held him more firmly when he tried to pull back from her hand on his arm.

"Fuck," he said, blinking. His voice was thick.

"Tell me."

Suddenly, he rocked back on his heels, naked there beside her, his arms raised. He looked furious when he pounded once at his chest, a single thud. "Hurt!" he roared, like she had caused it.

Henrietta wasn't afraid of his anger but was totally confused. "Hurt? Like physical pain?"

He shook his head angrily.

"Grief?"

He nodded violently then, his neck straining, his eyes feeling wild like they didn't know where to look. He tried once, tried again. "My momma, my life—" he choked out.

"What?"

"Died!"

Henrietta rose onto her elbow, her brow wrinkled. "Your mother died?"

He didn't move for a moment, a wave of utter self-disgust wrenching his heart. Then he blurted, "Fuck!" like he'd made some awful mistake, and he spat a little when he said that, so he lowered his head in embarrassment, and then as if his bowed head were granting permission, he began to cry, first with a strange, strangled sound and then huge sobs. Henrietta was off the mattress in an instant like an animal taking flight; she grabbed at Allmon, half in alarm, half in affection, but that only made it worse.

He was losing control, the reins slipping his grasp. He was almost incoherent when he spoke through the tears that flooded his cheeks. "I don't know . . . why you even want to be with me. They broke me. I'm fucked up. Prison fucks you up. I can't tell you what I did . . . I'm broke."

Her arms were around him like iron bands, but they didn't feel like a constraint when she said, "I don't think you see what I see."

He couldn't stop the horrible, stupid words as they began to run as furiously as the tears. "Why? I'm poor. I'm fucking ugly. They used to call me old-man Allmon. All anyone sees is black. I wish I was smarter . . . had money. I'm just average, you know." He laughed bitterly and made a downward sweeping gesture toward his lap. "I didn't get nothing good in this life. I didn't get nothing that lasts. Prison killed me. You're fucking a dead man."

What Henrietta said next shocked her, because she once believed its very opposite, but she recognized the truth of it as soon as it was on her tongue. "It's not the body I want; it's the man. And that man is not dead."

Allmon shook violently once as though he might cry forever, but then he stopped suddenly and laughed a rueful laugh of total humiliation, and was finally silent. When Henrietta heard that laugh, however minor the key, she scooted back onto the mattress on her back with her arms open. "Lie down with me," she said.

Allmon looked toward her once, warily, wishing to escape. He was hor-rified to the marrow of his bones that he had cried in front of her.

"Come here," she said again, and patted the mattress.

Gingerly, reluctantly, like he was testing broken bones that had only recently begun to knit, he rolled onto his side next to her. Everything hurt.

Henrietta placed her head next to his on the pillow, twined one leg over his, and held him fast until she felt certain he wasn't going to roll away or get up.

"What's the best thing you can think of?" she said.

He was surprised by the question but responded with surety. "The river."

"The Ohio River?"

Allmon nodded, and in his exhaustion closed his bloodshot eyes to savor a private vision. "Because my momma . . . I know she's on the other side. It's like she's alive and just waiting for me to come home." His words drifted away. Quietly, he said, "What about you?"

"Me?"

"Yeah. What's the best thing you can think of?"

Henrietta's face, as always, was serious. "Don't you know?"

"What?" He turned finally to look at her, quizzical.

"You," she said. "You're the best thing I can think of. I feel like the real me when I'm with you, and I've been waiting my whole life for that."

He's asleep, and she isn't going to wake him. She's leaving, but it's impos-sible to return to the house, impossible ever to return to her old self. There's a new spirit transplanted into the old, worn body. So, she wanders away across the grounds, which are her father's, through a brand-new morning under a brand-new sun. Born out of his grief, which he planted in her with his words, she can feel ecstasy growing.

The truth? His nakedness—the nakedness of his heart—is her first happiness.

The world is busy rearranging its terrors and its joys, and something in her quickens. She's aware of herself, perhaps for the first time, as constantly varying, no longer separate from nature, no longer the watcher.

She feels like a woman—or like more, like she herself is the spring, which once seemed like something outside of her: force and violence, charging the barren landscape and murdering winter, beholden to nothing—certainly no human or animal. Spring comes as a reconnoitering scout, a first slip of green peeking from the very bough tips of the oaks, barely there at all, just a weighted abeyance. Winter is damaged but still dreadful and full of poison ice and useless powder; every human heart senses that brief lull; it's only a first flirtation, but they're raw with expectation, impatient after the long revolution of the year. They let their stoves and hearths go cold. They turn their animals loose as a prayerful incantation. Then the air fills with a natural heat as if from many bodies crowding close. The birds trill early and through the night. The hours quicken in their clocks, then a late March blooms gulfstream heat, then the lead goose returns with its followers, and suddenly, the season emerges, an influx of green overlaying the old, dead architecture and breaking through fading, whitened scars. The green comes up and out, like a river that's been running under everything, rising, swirling, and pressing out of every living thing in wet, ripe presence, so the gushing river is in everything and covering everything—in the vasculature, the buds, the bark, the veins, the teeth, the tendons, the marrow. Up and out and over. This green burns the human eye. She isn't adornment; she doesn't care what you think of her beauty. This isn't a gift; it would burn you if you held it. She's brilliance without intellect, mother without love, a lover with two differently colored eyes: comfort and disaster. She destroys animals in their birthing, she floods the world, makes youth hasten out of itself, ripens everything to rot, she makes the graves warm.

This and more: viburnum in the yards, pungent as an ovulating woman, pink labial pistils, the leaf bottom shaped like a heart; fresh sun knocking down every shadow; the overeager daffodils, early every time; infantry grasses storming animal blazes and human paths; the lilac buds of the redbuds; pendant racemes of black locust; sumac's lip-red fruit; mosses on bleachy bones; mosses on the hunched river stones; mosses on man's abandoned hunting huts; also the drone of carpenter bees; bobbing nine-pin tails of deer; red-hooded woodpecker alighting; all the small animal bodies bathing in the sweetgrass; the green foliage glazed with yellow; new life in the old ossuaries; there's the frog in the muddy shallows, gripping a twig with one splayed hand and floating loose and easy in the shallow waters; tiny penile head of the turtle poked from the depths of the pond, auras of water rippling from his briefly borne movements; turkeys in their heavy, improbable flight; crickets; gnats; flies.

Everything comes from everything and nothing escapes commonality. I am building a house already built, you are bearing a child already born. Everything comes from everything: a single cell out of another single cell; the cherry tree blossoms from the boughs; the hunter's aim from his arm; the rivers from tributaries from streams from falls from springs from wells; the Christ thorns out of the honey locust; a word from an ancient word, this book from many books; the tiny black bears out of their durable mothers tumbling from dark lairs; eightieth-generation wild crab abloom again and again and again; your hand out of your father's; firstborn out of firstborn out of firstborn out of; the weeping willows and the heart leaf, the Carolina, the silky, the upland, the sandbar willows; every tart berry; our work, which disappears; our mothers' whispers, which disappear; every Thoroughbred; every violet; every kindling twig, bone out of bone; also the heat lightborne, the pollen airborne, the rabbits soft and crickets all angles and the glossy snakes from their slithering, inexhaustible mothers, freshly terrible. When you die, you will contribute your bones like alms. More and more is the only law.

Or is all this too purple, too florid? Is more too much—the world and the words? Do you prefer your tales lean, muscular, and dry, leached of excess and honed to a single, digestible point? Have I exceeded the bounds of the form, committed a literary sin? I say there's no such thing—any striving is calcined ash before the heat of the ever-expanding world, its interminability and brightness, which is neither yours nor mine. There aren't too many words; there aren't enough words; ten thousand books, all the world's dictionaries and there would never be enough; we're infants before the Ohio coursing its ancient way, the icy display of aurora borealis and the redundancies of the night sky, the flakes of snow common and heartbreaking; before the steady rocking of a man and a woman, the earthworm's curling, the leopard killing the mongoose killing the rat over the ant in its workmanlike machinations, the anonymous womb that knit the anonymous, the endless configurations of cloud, before the heron, the tern, the sparrow, and the wily peacock too, the peacock turning and splaying his designs, each particular shimmering feather a universe invested with its own black sun, demanding, Look before you die, Look—Don't turn away for fear you'll go blind; the dark comes down soon enough. Until then, burn!

It sounded like a bad joke, how Mack came from a place called Holler—too backwards to even have a proper goddamned name. Way out in Letcher County past Whitesburg under a ridge as tall as any New York skyscraper. Holler. I mean, goddamn. Holler for help was more like it. Too far in to get penicillin when you were sick or to get out when your daddy was drunk and tumbling down Jericho. He came from a family where almost nobody gave a damn if you didn't go to school, where you were eight the first time you got sick on spruce moonshine. Excepting his dear mother, who loved all her children gay or straight or green, his clan was full of shrew-faced ma-maws that ruled the roost and men so cowed they could have been cattle. A stereotype of a stereotype, that was Holler. Even the word was arsenic on his tongue. Of course, it wasn't politically correct now to talk about the mountains that way—a bunch of self-righteous cockroaches would crawl through the Internet and infest your inbox, call you a traitor to the ones you left behind. But that was all a song and dance to look better for the Yan-kees, and Mack liked Yankees about as much as he did mountains. Sure, people liked to wax romantic about down home, about places like Holler or Crine or Sundown—Mama's cooking and eighty-seven-verse ballads and awshucks I ain't knowed we was poor, that whole whitewash—but they only indulged it once they'd got out. Then they'd forget about the beatings, everybody dying too young from drugs and car crashes on mountain roads, the hellfire, the damnation, the everloving ignorance. Sentimental memories were just a way of apologizing for being the kind of asshole who escapes. And escape Mack had.

He was pretty sure they'd flung him up on a nag straight out of the womb. Just a spraddle-legged little fucker on the back of a bow-back mare, taking jam and pork cuts to his cousins over in the next holler, fetching mail in Holler proper for Mother and Daddy, making himself a general nui-sance by egging on anyone with a horse or a mule to race down the length of Big Hammer Holler, from Mine no. 11 down to the cluster of Union graves at the far end (his clan ran Jefferson, opposition to most of the county, which just figured). He was always sneaking up on somebody's horse, riding hogs for fun, telling folks he tamed a deer and rode it too, which was bullshit of course, but the story got so big, so reckless, he couldn't remember if he'd rode the thing or just told the tale. Didn't matter. It made him a minor legend, so somebody had actually heard of him on the Alabama Circuit when he went down there begging to ride—a fourteen-year-old with cannonballs in his Wranglers. But he conquered that rinky-dink show pretty fast and then headed west with a boyfriend who only made it as far as Peoria before Mack left him on the side of the road, and then he rode quarter horses in Wyoming until he got thrown hard and was busted up for three solid months. That's when he switched over to training, which was a natural progression, seeing as he was constitutionally incapable of getting along with people, much less taking orders from them. Soon enough he tore the Old West a new asshole and got bored again, ended up back in Kentucky. Of all places. Eating where he used to shit, he supposed, but he never went back to the mountains. He stayed in Lexington with his scratchy, undiluted Letcher County accent, and when people called him a hillbilly, he flexed his wrist under his Rolex and curled his toes in his custom Lucchese boots and thought, You have no fucking idea.

Mack slowed down for nothing but whiskey and his dear mother, whom he'd brought up to a Lexington retirement home pretty much the instant his daddy died, and just now he was charging at his customary speed through Henry's stallion barn, looking for the manager's office. Henry had said he would be there first thing in the morning. They were planning to roll through footage together, debate the new prospects for Seconds Flat, talk about siblings going to stud. He didn't do it like this for everyone; he was in the enviable position of choosing whom to work with so closely, but few were as driven as Forge. Henry was a man who never called it "the game," and Mack appreciated that. If you were born in Letcher County, you knew that nothing involving more than fifty bucks was a game.

He heard the sounds before they registered, but hell, it was February and every horse he encountered was cock-addled or in estrus, and his poor brain was echoing with the sounds of breeding or grooms talking about breeding or his own thoughts on breeding, so he didn't realize what it was until he saw it, though he certainly should have; his body already knew. He heard that sound of someone moaning low, and the slapping of skin that made his dick move before his brain could get involved. He only stood there at the office door for maybe two seconds—the fools left it cracked! Or maybe they got off on that, who knows—but it seemed just shy of an eternity: the black guy moving over a white woman who had turned her face away, but whose hair was unmistakable as she moaned and gripped the groom's buttocks, so it stood out in his mind later with all the startling, upending stark of a photographic negative. It was only when he had stepped smartly and immediately away, when he was marching off to the house, realizing Henry had meant *that* office, that he understood exactly what he'd seen.

At the far end of the shed row, he laughed once, a harsh, surprised sound. Mack wasn't a cruel man—well, he'd been accused of cruelty by a couple of employees, but mostly he was just impatient—but, more to the point, he appreciated a good joke. Especially at another man's expense. A wealthy man? One who paid him to be the best, all the while thinking he was a step above on the ladder? He felt a twinge of compunction when he thought of those kids just having their suds-in-the-bucket fun . . . But yeah, this was pretty goddamn irresistible.

Which is why he was grinning over Henry's head when he stepped into the house office, why he could barely tuck away that grin as they watched the seven prospect videos, and why he ended up saying something, even though he really knew he shouldn't, even though he felt a tiny twinge of almost-regret.

It didn't stop him. He was a risk taker, just like Henry Forge. "Tell me again the name of that black kid you got working for you, Henry."

"Allmon. Why?" said Henry from where he was switching off the DVD player and straightening up to see him out.

Mack tapped his Stetson against his thigh and torqued up his lip. "Well"— the world in the pause—"I know you watch your investments, Henry." The words were just barely weighted with the drag of meaning, but Henry looked at him sharply.

Henry paused before he spoke. "That's right."

"And you no doubt got big plans for your daughter."

This time, Henry didn't answer, just looked, and Mack played it easy, played it cool. He knew how to handle a whipsaw. "I can see how you've been grooming her to take over this operation. She's a talented lady, for sure. But things sure can go wrong in a hustle. All sorts of things. A girl headed for the big time can end up hauling coal. It's a crazy world."

The meaning settled and the sclera of Henry's eye brightened with blood. He said, lowly, "And you speak from experience? You've seen that sort of thing happen, I assume?"

They were standing at the side door to the el porch now, looking out over the acreage, which men like Henry were handed on silver platters at birth. Mack said, all casual, "Yeah, sure. I've seen it myself. It's just a reality of life how even the best-laid plans can get fucked. Funny how that can happen." Then he popped his hat back on his head and said, "It sure is funny."

"Henrietta!"

Henry made a hard knot of his Burberry tie and dragged a comb through his silvery hair, but his pugilist hands trembled in the mirror; there was disturbance beneath the water.

"Henrietta!"

Careful, Henry. The overeager go out in the first round, and the obdurate are softened by something other than hard blows. Night was encroaching and Kentucky was folding in on itself and, with it, untold possibilities for a man who couldn't manage himself.

"I'm right here." Henrietta was just outside the door of the bedroom, standing before the hall mirror in a red silk dress he'd bought her seven years ago for a Derby run—the year Hellcat finished second. He remembered the race; he remembered the red dress.

"You look beautiful, daughter."

Henrietta smiled, not turning from the mirror as she clipped her grandmother's pearls to the lobes of her ears. But Henry could see her eyes were too alive and elsewhere—the look of a woman only recently visiting foreign countries, her mind not yet returned home.

"Where have you been?" he said easily.

She stiffened, the old steel in her eyes again. "What am I—a child?" she said.

A cock of the head, a curb of the mind's tongue. It was Henry's turn to say nothing.

As she pinned up her hair, Henry stepped in and kissed the back of her neck. But his gall rose: from her shoulders drifted the heated smell of woman, that wandering sex; it was a noisome stench. "Your grandfather would be very proud of you," he said, and watched as her glance stalled, seemed to catch the waft of meaning almost after it had drifted past. She shifted in her low heels, adjusted the dangerous bodice.

"Are you ready?" she said.

He was ready.

Across the black expanse of farm, across the farrow winter-world of Bourbon County in January, across town, the old Tavern blazed. The centuries-old building, a gray limestone structure as pale in the night as the adjacent courthouse, built by pioneer hands and maintained by Old Dominion faith, stood festooned with stringed white bulbs and garlands. A round, hyperfecund moon loomed over her slate rooftop, and the stars were all dimmed before the overbright, nettling lights of Paris.

The old tavern door was manned by a wizened groom in age-old livery, bowing at the waist as he ushered them into the dark, cramped space of the low-ceilinged foyer. A single sconce twinkled. With his hand at her back, Henry steered his daughter through a narrow hall toward snapping candle-light and high, sharp chatter, voices like breaking glass. They descended three stone steps into a small banquet room.

Now they all turned as one, forty or fifty heads as a single body, conver-sation halting, all eyes on the lamplit pair. Henrietta clutched once at her bodice, sensing the almost irresistible draw of the passage behind them, the aloneness it offered, but Henry stepped smartly into the room ahead of her, a childish grin of delight on his face.

A smartly dressed woman of sixty disengaged herself from the crowd, setting aside her glass and reaching for Henry with both hands. Her eyes were rimmed with blue kohl and her feathered blonde hair reached im-probable heights in all directions. Her long bejeweled earrings swung to and fro, snatching the light as she turned to the small crowd, crying, "The guests of honor!"

Henrietta barely heard the cheer that followed. She'd been here before, but never at night, never when the scarlet walls were turned to swampy blood by flickering lamps and candles, clashing with the swagging salmon drapes. The woman was speaking into her face with boozy breath when someone pressed a chilled tumbler of bourbon into her hand. She took the thing as a shot.

"To the memory of John Henry, that Old Regular sonofabitch!" came a rallying cry, and she knew there were no strangers here. These white, warm faces, pink with alcohol, all possessed surnames that had struggled over the Wilderness Road to this bloody ground, naming it Paris after other trodden and trammeled wildernesses. Kentucky had folded all their lives together into a tight braid.

Look at them all raising glasses to her munificent grandfather, her ambitious father—panegyrics for the living and the dead. The bourbon Henrietta was drinking was florid and complex, but she tasted only confusion. She had lain under Allmon just this afternoon, cursing with want and wanting his need. She was in love, but maybe she was also hopelessly naïve. She blinked. Did she actually think that love offered some kind of escape? There is kingdom, class, order, family, genus, species. You could step out of your heels, walk backward along the hall, recede from their collective gaze, but you could never escape the category of your birth and all the morphological categories which precede it.

The garish mouth of the woman cried, "Come on, y'all! Dinner awaits!" and they were ushered to their tables, where gold flatware, crystal goblets, and old china sparked under the low lights. The woman raised a glass and knocked the tines of a fork against its faceted side. "We are here to celebrate the new Genealogical Museum of Central Kentucky"—applause all around— "funded in large part by a towering donation from the Forge family in the name of John Henry, whom we all remember as a treasured member of the community, deceased now more than thirty years. We wouldn't be—we couldn't be—who we are without men like John Henry and Henry Forge, men who preserve our past and guide us into a future where the past still matters. The Forge family is one of the crown jewels of the Bluegrass and, though they probably would have preferred to give anonymously, we just couldn't let them do that. We want to polish the jewels of our hometown. Now give a big Kentucky thank-you to Henry and Henrietta Forge! Join me in raising a toast!"

One long swig of bourbon and Henrietta's tongue was dry and bleached as a bone. There was raucous cheering and faces were speaking at her, but all she could think was: God, we all look alike, as if they'd crawled from the birth canal of the same remote ancestor. Love was an in-house project. When Judith had left, it was almost as if she'd never existed. Her bloodline offered no lifeline.

They launched into the repast: encrusted scallops with a mango spice reduction, roasted parmesan asparagus, local greens with raspberry vinaigrette and crème brûlée.

"Drink up," her father said, and she did. Her third.

Through the warbled glass at her nose, she watched Henry assume his stance at the lectern, his drink wobbling in his hand. Or was it her eyes that wobbled in their sockets? Another swig would answer.

"I want to tell you a secret!" Henry said. "A secret that not even my daughter knows." The room leaned forward, smiling. "It may surprise you to hear that as a young man I was disinherited by my father."

Disconcerted laughter thinned to a trickle, then ceased. Glasses half-raised were lowered. Henrietta sat up straight in her chair and tried to rally her focus.

Henry's gaze was steady on the room. "As you probably know, my father, John Henry, was a man of rigid principle, unbending in ways I couldn't understand when I was a young man. But what did I know? I was just a callow youth. When I looked out over our corn farm, I saw a pathetic, conservative misuse of land. When my father imagined a horse farm, he saw nothing but ostentation; he thought his son would forget where he had come from, where his allegiance ought to lie."

Henry folded his arms across his chest. "So we were at odds, you see, my father and I. I detected in him a failure of nerve, a fear of risk, and he thought my plans were beneath his dignity. Our dignity. Dignity that—like yours—was purchased at high cost over many generations. In short, he feared a reversal of hard-earned fortune in every sense of that word.

"My father was right, of course," he said, smiling into the shocked silence, smiling at Henrietta. "But please don't misunderstand me; I was right too. I'll get to that in a moment.

"My father, the man we are here celebrating tonight, saw my rebellion as a threat to something far more important than me: our family. That he was mistaken is now of no consequence. The important thing is that he would do anything to protect the family name, to protect the women in our house, to maintain the land, to store up honor for his children and their children. He understood that our lives are really lived in the minds of others. Their good opinion is worth more than gold. So, the most important thing—the critical component of my father's character—is a seeming paradox I didn't understand then, but understand now. He loved his family more than he loved his own child."

Henrietta choked down what was left in her tumbler, and it was instantly refilled.

"Now, my uncle never wanted to farm, and he returned the land to me. He understood what my father couldn't understand: that my plans for the land were no threat to the family name or fortune. And that's why my rebellion was never wrong. Because it furthered the cause of the family. And I know that's something that everyone here tonight can understand, because there's true-blue blood running through the heart of the Bluegrass, and that's been the case for two hundred and fifty years. We built this state brick by brick, and we saved it twenty times over from the riffraff that would unthinkingly tear it down. Why, families like all of ours are the only reason we're not . . . Mississippi!"

Laughter erupted in the room, brightened by the high, sharp overtones of relief. "We were the Old South and, unlike most of our sister states, we still are!" Henry raised his glass. "So let's drink to John Henry!"

The room exploded, but when he turned to Henrietta, his gaze was a kill shot.

"And let's drink to Henrietta Forge. I want you all to look at her, how beautiful she is tonight. If you ever want to see the pride of my life, look at her. I've done everything for this precious woman and, as far as I'm concerned, she's the crowning glory of the family. She's never done me wrong, and I know beyond the darkest shadow of a doubt that she never will. Because she knows what my father knew. She's more like him than she can even know."

The room turned to look at her.

"Henrietta, I'm drinking to you, my Ruffian," her father said. "We're all drinking to you."

She raised her fourth glass.

"To you!"

She hesitated.

"To you!" they said as a single organism.

She quaffed the shot, her eyes stinging. The hideous pink of the curtains swam before her. She tried to hang on to Allmon's name as a bouy, but it was slipping out of her grasp.

"And let's drink to Hellsmouth, my favorite racehorse." Without taking his eyes from Henrietta, he said, "A fine example of controlled usage, of taking great chances with breeding. We're going all the way with this one!"

The waiter was behind her, reaching around her, so she could smell the rank odor of his underarms, and even before he was done pouring, she was raising the tumbler again, they were all raising their glasses to Hellsmouth, the promise of Forge Run Farm, of Henry. A quintet was tuned, and now their chords were flushing the diners from their velvet seats to take the parquet dance floor, which was too small for their numbers, but they crowded there anyway, glasses in hand. It was much too much of too much—dancers filmed with sweat, low, guttural laughter, the stridency of some woman's voice too loud for the environs, shoved here by a body and there by another, until her father was wrapping her up in his arms and swept her down a slim corridor between bodies, so the fishtail hem of Henrietta's dress flared, and they were eye to eye.

As they turned on the floor, Henry breathed in the bourbon on her breath, strong enough to make a man drunk. He gripped her drinking hand and raised the tumbler to her lips.

He said, "Henrietta, young people think life is just a game. A sport."

She tried desperately to focus her disobedient eyes on the buttons of his collar.

"But you're smarter than that."

The scooping of his vowels was broad as a river. They all talked like this, she realized with a start, as if life were happening in slow motion, their words a hundred years behind the times. She wanted to put her hand to her hot forehead, but she couldn't, because it was raising her drink to her lips. He was.

"I love you, Henrietta."

She was nauseous. She was revolving on the axis of him.

"But I also love perfection."

She nodded slowly, his due.

He drew her tighter than a bow. "And perfection is worth every risk."

The knock came when she was half stumbling out of her dress, her hair fallen around her shoulders and her mascara smeared from rubbing. She turned clumsily in her drunkenness, gripping the bedstead to remain upright.

"Knock, knock." His voice, that old familiar, almost her own.

The ceramic knob turned and when the door opened, it creaked on its ancient hinges.

"Knock, knock," he said quietly, all eyes.

She turned half-naked in the dim light.

"Come in, Daddy."

Success: wealth, status, fame; involves the attainment of the worldly good only insofar as these attainments ensure the survival of selfish genes; autologous continuation; not merely survival but increasing complexity, including larger cranium or diminishment of dangerous vestigial organs, such as appendix; dependent upon genetically mutant transitional forms; see evolution of theropods & Etc for evidence of speciation and other deviations from ancestral forms; dependent in ancient thought upon the leniency of the gods and the mastering of fate; or, predestination generally requiring a supernatural agent (i.e., fate as a spindle, around which Clotho, Lachesis & Atropos wind an individual's thread, analogous to fate as the spindle in the cell); *archaic*: the good or bad outcome of an undertaking.

Now Henry was like a teenaged boy, bouncing on his heels, his strength renewed by a bold new diet. He was seeking out the groom, the antiphonal calling of mares and foals ringing over his head like church bells, celebrating the hour. He smiled. The other groom was late to the church, entirely too late.

Their regular farrier, a mustachioed man with hair the color of a chestnut roan, was exiting his Nissan and moving in the direction of the stallion barn.

"Have you seen Allmon?" Henry asked.

The man raised his darkly red brows. "Which one's Allmon?"

"Stallion groom. Black."

The man shook his head. "Not yet, but I'm headed up there directly."

"Well, when you do see him, tell him to come meet me in the back office. I'll be expecting him."

Now, Allmon's waiting had long turned to dread. When the farrier relayed the message in his disinterested tone, he remained rooted in his spot for a long time, bent over a grain bin in midmotion, barely breathing until black speckled at the edges of his vision. Electric alarm had shot through him— what should have been excitement, what should have been the gambler's triumph at holding an ace hand, stalled when he flipped the card and found it was a portrait of the boss man's daughter. He felt . . . sick. He turned and faced the tack room and could not make himself move for the longest time.

But he did move. He started before indecision could freeze him again. After all, you got your foot in when you got your cock in. That was the whole point, right? Yes. Exactly. He gained momentum as he moved across the yard.

Then, for the first time since that day he was hired by the woman who was now his lover, his first and only, he was standing in the kitchen of the big house. High coffered ceilings, brass fittings, white molded cornice, glimmering appliances, sienna tile floor, all laid-back, rich. But he found that he couldn't associate Henrietta with it anymore, not exactly. She had been some stony figurine initially, something glossy and cold, but now she was a personal warmth that enveloped him in his room, the hair that washed over his face when she was rocking over him, the— He had to stop thinking. Jesus Christ.

A wide hall paraded out of the kitchen toward the front, western half of the house, but as if he'd been there before, Allmon turned instinctively to a narrow perpendicular corridor, which ran alongside a staircase to the dark second floor. At first, he stood quietly at the door, able to stare in for a moment at Henry sitting at his desk and absorb the principled beauty of the man. Henry glowed in the fall of sunlight streaming through the double six-panes, the drapes drawn away as if to purposely frame him. He was golden as the calf at Mount Sinai. If the light had been lower, if the hair had been darker, it could have been Allmon's own beautiful father, but Henry was thicker, redder.

"Come in," Henry said without looking up from his paperwork. "Come in and sit down."

Allmon hesitated, feeling something good twining into his dread—yes, what he initially wanted was about to happen—and the future before him. He entered and sat.

"I've been mulling over a conundrum," Henry said when he finally looked up. "But I think I've solved it."

Allmon held his power in his mouth, his chin slightly lowered, eyes unblinking.

Henry muttered softly, "What to do with Allmon . . . What to do with the stallion groom."

Allmon couldn't move an inch, lest he betray something.

Henry said, "I asked you once what you were here for and now I know. There's nothing new under the sun. And I'll hand it to you—you've maneuvered your way in in a manner of speaking. But let's be clear: I'm not going to tolerate you near my daughter any longer."

Now Allmon's mouth slid open like a fish for the bait, but Henry was there first: "I'm no fool. I know I can't make you stay away from her. But I can offer a proposition that I doubt you'll refuse, and that could be to our mutual benefit."

Allmon had to drag the words forcibly out of his closing heart. "Like what?"

"I have an extraordinary horse," Henry said. "I know it like I've never known anything before in my entire life. I've been doing this since I was half your age, and, believe me, I know I'm right. What I propose to do is send you with Hellsmouth to Mack's training facility, let you oversee her conditioning. I'm saying I want you to be her personal groom. You'll have a groom's pay, but I have a contract here promising you five percent of the purse in her third year, payable upon her retirement. After the third year, you'll get your payout, and then you move on. End of story."

"No," Allmon said abruptly. "No deal." And as soon as he said it, he felt sudden, yawning relief, like there was still a way out of the madness. He could walk right out the door. But in reality, he could only fool himself for a brief moment. With a finality like fate, he knew they would work a deal. It felt beyond his control.

Henry sat back in his chair, incredulity smudging the veneer from his beauty. "Please don't try to tell me you're in love with my daughter. I wasn't born yesterday."

Allmon leaned forward suddenly toward the desk, his face shining with purpose. "Ten percent of earnings."

"Ten percent! For a groom? You're lucky Mack will pay you three-fifty a week!"

"You think I intend to do this my whole life?" Allmon hissed, and now words began to roll out with momentum, words that had been trapped in him for far too long. "You think I ain't got a vision? What do you care about the money? It's not why you do this! I want two of her foals—fifth year and sixth year and a breeding share every season for five years on your best stallion when he goes to stud. That's what I want. What you got?"

Henry struggled for composure as he took in the sight of this youth practically foaming at the mouth for the same things he'd spent a lifetime striving to achieve. His derision was plain. "Why am I not surprised that you want a handout?"

Allmon stood up from his chair, his height seesawing the room. He glared at Henry, his blood thick: On my seventh day in I saw this white dude stomp this black dude, and his jaw folded under his boot like you fold a piece of paper, his tongue sticking out like a dead dog's tongue. One of his eyes was lying on the floor attached by the root. He didn't die right away; it took him five days. You really think what I want is a handout?

What he said: "You need to learn what reparations means."

Henry was visibly startled. "Sit down!"

Allmon took a single step back toward the door, reaching blindly for the knob. Again, he suffered the wild sensation that he could simply walk out, that this would collapse like a house of cards, that he could go back to his room and life would continue on. But no. That's not what was going to happen.

"Sit down or there's no deal at all!" Henry barked.

Very slowly, Allmon laid down his bluff and returned to his seat, but he said, quietly, wondering at his own ability to play this cool and contained part, "You got no idea this horse is gonna make it . . ."

Henry nodded curtly and waved his hand. "It's a gamble. But given the stakes, it's one I'm willing to make."

Allmon curled his hands into fists and waited.

Henry went on, "All right, I will offer you ten percent of earnings—listen to me—*only* payable at her retirement at the close of her third year.

What I'm saying is you have to keep her healthy through the end of the Triple Crown or you get nothing at all. Nothing. You hear me? And then you'll get two of her foals and two stud shares. Take it or leave it, I will not negotiate further. But be warned—all of this is contingent upon no more contact with my daughter. I mean not one sideways word between the two of you. If you agree, you'll be employed by Mack Snyder from now on."

Allmon didn't need cash in his hand; horses were banks. "Deal."

Henry sat back. "Excellent."

"Where do I sign? We're signing, right? No deal if I don't sign." He sounded eager, naïve, ridiculous.

Henry cringed at the thought of this man and his daughter. "Sign Monday morning in this office at nine o'clock."

Then Allmon was moving out of the room, a light beginning to show in his mind, and there was a brief, triumphant elation. But then he realized how quiet his chest was, as if his heart had stopped beating, and he paused at the door and looked back with his hand on the knob. He said quietly, "You really hate me this much?"

"Hate you?" Henry said without looking up, his attention returned to the papers in front of him. "I don't even remember your name."

There is an old story of the seven hills. A great lion lived there, and he ate up other animals every day to build his strength. So the animals banded together and sent a representative, who said, "It's not good for a great lion such as yourself to waste energy on catching food. In exchange for eating only one of us a day, we will send you your food for dinner."

"Fine," said the lion, "but let's begin now."

They did as he bid them, and they sent an antelope the first day. On the second day, they sent a goat. But the animals were all worried, because they knew it would soon be their turn.

One day it was the hare's turn to be sacrificed. But before he went to the lion, he walked down to the river and rolled in the mud. He was filthy when he appeared before the lion.

"I'm not going to eat you!" cried the lion. "You're dirty!"

"Oh, I did not come to be eaten," said the hare. "I was bringing you a hare, but a great lion came, wrestled with me, and snatched it out of my arms."

The lion was astonished. "Is there another great lion roaming my seven hills?"

"Yes," said the muddy hare, "and if you will follow, I will show him to you."

So he led the lion out of his lair and across the savanna to the site of a deep well. The hare pointed down into its narrow depths.

"Look!" said the hare. "The lion is there and also the hare!"

The lion looked and saw that this was indeed so. Forthwith, he jumped into the well and

It began with one bad glass of wine she was served at a fund-raiser on Main Street, a wine so corked or old that it tasted not like berry or oak but only astringent, like sake, so she held out her glass and chided the server: You offered me the dregs?

Then, two days later, she stopped at Windy Corner for lunch, and no sooner had the screen door slammed behind her than the scent—stench— of barbecued pork came rolling over her like a rogue wave. Her body had ushered her away in immediate, instinctive retreat, and she'd stood on their porch before God and Thoroughbreds until her stomach settled, and she'd been able to return inside and eat, but not the pork.

Chicken. Which is what she was vomiting down the side of the 250 in twenty minutes' time, sickness wracking her with such suddenness and force, she had no time to pull over and could barely slow down before she was retching out the window, the truck wobbling madly between the lanes until she floored the brakes and came to rest like a shoaled boat between the road and a ditch carved by a shallow creek. Now she was scrambling from the seat, vomiting onto the tarred road; now she was leaning on the hood, expelling what felt like the insides of her insides; now she came to rest on her hands and knees on the road as the hard reckoning finally struck home.

There are no new stories, only new generations. Her nipples hurt. Her head was light and unfamiliar, unfocused, and she had been recently lain low by fatigue. For the whole of this past week, she'd been moving through her life as if under the influence of some ominous, waking sleep. She'd thought it was a result of not seeing Allmon, who'd been strangely absent all week, but then the wine had tasted bad and now—

A truck carrying an elderly couple pulled alongside her and almost before they could roll down the window, before they could say in wobbling, age-softened voices, Are you all right? Can we help you, miss? she was howling like an animal from her hands and knees, "Go away!"

Then she was pulling herself up onto unsteady legs, one hand to her clammy cheek, one hand to the white hood for what little support it could offer. She could smell her foul breath. The deepest kind of surprise flooded her, the age-old surprise of alien life, of life uninvited. She stared up at the sky, but it was unforgiving, as if even it had triumphed over her. The sun beat her face. For a moment, the defeat was gilded with excitement. She thought of Allmon, and her chest opened. Except: nothing was so simple. There was entrapment. Invaded by life, because you were born into a body with breasts and a uterus and the curse of fertility. She'd always thought pleasure was a simple thing to be had, like a meal or a conversation. She had been wrong.

She shook her head, she moaned out loud. The father . . . who could say? She pressed both of her palms to her enflamed cheeks. "Oh," she said into the emptiness of her predicament, and stumbled unseeing toward the little stream, barely book-deep, walking straight through it to the white fence on the other side, disregardful of the bracing water discovering the seams of her boots. She draped her body against the upper planks of the fence, staring into the pasture in front of her.

She pressed a hand to the flat terrain of her belly, mindful of the pained irony, the flatness there a coy contradiction of the changes taking place. It left her mind spinning. Sneaky thought: Wasn't it inevitable? The body making the body . . . Hadn't this been destined to occur from the moment she had pulled Allmon over her for the first time, at first desiring him, but then desiring to give herself away with increasing fervor, day after day, week after week? But the father. Oh God. With an intensity that surprised her, she wished suddenly for her mother, for her counsel. But Judith was far away—had been far away for many years now, and the distance was more than physical.

The most tiresome question of all presented itself: What now?

She blinked rapidly, trying to clear her vision. All her life, she had trained her eye upon this, the natural world, the land she was surveying over the top plank of a fence. The numbness of shock was wearing off, and she gathered some tattered remnants of ordered thought. Because she didn't know who the father was, her immediate impulse was to get rid of it. What on earth had come over her? She'd lost herself to some urge or some forgetting; she thought she was in love . . . she'd been preventing this very scenario for more than a decade, and here she had simply failed. Or. Or, she couldn't help but think, the biological destiny of the organism is to reproduce, and she had not even mentioned a condom to Allmon and then let him lie over her; she didn't even come half the time, and it hadn't mattered, because . . . yes, just like Allmon, she wasn't free. And then with her father, because . . . She shuddered. She knew with absolute certainty that there was no animal on earth less free than herself. But the question remained: What was her duty? Well, she had always said her duty was to Henry, and from that duty, she had excused herself only for pleasure. With some surprise, she realized that she had never indulged the question of what her duty to others might be. At another time, the question would have been merely an abstraction, but now the radical force of life was imposing itself, and she couldn't suffer any sophistry. She wanted desperately to think this emergent thing was not life—and she would have argued it vehemently at one time—but now it would be only a conceit of the intellect. She knew it with her mother's mind and an older, ancient, original mind, which was maybe the same thing. This was stupid, blunt-force life. Only women—not science—knew how the species reproduced: the next life nothing new at all but an undulation, a spillover from the abundance of the last. The earth and its living were not created in seven days by some sky god; the earth was an eternal birth canal, mediating energy in surge after surge of transmuting life. The question was not when does life begin, but does life ever end? To have not seen it before was to have lived under a veil of illusion. She didn't want this knowledge or this change. She wanted to be left alone. Yet her want was nothing but a speck of cloud, because here it was, her estrogen rising, her progesterone rising, her uterus distending, life bending and molding her to its will, as she had always been bent to someone else's will. They were two prisoners trapped in one body, two wills diametrically opposed. The irony was bare and bitter and unavoidable: she was a woman, so she was a slave to life. Never before had she understood the brutal actuality of life in a body she didn't choose. She stared hard across the rise of the pasture to where a cluster of bay horses stood like statues in a grassy museum.

What was her duty? Now she thought of the mountains, the prairies blanketing the earth, which she loved; she thought of mustangs in the wild and fields of bison carcasses like shed snakeskins, useless on the plains; of dull Galápagos finches and kiwis in cages; of pinhead barnacles splayed on a table in Downe, their sex organs poked and pinched; and she thought of the last tiny passenger pigeon with its foreign burden, the way it perished in bizarre servitude. She thought finally of herself. What was her wish for this endlessly replicating, wild world? That it be left alone. So what was her duty to this being and its natural wild? She realized there was no duty, only choice, and choice was the heaviest burden. Duty was for priests and other fools. So, what would she choose? She would revoke her will and permit it to be. Her shoulders slumped, her lips parting in stupefaction. The war of organic beings might do its part later, but for her there was a conflict of interest, and she was in no position to judge. She must recuse herself. Then she was on her knees again, clutching the fence post and vomiting.

Allmon. The word wound round a whole new, gut-wrenching desire, because the whole of life had changed in a day. Pale as paper and eyes full of unshed tears, Henrietta half ran to the stallion barn. She was almost desperate to see his face—or more, to feel the full length of his body against hers, not for sex, but for something more important: assent.

But there was no man, no lover, no father of her child in the barn. Not even the scent of him. God, that scent had been such a drug! It had caused her to strip herself bare, spread herself, and grasp tight the arrow. For a brief, wild moment, Henrietta felt undone by panic. Women invited death when they let men inside their bodies! Why did they do it? Love couldn't possibly be worth it. All those dark morning meetings and the harmony she heard in their twined cries . . . that music was nothing but a meaningless ditty finches were singing from the tree of life.

And yet she wanted the whole of him more than she wanted air.

She saw the bedazzling horse before she saw Allmon—the pert power there was in the yearling's body, gleaming like new silk, spirit unbroken despite the halter. Then she realized the filly was being guided toward a waiting trailer by Allmon's hand.

"What are you doing?" she said, her voice sharp, her predicament suddenly secondary; Hell was still months shy of transfer to Mack's training barns.

Allmon swung round with a guilty start, the lead shank swagging loose. He registered the pale face, the bold, fearless, almost otherworldly gaze, and nearly lost his sense of place, of time. Then he drew a curtain of reserve down across his own face, so Henrietta could read nothing there.

"Heading out," he said cryptically.

Henrietta reared back in surprise. "What do you mean? You and Hell?"

"We're going to the training center." Allmon glanced nervously at the groom manning the truck; he could see the man's concerned eyes trained on them in the side view.

"What?" Henrietta said, her voice rising against her will. "What are you talking about? I didn't arrange for this." She reached out now to grasp hold of the lead shank, but Allmon only redoubled his grasp and made his shoulder into a kind of blunt wall she couldn't pass. Henrietta gasped audibly.

He wouldn't look her in the eye. "I'm her groom now. I'm going with her."

Stunned, Henrietta stared at his impassive, reserved, stony face. That withholding suddenly struck her as the worst thing she'd ever seen. "Why? You work here. Here. *With me.*"

He turned his face away from her.

She pressed forward. "Who authorized this? What on earth is this about?"

Against the closing of his throat, Allmon said three simple words: "Ask your father."

Henrietta stood there with a bewildered look on her face, trying to con-figure it in her mind. Then she reached forward, and with the strength of both hands grasped Allmon's face and forced it toward her, so her gaze was inescapable. He might have come apart, might have yielded, but Hellsmouth skittered to the side, sensing wild woman's energy loosed all around her like snakes coiling and weaving for a strike.

"I'm pregnant," Henrietta said.

For a hundredth of a second, she saw pure, unadulterated wonder in Allmon's eyes before he used his forearm like a cudgel to push her back or to push himself away, and blurted, "No, no, you ain't, no."

"What?" she said, stricken, the shock worse than any physical blow.

He was shaking his head, looking confused, then belligerent, then confused again. "No, my whole . . . I'm broke. No way . . . It's too late." He wasn't making any sense.

"What's too late?"

"No."

"What do you mean?" she cried.

"It's too late," he said very simply, hopelessly.

Henrietta stared at him in absolute silence, as if he'd transformed before her eyes from something familiar to something ghastly. Then disbelief at his response loosened her hand, and she reached forward and slapped the left side of his face.

Now the driver, who'd been sitting nervously with his hand perched on the latch, came rounding out of the cab, crying, "Whoa, whoa, whoa there!" and Hell skittered and neighed, straining against the shank, her tender neck wrenched by her own attempted flight, so Allmon was forced to step off to the side with her. The driver stood to the other side with his hands up, unsure what to do now that he was there, his wary face an apology.

"I am pregnant with your child!"

He'd been desperate, looking for an out, something immediate, something sure. When he found it, a grotesque calm flooded him. He turned to her with one brow arched. "How do I even know it's mine?"

"Holy shit," said the driver, eyes wide, trying to look nowhere at all while reaching blindly for the lead shank.

Now her screws came loose, the nails clattered to the ground, the joints that held her joists weakened, and she fell upon Allmon's person, beating his chest, his shoulders, reaching for his face, which he tried uselessly to shield with his one free hand. But the driver was scooping her up, banding her with work-strong arms and caging her.

She screamed, "You know what you are, Allmon Shaughnessy? You know what you are? A stereotype! Are you really going to walk away? You want to live your life like a goddamn fucking stereotype? Fuck you!" Then invective and senseless wounds flowing out her mouth and then that one vile word, coined long ago and wielded like a white man's axe, so the groom holding her lifted her bodily from the ground, yelling over her, "Jesus Christ, lady! Hold up! Shut up! Just shut up!"

But Allmon didn't respond visibly to the word; he crawled behind the hard wall of that old, familiar, stoic face, and her words hit that wall seemingly without a bruise. "You got what you wanted," he said, but very quietly. To his own ears it sounded unsure.

"What? No!" Henrietta cried, "No, I didn't!"

Allmon began to rush now. He guided Hellsmouth into her trailer, and when Henrietta realized there was nothing left except the small, intransigent life in her, which she would be growing alone, the fight went out of her, and she sagged back against the chest of the driver and said, "Why?" The question small, sad, girlish.

Allmon's hands were shaking when he tied the horse, and he could barely get air into his lungs. But he had made his decision. No one had ever offered him any quarter, and he didn't have any to offer. He turned to Henrietta, and though he couldn't meet her eyes, he was honest with her once again like he'd never been with another person. " 'Cause I'm out to win."

Bewildered and exhausted, she said, "What could you possibly have to win?"

Allmon was done tying Hell. The trailer was closed, and he was walking to the cab on legs he couldn't feel. He didn't look over his shoulder when he offered up that old chestnut, which suddenly tasted rotten in his mouth: "It's a black thing, you wouldn't understand."

Father, Father, Father—

She gathered herself up, her skeleton clattering painfully under her skin. She stumbled into the house, her lungs on fire and her tongue burning.

He was there, of course: Father and Lover. He was always there. He had given birth to this house, given birth to history. He had given birth to her.

She leaned against the kitchen door, her face blighted by pain. "I'm pregnant," she choked.

"Good," he said, and enfolded her in his arms—old man, still strong, still life giving, guiding, knowing, encroaching, forcing.

Her tongue was scooped out, the empty place filling with tears.

He said, "I'll take care of you just like I've always taken care of you."

She was beginning to cry. The Forge endurance was cold comfort, no comfort at all.

"Calm down now," he said.

"I hate him."

"Calm down, or you'll hurt the baby." And he laid a sunspotted hand over her flat belly.

She flung his hand away and stepped back, unsteady on her feet, nearly hissing as she spoke, "You better pray it's not yours—don't you know old seed produces weak plants?"

Now Henrietta finally cried. She cried as she had not even cried as a young girl when her mother left. She cried with such passion that she could barely manage the old slave staircase that led to the upper hall, at one point sagging like a broken, discarded doll against the banister, then sinking to her knees on the landing and sobbing in utter, encompassing sorrow. Until this moment, there had been some kind of hope that love would be requited like a priceless gift returned to the giver. But now that shadow hope was dead in the daylight while the fetus went about its triumphant business, not giving a damn. Her wails rang through the house, that colossus trophy waste dream cenotaph bore. She couldn't find the strength to rise; she crawled pathetically on her hands and knees into her bedroom. But at the sight of her highboy, her old notebooks, her tattered books—remnants of the old life—the constriction of her clothing was too much. She tore her tank top over her head, she wrestled out of her jeans as if they were on fire, finally rising to get out of her underwear and socks and stumbling into her blindingly white bathroom naked.

She gripped the very real, very cold ceramic of the bathroom sink, but could not bring herself to look in the mirror. What now? Her actions were a mystery; she was a mystery. With anguish, she sensed that time's blood had been merely passing through her seemingly discrete existence, her temporary form, and that when she was gone, time's blood would flow dispassionately on. She was beginning to think she had spent her time badly.

Remember the old books, Henrietta? She recalled the private education of her youth, the one sought by her own insistent will, not the one forced upon her by her father. Think. Perhaps the very point of education was to discover the world beyond the self. Think, think, think . . . God, how she struggled to rope her discursive, selfish thoughts.

Her mind began to unfold like a late-summer blossom.

Within her, life was busy with its divisions and multiplications. But she knew that the machine, with its supposedly higher mathematics, only manufactured mystery. The principles of organization were still cloaked in darkness. She contained so much—so much, in fact, that she couldn't contain it at all. How was it possible to live so many years in a body, not knowing yourself to be a small everything? She had been so busy consuming without digesting, absorbing what she wanted and shitting out the rest, too numb to see that her hair was streams, her bones stones, her breath humid weather, her heart soil, her veins endless waterways that coursed through the earth she walked upon. She should have spent more time looking not at the earth but at herself. Maybe she had known this once, but something, someone had driven her to bed on her back, where she could see only four white walls and a low white ceiling. Then somehow, she'd worked a self-deluding magic, deciding she had always wanted pleasure above all things, and had gone about it as men said you should, with abandon, never asking whether abandon was the mother of satisfaction. Who enjoys sex more? Why, Teresias, I say it's the woman! Nine times more.

A little bit of strength returned, and she looked down out the window at the grassy paddocks with their horses, her father's bucolic charms. Yes, she had been with men of all shapes and sizes, easing onto them, sliding with a timeless force, an urgency not even her own but nature's, nature who she had always felt held a gun to her head. The men were reduced under her body to hard statuary, marble men with marble cocks until she was coming and in that nothing, the bliss of absolutelynothingandnoplace, where her father could not exist or ever have her, it didn't matter what they were. That had seemed so easy. Yes, back then—was it only weeks ago? Twenty lifetimes ago?—back in the halcyon days of her ignorance, her monthly period had been only a nuisance. Her pussy like something she had invented—sui generis. There's no business like my business! But, pregnancy shattered that illusion like so much cheap mercury glass. What differentiates man from animal is deferral of appetite. And here was the real silver that turned the blood blue: Each menstrual period was a bright reminder, a clotted remainder, a libation to the gods on behalf of every child unborn, those quietly waiting in the hidden place where the waiting gather. Woman was a tensile thing stretched taut between generations. So no fucking was casual and, further, there was no such thing as a free body in this world, our occasional choices laughably, infinitesimally rare. Each was born squalling and covered in blood with a bill coming due in her clenched hand, her tiny ovaries constellated with potential life, floating there in the warm, watery dark. The world, in fact, existed. She thought a woman's body was then and now and forever beholden to an invisible First Cause— the unknown, unchosen, brute mistress, the goddess—yoked to it like a dumb, intractable mule, wrestling uselessly for freedom to the point of shredding its stubborn neck and letting its own blood in a vain effort to free itself, too ignorant to even know its name in the world: mule. A mule is not a hemlock is not a hame is not an ear of corn or a shot of bourbon, but a manifestation of fact called species: Equus mulus, a hybrid of the genus Equus of the tribus Equinii of the subfamilia Equinae of the familia Equidae, possessed of neither the sixty-two chromosomes of its ass father or the sixty-four of its horse dam, but a strange sixty-three, damned to a life of physical obligation through no fault of its own—a life of unmerited suffering, doomed once in a while to produce a little foal.

And yet . . . this was not exactly right. She was mired in self-pity, her conscience moving and wrestling within her like the baby soon would. She wasn't crying now; she was dry-eyed. There was some poison in the pie; she wanted the treacly sweet of determinism with its aftertaste of martyrdom, but that came at too high a cost. Easy answers required a death of the mind. Yes, thinking was hard physical labor and nowhere near as pleasurable as sex, so she had abandoned it long ago. That was the pitiless truth. All the distractions of workaday life were so much easier than thinking, because thinking's consequence—belief—made unceasing and terrible demands. It spoiled every pleasure. Yet, to live with half a mind, lobotomized in the peerless world, was to be a dead woman walking.

What she finally knew was shocking, even ugly in its power, but it brooked no equivocation. She took the leather strap between her teeth and sensed that she would survive the sawing off of an old, diseased limb. All of her life she had imagined herself a slave to a body she hadn't acquired by choice, but this was only half the truth. Nature had never overridden her will. The gene is not the judge, only the court reporter. Or further: The gene is the prisoner trapped in an organism, which can reason and plan. She, Henrietta, had made many, many choices. Her body was female, but she was never a slave. Never that. She had only imagined herself so.

———

And now, poor Henry—the victory should have been his! This was the triumphant first month in the busy factory of his daughter's womb. Yet he
couldn't discover an easy satisfaction. He listened to Henrietta's animal
howls on the stairs, and his ears bloomed with home blood. A worrisome
worm wriggled: What if the child was, in fact, not his? An unfamiliar, seizing sensation took up residence around his organs. He realized it was
simple fear. What if it was not Henrietta but Henry himself who was under
harness and curb? No, no, no—he knew that the great machinery of life,
the mechanical divisions in her wailing wall, the water sac and the placenta
emerging as globs of cell and the splashing of three translucent layers, had
been set in motion by himself alone. His daughter was manufacturing not
her own fresh, originating dawn horse, and certainly not a dark Barb, but a
pure Thoroughbred, the line of which could be traced back generation by
generation through the age-old stud book.

So in the second month our Kentucky Colonel is soothed. It's surely emerging, the tiny, twinging child: come, apple seed, tiny globular thing, shiny as
mail and newly recognizable—ancestor in egress; a simple fish, then a tad-
pole, which crowns and rears, reptilian eyes engorging, then the smallest
horse. It makes imperceptible movements full of meaning. Its heart beats
time on Henry's drum. It will fill the frame of hope.

In the third month, fact asserts itself through the flexing wall of
Henrietta's belly. But Henrietta herself is now marked by a strange and pre-
ternatural calm, a deep silence roosting in her bones. It's like the glassy
calm that surrounds a ship on a windless day, and her lassitude is worse
than her previous anguish. What does she know that Henry doesn't? What
secret is she keeping in that growing belly? Does she actually think she's
growing a brand-new thing that will burst into life's bright pavilion? Warm
blood doesn't spring from cold, nor bronze from gold—
    Henrietta: Oh, come on, the Thoroughbred was a late hybridization, a
mongrelization. That's why they're so strong.
    Henry: The breed is genetically pure.
    Henrietta: No, they married the sturdy English mares to the fast Moors—

Henry: Blood will always tell.

Henrietta: They were looking for free forward motion! Don't you understand?

Henry: Purity builds the empire.

Henrietta: They made the world modern!

In the fourth month, Henry stubs his hotblood fingers deep into the curlicut channels of his ears, where no anxiety can wend its way into the old family brain. In that darkling matter grows a perfect, unalloyed specimen of his own making—now a pale clenched limb beginning to sprout hide, lengthening and straightening, testing newfound muscles from neck to wet tail, now wriggling here and there and growing heavy as platinum, waiting and preparing for the blast of life when with new-sprouted wings, which unfurl like translucent flags—vestiges of divinity—Pegasus will leap from his mother's neck, whose spilled blood frees him to fly.

In the fifth month Henry's terror grows steadily in the womb of his mind. What if the Blood Horse is born of Soured Milk? What if there exists no vestige of divinity at all but only a satyr, that beast of horsetail, cloven hoof, and black, pugnacious eye? It's all her fault—seductress! She was too voluptuous, too hot-blooded and luxuriant. She lay in the undulatory grasses under green, fireworking trees, drunk on the liquor of Nature when the Other pricked her lip and butterflied her and split the red carbuncle. See how the ordered marvels have been made vulgar! Now the invasive little goat floats in the tendrils of his sodden horse's tail; he is swilling her dark wine, strangely robust and grinning, that swarthy little fiend already stroking himself erect, good for nothing and unfit for work, a mother's trouble and Nature's excess, the child of a warmongering Orangutan and a woman, *Simia satyrus*. The bestiaries will designate him an indolent cline.

And now the thing is kicking her in the sixth month—she's doubled over, a portrait of suffering. She grips her belly and moans, but all with the detached resignation of a fettered stock animal at the plow. Oh, Henry Forge, what have you wrought with your diseased imagination? What grotesque develops in that belly, bred by the convergence of father and daughter, that

crime against Nature: hairy, fully grown ghouls with legs for arms and lips
for eyes, sickly, feeble children with horns, perversions with four hands or
as many flippers, beaked or tailed, fused ass to ass, a brand-new generation
of evil so incontrovertible it should be killed at birth like the monsters of
Krakow or Ravenna, disfiguration bequeathed upon them by the sins of the
father—

NO. Stop, Henry. STOP STOP STOPSTOPSTOPSTOPSTOPSTOP

Lou stood with her arm thrust up to the elbow in the uterus of a bay mare.
Her neck was loose, her shoulders free, the silver in her bun sparking off
the sun just now peeking out from smoky shower clouds. She squinted under
a skylight, stinging tears coursing along her cheeks, her sunglasses accidentally smashed on the floor of her truck. But her eyes weren't really necessary
for this work, her hands pressing right and left for the pulse of life. Finally
she detected them—not one but two.

In her awkward position, there was nothing she could do but tilt her
head away from the light streaming through the skylight, one of dozens
Mack had installed in his training center's barns to increase the tidal sloshing of the mares' hormones. Pretty extravagant, some might say, but she had
no opinion on the matter. She cared only about the animals, not their surroundings or their owners and their accomplishments. Some despised the
industry for its abuses, some pursued its glories thoughtlessly, but so long
as horses existed in proximity to humanity, the industry wasn't going
anywhere, and neither was she.

Horses had always been deeply compelling to her, still were. She could
find few points of connection between herself and these animals. Her favorite professor at Cornell had always emphasized this. Every day, your job
will be about another animal's body. Never confuse it with your own. Approach every animal as though you've never seen the species before and
nothing will ever get past you.

She'd always done her best to abide by this truth; in the barn, as in
life, she tried to approach things unhampered by the baggage of exces-
sive opinions. What good were they anyway? Opinions broke up mar-
riages and started wars. Her husband sometimes accused her of being

stubbornly apolitical, but what did she—one woman in Bourbon County, Kentucky—really understand of anything? And who cared what she thought? She didn't need opinions to convince herself that she mattered. When you grow up the last of six children, you know your place in the world.

I do not understand what I do not understand.

Her right side was fatigued from work with the mares, so it was a good thing her palpating side was so strong and her hands so nimble. She managed to separate the two embryos instead of accidentally swooping the whole package into one hand and killing both. Her fingers separated out one twin and pinched hard until its tiny burgeoning life was aborted. The risk, of course, was that you might be pinching the next Man o' War or Seattle Slew, but that was just part of the gamble. Spare them both and you'd end up with two weak, undersized foals.

Lou withdrew her arm and patted the mare once on the round of her rump before peeling off her lubricated glove. Light-drawn tears were still streaming down her cheeks when she detected a presence behind her. She turned and saw a distorted shadow swimming in the pool of her tears. With an ungainly gesture, not unlike a cow swiping at flies, she wiped her eyes with the cotton on her shoulders and looked up again to see Henrietta Forge standing in front of her, her belly bossed out, heavily pregnant. Lou couldn't swallow her surprise: "Oh!" The bump was incongruous, as unexpected as a dirty joke on the lips of a child.

"Hello," said Henrietta, unmistakably tired, the voice of a woman carrying an enormous burden. The sound alone made Lou's hips ache in sympathy; she instantly remembered her ninth month, when the fun was over and the anxious desperation had set in.

"Let me wash my hands," said Lou. She untied the mare, scooted her gear bag out of the stall with the toe of her hiking boot, and moved without rushing to a barn sink, where she soaped up to the elbows. She cast a curious glance at Henrietta, who remained where she stood in the streaming light, a rustic Madonna in the sun-splashed shed row, her belly all aflame. Lou said easily, "How old are you now, Henrietta?"

It was as though she hadn't heard; she just stood there like a deaf-mute, seeming utterly innocent, then her hands twitched, and she said abruptly as if jerking awake, "Twenty-nine." Lou thought, My God, she had to think about that; she had to count.

"I guess I haven't seen you in a while," she said gently. "When are you due?"

This answer came quickly. "Five weeks."

"Boy or a girl? You're carrying pretty low." Lou resisted the urge to reach out and touch her. Though she sensed some of the girl's ice was melted, that was not the same thing as warmth.

"I don't know," said Henrietta with an eerie, imperturbable calm—not exactly despondent, but low. Hard fact had come to roost in the girl's mouth, and it crowded out small talk.

Lou said, "Would you care to sit outside? There's a bench under a tree at the end of the barn. It's a nice place to take a minute." Henrietta just nodded and followed, and they settled themselves there, the September sun as warm and comforting as bag balm on their faces and necks and their hair, one redheaded, the other early gray—or, not so early; Lou was now forty-five. Neither young nor old, but right in the middle of things.

They sat in silence a while before Henrietta said abruptly: "How do you figure out how to be a mother?" She could have asked her own mother, but why would she?

Lou didn't have to think on it. "Some of it comes naturally. The hormones help, a lot of it will feel instinctive. But not entirely. I can tell you the worst day of my life was the day after my daughter was born, when I was exhausted and she wouldn't breast-feed. I thought I was going to have a nervous breakdown." Lou leaned back into the bench, remembering. "You know, babies are pretty shocking. No one ever tells you how hard it is to have small children, how utterly consuming. I remember feeling kind of angry about that—that other women hadn't told me how tough it would be. They only shared the good stuff. Plus, babies are really disruptive to a relationship, even a good one." She glanced at Henrietta sideways, carefully.

Henrietta nodded curtly, her face inexpressive. Then: "Will I be a good mother?"

Instantly, unbidden, Lou was charged with a sense deeper than knowing that this woman—this girl, rather—had never been properly loved, that she didn't know the first thing about real intimacy. It cracked Lou's heart. But the awareness was fleeting, and she said, with the equanimity of a counselor, "You'll do just fine. I can tell you the titles of a few good books. My only real advice is don't leave the hospital until that baby's latched on good and tight."

When Henrietta said nothing further, an easy silence washed in like a gentle stream that carried their conversation away. Lou fought the urge for further niceties: How is your father? How is that magnificent filly, that two-year-old everyone is talking about? She's showing awfully well against the boys, placing four out of four and inspiring talk of greatness. But Lou waited. She waited, because she was quite confident this girl had never delivered a social call in her life.

Then Henrietta cleared her throat and said, "You told me something once. Something I didn't understand. I remembered it the other day."

Ah, here it was. Lou turned her palms up to the warm September sun and waited.

"It was the day Hellsmouth was foaled. You said something about every horse being the product of evolutionary failure. Something to that effect."

Lou stretched back her head a moment, looked up at the sky. "Yeah, sure," she said, "I guess it's kind of ironic."

"What do you know that I don't?"

It struck Lou as a funny phrasing, and she smiled. Then she turned toward Henrietta, who turned toward her, so their heads almost touched, and they spoke in quiet tones, the red, desiccated leaves of the tree falling all around them, a few onto their laps.

When Henrietta straightened up, her face was pinched with consternation.

"Then why are we chasing the perfect horse . . . ?"

"Who knows," said Lou, ticked her head to one side. "There's no such thing. Beauty, maybe. We always seem to get sidetracked by that. And horses are such beautiful remnants." She glanced sideways at Henrietta. "I thought you would have learned all this in school. Horses used to be the model for evolution, at least when I was a kid."

Henrietta flushed. She suddenly looked angry, but not at Lou. She stared out over the black, peeling fences, the green bluegrass under the sun with its tireless recapitulations, over the many fillies in the field before them. She was struck by a sudden lash of jealousy. These imperfect little fillies would be protected, coddled, and prized *in aeternum* if they proved themselves in the sport of kings—what strange luck to be a thoughtless horse. What woman could hope for half as much in this world? Suddenly, she began to laugh. It was not the sound of amusement. It emerged as a confused cry, a conflicted cry. Then it boiled up and spilled out from the center of her with absurd force. She leaned forward, and the sound crashed like cymbals in her mouth. My God, she was laughing so hard she was gripping herself as if in pain, her shoulders heaving with grieved humor, tears spilling from her eyes, but then she was suddenly quiet with her head bent, so it seemed at first she was merely spent, having released some demon from her imagination. Lou realized she was hunched over herself, looking down at her protruding belly.

"Henrietta, are you all right?" said Lou.

She couldn't speak. The seizing was strong and swift. It gripped her with such ferocity that she seemed mildly surprised to see her belly wasn't actually moving, though she'd sensed for days that something indeed was gathering its energies within her. It was coming as sure as the change of seasons, shifting from elegiac autumn to hard winter.

Lou was watching her carefully. She counted in the habit of her training. "Well, that's a long contraction," she said in an even voice. "Are you sure this is your first one?"

It was a moment before Henrietta could raise her head. A fine film of sweat had formed on her upper lip, and her cheeks were flushed with a ruby color. She shook her head. "I don't know. It's been . . . shifting."

"Have you felt crampy . . . ?"

Henrietta nodded weakly.

"For how long?"

"Three days."

Lou didn't ask, she just tightened her arms around the girl's shoulders and said, "Okay, sweetheart, up you go. Let's get you to the hospital just to be sure. Just to be safe."

Henrietta said, "University of Kentucky."

"Okay, no problem. I'm going to take you right there."

"I'm not afraid," said Henrietta.

Lou smiled. "I've been afraid every day of my life," she said. What she did not say: When my own labor started, I thought I was going into battle, but, honestly, it wasn't anywhere near as bad as I thought it would be. I've had ruptured cysts that were worse. But even as she thought the words, making their way to her truck, Henrietta's arm was slipped through hers like a fish through a holey net, landing on the ground, where she moaned steadily, steadily as a song, a dirge, an incantation. She sat there on her crossed legs, her hands grasping at her belly, simple suffering on her face. Lou could do nothing but kneel beside her as an attendant, patting her back.

When Henrietta's face finally loosened, Lou helped her to her feet. A few tentative steps and she was walking easy again, helping herself into the cab of Lou's truck and waiting there for Lou to slip in behind the wheel. Only then did she say, "Will you call my father?" which Lou did, saying they were headed to UK and detecting panic there in the man's voice, so different from the low, even, steady, unmoved, resilient, enduring voice beside her. It made the hair stand up on her arms.

Lou thought to soothe her, wanted to say: Don't worry. My mother filled my head with all sorts of fears—how she bled, how she was cut and couldn't feel pleasure properly afterwards, and how her last, which was me, had led to a hysterectomy. But all Lou said was, "Hang in there, sweetheart. It's worth it. I ended up with a child I love more than I love myself. She's one of the best things that ever happened to me."

They were some way down the Paris–Lexington Road when Henrietta was once again clenched over her belly, deep in communion with this emergent, wrestling thing. She lost her sense of travel, of Lou at her side. Her baby argued viciously with her body, and she grimaced in complicated pain over it. When the baby's demands eased, she laid her damp head on the headrest and looked out at the virginal white barns, the cupolas with their vanes pirouetting in an insistent wind, the horses with tangled manes fallen over bulbous eyes. History like floodwaters swamped them to the pupils. The stone walls began to totter and disintegrate even as she looked; the karst caved into sinks and ponds, and she laughed again through the pain, atop the pain, in the face of what was to come.

She saw Kentucky as a land of country contentments, rolling like an ocean in the sights of a ten-gun brig. The ocean reveals the most distant, dazzling islands to honest ships only after strenuous searching—by that worst journey, which is the ascetic's choice. A midshipman's boat is a cell, and a cell is the mind's spyglass. You are a measurer of the winter farrow and summer effulgence and everything in between: girl turned fearless sailor. When you grow up and become a mother, never forget the delightful, early days of discovery. Remember the green, milky constancy of the ocean, the sturdy ship of your body with unsuckled breasts masthead to the wind, how you spied green, glossy life on basalt shores, how birds trilled the infinities for you. Remember how you journeyed in your body across the world only to discover that you were the original uncharted topography.

Disconcerted by Henrietta's laughter, Lou said, "Are you breathing? Are you keeping your breath deep and even?"

"Yes," with irritation now, "yes!" She was breathing out the last of the Old Dominion air her father had blown into her lungs and looking past the farthest row of white plank fencing: the rolling bluegrass has turned to bottle-green waves, and she can see ten volcanic islands rising in the wriggling heat. This is fresh, unknown land and so beautiful, though the islands appear to be divided, barren, and lava-scarred below the hanging clouds and above, ensconced in the damp humor of the heights, crudely efflorescent with life. As they draw near the first mass of land, she can see, amidst the many black conicals, reptiles hissing and dull-colored birds who care no more for her than they do for the great tortoises.

My God, the great tortoises! Heavy, lumbering giants. The second island is striated with crisscrossing blazes that the ponderous beasts have cut across the sloping green hillsides. Tiring of succulents in the fire-pit districts, the tortoises travel day and night for water, their crepey heads thrust before them up the precipitous slopes until they discover the springs where their kin are just now returning, moving with the stolid gait of those obedient to nature. They pass one another as they've passed before and will pass again. Now, the newly arrived slip into the crystalline pool past their heavy-lidded eyeballs to drink and drink and drink.

Henrietta's guts reached around her lower back and wrenched hard. The grip was so strong, so quick on the last that Lou, who had been watching the dash clock, said, "That was awfully fast." Henrietta's answer was silence, because it was too strong for words. Now there was no doubt in Lou's mind: The child wanted out. And soon.

Lou's voice was calm but urgent. "Henrietta, I think you may have been in labor for the last couple days. You may be active right now. Promise me that if you feel the urge to push, you're going to resist. Okay? We're almost there, so just hang on."

Henrietta wasn't listening. The sea of volcanic islands came to an abrupt end, and the city flashed before her with its gaudy distractions—aluminum siding, pocked roofing, garish billboards, trash aflutter in the streets. Yet, there were still snatches of green grass under the vivid noon. Century-old trees with ancient memory. And there, perched on roofs and wires, arcing over the truck, commenting upon the sprawling growth of the city, were the daring little perspicacious finches, dull but quick, at first darting at the corner of her eye, then everywhere she looked congregating on porches and porticoes, strutting for worms and berries, swooping on the wing, staring black-eyed into the truck. They were of a family, yet they varied enormously, thirteen species all peculiar to the various neighborhoods of the city. Amazing how tame they are, how unafraid, so this one—with its abrupt tail and modest beak; *Geospiza parvula*, so tiny and pert—alights on her hand, and after observing it a while in curiosity and admiration, Henrietta snuffs its life with a single blow. Now she opens its chest with the obstetrician's scalpel, while all its kin crowd around, perching on the hood of the truck, the ashtray, on her shoulders, observing with beady curiosity as she makes her careful incisions. The feathery flesh is spread, showing the small veiny networks and coiled viscera. The finches chatter with great vivacity, their talk overwhelming the honking horns, the squealing tires, the radios, as she cracks open the fragile rib cage and exposes the organ of animation. Like a wet treasure, here is the mystery. It's too hot to touch with her hands. Now she realizes that along with its endlessly varying kin, the dead bird is still singing, its throat pulsing with blood and sound, and that the song is for her.

She lays the carcass down and is fully persuaded. Hadn't she always been like a ripe fruit even when life was hell? It was perhaps true that she had never been happy, but happiness was a cheap, ephemeral thing brought on by novelty or chance; happiness was a trinket from a fair; inevitably the fair moved on, and the trinket was broken, stolen, or lost. Only joy abided. It was like blood, and as long as blood flowed, joy flowed, intrinsic to the organism. She looked at the wild and abundant world, the new and old species forever mutating, the violent sun and its cool hanger-on the moon, which she knew remained in the sky uncaring whether seen or unseen. She had joy. If you carry a hardy pagan god in you, no parent or enemy can kill it. She realized with surprised relief that someday in the distant future when this day of great pain was long past, they could raise a monument over her bleaching bones that read: Accomplished.

And that was her last thought before the work of her body engulfed her and this time would not let go. In the midst of that overriding pain, hands were trying to ease her out of the truck—were they at the hospital already?—yet she couldn't uncurl, her body wouldn't allow it, so they brought a gurney and now Henry was before her, his beloved face twisted with worry the way her guts were twisted.

"I'm here, I'm here," he said as they eased her onto the gurney. They were wheeling her now, Henry trotting along at her head, listening to her moan, "It won't stop."

"Your contractions won't stop?" But her answer was an animal's panting and groaning, her hands a knobby lace over her distended belly. Henry saw how her hands were distorted with swelling. In these last weeks, her skin had been scorched by itching. Her belly, too big for her slim frame, was bursting like a late-season watermelon. It stretched so taut that raw fissures opened, and he was sick with guilt. In the unnaturally aseptic light of the hospital corridors, he was stricken with the memory of when they had first handed her to him swaddled in a pink cotton blanket. This is mine? he had thought. I made this miracle happen?

In the birthing room, the questions came furiously: Were you having contractions for the last few days? Mild ones? Are you sure your water didn't break? Bloody show? Is the father on his way?

But Henrietta remained clamped in the vise of her pain, sweat tracking down her red, brutalized face—and bland tears too—as the contraction refused to release her. Pain was a hideous symphony, every note sounding at once, and it didn't matter if every pitch was labored, slaved over, overwrought, caressed, or hated. I don't care whether you can detect the fruits of my labor! I can't hide anything, birth is breaking all of me. Sounds emerged from the deepest part of her.

Henry's face was close to hers, almost against hers, almost kissing her cheek, saying, "The doctor's here," and then the man was gently prying apart her clamped legs.

"Should it be this hard?" she cried out in bewilderment. "Should it be this hard?"

"Goddammit," hissed Henry. "Give her something!"

The doctor dispensed his obfuscations: "Dilated to five, but hypertonic uterus." Henrietta interrupted: "I'm peeing." The seep of warmth turning instantly cool in the mortuary chill of the room.

The doctor placed a gloved hand on her knee. "Miss Forge, your water just broke. I'm concerned, because there's too much blood in your fluid, and you're just starting to spike a fever, which we want to contain. Your uterus is hyperstimulated; that's why you're not coming down off these contractions. We're not going to use an epidural, because—"

Henry's eyes were wild and he gripped the plastic edge of the bed rail. "Why on earth?"

A nurse's voice then and a whirling from the periphery: "Flat strip—"

"What is that? What is that?" Panic made its own contractions on Henry's heart.

The doctor remained maddeningly calm. "It means there's minimal variability in the fetal heart rate. I suspect abruption. This is something that requires immediate intervention. But there's no need to panic." He turned to Henrietta. "Miss Forge, we'll need to give you general anesthesia, because I'm concerned about your baby and need to expedite the delivery. Placement of a spinal will just take too long. We're going to move you into the pre-op room now."

To a nurse, he said, "I want Miss Forge hooked up as well as the baby."

Henrietta nodded weakly with a face that looked like doubt but was all pain. Why were they breaking into her private world? She was busy with her hurting, which was immutable and constant, pain breathing in, pain breathing out, pain eclipsing her mind.

Her eyes were glassy, and they were instantly moving again, the ceiling passing her, this must be the operating room; she knew because she recognized the many-bulbed lamps like blinding, wide-mouthed carp. Her father's face—comfort, intrusion, her everything—interrupted the light. Someone said, "Sir, you can't be in here," and yet he remained. Henrietta's eyes focused suddenly with a consternation so savage that Henry felt her pain move all along the length of his body like a lightning strike. For a brief moment, she abandoned her struggle. She said, "You never loved me."

All he could do was stare at the garrulous shock of red on her cheeks. He struggled for language. "How can you say that?" he whispered. "Everything I've ever done is for you."

"Lou said . . ." Her words drifted, evanesced, vanished into pain.

"What?" he said. "Lou the vet? What did she say?"

She could hear someone speaking to her father, but she was sunk down into her body again, any words elongated into wails by the pain wracking her, pressing her with the weight of oceans and mountains. Her face grew hideously pale, even her eyes appeared blanched. The relentless contractions were reshaping her into something foreign and alone.

The tenor of the room changed. She had no words now, all of herself concentrating on this pain. Language was done. The anesthesiologist was wrestling with the IV catheter as she made deep, guttural wounded sounds. But under it all she felt—far beneath the wretched pain and the fear—a deep and primitive excitement. It came from her bedrock self. Soon her child would appear, and everything would begin again.

In the first miracle, the universe created itself out of nothing. So there is always hope.

When the anesthesiologist moved in with the oxygen mask, she gripped his arm to stay him. Her voice was barely recognizable now, chafed and roughened by labor. She gestured, rolling her hand, so her father leaned in, and she laid her hand against his beautiful, weathered, beloved cheek. "Father . . ."

"What, darling?"

She grinned an ugly grin. "Every animal knows more than we do."

"Someone get him out of here," said the anesthesiologist, but Henrietta was already drawing her hand back to her chest, and because she needed to release the burden, she said, "Quick. Quick!"

The mask was fitted to her face, and she drew deeply from its clean breath. Perfect. Her eyes were washed with calm, it was effacing her now. Henry could see she was still speaking under the mask, but he couldn't hear her words. He leaned in as though they were still conversing, but then her mouth stopped moving, and they only looked at each other gently before she closed her eyes.

Then she was drifting, the anesthesia washing in like a low and lovely tide. The lines on her brow eased and her mind softened, and her hands were very comfortably arranged like weights under her breasts. A wave came and she sensed it pulling her in deep, like an undertow, but it was pleasant and she didn't mind. She smiled. She felt as though she were saying words, but it was more like dreaming in her mouth. They were going to free the child from her any moment, and she was so grateful. The child needed to be free. Deep in the water she could see a light, and that seemed no contradiction at all, only a curiosity. It was marvelous.

"Flatline!" The nurse's voice, a crashing cymbal. "The mother has flatlined!"

There was a bustling in the world that Henry didn't understand, and someone was gripping him by both shoulders, trying to pull him from the room, but, suddenly realizing, he flung them off with a ferocious strength, unable to take his eyes from his daughter's face, which was changing and emptying as a room is emptied. The change was subtle but sure; all the minute and incessant activity of life ceased suddenly. Some old bitterness slid from her as her muscles went slack and her lips parted without emotion or word. There was nothing there. Henry could not move, he remained where he stood, gazing upon her in horror until horror was replaced by a grief so entire, so absolute, that he could think of no other option but to die himself, to lie down next to his daughter's body and end entirely and perhaps would have tried, except they were yelling, were placing the paddles on his daughter's naked chest as a new doctor labored and tried to break the hold of death with useless and violent electricity, so her dead, absented body convulsed violently, horribly again and again until the truth was called a fact: she was dead, and the obstetrician, who had labored on her behalf while they strove mightily with her body, held a brand-new baby aloft and in a voice strained with shock said, "He's alive. He's perfect. He's perfect." The words—so impossible—broke through the brilliant white light of Henry's horror. He turned in confusion, having forgotten a child was being born, and with convulsive, confused motions, he moved down the side of the bed where the exhausted body of his daughter was exposed, where he could smell the private blood of her belly, where her lifeless limbs were slack. The nurses were an agitated stream rushing past him toward something he had left behind, and again someone was trying to wrestle him away, but again he shook them off with unnatural strength. His daughter was gone; she would never speak again. He barely sensed the tumult and noise now as he turned to the child. At first he recoiled, his mind rearing like a frightened horse. Then, with shaking hands, Henry drew the tiny, perfectly formed brown baby to his chest and looked in astonishment at the only family he had left.

INTERLUDE IV

One day, after he had whipped up a batch of ocean and scattered stars and a sun for light, the Great Big God of Pine Mountain made a man. He wasn't the smartest creature on the mountain or even the strongest, but he was a hard worker and he did what he was told. The God said, "Name all these animals here," and the man named the red fox and the bobcat and the mountain vole and so on and so forth. Then the God said, "Have at these plants," and the man named the hickory tree and the nettle and the wheat berry and the God was impressed. He said, "You're not half as dumb as you look. I hope you like having power over all these plants and animals just as I like having power over you. All I ask is that you not eat the pawpaws. I don't want you to get too big for your britches, and I don't want you to sass me."

The man obeyed the Great Big God of Pine Mountain, though after a time the God could see that the man was out of sorts: he mumbled to himself a good deal and appeared disgruntled, and coitus with goats grew tiresome. It was clear the man was lonely.

So the God of Pine Mountain laid the man down on the loam and fed him corn liquor, so he would fall asleep, and then he rooted around in his chest until there was a great crack. He removed a white and bloodied rib. From this he fashioned a woman. When the man awoke, he saw that her eyes were bright, her breasts were heavy, and that between her thighs was a thatch of unruly, scratchy hairs. All of this sparked his interest. In fact, the man felt a lurch in his loins when he gazed upon her and his mouth was dry when he said, "Whatever you do, don't eat the pawpaws. If there's one thing we can't stand around here, it's a uppity woman."

So for a time they walked hand in hand on the springtime side of the mountain and they were happy as far as it went, but the man could not escape the feeling that something was missing from inside of him. He was sure that the God had stolen something from him while he was drunk and had hidden it in the woman, so one day he laid the woman down on the grass and pinned her there, so that he could better and deeper seek for his spare part within her. But no matter how he rooted—and he did it more and more often with less and less patience—he could not find what he was missing. And the woman, who at first wound herself around him in surprise and gratitude, became confused and weary of his mean pressing, which made a depression of her in the grass like a grave. So she snuck away and wandered around the slopes of Pine Mountain. She beat blazes in the pastures with her bare feet, she swam in the mountain streams, she petted the animals and named the stars. Eventually, she stumbled upon the pawpaw stand.

Now, out of a blackberry patch came a wily rabbit wearing a woolen jacket and crisp pantaloons, though the woman didn't know what those were, because she'd never seen any before. She stared at the rabbit in frank alarm when he spoke: "How do, missy?"

She couldn't remember if the man and the God allowed her to speak to strangers, so she only nodded.

"Oh Lord," said the smartly dressed little rabbit with a sigh, "I sure wish I could reach me some of them pawpaws up there. God played a mean old nasty trick when he made me this short."

The woman looked down at him with concern. It was true; he was a right midge, even as far as rabbits went.

The wily rabbit began to cry big, fat crocodile tears. "All I want"—he sobbed, glancing at her out of the corners of his eyes—"all I want . . . is a little pleasure."

The woman's heart swelled with compassion. Surely, it could not be wrong to soothe the suffering of such a tiny, unusual creature? She plucked a pawpaw from the branch and handed it to the rabbit, who gobbled half of its yellow fruit immediately. Then he held the rest up for her to try, tears still wet on his fuzzy cheeks. "Eat with me, gal."

"Oh, I can't," she said. "I'm not allowed."

"Who says?"

"The Great Big God of Pine Mountain."

The rabbit looked at her and said, plain as day, "But your God is a tyrant." Then the woman saw the simple truth of the statement and ate the rest of the pawpaw, seeds and all. It filled her with delight, a delight that she immediately wanted to share. So she plucked a second pawpaw from the branch and went in search of the man.

When she found him, the man suspected what the fruit might be, but it smelled so sweet—like raspberry and pear and honey all in one—that he ate it without asking any questions. Then a strange thing happened. Clouds the color of hearth ashes rolled in from the east, and a new, chilly breeze blew over their heads. The God, who had been busy with his whiskey stills, marched down the mountainside and his voice rolled out like thunder. "What in creation have you done?"

The man turned on the woman. "It's the woman's fault! She ruined our good thing!" he cried.

"You didn't have to listen to her!" said the God. "I left you in charge!"

"Well, you made the bitch," muttered the man.

"Yes, it's true, it's true! It's all my fault and only mine!" cried the woman, who, like her many daughters to come, drank down blame's poison like clear mountain water. Then she began to cry, but she cried so hard it caused her skin to wrinkle, and the first gray hair of worry sprouted from her head, which the man noted with disgust and alarm. He decided he had never loved her.

But the God just shook his head wearily. "One rule . . . ," he said. "I gave you one goddamn arbitrary rule but apparently it was one too many. Your eating of the fruit is so vile, so unthinkably evil, you're no longer worth the manure under my brogans. So get out. Go on and get off my mountain."

Stricken, they prepared to leave, though there was little to take with them. The man was so ashamed of himself that he could no longer look at the body of the woman, so he killed his first animal, a cow, and covered the woman with its hide. He also covered himself in case he got cold on the journey. Then he led the woman across the cooling fields of Pine Mountain, while all the animals trailed behind them in curiosity and dismay, the chipmunks and the black bears and the deer alike. Soon the man stood on the edge of the future and he saw it was a broken and desert place. There were screwworms in the corn and weevils in the cotton. Kudzu choked the trees and the tobacco fields were cracked with drought. Even the light, which fell on the wasted land, was like weak beer. The man shook his fist and cried out, "I don't deserve this fate!" But the God of Pine Mountain was already busy in his barns and he didn't hear, or didn't care. Either way, he would ignore them for the rest of time and leave them to their own devices.

The man was really angry now and looked behind him, realizing he would need a better companion than the woman if he ever hoped to find his way back here. Clearly, the woman could not be trusted. Without hesitation, the man stepped up to the tallest, strongest animal he could find—a horse—and grabbed it by a hank of its mane. Then with resolute steps, he led the woman off the verdant slopes of Pine Mountain, and the wide-eyed horse, bewildered by dislocation, followed behind.

HELLSMOUTH

Nor ought we to marvel if all the contrivances in nature be not, as
far as we can judge, absolutely perfect; and if some of them be ab-
horrent to our ideas of fitness. We need not marvel at the sting of
the bee causing the bee's own death; at drones being produced in
such vast numbers for one single act, and being then slaughtered
by their sterile sisters; at the astonishing waste of pollen by our fir
trees; at the instinctive hatred of the queen bee for her own fertile
daughters; at the Ichneumonidae feeding within the live bodies of
caterpillars; and at other such cases. The wonder indeed is, on the
theory of natural selection, that more cases of want of absolute
perfection have not been observed.

—CHARLES DARWIN, *On the Origin of Species*

Again, they came out of Albemarle and Fauquier and Orange with
spinning wheels and flintlock rifles strapped to mules and mares, a
cavalcade over the folded Blue Ridge and smoky Shenandoah, fording
countless streams until they arrived at the disputatious Clinch with its cur-
rents of cuss and complaint, then slept their wolf-encircled sleep and resumed their trek along the path of empire until they reached the midmark
block house, where behind them teased two roads back to Prince Edward
and Carolina, where proper cabins awaited with dogtrots and puncheoned
floors, also ordinaries and steepled chapels and girls in laced corsets,
whom they forsook for Indian Country across Clinch Mountain, Big Moc-
casin Gap, Powell Mountain, seemingly minor foes before this power of
great white mountains insurmountable but for a high gap, the Gateway,
which led to more and more earth, more rived ridges and black recesses,
and ultimately the Kentuck, where the Indians and wolves were rivals for

scalps, where the pack animals began to droop and die with Pine Mountain finally in view, where the men ate without benefit of fire until they passed through the virgin forest, through the outlying knobs to meadows of herbage and buffalo grass under pigeons in their thunderous passage over the Rock Castle River, where they decided to walk to the caneland in the north, where they tamed the grassland and timbered the chestnut and hemlock, plucked stones out of the earth for fencing, fired soil to brick, raised up houses out of the old growth while their cattle cropped the meadows, and after they became rich as Boaz on the fatling land, built a church of blue ash on a windy upland slope and christened the place Cane Ridge, where, when the old century spilled into the trammeled new, sinners trickled down from Ohio, up from Tennessee, and from all over the new state, where preachers ascended platforms, proclaiming Christ to the conquerors, who had traded their buckskin and coon caps for brooches and prunella, capes and velvet mantles, all converted now, faces to the bloody soil, trading earth for sky as they once traded baubles for earth, forgiven surely their success, jerking and calling with abandon, unrestrained now, the crowds pulsing and babbling as if carousal could render fool's fat from the hard bones of history—

No. The old language is dead, as is Henry's daughter, who lies in that storied tabernacle built on the ridge, where the cane once grew thick. In the shadowy reserve of the room under the old slave gallery, Henry senses an astonishing light beyond the log structure with its surrounding stone shrine, but looks away from the open doors. He hasn't been able to bear the light these last two weeks—two endless, unendurable weeks. The funeral was delayed, because Judith requested time to return from her home in Bavaria, and because the confounding, surviving infant—his daughter's son, his own blood—required a week in incubation. But Henry waited, most of all, because his grief was beyond the capacity of his flesh.

Now he could hear them: all the people filing into the church, the clacking of smartly shined shoes; he could hear their averted eyes. Yes, it was right that they should come; he wanted every house to be present. Fill the pews, pay their dues! He managed one look around at the subdued figures, but their somber faces, even their expensive black garments all seemed an affront to the reality of death. The very fact of their living offended him.

Now the pastor's gentle hand was on his shoulder, now they were on the casket, and Henry's stony calm was swamped for a moment by panic— *Don't do this! Please don't do this thing!*—but the words just echoed in the hollow of his mind, which seemed now like nothing but an antechamber for death—and then the lid was raised. He heard Judith cry out behind him, a sound of despair and recrimination. He wanted to stand up and say I didn't kill her, I wasn't the father! But the child in him was not so sure.

God, look at her face. In two weeks death had made no inroads, done no damage at all. Man truly is the measure and maker of all things, Child Henry thought wildly. Even industrious death is no match for his craftiness! His daughter appeared perfect and untouched, her hair lustrous, some blush color enduring on her cheeks and lips. She'd even assumed a restless beauty in her two weeks of tiresome solitude, time spent wandering aimlessly over the dark, purling river and under the tree of dreams, as if at any moment, she would rise with her innate disdain and dismiss them all with a withering glance and a flick of her hand. Then she would look Henry deeply in the eye, and he would know that all this suffering had been unnecessary, just a sickening dream. And he would forget it. Yes. There could be no greater prize on earth than to forget one's suffering.

Once the lid was raised and the fact of Henrietta's death made indisputable, the pastor slowly ascended the three wooden steps to the dais and regarded the familiar, monied crowd with a solemn, mild eye, one that had learned calm in the face of disaster over the course of a long career. When he intoned quietly, "We have lost a member of the Paris community, Henrietta Forge, the daughter of Judith Schwebel and Henry Forge," Henry started visibly in his pew. He retightened the fold of his hands.

"When I asked Henry how he wanted his daughter to be remembered, the first thing he said was that we should remember her as a good horsewoman." The room smiled; it shifted and relaxed. "I'm told she was capable in the saddle, capable on the track, capable as the manager at Forge Run Farm. As Henry will be the first to tell you, his nickname for her from a very young age was Ruffian. Tough and strong in a very competitive business, she was a steady presence in the community, and her experience—though she was only twenty-nine—will be sorely missed."

The man brought his hands together and gazed down at Henry and Judith, who sat directly behind him. "But Judith and Henry, she was more than that, wasn't she? She was a wonderful daughter, a beloved child. I know with perfect confidence, speaking as a parent myself, that she was the principal joy of both your lives, that she didn't just bring honor to you with her accomplishments, but that you were honored to discover who she was and to draw her out into the fullness of her life and unique being. You were honored by the miracle of being her parents."

Don't speak. Don't say another word. Henry could hear Judith's unmerited snuffling behind him; he could hear the sunlight outside banging brutally on the roof of the shrine, demanding entrance.

The pastor continued in his measured and steady way. "This is the worst grief we can bear as humans, the loss of a beloved child. It feels unendurable. I want you to know—I want you to hear it from me—that this crowd is here today to bear witness to your suffering. Their presence is a confirmation that while no one can be inside your grief, a thousand can walk along beside you. No one is asking you to bear this alone.

"Now, some will say that death is God's will and when he takes us out of life, he delivers us to a better place. But as I've sat with others in their grief, I've come to believe beyond a shadow of a doubt that death is the enemy, the opposite of everything good. It's why I'm a Christian. To be a Christian is to be with others in Christ, the memory of what lives on. *Do this in remembrance of me. Gather in remembrance of me.* If there is one thing the unnaturalness and finality of death teaches us, it is that we were never meant to be alone; we can't bear it. Our stories about life and death are meaningless if they aren't shared. Community is what religious faith is all about. Believers are persistent, they refuse to forget. Without believers, the sacrifice of Jesus would have been forgotten, a lost relic of history, just a story of a wandering radical with a vision for the new kingdom. It was only the witness of the community through storytelling that transformed Jesus' tragic death into Christ's ultimate sacrifice. In their retelling, he was no longer a political dissident put to death by the state, but a hero. They used the language of meaning, because when someone extraordinary lives and dies, it's not enough to recount the facts. The community and all succeeding generations need to tell a truth which transcends."

Now the preacher looked gently but firmly at Henry, then at Judith, allowing them to shelter under his gaze. "So Judith and Henry, in the presence of Christ's community, how do we begin to cope with the death of a beloved daughter? We have already been given the facts. Henrietta had a difficult labor that required general anesthesia when her son's heartbeat began to falter. Under anesthesia, Henrietta experienced sudden cardiac arrest and passed away. Her child survived. These are the facts as they've been told to us." He paused, leaned across the lectern with his arm outstretched so he appeared to be gathering something in the air over Henrietta's coffin. "*But her child survived.* This is where we must let go of the facts and begin to tell the truth. Henrietta wasn't the victim of a medical mistake, Henrietta didn't have a defective heart, Henrietta wasn't in the wrong place at the wrong time—don't relegate her to that, which is what the materialists want us to do, all those trapped unwittingly in the prison of the physical world. They want you to call this an accident. But believe me when I tell you that if she'd wanted to, Henrietta could have continued on with a regular labor, even though it was threatening her son's life. She could have waited longer before beginning anesthesia, or she could have refused it altogether. But she chose not to, even though she knew the risks. Instead, she said, "Quick. Quick." Henry told me that; he was there with her in the operating room. Henrietta told the doctor, "Quick. Quick," and when she said that—make no mistake about it—she forfeited her life for her child's. She suffered mightily in Gethsemane, but when the soldiers came, she stood and said, "I am she." As a result of that choice, we lost her in the physical world but see her transformed in the spiritual one, and we gained her beloved son, who now possesses the gift of life and more than that, the knowledge of his mother's gift, which will form the foundation of his own life and self-understanding. A double blessing has been bestowed upon this new life, one that we can barely comprehend with our worldly minds. Isn't love a mystery?"

The preacher leaned further into the room. "Judith and Henry, I know your hearts are broken. Sometimes it seems as though children are born to break their parents' hearts. But Henrietta was a parent too"—his voice was barely a whisper—"and Henrietta's heart just broke a little sooner. Isn't love a miracle?"

Henry stared at him, stricken.

"Now, your daughter isn't here today to hold her baby, and she won't be able to watch him grow up, but I already know everything I need to know about what kind of parent Henrietta would have been, the parent she *was*.

We call God the Father because, like a good father, there isn't anything that God won't do for his children. And if we are truly made in this image of God's love, then, accordingly, there isn't anything a parent won't do for a child. Even accept death."

Behind him, Judith was silent as the void. Her crying had stopped. Henry's hands parted at the word "death" as if, perhaps, he might grasp hold of the thing and contain it, stop it, but his hands held nothing, less than nothing. His face twisted with confusion.

"Even accept death," the preacher repeated. Then he looked up from Henrietta's peaceful, final face, where he had been gazing. "Now, as a community, can we begin to retell the story of Henrietta's death? Can we talk about the ultimate sacrifice she made, which shows us what love really is, love which requires nothing in return, love which promises nothing for the lover, but which gives everything to the beloved? Can we now stop talking about the terrible accident of her death and speak instead about her hero's death? We, as a community, have the power to do that. We were the ones who knew Henrietta, and only we can rewrite the story to tell the truth."

They were rising and singing. More words were spoken, but the only thing Henry understood was the too-awful truth that his only child was dead. When the mourners had filed out, when he had shaken three hundred hands, when he stood with Judith beside the silent remains of their daughter, there was finally that cold reckoning. The peace of her perfectly preserved body was false; she had never been placid in life. Makeup was visible on her pores; she had never worn it. He stared hard for her breath, thinking the agony of his effort might force oxygen into her lungs, but it wasn't there.

The preacher placed his hand on the casket lid with a question in his eyes, but Henry could not answer it. His entire being was overwhelmed by grief. Suddenly into his mind came sapphirine skies, mineral-green streams, tilled soil, and endless vistas. The casket lid threatened the significance and integrity of the natural world itself. He began to shake visibly.

The preacher's voice was low. "May I close the casket, Henry?" Henry could not say yes. How could he? His lips were frozen, his mind harrowed, his tongue paralyzed in his mouth. As the lid was gently lowered, it cast his darling daughter first into a shadow, which grew gradually deeper, then her

features were eclipsed, inch by inch, until her physical form vanished forever, and the casket was locked. Henry realized with horror that he could
not recover the key. There was no key to the world.

Far across the road, cattle moaned with longing for a night coming in fits
and starts. The air was restless and the crickets thrummed. The hot,
humid breath of October was lifting now from the ground, where it had boiled
all day, rising to meet the cooler streams of air that hovered over it. Airs
kissed and stratified, whitening and thinning as the sun slipped its moorings and sank to the bank of the earth. Its center was as orange as its umbral
rim was black. The sky grew redder and redder as the sun turned an
earthier orange and less brilliant. Above it, purling clouds showed terraced
bands of dark against crimson, and the rungs spanned the breadth of the
sky. They stacked one upon the next on and on above the sun until the
highest bands stretched into interminable shadow, darkening as they
reached the top of the bow of the sky, then drifting edgeless into the risen
evening. Blackish blue emerged from the east and stretched over the house
like an enormous wing extended in nightlong flight. But day was not done,
it shook out its last rays, and as low clouds skimmed before the spent sun,
the roaming, liberal light was shadowed and then returned like a lamp
dampered and promptly relit. The westernmost rooms of the house registered this call and response—walls now flush with color, now dimmed,
now returned to red, the orange overlaid with gray, molten color penetrating the sheers and staining the interiors. Walnut moldings and finials and
frames were all cherry-lit like blown glass—
    No. The old language is dead. Henrietta is dead.
    Henry stood in his foyer alone. He had invited no one back for supper
after the funeral; he couldn't bear the thought of polite company, how
everyone would invade her home, chatter in her living room, sit on her
sofas and wing-back chairs, all while he stood there, listening to the relentless ticking of the tall clock in the hall. It was impossible.
    When a hand reached out gently to grip his elbow, he turned slowly as
though moving underwater. The nurse, whom he'd hired for these few
weeks, was beside him, whispering in her gentle voice: "He fed right on
schedule and slept until you walked in the door."

He? Who? The child, wrapped tight in a blanket of lilac cotton, one creamed-coffee fist escaped to find the plush petals of his lips and wave smally in the air. He was fat and ancient-looking, smelling vaguely of sour milk and sweet, warm skin. Dark skin. Henry's breath hitched. Beneath that brown, he could detect the sure set of his daughter's brow, the shape of her eyes. This black child was like the living memory of her, but altered. Henry wanted nothing more than to push him away even as he pulled him close, his mind churning with the new reality.

Bearing the mewling child carefully away from his body, as if he were a fresh-baked loaf from the oven, Henry ascended the evening-strewn stairs. He peered down his own hall, which had once held his wealth but now only echoed his bankruptcy. He remembered purchasing the Oushak on the floor; had he really spent the precious moments of his life in a store purchasing a rug? And here was his daughter's room, which had once been his and his father's before him and before him NONONONONONOSTOP

Time, that old murderer, was now the room's only occupant.

Henrietta's beingness, her recency was lodged in every object; it permeated the air. Henry took dazed survey of his newly unfamiliar surroundings, and an old, confounding gear ground into motion: life would continue on somehow, but as long as Henry lived, rotary grief would come round again and again like a nail on a wheel.

He moved at a stuttering pace along Henrietta's bookcases, tracing a single finger over the spines of books that had furnished her life—scriptures to which he had given no prior thought. Bartram, Lyell, *The Birds of Kentucky*, *The Descent of Man*, *The Diversity of Life*. He hesitated over a uniform row of black, unmarked spines, her old notebooks. He touched one lightly as if touching a relic, then slid it free. First arranging his sighing, squeaking grandson on the bed, Henry eased onto the bed beside him and read sentences at random:

Shy fish and bold fish; inborn temp; Journal of Fish Bio; Apr 2003. Are genes determinants, or are they merely expressed? Black box or . . .

For a long time, I thought I was nominally a body, really just Father's idea, a meme produced by his brain. But no one can invent a human wholesale. Why else would we have invented a god? Being is too great for

a single mind, because it did not emerge from a single mind. Mind itself
is an epiphenomenon of changing nature and the contingencies of
history. That's why I don't know if I am free, or to what degree I can
experience freedom.

Having found the generation distance between A and B via a particular
common ancestor, calculate that part of their relatedness for which that
ancestor is responsible. To do this, multiply ½ by itself once for each step
of the generation distance. —R. Dawkins

Am not the center of the universe. Am a speck of matter so minuscule as
to be almost nothing—a no thing, less than a no thing, a space between
subatomic particles, which have no name and are themselves divisible
into infinity and forever vibrating.

Is there a difference between happiness and joy, and why can I feel neither?

The appearance of man is the last phenomenon. —Lyell

What strange creature had jotted down these notes? Henry held the
notebook away from him in consternation as he disentangled the scratchy,
idiosyncratic cursive of a girl pulled out of school just as her formal education had begun. Yes, it was Henrietta's hand, but . . . who exactly was
that?

He realized with a start that death and perfection could not both exist.

He gazed down at the baby. This child had killed his daughter, this
dark thing, this emblem. The old hateful designation tried to return, but it
was distorted by distance, wriggling in the heat of time. It still lived in
Henry's heart, but not in his mouth. This was his . . . grandson? God, how
he wanted to hate him! Henry's mind fumbled, and there was a panic born of
loss and change. Was there some other word—a replacement—for the
strangeness, the difference, the not Henry? He didn't know. It occurred to
him that it wasn't really a problem of words.

For the first time in his life, questions yawned before him like open
graves.

"Henry Forge! Henry Forge!"

His old man again, forever angry about something, yelling up from the foot of the stairs. Henry snatched up the sleepy baby and rushed to the landing, an argument already rising like a bruise on his teenaged lips, ready to shout or spit or draw his bow—

"Henry Forge!"

It was Ginnie Miller from across the road, no longer a redheaded child in pigtails but a woman well into middle age, standing with one foot planted on the first step and holding a foil-wrapped casserole in both hands. Her hair was all gray curls about her pink, farm-worn face, but her eyes were the same piercing blue of so many years ago. Without apology, as if it hadn't been years since they last exchanged words, she announced, "Henry, I just let myself in when no one answered. My husband said I should leave you be since you're probably exhausted, but when I heard there wouldn't be people over after the funeral, I thought, that can't be right. It's not good for you to be locked up in this big house all alone. You need to keep your strength up what with— Ooooooh!" Her remonstration collapsed into a soft cry. She deposited the casserole on the second step and hurried up the steps with her arms outstretched. "Oh my goodness, here he is . . . !" She swept the chubby swaddling right out of Henry's arms, gazed down rapturously, then cocked her head slightly. "Why . . . well, you're not exactly what I was expecting, but . . ." A slightly perplexed smile wavered on her lips, then broadened: "Oh, aren't you just the most perfect little man! So handsome—just look at him, Henry—isn't he just perfect?" With a kiss to his downy forehead, Ginnie ferried him down the staircase and over her shoulder said, "What's his name?"

Henry peered at her from deep within the geography of his shattered mind. He shook his head faintly.

"Well, there's no rush, I suppose," Ginnie said. "The right name will come when it comes. Until then, I simply can't allow you to eat alone. In fact, why don't we just go over to the house. Leave the casserole. There's plenty more where that came from."

Henry wanted to retreat—his whole body was an open wound without hope of a scab—but he lacked the strength or volition to withdraw; he allowed Ginnie to guide him through his own front hall, down the sloping lawn of his childhood, across the black ribbon road to the Miller property. He hadn't set foot on their land since he was ten. God, had he once been a little boy with a father and a mother still alive? The years had flung themselves past him with stunning certitude and no mercy at all.

"Go right on in," said Ginnie, bracing the screen door with her shoulder while snuggling the now sleeping child against her chest. Henry did as he was told and saw the inside of his neighbor's house for the very first time: the low ceilings and thread-worn furniture, pleasantly tattered Persians on the floor, pictures plentiful and cheaply framed. Two Cardigan Corgis charged from an inner bedroom and circled their legs with frantic joy as room followed upon tight hallway upon room—all dark and comforting as a rabbit warren—until they emerged into a kitchen, which glowed with soft lights. At a kitchen table pressed to the wall, a tall man sat stooped over a disassembled radio, his long fingers sorting rivets and washers.

"Really, Roger? On Rosie's tablecloth?"

The man glanced up, startled, then rose from his chair, standing nearly to the low ceiling at his full height. Whereas his wife's gray hair sprung from her head with all the vim of a forsythia bush, his was nearly gone, showing only thin, sun-battered scalp. Behind his head hung an engraved slab of cherry wood, which read, *Ruby Anniversary—Congratulations, Roger and Virginia!* This was a man whom Henry had seen for many years passing in a red pickup truck, but whose name he had never known. He seemed quiet, though not exactly shy. "Mr. Forge," he said, "may I offer my condolences."

"Look, Roger, look," said Ginnie, wading through Corgis and holding out the baby in her arms. "Tell me this isn't the most darling thing you've ever seen in your whole life."

Roger peered down his nose, considered the napping child, then the couple exchanged a long, signifying glance. With a voice so deep it had made dogs crouch and roll and whimper all his life, Roger said simply, "Very cute, indeed."

"Here," she said, passing the baby carefully into his arms, "I told Henry I couldn't bear to leave him over there to eat alone, so I dragged him over. Neighbors should support one another, you know." She glanced meaningfully at Roger, who met her gaze with barely arched brows. "Now, I intend to feed the man. It's the very least we can do."

"Certainly." Roger cradled the child in the crook of his arm and swept the innards of the radio as well as a checkbook and bills and various pens off to the side of the table. With his free hand, he indicated the chair opposite. Then he and Henry sat while Roger rocked the child with the easy, practiced arms of a man who'd raised two children.

"Was your daughter married?" he asked with a glance down at the child.

"No," Henry said, his voice barely a whisper.

"So, she was dating an African-American gentleman?"

Henry nodded dumbly; he didn't know what to say.

"Well, it's heartening to see the way times have changed," Roger said, dandling the child. "The world used to be so ugly about these things. Even good folks . . . well, your father was a bit of a racist, wasn't he, Ginnie?"

"Oh, Daddy was a good man," Ginnie said, "but yeah, maybe a bit. Nothing too crazy."

"My folks were Quakers," said the man, turning his warm eyes on Henry and not waiting for his response. "They taught me that God made of one blood all peoples of the earth. My mother actually had a cross-stitch of that, which hung in our foyer. And they lived that verse. Especially my mother. She was a very politically active woman."

Ginnie moved smartly about her kitchen until she returned with plates heaped, saying, "But my daddy was kind too, Roger. He was. He just had some backwards ideas. You can't help the way you were raised."

"Ah," said Roger, and cocked his head, "but when you grow up, you have to take responsibility for your adult mind."

"Well, anyway, enough about that," Ginnie said, reaching out, "give me back that baby." She situated herself at the corner of the table, where she could dandle the child with one arm and eat with her free hand.

Henry stared down at his plate piled high with beet salad and venison casserole, buttered sweet potatoes and rosemary bread still steaming from the oven. Ginnie had filled his glass with sweet tea. It occurred to him that he had not been hungry in a long, long time. Then hunger moved him, and he fell on his food like an animal, even though he felt it as a betrayal. His heart was broken, yet his body was ravenous. He ate and ate and ate. After some time, he sat swaying over the remains of stew and bread, his eyes glazing with tears that pricked like a thousand needles. He wanted to say something, but he could not release the clamp on his throat.

Roger stood to offer privacy and moved to the rear door, both dogs at his heels, and slipped a pack of American Spirits from his breast pocket. He wavered on the top step, about to move down onto the grass, but when his wife appeared not to notice, he remained where he stood and lit a cigarette.

Ginnie, who was planting kiss after kiss on the child's sleepy forehead, said, "Why, I believe he has your nose. Yes, if I'm not mistaken, I believe so. Roger, I can see you standing right there. Don't think I can't." Then she looked up at Henry with unvarnished delight. "You always did have a proud nose like the horses we used to have, those Walkers you sold Daddy back in the day." She hefted up the child, who swooned with his lips pouted out. The sloped nose was indeed a miniature replica of Henry's.

Ginnie gazed with unblinking eyes at Henry. "I do wish I had known Henrietta better. Perhaps I could have been . . . a better neighbor."

Under her bright, direct gaze, Henry was silent. How miraculous that Henrietta could be spoken of and yet not exist. Remorse had become more real than she.

"I didn't see her very often, but I always found her to be"—Ginnie seemed to be rooting about for the right word—"very interesting. And just look at her baby. What a treasure." Flicking his half-smoked cigarette into a Folger's can, Roger returned to the kitchen, gazing steeply over his wife's shoulder at the child in her arms.

Ginnie waved one hand irritatedly. "Roger, you smell like cigarettes. Good Lord." Then, turning to Henry, she said, "If you ever have some trouble with him, you just bring him over. Roger has a way with colicky babies."

With a glint in his eye, Roger said, "I know when to be quiet."

Ginnie made a dubious sound in her throat.

"Well," Roger said, "I'm glad we had this . . . supper together. Neighbors should break bread together."

Ginnie nodded firmly, while Roger settled himself back into his creaking Windsor. Stroking a Corgi on its head and gazing curiously at Henry, he said gently, "So, how's that fine horse of yours doing, Mr. Forge?"

Henry, who had been absorbed in the mysterious face of his grandson, could only look up at Roger in astonishment, as if he couldn't remember his own name or how he had come to be here. When he spoke, his words were rusty like the hinges on an old door. He whispered, "My horse?"

One little jockey in the hot tub; one little jockey on the phone.

One little jockey in the kitchen; one little jockey still at home.

One little jockey with his agent; one little jockey in the box.

One little jockey puking salad; and one little jockey—imp, raconteur, pissant, tricky truculent slick, Reuben Bedford Walker III of provenance unknown and character indeterminate, five feet three inches tall, 3 percent body fat, and 118 pounds—barreling out of the jockey room, his valet hollering at his back, in search of the animal only seen from a distance under other jocks, but what an animal!: sixteen exquisite hands at the withers, a deep barrel chest with iron shoulders, and a head of black chiseled marble cracked by a white chine blaze; black satin tail and legs that screamed RUN MOTHERFUCKER. She was a black, cresty-necked filly who bit handlers, broke jocks, and rammed in fractions like a new Secretariat, what Mack Snyder called his perfect thing, the kind of filly that got hotter and hotter until she burned up the Triple Crown and retired to the mommy track; wife, mother, and one-night stand all in one.

Reuben careened along the back stretch, that theater of quarrel and striving and hungover work, of labor white and brown and poor all over, of motormouth agents and trainers chewing out assistants, of milkshaking vets hauling gear bags—

"Heya, Reuben!"

"Why you back here? Ain't you got a race?"

"Your valet's looking for you!"

He acknowledged them with not so much as a flick of a hand, or a cock of a brow, but slipped the corner of Barn 23, the first of Mack Snyder's four. Along the sun-dappled shed row above all the pillow talk muttered into equine ears, he could hear the big filly knickering her pleasure as she was combed.

"Hail, fine Ethiope!" cried the tiny man, and Allmon spun where he stood at the rear of the filly. In that most reliable of stage moves, he looked forward before looking down, and in the delay the jock had slipped under his arm like an otter in silks, crying, "What a balm for the old cryballs you are! A noble Ebon tires of these Caucasians with their corpsy skin and tea-stained hair, their awshucks and awdangs, their pallid faces—fucking

tallow! Don't get me started on the wetbacks. Oooooh . . ." His words whistled up the flue of awe: "Hellsmouth, as I live and breathe."

Pure instinct caused Allmon to grab the man by his wiry arm and haul
him hard round. Hellsmouth stirred sidewise as Allmon took stock of the
man's face: hard as a train with a tough jutting jaw like a grille. Lips curled
churlish and coy under deep-set eyes with mini-Hells spangling in their
depths. All muscle and barely more, he was eight feet packed into four, his
sharp body sinewed by starvation and the sweat box.

"So intimate?" the jock snarled. "You don't even know my name,
soldier."

"Get out," said Allmon.

The man jerked back his arm. "Oh, you don't get to tell Jimmy Wink-
field to get out, no sirree. You don't tell Isaac or Oliver to skedaddle!"

Someone tossed over a stall: "Don't listen to that fucker, Allmon!"

The jock tossed right back: "Hush, vile and greasy interloper! You
stink of river water and *queso*!"

From over the stall: "Listen, asshole—"

"Coital sludge! Slander not this ancient tongue! I am presently engaged
in the business of horseflesh and perhaps other flesh, and your intrusion is
an unforgivable offense!"

The little man whirled back to Allmon, his hard eyes aflirt as he thrust
out rough rider's hands. "Reuben Bedford Walker," he said. "The Third,
mind you. Not the first, a pederast, nor the second, a wife beater, in fact
none of the priors, but in all likelihood the last. Until men grow pussies.
Which, Lord have mercy, they might! It's a fabulous new age. Pleased to
make your acquaintance, Allmon Shaughnessy."

Without a clear course of action, because the man's voice was a wily
wend of place and time, threading old centuries up through the chinks and
fissures of newer ones, his words swift in one ear and then tangling in the
disordered avenues of the other, Allmon took the hand up automatically,
but it turned soft as a silk scarf caressing his inner wrist even as he was
saying, "Where'd you get my name?"

Reuben grinned. "Don't be so modest, little Almond. Everyone knows
the prison kid with the good hands and the sorrowful face. Carrying a burden of mysterious origins! Nigh on a horse whisperer, they say, an old
island conjurer, got the Nawlins voodoo touch, one of those old 'tation

niggras—a natural! Where do you come from, and where have you been? We all want to know. You're a curiosity, my man!'"

As he pattered, the jock, dressed only in his silk breeches and a white tank, was squeezing past Allmon toward Hellsmouth, inspecting, mean dreaming, and counting coins.

"The fuck you think you're doing?" said Allmon.

In his finest Tom, Reuben drawled, "Me and dis hoss here, we gone cut us a fine caper, Lawdy yes! I jess been beggin' ole Massah Snyder, lemme leg up dis pony! And now I gone do it! So liff a poor niggra, son."

Shapes were shifting in the man's mouth. Allmon could only stare at him in alarm and distaste.

"Did you hear me, young man?" said the jock with a voice fresh, level, and boss. "Offer your superior a lift."

"You fucking kidding me?" said Allmon, incredulous. "She broke the leg on her last jock in the gate at—"

"I am perfectly aware of Señor Alano's miscalculations, believe you me." Reuben's voice devolved to hiss, "Now toss, Hoss."

If he'd looked a grown man, Allmon would have bristled. If there'd been actual physical threat behind the words, he would have fought. But as it was, he knew this was the jock who'd missed the morning breeze because of a delay at the Los Angeles aiport. Not sure what else to do, he lifted the man onto Hellsmouth as if he were no more than a sack of cornmeal.

Now it was Hellsmouth's turn to object. The two-year-old was already expert at shedding riders with a lightning-strike hump and dump. Now, true to form, she bristled and jumped like a goat, but the jock went nowhere at all, stuck like glue. When she went to rear, Allmon's hands were quick at her mouth and her neck at the withers. Bracing the wide brain pan, he caught and calmed her, though her mouth continued to work suspiciously, snarling.

The jock leaned into those pinned-back ears. "Hush, my sweet little horseypie," he whispered in a voice like chiffon, "you're gonna win big for this here jock, or I'll cut your throat cheek to jowl."

Allmon reached up and dragged off the man who weighed no more than a girl, delivered him hard to his feet in the straw. "Get the fuck off my horse."

"Your horse?" Reuben flickered his spiky lashes in astonishment, his hands on his bony hips. "*Your* horse? Don't forget, Almond Joy, that three people make the money around here—Henry Forge, Mack Snyder . . . and Yours Truly. Your horse, my ass." He reached out and pointed at Allmon's face. "Mind your tongue, young man, saddle up in an hour, and let old Reuben show you how the doing gets done."

Champagne Stakes, Belmont, October 2005, cloud-churning sky over an Indian summer, Mack marching at Allmon's side, his lips blanched white with game-day strain, his cheeks ruddled as ever. The will to win rendered the man a permanent blustercuss, and Allmon had learned quickly to wrap himself back up in a shroud of silence. It was easy. He was cold, permanently cold since the day he left Forge Run Farm. He marveled at how easy it was to look like a statue again, one that didn't look left or right. Except this statue had a mind, and it poked at him, whispering, She must be having that baby any minute. Your baby.

The day, the race, the horse. Hellsmouth was dancing up on her hoof tips, cresting her neck into a fulminating wave as she approached the other mounts in the emerald-green saddling paddock. "You got nothing," Allmon muttered at them under his breath, knocking his mind into place. It was easy; the horses were an astonishment. Among the antic fillies and nerve-addled colts, there was charm and brio, founting talent and flaming speed. Skulls carved neat by nature, legs bred bold by owners, hides like autumn leaves. Here was the bay Wagnerian bass, the Carl Lewis sprinter, Sarah Bernhardt so divine, Solomon's gold, and Tesio's dream. But, listen, as sure as I write this, with Hell's perfect limbs and her big motor, they were just whistling in the dark.

Diminutive even among his coevals, Reuben was ready and waiting, turning this way and that with his crop in his hand, a tightly muscled bundle of expectation, bright and beady-eyed as any peacock. But he ceased all motion when Hellsmouth appeared, his gaze trained on his mount with an unearthly concentration, mean mirth all absent.

Allmon couldn't help himself. He said with a terse, dismissive gesture, "This new jock, I don't like him."

Mack said, "If I had to like any of you sombitches, I wouldn't be in this line of work." He pointed at Reuben. "That's the best rider you'll ever see

on the skin of a horse, and don't you forget it." He raised a hand to the paddock judge, then stepped to Reuben, over whom he towered at five-ten, and,
with one hand to Hell's withers and his other slicing the air like a toma-
hawk, said: "Now do exactly how I said. Let her flop around out of the gate,
that's how she goes. She likes to eyeball ass for a bit. You can hit her around
the curve, but don't crop till you're solid. DO NOT CROP UNTIL YOU'RE
SOLID, REUBEN. You got a rocket here, a classic deep closer, understand
me? Not until you're solid."

Reuben nodded once, his lips a firm line. Allmon saw none of the mean
mirth he'd detected there earlier.

"Riders up!" The marching stopped, followed by a flurry of activity
around each mount. Mack cupped his hands and tossed the jock onto Hell's
back, where he landed with practiced ease, hands snapping up the reins
and gleaming boots cocked acey-deucey. Mack said, "I wish to hell you'd
got up here for a morning gallop. She's a handful. Tricky."

Reuben leaned into Hell, nostrils widening as if inhaling the very stall-
born essence of the horse. He said, "Oh, I'm trickier by half."

Mack just ignored him. "Post assignment to good advantage. Four."

The jock's carved face finally cracked a brittle grin of surprise. "Four!
'Twas ever thus!"

"No time for superstition, Reuben," Mack muttered, but his brows drew
tight as if to secure his eyes against the explosive pressure of his nerves.
"Just keep your head in the game, and don't bring her back here without
the mile."

With a mock salute, Reuben said, "Me and little gal, we'll make a mockery of their bestest efforts," and Allmon led off horse and rider under the
ivied clubhouse into the shadowy tunnel. At the far end, the track loomed
like a handicapper's heaven, lit by a sun just now punching through rarefy-
ing clouds and turning the hoof-churned track to silver. Allmon's blood
quickened, his stomach a fist of fear. One wrong step on that track, one
hard bump, and his whole life would break down with the horse. He swallowed hard to keep his lunch from flipping.

As the first mount emerged from the tunnel, a terrifying rumble rushed
slowly through the grandstand, gathering force as it went—the sound of a
thousand ships shattering at once, louder than God—so the horses danced
in distress, pulling left and right or cantering forward, with only Hellsmouth

displaying no signs of alarm. She raised her head and worked her capricious mouth, taking the crowd in round. *Vox populi vox Dei.*

Against the roar and against orders, Allmon suddenly blurted, "Look, this horse, she's got a sensitive mouth. See her talking around her bit? She's always been like that, even when there's nothing stressing her. Lay off her mouth much as you can."

His lashes fluttering, Reuben leaned down with a hard note of surprise. "And hark! I did hear the prattling of the American youth."

Allmon ignored him. "No need to crop her. Every jock'll tell you the same thing—she runs hard when she wants to run and if you hit her, you just piss her off. She don't need pain to run hard."

A grin, but Reuben's eyes narrowed to slats. "Where exactly are you from, little catfish?"

Allmon looked straight at Hell's billet strap, said quietly, "Cincinnati."

"Of course!" the jock said. "I can hear the river in your mouth! It sounds just like the South."

"Cincinnati ain't the South," Allmon said briskly.

Reuben returned upright on his slip of a saddle and cackled to the crowd. "Not the South, folks! Not the South!" A slicing glance: "It's all the South, son."

Then he winked and with a flick of his hand, he and Hell were parading to the gate on the far backstretch, a stolid palomino pony leading the way. It was only when Allmon and Mack stood aside so the next horses could pass that, suddenly released from the severe focus the Thoroughbred required, Allmon realized something was amiss.

"Where's Forge at?" he said. But he didn't really want to know. The sight of the man elicited a surge of feeling so complicated, it didn't have a name. And the thought of Henrietta was a one-two combo: desire and repulsion.

Mack, his eyes trained on the post parade, waited for the bleating of the bugler to quit. Then he placed his thick fists on his hips. He didn't look back at Allmon when he said, "I track the man's checks, not his whereabouts."

Across the field, as mounts were slotted one by one into their stalls and while Reuben was drawing down his goggles, Hellsmouth skittered back with a violent shake of the head and a fractious cry. She wasn't some bird content with its cage, some laboratory rat. She was one thousand pounds of propulsive muscle, suddenly shadowboxing the sky and scattering her handlers like pins. Reuben was quick, he poured himself across her neck and rode the bucker as ably as any ropey rodeo kid from Cody or Cheyenne. When the green-jacketed handlers regained their feet and dusted themselves off, they placed all hands on her ass and shoved her into the metal stall. The crewman held her head with both hands and smiled nervously at Reuben. "Now you're in a tight spot," he said.

Reuben ignored him, perched and ready for an emergency scramble to the side bars. The reins in a cross, he turned left and right, surveying the ranks: Peru, Guatemala, and Mexico; Colombia, Argentina, more Mexico. "Why, it's a brown battle royale!" he muttered, then tucked his face against Hell's neck, and the gate sprang.

Breaking from the four hole, Hell slopped and thrashed into the race like an overexcited dog, then settled straight away into a loopy, loping, embarrassing last. Even as the field began to jostle and strategize along the rail and the far outside, the filly couldn't be bothered and expended no run at all. Hell was smoking in the ladies' room and didn't give a damn.

On the far side of the track, Mack placed a hand over his heart and muttered, "So help me Christ, this horse is gonna kill me."

Heeding instruction, Reuben rode calm, rump high, head low, a silhouette of hardboiled patience. At the quarter-mile pole, Hell had overtaken only one contender—and that a mere matter of chance as a gray pulled up favoring a leg—and was just beginning to angle wide. Reuben clenched his crop, flipped his filthy goggles, and growled once, "Come on, sister woman."

But Hell just rolled along on her lovely little pleasure cruise. The air was fine with the lushest of breezes, the waters glassy and dotted with befruited islands—

"Goddammit!" Mack hollered from the rail. "Fucking graze for all I care! I fucking bought this pasture for you, asshole!"

It was a fast half mile when the pack passed the pole at just over 0:45. Angelshare, a rangy Runnymede colt, led by two lengths on the inside as Hellsmouth eased her way into ninth along the rump of Play Some Music. Boomie Racz, the curly, blonde up-and-comer, stooped over Music and whipped him when she suddenly sensed Hell at her heels. She flipped her goggles and doubled down, straining for a path through the traffic.

Now the school of horses swung around the turn as if caught in a sweep net, Angelshare faltering off his pace for a moment as he changed leads and Scintilla charging to overtake him with Chief Contender hot as breath on his neck. Only now, as if realizing suddenly that she was hungry and food awaited, Hellsmouth began to stretch out under Reuben and reach for sunlight as she curved around the field. Wary and shrewd, Racz stayed so close that Play Some Music bumped Hellsmouth, shoulder against shoulder, not once but twice. Reuben snarled and shoved and battened down the hatches just as the group emptied into the stretch for the final quarter mile, the four leads now charging neck and neck.

Reuben was done waiting. With an electric strike, he flung back his crop, and with a single stinging lash made contact with the filly's rump. Her muscles leaping beneath her skin, Hellsmouth exploded out of her gait with such vicious power, her first free stride made the previous three-quarters of a mile seem nothing but a lark. As she shot forward she bore in toward the rail and delivered one fast, teeth-rattling bump to Play Some Music. While Racz cropped and corrected her faltering bay, Hellsmouth drove to the wire with a stride so long and self-assured, so dazzlingly late, that the grandstand rose as a single entity, driven up by a surge of energy that seemed to come from the very center of the earth. Farmers three miles distant heard the cry when, fully extended with her limbs threatening the limits of form, Hell shot under the wire. Play Some Music followed in two solid lengths, but as the crowd threatened to deafen man and animal alike, Mack was already clutching his skull at the sidelines.

"Don't fuck me, history!" he cried. "I'm too old for this!"

The inquiry sign began to flash.

"No! No! No! No!" His fists were uncorked grenades, the crazy in his eyes unleashed. "NoNoNoNONONONONONONONOOOOO!!!!!!!!!!!!"

Reuben and Racz were off their mounts in a second, hustling, then running, and now sliding through the office door of the stewards, side by side, panting and pointing.

"He bumped me hard on the straight!"

"She bumped me twice in the turn!"

"We'll watch again," said the steward from the Jockey Club.

"We barely touched him on the turn!"

"I can't prevent a lead switch!"

"Hold on," said the steward from the Racing Association.

"It's a miracle Hellsmouth even stayed up!"

"I couldn't take down your filly with a bulldozer!"

"Ruling stands," said the steward from the Gaming Commission.

Aboveground, the lights stopped flashing and the crowd lost its mind.

Which is how Reuben came to be photographed victorious atop Hellsmouth in the winner's circle at Belmont, Allmon at her halter. In the photograph, Allmon looks taller than he is, chin high and proud, but eyes like dark wounds, peering through the camera, past the trainers, the jocks, the drunks, the bettors, the stoopers, the stewards, to a woman he can't see, but whose details can't be erased. He shakes his head, so the image is blurred.

"Just like 1972," Mack mutters. "I thought history had us by the short hairs."

Reuben puffs out his bird chest and stares down his nose. "I don't repeat history," he says, "I make history, and I'm never riding the bitch that easy again."

There's the front of the house, and there's the backstretch, and never the twain shall meet. Allmon was no more than a migrant worker, no different from the Guatemalans and the Peruvians he groomed with, moving from track to track, following the racing season, following Mack. Like all the rest, he slept in unventilated cinder-block dorms with dingy, mold-streaked walls and sputtering lights, quarters where you couldn't run an air conditioner, because the barns weren't set up for the voltage, so you sweated in the swampy ninety-degree nights and watched the other grooms swoon and puke from the heat. You drew flies like any other animal. A couple of the skinnier guys ended up with dysentery. There were track doctors, but they basically dispensed Vicodin and sent you on your way, and unless you were dying, you didn't get a day off. So you slept in your sweat, bought your food at the 7-Eleven or some Mexican dive, and you worked.

The filly was winning stakes races, but that didn't change Allmon's four o'clock mornings at the barn, going round on a carousel of tack and groom: bandage work, leg checks, scrubbing off poultice wrappings, taking temps and mucking, filling waterers and haynets, laying down fresh hay. He passed mounts to exercise riders, tidied the shed row, washed and groomed again, iced and rewrapped million-dollar legs. If it was race day, that meant rounds after lunch. Otherwise, the vets came in and doped the horses from their grab bag of steroids, then there was more schooling and walking and feeding, and when evening rolled around, Allmon draped them with blankets nicer than any he'd ever owned. For doing this, he made $350 a week, maybe a hundred extra when Hell placed. He spent his first paycheck on a sleeping bag and a .45 1911 automatic he bought off a guy at the track who used to be a marine, just something cheap he could keep close. You couldn't trust anybody anywhere anytime; he knew that. Though sometimes he also knew in the subterranean passages of his heart that he was the least trustworthy of all.

"Hey, kid. Decent job today." Mack was standing there in the stall door, arms folded across his chest, his white Stetson cocked back. Allmon looked up, startled, from where he'd been staring down at his own hands in mystification, lost in thought. He said the first words that came to mind: "My hands feel broke." As soon as he said it, he wished he could reel the words back in.

"Your hands, huh?" Mack's eyes narrowed and he cocked his head. "Okay, listen. I've seen you doing your work around here for a couple months, and that's real good. I mean it. So I'm gonna give you some advice, but don't ask for it again."

Allmon with side eye: "I ain't even asked for it this time."

"Which is why it's amazing I'm giving it to you for free." Mack cleared his throat. "Kid, you know what possum and pepper pot is?"

Allmon didn't bother to shake his head.

"Of course not. See, I grew up in the mountains. Crapalachia. I didn't have two nickels to rub together, and the only roses I ever saw were coffin roses. Never even heard of the Derby till I was thirteen. Somebody once said to me that if you weren't born into money, you couldn't ever be truly wealthy. Do you think I gave a fuck?"

"I'm guessing you didn't give a fuck."

"I didn't give a fuck." Mack recrossed his thick arms. "You ever wonder why horses like me?"

Allmon shook his head.

"They don't, so don't worry about it. There's a lot of things in this world not worth worrying about." Mack peered carefully at Allmon. "So, I noticed you don't drink."

"Nah." Allmon shrugged. "Not really."

"Well, that's interesting," Mack went on. "Every black old-timer I ever knew, and I knew a whole mess of them when I was coming up on the track, they could drink you under the fucking table. Well, go ahead and drink if you want. No law against." He gestured out toward the broader barn. "You think I don't know these banditos put tequila in their coffee every morning? You think I don't know that? Only one rule." Mack held up a single finger. "Don't ever let a horse get hurt under your watch. Or I'll make it my personal mission to put a bullet in your hide."

Grown impatient, it was Allmon's turn to interject. "See, you don't know me," he said. "Or you'd know I don't intend to fuck up. Ain't no horse gonna get hurt under my watch. I lost everything; I don't intend to lose this."

Mack was quiet a moment, took stock of him; he set his legs apart and appraised this young man who—goddammit—he had to admit, reminded him of his own younger, hungrier self. "What have you lost, kid? I know you were in Blackburn."

Allmon lowered his chin; his eyes burned holes through Mack's face. "I. Lost. Every. Thing." And it was God's own truth. There were tears at the back of his voice, the place where Henrietta's name lived.

"Huh," said Mack, nodding, and crossed his arms. "Well, let me tell you something. I'm nothing. I'm nobody. From nowhere. I'm not even going to tell you the name of the town I grew up in, because you'd think I was shitting you. Who the hell am I to be a millionaire five times over? In the hunter jumper world and all that fancy boondoggle bullshit, you can't rise. But here—in this world, in the blood horse world? Sky's the limit. We don't care who you are. We don't care if your daddy hit you, who raped you, who you sleep with, what prison you came from, understand? All you got to do is work. I want you to remember that."

Allmon held wide his arms, affronted. "I been working since I was twelve. I know how to fucking work."

"Well, then, here's my advice."

"I thought you just gave me your advi—"

"Number one!" Mack snapped. "Don't smoke pot; it makes you stupid. Number two, cut your hair; they're looking for reasons to hate you."

Allmon sighed, swagging his head.

"And number three," Mack bulled over his objection, "don't ever loan out your sleeping bag."

Allmon looked up, eyes narrowed. "Why?"

"Crabs. Now get back to work. I'm not paying you to work your mouth."

"Henry Forge, a lifelong devotee of racing and one of its steadiest breeders, is finally putting his name in lights with his big black filly, Hellsmouth, who trounced the field this October at the Juvenile Fillies Stakes. Close readers of *Blood Horse* will recognize the marks of her predecessors Hellcat and Hellbent, but even the most casual racing fan should detect the imprint of Secretariat. This horse is a living, breathing manifestation of the old adage: the best horses come out of the best horses."
—Burrow, *Blood Horse*

Father has spent his life under a bright light in a narrow hallway, repeating names he memorized long ago. But I looked out the window, looking for the ideas that underwrote nature. The problem: what I really saw was my own imagination written onto the landscape of physical matter over time. Self on everything.

"In a long career as a track writer and as witness to some of the greatest horses this sport has ever seen, I can say with absolute certainty that this is the first horse that's eclipsed the great Secretariat in my mind. And it's a filly—if that don't beat all."
—Greeney, *Racing Form*

Then I met someone I wanted more than the idea of him, and I began to think: another also thinks. An equivalency began to assert itself. I sensed the enduring mutual affinities. But until that moment happens, it's impossible for the mind to accept that the self is not the center of the universe, that the center is everywhere, that the universe is always expanding, that there is, in fact, no limit to the universe at all.

"The King is dead. Long live the Queen!"
—*The New York Times*

The movement of evolution is from simple to complex.

The queen knew what she was—something royal, a bold ruler—and she liked nothing better than to show out. On her early morning walks with Allmon, she would showboat among the riffraff, spinning her black tail and crow hopping on her perfectly turned hooves. She mugged for the cameras like her grandsire had done thirty years before, tossing her bull head and rippling her withers like a colt shot up on elephant juice. But Allmon knew she was clean; no one was sneaking in Regu-Mate or Equipoise, Lasix or milkshakes or anything beyond the standard regimen of anti-inflammatories. All the coltish conformation she displayed, the thick, bundled muscles of her quarters and the long, aggressive neck, was her treasure by birthright. Some fillies were just like that—better than the colts at their own game.

Henry. The sight of the man was a shock. Allmon reared back, not recognizing him at first, the way he leaned against Mack's barn as if it were the only thing keeping him from toppling into his own grave. Allmon blinked, as if to clear his vision of a mirage. Where had all Henry's physical beauty gone? His face was the color of old ashes, his once red-gold hair visibly thinner, and he had lost twenty pounds he couldn't spare. He looked to all the world like a handicapper down all his profit, all his luck.

When Henry felt the weight of Allmon's gaze, he straightened up, looking right at him. Then he pushed himself away from the barn wall, turned, and walked with visible effort through its rolling door.

Dread moves swift as blood through the body, from the heart to the distal extremities. For some months, the baby had existed only as a strange muscular tension that wrapped itself now and again around Allmon's brain, but suddenly it was as present as the blood in his veins. Yes, it had surely been born by now. Sweat prickled at Allmon's neck. He walked slowly toward the barn, a knocking in his chest. It was like the blow of a pick against an ice block.

Hell was rank for the lead, shouldering past Allmon into the barn, passing through golden streams of morning light, so chaff particles swam and eddied around her in a liquid rush. Henry watched his filly pass into her stall—his winning girl, his thousand-pound trophy. He could detect no flaw in her at all. She was perfection. A furious, wasting anger blew through him. How could that illusion be so enduring?

Henry looked at Allmon and cleared his throat. "My daughter died."

Allmon came to a complete standstill, body and mind. Then he drew back with a stupid expression on his face.

Again: "A month ago, my daughter died. In childbirth. The child survived."

The color drained visibly from Allmon's face.

"The child is small but healthy." Then he said hesitantly, as if he'd been asked a troubling question, "Some produce better than they run."

Allmon searched Henry's eyes, desperate to comprehend, yet desperate not to comprehend, now or ever. There was madness in the words. The edges of the world were crumbling off the map.

"This horse is all I have left," Henry whispered suddenly, but even as he said this, he felt the falseness of it immediately. He also had his name, he had that.

The words helped Allmon recover himself, if only slightly. He leaned forward, his face jutting into Henry's space. "You don't even know what nothing is."

A flash of a despondent grin.

Allmon didn't even know how he found the strength to speak, it was like the devil swept up through his body to wag his tongue. "The deal still stands, old man. Don't try to play me now." But through the anger flashed an old, wilding, reckless sorrow: God's finger touched her and she slept. It threatened to upend him; he was breathing in panic, not air.

Brief confusion slashed Henry's grief-lean face. "Yes, the deal still stands. We will take this horse all the way. Give her the best possible care. Baby her, feed her by hand, sleep outside her stall, do whatever it takes. I don't want another pair of hands on her. Protect her by any means necessary." Allmon had some sense that his head was nodding, playing its part, nodding because there were all sorts of sabotage afoot in barns like sponging or slipping blistering agents into a horse's mouth, agreeing because this was a conversation any two horsemen would have, but then the horror of the thing began to break forcibly through his thoughts, and he said, "The baby . . . it's mine?"

Henry paused. He felt his father pulling on his right hand, his grandfather pulling on his left, dead weights both. He straightened up. "No," he said suddenly, surprised as the words spun like silk from his mouth. "It's not."

Allmon drew back jerkily, a look of pure astonishment on his face. There was a rending of the temple cloth. In an instant, furious tears filled his eyes, and those tears turned to hate even before they touched his face. He could find no words as cutting as the betrayal that swamped him.

Henry stepped back, half turning to exit the stall, but confusion stayed him, as well as a complicated weight of regret that he immediately sensed would only grow, but he couldn't correct. The child—the wrong color but the right blood—was his. His family.

"The child's name is Samuel," he said, surprising himself.

Then he left Allmon alone in the stall, Allmon who now had nothing in the world but a horse that didn't belong to him. He took one step forward as if he intended to follow Henry and demand some different truth, an altered past. But he just sank to his knees in urine-soaked hay, a howl of grief and rage filling his mind. Fool! And he thought he had known loss!

Laurel Futurity, November 2005. The trees were bare, and like the leaves, the bright crowds were thick on the ground, turned out in their Saturday color jostling for position at the saddling paddock, where the grooms managed the mounts and the trainers sprang jocks. Henry stood among the Laurel Park spectators but they, as if by instinct, offered him a wide berth. He was an emaciated version of his old self, a hack among Arabians. A month along, his grief was still so fresh that no one could look at it. It traveled as a bright sparkling acid all along his capillary rivers; his skin was so thin, it shined right out of him, a gorgeous, harrowing thing. It was like the angels of old: it stunned everyone into silence, and they averted their eyes.

Only Reuben—a Currier & Ives on his pert Hell perch—stared openly.

"What ails the money man?" he whispered down his mount's neck.

Allmon's hands were visibly shaking as he struggled to adjust the bridling over the bridge of Hell's velvet nose. Reuben peered at him with shrewd, hooded eyes. "Why, Allmon, you're white as that bridle," he said. "Perchance you've seen a ghost?"

Mack looked up from where he was adjusting Reuben's stirrup higher. His eyes were narrow. "You and Henry have a chat?"

"Whatever do you mean? Is there a mystery afoot? Pray tell." Reuben's marionette head snapped back and forth from Mack to Allmon, its blunt jaw snapping.

Mack said, "Forge's daughter died in childbirth. Lift your boot a second."

Reuben's eyes popped with delight, and he raised one rein-roughened finger to his lips. "One of their own died? Drama!" he whispered as they guided his mount out of the paddock, a man at each side. He leaned down and whispered into Allmon's air. "I do believe this is what white folk call a Tragedy." Allmon's head was bowed as his hands trembled on the girth strap, so Reuben popped back on the saddle, swiveling in amusement. "Remember that time there was a big ole fire up at Garden State—remember that, old man? My, wasn't that a big time."

Mack grunted, his eyes trained ahead of him at the track where the sun threatened to warm the chill autumn day. "Be careful how early you rally, Reuben. She slowed up yesterday morning during exercise. Leave her some juice." He tugged for the last time on the billet strap.

"Oh yes, Mr. Mack, those sure were the times," Reuben said with a smile of sweet reminiscence. "Some kitchen critter lit up the place in the middle of a race, and that old wood grandstand, why, it went sky-high like a firework stand! Some folk died—oh, just workin' folk, don't let it trouble you none—but the take was still in the vault. Yes, indeed, Reuben's purse was snug as a bug in a rug. Why, hello brute bettors, butchers all!" With a wave of his rough hand to the grandstand and his nose curled up in distaste, he was off with the lead pony, head high and shoulders square. Far along the curve they went, funneling one by one into the green and white clanking gate. When a green-jacketed handler secured the latch on the gate, he whistled in admiration at Hell and smiled up at Reuben. "You're in tall cotton now, Reuben."

"Cotton?" Reuben tucked into position, his eyes turned to sharp, side-slicing daggers. "Remember Fort Pillow, motherfucker."

They exploded out of the gate like doves from a cote. Down the far stretch they flew, Hellsmouth flapping around at the rear, spending energy and spending time. Dragooned for the third time into this public humiliation,

Reuben tucked his crop and let her drag her feet all the way to the quarter pole; he understood now she was just stalking her prey.

At the sloping curve, the bundled pack switched leads as one, shifting and settling out of their steady pace for a brief moment. A mount or two fell away or bore out. Reuben had been waiting lynx-eyed for the speed shift; tucked close to Hell's withers, he staked a tenuous balance atop the brief irons and, with his silks billowing, flashed back the crop so it struck with a single, smart snap. Two things happened at once: Hellsmouth jetted forward with a locomotive force so sudden and propulsive that Reuben's boots slipped the irons and he thumped onto her back with a jarring, graceless plop; and a shoe dislodged from the hoof of a bay colt ahead of them in traffic, so the aluminum ring flung threw the air like a boomerang, and just as Hell stretched low in her deepening forward lunge, it spun over her head and struck Reuben in the nose where he sat without irons on the filly's back. In what the Laurel Park announcer would call "a testament to Walker's athleticism and training and not impossible for competitors of this caliber" and what the backstretch would call "A GODDAMN FUCK-ING MIRACLE," Reuben remained upright in the saddle, though his eyes rolled back to white, his head flopping grotesquely on his neck as the world went absent. Somehow his hands maintained their death grip on the reins and in less than two seconds, he was coming to, his feet reclaiming the irons by instinct, his bony rump risen high, his broken nose gushing blood down the front of his purple Forge silks. "Haw!" he cried woozily, and Hell responded to his fresh balance. She opened up beneath him, her stride extended to an almost magical length, so she was airborne a split second longer than any horse Reuben had ever ridden or the crowd had ever seen. She didn't run at full stride, she leaped, her long body an airfoil. The horses around her—confounded colts under their desperate, whipping jocks—appeared to slow against her blistering speed, which only increased as she burned through the remaining pack, war-striped with Reuben's blood and streaking over the line a full seven lengths ahead of the pack.

Pandemonium erupted as the rest of the field trickled under the wire. The crowds rose in a screaming burst and flash bulbs exploded, so Laurel Park was bright as a sun. Hellsmouth had barely broken a sweat under Reuben, who was busy recovering himself, swiping at his nose with his sleeve and neglecting even to raise a hand in victory. When they moved into the winner's circle, he slapped away concerned hands, accepting only the silken houndstooth handkerchief of a competing owner, who said, "Well, there's a broken nose and no doubt about it."

Hermès silk was soaking up the crimson flow when Mack made it to his side and placed a steadying hand on his boot. Reuben leaned down, his eyes all business even as he fought a hard faint, his wide pupils black bottomless pots. "She look okay? She pull? Felt something funny at the wire." He was slipping in a daze from the saddle.

Mack pushed him back upright with both hands. "She looked good, but it's one hell of a picture you're gonna take. You got goddamn mettle, Reuben, I'll give you that."

They were a strange admixture of animal and man: a gleaming thousand-pound horse topped by a bleeding bird of prey, stars whirling in his eyes, a trainer scowling under a white Stetson, and Allmon at Hell's foamed mouth. His face conveyed not victory but a bleak abeyance, as if he didn't know where he was, or how he came to be here. "Look here, look right here!" said the photographer with some impatience, because Allmon kept turning aside. He was looking for Henry Forge, who was nowhere to be seen.

Barely leaning, lest he faint and tumble into a heap of anorectic limbs, Reuben whispered from the catbird seat, "What do you say we have us a drink, soldier. Swap prison tales!"

Allmon shook his head faintly, his face whitewashed. "I don't drink . . . ," he said, but the hesitation in his voice was plain.

"Malt does more than Milton can to justify God's ways to man. Smile for the camera, all and sundry!"

The eye of fame blinked and captured them.

"Sir, what can I get for you?"

Henry was staring past the stewardess, his gaze fixed on the fat, white cotton boll moon. It filled the whole of the opposite window, its planar seas and gradations clear in the rarefied heights of their flight. A jagged line was scribbled on its surface, a question that repeated itself again and again, scrawled in his daughter's hand: Is there a difference between happiness and joy, and why can I feel neither?

"May I get you something to eat or drink?"

He should have been celebrating with Mack, holding court with the local news station, fielding questions from the *Times* and the *Racing Form*. He should have been telling Allmon the truth and setting the world back on its axis. Instead, he was returning to his grandchild as quickly as technology allowed. There was no time to waste. His life was caught in a war of attrition and Death was scattering his strongest troops: his singular focus and his old convictions.

"Sir, is there anything you need?"

Need? Yes, he needed to know that his grandson had eaten well, that he was sleeping in peace, that he would be kept safe from all the dangers of the world. To his own astonishment, his chest was full of the most blissful emptiness, wherein he discovered only one thing: Samuel. He realized this was love. It had nothing to do with his happiness, which was nonexistent. He wasn't sure yet about joy.

In a Thunderbird the color of money, Reuben rolled them round to a shack way out in the deeps of Howard County, west of Clarksville, what might have been a speakeasy or a juke joint back in the day, but aslant now and barely standing, filled to busting with grooms, hotwalkers, and a few slumming jocks. Thick light streamed through frosty porthole windows and a general din pulsed the walls. When Reuben burst through the tavern door with Allmon at his heels, reluctant and wary as a deer, they were nearly thrown back by an odorous wall of rank armpits, sodden bar mats, urinal cakes, and unmopped floors. At the sight of Reuben's wizened mask of abuse—grotesque purple nose and great slices of bruise beneath his eyes— all heads swiveled round. Then the room loosed a drunken roar, raising fists and pint glasses, and Reuben raised triumphant matador arms.

"Doo-dah!" he cried, sashaying into the crush of handshakes and shoulder slaps. He tossed back a sly whisper to Allmon, "Tap, tap, Endman. Give them what they think they want, but keep your eyeballs open."

As expected, theirs were the only black faces in the room.

"How's that nose, Reuben?"

"Nought but a scratch!" he said, squeezing his way toward a tiny four-top.

"Had it coming, Reuben! No broke bones in two years—"

"Them's the wages!" He pointed an impossibly misshapen finger at the nearest barkeep. "Whiskey for my men, beer for my horses!" Allmon had barely found a chair when sloppy shots were slung before them. He eyed the glass, eyed Reuben's dangerous grin, and, with the new reality snapping at his heels, drained it. What else was there to do? He felt smoke curl out of his nose. When the smoke cleared, there was only Henrietta's face before him. Allmon bowed his head, breathless.

Reuben leaned across the table, the dim overhead lights casting mean shadows across his mangled face. "How are you liking our dirty business, prison kid?"

Allmon remained motionless, his eyes down. "On my way up." The words were outside of him as if belonging to someone else. He suddenly wanted his own mind, and all of its life-roughened texture, to be shredded away. He wanted desperately to be drunk.

"On the house—congrats, Reuben!" The barkeep sloshed down a second round.

Shot glass to his puckered lip, Reuben said, "Well, tell me then—why dost thou bow thy head and wring thy hands thusly?"

Allmon looked up; he'd been unaware of the clustered knot of his fingers, how he kneaded them from the thick knuckle to the nail tip. There was a tiny fissure of anguish between his brows.

Reuben narrowed his sly eyes. "Do I detect a note of worry over the death of . . . hmmm . . . a little white gal, perhaps? I swear you went pale as a paddy earlier today! Was she your precious little fig? Did she catch your cock one day when she was out angling for exotic fish? You know how white girls love to gnaw on Negro dick now and agai—"

"To Reuben!" someone cried before Allmon could rise and separate Reuben's head from his neck. Reuben smiled into the crowd with wide eyes and a feint of delighted surprise. But the smile was cut from cruel cloth.

A man stumbled into his side with a bear's embrace. "Nobody can bring down this son of a bitch, not even a flying horseshoe and Boomie Racz! Toast! Toast!" And the cry was raised again, and now two grooms— Barney and Truss—slid into the other two empty seats with yet another round, but even as their glasses sparked empty beneath the tavern's grimy lights, Reuben leaped to the seat of his chair and, with hands to his Pan hips, cried, "Toast? Why, sure! I'd like to take this opportunity to praise an old friend who holds me tight and never lets me go! Raise a glass to Jeff Davis—may he be set afloat on a boat without compass or rudder, then that any contents be swallowed by a shark, the shark by a whale, whale in the devil's belly and the devil in hell, the gates locked and the keys lost, and further, may he be put in the north west corner with a south west wind blowing ashes in his eyes for all ETERNITY. Say aye if ye mean aye!"

"Aye!" Sloshing glasses punctured the smoky air above their heads. Reuben perused the scene with a sharp, slaten eye.

"Are you happy, Reuben? Your purse is getting fat!"

He grabbed at his cock. "It is!"

"Speech!"

He leaned down and pounded his fists once, twice on his table and rocketed upright. "Speech?" he cried. "Why, no soul wants to hear a speech tonight! Let's play a game instead!" He swooped up his drink, threw it back, and the bar followed suit. With flint whimsy, Reuben hollered over the din: "Fellers and fellerettes, free shots for the winner of the interlocutor's quiz!" He stomped about in a small circle on his chair as if it were a dirty shingle. "Tell this here jock, why are there no Thoroughbreds of ebon hue?" He gazed around, then tossed up his hands. "Black, you idiots, black!"

"There are!" called someone near the tap.

"Nyet! Not jet! Not one of you critters has seen a true black on the track!" And it was true; they hadn't.

"I'll drink it myself, then," he snarled, and upended his shot. "All the pretty horses descend from the black, but interbreeding dilutes the majestic purity! Now the blackest black is merely muddy brown!" His chin crumpled under a swooping fishtail frown, but he winked at Allmon.

"Another!" someone yelled. "I ain't drunk yet!"

"Yes, yes, let me amuse you, please," Reuben hissed. Then, trumpeting through the tight embouchure of his lips: "Yokels! Riddle me this: How came I to be a tin soldier? Where are my esteemed brethren? Black predecessors once ruled this unruliest of sports!"

Proudly, as if coughing up a pearl, their neighbor slapped the table and blurted, "Jim Crow."

A flap of a disdainful hand. "I see you know your minstrel show, but no, no, Paddy, no. Once upon a glorious time, we won every Derby, snatched every purse. But the vain rascals of the North conspired against the Sons of

Ham. They staged a coup! And the Negro, once so dominant, was ousted! Why, Willie Sims himself had to grovel for a ride! Sorry, no shots for my dear friends . . . not tonight anyway!"

"Ahahahahahaw!" The room roared and they drank and Reuben glowered through snaky eyes, slipping down from his dais perch and plopping into his seat.

The room was full pickled, and Allmon too. Five shots in, there ensued a fabulous unraveling. As he sat marveling at the curiously dead weight of his tongue, thinking it a relief to be freed from memory, he was dragged up from the table by one elbow and yanked gracelessly again through the roiling, rowdy crowd. Reuben was a tiny man, but all muscle and trouble.

Back at the half-empty table, Truss shook his head and leaned blearily toward his companion. "Man, I get sick of that shit."

"What?" said Barney.

"It's always black this and black that," said Truss. "Like bad shit didn't happen to anybody else."

Barney nodded. "I know. Things have changed."

"I mean, there were white slaves too. People forget that."

"Yeah, people totally forget that." They clinked their glasses and sloshed whiskey.

The season ripped the door from Reuben's hand, the wind as cold as Christmas. He and Allmon stumbled into a night of river-bottom black; yes—overhead the faint stars wobbled like the light of steamboats spied from below. Allmon looked at their vague and nameless number, his head beginning to spin on what remained of his sober sense. Ungoverned, his tongue blurted, "Eight years ago, I lost every . . . but I got a deal . . . I'm the devil."

Half-distracted with machinations and manipulations, all manner of chaos on the tip of the rapscalliest tongue, Reuben swung round in the dark and peered hard at Allmon. "Come again, little nut? What business is this? Are we speaking of the pale lily and her get? Were you by any chance the sire?"

Allmon weaved and stumbled back against the aluminum siding of the building, huddling under the meager eave, burrowing into his jacket against the weather, against reality. He shook his head.

"But . . ." Reuben sidled. "You expected you were?"

To nod is to die. Allmon nodded.

Reuben hopped forward one step with utter delight. "The bitch! The lascivious cotton candy cunt!"

Allmon mumbled, "I signed papers . . . with Forge . . ." He wanted to stopper his mouth, stop talking, but was wholly unable.

Reuben inched closer, his voice careful, but his blinks rapid as a hummingbird's wings. "You made a deal with the White Father? Of what nature, pray tell? Blackmail? Revenge?"

Allmon felt too sick to respond; he stared down at the ground, which could be a bed if he would only let his knees buckle.

Reuben winks at you: "Revenge it oughta be."

When Allmon spoke, the world whirled. "Stay away—from the . . . Henrietta. Something wasn't right between . . ."

Reuben leaned close. "Henrietta. This was the nubile Aryan?"

Allmon's hands were a horror when they gripped his head. His hands nodded his head.

Reuben reared back, his eyes all astonishment and his breath blooming white in the gelid air. He made a sputtering noise of pure delight. "By God, Almond Joy's got nuts! You're a meddler and an entrepreneur—more enterprising than a soul might have guessed! See, my brother, you had a dream. First you rifled for it in the silver drawer, then you swallowed it down with a dry little cracker! Impressive, I'm sure." He cocked his head. "Twilight striving notwithstanding . . ."

Anger suddenly doused grief and drunkenness. Allmon lurched around toward Reuben. "How come you can't talk like a normal fucking human being? Who the fuck do you think you are?"

Reuben waved a dismissive hand. "Oh, I ain't what I am—unlike you, so faithful and true, even in your conniving! But never mind, the hygiene of your heart is questionable, and I wholeheartedly approve! Did you study the art in prison, or did you come by it naturally like an atavic tic? From the dam or the sire, pray tell?"

Jesus. Jesus Christ, he was drunk. He—

"Use your words, soldier!"

"My momma died when—"

"Died! Of what? Tell Reuben! Was she murdered? How marvelous!"

"Lupus. Kind of like lupus . . . We ain't had health insurance."

"Murder, indeed! Give me every gruesome detail! And tell me all about prison while you're at it! I'll have no more of your wily reticence. I just love a good comedy."

But even four sheets to the wind, Allmon wouldn't go there. That's where they tear out your heart and stuff you with newspaper and wood chips. No. He tried to stand tall against the aluminum siding, and when he inevitably began to tilt, Reuben was suddenly there like a post beam to prop him up with both hands. Allmon was sloppy and spitting as he spoke. He tried to dredge up something old, something sure, something that would tether him to life. "Ten years from now, look for me. I'm gonna make something of myself. You know what I'm saying? I'm making . . . me, there . . . this world, all these racist motherfuckers—"

"Their very lives do learn us hate," Reuben chided, "but you're behind the times, my friend. It's no longer the man but his very house."

"I'm gonna be standing in the front of the house—grandstand. You see the suits they wear? When's the last time you saw a black dude with money—"

"Why, last time I gazed upon myself in a limpid pool."

"I'm serious—"

"Yesterday, I'm sure." There was flint about Reuben's amusement.

"Well, not me!" Allmon cried suddenly, anguished. "Not you!"

Reuben reared back. "Not me? NOT ME?" Now he leaped away from Allmon's side, so he nearly collapsed to the ground before he could catch himself, stumbling and clutching at the corrugated siding. Reuben pointed a finger in his startled face. "Mind now, young whippersnapper, I'm richer than Mansa Musa! I'm stronger than Shaka! Wise like the magi! The only irons near me are under my boots!"

"You ain't nothing but a jock," Allmon snarled.

Reuben's wily face was distorted by mortal offense. "Nothing but a jock? I'm nothing you can even imagine, you fucking river rat! Not with your borrowed dreams! I am the Defender of Myself, wizard of the saddle, untutored genius, the first with the most!" He thumped his pony keg chest, strutting before Allmon. "You've never seen mischief like me! I subvert and invent! I never relent! I resist and supersede! Confabulate and fabricate! No one knows my name—or my history! Hallelujah and fuck you! I piss on family and order, I lie and I counterfeit! No mother made me, I bore my own damn self. I got a contraband brain and Napoleonic balls. Twenty-nine

horses shot out from under me, and still I ride on. Can I get a goddamn
Amen!"

"Amen!" came a shout.

Allmon tried to formulate a vicious reply, something to put the arrogant
jock in his place, but he was suddenly riding wild waves of resentment and
nausea. "Oh shit," he gagged, and began to stumble forward, away from
the building.

"Heavens to Betsy," said Reuben mildly, stopping short as Allmon
dropped to his knees, coughing at first, then retching the contents of his
stomach into the dry winter grass.

Reuben blinked a few times, then edged over and leaned down. "Oh,"
he sighed, patting Allmon absently on the back, his speech gone suddenly
cool, "what am I going to do with you, my little wingnut? What am I going
to do with you?" He looked out into the surrounding woods, which were
pitch-black, laced with frost and punctuated with the yellow eyes of animals. "I'm sure I'll think of something."

Finally, Samuel in his arms. It was true that at first he had seen only his
color—a dark shock, an intrusion. But day after day, the more he stared at this
child, the more he found the old revulsion shifting. Dark, unformed flesh
transformed to something more complex, more significant than a mere
body, transformed into a structure yielded by human effort but sui generis in
its construction, a product of ingenious architects. Look at the smooth stone of
the forehead, the nave widest at the fat cheeks, the flying buttress nose, stained
glass eyes. Admit it, Henry, you stand before a mystery, an immensity, and
inside this building you will find something previously unnamed, something
that until now you never wanted to know. Something other than yourself.

"Oh, just look how happy he is to see you, Henry! He certainly recognizes his grandpa."

Henry blinked unsteadily in the warmth and glow of the Miller kitchen.
Ginnie was preparing him a cup of peppermint tea as he cradled Samuel
after his two days of travel, what had seemed like a two-year separation.
How his life had changed in such little time. He was nearly stupefied by it,
but it was there nonetheless, as plain as any other fact.

As she dropped a tea bag into a mug, Ginnie said, "Henry, you can leave Samuel with us anytime. It was wonderful having a baby in the house again—wasn't it wonderful, Roger?" She turned to her husband.

"It was." Roger nodded.

Uncomfortable color rose into Henry's cheeks. "I . . . I can't impose upon you more than I already have." He turned to survey the room, possibly seek out Samuel's overnight bag, but Ginnie just batted at his hand. "Oh, I'm not letting you run off just yet. You need to eat after traveling. Plus, I need someone to play checkers with. Roger has a three-game limit, and that just won't suit."

Henry noted the red and black game board on the kitchen table, its checkers scattered and glinting under the porcelain table lamp. "Checkers . . . ," he said blankly, as he shifted Samuel from his right to his left arm.

Ginnie cocked her head to one side. "Checkers," she said slowly, then she and Roger exchanged a swift glance. She cleared her throat. "Do you . . . not know how to play?"

Henry stared very gravely at the board. "I don't believe I do. My father started me off with chess."

"Oh!" said Ginnie with a decisive nod of her head. "Well . . . it's never too late to learn. Just sit yourself down right here." She gestured him into one of the well-worn tavern chairs and went to swoop Samuel from his arms and into her own, but restrained herself; their reunion was something to see. Samuel's face had turned bright at the sight of his grandfather, and now he cooed under his chin, busy pressing into Henry's hollow cheeks with his soft, chubby hand. He was making a new sound that was very much like a laugh, his delight filling the room.

"Well," Roger said, moving toward the hall, which led to the back recesses of the house, "I shall leave you to it. I'll just be taking this tea with me to bed."

"Why don't you leave it out here," Ginnie said with a wave of her hand, "and save me the trip of bringing it back. It's not like you ever drink it."

"I often drink it," Roger corrected her.

Ginnie looked up. "Never once have you drunk your evening tea. Not once."

Arc of a gray brow. "Woman, you do not know me."

Ginnie snorted, but before she could utter a retort well honed from decades of use, Roger leaned down and kissed her on the forehead. "Good night," he said, and, "Good night, Henry. We enjoyed having Samuel. The Corgis especially. They love children."

As he disappeared around the doorjamb, Ginnie called out, "Don't forget to leave the hall light on. You always forget, and you know the night-light's been burned out since forever."

"I will not forget, woman."

"Okay," said Ginnie, then quietly so only Henry could hear: "He always forgets." She settled back into her chair, scooping all the discs to the center of the board before she began to sort them with two fingers. "Henry, you'll be black, and I'll be red, the goal being to advance across the board, capture the other's discs, and make it to the opposite side first."

But Henry was barely listening. With Samuel cradled against his chest, he had turned to watch Roger's retreat down the frame-lined hall to the back of the house. When he came slowly right, he said, "You seem to . . . suit each other very well."

"Who? Me and Roger?" Ginnie looked at him in surprise, as though he had said the most absurdly obvious thing. Then she shrugged. "The annoyance of my days and the love of my life."

Henry smiled sadly and clutched Samuel.

Ginnie noted that smile as she arranged the checkers and said, "Did you have a great love in your life, Henry? Someone who gave you a reason to live when the going got rough?"

The question startled him visibly. He blinked and then a chaos of feeling washed over his features, so that he didn't know where to look—at the game board, around the room, or at the boy in his arms. Suddenly, Samuel yawned with all his might, and his entire body shook, including the fists he drew to his wobbling chin. Then he smiled.

"I just can't wait," Ginnie said softly, freeing Henry from the burden of answering, "to see who Samuel will grow up to be. I have a feeling he's going to be extraordinary." She glanced at Henry, lamplight in her eyes. "But then we all are, aren't we, each in our own way?"

In the morning, Hellsmouth seemed healthy as—God, sorry—a horse, so they wrapped her limbs in white cotton traveling bandages, loaded her into the custom Turnbow, and headed for home. While she swayed, dreaming her bluegrass cockcrow crooktree dreams, Allmon's companion smoked and chattered on for twelve hours straight. Trying not to puke, Allmon just leaned his tender head against the window and slept a liquor-thrummed sleep, his sleep the thinnest veil over the horror of the new reality. Not his? How was it possible? The way she had clung to him in their lovemaking—and it had been that, he knew it had. Or he had known. He drifted on waves of sleepy fright. He saw a baby's chubby hands reaching out to grasp hills like tits that rose across a shimmering river, water waving like the flag of conquerors. The baby looked just like him.

Wake up! the Reverend whispered. Human love ain't nothing but a halfway house, where we prepare our criminal nature for the love of God.

AMEN!

NO! His eyes snapped open. She had cheated, cuckolded him, lied through her thin, white-girl lips. Never forget.

The road had led them back to Kentucky and Mack's training center, where Hellsmouth would overwinter in her own paddock, undapple her mottled black, and rest easy. The driver shifted down on the sunny side of the broodmare barn to unload their half-ton cargo, but Allmon never made it to the back of the trailer. He had only the briefest moment to note the dull ache in his hips and knees—surely the result of too much alcohol and lack of sleep or his fresh horror—before his legs collapsed and he slumped to the ground, appearing like a man who'd slipped out the door into a deep pool of water. The man came sputtering out of the driver's side, hand tracing the nose of the truck as he doubled over with laughter, trying to wipe his eyes even as he was hauling Allmon to his feet. "Oh shit!" he cried, not even trying to rein in his amusement. "Oh shit, man! You all right?" But Allmon wasn't laughing. Pain was poking mean fun in the joints of his legs and hands. There was the briefest moment when panic came bobbing up, but he tamped it down. You could not think of your life in time—or your mother's. He took Hell's lead and moved forward, his eye trained resolutely on the horizon beyond the barn, a vain trick to foreclose on the near.

But in the stall, he sensed it, a subtle but sure shift in the space, like a ghost in the room. He looked at Hell, at her mouth and into her vitreous globe eye, and pressed his aching, hungover hands to the flat plains of her jaw. Her pupils mere millimeters wider than placid; a whisper of too-warm heat drifted from her flanks. Suddenly, undeniably, she was idling high.

Allmon didn't have to be told what to do; he limped, then ran, beelining past the farm manager, and barreled straight into Mack's office. Mack was only a half hour home from Newark, leaning over his desk, peering at his winter colt list, when Allmon skidded across the threshold. Two words: "She's off," and Mack was barking like a Doberman into his cell, so not fifteen minutes later his eighteen-year home vet, Don Patrick, was striding down the shed row, chin tucked into his neck, gear bag in one hand, silver La Boit case in the other.

Mack was utterly useless before illness; he could do nothing but pace the row, sweating pungent sweat, muttering at his second-tier fillies, doing what he never, ever did: praying to the clerk of the course, the patron saint of the horse, and various other minor gods, Take any filly you want, but not this fucking one.

"Her temp's a little high," said Don. "She break funny up in Camden? Finish funny? Go off her feed?"

Allmon shook his head, confused.

"Nothing?"

Mack said, "Reuben said he felt something at the wire, but she touched cool and looked good."

Don sighed. "They're like cats, these horses. They'd rather die than let you know when they're hurt. Let's start with distal extremities, lower left first. Let's just get some shots."

Allmon was desperate for something to do; he couldn't indulge in the luxury of Mack's rabid pacing. He carefully stood his meal ticket in her stall, arranging her hooves in a position she had at least a prayer of holding. He stared at her in desperation as if she was the only thing separating him from the void—and she was.

Mack quit his pacing to struggle into the lead apron Don handed him. "Hold her still," said the vet as he clicked open his case, sliding out the laptop.

"Mack, hold the plate." Mack squatted down around her rear left pastern and balanced the radiographic plate on the hay-strewn row, while Don stage-managed the shot.

To Allmon's eyes, the laptop screen showed nothing but the ghostly haze of the inside of the filly's leg—her beautiful bones glowed in photographic reverse like the dream of a horse—but Don stared long and hard. He made a clicking sound in the back of his throat.

"Goddammit," said Mack, "what?"

"One more round on this leg," said Don cryptically, and then the gods or Saint Eligius or some other rough divinity coughed up a small curse. The second round of shots showed a soft, snowy dusting of white on the thick, clean cannon bone near the hinge of the fetlock joint.

"Hairline fracture," said Don, nodding grimly.

Mack said, "Do I shit or go blind?"

The vet was already emailing the images over to a colleague at Rood & Riddle, and two minutes later he was conferring with her on his cell. When he snapped it shut, his brows were drawn together, and there was little room for doubt in his voice: "Okay, two months of stall rest. That's the deal. I don't want her to take a single step anywhere, not one—do you hear me?"

"I'm not new here," Mack snapped.

"I'm saying not a single step, Mack," Don said, holding up one work-roughened hand to preempt argument. "Yeah, I know, buddy. But to be frank, you're lucky it's not a splint bone problem. We all realize you're sitting on a king's ransom here, but don't push your luck. Two months. Even that's a gamble."

Allmon turned toward his filly and looked in one grave, rheumy, bitter chocolate eye, then the other. I'm gambling with my whole life here, you motherfuckers, he thought. Then he imagined Henrietta, and his heart burned with grief and betrayal in equal measure. But not guilt: guilt was dying with every moment, as surely as she had.

"Two months!" Mack moaned, as if the words were just now piercing the concrete of his skull. The blood vessels in his eyes looked fit to burst.

Don Patrick sighed. "Listen, we got a problem that we can't control, but what we can do is throw money at it. Let's do green juices, everything organic, some acupuncture, massage, electromagnetic stimulation, read to her," he said, looking at Allmon, "and give her some treats, sweet-talk her. Do it all."

"Fuck horses," said Mack. He puffed out his cheeks, looked up once at the rafters of the barn as if for help, but apparently the gods were all ate up with bullshit today. He exhaled roughly. "Okay, well, I'm gonna go deal with Henry. Right now. It's not gonna be pretty. But okay." And then he was gone as quickly as he'd come.

Don Patrick stood in his wake and sighed. He took stock of his patient.

The filly was eccentric, sensitive, bold, petulant. A horse was a code of laws that few could read. On this one was written: Ultra.

"You know what?" he said suddenly. "I've been doing this a long time, and sometimes you just get a real good read on a horse. I'm gonna put her in an air cast. I'm not even going to bother with plaster of paris."

"How come?" said Allmon. He could already feel Hell's fresh unhappiness in the air, and it matched his own. He knew he'd have to be more angel than groom to tend the devil of her dissatisfaction.

Don smiled wearily. "Because damned if she won't go in that stall and break her leg or worse trying to kick it off. When you've got a diva on your hands, it's always better to face facts. This here's a Scarlett, not a Melanie. And it's nothing but trouble when you trap an ultra in the middle."

It wasn't something he was going to say over the phone, so he drove his blistering ass over to Forge Run Farm, rehearsing various ways of saying We're fucked You're fucked The filly's fucked I'm fucked You're fucked & Etc. He couldn't remember—truly could not recall—the last time he'd been this angry, fury stoked in him like an August barn fire. It was a fury brought on by stifled tears, not that he even realized that. Mack didn't do sad. He hadn't even cried at his dear mother's funeral, mostly because she'd looked better than she had in fifteen years. That mortician had been a wizard.

What he ended up saying, standing there in the Forge kitchen with his hat band-up in his hand, was very simple. "Hairline fracture on the cannon bone. Bad news but could be worse. That's the deal." He had made a straining, sideways gesture with his mouth. He could barely meet Henry's eyes. He felt gutshot.

Henry reached out with both hands and clamped them on Mack's shoulders. With the scorched-earth eyes of inconsolable loss, he said, "Fix my filly. Do whatever you have to do to fix her."

Mack nodded hard. He figured it was all fucked and dandy, but he said, "We're gonna rest her up. We're gonna baby her—"

"Fix her. Do you understand what I'm saying? Do whatever it takes to run my girl in the Derby. You and I both know what she's capable of."

The air in the room stilled. Mack narrowed his eyes, slyly rooting around for permission. "Anything it takes?"

"Anything." Henry said it as two implacable, final words.

"Goddamn right," said Mack, and he popped his white, off-season Stetson back onto his graying head. "I'll get your little girl up and running."

Mack was looking for an excuse and it didn't take him long to find it. One look at the kid made your own temperature go up. He was a walking fever—unsteady on his feet, his hands limp as rub rags; he was leaning into Hell like she was the support post and he was the sagging roof. Mack surveyed the situation with distaste, his lip curled, before he said, "I had no everloving idea black boys could turn pink. What in the name of God's wrong with you?"

Allmon didn't dare look up or the whole barn would swirl the drain. He still felt sideways with alcohol, but that didn't make sense. It had been too long. "I'm off," is all he said.

"Well, don't lean on my goddamn broke horse, kid. If you're sick, I don't want you in here. They can catch what you got." His voice was hard, but when Allmon turned his watery, febrile eyes on him, Mack didn't look angry. "Get to a doctor. I can't even believe I'm fucking saying it, but take a couple hours and go to a doctor."

"I can't afford it." Allmon didn't even have to ponder that.

"Well," said Mack, and it bothered him a bit, the kid didn't look right, but he wasn't going to back down now. "Get out of here either way."

Mack stood there in the stall and watched him limp off. Then he finished up the rub job with cursory movements and cogitated on the issue a bit more, took stock of the blue air cast around Hell's leg. He scratched with some irritation at his three o'clock stubble. On the one hand, things were getting tighter around the track, and you could feel it gathering like a storm; there was railbird chatter about a congressional crackdown right around the corner. On the other hand, that was Later and this was Right Fucking Now. On a totally different hand, this stuff could shrink up ovaries and screw up estrus, but on another hand, that's what long-term infertility insurance was for. On the fourth hand if you were counting: Hell was a filly; it wasn't as if Mack was risking his share on some hot stud. But on the most important hand of all, while it wouldn't make her run faster, it sure as shit would speed recovery, and recovery was half the game, especially for the Preakness. Besides, Hell didn't need more speed; she'd already bested the best. There simply wasn't another horse like her, and everybody knew it. But—goddammit—that's exactly why Mack just stood there motionless with the syringe in his hand instead of jabbing it into her rump and pressing the plunger. He'd perfected the art of bulking his ponies way back when he was running quarter horses up in dusty, middle-grade Wyoming, his motto: What separates the best from the rest is the best don't get caught. But the fact was he'd never seen a horse like this, at least not since 1973. She made him feel like a kid again, idealistic. He couldn't help but want to see what she could do on her own, without any help. So, against his better judgment, feeling like someone entirely unlike Mack Snyder, he repocketed the syringe of Winstrol and stepped out of the stall.

A year ago, there would have been a winter to describe—a palace of ice, hoarse winds that wound white ribbons around the houses with strange gunslinger lightning at Christmas. But this was a new year. The winter was unusually cold. It snowed heavily. That's all I can tell you.

In the dark heart of January, Henry was startled awake by a shrilling phone. Mack on the other end, his crude holler of triumph nearly indistinguishable from anger.

"Henry!" he barked. "Henry, we got it!"

Henry worked to draw his mind round. "Got what?"

"Eclipse Award! Two-Year-Old Filly!" The air was charged with his waiting, but when Henry didn't speak, Mack barreled on. "Awards are in Beverly Hills on January twenty-second. I'll be coming from Sarasota, so I'll meet you there. It'll be at the Wilshire Hotel. They make a damned good old-fashioned."

Henry cleared his throat. "I won't be there."

Now it was Mack's turn to be silent. He stopped pacing to peer mystified around his office, as though it had vanished before his eyes and he'd suddenly found himself in a bleak and barren wasteland.

"You're staying home," he snapped shortly. "You—why?"

"Samuel."

"Samuel fucking who?"

"Samuel's having recurrent ear infections and until that's cleared up, his pediatrician advised that we not fly. He goes where I go. Period."

Mack tried twice to speak and failed. He tried again. He sounded like a jalopy engine sputtering. "You're staying home from the Eclipse Awards to take care of a baby?"

"Yes," said Henry.

There was a silence as beautiful, delicate, and clean as Venetian glass. Then: "Okay!" Mack snapped. "Okay! We've worked for this for ten fucking years. Yes. WHAT???" And he flung down his cell phone with such force that the casing snapped and the battery went spinning out his office door like a small satellite careening out of orbit. Stalking to the row, he made a crazed, animalistic sound deep in his throat and grabbed his startled assistant trainer by the lapel so the young man flailed, thinking this was it, this was the moment when Mack would finally haul off and punch him in the fucking throat, but Mack just hollered, "Will someone please tell me where the fucking sane people live?!"

Which is not what he said into the cavernous ballroom at the Beverly Wilshire Hotel standing before thirteen hundred of the country's wealthiest and most ambitious horse trainers and owners, circled by the track writers and videographers who recorded it all for posterity.

Mack stood in the glare of the evening's lights, the whole fancy boondoggle sparkling in its black-tie finery, all those acquisitive eyes focused on him, his Zuni bolo tie suddenly feeling not unlike a noose. God, how he hated this primped-up bullshit, and he'd never forgive Henry for making him puke up a speech on his behalf, but Mack knew that horse better than anyone else, so he guessed he was the only other man for the job. He shifted at the podium, put those red, perma-chapped hands to the hips of his pressed jeans, and said, "Y'all know I'm no speech giver. I don't care for talk if there's horses to be trained and races to be run. But, it's January, there's nothing going, it's the Eclipse Awards. I'll talk for a spell."

He sniffed hard, looked out at those expectant faces, all of whom had seen the filly run her races and knew what kind of extraordinary thing he was dealing with here. She was more than high-quality stock, more than good legs, more than brass lungs. She was hunger, and you couldn't buy that.

He said, "I've been running horses since I was yay high, and I've been training them since I was twenty and a half. Let no man say that I don't know a great horse when I see one. And by love of God and money, Hellsmouth is a great horse."

There was rambunctious applause and hollering, but he just talked right over it. "This big black filly isn't just the best horse I've ever trained. She's the best goddamned racehorse I've ever seen. And she's just getting started." He paused. "That's all."

He stepped off the podium amidst the clapping and not a little eye rolling from those who'd rather have seen him shot than win another purse, and the genuine applause of the men and women he'd made rich. He shook a couple of hands on the way back to his table, where his drinking could be resumed, and he didn't think, How the hell did some poor Letcher County kid end up here with the brightest and best, but: They ought to pay to eat the dirt under my boots. I turn the mill wheel. Blue-blood silver-spoon trust-fund bastards.

As if on cue, Stu Penderson, a Woodford County acquaintance of some forty years, clapped him abruptly on the back and said, "Where's that old rascal Henry tonight?"

Mack scowled openly; he didn't even try to hide his disgust. "You don't want to know," is all he said as he tugged loose his bolo tie and returned to his drink to suffer the rest of the banquet alone until he found some lonely desperado who would suffer him in turn.

I don't care who you are—a breeder of champions, the scion of scions—a crying baby can bring you to your knees. Henry was snatched from sleep for the third time that night, prisoner to Samuel's wailing. Nothing in the world could soothe him, not the whirring of a fan, no amount of sweet talk or pacing. He refused the bottle, he struggled righteously against a fresh diaper, he waved his fat arms in fury, and screamed over Henry's lullabies as if to wake the world with his frustrations.

After an hour of it, Henry was nearly in tears himself, and there was nothing left to try but read from Henrietta's notebooks, the soft roll of his reading voice serving as a balm, the words a communiqué from another world. Henry arranged Samuel, beet red and squalling, in the valley of his lap, then flipped through the pages. This was a shared habit of their mornings and nights, looking for something he hadn't yet read. Here was a chart of worms in Kentucky soils, a diagram of the Cincinnati Arch, a quote about the men of Tierra del Fuego killing old women before dogs, because dogs are more useful. Finally, he found a fresh page and read over Samuel's cries: "Gene Schwartz Jefferson Lecture, transcribed from Penn's tape."

The speech was scrawled in excerpts that covered a half dozen pages. Henry transformed the words into a parent's singsong as he read: " 'I am a farmer and always have been. When I was born, this country supported thirty-two million farmers. My mother used the *Farmer's Almanac* to teach me to read, and my father took me out in the fields before I was even able to walk and instructed me properly in the art of plantation. I was educated in the very best sense of the word.

" 'But something has gone amiss in the almost sixty years since I was born. Today, America has only four million farms. That is less than two percent of the population—less than two percent! Can you think of anything less significant than that? Yes, one percent, and it's coming. We're on a slippery slope to a postagricultural hell. The how and why of this turn of events is a painful story, and a portentous one if the best predictor of the future is the past.' "

The singsong lilt slipped from Henry's voice. Samuel was hiccupping his way into calm, listening now with rapt attention, his wide, deep gaze locked on Henry's face.

" '. . . We live in a consumptive world, where we consume more food than we need, where animals are forced to consume our cast-off poisons and the bodies of their own species, where we use more of the world's resources than is right, where we empower corporations, which consume the lives of their workers with all the blessings of our government, which grants them the same rights and recognitions historically reserved for humans by the Fourteenth Amendment—the amendment designed to guarantee slaves their status as human beings! This, my friends, is consumption. And if you will recall, consumption is an insidious disease, creating for much of its progress the illusion of increased vitality. It promises health, but it delivers death.

" 'We founded this nation under the illusory notion of independence, and we have suffered from that disastrous ideal ever since, this notion that a man's life is entirely distinct from the life of his neighbor; that the poisons in his water have no bearing on the cleanliness of his neighbor's water; that the suffering of a laborer has no direct relationship to the purchaser of goods; that animals are objects for sale; that the health of the land is divorced from the health of the collective. We've turned freedom from tyranny into freedom from each other.

" 'In the 1700s, when we fought our war for supposed independence, we were actually securing our rightful dependence upon the land, upon each other, and upon our deepest religious impulses, which cannot be governed by a king, but only by mystical union with . . . We have always been trying to establish a mystical union with what is ultimately ineffable. This invisible reality leaves its mark everywhere; in friendship, intimacy, prayer without dogmatism, laughter, compassion. Camus said man's only real choice is whether or not to commit suicide. I say when we choose not to commit suicide, our reasons for living divulge the meaning of life itself. They give voice to the ineffable. And all of those reasons for living point us toward community, rather than singularity and division.

" '. . . These days, I'm often accused of being a moralist, but if this is a critique, if being called a moralist is now an insult, then it merely indicates how far we've fallen and how resolute and inflexible our relativism has become. Unlike many of you, I was born immediately after the Second World War. If the twentieth century was not a clarion call for humanity to awaken and choose sides, what could possibly wake us? It was a time for staking moral claims. Yet our sleepwalking culture persists in looking for the easy answer, waiting for someone to tell us what to think. I'm not here to tell you how and what to consume, what technologies to embrace or avoid, how to organize your communities, how to vote, how to live. America has many ills, but none greater than the refusal of so many to think long and hard, to think critically. We must learn to be choosers, not merely receivers; to be self-critical; to cast a suspicious eye on the powers that be, including one's own unearned power. We want easy answers, but we must refuse them. The only true answer is to think.' "

Samuel was finally deeply asleep. He lay there, Henry's right hand a warm cradle under his head, his breath coming in even passes and collecting around them both as a pocket of warmth. Looking down at him, Henry's heart beat a complicated rhythm. He remembered suddenly his own daughter as a child, so flush with life, a life he had always assumed was indistinct from his. Yet, here he was holding her difference in his very hands even after her death. In life, he had held up her flesh only as a mirror. Now a complication was rising like bile; it was bitter with the first taste of regret.

Barely able to turn his gaze from Samuel's face, Henry fumbled back through the leaves of the notebook, looking for something he had spied earlier. Yes, there it was: a Sandgap address for Penn, presumably the same one who owned the tape. An 859 telephone number. Under the number, scrawled in Henrietta's impatient handwriting, he read the sentence again: *The movement of evolution is from simple to complex.*

Animalia—Chordata—Vertebrata—Aves—Passeriformes—Hirundinidae— Progne subis: In one of the many mysteries of spring, the purple martins, our loyal, royal swallows, return in pairs to their high nesting grounds in the hills of Kentucky. Here, their young fledge every year. They come in monogamous pairs as if a compass were guiding them, driven forward by a wild, inborn sense of the sun and the poles, a knowledge deep within the eye that has little to do with sight.

I was and am forever trapped not by Father, but by myself. Until I become a god or a bird. Irony is life's central condition. A god experiences no limitations, which is why it cannot exist. Or if a god exists, you cannot experience it or think about it or know it, because it has no explicable border. What can't be talked about is not worth talking about. That's what I mean by irony.

She followed him everywhere, even as he traveled like one of those martins, drawn inexorably back to his place of origin. The farm he found—if you could call it that—was a humble copestone atop the outer fortifications of the mountains. A proper gentleman's farm perhaps fifty years prior, the white farmhouse long shorn of its beauty, and the Lincoln log corncrib slumping to rot in the rocky soil. Of the numerous pastures fitted onto these high flats, fully half were unturned, and Henry soon saw why. A man— presumably the man he sought—was struggling in the right field with a plow and two thick-necked oxen. What old-time conceit was this? They seemed ghosts of the previous century, now stymied in the mud, the blade of the plow lodged in the late February muck, the oxen sunk to their fetlocks in the mire. One ox brayed heavily as if in warning when it spotted Henry's car. Like an animal sensing danger, the driver remained very still for a moment, shielding his brow, then he raised one muddy hand in greeting, and Henry returned the gesture.

The man called out across the pasture, "Boots on the porch!"

There were old, weather-crackled LaCrosse hunters behind Henry on the warped porch boards. He slipped off his fine loafers and pressed his feet and wool trouser hems into the mud-caked boots. Then he trudged out into the early-spring fields, feeling foolish and vaguely abused. But this man had known his daughter.

The man had gray and black hair, thick as a barge rope and cinched by an elastic at the nape. Gray-green eyes and freckles, incongruous on a face so lined—lined less by age perhaps than a life spent outside hunting and drinking and doing this, tending to a thankless plot of land attached to a threadbare home. Couple of curs for company. A talent for home brew. An old truck, some pornography, some pot. It wasn't hard to imagine.

Before Henry could introduce himself, the man pointed to the ground where the old moldboard plow was lodged and said, "Not much rain this week, but there's this funny spot"—he gestured at the declivity where the field sloped gently like the sides of a French salad bowl—"and I forgot . . . it holds rain. I fill it every spring and harrow around it . . . but it sinks again every winter." The man had something slow and untutored about him, or it seemed that way because of his measured speech, but he had wide, watchful eyes that took quiet notes on everything around him, even as his mouth was busy with something else.

Henry said, "You should have plowed in the fall." It startled him that he remembered that; it had been over forty years since he'd last witnessed a laying-in.

"Had pneumonia," the man said simply, then gestured at the coulter and share, wedged deep in the mud. "You guide these guys . . . and I can press the plow. Straight like an arrow now."

Henry did as the man asked, standing at the shoulder of the enormous lead ox with one hand to its bridle, and when Penn gave a heaving, half-angry cry of encouragement in the plow lines, the oxen impended forward as one, and—twice, thrice, four times, they did this until the man's voice was nearly wracked with calling "Git up!" and, with a sucking slosh and a spattering of fresh, clean mud, the plow moved forward and continued to trundle along the earth. Down the row they went, unfurling a slow wave of brown soil, the traces tinkling. Henry let loose the bridle of the lead ox and Penn drove the train with ease now that they had achieved level ground. Comparatively free, the oxen moved swiftly along and Henry watched as the chest of the earth was sliced open. The exposed earth wriggled with life: *Lumbricus terrestris, Narceus americanus, Procellio scaber, Armadillidium nasatum, Talpa europaea, Walckenaeria acuminata*, and all the *Kingdom Monera* and all the *Kingdom Protista*. His daughter knew them all by heart. These bottom-feeder servants would now feast on the remains of the supposedly higher plants.

When they cleared the last forty yards of the row, Penn called "Gee!" and the team made the lumbrous turn onto the next unriven row; they moved as the Greeks had written their language. But Penn pressed back with the full weight of his body, crying, "Whoa!" which Henry mirrored instinctively with a soft "Whoa," and the whole rattling configuration came to a halt.

It was only now, with the leggy oxen resting idle in their harnesses, that Henry could take a proper look at them. They stood to his chest, their enormous white bulk—solid and stolid as if carved from marble yet radiating heat—brockled thick with black. Upon closer inspection, one ox's black was more like midnight blue with white showing through like fat stars. Their long backs were plain with white but without the black that peppered their blockish heads. Their points too were black. They were animals of distinct stature, boasting a heavy, bulky dignity even as ropy mucus strings spooled from their nostrils and eager flies pestered them. Henry had never seen anything quite like them before.

"Randall Linebacks," Penn said, approaching the blue and patting it where the yoke beam pressed into the heavy flesh of the neck. "America's rarest breed. Colonial cattle. They came out of a closed herd up in Vermont. I got these two, because . . . I can't work on tractors. And I can't afford a tractor. Repairs are too expensive."

As if in response, one ox lowed and stamped and rubbed with irritation against the curves of the oxbow.

Penn swiped at his sweaty face with his sleeve, but just smeared warrior lines of sweat and soil. He said, "They weren't worth a damn when I got them here . . . Barely plow trained. This one especially, Boss"—he pointed to the steer with the blue buckling—"was just ornery. Every time I'd say gee, he went left. Every time I said haw, he'd go right . . . I could have got more done with a team of fainting goats." He indicated with one hand. "That black one's Taurus. She named them."

Henry said nothing. He just listened.

Penn shoved his hands in his pockets and fixed Henry with an unblinking stare. "Thanks for calling me. I wouldn't have known . . . Sometimes she just didn't show up here for a long time."

Henry nodded once.

Then Penn said, "I loved your daughter," and the man's forthright declaration startled Henry into looking into his broad face. Dappled spring sun was playing with shadow there like fleetings of emotion. The man said simply, "I really did."

It seemed Henry could actually feel the spinning of the earth as he said, "And did she love you?"

"Eh, you know," the man said with a dismissive shake of his weather-roughened hands, then, "Let me tie up these guys . . . I'll show you a place she liked."

With some effort he led the oxen to a line of old chestnut fencing that separated a fallow pasture from the clodded soil they had just turned. Using the plow lines, he secured the pair to the upper plank, which they sniffed and tongued with their ropy, inquisitive tongues, turning the wood dark with saliva.

Penn patted a sloping haunch and then they were off along the northern edge of the unturned field. At one point, without stopping, Penn grasped up a small rock from the soil and flung it out as far as he could into the field, the way a boy hurls a stone into a river to savor the violence in his own arms. He said, "I trusted Henrietta. She wasn't always nice, you know? You can't really trust anybody who wants to please you all the time— Hey, arrowhead."

This time he stooped and grasped up a slate-gray chipped piece of flint, ancient and smooth-sided but still miraculously sharp. He handed it to Henry.

"Maybe she was kind of messed up. I don't know. No offense. I went in the marines when I was still a kid, and I came out just . . . Most people probably aren't worth much till they're messed up. But I could be wrong about that."

The pair passed a black, sagging tobacco barn, a sink like a meteor hole, and trees skirted by bushes. There came a rustling in the depths of one thicket, then a dog leaped onto the path, bounding toward them with his tongue a loll and his tail a banner over his back. Penn patted the dog and pointed up ahead of them where spindly trees clung to a rocky outcropping. "Your daughter liked this spot. Jack, stay. Stay."

Henry stepped carefully onto the rock outcropping and stood very still, gazing straight ahead into the bliss or abyss, feeling his feet on the earth even as his forehead penetrated porous clouds. The green earth sprawled before him, but it seemed more like mockery than beauty. He felt dizzy and barely rooted as all of space went sheering past his body with a horrifying velocity, which he'd not understood before. He sensed it now because grief had rent the beautiful fabric of his former self. He could hear time whistling through the hollows of his bones. Grief had sucked out all the marrow.

Henry swayed precipitously, so Penn reached quickly for the point of his elbow, then placed one steadying arm around his shoulders. They stood side by side like father and son, one just approaching old age and one middle-aged, both staring into open space.

Penn cleared his throat. "But me," he said, as though the conversation had not stopped. "I just like to stand here and think. Standing up high like this, I feel like I can . . . like up here, you can see everything. It's the big view, you know. I feel lucky to have it. But what are you gonna do with a view like this? That's the question."

It felt like a dare, a challenge between men, regardless of how gently, how thoughtfully it was proffered. Henry shrugged off Penn's protective arm and stepped out to where the rock and soil crumbled away and looked down over the careening edge. He looked and looked and looked. But in the interstices of the rock formations, in the distant canopy of the trees, in the land, he saw nothing, not even history. The entire natural world was composed of dirt and its senseless inhabitants. His frustration mounted to agony.

He whirled around, his face stricken, and he cried, "What did my daughter think of?"

Instinctively, Penn grasped Henry's forearms and pulled him in toward him, asking sharply, "What? Here?"

"Yes!"

If Penn found the question odd, he didn't show it. He continued to grasp Henry's forearms as he considered this very seriously. Then his face brightened with remembrance and he said, "She thought of you. I remember now. She thought of your family name."

The fevers came and with them the dreams, so once the stars began their sardonic winking, he was rolling in her arms once more, his hips cracking against her coffin box, the lily-white baby hard as a bomb between them, then she was crying his name, which his dead mother had given him, or it was the sliver moon catcalling through the prison bars, and he was moaning himself awake in the jittery space between fever and wakefulness, thoroughly confused and baptized in sweat. He lay with dry eyes pressed to the crook of his arm, riding the tides of Hell's night breathing, the sound of her entrapment, his own: Get me out of this nightmare.

But there was something on the scent of harvested hay this early morning, a sharp, strange tune adrift on the barely moving air. He knew the source before his eyes could discover it in the dark—the little jock perched on a farrier's stool, an unlit cigar tilting jaunty from his lips, his hands patting a rhythm on his thigh.

"Reuben," Allmon said confusedly, the dream of alarm still in his mouth. He sensed the great shadow of Hell's head as it swung, curious, over the door.

"Fret not," said the jock, crossing his wiry legs. "I was just a-wandering through on my way to Hialeah, thought I'd say hello to the Barbary horse and the Cincinnati Kid—and here I find you just a-moaning and a-crying in your sleep, a right sorry sight to be sure." Reuben scooted his stool closer, his eyes shining in the moonlight. "What ails you, my little nut? There's a rattle in your chest and a tear in your eye."

Allmon's tongue was thick, a grotesque muscle suddenly unfamiliar in his mouth. It required all of his energy just to mutter, "You got something for pain?"

"Do I have anything for pain!" Reuben chuckled. "I am La Pharmacie du Quartier Hoss, but, why should I share with you? I came by my contraband honestly. Anyway"—a pinch of a grin—"are you not by your own admission a confidence man of great renown? Surely you have your own pick-me-ups?"

Allmon just groaned in frustration, one hand a hard lace over his forehead.

"No?" Reuben turned his head practically on its side. "Forsooth! What kind of deal did you strike with the old boss man, anyway?"

"No money till the end of the season."

Reuben's voice was low and without game. "How much exactly?"

Allmon told him.

Reuben crowed. "I wipe my ass with that!" Then he fairly tripped coming off his stool and stood tall, which wasn't tall at all, barely a child's height under Hell's chin. He held his arms wide, and Hell knocked her teeth once in irritation. "That's your infamous deal? That's what they taught you in the cement tower? No cash on the barrelhead, and gain all a gamble—on a persnickety bitch with a monster-truck ass, but toothpick bones and a bad attitude?"

"She's going all the way, and you know it," Allmon snapped, because she had to, and she would. For a moment he looked up at her towering darkness in the night, her breadth and height. He felt that for all his lifelong striving and desperation, he had nothing comparable to her enormous, innate power. All he had was his biography running through his veins, a biography that consisted of a single word: *Want*.

Reuben sighed. "Well, you've upset the apple cart, Allmon, yes indeed, and made yourself a wen on the scalp of a founding father." His voice grew cold as he sidled over. "But you're like the hillbilly who kills Old Master for forty swampy acres and a half-starved mule. Was that your biggest, baddest, blackest, ballsiest dream?" He looked down his nose in disdain.

"You don't know nothing." The words emerged as a deep, furious growl.

Reuben wagged his finger. "Nothing? You sure? I see the pink in your cheeks! The limp in your gait! Something tells me you've got the flushing disease—a precious gift from your mama, perhaps?"

"You best back the fuck up." This time the growl was deeper, crueler. But rough words couldn't erase a knowing that was very deep like bones at the bottom of the river. The movement of the river passes through their hollows, leaving them undisturbed, witnessed only by bottom dwellers. But Allmon hadn't reached the bottom yet.

"Admit it," Reuben hissed. "I know what I know! Yet here you are waiting for money like some brother on a street corner begging for change, when—ye gods!—time itself is the only currency! You ain't earned your black badge, Boy Scout! Sitting here like a goddamn naïf!"

Allmon actually made a move to rise, but he was so woolly and woozy with fever, Reuben required only a hand to his shoulder to press him back down on his cot. "Busy playing the horse's mammy," he continued, "thinking you got years to eat and ages to shit! You need a better dream, young man, one that won't fester, that won't start to stink."

Allmon slapped his hand away. "I lost everything! My momma died, my granddad! My . . ." He paused, whipsawed by the hellish feeling that consumed him at the thought of Henrietta. It had been sickeningly hard to learn any delight. And now delight had become the mother of rage. He held his arms out to either side. "They sent me up for trying to survive! For trying to make my way through their white fucking maze. You understand what I'm saying? They made it a crime for anybody to survive in the world they made!"

"So, why hasn't your suffering schooled you? Because you won't tell the tale, that's why! You're too busy trying to shit out prison instead of digesting it, letting it make you stronger! You got to build your blood, son!"

"I ain't your fucking son and my life ain't your business," Allmon snapped.

Reuben sighed. "Really, why must Queen Reuben come and do the dirty labor for the hesitant, lumbering Sons of Ham? Good thing Reuben's a practiced critter! Good thing he always has a stump speech at the ready!"

With gutting purpose, Reuben peered into Allmon's bleary, feverish eyes, and the groom sensed suddenly that the little man before him had changed not merely in demeanor but more fundamentally in appearance, having grown so that he was staring down at him, a man on stilt legs his tongue had constructed. Here was not the grinning jock of jokes and jabs but the calm, cold preacher on the circuit, cruel as God. It silenced whatever retort was forming on Allmon's lips.

Reuben said: "Now listen and listen good because I'll only say it once: I am the devil's midwife, the Messiah come in shape no bigger than a black man's fist in the face of the Kentucky colonel man. Drawn darker than a stub of burnt cork, he straddles the black brain as it sleeps awake. His silks are sound from the pickers' jubilee; the fine helmet of the overseer's skull; reins from the braids of white bitch bitties; black boots from the flays of baying backwater hounds; his crop right snatched from the Southern whipping hand, its handle fashioned from fingers that when felled, grabbled up Mississippi mud like velvet cake."

"What in the holy fuck," said Allmon, his anger stalling.

"Shhhhh," hissed Reuben, slipping closer with a finger to Allmon's lips. "He speeds upon a filly dark as lampblack made by some master behind hell's white fences, time out of mind the measure of all things. And on this destrier he gallops night by night through Jim Crow's brain, so he stills his pattering feet; so Brudder Bones and Tambo cease their infernal noise; over Miss Lucy Long's lips, those flaps of deceit that divest blackest words of their very meaning and whitewash thuggery with hijink cheer. Sometimes he gallops over Zip Coon's brow and then naked, Zip stands like a new man born of rage. And sometimes he comes with the great black book, bedeviling the black pastor, who, pilfering the plate, forgets the kingdom's to be had on earth as in heaven. Sometimes he rides like a dull knife over a soldier's neck and then he dreams of cutting fancy throats; of manacles, chains, whips, and iron collars; of ocean five miles deep. Awake, Reuben whispers in his ear, at which he starts and wakes and, imagining he is going somewhere anon, sleeps again."

Allmon shook his head. "You need to recognize you're crazy."

Reuben just batted away his words. "You are the benighted soldier that plaits the manes of horses even in the night, mere servant of the pale king's tresses which once untangled some reparation bodes. You are the one, when daughters lie on their backs, who frightens, fucks, and forces them to bear, making them mules strapped to their heavy carriage. It is you—"

"Fuck you."

Reuben rose abruptly. "I speak of your ambition, which is the heap of a moving bowel, bleached white at the core as Dinah Roe. Horseshit has trampled old memory, which woos even now the black bosom of the North, but you, being angry, stiffen your resolve and turn your face to the fruit-swinging South."

Allmon laid an arm over his face, pressed a hand to one ear. He couldn't tell whether he was asleep or awake. Maybe he'd never emerged from sleep at all.

Reuben just leaned down and whispered his conspiracy: "I hope too early, for my mind imagines some marvels soon hanging from those boughs, shall perfectly begin this late, aggravated date with Reuben's stump speech, and expire the term of some regnant lives, closed in a white breast, in some show of consequence or fate. But the devil or Christ that steers the course, direct his sail. On sleeping soldier!"

And then, laughing, Reuben hauled up his duffel bag, which was nearly as large as he was, and left, waiting until he was safely outside the dusty confines of the barn to light his Cuban cigar.

Even after six weeks of incarceration on limited rations and no exercise at all, the filly's self-possession was total, unwavering, and irritating as all get-out. She snapped at anyone fool enough to walk down her shed row, butted her head against her stall wall, and snarled out her window at each passing February day. This horse knew who she was—and she'd had more than enough.

"Oh, fuck it," Mack said, tired to death of his role as martinet. "Get this peccary head off her lead and into a porta-paddock. No more handwalking, no more coddling. I can't take this crap anymore."

She trained one wicked eye on Allmon when he entered the stall, but she didn't bite. Still, Allmon managed her head, through which coursed a high, almost electric energy. She was a hurricane in a black barrel.

"Goddamn," said Mack as he eased down slowly to a squat beside her, careful not to make a sudden movement. "Goddamn if I'm not a little bit scared of this filly. That's a first."

But the long, knobby leg was cool, and Allmon limped alongside Hell to a paddock constructed on the back of Mack's broodmare barn, where a sun the color of old lemons was shrinking the snow. The instant she felt the bite of the February air, Hell's nose rode high like a schooner on waves, and she began to skitter and dance to an old, unheard tune. Her tail snapped and her eyes shined with the bliss of the cold.

"Turn her loose," said Mack.

"Really?" said Allmon, pausing at the paddock gate.

"Can't never could," said Mack, flanked by two assistants. Then he reached forward and unclipped the shank to turn Hell loose.

For a long moment, she stood perfectly still in the paddock, her black mane waving and twisting in the squirrely wind, her nostrils wide as the world, her ears pricked forward toward something far beyond the confines of the paddock.

"My God," one of the assistants whispered. "Her legs are magnificent." The filly's ears swiveled back, then without so much as a tinge of hesitation denoting pain, she sank into those magnificent legs, her rump a boss of rippling muscle, and leaped forward like a deer from her quarters. Two strides and Mack was beginning to yell; three more and, without altering her speed or veering, Hell crashed chest-first into the metal rim of the pen, sending ripples of shock along its length until it bent under her force. She stumbled heavily against the resistance as if startled, then jerked away and spun around toward her handlers, her eyes lined with high white. Lips furled back nearly to her tattoo, she cried out a wild, shrill, enraged sound that pinned them all, except for Mack, who had flung his hat from his head and raced into the paddock, hollering, "She's gonna charge! She's gonna break her legs!" Allmon didn't know whether it was an honest escape or merely to exercise her natural strength, but he was there inside of two seconds, ready when she leaped forward again, strings of saliva swooping from her bared teeth, her breath a wind shear against his face. She feinted left, then dodged right, but they had her circled. Allmon snatched hold of her halter and drew her head savagely around where he could gain a proper hold. Only then did he see the jagged wound that had opened across her breast, the thin marbled fat exposed beneath. With a start, he realized that Hell—competitor, champion, beauty, his future—was raw meat.

They managed two lunging steps forward with Allmon at the halter, whispering and cajoling and petting her with his voice. But Hell didn't want sweet nothings; in a flash she traced a swift circle with her head and butted him with the long, blunt ridge of her nose. She sent him sprawling elbows akimbo into the dirt.

Allmon cried out, more from surprise than pain as Mack scrambled to restore a hold on the halter. She'd never snapped at Allmon before, never once tried to best him. Now he rose to his feet, his face twisted up with swift, furious offense.

It took the strength of seven to wrestle Hell back to her stall.

While Mack went sprinting for his cell phone, she stood there with her head high, blood running tracks down her front legs, squaring eyeball to eyeball with Allmon, who stood safely on the other side of the stall door. They both shook with grievance.

"Is that how it's gonna be?" he hissed. "I'm the enemy now?"

She raised her lip.

"Well, then this is what you get!" He gestured with a lashing motion at the hay, the dim light, the stall, knowing full well that until the day she quit racing, when they retired her from the track and began forcing select stallions on her, that long-awaited moment when he, Allmon, would make a real life for himself with one of her foals, she would never experience a moment of freedom again.

Copied into the fourth notebook, from K. Aubere's *Limitless Variation and the Advent of Life*:

> *For a billion years, there was little, only the brownish green scum of the seas. Nothing but basalt rock existed on a land deprived of oxygen and blasted by ozone. In the waters, life was a thin, primitive, fragile sheet. Single-celled, prokaryotic organisms clung to one another like magnetic bits of thread, accreting and forming these microbial mats. Photosynthetic organisms crowded to the top, striving for light, while their buried peers split the weaker sulfide bonds to survive.*
>
> *But the wheel of the world was spinning, the mats mutating and diversifying, spreading throughout the seas. In a blink of the earth's basalt eye, eukaryotic organisms emerged, algae-like with their organelles, tiny harbingers of complexity. Tissues and organs soon followed.*
>
> *540 million years ago, Nature reached down, took up all her organisms, and cast them like dice. Invertebrate life tumbled throughout the seas, and in wild radiations, the ocean phyla appeared in startling profusion. Soon, the algae blossomed into plants, which marched out of the waters onto temperate land and blanketed the terrain from sea to sea with vegetation. Tiny animals then emerged to*

*burrow and tunnel through earth's undiscovered soils. The world was
redolent with new bodies.*

*But why the sudden and dizzying acceleration of life in the
Cambrian? Why then and not before? For 4 billion years, the rate of
expansion had been placid, steady. The fossil record is slim, the
cupboard nearly bare.*

*Freedom. Oxygen levels rose in the Cambrian, there was a cooling of
the earth's simmer, followed by a sudden, sigmoidal rise. In land's
abundant light, single-celled life strengthened and augmented,
occupying new adaptive roles. The first land plants became coal forests
that grew taller with each generation. The denizens of the seas grew to
an inch, then a foot, then a meter in the form of terrifying fishes that
established suzerainties in the depths. Extinctions shook the dynasties of
the earth, cutting down classes and orders—though the phyla never
vanished. They simply regathered their troops and when the Age of
Reptiles began, dinosaurs thundered over carpets of insects and beetles,
flowers and ferns. Mammals broke the trees and cut blazes, and then the
apes appeared, and the ape men eventually stood up. They spread out
from the bowl of Africa to Europe and Asia with crude tools in their
hands and eyes evolved to gaze ahead at the horizon. But then Homo
emerged out of the family Hominidae, and brought with him that very
late and crude invention, the human brain. The rest, as they say, is
history.*

She wasn't green anymore, she was seasoned, and she was enormous. The
turf writers flocked around her at Gulfstream—Todd Greeney from the
Racing Form, Jeff Burrow of *Blood Horse*, and all the rest. Mack hated
the press; as far as he was concerned, fielding a single question was an unforgivable waste of his daylight, but the track management had requested
it—hell, they'd all but demanded the press conference, so here he was,
every pugnacious, impatient, hypertensive, contemptuous ounce of him.
While Hellsmouth stood at attention with Allmon at her chin, Mack barked
out her numbers in a blunt staccato:

"Height: 16 hands, ¾ inches.

"Point of shoulder to point of shoulder: 16 inches.

"Girth: 74 inches.

"Withers to point of shoulder: 28 inches.

"Elbow to ground: 37½ inches.

"Point of shoulder to point of hip: 46 inches.

"Point of hip to point of hock: 40 inches.

"Point of hip to buttock: 24 inches.

"Poll to withers: 40 inches.

"Buttock to ground: 53½ inches.

"Point of shoulder to buttock: 68 inches.

"Circumference of cannon under knee: 8¼ inches.

"Point of hip to point of hip: 25 inches—she's got a big ass.

"All right, now you know the numbers. Clearly, she's huge."

Greeney squinted, tilted his head, and said, "Mack, you've waited for the Florida Derby to race her. It's pretty clear you're going straight for races that offer you a hundred points and not messing around with smaller stakes. Why are you getting such a late start? Is there something we don't know? You're not exactly known for being conservative."

Mack reached up and touched the pale brim of his hat, forming a brief shield over his features, then he squared up and stared down his interlocutor as though an epithet had been hurled in the general direction of his mother. "First off, I'm a registered Republican, and I'm conservative as fuck. Second, there's nothing wrong with my filly. She's a hundred percent. Actually, this filly's two hundred percent."

"Then why'd you—"

"Because," Mack said, his lips thin, "I've got nothing to prove. I know where she's headed."

"Is she breaking from the gate any better?"

Mack grimaced. "No, that's still a shit show."

A writer from the *Herald* said, "She's still running from behind?"

"Listen, yeah," Mack said, then sighed, hands to his hips. "What you guys don't understand about women is a lot. Smart women, they get bored easy. This one here, she's so much better than the rest, she has to manufacture her own challenge. If she didn't come from behind, she'd fall asleep on her own goddamn feet."

Greeney again: "But do you feel she's gotten enough conditioning to come back with the kind of performance she was capable of last year? We've all watched a lot of juveniles burn out in their third year. You think she'll be ready without warm-ups?"

Mack's patience was about sapped. He jutted out a blunt finger into the air in front of his chest with all the cocked force of a small revolver. "This filly just burned up five furlongs in fifty-eight and a half," he spat. "You could cut off one of her goddamn legs and she'd still run faster than that bowlegged hack Angelshare."

Greeney was shaking his head, a grin twitching about his lips. "Can I quote you on that?"

"Go ahead and quote me. I think we all know I'm not gonna die of natural causes."

They broke up laughing.

But one voice pierced the laughter. "Yeah, I'm not buying it." It was Jeff Burrow, tipping his ball cap up from the springy mass of his graying brown hair. He'd worked the track for thirty years, and there were numerous things he was afraid of, including his semper fi father-in-law and butterflies, but Mack Snyder was not on that list. "Let's stop beating around the bush. You're hard on horses, everybody knows it. Your filly's big as a boat, that's great, it's impressive. But she skipped all the spring prep races, and now you bring her to Florida with a busted-up chest. How do you know you're not setting her up to be another Ruffian?"

Mack started at the reference. Everyone could see the war on Mack's face as he struggled to manage dueling armies of blustercuss and knickertwist. His normal raw porcine pink bloomed to a beefy red. He stepped toward Burrow with that finger still extended and the safety off, but, as if on cue, in a massive show of bravado, Hellsmouth sank into her heavily muscled quarters and reared high, rolling her hooves above the heads of the gathered men. Without a beat, Allmon scrambled to manage her.

Mack laughed a gravelly laugh and turned his pointing finger toward his horse. "How do I know? I know because I'm in love with her. And I never loved anybody that didn't know how to fight."

She was frothing in the post parade and fractious in the gate, whinnying for free rein and snarling at the bars of the five slip. Reuben eased his bones off the rails and situated himself on her back, snugging up his knees and fixing tight his goggles. He pressed the red crop under his arm, licked his lips, and surveyed the dirt track before him. He'd been waiting all winter like Hell's war wife and here they were, reunited at the edge of a triumphant future. Hell had been crushing furlongs—absolutely demolishing them—in her morning workouts all week. She'd drawn the faithful railbirds with their cameras at dawn; she'd made the chief clocker stutter with excitement. Now she was tossing her black braids, banging her rump once against the rear door. She was more than ready, she was bursting out of her skin.

"Come out," Reuben whispered, staring through the crack in the gate. "Come out for blood." Now the jocks balanced their mounts. The sun was streaming light so loud they could hear it like a banging drum. When the burn of expectation mounted to out-and-out pain, the bell shrilled, and the gate clattered wide. An earthquake cracked through the stands, and the Florida Derby was on.

In a move that made the announcers shout, Hell broke clean as new glass beneath Reuben. She sheared out so suddenly without her usual sink and bob that he had to snatch manically at the roots of her braids and tuck hard to remain aboard. Was it only yesterday morning that she'd shambled out of the gate with her old loose-limbed stride? This was altogether new, how she plunged past the charging field inside of three paces, long before the first turn. Gone was her adolescent chop and her early wastrel furloughs. In their place a deep and powerful lunging had asserted itself. With every stride, she reached further forward, her nose piercing the air with a fresh and dreadful aggression. It was as if a new horse were unfurling under Reuben; he recovered his wits, doubled down upon her, one ear thrilling to the warrior report of her hooves.

The crowd didn't wait for the turn, they rose in a jolt at the ⅞ pole, every eye locked on the charging filly as she took possession of the field. She was too strong to be pretty, but she had something in her new maturity far better than beauty: dignity. The colts all felt her occult energy; they sensed it like a shadow tilting over them and dropped away as if they'd slowed up, though in reality they only charged the harder. As the stunned field wound out of the turn and into the straightaway, never once did Reuben think to raise his crop to tap her on a shoulder or quarter. Hell was riding a wave of her own power and needed no spur to draw the first four lengths between her and Angelshare, which was when Reuben first became aware of the unearthly roll of sound ripping across the grandstand. "The devil's on his long black train," he muttered as four lengths turned to seven. Seven to ten, and her wave began to crest and unfurl with unmitigated strength. She was pulling further away and the words of the announcer were unclear, but Reuben knew the man was yelling. Poured across her back, he spared a thought to reserve her—go easy on that delicate bone— but he didn't or he couldn't as she rolled out her most destructive, punishing stride, now extending sixteen lengths from Angelshare and closing in on Secretariat's coppery ghost, so she was practically on his tail when she rolled thunderously under the wire twenty lengths ahead. She had slain the colts and flung dirt in their eyes, but her victory and Reuben's wild yell and the shattering cries of the crowd didn't alter her course; she continued to accelerate past the wire, her sweat unbroken, her huge heart untested. Reuben cawed and whooped and finally had to stand in the irons, hauling savagely on the reins. Hell whinnied and jerked her neck, arguing strenuously against her restraints, but finally, with an angry cry and a churlish toss of the head, she eased to a hard gallop. Now Stop the Music, poor fool, pulled up alongside her in his cooldown loop. Hell turned to him, her lips curled, her eyes like globes of a newly charted world. As the cameras rolled, she snaked out and bit the gelding savagely on the tender flesh of his ear. Both jocks cried out, wrestling for space, until Hell finally galloped away, a spring in her step and blood in her mouth. The season was on.

Old-timers were rooted to their seats that day. Tip-sheet hawkers gaped and the railbird kids were half-cracked with joy. The seasoned press? Some shed tears they'd held in reserve since 1973. Greeney, hunched over his laptop with his *Racing Form* deadline like a hand pressing on his chicken-fried, middle-aged heart, typed a sentence with stubby fingers, then erased it, typed, dragged, typed, erased. Finally, tapping his electronic cigarette against the black rim of his laptop, he could find nothing to declaim but this: They said it was an impossibility to rediscover the speed and poise of runners past. They said the golden age of racing was over and gone, the sport nothing but a relic from a forgotten time. But Hellsmouth, the unbeatable filly bred by Henry Forge of Paris, Kentucky, trounced the field here today at the Besilu Stables Florida Derby. The big girl did it by a towering twenty lengths at 1:44, destroying the standing record of 1:46⅘. To all the lucky fans who witnessed this historic Gulfstream race, one thing was perfectly clear. Hellsmouth didn't win because of Forge's brilliant breeding choices; she didn't win because of Snyder's unusually strict racing regimen or because she finally broke from the gate like a world-class athlete. No, reader, this horse won because she's a monster. My eyes are on the Triple Crown, and my money's on Hellsmouth. The superhorse is back.

No sooner was she crowned with laurels, no sooner was her name in lights, than she went hot. When Allmon's hand first touched her leg, he couldn't tell whether it was his own high fever or hers. But no—she was a burning stove compared to him. In an instant, Allmon's heart was lodged in his throat, and sweat prickled at the corners through his eyes. His hands fumbled again at her leg, but no doubt about it now: she was swollen along the old injury.

Two minutes later Mack was careening into the stall, his cell in his hand, steam pluming from his ears, his white-man lips gone even thinner. Another two minutes and Jameson was there, that old vet, that adminis-trator of milkshakes and cobra venom, of steroids and Equipoise. He and Mack conferred, they rubbed their stubbly jaws with lined hands, their hooded eyes met, and they nodded. Then Jameson, who had advised his multitude of like-minded hacks in other barns, who then churned out simi-lar prescriptions like monkeys at typewriters, reached into his gear bag and produced a syringe. Allmon stood there, eyes wide, not sure yet what he was watching.

Sensing his hesitation, Jameson looked up from where he was tapping the syringe. "It's just painkiller," he said. "We should all be so lucky."

There was a tiny, sharp moment, like the head of a pin, when Allmon felt an almost insuperable urge to reach out and stay the man's hands, and thought: Not this way. If she's hurting, don't run her. But then the pin dropped, and the whole of his history rose up and his eyes grew hard. Yes, it's better to not feel. Absolutely. Then Jameson jabbed the syringe into Hell's warm flank, rubbed the spot with a practiced, calloused hand, and grinned a knowing grin. Allmon couldn't return the smile, too busy strangling the

voice that asked, Is this really what you want? To crouch in the shadow of
that tree and divvy up her earthly possessions: her bridle, saddle, her blanket, and her whale's heart? Is this really what you want?

Jeff Burrow had only one simple question: "Is she sore, Mack?"

Mack said, "Nope."

Burrow said, "Well, that's interesting, because your hotwalker said she
was limping."

Mack said, "Thanks for the tip. I'll fire my hotwalker."

Burrow said, "You gonna keep her nominated for the Derby?"

Mack said, "What do you think?"

Burrow said, "I think she might—*might*—make it through the Derby,
but from what I hear Jesus doesn't hand out Derby wins like party favors.
Even for those who pray at the altar of cortisone and Winstrol."

Mack sniffed hard, scrunched up his eyes. He put his thick hands on
his Wranglered hips. He had a backcountry bon mot just waiting there on
the tip of his tongue, but when he opened his mouth, all that came out
was, "Fuck you, Jeff. On behalf of my horse, who has more talent in her
hoof than your entire family tree. One hundred thousand fucking percent
fuck you."

A wild desire had overcome Henry Forge, as strong and strident as the
surges of spring. The hard labor of winter was done, and the sun was beginning to ripen the world. When March winds were winding up and early
daffodils punctured the fluorescent soil, Henry could contain the urge no
longer and called Penn, who said, "Yeah, I've been a little covered up, but
this is good timing. Now's sort of the sweet spot."

He drove up on a Saturday afternoon, his rust-scabbed Toyota coughing exhaust up the long Forge drive. The closer he drew, the slower he
drove, eyes widening behind the wheel as he absorbed the patrician heights
of the house, the barns bright like snow blindness, stark equine silhouettes
in the distance where the land swept down into a bowl bisected by a stream.
Holy shit, he thought, taking it all in. She really did come from money.

He found Henry waiting there as still as a cenotaph on the el porch as if he'd been standing there the whole day, or possibly his whole life. At first, Penn was struck by the similarity again between this father and the woman he had known—the slim, elegant frame, the coppery hair. Then he noticed the child in Henry's arms. From his erect perch against Henry's chest, the boy sported all the wide, bright-eyed curiosity of a seal. He was fine, fat, and waving his chunky arms at the sunshine in obvious delight. Penn didn't care one way or another about babies, and yet . . . this was Henrietta's child, all that was left of her. She had died bringing him into the world. Should he hate it? Perhaps. But when he approached and the child laughed at him for no reason that any grown man could grasp, Penn smiled. He couldn't quite muster a laugh.

The two men met again, and they shook hands properly this time. Then, in silent, mutual agreement, they walked southward, Henry on the el porch and Penn along a tended bed of eager, nodding daffodils. When he reached the banister, Henry lowered Samuel so he could stand his slippered feet against the wood and said, "This is the space I described on the phone." Then he bent to kiss Samuel's curly head and, at the same time, pointed out toward the apple orchard and the slim clearing between the last budding trees and old windbreak, forty years in its growing, durable now as any chestnut fencing.

Penn stood there with his hands on his thick hips, chewing his lip and taking measure this way and that. He said, "Well, if you want to grow your own food like how we talked about, you've got plenty of room."

"I've thought about it, and I've decided I'd like to do more than that. Feed more than us."

"Really?" said Penn, dubious, looking around and wondering, How many folks could there be to feed? Forge didn't seem like the type who wanted to start a CSA or something.

"And flowers," Henry said.

"Flowers? Sure, well, it's March, I could . . . maybe lay in some pansies if you want."

"What else?" Samuel raised a sudden squall, so Henry drew him back to his chest, where he was nestled easily, his little cherub's face turned into his grandfather's chest.

"Well . . . ," Penn said, studying the idea for a moment. "You could maybe transplant in viola, some Lenten rose. But most early flowers . . .

they're bulbs, you know. You plant them in the fall when everything's going to seed. Now in a month . . . I could lay in just about anything you want. Make a real flower garden."

"Yes, I want a field of flowers. My grandson will like that."

Penn smiled, but he was silent as he looked on the pair. There was something he didn't quite trust about the older man. Not that he was a bad guy necessarily . . . just not fully formed or something. Did he want to grow a garden, or did he want to be the kind of guy who grew a garden?

Eh, what did it matter? Penn shrugged in his mind. He was watchful and methodical, the guardian of his own opinions, of which he had more than a few, but ultimately he would help out anyone in need. It's how his dumb ass got sent to war.

"And I'd like to prepare additional space for next year." Henry stepped down off the porch, so that he stood shoulder to shoulder with Penn. "Put marigolds and petunias in after the freeze."

The younger man's head ticked to the left. "Sure," he said, "but if that's what you want, you're gonna need more room. What's with these bushes?" He gestured to his right.

"That's a windbreak."

"Well, it's in the way. You need it?"

Henry hefted his grandson higher onto his chest and, brow crumpled, watched as the boy busily gummed his own fist. He smelled like sunlight and the warm, particular, inimitable scent, which was his own person. His eyes were bright and impossibly untroubled. "Perhaps not," Henry said softly.

"But you'll need a backhoe."

"I have a backhoe."

"Well," said Penn with a smile, shaking his head slightly. "All right. Show me where the backhoe's at."

So, they worked together, he and Penn. First Henry laid out a checkered tablecloth upon which Samuel rolled and made his froggish motions in the sun, a shaker clutched in his hands. One eye to Samuel, Henry helmed a rototiller that chewed its lurching way through the tender lawn, as Penn, perched on the sun-busted seat of the backhoe, began to extract the edges of—

—my God, I get so tired sometimes, I can't tell you how it was. I try to cut to the pith with the blade of my life, but it's a dull blade from a common kitchen. My people came out of the mountains to Ohio; my grandfather was born in a tent near the oil wells, and my parents were poor. I'm not beautiful or clever; all I can offer is the brief portrait of a spring's plantation, the smell of the sweat of labor, the color of a child's eye, and sometimes not even that. What can you do? You can't pray for yourself. The gods disallow it—

"Hey! Henry!" Penn had ground the backhoe to a halt and was twisted back and around with one hand gripping the bucket seat, the other on the wheel. "What is this? You want it out?"

Henry left his post at the rototiller and picked his way along the fresh soil until he rounded the edge of the remaining windbreak. There the thing jutted out of the earth like an arrow pointing to the sky. For a moment, Henry could not configure the object in his mind, could make no sense of its height, its brown hue, the wood patina like rot. Then, when memory finally slid home and he realized it was the old whipping post, he couldn't speak, couldn't blink. Time rolled back his eyelids and pinned them to his skull.

He whispered something barely intelligible.

"What?" said Penn, leaning down. "You want it out . . . ?"

Henry drew in one tremble of breath, made a roundabout gesture with one hand. When Penn just shook his head in confusion, Henry raised his voice. "Leave it there," he said. "Make a scarecrow of it."

Penn grinned slowly, then nodded. "For the garden. Right. Yeah. We can dress it up in some of your old clothes or something." Then righting himself on the seat of the backhoe, he brought the engine back to life and managed to uproot the rest of the tangled thicket without disturbing the post where it remained, leaning like an old ruin, dark and scarred, a remnant of centuries-old hickory and hurt.

But Henry could not continue in his work. He turned his back on the post and walked the freshly fertile ground to Samuel, who was now gnawing fistfuls of fresh grass. As Henry plucked grass from his lips, the child began to whimper and then wail in outrage. Henry lowered himself to his knees, grasping the child's crabby face in his hands and looking down at him with bright sadness and satisfaction. Again, he reckoned with the full enormity of the change in himself. The change was a disturbance and more: a deeper, astonishing resolution. For a moment, in the golden almost-liquid beauty of the afternoon, he felt that his daughter had finally fallen silent. Her mouth was shut, the ink in her notebooks dry. His grief felt less like the crushing of his chest and more like the memory of the crushing. Was the worst of his pain over? Was that possible?

Henry walked to the kitchen to make a gold rush for two: bourbon with lemon and honey over ice. He passed the site of the original kitchen fifteen yards from the house, a kitchen that was razed when they filled in the old ice well. He had been seven then, just a kit in the yard, his mother a minx. He passed a hand over his eyes, weary and wary of his old mind.

As he arranged two icy tumblers on an old silver tray, a gem Lavinia had bought at auction in Nashville on a horse-buying trip, the landline shrilled. His hand jerked, and a tumbler shattered to shards in the white ceramic basin of the sink.

When he grasped up the receiver, the voice—firmly lodged in the nose and unmistakably northeastern—said: "Mr. Forge? Hello, I'm so glad to have reached you. I'm the assistant to M. J. Deane. I'd like to congratulate you on your amazing horse."

"Thank you very much."

"I'm sure you're getting more interview requests than you can field, but my employer would very much like to interview you for a book on Kentucky history and horse racing. Would you be at all interested in participating?"

Henry was silent for a moment, trawling through the recesses. The name flicked at the edges of familiarity.

Into the silence the woman said, "Deane writes mysteries, but also general nonfiction. Perhaps you have read some of the books, or at least seen them around. Or articles in *The New Yorker*. On cuisine, mostly."

The food articles—yes, that rang a bell. And, of course, he realized now, he'd seen the books in airports. With one careful hand, he reached down to arrange the glass shards, which littered the sink. "Yes," he said. "Yes, I believe we can work something out."

The assistant said, "Wonderful. Well, an interview on the morning of the Derby would be perfect, if that's not too much to ask. I'm sure that will be a crazy day for you, but we figured there's no harm in asking."

"The morning of the Derby?" It was an odd, even improbable request. He hesitated. But this wasn't a journalist from a local paper or even the *Times*; this was something more intriguing, potentially more durable. A book featuring the Forge name. It stirred him. "Yes," he said slowly, "that might be possible."

"Will you be in Louisville or in Paris that morning, sir?"

He was startled to discover that he had no ready answer. Of course, he should be in Louisville—for the parties, the glad-handing, the carousing that would precede the running of the race. And yet . . . he gazed out the window, his heart a tuning fork tuned to Samuel. He watched his tiny grandchild on his fat belly, grasping again at bunches of grass; he was like a foundling who had arrived with a message for change from the deep underworld, a note passed to him from his daughter. So she was not silent after all. A knowing pressed up into the space where his heart had been knocking about uselessly for so long. It was both a blessing and an affliction. Relaxation flooded his body as if his old, worn organs were being replaced with an emptiness that was not terrifying but delicious. Into the emptiness wended a pride—yes, he was proud of everything he had accomplished, his farm and his horse, his new feelings for his grandchild, how he was transforming the family name. His smile was broad when he said, "Yes, I will be right here at Forge Run Farm on the morning of the Derby."

Ever the good doer, Hellsmouth downed three quarts of oats and snatched at two proffered carrots on the morning of the Wood Memorial. She traced her rounds and lay heavily down in the stall to rise knuckering four times—nothing out of the ordinary, her usual race-day routine. But as Allmon stood there at the stall door watching her rise like a black wave for the fourth time to level him with the watery burn of her lucent eyes, what he found was only a flat, uninviting darkness, interminable night sky between stars that had flamed out; in the place of her personality, there was nothing.

His own body was on fire in every joint, his hands woolly and too warm as he slipped into the stall, patted from the bunched shoulder to the coronet of the hoof. He was nearly disabled by fatigue but could tell the leg seemed good and cold; they'd drawn out the heat with an old-time poultice of bran, Epsom salts, and clay. Now painkillers coursed along her ropy veins, pulsing through each chamber of her overlarge heart, sloping down her gaskins, softening the tips of her ears.

Though something was rubbing her soul against the grain, all he said as he stared into those altered eyes was a dull, blunt, "You'll be fine."

When Mack turned down the row, Allmon made a sharp, beckoning gesture and said under his breath, as though the filly could hear and understand, "She's not happy."

"Who the hell is?" Mack snapped, but he squatted and turned his own hands down the length of the leg. "She's cold," he said from his stoop. "I'm getting nothing here." He leaned back on his haunches then, braced on one ruddy hand in the hay and peering up along the steep, sloped band of her nose. He sighed. "Give her some scotch. That'll turn her up."

Tucked behind posts draped with saddle blankets and a row of black velvety riding helmets, a smoky bottle of Caol Ila was kept on a shelf for just such a purpose. But when Allmon poured the scotch into the trembling scoop of his palm, which seemed so hot it would boil the liquor away, Hell just swung her head wide, and the tinkling of her stall bridle, very faint, was like Christmas sleigh bells without cheer.

"You'll be fine," he said again, but he didn't know whether he was talking to himself or the horse. All he knew was he didn't believe it.

Then Reuben; he sensed it in the saddling paddock when he was hoisted onto her gleaming back. Slipping his boots into the irons, he stopped suddenly as though listening for the faint beating of his own heart, then stooped in the irons, gazing bug-eyed down both sides of Hell's long face as she stared straight ahead, blinking sedately and swishing her tail once. He detected the pulse in her articulated runner's veins, then turned to Mack, his eyes narrowed. "What ails my black beauty?"

"She's cold," said Mack, but his brow was puckered. "She walked easy. You saw her."

Fraction by fraction, Reuben eased down, reassuming his wary spot on the saddle. "Oh girl, this ain't the time," he whispered. The diaphragm of his eyes constricted, so the nervous colts and that worser animal—the ungovernable crowd—faded to a blur. He said nary a mischievous word as Allmon led them away. Reuben looked nowhere but down, his eyes bending pencils of light as they emerged from the tunnel, so he took in only the shortest field—Hell's tented ears, and the gathering and releasing of her shoulders with each step. She came along sure, she came steady, but she wasn't a horse who was born to just come along.

Reuben's mouth was dry with determination, his hands clamped on the reins, his heart slowing: visions of paralysis, of death on the track under half-ton horses, his spalled flesh ground into the very fibers of the racing world. But then he straightened up. Whatever. His horse wasn't right, that was for sure, but one minute on a half-well Hell was worth ten years on these other hacks. His grin bared his teeth.

The bell clanged, and for a moment, fresh out of the gate, all concern seemed unfounded: Hellsmouth rocketed from post position, instantly strong and upright; she broke with stomach-flipping loft in her three-year-old stride, her newly elongated signature. Inside of four strides, she separated herself from the field just as the bettors had banked on, as the oddsmakers had predicted. She was the fulfillment of every Saturday promise—inevitability itself—so the stands didn't wait for her to roll into that first turn; they rose headily, drunkenly in advance of their sure thing, their cries rolling out across the infield like thunder before the storm. At the sound of their jubilation, Reuben, already tight with the hope of victory and plastered over her withers, twitched the crop back and delivered a perfunctory tap to Hell's flanks just as they angled into the turn. Now the rude truth reasserted itself. Hell took the crop with a gathering of her muscle and a straining of the head, but her body delivered no burst of speed. She didn't advance through the turn as she always did, the filly braggart who could walk on water as lesser horses slipped under the waves, the filly who rolled effortlessly around a curve on the strength of personality alone. And not only did she take the crop without a surge, but when she switched leads on her bruiser's legs, she faltered. The tectonics shifted.

Stop the Music pressed past Angelshare and Loop de Loop, crabbing out of the curve so his bulky ass moved up on Hell's right shoulder. Another second into the straight, and there commenced a violent bumping and jolting as the other colts circled their wagons, boxing in Hellsmouth, so Reuben was forced to wield the whip again to spur her into any possible pocket, real or imagined. He snapped her flanks, then he bashed her flanks, calling out encouragement and demand, the crop suddenly electric as any cattle prod, but though she tried and tried, she couldn't advance. Neither left nor right, the colts left her no avenue. Now her effort became an ugly thing to see; blood spurted from her nostrils despite the Lasix, the proud flesh on her chest pulsed white against her black.

"Haw, little bitch! Bring it home!"

How she strained and lunged under Reuben on the straightaway, sling-ing saliva back onto his shoulders and face, digging deeper than deep, but her pace was a sickening diminuendo, a single discordant instrument in the orchestra. When the wire approached, despite the desperation in her limbs and the agonized shearing of her lungs, there was nothing left to muster. She came in third after Stop the Music, her archrival, and Possum, a fat-nosed al-lowance horse born on a Tuscaloosa farm with a plastic spoon in his mouth, a colt with no fashion in his pedigree whatsoever, not a single placer in his line.

Jeff Burrow: Well, the 2006 season is no longer a done deal, a fixed race between perfection and a middling field. The almighty Hellsmouth, a filly all but guaranteed to wrap up the Derby in a rose-red ribbon, is no longer a sure thing. Horses lose every day in this sport, but there was something different in the air after Hell's defeat on Saturday. Her loss seems to have peeled back the layers to reveal an unspoken truth just under the surface of this testosterone-fueled industry. Hellsmouth has never been just another equine athlete. In a sport overrun with huge colts and powerhouse geldings, she's a filly, and a tremendous one at that, and that makes her unique. If, despite this loss, she manages to conquer the Derby's mile and a quarter, it won't just be a win for Hellsmouth, but a testament to the power and potential of her sex in the sport. In a world that downplays the accomplishments of women at every possible turn, a great female athlete is representative, whether she likes it or not. They change their sport and public opinion. So when May sixth rolls around, let's not forget the much larger truth at play on the dirt track at Churchill Downs: this big filly runs for all fillies, and the distinction still matters.

Henry jabbed at the remote control in a daze. He rewound the DVR again and again, Samuel gnawing sloppily on a teething toy at his side, oblivious to what had just occurred. The last time Henry had felt such stupefaction, they had heaped dirt on his daughter's casket. With this race, he'd been so close to the maximal, he'd felt victory was already accomplished. Now the vagaries of chance circled round him once again, chirping and pecking at the pebbles under his feet, their musty wings unsettling the dust and leaving him to shift with apprehension. Hell's perfect record was broken. Someone help Henry: If Hellsmouth is not his perfect thing, then what exactly is she? What if she isn't his at all, or worse, not a thing at all? What if she—

Did you see her body tumbling from orbit, all out of order? Call it a loss if you want, but did you notice how, like something breaking apart upon re-entry, she grew even brighter as she came apart?

> This many times my heartbeat
> $16\frac{3}{4}$ 16 74 28 $37\frac{1}{2}$ 46 40 24 40 $53\frac{1}{2}$ 68 $8\frac{1}{4}$ 25
> an ungoverned thing,
> when I end circles,
> there is a remove like sleep but
> I am still the center
> I am worse
> I am undivided

I'm sorry, I know you want more and there *is* more and you deserve it, but this is all I have. I'm a beggar. I was pitched out of my mother onto a dirt floor, and all I was given at birth was two fistfuls of language.

HawHaw! cries the half-cocked jock. Y'all think I'm down for the count, this little coyote? Why, my filly's tricky, there's gunpowder on her breath! Your story's a bore, your limits my delight! You set out your words like the farmer sets out his traps! But my eye is keen and my sense is uncommon; I watch the other kits get snatched up in your traps. They wail and moan and gnash their foxy teeth. They chew off their own limbs for freedom, the fools! But me? I'm mind, I'm wind! I'm wise, little girl, you can't fathom me! I turn tables, debunk, redefine, and rout. I slip your constraints and shit on your traps! While you tipple your applejack and tap out your tale, I feign, fib, fabulate— How now, I climax revenge! Contradict, appall, instruct, assassinate! I rise like a raven from the black of your page. I'll strip the very meat off your aching hands, little scribbler!

· · ·

Mack: Okay, everybody calm the fuck down. I never wasted a minute of my life on worry and neither has that goddamn horse. Buy your burgoo, place your bets, and watch her do what she does. Jesus Christ almighty— Enough.

The tall-case clock announced noon.

The writer didn't come to the kitchen door as Henry had instructed, but parked at the front entrance of the house and knocked on the front door shining with spar varnish and crested by high mullion glass, cut to fit perfectly two hundred years before. Through the rilled sidelights, Henry detected a figure. When he drew open the door, a black woman stood there.

She was short as a child but held herself with a military erectness. Her face was plain, severe, falsified neither by smile nor makeup. Perhaps seventy, perhaps more, she cut an unforgiving figure—gray hair scraped back into a tight bun, cheekbones made for cutting glass. Her shapeless gray silk blouse was buttoned to the neck and tucked into an equally shapeless black skirt that fell without a hint of sensuality to her calves. On her feet: black orthopedic shoes with fat soles. She looked like a nun.

"You are M. J. Deane?" Henry said, a soft suspicion that looked very much like humor wrinkling his brow.

"I am." Two little words, but all of the South.

"I'm Henry Forge."

She looked steadily at Henry with eyes so dark it was impossible to determine where the pupil ended and the iris began. When they shook hands, the woman's hand was cool, dry, and weathered as an old cornhusk— but firm, almost too strong. The intensity of her gaze bordered on the familiar.

"I'm afraid I have only one hour," said Henry. "I'll need to get to Louisville as I believe I mentioned to your assistant."

"Hellsmouth," the woman said slowly, her voice low and throaty with age. "I have followed your little horse very closely."

"It's been a good racing season. Two good racing years." Even as Henry smiled, sweat sprung prickly across his back and under his arms. Outside, there was an urgent, early heat. His May dams drowsed with foals in thick shade, the tack already sprouted mold, the pawpaws were coming on. Kentucky was overripe and it was only the sixth of May.

The little woman moved past Henry, a large purse swinging from her arthritic fingers by glossy straps, a purse that even he, who knew nothing of fashion, recognized as an artifact of tremendous luxury. The boxy satchel—perhaps alligator—was secured by a small gold latch and stamped with its provenance in gold letters too small for him to read.

The woman stepped smartly into the parlor, then paused at the coffee table set for tea that separated the two Chippendale camelbacks. She took slow survey of the room, especially the Aubusson beneath her feet, its dun, gray, and tawny Gallic medallion edged with aubergine like bloodlines running through its pale arrangement. Then she lowered herself onto the divan.

"What's that?" she said abruptly, pointing with a knobby finger above the hearth.

"Columbia jays," Henry said, but looking at her, not the print. "Audubon, first folio. I bought it in Philadelphia and brought it back to Kentucky."

"Is it a real one?"

Henry was almost too distracted to be offended. He was realizing suddenly that she'd walked ahead of him into the parlor prior to any invitation. He suffered a strange and phantom sense of displacement, as if he had suddenly walked out of his own story and into someone else's.

He didn't serve her. He merely gestured at the tea service, which she also ignored, the exquisite purse now perched on her knees with all the stately presence of a sleek black cat.

Henry said, "So you've written books on horse racing . . . ?"

"No, I have not," said the woman. "I spent my life writing mysteries. And I made a king's fortune doing it. Then, one day I decided it was time to write nonfiction." She looked at him evenly, coolly. "It was time to tell the truth."

Outside the willows and the lilies and the buck roses were drooping in the voluptuous air. Henry said, "And where does your family come from?"

A cocked brow. "They come from here. But I would not call this place my home."

Jarred by a distinct sense of unease, Henry crossed his arms. "And why is it that you publish under your initials?"

Now the woman stared directly into his eyes. "'Cause I ain't nobody's business." The drawl, the slide into dialect, caused his hair to stand on end.

Henry said very slowly, very clearly, "You came to talk to me about horses and the racing life. Well, now you're here."

"I never said that."

"Your assistant told me—"

"Henry Forge," she said, and she cocked her head ever so slightly, "do you not remember me?"

Henry sat back into a moment of silence. From somewhere distant came the quiet inflection of hooves passing along the earth, then nothing. The woman smiled a smile that became colder as it grew, the shape of hate nursed over the course of a long and difficult life. Then she said: "Your father, John Henry Forge, was responsible for the death of Filip Dunbar; I know this because you told me yourself on the morning of January second, 1954. Filip was the lover of your mother, Lavinia. I know this because I saw them with my own eyes. You could never be convicted of anything in a bodyless crime; I realize that. It was your father who committed the crime. But I have the power to ruin the Forge name. That I can most certainly do. And I suspect for you that would be an end more permanent than actual death."

Time distended to the point of bursting, and nothing made a sound. The clock yawned. The drapes stilled in midbillow. The tea leaves settled in the pot. Nothing moved except Henry's blood, which was older than time and could only be called by one name, a surname, which was a useless thing really, signifying nothing, a word that began with force in your ancestor's lungs and died with a curl of the tongue behind your teeth.

The words did not register at first. Henry peered at her as though her very person were impossible. "MJ . . . ?" he uttered.

"Maryleen Jesse Deane," she said.

The name shot through him, but Henry gathered himself, refused it, said evenly, "I don't know what you're talking about."

Maryleen just lowered her chin, leveling him with a stare. "I plan to publish a book in August, just in time for the Belmont. I intend to tell the real story of your family, of this house, of Kentucky. I intend to tell the truth."

As if finally realizing the import of her words, Henry leaned forward suddenly. "Do you actually believe that you can piggyback on our fame and libel my family because a man who worked here once disappeared under mysterious circumstances? A man who was the town drunk, someone my father and grandfather had always supported?"

"The truth, I said." Her voice was steely.

Henry's own voice grew low. "Then I will take you for all you're worth."

"You could come after my money," the writer hissed, leaning forward too, "but you wouldn't know how to get at my worth."

Suddenly, teetering on an edge, Henry pressed a palm to his chest, his face wrenched: "I lost my daughter this past fall. Do you understand that my daughter died, and here you come . . ." But instantly, he wanted to reel the cheap words back into his private heart; for the first time in memory, he was swamped by shame.

The woman slowly shrugged, her face cold. "I am the bill collector."

Trembling, Henry said very quietly, "Get out," but it was too late, she had already risen, and he could see the pleasure on her face as she stood there eyeing him, calm hands gripping her purse.

So the words erupted from him again, coming not from him but through him, rolling down the endless corridors of time and memory. "Get out of my house!"

But no sooner had the woman turned away from the davenport than she nearly collided with Ginnie Miller, who appeared suddenly in the doorway, Samuel hauled up against her shoulder and her face a portrait of alarm. "We were in the kitchen and I heard hollering—what's going on in here?"

"This woman was just leaving," Henry said stonily, his hand still over his heart.

But Maryleen couldn't move, much less leave. She stood frozen in place where she had turned, her face suddenly still, like a sheet smoothed, her eyes newly wide. A single finger drifted like a leaf slowly falling up to graze the air around Samuel's cheek, as he twisted round on Ginnie's chest to gaze, alarmed, at the ancient face hovering near his. "Whose child is this?" Maryleen said wonderingly.

Henry was silent.

The woman's eyes turned to Henry again, confused, wary. "This—this is your child?"

Ginnie answered for him. "This is Henry's grandson. He's the son of—" And then she stopped abruptly, sensing she had perhaps said too much. She glanced worriedly at Henry.

Henry drew himself to his full height. "I am raising my grandson," he said simply.

"Oh!" the writer cried, her composure pierced, and Samuel started, so Ginnie retreated into the hallway with a protective arm wrapped around him, her eyes all suspicion. Maryleen whirled around with a strange smile of bewilderment on her face. "Is this true?" she said, and then the air whistled out of her lungs. She inspected Henry's guarded face. "It is! Lord God! The truth really is stranger than fiction!" Then a laugh erupted from her tiny frame, a howl pinned between outrage and hilarity. Samuel began to cry.

"A black baby!" Maryleen cried. "Henry Forge has a black grandbaby! And here I come— Oh, maybe my daddy was right, that old religious fool. There's no such thing as earthly justice! No such possible thing— Forgive me, Daddy! You were right! I think I understand you now!" She was barely able to get out the words, laughing uproariously and turning back to the child who was staring at her in frank fear, his little mouth opening to cry, interrupted only by the bellowing of his grandfather, a sound he had never heard and would never hear again from him, the voice of pure rage:

"GET OUT OF MY HOME!"

The woman's laugh died slowly on her lips, her eyes once again impenetrable. She held up her hand as though swearing on the Bible.

"You may believe you can still order me away," she said, carefully enunciating each word. "But this time I leave on my own terms." Without haste, she walked along the richly appointed hallway and out the front door, the luxurious purse swinging from her right hand. She left the door standing wide open.

Henry was very late. He grasped up Samuel, this thorough innocent, who was now smiling as if his earlier tears had served no purpose at all but to wash his face clean. Henry had meant to leave him for the day with Ginnie, but now he couldn't remember why, couldn't imagine any other course of action. He would bring him. Henry stumbled down the el porch and into the firecracker sunlight, requiring a moment to remember where he had parked his own car alongside his own home, then half ran toward it, guided only by the need to get Samuel into that car, because the car led to the future, and the future was the safe house where he could escape his old self—the Henry of his youth, the Henry of even one year ago, the Henry of grief. And guilt.

The world existed before you, Henry Forge. Open your eyes.

Drive across Kentucky on the waning strength of your old self. Look at Paris, barely changed from the Paris of your youth. It's still your father's town and your father's father's town, and the Paris–Lexington Road is still a billion-dollar byway, the homes exquisite baubles designed to impress, a gorgeous necklace on the white neck of the state. The child in this car was disinherited from these holdings long ago, though his great-great-great-great-great-grandfather built this place with all the strength of his body. Your strength was never strength at all but bantam posturing over shame. Hate has always coursed through your line like a mutant gene.

And here's Lexington—once the perfect Southern woman, modest, discreet, and not very large—with her masses packed and huddled into her cinched inches, ringed by a lush green skirt, a pleasure garden for pampered horses and wealthy men. Sit up straight and peer beyond the colonnaded mansions with their mile-long lawns, beyond the words your father said over and over and over again. Repeated long enough, stories become memory and memory becomes fact.

A flash of panic lit Henry's wilding mind—what was he doing, what on earth was he doing? He should turn around, drive the child home and hide him away, but he could not. This was his blood, his line.

A reckoning was coming.

Henry, who built this state?

Quick! Quick! Henrietta said.

Why, the help, Father, the servants, the bondsmen, the chattel, that species of property, those dark machines in the fields, who came through the Cumberland Gap from Fauquier, Fairfax, and Albemarle, or from Forts Pitt and Duquesne down the Ohio into Virginia's pretty annex. They climbed the hills in iron chains, a premonition of the Cheapside coffle gangs to come; they felled trees and laid foundations under the eager eyes of rifles; they molded and fired red clay bricks and half slept on the ground or thin shuck mattresses. In a life of relentless labor with no hope of recompense, they plowed the karst fields and pastures, cut teepees of hemp, burned shives, cured tobacco, carded wool and dyed cloth, hauled salt, slopped hogs, cut back briar, tended gardens, cooked vittles, dried herbs, cured ham, dragged ice, polished silver, tended fire, wove baskets, caught babies, nursed them and rocked them, plaited hair, roached hair, beat rugs, brewed beer, stilled whiskey, pickled and preserved, made soap, worked leather, wove duck and fustian, darned socks, cobbled shoes, planed cabinets, fired iron, molded tools, picked worms, milked cows, raised barns, shoveled manure, skinned deer and slaughtered goats, drove the cattle from field to market, and, yes, managed the horses.

Henry's eyes snapped to the rearview again. Samuel's face had grown dreamy with a trace of spittle along his voluminous cheek. His eyes cast round once, focus drifting, followed by a shuttering of the lids in untroubled sleep. Henry said his name out loud to test the reality of the present time, because she was there—not beneath the color of the child's face but in it, her bones building his bones moment to moment, the fullness of her face fleshing his. Her blood coursing through him.

Henry, you spread your daughter's legs the way you split a tree to build a house. Was it worth it?

Suddenly, slowly, the line began to slowly flow backward like the Ohio, which reversed course after the great earthquake so many years ago. He couldn't fight it and in an instant, Henry's being was overfull; he began to drown with the new knowing. The earth was like a great king, and all the various beings in the world were only component parts of that majestic body. Henry had always imagined himself to be the king, but he was only the left hand, which had—in its madness—reached across and severed the right hand, thinking it would grow his station. And yet here he was bleeding out into endless space and time, because—Henry, now you know— the man who destroys another destroys himself. That is the taste of her blood in your mouth.

But, isn't it true that the great slay cheap morality in their quest?

That small minds spend lifetimes setting limits on their betters?

Now, the old language slips again through the fissures of time: There's shame hidden in the walls of the family house, Henry, so we will take it apart, dismantle the entire structure. Fling the shingles from the roof and crumble the old stacked chimneys, all eight. Strip out the pipery and haul out the case goods, the sideboards, the sugar chests and chesterfields, the old Jackson press; yank the moldings and the millwork down, hammer out the mantels and unhinge the doors from their sills, slide out their glinting windows. Now loosen the bricks from their old arrangements and toss them down in a heap where the cabins once stood, until there is nothing left but the cagework of the old homeplace, a chestnut skeleton of exposed raftery with nothing to stave off the frigid northern wind that comes rushing through in the form of a nameless, fire-blackened woman with singed wings striated under her gusseted corset under her tattered moiré gown under her gentleman's banyan of obscene color, who from a rotting reticule at her elbow withdraws an old promissory note and gives it a wild shake. The serpents of her dark hair sidle and weave, the irises of her eyes irrupted by arterial blood.

Take the note, Henry, take it and see that it's more than a promissory note, it's a page ripped from a ledger written in the language that begat him begat him begat him begat him begat you begat her begat Samuel

What do you know?

that old man

Who?

Forge.

that Edward Cooper Forge

walked the parlor, tears soaking his mustache and beard, his mind routed by grief. By turns, his hands clutched at his broad forehead, or were clasped trembling at his chest or hung slack at his side. They were now utterly useless, despite their dexterity and strength. He paced his rounds like a sick horse, round and round, the chestnut boards creaking and crying—no, that was the child upstairs wailing in Lessandra's spent arms. He gazed blearily up at the ceiling of the parlor, through it to the woman with her weak womb. One alive in sixteen years! So little to show. The nature of life was to take, take, take until it ruined you. Everything you built, everything you made, even your children, was sure to be ripped from you. Life is not a durable good.

The nature of nature is to kill.

He hadn't stood still for more than a minute since the boy died. His Barnabas. Barnabas Monroe Forge. Shock of thick blond hair and quick laugh. But a boy of action who lacks caution and doesn't always think—son, didn't I tell you to use your head? Never use a rifle as a tool! A firearm is only for shooting! But then your damn fool beloved son is chasing rabbits in the snow, their tiny madcap prints veering left and right in the pearly-eye blinding white until the worthless animal disappears into a rotting log without escape on the other side, so dear excited unthinking beloved son crouches and rams the butt of the rifle into the hollow log to flush a creature with not enough meat to feed a girl child, and the rifle discharges, and sixteen years is dead, its heart blown out in the snow.

Edward clamped his eyes as if to break them, organs that serve only one purpose: to make a grown, aging man cry. He could not tell his grief from his rage, together they seemed far larger than his physical body, larger than his home. The word "please" had died on his lips. No, he could no longer pray or his neck would break from the strain. How he had prayed to the God of Eternal Uselessness, raise up my son, because he cannot be dead! He must be only sleeping! Raise up my son, because the infant may not survive the winter and neither my wife! Raise up my son, because I obeyed your laws all my life and was like the good servant, not burying my talents but raising children and stewarding the property I was given. Raise up my son, I have cried over his wet, cold face! But God was silent, because God did not exist any longer. God was alive only until he was shot in the heart in the snow, and now it is the third day and still he has not risen.

It was clear that Death wrote the rules of life and a man was a fool—a callow youth—until he acknowledged it. But Edward's will musters against this ultimatum. Man spent himself in a war against the processes of entropy and, yes, it was a useless endeavor but to cede was to capitulate, to be a coward. It was to write Death a blank check.

He stops his pacing, his eyes suddenly bright. He has alighted upon something permanent. The only light in the darkness is life and more of It.

He snatches up the murderous rifle, which has lain on the floor for three days under the coffin box and its black silk drape—this thing whose propulsive force is stronger than even his own son's life, and not a minute later, Edward is in the cold yard in nothing but his black trousers and white poplin shirt, his breath huffing out in vaporous blooms as he crosses the attenuated lines of window light crossing to the cabins. The constellations are blurs overhead as he bursts through the door of the first cabin. The family of seven who are huddled before the fire at first stare up in mute alarm until they see the rifle at his side, gleaming like a scythe, then they scatter to the shadows along the dark walls.

His one word explodes into their dark and quiet space: Phebe.

For a long, agonized moment, no one moves or even dares to breathe.

Then into the cocked silence, out of the shadows, the girl called Phebe creeps forward, half-bent by fear like a crone. She moves forward, her eyes locked on the rifle.

Come.

Come now!

Marster! Her mother jets forward out of the swallowing shadows, her arms out. What you gone—

He raises the rifle and the shadows consume the mother, and the young girl proceeds out of the silence and into the night. She's upright now as if quiet obedience will save her from whatever unknown fate awaits, eyes moving neither left nor right. Across the barren, bone-rattling yard they go, and into a cabin, where three likewise sit round the hearth fire with their yams and cornpone and heated chicory. There is the sound of throaty laughter, of some story reaching its conclusion. Then all three men stand abruptly when Edward storms through the door, the girl stumbling beside him, her bewildered fear now turning to dread.

Benjohn there, his strongest and most beautiful. Edward says breed to this gal, and the other two creep first to the edges and then on out the door, looking at each other but not bothering with useless words. Benjohn saying, Marster, I's fixing to marry my gal Libby the next week over Drummer farm; you done gave permission two months ago, but Edward says, Increase my stock. The man only shies up into his shoulders, shaking his head, so Edward says, For every pickaninny you give me, I will reward you with dollars, then the rifle says NOW, and the girl is shivering on her hands and knees with her woolen skirt over her shoulders, then they are hunched and pressed together, and Edward is pushing her forehead into the dirt with his own hands to raise her haunches high for the take. Her tears mingle with the dirt. Edward says, Give me a buck, and then he is off to fetch Mim and Sarah while Benjohn recuperates in astonishment. The girl flees to her cabin as the others come, their eyes round with fear but not suspecting, and then again and again with his buck Prince because Benjohn is spent, then Edward himself is at his maximum with his own blood risen up into his feverish head, so he leaves the last two bred and clutching each other not in love on the cold, packed ground. At first he is merely walking, the rifle resting on his shoulder, but then he is running across the yard toward the house all lit up for the deceased—no, for the mourning—and he charges through the kitchen door, so that Prissey nearly drops the roaster with its hulk of turkey no one will bother to eat tonight. Edward twists up her wrists in his left hand, the rifle clattering down, yanking her from her task but not up the stairs where Lessandra, withered dry by milk and tears, is suckling a colicky, perhaps dying infant son, his own, but into the corn-meal and spice smell of his own pantry, where she is saying no no no no please no; Prissey, your beauty has saved you, I would never breed you to a nigger. Marster, you just undone! I am undone. Give me back myself. No. Give me back to me. No! Prissey, I have owned you sixteen years and never touched a hair on your head, been nothing but a loving master. I have of-fered you protection from the world and treated you as a favorite, better than I would have a daughter. But now, give me back to me. Spread your dark legs, Prissey, spread your dark hair, split your dark open, the center of you suckle me, give me back now what I have lost. Pinned against the butcher block, with her skirts shoved high, the sweat of terror and her day's labor and sorrow commingling, he breaks the tight prefloration and de-mands what there is, bruising the skin of her thighs and rattling her teeth until what's left of his life convulses into hers, and then he is weeping openly, crying like a wounded animal, and she sighs, which to him sounds like pleasure. With eyes to the sky, which is just a low ceiling, she reaches around his bulk and, with all the weary resignation, which seems the lone inheritance of woman, she comforts him.

Pain is an alien being in your being. You think: How did this other life get inside me? This isn't a stubbed toe, or indigestion, or the vigorous ache of a fever that rattles your bones but then passes in a week. No, you can't kid yourself any longer; this is permanent, this is disease. Somewhere in these last few weeks, knowledge has pressed itself through the cracks of Allmon's concrete heart, and now it can't be routed out, neither the knowledge nor the disease. The world took everything from you, then found more to take, and now it's going to invade your entire body, crowding your insides and diminishing what was once you until all that's left will be the memory of how it once felt to live as a self without pain in the body you possessed—or you thought you possessed—as a long-ago child. A child who still had a mother. Marie.

"Young man."

Allmon started and looked up from where he was wrapping Hell's leg with what strength was left in his wrecked hands. A small woman had appeared on the other side of the stall chain; she stood utterly upright with a stern, martial formality, a black handbag gripped in a hand that looked more like old, creased iron than flesh. Her eyes were strangely heated when she said, "You are the groom of Hellsmouth? You work for Henry Forge?"

If it had been a white person, he would have said, Who wants to know? But to her, he just said, "Yeah." And then he rose up slowly, a flicker of hurt on his face that appeared almost like anticipatory grief, as though the executioner had finally come. He took a hesitant step forward.

"Oh, young man." The woman lowered her chin fractionally and smiled up at him without smiling. "Do I have a story for you."

Allmon stumbled from the barn on inflamed hips and crumbling knees, desperate for air without chaff and mites, desperate for the cool remnants of the afternoon's light rain. Through his tangled, terrible, scorched mind he could see the horses crisscrossing the Downs, dark and rangy and terrifically strong, stark as ink stains in the mist. A sudden resentment rose for the freshness of their young, ignorant lives, and he looked down at his own blasted body with a wholly different wonder. Prison had broken him and though he'd patched his pieces together, the mortar was crumbling.

He thought of Henrietta, but he pushed her away. She hadn't taken his life, but she'd taken his fucking dignity. She was a cheap trick, a white slap, another humiliation to endure. He hated her.

Given a chance, these white motherfuckers will always take your black life. Always.

He began to stumble along after one of the sauntering colts, as though it offered escape, but there was no escape, not from the sick story he had just heard. Forgetting wouldn't work this time. You tried to close your ears to time, but it was louder than ten thousand horses thundering across the plains. Time told stories that busted your eardrums and made them bleed. The Forges had murdered a man, the woman had said. Of course they had. Of course! He felt the righteousness of his vindication like a sun in his chest; it

transformed and shined light on the guilt that had been torturing him. He
had always known what the Forges were, but in Henrietta's deceiving arms,
he'd allowed himself to ignore it! Of course, he'd known; he'd spent his
whole life on the run from a fucking lynch mob.

Allmon felt the vibration of the swelling crowds before he could see
them and veered away from the track toward the parking lot, but the crowds
were there too, chattering and smiling and moving along in their finely cut
suits, outrageous hats on display. Smug, self-satisfied, like they had actually earned their wealth honestly and not by standing on the necks of
others. Allmon stopped at a gate, breathless. None of them even noticed
him in his stained polo and manure-caked boots. He was a bland, brown,
weathered rock, and they were a gorgeous stream flowing past.

Allmon's features were wrenched by a wrathful pain so pure, so ultimate,
it was like the heat off a stove, so hot it was icy. He couldn't tell any longer
whether it was pain of the body or of the spirit. He fished in his pocket for
his Vicodin, and the tablets jangled there like chalky coins.

You got the flushing disease?

He needed a doctor; he knew that. But these disunited states had
turned the complex math of a human life into the simplest number: You got
enough money for insurance? Insurance cost what he made in two weeks,
and they made you pay a five-thousand-dollar deductible before you got
any help. Then you could only go to certain doctors or you had to pay even
more . . . He knew the fucking rigamarole. *He knew.*

This world breaks your bones, and some breaks are permanent.

He turned back toward all the barns, which were laid out all orderly
like graves behind the track. Hellsmouth was waiting; the Derby was only
minutes away. The critical importance of the race only grew in his mind.
Everything—his whole life—hinged on it.

Oh God, he suddenly prayed with every pain-ridden fiber of his being,
knowing full well God was Momma, because when he prayed to him now,
all he could see was her face in his mind, her nose, which was his own, and
her wide smile, her chestnut eyes, the face of her youth, which was his in-
fancy, the face he had loved above every face on the earth—even more than
the Reverend. The Reverend! He was there too, the hammer of his preaching, the unrelenting ground of his living. He hadn't thought of the man in
years, because he'd left them, and Allmon had never forgiven him for that.

Now they were the prayer, the entirety of his breath and blood: Please, God, let this horse win. Let me finally get on the outside. Winning is justice—my salvation and revenge.

The twin spires of Churchill Downs loomed overhead, their flags snapping with the brisk violence of the weather. There had been a heavy rain and now the day turned astonishing in its beauty, the clouds all piled and red-tipped like a sun-shot mountain range inverted, streaming red and gold in every direction. Under that play of light, all the minuscule players—the jocks, the trainers, the grooms, the fans, the horses—made their moves. When the human world is rotted away like an old walnut, that light will remain.

Henry had left the diaper bag in the car along with the stroller folded in the trunk, his suit jacket crumpled on the passenger seat. The ground was still wet, puddles everywhere, and it looked as though it might start raining again at any moment. Henry barely noticed. He simply held Samuel, the child sound asleep with his cheek on Henry's shoulder.

Twenty minutes to post. Where in this carnival was Hellsmouth, his darling destrier, brightest and best, his black beauty hopped up on pain-killers, his glory runner, model of the reliability of heritability, his once perfect thing? Where was his daughter?

Natural selection isn't everything. We still don't understand the principles of organization. The mystery is intact.

I am not a meme but a mutation.

Life is a chain of affinities.

Nature hath made of one blood—

In his mind, he cried out, Why are you torturing me, daughter?
I'm not torturing you—I'm at peace. Why are you torturing yourself?
"Henry."
"Henry!"

He whirled before his mind came round, his eyes confused and slow to discover a resting place: Louisa, his home vet, standing in front of him in the milling crowd, her face so easy and calm, as though life weren't a madhouse. Was it possible that anyone could actually be as untroubled as she appeared to be? At her side was her young daughter—maybe twelve and slender as a stalk—clinging to her side in a childish way, her limbs entangled jealously with her mother's, who managed her gently, one arm wrapped in a protective gesture over her shoulder. The girl's hair fell in a glassy brown sheet to her lower back as she gazed up at Henry in curiosity.

"Whose baby is that?" she inquired.

But Henry didn't hear. His dilated pupils took in too much light; it caused everything to grow distorted and overbright. "You talked to my daughter," he said to Lou. "You talked to her the day she died."

Lou's gaze was steady, level. "Yes, I did. She came to see me, and we talked for a good while. I often think of you and your grandson and wonder how you're doing. I'm sure it's been very hard for you over at the farm. I've been over a few times, but never—"

Her compassion was Confederate money. "Tell me what you said to her that day."

"What I said?" Lou's eyes assumed a distant look and her lower lip pressed out slightly as she turned her mind back to that autumn day. "She had come to see me, kind of a surprise visit."

"What did she come to see you about? I need to know."

Lou looked pensively at the ground as her daughter bumped gently, rhythmically against her side. Then Lou stopped the girl by holding her shoulders with both hands and, looking up with the light of remembrance on her face, said, "I had mentioned to her once that the horse was the remnant of an evolutionary failure, and she wanted to know what I meant by that. We talked for a while about the pregnancy and—"

"An evolutionary failure?"

"Well, yes," Lou said, clearing her throat. "It's really the first thing you learn when you study evolution in school, that Equidae was an empire—a huge family—in the animal kingdom, but most of its branches disappeared and its descendants died out until all that was left was equus: the horse, ass, the zebra, the—"

"Evolution is a ladder," whispered Henry, "a ladder to a perfect thing."

"Actually, no, not really." Lou shook her head quizzically, so her hair fell lopsided out of its graying bun. "It's not a ladder. It's more like . . . a bush." She raised her hands to mold a fulsome round in the empty air. "Think of it as a branching bush. A great, endlessly diversifying bush that gets stronger with each new branch, each new variation."

Henry stared at her without moving a muscle. Samuel chirped near his ear, slowly waking from his sleep. Henry's mind was filled with the memory of Henrietta, his child, his responsibility. His eyes filled with tears.

Then Lou said suddenly, as if his gaze were a question to be answered, "Henry, you should know that it was not a—a heavy day. I mean, I remember Henrietta laughing. And she seemed very ready for birth."

"Henry!"

Henry's head snapped round in the direction of the voice, a man calling for him in the midst of the crowd. "Henry Forge!"

"Where is he?" Henry said.

"Who? Henry?" Lou reached for him with one hand.

But Henry was already moving away, his body an automaton maneuvering his spirit through the crowd. Samuel wriggled, reaching up with one hand for Henry's right ear. His grandfather's ears were his favorite new toys.

"Henry!" Yes, he knew that voice—knew it like he knew the inside of his own mouth. He was peering around all the Derby hats, their absurd heights and ostentation impeding his clear view.

"Henry!" The voice was insistent, implacable, eternal.

And there he was, a shadow in the crowd.

Henry reared back suddenly, wanting to reverse course and disappear.

No, Father, my lessons are over and done.

Tell me, Henry, is man the measure of all things?

Father, I don't want to play this game anymore—I can't!

I am the pruner and you are the vine.

No, you are the tyrant!

Henry, you don't understand—

That's where you're wrong, Father! I do understand! Man may be the measure of all things, but no single man can be, because there's no such thing as a single man. Now I know you cannot kill a tyrant—he wrapped his arms tightly around Samuel—because the man who kills a tyrant becomes a killer and a tyrant. And that, Father, is why they call it the wheel.

Henry stands in the crowd, utterly still and sure. He finally knows what he is going to do, what has been rising in him like water set to burst its dam; surety overflows. He will pull Hellsmouth from the Derby and end it right here, right now. There are no bodies, only beings. That truth is the child in his arms, whom he will reveal to Allmon. The truth will not roll back time, but it will make the future. He turns around and begins to run with Samuel in his arms. He finds no argument in his heart.

But it's too late. Reuben has already swung up onto Hell's saddle, his hands like money clips on the reins. The sky begins to churn and drum with approaching thunder.

Henry cries, This is my Regret!

Allmon's stomach is in his throat as he leads the fearless filly through the tunnel and out onto the churned turf. When he lets go of the shank, the eyes of the crowd pass from him. As if he doesn't exist.

The Reverend says, Who shall uphold the cause of the needy? When shall the fatherless say Amen?

By the time Henry reaches the grandstand, when he finds a sightline, it's too late. Hellsmouth is nearly through the post parade with a palomino pony at her head and a vulture on her back.

The horses are in the gate.

The starting gun is cocked.

Wait, wait, stop their mouths and still their minds. Unseat the jocks, unsaddle the mounts, loosen the shanks, rewind the walkers. Once again and with care: In the green paddock stand the glossy blacks, bays, grays, and roans. In the bright and bustling paddock, it's May. Circling, the horses nod and pass, nod and pass. Listen closely and every sound is sovereign in its kingdom, the chains clinking, saddles creaking like winches, hooves knocking dully at the door of eternity, cries of hup!hup!hup!

The bright silk jocks are cardinals, jays, purple martins, blackbirds. Process, progress, mercenary plumage along the gray brick walk. Firing hearts scatter buckshot beats to delicate wrists, behind emaciated knees, along bony insteps. The youngest jock leans over the embankment of his horse and vomits into the dirt as they pass through the tunnel. On its axis, the grandstand tilts and the bettors tumble to the fore of the house—gripping the rails and vying for a view of the beasts as they emerge.

The horses pass along the gate like lanterns shining, lanterns that bathe the watcher as they pass one by one, dark lanterns swaying on their chains housing bold, interminable light; bright, brief lanterns in a round processing, swaying, passing one by one into the damping gate.

Motionless and massive, they stand.

Suddenly the bell rings, the gates are sprung, the sky hurls invective rain, and the horses unfurl their colors before the crowd. They move through the gray veil of rain, gathering speed, charging on brittle bones, swinging as a single body around the track, shod hooves spattering mud. The mud is inside of everywhere—mud slung under saddles, in the eyes of the horses, caking the goggles of the jocks, which are stripped again and again and again. The wind whips the group from behind, pressing them to greater speeds but in the downpour, so they run sloppily, jostling and bumping and sliding, crossing the track with their lungs bursting and their nostrils bloody. When one horse begins to pull away, it's colorless from the mud, as if the earth itself has risen up and begun to run, and the crowd can't tell which it is. With each amplifying stride, it drives free from the pack, first its nose, then its withers, its rippling quarters. The animal accelerates without seeming to labor, as if the agony of racing were nothing but a game. Now the crowd rises without knowing which horse it rises for, each indistinguishable from the other. One length becomes five becomes eleven becomes sixteen. The crowd is screaming in abandon with arms raised; their faces are glazed with rain, their hats are ruined. They're roaring for the anonymous gladiator as it crosses under the wire at twenty lengths, all four hooves free from the ground, its tail streaming behind it like a muddy flag. Now the field follows in a brown bundle, and the first horse is hauled up to a gallop, the jock standing in the irons. It's Reuben Bedford Walker III pummeling the sky with his fists, while under him Hellsmouth spins like a weathervane, wet earth fanning out from under her hooves like seeds from a sower's hand.

Mack was screaming himself hoarse. He hated the Derby—hated all the hats and the cheesedick celebrities, hated the dilettantes, the brutal distance, the field thick with worthless runners, and he really hated that his most prominent owner—the increasingly witless and unreliable Henry Forge—had not shown up to the prerace press conference, nor the morning workouts on the most important day of his entire life as an owner, and was now refusing to pick up his fucking phone. He hated to an almost biblical degree that he had to call any owner twenty times—it made him feel like a lovesick straight chasing a skirt.

The whole Derby rigamarole was a bullshit sham and a shitshow, except for this, this, THIS. And THIS is why he was screaming, his suit jacket threatening to rip at the seams as he reached his triumphant arms over his head, his mouth hollering gibberish, his Stetson behind him on the ground, band up and collecting rain. And now once again—still hollering like a bear—he was snatching the cell phone out of his jacket pocket and dialing Henry's number, his eyes bugging. Turning hard right and then hard left, he spat, "Where in the everloving fuck is Henry Forge?!"

Allmon was weeping openly, limping toward Hell on the dirt track as fast as his legs could carry him. She was victorious, unbroken, and covered head to toe in mud, but he would always know her amidst the field of pretenders. His scream sounded more like a war cry than delight. He caught her fast while Reuben was still standing in the irons, pumping his fists and screaming for glory. Barely able to control his hands as the blood of victory flowed through him, Allmon drew her round in a fast circle to bank her fires, then haltered her on the saturated carpet of grass. He would live, he would live, he could feel himself growing into a new being as Hell's eyes rolled with her unspent energy. Filthy and carved with proud flesh, she was an unholy mess, as battered as an old pot, but still shimmering with beauty when two men appeared with the leaden blanket of bloodred roses. She skittered once to the right as they approached, blowing air with bubbles of blood. Then Reuben sat down on the saddle and with his help, they draped the forty-pound garland of Freedom roses across her back. Instantly Hellsmouth stilled, then she bowed slightly as if surprised by the weight of the thing, then stamped her front hooves and hopped once to show that the weight was nothing—nothing at all. There are some animals that crumple under victory, but she wasn't one of them. She trampled the geraniums when Allmon led her into the winner's circle.

The whole of this wet Saturday had spilled into the circle—Mack and his assistant trainers, old friends of the Forges, the mayor of Paris, the governor himself. They were flocked by blue vests, the press circling the circle, cameras perched at the wing blade. But there was a rumbling among them, some confusion, some pointing. Reuben clutched his bouquet of sixty roses and turned to them with a brilliant grin. "Wherefore the wait, y'all?" he said.

They were waiting on Henry Forge.

Mack, his dripping Stetson returned to his head, made a rolling gesture with his hands, snapping, "Take the picture, take the damn picture." Allmon corralled what strength he had left in his body and stood tall. He could feel Hell's explosive breath on his shoulder and droplets of her blood on his polo. He felt like he would never die. The circle exploded in artificial light.

And then it was over, just like that. Allmon led the dancing filly away to the hermetic world of the backstretch, and everyone else trouped onto the pagoda and stood behind the rail, which, glossed with rain, shined like white ice under an emergent, hesitant sun.

One last time, Mack checked his cell phone. "Motherfucker," he snapped, and when Bob Costas shot a hard, inquiring glance in his direction, he just glowered and tucked his chin. Arms crossed to contain his bunched fists, Mack was fairly rippling with irritation. But was so blissed he could hardly stand up straight.

The chairman of Churchill Downs was saying something Mack didn't give a shit about—HE HAD WON HIS FILLY HAD WON—then the governor turned to Mack with the trophy in his hands and had damn near unrolled his entire speech before he blurted, "Where's Mr. Forge?"

Mack's lips blanched against each other for a second, then: "Don't believe I've seen him in the neighborhood."

"No winning owner has ever missed a Derby that I can recall," said Costas. "This would be an unusual first in the history of the sport."

In front of the crowd, in front of God and a live television audience,

Mack reached out and wrestled the cold, beringed trophy out of the governor's startled hands and said, "Well, it's hard as hell to find good help these days."

They don't even know who he is. He's not leaping up as a victor on Millionaires Row or spilling a julep down his shirtfront, he's not roaring beside an overpriced trainer like an Achaean in Troy. No one reaches out to pump his hand or clap his back. He's nothing but a common spectator on the ground floor of the grandstand—behind all the celebrants, back where they sell burgoo and beer on tap. He's standing on a bed of torn gambling stubs, and there's gum on the bottom of his expensive shoe. He's struggling to cover the ears of a smiling baby, but his eyes are trained on the horse, now being led back into the tunnel, the monster filly that has left the crowd delirious. Someday they will tell their grandchildren they were there the day the big girl won. They will say how they knew it was her, even though they all looked alike, how strong she was, how she danced at the finish and spun like a weathervane. They will make a legend of her simple runner's life. They won't understand that she was racing on a prayer of a leg. They won't know that painkillers were coursing through her gladiator's blood. And they won't understand what happened next. They'll think Henry was an idiot or a madman. But the madness had all come before.

New knowledge is sunflower honey on the tongue.

And so began the third and final movement of Henry Forge's life.

INTERLUDE V

There were voices on the river, and one was his own. It was a pleasing
baritone that chatted easily with the other picnickers and called out
greetings to a few acquaintances, but Scipio heard it as if from a great
distance, as if it had come rolling down a long corridor, startling him before
he recognized it as his own. This happened to him often. He would walk
into their home in Bucktown after a long day up at the Rankin house,
where he was busy constructing a new carriage house, and suddenly see a
woman standing there in what he knew to be his own little home, and
think: Who is this gal with the brown calico eyes and the heavy bosom,
who stands there so familiar-like? One time he had even said hello and embraced her before he remembered with the whole of his body, oh yes, this is
my wife. The woman I have sworn to love.

His family had brought him here today, but he hadn't wanted to come—
never ever wanted to return to the river's edge, even though his house
stood a mere half mile from its banks. Mercy had pleaded, as well as Joe,
who had recently begun to apprentice with the blacksmith on Liberty, and
then there was little Laney. Little Gal, Big Trouble, that's what he called
her. Such a bold child and only eight years old. It stalled his heart to think

of her lack of fear—always beating up on boys, even those a few years older than herself, showing up afternoons at the Rankin doorstep, having dodged wagons and herds of swine and God knows what else to escape her mother and arrive there alone. Where on earth had she gotten such unvarnished force? From him, of course. Once upon a time, he too had been without fear. Back when he lived in the body he had been given at birth, back when he had belonged to himself even within the devil's system of slavery, back when he did not wait for voices—his own and many others, all lost now—to roll down time's corridors to confuse his ear.

The voices on the river belonged to the church all gathered there for the Fourth of July celebration. Scipio did not believe in anything resembling a god. How could he? But Mercy was a good, obedient citizen of the Lord's free city, and she believed. Scipio had met her the day after he stumbled wet and half-mad into the black district and found the safe haven of the A.M.E. church near Broadway and Sixth. The door was opened by Mercy's sister and brother-in-law. They soon took him into their own home, where he recovered for a time, and a young Mercy had been waiting there for him with her beautiful name, which he didn't deserve, and her loving arms, which he didn't deserve, and in time, she had brought forth two babies—nature's blessing, which he knew deep in his broken heart he could never deserve.

"Laney, behave yourself!" Scipio cried out suddenly, almost before he realized he was crying out. He looked around guiltily. The anger in his voice frightened him. Laney, who'd been yanking a younger child along by a braid like a farmer pulling a mule's reins, whipped around at the water's edge, her linsey-woolsey pinafore swinging around her scabbed knees. She lowered her chin—more bull than child, he thought—hands to her hips, so that even from a distance, he could read the obstinance there. Scipio glanced about for Mercy, but she was deep in conversation with another woman and there was only a single elder close by, smiling and saying, "She got the Lord's own fire, she do," and Scipio muttered, "She 'bout to get the Lord's own punishment." But it was just talk. He couldn't control his own child. And it troubled him. He looked past her at the river—the hateful, swollen, sickening river with its view of the Kentucky hills—and thought, Our children, they get spoiled by freedom. Laney don't even understand they kill girls like her over there—high-spirited, bold. Dark.

And that was his last clear thought before the incident, though prior to her fall there was a hazy swinging time, through which he waded, confused and sweating under a sweltering July sun that melted his mind and what remained of his will. He drank lemonade; he remembered later how it puckered the edge of his lip. There was a mélange of berries and apple that he knew he should enjoy, but it just reminded him how fruit inevitably rots, and all the while he tried not to look at the river, which hastened any dead thing into its decay. Finally, he looked at his wife to make sure of the time and place, and counted back fifteen years to their marriage day, also in July. When he couldn't remember where he was, he looked at her. And prayed he remembered her.

Then Laney fell in. She fell from one of the three mighty old-growth oaks that had fallen over in a terrible lightning storm the previous spring and landed like partially collapsed bridges in the shallows of the river. Like a bandleader, Laney had been guiding a small line of children out onto the slick, bark-stripped trunk of one tree when, irritated by the whining of the younger and more hesitant, she had turned to scold them, lost her footing, and slipped from the tree, sending up a small rictus like a white crown when she struck the hard water.

Scipio jolted forward instantaneously before the impulses of his body made any sense. He was running across the pebbly mud of the banks before he even realized it was his own daughter who had fallen in, his very own lifeblood subsumed by the waters. When he did realize it was Laney—his usually slow mind snapping puzzle pieces together with the speed of the lightning that had riven the trees—his only thought was: My baby can't swim. Because he refused to let his children anywhere near water.

Scipio flung himself into the river. His arms were an axe chopping it down, splintering it apart. Blood nearly burst the boundaries of his veins as it rushed through him, firing him through the shallows to the place where the cruel white crown had briefly appeared. With a madman's strength, Scipio dove straight down at the spot, while above him the children clung to the fallen tree, weeping and shrieking and pointing down where Laney had disappeared. Down, down he dove, his work-hewn arms fanning wildly in all directions, searching blind in the thick river waters, where the catfish lazed and the eels sidled, where bits of the further north drifted

past on their journey to the Deep South, where the dead watched with be-
musement or—he wondered—vindication. He could feel the river in his
mouth, threatening to fill him.

Then he found a snatch of wet linsey-woolsey. When he tugged, it threatened to tear, so he jetted forward, found Laney's little waist, and while she
struggled against him, her elbow finding his eye, he struggled mightily to
rise, dragging her toward the surface. His little girl kicked and fought like
a first-round prizefighter—radical strength and determination in such a
small, wiry body—unable to understand her fighting was her dying. She
jerked away and he pulled, she twisted and he wrestled her to him, and
somehow against the odds of water's gravity, they rose and rose until with a
great angry burst like two fishes in a death struggle, they breached the surface of the river, Laney sputtering and flailing in all directions, and Scipio
grappling for her arms and inching them toward the bank. He employed no
gentleness, simply dragging her by any means, but Laney had found oxygen now and began to scream in her husky, distinctive voice, in offense or
fear or both, she didn't know and would not be able to reconstruct later.
She only knew that she was dragged bodily toward the shore with her whole
life rising up in her throat, echoing on both sides of the river.

Once on the safety of the bank, Scipio began to beat her. He whipped
her around, his face a foreign mask of rage, and yanked up the sopping
pinafore and began to smack her behind, but sloppily, hitting like a brute,
like a wild man, so Laney was twisting and howling, causing his blows to
land on the small of her back and her hip. When his open hand abruptly
found the side of her face, she went sprawling from the blow, landing like a
bedraggled doll on the bank, and in an instant Scipio was grasped and
pinned down by what seemed like a thousand hands, and then the voices
rolled down the corridor Brother Scipio Brother Scipio Scipio Scipio
Scipio She all right The Lord is good Scipio Scipio Scipio
    Scipio.

The world began to return and pixelate around the edges of his vision,
then the light creeped inward, and he saw his little girl raised up off the wet
earth where he had flung her. I don't deserve my own child, he thought,
dazed. He watched as she was embraced and petted by two elders, watched
her try to shrug them off, her dark, wounded, angry eyes turned on him.
Mercy was behind him, he felt the distinctive touch of her hands even

amidst the other hands, the voices now saying, We got you, Brother Scipio. Everybody all right. Quit your struggling. Quit now.

Quit now? Someone began to pray even as he struggled to understand what quitting was, and he was reminded of that first prayer meeting he attended as a free man in Cincinnati, how he'd looked around at the worshippers gathered in the church, holding the borrowed Bible in his lap, thinking, You ain't safe here, even in the North. If the Lord even exist, he can't offer nobody safety nowhere. He knew that because the shore of Kentucky was always visible, a permanent reminder. A forever place.

Then he grew confused as to the year, as to whether Miss Abby was alive, or whether he had killed her in the river yet.

Again, he looked at Laney. No, he would never deserve any good thing. The devil didn't need to do his work on earth so long as servant Scipio was alive. A keening sorrow rose up and filled him. He felt his bones collapse in the building of his body, his lungs empty of air. And in the moment before he sputtered for breath, he knew suddenly and with an unshakable certainty, a prescient knowing, that soon his worn-out soul would go to the Rankins' house—a house he had built with his two hands—and he would say his final prayers to a God he did not believe in, a God who had abandoned him to a white world that extended far beyond the physical borders of slavery, and he would steal away to the attic where he had strung rope and placed a ladder. Then he would ascend the ladder of forgetting.

Scipio began to cry, and the sound snuffed Laney's tears in an instant. Her anger and self-pity evaporated as quickly as her clothes were drying in the July sun. She stared in open-mouthed astonishment as her great, gruff father, usually so still and stoic, a man in residence many miles behind his eyes, began to cry like a child in the arms of the elders as they prayed over him, their voices a gentle stream like the burbling of the river.

"Daddy," Laney said, struggling against some old woman who was holding her. "Daddy!"

Scipio didn't look at her, didn't seem to hear her; his weeping eyes were trained on the far distance. Abruptly, confusedly, Laney turned to see what he was staring at. What she saw then she would never forget: It was not just the expanse of Kentucky with its fine gradations of summer green, the sloping rise of gorgeous hills that led to a graceful interior. This time she saw something inside of the prettiness, something that had captured her father's gaze, or perhaps captured him. She saw the shadows between the trees, the grave-black spaces that could harbor secrets. Or people. They were natural hiding places. Your father is still hiding there, a voice inside her said—not her own voice but many voices, like the elders were speaking in the round of her heart. Your father never escaped, he couldn't. White folks won't give you nothing you don't demand, and you got to demand your soul long after the body reaches freedom. Then, like a good soldier, you got to fight for the souls of others, and if necessary you offer up your most precious thing—your life—to do so.

Laney whipped back around, facing the church crowd, full of new and sudden understanding. Then she took off running, stumbling briefly on the uneven ground of the riverbank, and slapping away the elderly hands that would hold her. She ran with arms outstretched, asking for what was not in her nature to need, something she would never again request, not even as a ploy when she was once captured guiding slaves out of Kentucky to the promised land. She asked forgiveness of her beloved father for the sin of ignorance, for wasting all the fight in her heart on foolishness, for not taking up arms in God's great war. She would never make that mistake again.

THE INTERPRETATION OF HORSES

For although God Gave unto Horses such excellent qualities at their Creation, now are they changed in their use and are become disobedient to man, and therefore must be subjected by Art.

—MICHAEL BARET, *An Hiponomie* (1618)

Moderator: Ladies and Gentlemen, I want to welcome you to the 2006 Kentucky Derby press conference featuring the connections to this year's winning horse, the 2005 Eclipse American Champion Two-Year-Old Filly, Hellsmouth of Forge Run Farm. We'd like to introduce trainer Mack Snyder, owner Henry Forge, and jockey Reuben Bedford Walker III, a trio of horse racing's finest. We'll start with a few questions for Mack, a four-time Derby winner, two-time winner of the Breeder's Cup, and all-around master of the three-year-old classics. Mack, can you say with confidence that Hellsmouth is the best horse you've ever brought to the Derby?

Mack: I sure as hell can.

Mod: She's shown a lot of personality and quickly become a crowd favorite. Has she also become a Mack Snyder favorite?

Mack: Well, the love of my life is always the one in my bed.

Mod: Now, it's a win but not a Derby record. Were you hoping for better speed today?

Mack: Records are nice, but time only matters in jail.

Mod: But can she take the Triple Crown? We've never seen a filly go all the way—Genuine Risk came closest—but then I think we can all agree we've never seen a filly quite like this one.

Mack: I'm standing here today to tell you this filly can and will go all the way. You can take that to the bank.

Mod: Now turning to the owner of Hellsmouth, a very familiar face in the racing world and one who's been chasing a Derby win for more than two decades, Mr. Henry Forge. Henry, do you feel that despite last year's injury, your filly can be ready for the Preakness in two weeks, then the grueling mile-and-a-half Belmont Stakes?

There was no immediate reply. All eyes turned to Henry, sitting stiffly in his shirtsleeves before the black YumBrands!YumBrands!YumBrands! banner that rippled faintly in the breeze from a fan. That same breeze prickled the sweat on Henry's forehead as he looked from one camera lens to the next, a sea of dark apertures narrowing on his face: age-freckled, quiet, haggard. He opened his mouth, closed it, opened it again. Then he said, "As of today I am pulling Hellsmouth from racing."

He wasn't sure at first whether he had said the words aloud, because no one moved. The room pitched into a Quaker quiet. It was as though they were waiting for the joke to crack, but Henry didn't even crack a smile. Beside him, Mack suddenly turned toward him, blooming pink, which turned to blustery red as his lips thinned. Then a single camera clicked, and the room came suddenly alive with the mad, syncopated clattering of a hundred cameras.

Mod: I . . . are you . . . . I'm sorry, I'm not sure I understood you properly. Are you intending to pull Hellsmouth from Thoroughbred racing altogether, or . . . ?

Mack: What? No, he's— Hell no—he's—

"Yes."

The word was uttered and then another Yes followed on the first, but louder this time and more resolute. Yes and Yes. The flashes were blinding; Henry grimaced, unable to open his eyes against the onslaught. Yes, he was certain. When he earnestly tried to recall the force of the old passions and antipathies, he could not; he could barely remember them at all.

He opened his eyes and sought out Lou in the crowd; she had lifted

Samuel out of his arms just before they'd taken their seats. He detected her on the fringe of the news conference, watching the event as it unfolded, alarm visible in her eyes. She shifted Samuel higher on her hip and—Samuel, yes, that child was the length and breadth of it now, the new world, his future, the whole future. His choice wasn't shame now, it wasn't even regret, though he had too many regrets to count; it was life.

It was rising in him—It—It could buoy him now, because it was no longer a chain. Henry came to his feet, knocking back his metal chair and pushing away the banquet table with a rough squawk, so that Mack and Reuben both scrambled backward, astonishment written in their every movement. Henry said, "I will contribute no more horses to this sport."

Belatedly, Mack's sense knocked back into place on his tongue. "Henry! Have you lost your goddamn mind?" But he was just biting air. Henry didn't acknowledge him—was either unwilling or unable to hear him—amidst the sudden pandemonium that erupted in the room. Mack grabbed out wildly for his arm, but Henry slipped from the table, a gray figure flashing briefly before the YumBrands!YumBrands!YumBrands! banner before stepping directly into the press that swarmed around him.

Behind them all, abandoned, Reuben remained exactly where he sat, eyes unblinking with his fingers knotted at his anorectic chest as though the banquet table still remained beneath them. He blinked rapidly, trading the mask of victory for one of a different kind. "Don't do it," he said on the barest whisper of breath. "Don't do it, old Paddy, or you'll be sorry."

Henry pressed into the frenzied crowd.

"Mr. Forge, what's brought about this abrupt change of direction?"

"Have your personal losses this year had any bearing on this turnabout?"

"Mr. Forge, are you one hundred percent sure?"

The feet were thunderous, the flashes a lightning storm. There were many voices in the storm calling out his name, but they didn't matter at all now, because there was no chaos in him any longer. He simply shouldered his way through them with a steadfast impassivity, his face a cipher. He walked straight to Lou and touched her elbow, and together they moved toward the door. Though her eyes were full of unasked questions, she didn't say a word, only switched Samuel to the opposite hip and kept pace as Henry began to hurry now with the sudden lightness of his release. His denial was an assent, and it was total. He was sure he was doing the right thing, though it was the hardest thing. The sensation was deliciously unfamiliar. Was this finally joy?

They attained the cooler air of the outer hall and passed through the main double doors where the sky yawned empty of rain, where the soaked ground glittered, and the dusty smell of horseflesh was swamped by the damp breeze. In the distance, beyond the roiling press, straggling fans still walked the grounds, boisterous hats weaving through the parking lot, where drunks were draped like amorous ragdolls on tailgates. Henry knew somewhere, probably in the back of some van, the garland of red roses was beginning to brown. Time is a horse you never have to whip.

As they pushed through the turnstiles, Lou finally gripped his arm, saying, "Henry, are you really doing this?"

Henry's mouth was empty as an urn. He kept walking in the direction of Barn 23.

Hellsmouth sensed them through the ground before she saw them. She'd been hotwalked and cooled out and was now done with her photos, all her showing out. Something was over. Her body was loose-limbed, sleepy, yet she wasn't exhausted, only resting. She was drifting in and out of fleet dreams under the hands that dried and curried her, that rubbed cream into her hide and made her shine.

Suddenly, her ears straightened and swiveled. Her tail twitched minutely, then whipped, and in a single agitated movement, she swung her dark, articulate head across the chain at the gate of her stall, her lips risen fretfully over her teeth, her mouth working.

Henry Forge and the horse stood eye to eye. For a long moment, they breathed each other's breath. Henry fought the urge to draw back away from the reality of what he saw, the reality of this horse, what he had not let himself see before. Hellsmouth was bold as life, but her brittle bones were no match for her power. The creative vitality of her gait, the tremendous heat of her racing engine fueled by her competitor's blood, that fierce physical ambition, which was wholly natural to her and as inextricable as her limbs, would come at the expense of her life. She would break. A competitor like Hellsmouth could never stop of her own accord. She was not just unwilling but actually unable to save herself.

"Load her up," Henry said.

Allmon, standing at the filly's head, made no immediate move. He'd also sensed Henry's approach, watched his whiteness intrude on the private warmth of the stall. Now his eyes were locked on Henry's, but he wasn't watching the realizations coalesce moment to moment in the man's eyes; he saw the darker shadow of a man dangling in his pitch-black pupils. Allmon flushed with hate that rose like a cold fire from his feet to the very follicles of his hair.

"Load her up," Henry said again. "I'm taking her home."

But Mack was there first. "No, no, no, no, hold on!" He was shouldering his way through the press, which had gathered, bearing down on their small circle of man and beast. "Nobody's going nowhere! Just hold on one fucking minute!"

"I said load her up!" The words erupted from Henry, startling Allmon from his hateful reverie. He realized quite suddenly what was being demanded of him and he stepped forward, his movements a rude assertion, eyes wide and lips parted for rebuttal, but Mack was on the warpath.

"Don't do this, Henry," the trainer said, grappling for Henry's elbow. "Just calm down—"

Henry whirled on Mack, his face finally ablaze with all the passion absent ten minutes before. "I won't race her anymore, Mack. You'll break her!"

If Mack was looking for acquiescence, he wasn't going to find it. He stepped into Henry, his bewilderment wrapped in rising anger and his hands working wildly, uselessly between them as if gesturing for words out of the charged air. "Nobody's breaking anybody!" he spat. "She's a goddamned racehorse! Let her do what she does best!"

"Not like this! Not this . . . !"

"Yes, yes—actually, fucking just like this!" Mack rejoindered, his head hobbyhorsing on his ruddy neck, his arms wide so the press nearest him could smell his sweat. "Henry, this horse was born to run! What the fuck are you talking about?"

Allmon looked from Mack to Henry, then back to Mack. Systolic waves of shock began to roll through his torso. It began to dawn on him what was happening here, what Forge was doing. This wasn't the plan, this sure as hell wasn't the deal, and if what seemed to be happening actually happened, then he had survived his fucking life, had scrambled and fought, for nothing. Nothing.

"She runs because we made her to run," blurted Henry, "not because—"

"Made her to run . . . ?" Mack snapped, sputtering like a jalopy. "Okay, Henry, okay, okay! Maybe because we"—he fumbled wildly, he couldn't wrap his mind around the goddamned absurdity of the foreign words about to come out of his mouth—"because we made their nature, doesn't make it any less their . . . what the fuck, Henry! What are you doing to me here?"

But Henry had turned his back on Mack, stonewalling him better than any ex-boyfriend ever had, and now the damn baby was whimpering behind him, and the press, those jackals, didn't know where to look any more than Allmon did, and Mack's eyes were apocalyptic as he tried to discover the final word, the persuasive knife that would slice straight through the insanity to the common fucking sense. "Henry Forge! Listen to me now! A filly like this—she's a bullet out of a gun! You pulled the trigger three years ago and you cannot—LISTEN TO ME, YOU CANNOT STOP THE BULLET NOW! All you've got to do is just stand back! Stand back and let her happen, Henry."

There was a long moment of silence as Allmon and the press leaned in, collective breath on hold.

"I'm asking you to load my horse," said Henry, very steely and very quietly in Allmon's direction.

Allmon, silent until this very moment, leveled Henry with a brute stare. "Over my dead body." But the words were stronger than his hope and crumbled on his tongue like old tabby, because two things happened at once: he realized suddenly that his previous maneuvering was a farce, that his name on a dotted line was worth less than an afternoon's dream, that it was always men like Forge who controlled everything in this world; then Lou stepped into his line of vision, baby in her arms. At first Allmon spared only a fleet glance for the way her right hand cradled the child's head all sprung with plump curls that framed his wide-eyed face. But then he noted the soft darkness of the face. Blood stalled in Allmon's veins. Instant recognition: loose curls and those eyes. He knew them from photographs of himself as a baby, photos that had disappeared along with everything else, thrown away by strangers when his mother died. His lips parted in shock, and his wide eyes slid back to Henry and locked in place like the old prison door.

Henry had been watching. They shared a long stare in which a hard reckoning began to unfold, and then Henry said, simply, "Yes." Henry reached forward and slipped the reins from Allmon's hand, but Allmon jerked his hand away as though Henry's touch were a snake. The purity of his astonishment transformed his face into that of a child's, the Allmon of a hundred years ago.

When Henry spoke again, his words were softer. "I'll load her," he said, and then he passed a cold, hard ring into Allmon's trembling hand. His car keys. "Why don't you bring my car to the farm tomorrow. I'll do my best to explain."

Without further ado, he left Allmon where he stood frozen and led the big girl out. Though her ears were plastered back and her lip curled, she strode purposefully from her confines, her head high as the cameras captured the cut of her balletic leg, the muscle showing stark from the day's dehydration. She took all of Allmon's breath with him as she went, and he fumbled without oxygen for the scraps of truth to form the whole. But the whole was hell. If this child was his, then Henry had lied to him for six months. If this child was his, then he had never been betrayed by Henrietta; in truth—*in truth*—the betrayal was all his own. He had used her like meat and then left her to rot. I am Mike Shaughnessy's son after all. Suddenly, woodenly, he began to move in the direction of the baby, of the horse, of whatever remained of his broken and blasted life.

When Hell was tied and secure in the trailer, she lowered her head to gaze out the slide window at the cameras. She raised her lips at the press and stamped dreadfully. At pasture, on the track, or tied in an aluminum box, she knew she was the gift. And she knew they knew it too.

Henry turned to Lou and lifted Samuel out of her arms. "Thank you," he said simply, then hauled himself into the Chevy's bucket seat and looked at Mack and said, "We're done here, Mack. You're too hard on horses."

Mack, who had charged after them, raised one red hand, as rough and cracked as an old, worn baseball glove, and pointed directly at Henry. "You listen to me good, Forge," he said, then made a circling gesture at the press. "Listen, all you assholes. You think I'm hard on horses? You think

I'm tough? Well, I'm the only one in this fucking place who knows what respect looks like! All you critics writing your shitbit reviews, you Monday morning quarterbacks that can't even throw a spiral, you actually think it's a *virtue*"—his lips trembled—"to coddle a great talent? To rein in the best of the very best? Listen to me, if you got the fire, then you burn! You don't throw fucking ashes on it! You don't tamp it out!" He pointed into the trailer at Hell, and she looked right at him with one black, half-wild eye. "It's better to be great and break down than to never be great at all. She knows it, I know it, and anybody with any goddamn courage knows it. That filly's got bigger balls than the rest of you put together!"

Henry settled Samuel on the seat beside him and inserted the key. Allmon pressed against the crowd—that is my son, that is my child—but try as he might he couldn't get through the crush of press that surrounded the trailer like a security detail. Panic flooded him.

Mack stepped up to the driver-side door. Even as his head seemed to balloon visibly with a fury that threatened to burst his eyeballs, his voice was steady and hard. "Don't do this, Henry," he said. "Don't you turn on that goddamn truck. Listen to what I'm saying. Listen to what that horse's body is saying."

The truck engine roared to life.

Mack punched at the air and took a single step forward. His voice was so loud, they damn near heard him on the other side of Churchill Downs. "You bring her back to me, Henry!" he yelled as the truck pulled out with the trailer. "Either she's on my farm in one week for the Preakness, or I'm gonna come get that filly myself, and she's going all the fucking way! Do you hear me, HENRY? ALL THE MOTHERFUCKING WAY!"

Henry sped eighty miles an hour down I-64. The Kentucky acres sweeping past, he was buffeted by wave after wave of realization. This horse—this life—was his patient, always had been, always would be. The soul was not an essence but a doctor. The salve was not medication or temporary rest or painkillers, but his action in the world under the aegis of his will. Yes. I, Henry Forge, swear by Apollo, the healer, Asclepius, Hygieia, and Panacea, and I take witness to all the gods, all the goddesses, to keep according to my ability and my judgment, the following oath and agreement: I will prescribe regimens for the good of my patients according to my ability and my judgment and never do harm to anyone. I will preserve the purity of my life and my arts. If I keep this oath faithfully, may I enjoy my life and practice my art, respected by all humanity and in all times; but if I swerve from it or violate it, may the reverse be my life.

Henry looked toward the bloodred sky of diminishing day and wondered whether there was forgiveness in it. Who was his doctor? Did he even deserve one? His eyes filled with tears and they turned the sky to a crimson wash, so it seemed he was peering through tears of blood. He would be home in an hour.

They were gone—the cameras, the press, the crowds. It was so quiet now you could almost hear the monarchs winging over the milkweed and wallflower and the pollen tumbling through the breeze. Allmon was squatting with his palms flat against the outside wall of the barn, the exit to nowhere within his sights, when he detected the distinct patter of a featherweight approach, fleet feet ferrying a man on the run. On those feet followed an unmistakable voice, a squeal on gravel with its faux jaunty no-care air: "I jumped in the seat and gave a little yell; the horses ran away, broke the wagon all to hell; sugar in the gourd and honey in the horn, never been so screwed since the day I was b— Allmon, as I live and breathe! Why so forlorn, my man?"

Allmon didn't look up, he didn't have to. His head remained bowed, as if the crumbled mulch between his feet required the whole of his concentration, but all he saw before him was his son's face. "Go away," he hissed. It was barely a whisper, but the force of hate in his words surprised even him. He couldn't take any more today. He couldn't take any more ever.

Reuben reared back. "What? Who? Me? What has dear Reuben done?"

Allmon came up unsteadily from his crouch, so he rose with the height and clumsy movement of a bear to turn heavily on Reuben. "Forge left. He took Hell and left." There was more, but he couldn't form the words.

Reuben's mouth smiled slowly with a pained draw, and a single veiny hand drifted to his chest with cold, calculated surprise. "Withdrew her out from under this here jock?"

"Withdrew." The word was disgusting, vile. It was violent. It smashed the whole of hope.

Reuben shook his head and whistled softly. "Jockey claims foul . . ."

Allmon practically spat words through rising grief. "Nobody's running that horse again, not even you—the great Reuben Bedford Walker III!"

"Are you sure about that?" Reuben's slaten eyes never wavered from All-mon's face.

"I'm done!" And then Allmon forced the worst words. "He took my son!"

Reuben cocked his head. "Your what?"

"That motherfucker lied to me! He's raising up my son!"

Now Reuben reared back cartoonishly with a surprise that even he couldn't hide. "By Jove and Elegua . . . ," he whispered.

Allmon stretched his arms wide. "My fucking child! My child's in his house! I'm standing here and all I got in my hand is the keys to his fucking car. I'm sick, I need money. I need my own child! And all I got after all this, *all* of it—is some keys." He stared down at the keys, heavy as a heart in his hand. Yes, men like Forge had the keys to everything.

Reuben shook his head and regained his bearings; he leaned forward with narrowed, coy eyes. "Out of the saddle and into the dirt—thereby hangs but not ends a tale. Snatched swaddlings aside, what about the horse? Riddle me this—do you or do you not have a deal with Mr. Forge? Surely the deal still stands and the filly must race to the end of the season. Of course"—Reuben cleared his throat—"Mack would take the reins if Forge were to become . . . indisposed. All's well that ends well, isn't that what they say when there's something rotten in Kentucky?"

Now the impossible highs and lows of the day had worn Allmon's self-control to a bloody nub. His child's face swam before his aching eyes. It was all he could do not to shake the jock right out of his simpleness; he wanted to pick up his scrawny 118-pound carcass and separate it from his chicken neck. "I made a deal with the devil!" He said it too loud and too slow, as if the jock were not only hard of hearing but stupid too. "No clause for with-drawing the horse! All I was supposed to do was keep her healthy, but no-body never said he couldn't pull her. I got nothing. You hear me?" Then a sneaking thought: Forge lied, but I sold my child. My soul is as rotten as old fruit. He wanted to weep, but this was grief beyond weeping.

Reuben's whole body grew utterly still, except for his fingertips, which twitched, and his eyes, which grew full of unfathomable things. With the speed of a striking snake, his arm swept through the crook of Allmon's arm. The taller man was jerked from the barn wall with a hissing command and inhuman strength, which was the hard secret of the jock's body: "Come along, my little wingnut. Come with me." A mismatched pair; Reuben tugged him toward the border of a parking lot, away from prying eyes, but no one was watching them now, they were of no interest to anyone; no one cared now that the superhorse was gone.

When Reuben spoke again, his voice was winsome and savage in equal measure. "Now hear this," he said. "The story's not even over and you're already telling it wrong! That's the problem with you—you never learned to tell a story slant, never learned to tell your own. Why, not once have you wooed me with swashbuckling tales of your days on the streets, your adventures in prison! You're too obedient by far, dragging your chains in resignation! Even when they've snatched your darling mtoto!" The jock shrugged and sighed. "But what can old Reuben do? Some are born to be kings, and some are content to be jewels on the king's sleeve. Maybe it's in the blood."

Allmon didn't listen with his old defended silence, his brooding brow shielding his eyes and overhanging his heart. He whirled to face the jock. "Why you always schooling me? I don't need your fucking lectures! Do this, do that, talking nonsense. You don't know shit about me!" But behind his words, he thought: Blood? My blood is poisoned. Momma gave me bad blood. A dying man wouldn't drink my blood to save his own life.

Reuben reared back on his booted heel, the lines of his starved face like knife tracks down brown bread. "Is that right? I don't know you? You think Reuben is a four-foot fool and ignorant as all that? Why, you're transparent as glass! You're nothing but a little nug of amber, and old Reuben can see clear through you to the other side!" He pressed his face up toward Allmon's. "You think I don't know the sobstory streets you grew up on? I smell government cheese on your breath, you got blisters on your thumbs from selling cut-rate crack! Concrete clefts in your eyes, bones broke by the police! Your daddy's fled and your mama's dead! You turned your back for one second and they stole your baby just like they always do! You think Reuben's ignorant? Well, maybe you need to recognize just how much I recognize!"

Allmon was already talking over Reuben's talk, features smeared with disgust and alarm. "That's all you think I am? That's it?"

Reuben waved a dismissive hand. "One man's stereotype, another man's award-winning performance. So you followed the script designed to mold you. They call you a brute born to a single mama, raised on welfare, sent to juvie, then prison, a man who walks out on his child and now shovels shit. Oh, you want their approval, but from now till eternity, they'll feed you just enough scraps off their plate to keep you hanging around their knees with your tongue lolling out. You won't starve to death, Allmon, but you'll always be their bitch."

Allmon roared, "I got nothing! All I've been doing, I've been trying to survive! The rules help them, not me! I didn't make this world, but I got to survive in it! The game wasn't designed for nobody but them to win!"

"Shhhh, I get it, I get it," Reuben whispered, glancing over his shoulder to determine the limits of their privacy. Then with something that looked like compassion, he said, "You think I don't understand the dreams you nurse in that big old coxcomb of yours? Think I don't know you pissed your drawers the first time you laid eyes on these big old Kentucky mansions with their pretty horses running rounds? Their frosty girls and money-colored grass? Oh, but you didn't just want the money, did you, my dear? Oh no—Allmon Shaughnessy wanted the dream!" Reuben searched for ammunition in Allmon's distressed face. "The dream of the Deep. Dark. Southland." He paused with the tip of his pink tongue between his teeth. "Well, has Reuben got the shock of a lifetime for you, Yankee Doodle Doo. Kentucky ain't the Deep South; it's the minstrel of the United States! Just a white nigger dandied up and trying to pass as an aristocrat! Haw!"

Allmon pressed a hand to his forehead as if to ward off the dim aura of a migraine. "I don't even want to know what you're talking about now."

But Reuben was six feet tall and rising. There was no stopping him. "This land right here under your clumsy-ass feet? Why, this here's the No-Man's-Land, the Borderland, the Dark and Bloody Ground, the In-Between, the Slaughterhouse, the Wild Frontier—the original Nameless Place! But they won't tell you that in school, no sirree!" Reuben spread his skinny arms as if to gather his powers. "See, back in the good ole cotton-picking days, all these plantations here—yes, my little almond, these plantations you so lust after—they grew corn to the eye and horses to the sky. Hickory-boned colts put cash in Kentucky coffers. But this here Commonwealth had a PR problem, didn't they? The piss-yella Yanks were scared to death of our dark idyll, our low-down disordered hell! A hundred and twenty counties of bourbon and murder, thick with backward woodsmen and outlaws fond of affrays and fucking, an uncivilized land of barkers and daredevils and gunslingers, horse raiders and assassins, barn burners and Klansmen. A damnable district of dopers and dastardly deeds—whippings and murders and baleful butchery! Kaintuckee meant scrapings from the devil's boot!" He yelped a sharp rebel yell.

"Why, there wasn't one man in a hundred willing to brave our races for fear of getting shot, so they started building tracks in New Jersey and New York. Pimlico purses got plump, Saratoga got sass, and the races ran like a Longines. Now, the perfidious paddy jocks wanted their share of the take, because we brothers were the best, and they couldn't gain a nose against us. So what do you think they did? Why, they staged a coup, of course, and blocked us from our own best game—they ousted us! Soon money was a river running north. Woe and lamentation! The Borderland went bust!"

Reuben leaned in. "So, what's a sweet little state to do in the face of bad press?"

Allmon didn't want to hear any more. He was growing increasingly ill with every word.

"Why, you spin, my little catfish. You spin like an ad man on Madison Avenue. Slap some columns on your farmhouse and paint it all white, get you some Spanish moss, rustle up an ancestral line and hire a noble Negro for a portrait, a sorry brother still bowing to the Lost Cause, scraping his bitchass snout on the ground. And marvels never cease! It works"—Reuben hissed and winked and drawled slow—"'cause don't nobody know they history."

A pinprick pierced the skin of Allmon's mind. The Reverend was right; I never should have crossed that river.

Reuben crowed in delight. "Yes! The Confederacy rose again for the very first time! Everybody forgot the Dark and Bloody Ground wasn't ever the Deep South at all, just a yellowbelly borderland of hellraisers and cowards. Most never fought for ole Jeff Davis a day in their lives! Kentucky didn't secede till the war was over! But hang your stars and bars, muddle a mint

julep, stick a lawn jockey on the drive, and everybody forgets what there is
to forget! The revelation of reinvention—it's the great white hope! The real
American dream! Ain't no fact in this world like a white man's tall tale!"

Allmon stared down at the ground in wonder, the words transforming
into fresh horrors in his mind. Reuben reached up one iron-rough hand
and grasped his shoulder. It remained steady as he spoke, his voice now thick
and heavy as a comfort. "But you didn't know, my friend. For that old fiction,
they got a man to sign away his life. Got him to sign away his baby boy."

Allmon shook his head to stave it off, but a soul sickness was rising up
and he couldn't stop it. "I signed my name," he whispered.

The jock waved away this objection with a brush of his other hand.
"You need to unass that notion! Your black vernacular ass ain't signed shit.
X don't mean nothing. Learn your history! White lies don't add up to the
truth! Your only choice was no choice!"

"I made a choice." Allmon's throat was full of shame, he was choking
on it.

Reuben tossed up his hands in frustration. "No, goddammit—you keep
telling the story all wrong! You think little sister had any choice when Massah sold her baby off the auction block at Cheapside, not seventy miles
away from this here horse track? They call their madness logic, but that
don't make it logic! Your life or your child? You call that a choice? Why, it's
fuckery and perversion, the cant of the Kaintuckee! History, Allmon—
learn your history!"

Allmon turned to him slowly like someone waking. "I know shit about
them you don't even know."

"Then use it! Tell the tale! Throw open the doors of that prison!" The
grip of the jock's hand and grin grew monstrous. "Get loose and dark, get
unruly and rank! Look at me—I'm black as a train and twice as fast, I'm
gonna run you down with the new reality! The man that stole your child is
the same man that killed your mother, the man that put you behind bars,
that's the same man that's been stringing up the black brother since time
immemorial. Think about that, Allmon! How you like them rotten apples?
I picked them just for you."

Allmon made an inhuman sound deep in his throat. Everything that
had come before this moment was creating a bursting pressure in his chest.

Reuben raised one triumphant finger. "Let it penetrate your sticky ear! If that is not the truth, then they changed the definition of truth. What say you? Is it the truth?"

Allmon was dizzy with a swirling sensation, the muddy confluence of one will slipping into another.

"Tell me for the sake of that child! Yes or no?"

It shot out of him. "Yes!"

"Then cut your jesses and burst your bridle! That child belongs with its rightful owner!"

Mother and Momma. Her name was Marie.

Reuben's whisper was harsh. "This is your time, Allmon . . ."

No, wait, wait, wait—

"Allmon . . ."

Allmon shook his head.

"Be a man."

Allmon drew a harsh, sudden breath. Then he straightened up and turned an unblinking eye on Reuben. He stared disdain down his nose. "I don't need you telling me what to do."

Reuben blinked then and reached out to place a palm firmly on Allmon's chest. "No," he said, shaking his head as if weary. "You don't. Your mind was made up before I turned the corner. I can see that now. You are the superior man in every way."

Allmon shrugged off his hand. "I got to go."

Reuben made a faint gesture toward Allmon's hand. "And now you have the keys to the kingdom."

Allmon said nothing in response. He had already turned away to scan the massive parking lot for the Forge Mercedes, a silver fish in a lurid sea of luxury cars. First he limped along on his aching joints, then he was running through the pain to get where he knew he had to go, where he was meant to go, where his child was being held hostage. Reuben watched him weave unsteadily between cars. He muttered, "A late response is still a great response." Then he turned his back and thumped his chest once to clear the phlegm, realizing that the after-parties were elsewhere and soon to commence. He grinned.

Henry stared over the dash at the undulating expanse of Forge Run Farm, the filly behind him in her trailer, Samuel asleep on the bucket seat of the dually, content in the farm dust and the animal dander. With some shock, Henry realized that despite the uproar of the day, the farm—this world he had created—was still in his possession and nothing could change that. Here was the two-hundred-year-old house, which had been the dream of the first Samuel; here was the crumbling fence and the perpetual stream. Here was the overgrown orchard and the old barns converted and stocked with horseflesh he had bred.

It struck him as preposterous, impossible, that in short order his family would be exposed and naked to the world, that the taproot name, from which all their brief names had sprouted like a season's leaves, would be ridiculed as some kind of fraud or, worse, would become synonymous with the way things fall apart, how autumn follows on every fulsome summer. Henry replayed his choices at the track, including his abrupt decision to bring Samuel and reveal him to his father. Allmon was a man he barely knew. Henry had imagined himself as stepping out of his family like a man emerging from shadow. But now on the firm ground of the farm, his resolve wavered, his old truculent defenses ever at the ready: if any crime had been committed, it was his father's doing, not his own. Yes, Henry had lied stupidly, but he'd merely been a prisoner of another man's ideas. His father had been the progenitor of hate and disunion, his father would have had half the world hanging from the boughs of a holly tree, his father was the one who—

His own thinking degenerated to white noise in his mind.

He could no longer convince his most faithful audience, himself.

Henry looked around helplessly, his old passions like vestigial organs. They couldn't fill the vacuum created by the lost generation. It was breathtaking: Once his daughter had been a little girl on this very ground, her ring finger crooked, her legs bandy, her face configured by irreplaceable, unrepeatable bones. She had held her hands to her hips in a particular way. She had frowned like this, tilted her head like that. She had emerged as a singular mystery, sui generis, from the womb of the woman who had once been his wife—a woman with red lips he'd met on the track, a woman who had left after many, many arguments, none of which were more important than the gum on the bottom of his shoe. He still recalled the set of his young wife's chin and how the iris of her eye soon turned the color of dissatisfaction. Now the little girl they had created was vanished. Her death was a marvel, a mystery, the ultimate school.

Henry raised a trembling hand to his brow as if shielding his eyes, though evening's evanescent light streamed from a distant eternity behind the truck. His heart beat terribly. How could life be so boring and terrifying and exhilarating and confounding all at once? Its contradictions did not seem possible. He felt so old suddenly. Yes, he *was* old. But this was newly unobjectionable. Cut the throat of *puer aeternus* and bury him in a vacant chamber of Henry's heart.

He watched with a kind of bland, uneventful horror as years of ambition swirled and washed rapidly down the drain.

My God, he had to get out of the truck or he was going to have a stroke, be laid down in the dust like his father had been that autumn day so many years ago. He eased his road-weary bones out into the dwindling warmth of the day. He needed the fresh breeze to clear his mind and strengthen his body. He needed his feet on the ground; he needed, most of all, to think.

So now there was nothing between him and the land. He saw that imminent change was all around him. The ragged and unattended orchard could be curated, its trees trimmed and grafted to produce a bounty of apples again. That could be enough to slake the thirst of a thousand people, and maybe it would. The breeding operation could be slowed, or halted— yes, even halted—and some of the paddocks returned to pasturage. After all, this was the finest growing land in the country outside of Iowa, and treasure troves of produce could be cropped. Even their new, relatively small garden could feed many more than Samuel and himself. Maybe, when all was said and done, he would return some of the land to its original wildness, something his daughter had seemed to value. Land needed no purpose after all. Land was an end in itself. Now to the barns—his excitement rose, he realized he could use them as they were. He could shelter and reschool retired Thoroughbreds. He had the permanent wealth to do so; racing had never been a moneymaking venture for him. Forge Run Farm could be a place of renewal and rest, where something old and broken could become fresh again. The very idea filled him with sober joy.

Hellsmouth interrupted his planning. She was stamping her impatience on the aluminum floor of the Turnbow, jutting her nose against the glass of the window. She swung her truculent head toward him when he pulled the ramp and unhitched the swinging door. She was here in this world as much as he was, and he would do well to remember it.

As he guided her out—and how good it felt in his shoulders, his hands, his whole being to handle his animal, the way it had felt when he was a younger man and racing was new to him, when the adventure of life was still largely to come—Hell seemed to have grown a hand on the journey. She loomed over him, her head swiveling on the tower of her neck, taking the farm in round. An uncontained shiver looped across her withers and under her girth. This was her old playground, and she recognized it, so she wouldn't come placidly. She was barking like a seal, dancing up on springy legs that reminded Henry, not for the first time, of dark and knotty rose stems.

Good sense dictated that he install his champion in the foaling barn far from the wild stimulus of the fields, let her recalibrate to the freedom of the farm, a freedom near limitless against her life on the track. But she had other plans and pulled Henry across the brick chip lane to the old paddock where she had once nursed greedily, where she had gamboled as a weanling in the simple restraint of a nylon halter, where she had gazed across rumpled earth like the sides of green bells to the eastern mountains with their black interstitial valleys and glinting rivers. She knew this was where she belonged.

When Henry clipped her off the lead, Hell rocketed out into the field, her aluminum shoes blurring arcs that trampled timothy grass and tossed turf. Reaching the center of the paddock, she kicked out with the silliness of a goat, then jumped once and turned, her conformation showing out speed and stamina, the Remus and Romulus of her sport. She snorted, then gathered herself up and, with a triumphant leap, began to run. Henry reached for the top rail, suddenly terrified that she would drive herself through the fencing into the safety lane and reopen her chest or break her own bones. Instead, she cut savagely left at the first corner and traced a round in the falling light, beating a retrograde path, brightening in evening's light and accelerating as she neared Henry like a heavenly body in egress. Her hooves reverberated into the roots of the trees.

Henry stepped away from the fence with his mind suddenly clear: If you closed every racetrack in the world, hung every bridle and threw open every paddock, horses would still race one another on the open plain. It was inevitable, undeniable, because their competition was innate. The greatest dreams of humans were nothing but clumsy machinations next to the natural ambition of animals.

Hell had barely slowed when Henry returned to the truck, where Samuel remained placidly asleep, exhausted by the excitement of the day. Henry drew up the bundled baby, but a question appeared suddenly in his mind, which had become like an empty room.

What if he had been born out on the tableland in a modest white farmhouse in Emerson, Nebraska, the child of landlocked Swedes, who told him, "This land will never make you rich. True wealth is in the hope for simple things. Son, work the land, dote on your children, and ease your elders into gentle deaths."

Or, what if he had been born a fisherman in Mobile? What if he'd folded himself into his boat every morning and pressed out against the tide, trawling for tiny swimmers to feed to his neighbors, and did this every day for sixty years until his anonymous death, knowing nothing resembling worldly ambition, only the land and the sea and the land and the sea, and wanting nothing more?

But he, Henry Forge, had not been born into those lives. He had been born into this indelible life. *This* was his grandson against his chest and *this* was his diaper bag in his left hand. And *this* here was his kitchen door, which his father, that old colossus, had slammed again and again in frustration over the course of decades. Henry could not now bring himself to walk through that door, to reenter history. Not yet. Evening flooded everything. Final ruby light plunged across the pastures. It filled every corner of his senses. He had been favored by fate to live on this plot of land his entire life, as rooted as any plant. But for the plant there was no ambition, and so no madness into which it needed to descend to cut through the confusion of daily living, the crass noisemaking of everyday speech, the rapidity of time's passage and its pseudolosses—what the human called its losses.

The flora and the simple fauna, they had no fathers, only genetic predecessors, and because they had no fathers, they had no stories, and because they had no stories, they didn't suffer any notion of themselves. In the landscape behind his eye, Henry fashioned a prairie of purple coneflowers, lovely and indistinguishable. He imagined the absurdity of one flower asserting its singularity, its glory, yearning to stand a hard-won inch above its nearest neighbors, straining on its flimsy stalk, flailing its petals, whispering in a hoarse, pollen-choked voice, "Me! Me! Me!"

Ambition is a form of suicide if it kills the simple self.

He looked down into Samuel's face. What do you know, Henry? His mind no longer howled with a grief that obscured fact; he had no more strength left to resist naked realization. There were galaxies in the body of every man and woman; Henrietta's had gone unexplored. He had flung her life away before her death. And he had mistaken the black body for a beggar's suit. Until today, until he had brought Samuel into the rain-washed open air of Churchill Downs, he had never rebelled against his father, not really.

What he knew could barely fill a teaspoon, and it looked mostly like hope: Samuel's diaper would be dirty again shortly, he would wake once during the night, there would be a few more ear infections, then he would begin to crawl and come rounding along the el porch on a shiny red bicycle his grandfather had bought him, he would read many books full of useless information, then make love with a woman and have a child, succeed at something, fail at many more things, argue perhaps to the point of breaking with his own child, then stoop and shrivel and go slack on some hospice bed somewhere, his eyes wide with Lavinia's disappointed wonder.

Still, Henry did not reach for the door. Though his body was exhausted—never more so—his mind was not fatigued. In his arms, Samuel was making the kittenish sounds of waking. In a minute or two, they would pitch headlong into a darkly blue night. But Henry's race was not yet run. There was still something to be known, something that arrested his movement. His mind pressed forward, grappling for it; he could feel the ache of its muscular exertions.

He might be a fool, a climber, a dreamer, supremely guilty, maybe he was even evil, yet hadn't he preserved the perfection of this land? Who else but the Forges and their ilk had done this, could do this? The poor of the earth were the tramplers of the earth, and that was the truth. Give them a beautiful thing and they would foul and wreck it. One last time, the old fire reasserted itself: Why should he, Henry, restrain himself? He was not the child of immigrants, not a fisherman, not a simple, unremarkable flower in a field. Look at what he had built; look at what he alone had made from the mud of his will and the mortar of his desire! If he was indeed a member of the animal kingdom—and he would grant that he shared something with the crude and base animal—why should he restrain himself when restraint was required of no other beast? The dogs rutted in the yard and the lions slaughtered the antelopes. The owl was as ruthless as the rattlesnake and so on and so on. Even the earth obeyed the demands of its nature: it snatched everything, absolutely everything, whether mountain or beast or daughter, back to its breast. Human beings alone were capable of greatness. Only they could even conceive of greatness. So he had stomped on necks, so he had used his daughter. He had grown rich in the wild capitalism of life! Those incapable of greatness despise greatness the most; theirs were the loudest voices denying its very possibility.

Father, we are uniquely capable of morality. We must be moral, because we can be moral.

He stood very still as the words settled like silt to the floor of his veins.

We can snatch from the air the abstractness of numbers, adding and subtracting and making logic from magic, and because we can, we do, and we must. We can build pyramids and sky-piercing towers, so we must. We can wrestle language from our grunting, so we must. We can map our physical mysteries with machines of our own making. We can classify the species of the earth, name every stone and streamlet. We can run a hundred miles, and we can walk on the face of the moon, so we must—and then we must go farther.

We can, from the chaos of existence, extract meanings, which do not exist. We can make ourselves philosophers and scientists and priests. We can construct our unnatural civilizations—we can, and therefore we must. To starve our genes is to honor our genes. With fear and loathing we can stand on the necks of our parents and refuse them. We can evolve from simple to complex. We can choose survival of the species over survival of the self. We can say no to nature and form a conspiracy of doves.

We are uniquely capable of morality, therefore we must be moral. That *is* our nature.

Across miles of time, I am coming for you, Henry Forge, and I am coming to settle for my son. I'm taking from you what's not yours, what I had no earthly business giving away. My fingers are shanks, my arms are lead pipes, my head is a cinder block to your skull. My life is death.

It's the bullpen for you, Henry Forge.

Let me tell it to you straight. Let me open your fucking ears until they bleed. I'm going to rip your eyelids away. In your fancy fucking car, I've got a story to tell.

The holding cell is this: dumb, dirty, sick, tired, evil, bored motherfuckers—forty of them shoved into a cell built for fifteen. I'm a kid among men. It's crazy, terrifying loud, sound of a cranked-up soap opera with bad reception over the wailing honky-tonk singer on the guard's radio, and there's so much talk, high-pitched crank chatter, two dudes fighting and someone yelling nonstop at the guards, begging and pleading, then talking shit, then begging again, and somebody's sick, the noise makes your head spin. And the smell! You try to breathe without using your nose so you don't retch—it's cigarettes, urine tang, BO smell, whole place like a barnyard and shit, oh my God, the shit. Only two things nonhuman in this crowded, sweaty hellhole, concrete benches and a stainless steel toilet clogged with shit. You got to go so bad, you don't think you shit since Cincinnati, but you're not about to do that in front of these people. You know what happens. You've heard all the talk, half the brothers in Northside had gone up inside. So you know. And they're all watching. Big-ass black Gs with hooded eyes and tattooed arms like trees, and white, meth-addled motherfuckers, strung out with open sores and scabs all over and mean, you can tell, like raw pitbull mean, a few wore-out men smoking or muttering or coughing up spit, but all of them keeping an eye on you, because nobody here is white with money, so you're the lowest on the totem pole, just a kid, someone says,

"Young."

But you're too scared to look at who said it. You stare straight ahead, stoic, try to look tough.

"Cigarette?" someone says, and squeezes in beside you.

"Naw." You firm up your shoulder. You can't accept nothing from no one. You can't owe nobody nothing. But the guy isn't leaning into you, isn't pressing your space, isn't trying to insinuate. You realize it's some old dude, hopefully harmless. Maybe. But you don't look him in the eye, you keep staring straight ahead, because you can't trust yourself not to break down. Grief is blocking up every orifice—can't shit, can't piss, can't cry, you wouldn't be able to eat if there was anything to eat. Your mother is six days in the ground. Everything inside you is paralyzed.

"What they bring you in for?"

Grand theft auto, speeding, driving without a license, resisting arrest, possession of a controlled substance, there's more but the words are all running together and it's confusing, it's like you're trying to read left to right or something.

"You got previous arrests?"

"Yeah."

The man nods. "They gonna send you up then."

"I'm seventeen." The words jet out, almost indignant. High with disbelief.

Dry laugh. Then he just says, "Well, they gonna send you to juvie first. But then, you going in. Me, I been in and out since I was twelve. Trust me, you be all right if you play. But hear me, Young: Niggahs always gonna try. Got to be on the awares. Fresh meat. Know what I'm saying?"

Stricken, you dare to glance at the man.

The man purses out his lower lip. "You gonna figure it all out, but you got to be wise like a serpent. You ain't small but you ain't big neither. You got a hard face, that's good. That'll get you mad respect if your fists as hard as your face. So when you get up in there, you gotta act a man. Get some cat in your stride. Straight up rough. No motherfucking hesitation. Don't nobody care if you a teenager except the niggahs that aim to turn you out."

Then the man settles into himself, crosses his arms over his chest, looking sleepy. He's done, his wisdom imparted. But that's it? There isn't anything else? You turn and stare through the bars, but you're just one of a dwindling many—they keep getting hauled off for their arraignments or let out on bail. You stare in desperation at the guards like maybe they'll recognize you, see the little kid in you. But the guards are white, glassy-eyed, they've seen it all before, years and years of it. You all look alike. You aren't Allmon anymore, Mike Shaughnessy's son with the Reverend's hands and Marie's soft nature. You're just a black boy neither big nor small with a fat nose and 3b hair, a body with no past and no future. A notevenreallywannabe thug. Nothing. Less than nothing.

When they close that rumbling thundering deadening door of steel bars, you've officially passed through the gates of hell.

Now, today, here in this car on this May evening, all you got is the memories flooding in . . . and pain. Can't lie to yourself anymore. It's here. It

C. E. MORGAN

was always in you, Marie's lost life making a wild wail of your joints and eyes. And you thought you had got control somehow—in this world where they murder mothers! But, Allmon, Marie got used and abused by Mike Shaughnessy just like Henrietta got used and abused by you—no, don't think, can't think. This isn't even about that, it's not even about your child, who got tricked out of your arms; this is about simple survival now! When Henry Forge takes away the future, he doesn't just take away money, no, he takes away your chance to go to the doctor and say, "See I got this little problem, just a setback, but I know you got medicine for me. I know you can save me and you will save me. Because I got money now. That's the key to survival in this country. I got money, so in this great nation that means I deserve to live."

I'm talking to nobody at all, am I? No one in the living world is listening. They kill your most precious thing, then close their ears to you. But I'll say it anyway:

The trial is in a plain, nondescript room, nothing fancy, some grooved paneling on the wall under fluorescent lights, an oak desk—you're freaked out by how normal everything looks, how empty the room is, not like on TV—with a white guy behind that desk watching all impassive as the prosecutor argues and your attorney, who you never talked to before five minutes ago in the crowded hallway outside, counterargues, and you get on the stand for maybe four minutes and begin to haltingly describe what has happened to you, Northside, juvie, your momma, her dying—no, wait, I was something else before all that, I promise, the Reverend can back me up—but the man says, "If your list of infractions wasn't so extensive, I might be moved by your story. But, frankly, I am not. In fact, I'm tired of it. For the life of me, I can't see what distinguishes you from so many identical young men who parade through these chambers and ask for leniency, day after day, year after year, all with a sob story, all seemingly repentant but right back here in two months' time if I let them go, all a burden on society—or, as in your case, a threat to society. If your experience in juvenile camp did nothing to curb your . . . enthusiasm for criminality, then I see zero call for leniency. I have no more patience for so-called kids like you. I'm sentencing you as an adult. You made your choice, Mr. Shaughnessy. You made all of your choices a long time ago.

"You are hereby remanded by the Kentucky Department of Corrections for the term of twelve years. Because you are seventeen, you will spend four months in a residential facility, then you will be transferred to Bracken. You will serve six years before being considered eligible for parole. May you be an example to others."

Take it away. Clasp its ankles in manacles to hobble it. Place a chain around its waist. Now weave cuffs through the chain and secure its wrists in the cuffs. And drive it away just like you're driving now.

Ice is breaking on the surface of the river. Allmon wants to hold all the floes together, reassemble the solidity and stolidity secured by the dead cold, but he can't, it's coming apart under him as he's trying to cross with his son in his arms; he can hear it whining and moaning as it cracks. It's because he's running too hot with this disease his mother gave him, the disease maybe he gave to his son, the disease Marie was cursed to bear because of her black burden of a body, black as river as grave as starless sky

Allmon's mouth is filling with water, but there's still room for words.

The youth offender facility is: nothing really. Not scary, just boring, trifling, you've done this before. It's like being a senior in high school; nobody fucks with you anymore, and it's not as intense as you think it's gonna be.

But the penitentiary is: Anarchy. Your worst fucking nightmare, only all day every day, 24/7, no escape. It's not where they house men, it's where they make animals. After they wash you down, delouse you, spread your cheeks and root around in your anus, they walk you for the first time along the tier of the main line to your cell, and all those eyes, black eyes brown eyes blue eyes, from the dayroom up the four dizzying floors, turn to watch you, and suddenly the rooster crows, the dogs start their barking, there's sheep and screaming birds and yowling cats, the sound rises, shriek piling on shriek until it crescendos to pure madness and you're more than halfway to panic. The sound of wild animals is so horrifying, your body would run away out of pure instinct if you didn't have a guard right at your back. That cacophony is worse than the sound of your cell door closing the very first time, which is a casket closing.

Six years in a cage is six lifetimes.

Your body is eighteen years old

you say when your grizzled old cellie asks. Shakes his head ruefully, doesn't say nothing, ignores you thank you god thank you god thank you god thank you because you don't even know what it means to look tough anymore. You don't know what it means to act hard on the inside. Up is down and hell is on earth in this inverted world. For the first time you are thankful for your naturally unfriendly face—a tough face only a mother could love—but it's small change next to these dudes six-five and up, cannon arms, cockstrong terrifying motherfucking extraterrestrial power in barely human form. You force yourself to look right at them, show them you're not scared, but you've never been so scared in your life. Your time back in Northside when you ran with small-time thugs, that was just playacting. This is the worst, realest life.

That first night, you can't sleep, think you'll never sleep again, you're just staring out in the dark and trying to stay alert. It's not long before you hear some wicked sound across the way, across the open space on the opposing tier, scuffling or sobbing, gagging and retching, you have some idea and it's making you sick, you're sitting up on your mattress when a guard runs down the tier and shines his flashlight directly into the cell opposite yours and burned into your retina you see a big white monster fucking some skinny white dude up the ass, and there's blood on this big man's yanked-down drawers and his fat hand is wrenching open the mouth of the bottom, saliva glistening to the concrete floor, the man's terrorized eyes looking like they're going to fall out of their sockets. And now the animal cries are rising up the floors again, the jackals, the dogs, the crows. These two men—or one man and one animal—get hauled out by five guards, one sent to the hole, one sent limp as a rag to the infirmary. You think you're gonna throw up, but you don't, because you can't.

You make a decision right there: That's not gonna be you. You're gonna survive. Whatever it takes. You'll cut someone's throat if you have to. So first thing, you make a shank out of a soda can by folding it and wrapping it around itself and stomping on it. You keep it in your trembling hand. Until the first shakedown, which is when they inevitably find it. They give you a pass this first time, seeing as you're young and fresh, and they don't send you to the hole. They're barely out of the cell when you're busy making another.

You do it right there in front of your bemused cellie, who says, "Ain't got to worry about me, I ain't gonna fuck with you." It takes a few more days of unrelenting terror before you actually believe him, because he does in fact—thank you thank you thank you god—leave you alone. All he ever does is sit on his mattress and drink hooch. He works in the cafeteria and somehow manages to make potato wine without any actual potatoes. But he never seems drunk, just deflated as an old balloon. His cheeks sag down to his neck.

"How come that shit don't make you sick?" you ask him.

"Been drinking it for years. Till I get out."

"When you getting out? Where you gonna go to?"

"Heaven, dawg," the man says. "Or hell. Either one better than this place."

Yes. The forty-foot walls, cell blocks running the length of a football field, gun towers, razor wire, guards with their twelve-gauge shotguns who bang their flashlights on the bars all hours of the night, waking everybody up, plus the motion sensors and the shakedowns, the mad labyrinth of gangs and allegiances you can't navigate because you're nothing but a scrub fish. But none of that's the worst of it.

You're so used to thinking it's the white man who fucks you that it's just instinct to get under the wing of these black dudes. What your naïve ass doesn't realize is they fuck down color lines here; mad-dog Aryans on scrawny white boys and blue-black brothers on black. How the hell were you supposed to know? So the first black dude who's decent, who nods and says what up from a respectful distance in the cafeteria, is somebody you acknowledge once. Smile with one corner of your mouth while trying to look hard. Like that's possible.

But no, Allmon, you're an idiot, a fucking idiot a motherfucking idiot idiot IDIOT!!! That's the same man who just grabs you two days later and throws you against a wall like you don't weigh a thing—six feet and 185 pounds but you're nothing, there's always somebody bigger than you—and as your head cracks against the tile, he says, "Your cunt." Doesn't even have to finish the sentence. "Fuck you," automatic out of your mouth. But just as quick he punches your windpipe with one hand, slams your temple with the other. And walks away as you sprawl down the wall. And people are just standing there watching it happen, watching you ragdoll. Which is worse than the insult, you know that instantly.

Life inside the migraine. You can't go to the infirmary. You can't snitch. You can't confront him, he weighs like 275 pounds. You can't go anywhere but back to your cell, where your cellie knows, 'cause that's how it works here, everybody knows everything while it's still happening. He sighs like he's almost too tired to tell you anything, but finally says, "Talking shit ain't gonna cut it. Just feathers against bullets. He still gonna turn you out." And he points to the combination lock on your cell locker. "Put it in a sock," he says very quietly, and makes a swinging and slamming motion like he's bringing down a hammer.

You rear back. "That's murder one! They'll send me up for life."

Your cellie shrugs. "You in the slaughterhouse now. Cut or get cut."

So there it is. It's not a matter you need to consider deeply. Your body's going to go for the Hail Mary pass, and you know it, because to refuse to choose is also to choose. But here's the thing: You know if you do it in front of people, you're caught for sure. If you do it in private, that won't send the right blood message. In the end, you just pray a message you do send is loud enough. Like the loudspeakers that holler at the prisoners all day, every day.

So, you carry it on you, two socks tied together around your waist under your khaki shirt, lock just hanging there like a big, cold eye. You figure out quick you can't just go attack him in his cell while he's napping because someone will see you do it—plus, he sleeps on a top bunk. Your only option is to get him in the shower. He likes to be the first one in the showers in the morning. So, very next day, when the unit's still dark, he trundles down to the washroom, big, hulking beast in nothing but a snatch of towel, and you slip out of your cell as soon as you see him turn from the dayroom into the showers. You can't follow him in there—the cameras that point at the sink catch the silhouette and sometimes the face of anyone who enters. You need a blind spot. So you have to wait out in the dark dayroom by the trash can, praying no one else follows and catches sight of you. But you don't have to wait long, which is good because your terrifying reality is tightening like a noose around your neck, blocking air and blood and maybe your ability to act. You don't even know if you can feel your arms anymore, but, sure enough, the body does what's necessary. When that big motherfucker comes sauntering out of the shower, you step out of the shadows and bring a swift cracking blow to the back of his skull.

He drops straight down to the waxed floor, his cheekbone cracking audibly when he hits. You expect to feel an overwhelming urge to run, but you don't. You're steady and levelheaded, as if the first blow has strangely relaxed you. You raise your hand again. One more blow to the head would probably kill him. Hard blows to the body will put him out of commission and, if you're lucky, get him transferred. You land swift, sickening blows to his back, wracking that metal against his backbone, because you want to paralyze him, not out of revenge, just good sense. Five or six blows and your internal sensor says that's it—wrap it up. You fling the socks in a trash can and scoot back to your cell, draping the lock back on the locker. You slide right back in bed.

Your cellie is watching you, wide awake, just lying there. You can hear him breathing. You try to match your breath to his and pretty soon it's almost back to normal and then the uproar comes and it's crazy loud, so you run to the steel bars with him to peer out, and the two of you holler at the guards like everyone else, make all the mad animal sounds, and then you simmer down and act normal as can be all day, don't change your body language or any of your habits—except in the cafeteria. When you walk in there, you straighten up and stroll with a new confidence through that fraught gauntlet, looking every single one of those men in the eye—every single motherfucking one—and see how more than a few nod at you? Feel how the air is changed and silent? That's the sound of respect. Your ability to inspire fear is the only currency you will ever have in here.

And now you know how to survive.

Six years, six lifetimes.

You look around you sometimes at the living nightmare, at the blacks and the poor white trash so country they almost sound black, and you think somewhere out there it's not like this. There's black lawyers and professors and ambassadors and businessmen. Somewhere. But those are just words inside your mind and your mind is inside.

And even if those fancy blacks do exist, you fucking hate them anyway. You understand now why the Reverend used to rail against them. They don't give a fuck about you any more than white folks do. In fact, they're worse than white folks; they're traitors. The way you walk, talk, spend your cash, rent-a-center house you live in, tricked out car you drive, your whole life—it all embarrasses the shit out of them. You are their living, breathing shame. They're the ones who still call you nigger. The whites don't have to anymore, because the state does it for them.

Who's gonna change this world? Most of these inmates won't ever get out. The ones that do, most of them will be back.

They grow failure here like flowers.

They say there's gonna be a black president someday. Maybe. Or maybe just black skin. Either way, you won't ever get to vote in Kentucky. Won't have a place to live, 'cause you won't qualify for Section Eight housing to get your feet on the ground, won't ever serve on a jury to keep a brother out of jail, won't ever get a good job once you X the little felony box, can't legally carry a gun to keep some crazy racist from killing you, and there was never any protection against the cops to begin with.

Men like Forge can get away with anything. But you? It's over—no money, no life, no hope. But that was always in the script, wasn't it? That's how they wrote it. If anyone has eyes, they can read it. It's written in black blood on white paper.

No matter the crime, they sentence every single one of you to death.

There it is, the house. With its lower-story windows blazing, its upper stories loom like a grievous shadow on a foundation of pure light. Allmon abandons the Mercedes down at the foot of the drive near the road, the driver's door wide and the alarm pinging softly. He moves across the lawn in the dark, but he isn't headed for the house. His every move is deliberate and firm as he heads for the barns with his .45 in his hand—not just loaded but jacked with eight bullets at the ready. He's come for his son, but he has other business first.

The night is as dark as the inside of a box, and the night watchman is nowhere to be seen; he must be with the other grooms at the Osbourne house on the far side of the bowl, raising silver mint julep cups in celebration. Half the state is either drunk on bourbon or sick on Derby pie. The rest are asleep in their beds, oblivious as ever.

With an unearthly strength born of determination, Allmon slides open the great door of the broodmare barn so that it bangs home with a deep, metallic sound. He passes inside, his breath whistling through his clenched teeth. Where is she? Where is the champion filly? He has come for Forge's prized possession. They came for his long ago.

But my God, just look at this barn with its oaken stalls polished to a sheen, Forge's purple silks like royal insignia painted on all the doors. The chaff drifts like confetti under ceiling fans, the very walls insulated with dollar bills. It's sickening, a veritable temple of tack and flesh. Allmon stalks from one pristine stall to the next, but the filly is nowhere to be found. What he discovers: two prized breeders, Seconds Flat and Forge's Fortune. The real moneymakers. They were separated from their foals months ago in the age-old game of Kentucky usage, the foals whinnying somewhere else, confused and alone in the dark.

Knowing what he now knows, the whole enterprise is as bold as sin.

Forge's Fortune, nestled in her straw, is staring straight up at him with warm, curious eyes when he points the .45 at her forehead four inches above her eyes and with the simple draw of a finger delivers her. She droops without surprise or alarm or life onto the bed of hay on the stall floor, her beautiful skull perfectly intact, her limbs going gentle and limp beneath her.

But now Seconds Flat is panicking, rising up on her rear legs in the neighboring stall, whining in alarm, and suddenly Allmon's hands begin to shake—he has always been the protector, that's who he is, right, Momma?— he can barely recover his aim, can't manage the target, especially with the mare rearing and her eyes rolling, but when she launches high for the third time with her forelegs cycling, he finds mercy and shoots through the soft velvet crook where her tongue rises against the soft palate, and then she's choking and already bleeding out as she crumples onto her heavy quarters, slumping to the right and crashing her beautiful head against the oak of the stall.

But where is Henrietta—no, Hellsmouth! Where is Hellsmouth? A strangled sound emerges from Allmon's chest, the sound of a distressed child, as he moves from the barn across the lane, but he presses it down until it disappears. Allmon doesn't find her in the stallion barn, of course, only three yearling colts who swing their heads nervously as he moves out the back of their barn with his dreadful purpose. There are more mares, but eye for an eye, mother for mother is done. Now he has to find Hell. Allmon doesn't want to kill her, only hurt her enough to free her. No one will use her again, not even him.

It's when he moves out again into the moon-addled night, where the stars are slowly waking and stretching, that he sees her. She seems only slightly more real than the shadows around her, a flicker of blacker black in one of the paddocks. He knows it's her; she's unmistakable. Allmon is there in an instant, unlocking the gate and swinging it wide, stepping inside onto the soft carpet of pasture grass. He moves with unshakable resolve toward his decision, he can actually feel the revolving of the earth grating against the steadiness of his own body. But he realizes suddenly how light he must appear in the darkness, still wearing his gray Snyder Barns polo under the bright May moon with its mock shock face, how Hell is almost certainly watching him. No sooner does he realize this than he hears gladiator breath and her hooves on the ground, thudding a syncopation that coalesces to a duple rhythm, her war beat rising, rising until it's almost upon him, and he raises a blindman's pistol, committed, absolutely committed, but when he fires at her left leg, she keeps coming wounded or not, and he throws himself to the ground, so she thunders by him or over him, he doesn't know which, but he feels the heavy, fluttering weight of her passage as powerful as anything he's ever felt, and now she's gone, beating her drum across the brick chip lane and down the manicured lawn until she finds the concrete of the road, where she beats her drum out into the wider, waiting world.

Shaken, Allmon picks himself up off the ground with bits of timothy grass clinging to his clothing, gun still in his hand. Everything's all right, it's all right, whether Hell is wounded or not. *F* is for failure but it's not failure if she's free, and now he's halfway through his labors. He carefully eases the hammer forward and slides the piece into his pocket, moving out of the paddock with renewed focus, no trembling in his hands. He knows what he has to do. *F* is for felony, and felony is for fire. All he needs is an accelerant.

The sheds, the outbuildings, yes. He slips into the first and nudges the switch with a calloused thumb—no, this is hay storage, how could he have forgotten so quickly? It's in the second, the one immediately next door, yes, here, the building with the mowers and the old Ford diesel truck and the gasoline along the wall in bright red plastic cans. He looks around with cold calculation for an old jar, a bottle, something—or this, an empty glass juice bottle flung into a recycling bin. He tears a rag from his own shirt, soaks it with gasoline, twisting and pressing it into the bottle, using one of his own shoelaces for a wick. Now, revolver in one ass pocket, bottle in the other, and a gas can in each hand, Allmon is on his way out the door, un-relenting passage through the night, back along the barns, toward the rear of the house. But before he reaches his destination, he's suddenly stalled by a yawning sense of the unfamiliar, of something known once but now forgotten. The ground beneath him is spongy and forgiving, newly so. Didn't there used to be a windbreak here? Confused, he stops in the garden by the slight movements of a ragged, sun-bleached scarecrow. He realizes he's trampling new growth, all lined out in flowering order at his feet. Allmon stands in the perfectly arranged, greening rows. To his right he detects the familiar dark orchard, all the tender boughs swelling with potential. Something heavy hangs in the air like the scent of musk or myrrh. Summer is near.

Before him, the first story of the house spills a golden light so warm, he can almost feel it on his skin. It's like a gold dessert cup, in which the rest of the house rests. He thinks, they're so rich, they live their lives in that beautiful golden cup, but I never got to drink from that cup. All I ever got to drink was their spit.

The cool, seductive silence of the garden pulls him backward. Nothing bad can happen in this dark, amniotic space between bursts of sun. Do I have to go ahead, do I really have to go in there?

His mind reels back in time, fumbling for the moment when it all went askew, when his feet wandered from the path, when his world was wholly upended.

Why me, Reverend? Why now?

Because if they can't see color in the night, you got to light up the dark. Be not afraid.

When Allmon moves forward, his whole being is a prayer for strength. He places one gas can on the limestone steps and reaches out in the darkness for the knob on the back door.

Henry Forge, you are hereby sentenced to death.

He's prepared to jigger the lock or break the glass, but it's unlocked. Disgust overwhelms him. They're so confident, so entitled, they steal your child and then leave their mansions unlocked. They're so ignorant, they don't realize they're gambling even when they toss down the dice on the goddamn baize. He walks straight into the narrow back el of the kitchen, straight into the room where he first met Henrietta. He's almost swamped by the memory of her against him, open under him, of her presence accepting him into her. They were as real as life together, as real as children. But he presses her back violently, just as he did in life. And she's dead again.

The house is utterly still, even though the lights are on. They must be asleep upstairs, Henry Forge and Allmon's son. He pours gas as he walks right up the slave staircase that rises narrowly to the second floor. He won't bother with the attic. The second floor will rise up to kiss all the dry and dusty combustibles that lie just beneath the roof. Henry's stored treasures will make for perfect kindling.

Everywhere, everywhere the markings of wealth appear as he begins his work, splashing gas onto the waxed hardwood floors, careful to avoid the wool rugs that won't ignite as quickly. Big dressers to the ceilings and cabinets with lavish knickknacks hold no meaning for him, velvet drapes and old indigo coverlets, curvy cherry furniture that gleams dry but positively dances under gasoline. While one gas can waits impatiently in the hall, he enters every room with his revolver in hand, seeking that most precious antique, Henry Forge, and splashing gasoline everywhere he is not found. But he only encounters Henrietta in these private spaces. Here is a woman's bedroom with silk blankets. Here is a child's room, perhaps once her room, now their child's—oh God, for a moment he can barely believe the child is truly his—but the crib is empty. A mobile dangles above it. He was once that child; so was she; they made one of two. Against rising anguish, Allmon splashes gas across the past and then takes care to pour extra in the bathrooms, where the acetone and mouthwash and rubbing alcohol will pop their bottles like little bombs. Burn down this world. Burn down what I did to her—

Pour it out, Allmon, don't swallow it down anymore.

Pour it out so that light may shine in the darkness.

Bring me my child.

Allmon's blood begins to boil over flames of regret and fury, and now he's moving more quickly, jogging down the front staircase, and swinging around the carved newel with one can of gas remaining. He's getting close, but so is she. She's almost on him, and to his relief, he realizes he no longer has an out, or a choice. The moment has come. But he doesn't find Henry in the foyer with the gas-splashed clock, or in the parlor with its two divans huddled together and begging to burn, or in the formal dining room with its damask chairs now dark with stains, or in the second sitting room, where Allmon rips the drapes from the windows and heaps them for a pyre. Now there is only one room left unexplored, the old back study by the kitchen, the office where Forge keeps the books and ledgers, where Allmon signed the deal, where the devil snatched his soul. The door is wide open. In his hastiness, Allmon had passed it on his walk up the back stairs. Now he stands silently at the threshold. Inside on the long Chesterfield, his body curled around the form of Allmon's child, Henry Forge is asleep. A fan whirs. A bottle of bourbon rests on the desk.

Allmon steps into the room and raises the gun, but then realizes he hasn't cocked it. He pulls the hammer back with the thumb of his free hand, there is an audible click, and Henry's head rises from the pillow of his arm with a start. He turns confusedly toward the light in the doorway and sees the hard shadow standing there.

A startled, strangled sound escapes his lips.

"Get away from my child."

It takes Henry a moment to realize that this dream is not a dream, so at first there's only the relief of suspended time, wherein anything might happen, or nothing at all. The sheer unreality of it offers a brief chance at salvation. Then Allmon takes two steps into the room, aiming the gun at Henry's head with the advantage of the light behind him. Henry can't see the gun in the dark, but he knows it's there. Instead of rising and following orders, he half slides and half tumbles to his knees beside the sofa, and with his back to Allmon reaches his arms around Samuel, who is startled out of sleep but not yet crying.

"Don't hurt him!" Henry cries. Despite his age, his arms are like iron bands around the child. "Kill me—but don't hurt him!"

Words won't save you now, Henry Forge, the old language is dead.

Allmon's voice is steady, steely. "That's exactly what I'm going to do. Now get the fuck up."

Suddenly Samuel is hauling air, shrieking up at the ceiling and flinging his chubby arms out to the sides, and Henry refuses to remove the shield of his body from his grandson.

Startled by the sound, a sudden rage threatens to shatter Allmon's composure. He realizes he can't handle the gun and the baby at the same time. "Pick him up!" he barks, suddenly confused. "Pick him up right now!"

It takes Henry a moment to realize he's being offered a reprieve, then he clumsily sweeps Samuel against his chest, Samuel who is struggling in fright, pummeling the air with his fists, his eyes wide.

"Walk outside. Now!"

Henry does as he is told; he carries Samuel straight out of the study, straight through the blindingly bright kitchen and into the swallowing dark of the Kentucky night.

"Straight back!"

Henry moves as hastily as he can without dropping his grandson, stumbling back toward the garden with all of its geometric, fragrant rows, which he arranged in hope of a future. Its order seems an absurdity now.

Allmon looks wildly about, and when he sees the scarecrow, he points. "Right there, right there." His body has instinctively led them to this place. "Put him down!" he orders.

"No." It sounds like a one-word answer, but then Henry says, "You'll have to kill me first."

Now rage overtakes him. "I AM GOING TO KILL YOU!" Allmon heads him with the butt of the gun, not hard enough to knock him out, just hard enough to bring the older man to his knees. Samuel spills out of his arms like a sack of kittens and rolls facedown in the dirt, screaming, and in the light that shines from the kitchen door, in the finely carved lineaments of Henry's face, Allmon sees Henrietta staring up at him, blood trickling down one temple.

He rears back and gasps for air as Henry swoons, then reaches down and draws Samuel toward him, panic rising that he's hurt his child. Samuel's little white T-shirt separates from his diaper and twists up around his neck. His cries are ear-piercing, but he's unhurt when Allmon lifts him from the dirt with his free hand, clutching him desperately against his abdomen so the child is struggling and flopping sideways and screaming as the soil on his face mixes with tears.

Still on his knees, Henry says, "Careful with his neck."

Allmon turns on him, his eyes furious. "This is my son! You stole my son!" He can't control the sound of anguish, which echoes across the fenced fields.

Though dazed and broken, Henry's voice is almost absurdly calm, and from the calm emerges his eternal refrain, "He is my . . ." But he can't finish;

he chokes on it. New words rise with a will all their own, and he can't withhold them. "I am sorry." He feels their truth like another blow.

Allmon almost spits on him when he stares him down and blurts, "You ain't sorry; you ain't nothing!" But his son is struggling in his arms, and he doesn't know how to do this, he's never held a baby before. He lets Samuel slide awkwardly down his leg to drop unceremoniously to the ground again about six feet from Henry, upon whom Allmon now advances. His body is lethal, pure menace, and when Henry looks up at him, squinting through blood that oozes from a cut above his right eye, the fear on his face is clear as day.

The fear there startles Allmon, but his words are unrelenting. "Take off your belt!"

Henry does as he's told, and Allmon snatches it out of his hands so it whips and snaps like a snake. His motions are growing wild now. If he can move quicker, stoke more anger, maybe he can stave off what's rising, some change he senses. He shoves the older man backward, then kicks at him to get him moving, so Henry scrambles back until he runs into the old post on which the scarecrow hangs. Henry's eyes are locked on Samuel as he's bound to the post with his own belt.

It won't hold, it's not enough, so Allmon whips off his own belt and cinches it lower, around Henry's abdomen. Now he's tied like a beast for slaughter. Still, Henry's eyes are on Samuel.

"I'm taking my child," Allmon snarls, but it's not until he returns to the baby, drawing him clumsily to his chest once again and moving away, that a sound rises up from Henry. It's the sound of a mother howling, a woman wailing at the foot of the cross. The wail rises and encircles the farm, it grips Allmon's head round. It travels the rolling pastures, wends through boughs of trees, swings over the old graves and the heads of the dark, startled horses. But Allmon has lived for so long, for more than six lifetimes, he thinks he can move steadily through it. He advances ten paces before he discovers he can go no farther and stops. He removes the bottle from his pocket and has to put the child down yet again. Henrietta's child. He had a chance to learn love with her, but he destroyed it. He goes pale with the knowledge.

It's too late, it can't matter. He's taking what's his—his son and his revenge. When the lady publishes her book, the whole world will understand what this justice means. They'll finally know. He fumbles for the lighter now. He knows the bottle will do its work and blow the house to kingdom come.

There's a steady breeze tonight to turn a smoky flame into a conflagration. Allmon winds up and lunges forward like a seasoned pitcher and hurls the bottle through the back door straight to the front wall of the kitchen, where it shatters and lands in bright bits on a spattering of gasoline. So it starts. A swift, softly blooming fire line races up the back staircase until it diverges at the landing, traveling into the separate rooms where the beds and sofas, each in their turn, ignite. From outside, it looks as if gentle, flickering lights have come on in every room. Presently, the drapes go up with a willowing motion as if the fire itself is waving for help. Not a moment later, the bathrooms burst open like fireworks.

With a sudden whooshing sound, the Forge house goes up in a blaze, and Samuel stops his crying where he lies on the grass, turning his wide, frightened eyes upward. But he's not looking at the house, only at Allmon, because Allmon's arms are burning where he's been fumed by gasoline. In an instant, he's on the ground gasping and rolling, lashing his arms against the cool, dewy grass, flailing like a crazy man or someone trying to make a baby laugh. Samuel stares at him in alarm, and when Allmon finally rises, gasping and moaning with his own fire extinguished, burned flesh hangs in white tatters from his forearms.

The house drowns out the wounded sounds coming from his mouth. He reaches down and hauls up Samuel, who screams again, wriggling and striking at him. He stares at his own child with burning eyes—burning from the fire or from his mother's disease, he doesn't know which.

Now the sweat on his face is mixed with tears. Henry's howl still echoes in his ears, and Allmon's head swoons with sudden flashing lights. Don't hurt him, don't hurt him—hurt who?

Allmon stumbles sideways a few steps. What's happening? Is this revenge? There was a plan, but he's suddenly horribly confused and lost. He had a story to tell, but who will listen—really listen? Kill Henry Forge and they'll say you're just another black animal killing a white man. They always tell the same old white story.

But, Reverend, they made me a body!

He begins to sob from the center of his chest. He can't feel the pain in his scorched arms any longer; it's as though there's ice packed against his skin. He looks down at Samuel, his life on the outside. Son. It's a foreign word on his tongue with a meaning he's straining to understand.

With a start he realizes that the flashing lights aren't in his mind but on the road near the drive, and police will storm the property at any moment. He doesn't have to glance over his shoulder to see them; he knows.

Momma, I can't, I can't. I won't—

Allmon's hand trembles, and the .45 wavers. The fire is building to an inferno behind him, striving for the stars, and already he can hear voices at the foot of the drive. He looks up confusedly at the night sky with its fishes, lions, serpents, and hunters. He knows they aren't really there, they're just make-believe, a story. But the story matters. A story lives forever, longer than anyone's child.

Allmon's tears stop.

The lady's ending is up to him.

Justice is an ancient animal still taking shape in the sky. Draw it with her pen.

With a great, shuddering breath, he finally understands why he is there. They will either hang you from a tree or let you die on a couch or stick you in a prison to rot, but they will get you just the same. The world doesn't love us. The Reverend says, When they render you a body, they won't listen to words no more, so you got to let the body speak! Let it tell the terrible tale! Let them that have eyes see, and them that have ears hear!

The distance between Allmon and Henry is not so far; he covers it in a dozen strides to stare down at the bound man. At any moment, the police will surround him. He bends down and places Samuel carefully to the side like a treasure in the dewy grass. With the desperation of a drowning man, Henry strains toward the child but can't reach him.

Allmon straightens up and says, "You can't keep what ain't yours, Forge. I won't let you." But Henry won't look at him, only at Samuel.

The Reverend says, Pray with your every action and be not afraid.

"Look at me, Forge!" Allmon demands.

He raises the gun. Be not afraid be not afraid be not afraid be not afraid be not afraid be not afraid benotafraidbenotafraidbenotafraidbenotafraid benotafraidbenotafraidbenotafraidbenotafraidbenotafraidbenotafraidbe—

"Look at me, Forge!" Allmon cries so his voice echoes through the night, and Henry finally looks up, his eyes wide.

Four bullets blast a staccato rainbow around Henry's head—one for Marie, and one for the Reverend, one for Scipio, one for all the men and

women who pace on the bottom of the river, their flesh eaten by fish, and
the last is for

me, Allmon

the deserving and the broken, the guilty and the gift. I am a sinner. I broke
love and sold my child to the highest bidder, but I will ransom his life and
his son's life with my own. Reverend, lay me down gently. Please ask
Momma to forgive me. I forgive her. Dress my body in Sunday clothes and
anoint my mouth. Let my life speak, then they will finally know me. I am
not afraid any longer.

    Allmon turned the gun on himself. He left nothing to chance.

In the dark, there was nothing but the fire. Henry thought he was dead. By
all rights, he should have been. But there was a dead man before him,
sprawled on the ground, his arms extended wide, palms open to the sky.
Figures swarmed around them as night air rushed in from the west, feeding
the inferno and all that was left of Henry's home. The structure was disin-
tegrating before his eyes, the joists giving way, the stories collapsing in
great billowing bursts.

    Samuel's mouth was stretched wide with crying where he lay in the grass,
but Henry could barely hear him, half-deafened by the pistol reports. An
officer spied the child in the tall grass and raised him to her chest, stumbling back from the smoke and crying out, "Whose child is this? Whose
child is this?" but Henry made no reply.

    Then the earth began to shake as if Nature were banging her fists on
plains and mountains. From his perch in the officer's arms, Samuel abruptly
stopped his crying and craned his neck around in curiosity and surprise.
The fire brightened with a volley of fresh air. When Hellsmouth bloomed
suddenly out of the dark, she was gleaming with sweat and bright red with
reflected fire. Samuel screamed in delight as the filly galloped toward them
and then sank onto her haunches and reared, her legs cycling as if to turn
the very wheel of the sky. She was almost perfect. She was ready for more.

EPILOGUE

Because he was on the long, moonlit stretch between Millersburg and Maysville, the driver had plenty of time to stop his rig, floating down one gear after another in the thick fog, then gently braking to a forty-ton stop like a conductor pulling his train into a midnight station. John stopped, because even though the figure was wrapped in fog like a man in a dream, he could tell he was a young guy alone in this unforgiving land. It was foolish to stop, especially on a night like this, on a route like this; you never really knew who was friend or foe, but . . . yeah, it was definitely a young guy. What could you do? You had to help a brother out. He'd been two weeks away from Miranda and was ready to get home; he knew she was lonely and always worried about him when he ran his Southern routes. She'd be making him steak and kidney pie right now on the far side of this fog-strewn night, so he was smiling when the passenger door swung wide and a haunting face appeared, dark, severe, and streaked with black.

John tried to hide his alarm, and his amiable mouth made it easy. It was already saying, "You need some help getting somewhere, my man?"

There was no answer as the young man stepped up into the cab without visible effort at all, as though he were a weightless thing, the mere shadow of a man.

The driver cleared his throat. "I'm Mr. Parker, but you can call me John. And you are?"

There was a long pause, then the man slowly turned his head and stared straight through John with chilly, golden eyes like jeremiads. He didn't say his name; his face was expressionless. Fear instantly cinched John's throat. "Hey, no problem," he blurted with a wave of his hand. "No problem if you don't care to share your name. I got nothing against a private man. We'll just hit the road and be on our way. No problem at all."

No sooner had he said it than a shiver wended along his neck and John felt the sudden cold—my God, the cab felt like a freezer. He was about six gears into real foreboding when he suddenly smelled the subtle scent of smoke on top of the chill. Barely detectable at first, like a faint memory, then the strong, sure smell of campfire.

"You been camping, my man?" he said. Again, no reply was forthcoming, just swallowing silence. The man beside him stared straight ahead out the dash without blinking an eye, without even the whisper of visible breath.

A true frisson of nerves now, the old, instinctive part of the body that detects the presence of danger. But he didn't need to panic yet. Best to just settle back, keep your eyes open, and not say a word. Yes, indeed, just stay calm, don't provoke, don't question, not one single word—

"Young man," John said gently, interrupting his better sense, "I know it really isn't my business, but—"

The man raised a single hand and, without a word, pointed toward the long, dark road.

"You want to go north?" Parker expelled a breath. "Hey, that's cool. North is where I was headed. I've taken a bunch of folks up this way, yes indeed. Just follow the North Star and you can't go wrong, know what I'm saying?" His hands were shaking slightly as he gripped the wheel, but at the same time he suddenly felt reassured deep in his bones; he was going to be all right. Just like animals, most folks were only dangerous when they were afraid. So he was coaxing the gas and they were flying through the thick Kentucky night, rolling north out of the Bluegrass and into the counties that separated central Kentucky from the Ohio line, the counties where John always started to relax and feel safer, where the river was close at hand.

About thirty minutes down the road, he said gently, "Now, just so you know, I'm going north, but I wasn't going all the way into Ohio tonight." He hoped that agitation wouldn't pierce through the steadiness of his voice. The man's head turned slowly in his direction, but John was afraid to look into those fathomless eyes again. He added hastily: "See, I live in Ripley with my wife, but I've got to drop half this load tonight and half in the morning, both on the Kentucky side. Processing plant just west of Maysville, you know, where that famous singer lived, you know who I'm talking about?" And now he was really starting to relax, extolling the virtues of voices you couldn't hear on the radio anymore and talking about the housing boom and how it couldn't last, how it was going to be a disaster, and of course it would hit working folks the hardest—folks like the two of them—but what could you do, really, what could you do, rich men ran the world, they called the shots, all you could do was try to stay one step ahead. His passenger sat rigidly beside him, motionless, and never said a word, so John tried to not think about how his cab now smelled like a barn on fire, and how he was so cold that the hair was standing straight up on his arms, and that the man's face was stony like an Egyptian sarcophagus, the kind they had in the museum in Cincinnati. Why, oh why, had he picked this one up? Because . . . dammit. A human being is precious cargo, and you had to help a brother out. It was how his mother had raised him. She'd seen a lot of hardship back in Virginia, hardship like you couldn't even put in words. If you didn't learn to help others, what was the point of surviving suffering?

When they finally turned onto Route 8 west of Maysville, John said, "We're getting pretty close now," but it was like the man already knew; he was leaning forward in his seat, closer and closer to the edge, reaching out to grip the dash with granite-like hands—God, were they singed from a fire?

John gathered his courage as he was pulling onto Plover Road with its quiet subdivision, where the night was pulling down a thorough black around the houses. He hesitated, wondering if he should venture it, then said gently and very carefully, "Young man, it seems to me like you've come into some kind of trouble. Now it's not my business and I'm not asking you for details, but I'd like to help you out. I'm happy to get you to a safe place where nobody'll come looking for you, and tomorrow you can travel on—"

"The river," the man said suddenly, his first words, and the raw voice

nearly stopped John's heart. It was the sound of old, rusted machinery rolling into motion.

John whispered, "The river's right down this hill behind those houses.
And my house in Ripley is right across the river. It'll be easier to see in the
morning."

"Stop."

"Son—"

"STOP."

John couldn't disobey that voice, enormous as time and deep as a grave.
It filled every cavity of his heart with migraine, it made his limbs go rigid.
He was not even close to a rolling stop when the door was flung open and
the man floated out, first his dark head and boxy shoulders, then his tattered T-shirt snapping and disappearing, the blackened sole of one work
boot the last thing John saw of him.

Now the man was passing over a thick, shadowy lawn, around a swing
set and a shed of fresh sawn wood, straight through a row of hedges, away
from the rig and away from the South, away from the markers of civilization
until all the houses disappeared and the night swallowed him, the ground
sloping down and away.

It was dark as far as he could see. The world smelled like coming water.

The man discovered he was not alone. A steam calliope shrieked in the
dark; muskrats peeked out at him from the shadows, and in a great colli-
sion of sound, all the animals began to chatter at once—ospreys, papery
herons, belted and bearded kingfishers, bank swallows in their burrows—
but this time it didn't frighten him. The muskrats chirped and the turtles
whispered and all the white-tailed deer conversed as, far below, like music,
the river was running. The man could see it now—eternal and quick, and
on the other side, the luscious, original world, the place where he had been
made. High on that distant shore, far above the bottomland with its rushing river, a single light burned. He understood it was burning for him. He
passed down the embankment, the brambles parting before him and the
limestone earth making a way, little stones rocketing down before him to
herald his arrival. The calm, watchful moon shone on the ancient course of
the flowing river, which sparked and fired with its dark gems. He was racing toward it now with all the remembered strength of his body, wanting
only to wash the ash from his old skin, the burn marks from his clothes, the

acrid stench from his hair. There before him the northern side was dark and lovely. He heard a calling in the distance and his mind was filled with the wonder of expectation. The whole world was rising toward him. When he reached the mudflats and felt the cold river embracing his weary feet, he cried out, "Yes!" From somewhere on the other shore, she called to him by his given name, and the sound filled him with knowing. He raised his beautiful, burned arms in long-awaited greeting.

ACKNOWLEDGMENTS

My deepest gratitude to Will Guild; Jonathan Galassi and Ellen Levine; Adam Clay Griffey; Terry and Bernice Morgan and Max Schweitzer; my friends; Sally Rhoads; Eugene Startzman; Barbara Napier; the Lannan Foundation; the USA Foundation; the Whiting Foundation; the Cullman Center at the New York Public Library; the Kentucky Arts Council; and Hank, a great spirit who accompanied me along the way.